Detroit Studies in Music Bibliography, No. 67

Editor
J. Bunker Clark
University of Kansas

German Sacred Polyphonic Vocal Music Between Schütz and Bach

SOURCES AND CRITICAL EDITIONS

DIANE PARR WALKER
and
PAUL WALKER

HARMONIE PARK PRESS   MICHIGAN   1992

Front Endsheets:

(Left) Johann Rosenmüller. "Beatus vir qui timet." Manuscript from the Sächsische Landesbibliothek, Dresden. Courtesy of the Sächsische Landesbibliothek, Dresden, and the Deutsches Musikgeschichtliches Archiv, Kassel. Cover.

(Right) Johann Rosenmüller. "Beatus vir qui timet." Manuscript from the Sächsische Landesbibliothek, Dresden. Courtesy of the Sächsische Landesbibliothek, Dresden, and the Deutsches Musikgeschichtliches Archiv, Kassel. First opening, left page.

Back Endsheets:

(Left) Wolfgang Carl Briegel. "Sehet, wir gehen hinauf gen Jerusalem." *Ander Theil Evangelische Gespräch* (*Evangelische Gespräch II*), Prima Vox. Courtesy of the Deutsches Musikgeschichtliches Archiv, Kassel, and the Bayerische Staatsbibliothek, Munich.

(Right) Wolfgang Carl Briegel. *Ander Theil Evangelische Gespräch* (*Evangelische Gespräch II*). Courtesy of the Deutsches Musikgeschichtliches Archiv, Kassel, and the Bayerische Staatsbibliothek, Munich.

Printed and bound in the United States of America
Published by
Harmonie Park Press
23630 Pinewood
Warren, Michigan 48091

Editor, J. Bunker Clark, University of Kansas
Book design, Elaine J. Gorzelski
Typographer, Colleen Osborne

Library of Congress Cataloging in Publication Data

Walker, Diane Parr
    German sacred polyphonic vocal music between Schütz and Bach :
sources and critical editions / by Diane Parr Walker and Paul
Walker.
        p. c.m. — (Detroit studies in music bibliography ; no. 67)
    Includes bibliographical references and indexes.
    ISBN 0-89990-054-2
    1. Sacred vocal music — 17th century — Bibliography.   I. Walker,
Paul, 1953-   .   II. Title.   III. Series.
ML128.S2W34   1992
016.7825'22026 — dc20   92-18215

Contents

Introduction

The purpose of this bibliography is to catalog all extant German sacred vocal music for three or more voices from the second half of the seventeenth century. The period covered extends from the end of the Thirty Years War in 1648 to the beginning of the careers of Bach and Handel in about 1700, encompassing the much-neglected repertory of German sacred music between Heinrich Schütz and J. S. Bach. For composers whose careers fall on the borderlines of the period we have chosen to err on the side of inclusiveness. A few notable borderline cases have been omitted: Schütz himself, who by mid century was entering the twilight years of a long and distinguished career and whose music is in any case already well documented, and Johann Kuhnau and Johann Joseph Fux, both of whom seem to have written almost all of their vocal music after 1700. Geographically, the bibliography covers all German-speaking lands, including the modern territories of Austria and Switzerland as well as German-speaking parts of what is now Eastern Europe. Several Italian composers of the period (e.g., Antonio Bertali, Marco Giuseppe Peranda, and Agostino Steffani) who spent their careers primarily or entirely in German cities such as Vienna, Dresden, and Munich have also been included, but foreign-born composers who spent only brief periods in German lands (e.g., Vincenzo Albrici) have not. Perhaps our most controversial decision has been to limit the scope of the bibliography to music for three or more voices. We began the project with an interest in "choral" music of the period, but quickly recognized the problems inherent in the nature of that word as it relates to performance practice and the question of how many singers per part were "expected" for performance of a given piece. The answers to this question are beyond the scope of a bibliography such as this one, and in the end we chose simply to eliminate the solo and duet repertory and include everything else, a decision made all the more necessary by our growing realization of the enormous scope of the project. Furthermore, we have made no attempt to distinguish compositions intended for three or more soloists from those intended for performance by several singers per part. Finally, because the bibliography is intended principally for scholars who wish to study the music and for performers who wish to present it, we have omitted titles for pieces no longer extant (for instance, those found in contemporary inventories or performance lists) or that survive in a significantly incomplete state (for instance, in only one part book). Works that have only recently been found to be missing are included, however. Given the difficulty of dating manuscripts, anonymous works have been incorporated only when they belong to collections that clearly fall within the chronological and geographical limits of the period.

THE SOURCES

The extant sources for this repertory exist in three formats: manuscript; published collections of works by individual composers; and published commemorative pamphlets containing the text delivered and music performed for a specific occasion, most often the funeral of a notable citizen.

Individual manuscripts of German music for three or more voices are, as one might expect, widely scattered throughout Europe. There are, however, four collections of substantial size that together contain most of the significant manuscript sources of the period. Two of these, the collection of the Erfurt Michaeliskirche and that of the Königliche Landesschule in Grimma, represent working collections of parts that still bear the annotations of dates of performance. The other two collections, the Bokemeyer collection in Berlin and the Düben collection in Uppsala, Sweden, were gathered by individuals with a particular passion for the music of their time—true collectors who sought out their selections and left us with a representative body of the sacred vocal music from the 17th and 18th centuries.

The Erfurt collection is the smallest of the four and perhaps the most cohesive. Most of the manuscripts were copied between 1673 and 1683 for the use of St. Michael's church and school. They remained in the school library until the collection was "discovered" by the German Denkmäler commission in 1905. In 1914 the manuscripts were transferred to the Preußische Staatsbibliothek in Berlin and were cataloged and integrated into the music manuscript collection. Elisabeth Noack described the Erfurt collection and published a catalogue of it in the *Archiv für Musikwissenschaft* in 1925.

St. Michael's was not the most important of the Erfurt churches, but its association with the school gave it a heavy responsibility for the education of children and community. In 1667, the city fathers initiated a thorough educational reform that included a mandate for the improvement of church music. The cantor became both tutor and musician, and it was his responsibility to furnish all music for church services. The repertory preserved in the St. Michael's collection cannot perhaps be taken as representative of the sacred music heard in the most prominent central-German churches during the second half of the 17th century, but it represents the sort of music deemed appropriate for the edification and education of the populace.

The bulk of the music was copied for the cantor's use by one Johann Christian Appelmann, who taught at the school between 1678 and 1683. Central-German composers are the best represented: Johann Christoph Bach, Johann Michael Bach, Sebastian Knüpfer, Johann Philipp Krieger, Johann Rosenmüller, and Johann Schelle are among the more well-known. Altogether, there are 164 sacred vocal works in the Erfurt collection, of which 86 are anonymous.

Similarly, the group of manuscript parts collected by Samuel Jacobi during his tenure as cantor at the Fürstenschule in Grimma, near Dresden, was gathered to provide music for the school and church. Roughly 450 works survive from what, according to an extant inventory, was a much larger collection assembled between 1680 and 1721. Again, the music represented is primarily that of central German composers, and, although there are a few Latin-texted works, the majority are German. Names include Johann Schelle, Kaspar Förster, Johann Rosenmüller, and Philipp Heinrich Erlebach. While in Grimma this collection was completely cataloged, but at the time of its removal in about 1962 to the Sächsische Landesbibliothek, Dresden, it was reorganized and recataloged to fit into that library's cataloging scheme.

Jacobi demonstrated a particular penchant for symbolism in his composer attributions, frequently substituting a sign for the composer's name. For example, the common symbol for female, a circle above a cross, represents Venus, the goddess of love; in Jacobi's system, the symbol indicates the composer whose name is "Love," Christian Liebe. The corresponding male symbol is also the symbol for Mars, the god of war, and represents Johann Krieger. Schelle's name, which literally means "bell," is replaced with the drawing of small bell. Most of these puzzles have been solved by Friedhelm Krummacher and Wolfram Steude, but a few still remain. The symbol that looks like a

Z with a hatch mark through its last stroke (⅄) was thought to symbolize Friedrich Wilhelm Zachow, who is well represented in the Grimma collection. Ortrun Landmann, music librarian at the Sächsische Landesbibliothek, has informed us, however, that Steude has recently cast doubt on that connection. The mark is now believed to be the symbol for the god Zeus, or Jupiter, but to date no one has been able to match this representation with an appropriate composer's name.

The Bokemeyer collection, presently still divided between the Stiftung Preussischer Kulturbesitz in the former West Berlin and the Deutsche Staatsbibliothek in former East Berlin, is named for its second owner rather than its original compiler. Georg Österreich, who was a musician at the courts of Gottorf and Wolfenbüttel between 1680 and 1735, was a prodigious collector of music. In his case, however, the music was copied in score for study rather than in parts for performance. Österreich marshalled the assistance of a number of copyists who helped him amass a collection of a few thousand scores and books. It is thought that the over 1800 scores remaining represent only about one half of the original collection. Some 850 of these scores are manuscripts of German Protestant vocal music by about 300 composers and include a number of *unica* and most of the extant sacred music of Nicolaus Bruhns, Vincent Lübeck, and Johann Theile.

Österreich eventually sold the collection to his friend Heinrich Bokemeyer, who was himself a collector, and who added yet other materials to those Österreich had gathered. Later, Johann Nicolaus Forkel acquired the library, and from him it eventually passed to the Berlin state library. There, the collection was organized more or less alphabetically by composer, and the individual manuscripts were sewn into volumes. Although work with the collection now is hindered by its division between the two Berlin libraries, the thorough catalog by Harold Kümmerling published in 1970 serves to document and describe in detail the materials to be found there.

Gustaf Düben was born in Stockholm, Sweden, to German parents in about 1628 and pursued his entire career there as a court and church musician. Although himself a composer, he placed much more emphasis on gathering the work of others into a library of 1500 vocal and 300 instrumental works in manuscript that he compiled between 1663 and 1690. His international connections are evident in the number of autographs by foreign composers found in the collection. Dieterich Buxtehude's autograph of "Membra Jesu nostri" bears an inscription to the collector and is among the 105 Buxtehude manuscripts obtained by Düben. Other composers well represented in the collection are Kaspar Förster, Samuel Friedrich Capricornus, and Augustin Pfleger.

Düben, like Georg Österreich, collected to preserve and to study. He and his assistants in Stockholm copied out sets of parts for each of the works he obtained, but Düben also preserved many of the works in organ tablature in bound volumes entitled *Motetti e concerti*. Düben's son presented the collection to the University of Uppsala in 1732, and it remains there today. A typescript catalogue was prepared by Folke Lindberg in 1942 and is now available on microfilm from the library. A chronological study and detailed description of much of the collection was published by Bruno Grusnick in the *Svensk tidskrift för musikforskning* in 1966.

Most of the music found in these four collections exists only in one unique manuscript source. These pieces seem in most cases to have been written by their composers for the particular performing forces at hand in the local court or free city and therefore were not thought to be widely useful, although there are examples of such pieces that obviously circulated and were copied out by more than one collector or cantor. Of a different variety—and clearly intended for wider distribution and use—were the works of such composers as Wolfgang Carl Briegel, Johann Rudolf Ahle, and Andreas Hammerschmidt. They and several other composers of the period published sizable collections of sacred vocal pieces with an eye toward providing the parish church of modest resources with suitable and easily-accessible music for the Sunday services. Those collections intended for use in Protestant churches frequently contained settings of the Gospel readings for each Sunday and feast day of the liturgical year; the parish church musician had merely to consult the index or table of contents to locate the piece assigned for the day in question and hand the partbooks out to his singers. The same sort of collection was published for the Catholic churches as well; these, however, usually contained several settings of the ordinary of the Mass or the Vesper psalms, sometimes in sets for increasing numbers of voice parts. Both types of collections nearly always appeared in partbooks and apparently enjoyed a relatively wide circulation; each of the manuscript collections previously discussed contains manuscript copies of some pieces from published collections, and there is often more than one extant copy of such volumes reported to RISM.

The final category of sources comprises the *Gelegenheitskompositionen*, or occasional pieces. Civic ceremonies, weddings, baptisms, and funerals were then, as they are now, occasions for show. The keepsake or memento from such an occasion was not a program that enumerated what took place, but a small publication that included the texts delivered. Quite often, the music sung at such an event was also published in the pamphlet. These documents provide a very rich source of sacred music from this particular period of German music history, but they have received only sporadic attention from scholars. Bibliographic problems may be a principal reason for their obscurity: the pieces are often buried within the texts that they accompany, they frequently are not kept among the music materials in a library, and they sometimes are misattributed to the author of the speech or sermon with which they were published. It seems that such occasional pieces were as often as not composed by someone not otherwise known as a composer. Roughly one fifth of the names represented in our bibliography are for composers whose only entry is for one or two funeral or wedding pieces.

In 1966 Wolfgang Reich published a bibliography of all such funeral pieces housed in libraries in what was then East Germany. The Deutsches Musikgeschichtliches Archiv in Kassel also has a separate catalog in its office, listing the occasional music on microfilm in that collection. For the most part, however, this last category remains the least investigated and most intriguing of the sources for sacred vocal music of the last half of the seventeenth century.

THE MUSIC

The diversity in source material is matched by a wealth of musical styles, a wealth that is in turn at least partly a reflection of German political life after the Thirty Years War. The Treaty of Westphalia that concluded the war in 1648 reaffirmed the fragmentation that had been a political fact of life among German-speaking peoples since the late Middle Ages. Only on paper did the power of the Holy Roman Emperor extend north of the Alps, whereas in reality the small, territorial princes divided the land among themselves and ruled as they saw fit. Many important free cities that before the war had enjoyed real power wielded by a middle class of ever-increasing means found themselves in ruins without power, wealth, or middle class. At a time when France had finally succeeded in centralizing its power in the king, and England and Holland had developed an important, expanding middle class, Germany lacked both.

Much of the music in the bibliography was composed for the court chapel choirs and orchestras that were maintained by nearly every territorial ruler from the lowliest prince to the Holy Roman Emperor. Often such rulers were particularly interested in imported culture from Italy or, later, France, and nearly all of the Italian composers in our list served a German court, sometimes in alternation with local German talent. In Dresden, for instance, the Saxon Elector brought in a large number of Italian musicians in the 1650s, eventually causing Heinrich Schütz's assistant capellmeister, Christoph Bernhard, to abandon Dresden for the greener pastures of Hamburg. In 1680, however, the entire Italian entourage was dismissed, and Bernhard, who had since returned to Dresden, was appointed to the position of capellmeister. Other smaller courts were also able to support fine musical establishments led by talented German composers. One such case was the ducal court of Weissenfels in central Germany, where Johann Philipp Krieger not only wrote some of the finest church music of the period but also is known to have performed a great many works by other German and Italian composers.

Some of the best polyphonic vocal music to come out of Germany in this period was written expressly for the musical forces at one of these courts. Almost none of this music found its way into print, however, since it was intended specifically for the performers available at the court and would in most cases not be marketable on a large scale. Nevertheless, manuscript copies did circulate. The more ambitious civic church musicians eagerly obtained pieces for their own performances, and private collectors such as Düben and Österreich gathered as much of the repertory as their contacts allowed.

Although few of the free cities regained their former glory after the Thirty Years War, a number of them managed to support important and very fine musical establishments. Pre-eminent in this respect were the northern cities of Hamburg and Lübeck, which suffered relatively little during the war. The former could boast not only the first public opera house to open outside Italy but also a thriving civic church music program presided over for many years by Christoph Bernhard. In Lübeck, Franz Tunder and, after him, Dieterich Buxtehude offered a famous series of *Abendmusiken* concerts for which they wrote a great deal of vocal music and which attracted the attention of a number of musicians, including the young J. S. Bach. Central-German cities were slower to recover from the war, but their musical traditions remained quite strong in many cases. Throughout the baroque period, Leipzig could boast outstanding church music provided by a whole series of prominent Thomascantors, including Sebastian Knüpfer and Johann Schelle in the latter seventeenth century. Like the sacred music written for the courts, most civic church music of this period remained in manuscript.

A few composers attempted to provide sacred music of good quality for the more typical parish church. In terms of sheer numbers, the most prominent were Andreas Hammerschmidt, Wolfgang Carl Briegel, and Johann Rudolf Ahle, who among them published, according to our count, 1132 polyphonic vocal pieces. Briegel's career is representative. His most important position was as capellmeister for the court of the Landgrave of Hesse-Darmstadt. The Landgrave, unlike many of his ruling colleagues, focused much attention on the smaller towns and villages under his jurisdiction, and he assigned Briegel the task of providing them with serviceable music. Over the next fifty-seven years, Briegel published more than 600 compositions requiring forces of only modest size and technical ability.

Voices — Voice ranges are recorded as indicated in the source. We have chosen not to include indications of *ripieno* or *cappella* parts. Although such parts are often indicated on title pages, the music itself frequently fails to make clear exactly what they are to sing, and they would appear in a great many cases to be optional (as in Heinrich Schütz's performing instructions for his *Musicalische Exequien*). We therefore report soloists and/or a second choir only when such parts serve a distinct function in the composition and are clearly specified in the source. The designation SATB, SATB describes a piece for two distinct choirs, not a piece for four soloists joined occasionally by the tutti.

Strings — String instruments encountered in this music encompass members of the violin family (bowed and without frets, including violin, viola, and violoncello), the viola da gamba family (bowed and with frets, including viola da gamba and violone), and the family of plucked strings (including lute and theorbo). In the seventeenth century the expressions viola da gamba and viola referred to entire families of instruments of like construction but different size and range. The gamba could be found in treble, alto, tenor, and bass sizes, the viola in alto, tenor, and bass. In most cases, size of instrument is not specified in the source; in order to determine this factor, one would have to examine each part for clef and range. As a result, we have not specified size and have instead simply listed viola or gamba as indicated in the source. The designation *violetta* appears frequently and refers during this period to any bowed string instrument that plays a middle part, that is, either a viola or a viola da gamba of alto or tenor range. We have made no attempt to interpret the word, but simply reproduce it when it is found in the source.

Woodwinds — Those used in the repertory include transverse flute, recorder, oboe, bassoon, shawm, and *Schreyerpfeife*. The shawm (German: *Schalmei*; Italian: *piffaro*) and *Schreyerpfeife* are loud double reed instruments that became obsolete after the seventeenth century. The two are closely related: a *Schreyerpfeife* is simply a shawm with a capped reed and without a flared bell near the bottom. Like the gamba and the viola, both instruments came in families; again, we do not attempt to identify which member of the family is called for in a given case. The remaining woodwinds in their baroque manifestations should be familiar to the reader and require no further comment.

Brass and Percussion — Brass instruments include the cornetto, the trumpet (natural, without valves), and the trombone. The cornetto fell out of favor by the end of the seventeenth century, but is relatively well known today thanks to its revival for performances of early music. The word *cornettino* refers to a smaller version of the cornetto pitched in E rather than A. *Clarino* and *principale* refer not to distinct instruments but to ranges of the trumpet: the former describes a part that plays predominately in the upper range, the latter a part in the lower range. The range of a part marked simply trumpet can be determined only through examination of the music; this term appears in the bibliography just as it is found in the source. The Italian word *tromba* is translated here as trumpet. Trombones, like gambas and violas, were to be found in families of alto, tenor, and bass size, which information is likewise not specified in the bibliography. Like *violetta*, the term *trombetta* is problematic. It is an early Italian term for trumpet, and according to Michael Praetorius could designate the tuba minor, trombone piccolo, or trombone. It appears uninterpreted in the bibliography. The only percussion instrument called for in the repertory is the timpani, which has changed little since the seventeenth century.

Basso Continuo — Instruments playing the bass line include the violoncello, violone, and bassoon; chordal continuo instruments comprise the plucked string instruments and keyboard instruments. A particular keyboard instrument is frequently not specified in the source. We have elected to indicate simply *bc* for all continuo parts that are either unspecified or clearly intended for keyboard. On the other hand, designations of a member of the plucked string family are reproduced, as are designations of single-line continuo instruments. Performance of the continuo seems intended for the most part to be flexible and to make use of the instruments at hand.

Miscellaneous — The word *taille* designates tenor range but does not specify instrument. It could serve as an abbreviation for *taille de violon*, *taille des hautbois*, and so on. We have elected not to interpret it.

FORMAT

Each entry includes the following information:

Title
>performing forces
>liturgical occasion
>source location
>>number in RISM and/or Reich
>>format
>>availability on microfilm
>modern editions
>notes

The various items are explained as follows:

TITLE: Spelling is modernized to allow for interfiling of like titles. Alphabetizing of titles incorporates definite articles as is customary in German. For instance, *Das ist das ewige Leben* and *Das Leben unsers Herrn* will both be alphabetized under "D."

PERFORMING FORCES: These are listed in the order of voices, strings, woodwinds, brass, percussion, and basso continuo. See PERFORMING FORCES above for more specific information on the instruments, voices, and the conventions of the present bibliography. Abbreviations appear in a list below.

LITURGICAL OCCASION: The place of the piece in the liturgical year rather than within the service is indicated. In the case of *Gelegenheitskompositionen*, the particular occasion is designated. The information appears only when supplied by the source. No attempt has been made to assign possible liturgical designations based on text or other factors. Liturgical designations are given in English: for the Latin and German equivalents, see the accompanying chart.

SOURCE LOCATION: Each of the three types of sources requires a different kind of information on this line.

(1) For a piece in a published collection: the title of the publication and the number of the piece in the collection. The complete title, place of publication, date, as well as RISM reference and microfilm location for collections are given at the top of the listing for each composer.

(2) For a manuscript: library and shelf number, the collection of which it forms a part (e.g., Düben, Bokemeyer), and the date (only if a reliable one is to be found on the source itself). Items from the Grimma collection include their old Grimma shelf number to aid the user in matching up old numbers with new.

(3) For an occasional piece: city and date of publication. Manuscript copies of pieces that appeared in published collections are not generally listed. In virtually every case these are copied from the print, which thus serves as primary source. Library abbreviations are those used in *New Grove*; the names and locations of the libraries are spelled out in the accompanying index of manuscript sources.

NUMBER IN RISM AND/OR REICH: Unless otherwise specified, RISM alphanumeric sigla (e.g., K21) refer to entries in RISM Series A/I; dates with superscripts (e.g., 1687^{13}) refer to entries in Series B/VIII. Reich numbers refer to entries in Wolfgang Reich, *Threnodiae sacrae: Katalog der gedruckten Kompositionen des 16.-18. Jahrhunderts in Leichenpredigsammlungen innerhalb der Deutschen Demokratischen Republik* (Dresden, 1966).

FORMAT: That is, whether the source is in score or parts. "Choirbook format" refers to a format that is reminiscent of the common late-medieval method of writing all parts separately but within the same opening of the book. This format is seldom to be found except in published occasional pieces.

AVAILABILITY ON MICROFILM: Microfilm reproduction of many of the items listed can be found in the Deutsches Musikgeschichtliches Archiv (DMA) in Kassel, or in the microfilm reproduction of the Liechtenstein Collection of music manuscripts in Kroměříž, Czechoslovakia, at Syracuse University. DMA numbers with a single slash (e.g., 2/1521) refer to entries in the archive's published catalogs. Those with a double slash (e.g., 34//57) refer to reel numbers for items in the Archive that are not yet listed in the published catalogs.

MODERN EDITIONS: We have listed only those published in scholarly complete works and monuments or in performance editions for which some attempt is made to preserve the integrity of the original music and text. Choral octavos are not included, since they almost always reproduce pieces already available in scholarly editions and they frequently involve text translation or replacement (making identification difficult) and arrangement or reduction of performing forces.

CONCLUSION   It is the hope of the authors that the present bibliography will stimulate research into the development
of German polyphonic sacred music in this important but neglected period between the establishment
of the early baroque style and the late-baroque works of Bach and Handel. Many of these composers
deserve complete works projects, an honor accorded at present only to Böhm and Buxtehude. Many
aspects of performance practice raised by the information in the bibliography remain to be solved.
Certainly the manuscript and printed sources of this repertory hold some important clues regarding
number of singers assigned per part in baroque performances, a topic upon which scholars do not
currently agree. Designation of instruments is also frequently problematic and can only be solved
through musicological study. The authors are also painfully aware of the likelihood, perhaps even
inevitability, that more pieces remain to be discovered. With the recent political changes in eastern
Europe, it is quite likely that additional musical sources "lost" since the end of the second world war
will come to light. The authors would be most grateful to their readers for information concerning
works or composers not included in the bibliography.

DIANE PARR WALKER
PAUL WALKER

Charlottesville, Virginia
May 1992

Acknowledgments

We are grateful for the assistance of staff in all of the libraries cited who answered our inquiries by mail and in person over the course of the several years we have been at work on this project. We especially appreciate the assistance of Jürgen Kindermann and the staff of the Deutsches Musikgeschichtliches Archiv, who allowed us unlimited access to the microfilms in the archive in Kassel during the spring of 1983 and seemed undaunted by the number of rolls of film we sometimes asked them to retrieve and refile in a single day. The Deutscher akademischer Austauschdienst, the State University of New York at Buffalo, and the University of Virginia have provided funding and research leave at various times since 1982 to make the completion of the project possible. A number of colleagues have offered advice and assistance along the way, and to them all we express our thanks; in particular, we acknowledge Eva Linfield, Kerala Snyder, Angelika Schmiegelow Powell, and Heidi Synnatzschke-Cochran for their advice on the content of the entries and German translation. And, we thank Pat Dyjak, Christian Lehmbeck, Emily Powell, and Kristin Powell for their help in tracking down modern editions, indexing, and proofreading.

*T*he Liturgical Year

ENGLISH	GERMAN	LATIN
1st Sunday of Advent	1. Advent	Dominica I. Adventus
2nd Sunday of Advent	2. Advent	Dominica II. Adventus
3rd Sunday of Advent	3. Advent	Dominica III. Adventus
4th Sunday of Advent	4. Advent	Dominica IV. Adventus
Christmas Day	1. Weihnachtstag	In Nativitate Domini
2nd Day of Christmas	2. Weihnachtstag	S. Stephani Protomartyris
3rd Day of Christmas	3. Weihnachtstag	S. Joannis Apost. et Evang.
Sunday after Christmas	Sonntag nach Weihnachten	Dominica infra Oct. Nat. Dom.
Circumcision/New Year	Neujahr/Fest der Beschneidung Christi	In Circumcisione Domini
Sunday after Circumcision/Sunday after New Year	Sonntag nach Neujahr	Festum Sanctissimi Nomimis Jesu
Epiphany	Epiphanias	In Epiphania Domini
1st Sunday after Epiphany	1. Sonntag nach Epiphanias	Dominica infra Oct. Epiphaniae
2nd Sunday after Epiphany	2. Sonntag nach Epiphanias	Dominica II. post Epiphaniam
3rd Sunday after Epiphany	3. Sonntag nach Epiphanias	Dominica III. post Epiphaniam
4th Sunday after Epiphany	4. Sonntag nach Epiphanias	Dominica IV. post Epiphaniam
5th Sunday after Epiphany	5. Sonntag nach Epiphanias	Dominica V. post Epiphaniam
6th Sunday after Epiphany	6. Sonntag nach Epiphanias	Dominica VI. post Epiphaniam
Septaugesima	Septuagesimae	Dominica in Septuagesima
Sexagesima	Sexagesimae	Dominica in Sexagesima
Quinquagesima	Quinquagesimae/Esto mihi	Dominica in Quinquagesima
1st Sunday of Lent	Invocavit	Dominica I. in Quadragesima
2nd Sunday of Lent	Reminiscere	Dominica II. in Quadragesima
3rd Sunday of Lent	Oculi	Dominica III. in Quadragesima
4th Sunday of Lent	Laetare	Dominica IV. Quadragesima
5th Sunday of Lent	Judica	Dominica de Passione
Palm Sunday	Palmarum	Dominica in Palmis
Maundy Thursday	Grün Donnerstag	Feria V. in Coena Domini
Good Friday	Karfreitag	Feria VI. in Parasceve
Easter Sunday	1. Ostertag	Dominica Resurrectionis

ENGLISH	GERMAN	LATIN
Easter Monday	2. Ostertag	Feria II. post Pascha
Easter Tuesday	3. Ostertag	Feria III. post Pascha
1st Sunday after Easter	Quasimodogeniti	Dominica in Albis
2nd Sunday after Easter	Misericordias Domini	Dominica II. post Pascha
3rd Sunday after Easter	Jubilate	Dominica III. post Pascha
4th Sunday after Easter	Cantate	Dominica IV. post Pascha
5th Sunday after Easter	Rogate/Vocem jucunditatis	Dominica V. post Pascha
Ascension	Himmelfahrt	In Ascensione Domini
Sunday after Ascension	Exaudi	Dominica infra Octave Ascensionis
Pentecost	1. Pfingsttag/Pfingsten	Dominica Pentecosten
Whit Monday	2. Pfingsttag	Feria II. post Pentecosten
Trinity (1st Sunday after Pentecost)	Trinitatis	In Festo Ss. Trinitatis/Dominica I. post Pentecosten
Corpus Christi	Fronleichnam	In Festo Corporis Christi
1st Sunday after Trinity (2nd Sunday after Pentecost)	1. Sonntag nach Trinitatis	Dominica infra Oct. Corporis Christi
2nd Sunday after Trinity	2. Sonntag nach Trinitatis	Dominica infra Oct. Sacratissimi Cordis Jesu
3rd Sunday after Trinity	3. Sonntag nach Trinitatis	Dominica IV. post Pentecosten
etc.	etc.	etc.

General Abbreviations

A	alto (singer)
B	bass (singer)
bc	basso continuo (any keyboard instrument)
bsn	bassoon
clar	clarino
corn	cornetto
DMA	Deutsches Musikgeschichtliches Archiv, Kassel, Germany
fl	transverse flute
gamba	viola da gamba
inc	incomplete
instr	instrument(s)
MGG	*Die Musik in Geschichte und Gegenwart*
New Grove	*The New Grove Dictionary of Music and Musicians*
ob	oboe
piff	piffaro
prin	principale
RISM	*Répertoire international des sources musicales*
rec	recorder
S	soprano (singer)
T	tenor (singer)
taille	tenor range, instrument unspecified
tbn	trombone
tbtta	trombetta
timp	timpani
tpt	trumpet
vc	violoncello
vln	violin
vla	viola
vlne	violone
vltta	violetta

*M*odern Editions Cited

ABBREVIATIONS

Accademia musicale   *Accademia musicale*. Charles Sherman, general editor. Mainz: Universal Edition, 1969-.

Adler   *Musikalische Werke der Kaiser Ferdinand III, Leopold I, und Joseph I*. Ed. Guido Adler. Vienna: Artaria, 1893; reprint, Farnsborough, England: Gregg International, 1972.

Ameln and Kümmerling   *Spruchmotetten*. Ed. Konrad Ameln and Harald Kümmerling. *Chor-Archiv*. Kassel: Bärenreiter, 1972-.

Anthology of Music   *Anthology of Music*. Ed. K. G. Fellerer. Köln: Arno Folk Verlag, 1958-76.

Antiqua Chorbuch   *Antiqua Chorbuch*. Ed. Helmut Mönkmeyer. Mainz: B. Schott's Söhne, 1951-52.

Böhm *Vokalwerke*   Böhm, Georg. *Sämtliche Werke*. Ed. Johannes Wolgast and Gesa Wolgast. Vols. 3-4: *Vokalwerke*, ed. Harald Kümmerling. Wiesbaden: Breitkopf & Härtel, 1963.

Buxtehude *Werke*   Buxtehude, Dieterich. *Werke*. Vols. 1-8. Klecken, Hamburg: Ugrino Verlag, 1925-58; *Collected Works*. Vol. 9-, Kerala Snyder, general editor. New York: Broude Brothers, 1987-.

Das Chorblatt   *Das Chorblatt*. Neuhausen-Stuttgart: Hänssler-Verlag, series 6.

Chorwerk   *Das Chorwerk*. Wolfenbüttel, Berlin: Kallmeyer, 1929-.

Das Chorwerk alter Meister   *Das Chorwerk alter Meister*. Neuhausen-Stuttgart: Hänssler-Verlag, series 4.

ABBREVIATIONS

Danziger Kirchenmusik	*Danziger Kirchenmusik: Vokalwerke des 16. bis 18. Jahrhunderts.* Ed. Franz Kessler. Veröffentlichungen des Instituts für Kirchenmusik der Friedrich-Alexander-Universität Erlangen-Nürnberg, no. 1. Neuhausen-Stuttgart: Hänssler-Verlag, 1973.
DdT	*Denkmäler deutscher Tonkunst.* Leipzig: Breitkopf & Härtel, 1892-1931.
DEK	Fischer, Albert Friedrich Wilhelm. *Das deutsche evangelische Kirchenlied des siebzehnten Jahrhunderts.* Gütersloh: Bertelsmann, 1904-16.
DnM	*Denkmäler norddeutscher Musik.* Kassel: Bärenreiter, 1965-.
DT	*Denkmäler der Tonkunst.* Ed. Friedrich Chrysander. Bergdorf: Expedition der Denkmäler, 1869-71.
DTB	*Denkmäler der Tonkunst in Bayern.* Ser. 2 of *Denkmäler deutscher Tonkunst.* Braunschweig: Litolff, 1900-38; Wiesbaden: Breitkopf & Härtel, 1962-.
DTÖ	*Denkmäler der Tonkunst in Österreich.* Graz: Akademische Druck- und Verlagsanstalt, 1960-.
Düben-Sammlung	*Die Düben-Sammlung.* Ed. Bruno Grusnick. Neuhausen-Stuttgart: Hänssler-Verlag, series 22.
EdM	*Das Erbe deutscher Musik.* Kassel: Nagels Verlag; Wiesbaden: Breitkopf & Härtel, 1935-.
Federhofer	*Musik alter Meister: Beiträge zur Musik- und Kulturgeschichte Inner-österreiche.* Ed. Hellmut Federhofer. Graz: Akademische Druck- und Verlagsanstalt, 1954-.
Feininger	Benevoli, Orazio. *Opera omnia.* Ed. Laurence Feininger. Tridenti: Societas Universalis Sanctae Ceciliae, 1966-.
Geiringer	Geiringer, Karl. *Music of the Bach Family.* Cambridge: Harvard University Press, 1955.
Geistliche Konzert	*Das geistliche Konzert.* Neuhausen-Stuttgart: Hänssler Verlag, series 5.
Gottron	Gottron, Adam. *Dreihundert Jahre Mainzer Kirchenmusik.* Mainz: A. Gottron, 1943.

ABBREVIATIONS

	Handbuch der deutschen evangelischen Kirchenmusik. Göttingen: Vandenhöck & Ruprect, 193?.
Hirsch	*Veröffentlichungen der Musik-Bibliothek Paul Hirsch.* Berlin: Breslauer, 1922-.
Die Kantate	*Die Kantate.* Neuhausen-Stuttgart: Hänssler Verlag, series 10.
Lück	Lück, S., ed. *Sammlung ausgezeichneter Compositionen für die Kirche.* Trier: Leistenschneider, 1859; rev. Leipzig: Braun, 1885.
Meisterwerk alter Kirchenmusik	*Meisterwerk alter Kirchenmusik aus Sachsen und Thüringen.* Hameln: Oppenheimer, 192?-.
Die Motette	*Die Motette.* Neuhausen-Stuttgart: Hänssler Verlag, series 1.
Musica sacra (Bote & Bock)	*Musica sacra: Sammlung religiöser Gesänge älterer und neuester Zeit zum bestimmten Gebrauch für den Königlichen Berliner Domchor.* Berlin: Bote & Bock, 1842-96.
Musica sacra (Commer)	*See* Commer, above.
MWKF	*See* Adler, above.
Organum	*Organum: Ausgewählte älterer vokale und instrumentale Meisterwerke.* Ed. Max Seiffert, et al. 1. Reihe: *Geistliche Gesangmusik für Solo- oder Chorstimmen mit oder ohne Begleitung.* Leipzig: Kistner & Siegel, 1924-.
Organum (St. Louis)	*Organum.* St. Louis: Concordia.
Proske	Proske, Karl. *Musica divina.* Ratisbonae: F. Pustet, 1853-76; reprint, New York: Johnson Reprint, 1973.
RRMBE	*Recent Researches in the Music of the Baroque Era.* Robert L. Marshall, general editor. Madison: A-R Editions, 1964-.
SBuxA	*Stuttgarter Buxtehude-Ausgabe.* Ed. Günter Graulich. Neuhausen-Stuttgart: Hänssler Verlag, series 36.
Schering	*Musikgeschichte Leipzigs.* Ed. Arnold Schering and Rudolf Wustmann. Leipzig: Kistner & Siegel, 1926-41; reprint, Berlin: Merseburger, 1974.
Schütz	Schütz, Heinrich. *Sämmtliche Werke.* Ed. Philipp Spitta, et al. Leipzig: Breitkopf & Härtel, 1885-1927.

ABBREVIATIONS

SDM	*Samfundet til udgivelse af dansk musik.* Copenhagen: Society for the Publication of Danish Music, 1872.
SMd	*Schweizerische Musikdenkmäler.* Basel: Bärenreiter, 1955-.
	Stuttgarter Bach Ausgaben. Neuhausen-Stuttgart: Hänssler Verlag, series 30.
	Süddeutsche Kirchenmusik des Barock. Ed. Wolfgang Fürlinger. Altötting: Coppenrath, 1970-.
Winterfeld	Winterfeld, Carl Georg. *Der evangelische Kirchengesang und sein verhältniss zur Kunst der Tonsatzes.* Leipzig: Breitkopf & Härtel, 1843-47.
Zahn	Zahn, Johannes. *Die Melodien der deutschen evangelischen Kirchenlieder.* Gütersloh: C. Bertelsmann, 1889-93.

*L*iterature Cited

Albert, Hanns. *Leben und Werke des Componisten und Dirigenten Abraham Megerle (1607-1680).* Inaug. diss., Munich, 1927.

Anger, Erhard. "Christian Demelius." *Musik und Kirche* 29 (1959): 131-34.

Arkwright, G. E. P. *Catalogue of Music in the Library of Christ Church Oxford.* London: Oxford University Press, 1915.

Baab, Jerold C. "The Sacred Works of Kaspar Förster (1616-1673)." Ph.D. diss., University of North Carolina, 1970.

Barndt-Webb, Miriam. "Andreas Hofer: His Life and Music (1629-1684)." Ph.D. diss., University of Illinois, 1972.

Baselt, Bernd. "Der Rudolstädter Hofkapellmeister Philipp Heinrich Erlebach." Diss., University of Halle, 1963.

Becherini, Bianca. *I manoscritti e le stampe rare della Biblioteca del Conservatorio "Luigi Cherubini" di Firenze.* Firenze: Olschki, 1964.

Berend, Fritz. *Nicolaus Adam Strungk, 1640-1700: Sein Leben und seine Werke. Mit Beiträgen zur Geschichte der Musik und des Theaters in Celle, Hannover, and Leipzig.* Hannover: Homann, 1915.

Berg, A. "Katalog över samlingarna Barnekow, Engelhart, Hierta, Quillfelt, Svanberg, Wenster upprättad av. . . . " Unpublished ms., Lund, Universitetsbibliothek.

Bernsdorff-Englebrecht, Christiane. *Die Kasseler Hofkapelle im 17. Jahrhundert und ihr anonymen Musikhandschriften aus der Kasseler Landesbibliothek.* Musikwissenschaftliche Arbeiten von der Gesellschaft für Musikforschung, 14. Kassel: Bärenreiter, 1958.

Birke, Joachim. "Eine unbekannte anonyme Matthäuspassion aus der zweiten Hälfte des 17. Jahrhunderts." *Archiv für Musikwissenschaft* 15 (1958): 162-86.

Blessinger, Karl. "Studien zur Ulmer Musikgeschichte im 17. Jahrhundert insbesondere über Leben und Werk Sebastian Adam Scherers." Diss., Ulm, 1913.

Bohn, Emil. *Bibliographie der Musik-Druckwerke bis 1700, welch in der Stadtbibliothek der Bibliothek des Academischen Instituts für Kirchenmusik und der Königlichen und Universitätsbibliothek zu Breslau aufbewahrt werden.* Berlin: Kohn, 1883; reprint, Hildesheim: Olms, 1969.

_____. *Die musikalischen Handschriften des XVI. und XVII. Jahrhunderts in der Stadtbibliothek zu Breslau.* Breslau: Julius Hainauer, 1890.

Bolin, Norbert. *Sterben ist mein Gewinn (Phil. 1,21): ein Beitrag zur evanglischen Funeralkomposition der deutschen Sepulkralkultur des Barock, 1550-1750.* Kasseler Studien zur Sepulkralkultur, 5. Kassel: Arbeitsgemeinschaft Friedhof und Denkmal; Stiftung Zentralinstitut und Museum für Sepulkralkultur, 1989.

Braun, Werner. "Der Kantor Christoph Schultze (1606-1683) und die 'neue Musik' in Delitzsch." *Wissenschaftliche Zeitschrift der Martin-Luther-Universität Halle-Wittenberg*, Gesellschafts- wissenschaftlichsprachwissenschaftliche Reihe 10 (1961): 1187-1225.

_____. "Neznani Gallusov Autograf." *Muzikoloski Zbornik/Musicological Annual* 4 (1968): 50-56.

Brosche, Günter. "Die musikalischen Werke Kaiser Leopold I: Ein systematisch- thematisches Verzeichnis der erhaltenen Kompositionen." In *Beiträge zur Dokumentation: Franz Grasberger zum 60. Geburtstag*, ed. Günter Brosche. Tutzing: Schneider, 1975.

Buch, Hans Joachim. "Bestandaufnahme der Kompositionen Clemens Thieme." *Musikforschung* 16 (1963): 367-78.

Buchmayer, Richard. "Christian Ritter, ein vergessener deutscher Meister des 17. Jahrhunderts." In *Riemann-Festschrift.* Leipzig: Hesse, 1909.

Buchner, Hans. "Samuel Friedrich Capricornus (1629-1665), sein Leben und seine Werke." Diss., University of Munich, 1922.

Catalogo della Biblioteca del Liceo musicale di Bologna. Bologna: Ramagnoli dall' Acqua, 1890-1943.

Chafe, Eric Thomas. "The Church Music of Heinrich Biber." Ph.D. diss., University of Toronto, 1975. Printed as Studies in Musicology, 95. Ann Arbor: UMI Research Press, 1987.

Crum, Margaret. "Music from St. Thomas's, Leipzig, in the Music School Collection at Oxford." In *Festschrift Rudolf Elvers zum 60. Geburtstag.* Tutzing: Hans Schneider, 1985.

Davidsson, Ake. "Die Dübensammlung in der Musikforschung." In *Festschrift für Bruno Grusnick zum 80. Geburtstag*, ed. Rolf Saltzwedel and Klaus D. Koch. Neuhausen-Stuttgart: Hänssler, 1981.

Deutsches Musikgeschichtliches Archiv. *Katalog der Filmsammlung.* Kassel: Bärenreiter, 1955-.

Dürr, Alfred. "Eine Handschriftensammlung des 18. Jahrhunderts in Göttingen." *Archiv für Musikwissenschaft* 25/4 (1968): 309-16.

Écorcheville, Jules. *Catalogue du Fonds de Musique Ancienne de la Bibliothèque National.* Paris: Société Internationale de Musique, 1910.

Eggebrecht, Hans Heinrich. "Johann Pachelbel als Vokalkomponist." *Archiv für Musikwissenschaft* 2 (1954): 120-45.

Epstein, Peter. "Ein unbekanntes Passionsoratorium von Christian Flor (1667)." *Bach Jahrbuch* 27 (1930): 56-99.

Fellerer, Karl Gustav. "Verzeichnis der Kirchenmusikalischen Werke des Santinischen Sammlung." *Kirchenmusikalisches Jahrbuch* 26-33 (1931-38).

Fellowes, Edmund H. *The Catalogue of Manuscripts in the Library of St. Michael's College, Tenbury.* Paris: L'Oiseau-Lyre, 1934.

Fétis, François-Joseph. *Catalogue de la Bibliothèque de F. J. Fétis, Bibliothèque Royale de Belgique.* Paris: Didot, 1877; reprint, Bologna: Forni, 1969.

Forster, Karl. "Über das Leben und die kirchenmusikalischen Werke des Giuseppe Antonio Bernabei, 1649-1732." Diss., University of Munich, 1933.

Fuller-Maitland, John Alexander, and Arthur Henry Mann. *Catalogue of the Music in the Fitzwilliam Museum, Cambridge.* London: C. J. Clay & Sons, 1893.

Gagliardi, Ernst. *Katalog der Handschriften der Zentralbibliothek.* 2 vols. Zürich, 1951.

Geck, Martin. "Figuralmusik der Bachzeit in einem thüringischen Dorf." *Die Musikforschung* 18/3 (1965): 293-95.

Giebler, Albert C. "The Masses of Johann Caspar Kerll." Ph.D. diss., University of Michigan, 1956.

Gille, Gottfried. "Der Schützschüler David Pohle (1624-1695): Seine Bedeutung für die Musikgeschichte des 17. Jahrhunderts." Ph.D. diss., University of Halle, 1974.

_____. "Der Kantaten-Textdruck von David Elias Heidenreich, Halle 1665, in den Vertonungen David Pohles, Sebastian Knüpfers, Johann Schelles und Anderen." *Die Musikforschung* 38/2 (1985): 81-94.

Gmeinweiser, Siegfried. *Die Musikhandschriften in der Theatinerkirche St. Kajetan in München: Thematischer Katalog.* Kataloge bayerischer Musiksammlungen, 4. München: Henle, 1979.

Gottron, Adam. "Philipp Friedrich Buchner: Kurfürstlich Mainzischer und fürstlich Würzburgischer Hofkapellmeister, 1614-1669." *Würzburger Diözesangeschichtsblätter* 7 (1939): 69-87.

Gottwald, Clytus. *Codices Musici.* Die Handschriften der Würtembergischen Landesbibliothek Stuttgart, ser. 1, vol. 1. Wiesbaden: Harrassowitz, 1964.

_____. *Die Musikhandschriften.* Handschriften des Germanischen Nationalmuseums Nürnberg, 4. Wiesbaden: Harrassowitz, 1988.

_____. *Die Musikhandschriften der Universitätsbibliothek München.* Die Handschriften der Universitätsbibliothek München, 2. Wiesbaden: Harrassowitz, 1968.

_____. *Die Musikhandschriften der Staats- und Stadtbibliothek Augsburg.* Handschriftenkataloge der Staats- und Stadtbibliothek Augsburg, 1. Wiesbaden: Harrassowitz, 1974.

Gross, Eric. "Music Manuscripts in the Library of St. Bonifaz, Munich: A Preliminary Catalogue." *Miscellanea Musicologica* 8 (1975): 82-114.

_____. "Musik alter Meister in deutschem Kloster entdeckt." *DAAD Letter* 3 (1984): 10-11.

Grusnick, Bruno. "Die Dübensammlung." *Svensk tidskrift för musikforskning* 46 (1964): 27-82; 48 (1966): 63-186.

Günther, Otto. "Musikgeschichtliches aus Danzigs Vergangenheit." *Mitteilungen des Westpreussischen Geschichtsverein* 10 (1911).

_____. *Katalog der Handschriften der Danziger Stadtbibliothek.* Katalog der Danziger Stadtbibliothek, 1-4. Danzig: Stadtbibliothek, 1892-1911.

Haberkamp, Gertraut. *Die Musikhandschriften der Benediktiner-Abtei Ottobeuren.* Kataloge Bayerischer Musiksammlungen, 12. München: Henle, 1986.

Hamel, Fred. *Die Psalmkompositionen Johann Rosenmüllers.* Baden-Baden: Koerner, 1973.

Hartmann, Karl-Günther. "Musikgeschichtliches aus der ehemaligen Danziger Stadtbibliothek." *Die Musikforschung* 27/4 (1974): 387-412.

Hehr, Elizabeth. "An Anonymous Motet Manuscript in Brossard's Library, Partially Identified." *Music Review* 47/2 (May 1986-87): 77-88.

Hintermaier, Ernst. "Missa Salisburgensis: Neue Erkenntnisse über Entstehung, Autor, und Zweckbestimmung." *Musicologica Austraica* 1 (1977): 154ff.

Hirschmann, Karl Friedrich. *Wolfgang Carl Briegel, 1626-1712.* Giessen: Kindt, 1934.

Hochstein, Wolfgang. "Liturgische Kirchenkompositionen in Handschriften der Staats- und Universitätsbibliothek Hamburg." *Kirchenmusikalisches Jahrbuch* 70 (1986): 51-110.

Hortschansky, Klaus. *Katalog der Kieler Musiksammlungen: Die Notendrucke, Handschriften, Libretti, und Bücher über Musik aus der Zeit bis 1830.* Kieler Schriften zur Musikwissenschaft, 14. Kassel: Bärenreiter, 1963.

Hughes-Hughes, Augustus. *Catalogue of Manuscript Music in the British Museum.* Vol. 1: Sacred Vocal Music. London: British Museum, 1906.

Husk, William Henry. *Catalogue of the Library of the Sacred Harmonic Society.* London: Sacred Harmonic Society, 1872.

Ilgner, Gerhard. *Matthias Weckmann, ca. 1619-1674: Sein Leben und seine Werke.* Kieler Beiträge zur Musikwissenschaft, 6. Wolfenbüttel: Kallmeyer, 1939.

Israel, Karl. *Übersichtlicher Katalog der Musikalien der ständischen Landesbibliothek zu Kassel.* Zeitschrift des Vereins für hessische Geschichte und Landeskunde, Neue Folge 7, supplement. Kassel: Freyschmidt, 1881.

Jacobs, Edward. "Der Organist Joachim Mager in Wernigerode (1607 bis 1678): ein Beitrag zur Geschichte der Musik seiner Zeit, besonders der Orgel." *Vierteljahrschrift für Musikwissenschaft* 10 (1894): 146-202.

Jaksch, Werner. *H. I. F. Biber. Requiem à 15: Untersuchungen zur höfischen, liturgischen und musikalischen Topik einer barocken Totenmesse.* Beiträge zur Musikforschung, 5. Ed. Reinhold Hammerstein und Wilhelm Seidel. München: Emil Katzbichler, 1977.

_____. "Missa Salisburgensis: Neu-zuschreibung der Salzburger Domweihmesse von O. Benevoli." *Archiv für Musikwissenschaft* 35/4 (1978): 239-50. Nachtrag, *Archiv für Musikwissenschaft* 36/4 (1979): 305.

Johnson, John Preston. "An Analysis and Edition of Selected Sacred Choral Works of Johann Rudolf Ahle." D.M.A. thesis, Southern Baptist Theological Seminary, 1969.

Jones, Peter Ward. "The Fate of the Music Collections of St. Michael's College, Tenbury." *Brio* 27/2 (Autumn/Winter 1990): 48-49.

Jung, Hans Rudolf. "Johann Georg Conradi." *Beiträge zur Musikwissenschaft* 13 (1971): 31-55; 14 (1972): 1-62.

Kade, Otto. *Die älteren Musikalien der Stadt Freiberg in Sachsen.* Beilage zu den Monatsheften für Musikgeschichte. *Monatshefte für Musikgeschichte* 21 (1888).

Kaiser, Fritz. "Zur Geschichte der Darmstädter Musiksammlung." *Durch der Jahrhunderts Strom. Beiträge zur Geschichte der Hessischen Landes und Hochschulbibliothek Darmstadt*, 108-40. Frankfurt am Main: Klostermann, 1967.

Karstädt, Georg. *Thematisch-Systematisches Verzeichnis der Musikalischen Werke von Dietrich Buxtehude.* Wiesbaden: Breitkopf & Härtel, 1974; 2nd ed., 1985.

Kast, Paul. *Die Bach-Handschriften der Berliner Staatsbibliothek.* Tübinger Bach-Studien 2/3. Trossingen: Hohner, 1958.

Katalog der Königliche Regierungs-Bibliothek. Ansbach: Breigel, 1913.

Katzbichler, Emil. "Über das Leben und die weltliche Vokalwerke des Ercole Bernabei." Diss., University of Munich, 1963.

Kellner, Altman. *Musikgeschichte des Stiftes Kremsmünster.* Kassel: Bärenreiter, 1956.

Killing, Joseph. *Kirchenmusikalische Schätze der Bibliothek des Abbate Fortunato Santini.* Düsseldorf: Schwann, 1910.

Krummacher, Friedhelm. "Kantate und Konzert im Werk Johann Pachelbels." *Die Musikforschung* 20 (1967): 365-92.

_____. "Motetten und Kantaten der Bachzeit in Udestedt." *Die Musikforschung* 19 (1966): 402-08.

_____. "Die Tradition in Bachs vokalen Choralbearbeitungen." In *Bach-Interpretationen*, ed. Martin Geck. Göttingen: Vandenhoeck & Ruprecht, 1969.

_____. *Die Überlieferung der Choralbearbeitungen in der Frühen Evangelischen Kantate.* Berliner Studien zur Musikwissenschaft, 10. Berlin: Merseburger, 1965.

_____. "Zur Quellenlage von Matthias Weckmanns geistlichen Vokalwerken." In *Gemeinde Gottes in dieser Welt: Festgabe für Friedrich-Wilhelm Krummacher zum sechzigsten Geburtstag.* Berlin: Evangelische-Verlagsanstalt, 1961.

_____. "Zur Sammlung Jacobi der ehemaligen Fürstenschule Grimma." *Musikforschung* 16 (1963): 324-47.

Krummel, D. W. *Bibliographical Inventory to the Early Music in the Newberry Library.* Boston: G. K. Hall, 1977.

Kümmerling, Harald. *Katalog der Sammlung Bokemeyer.* Kieler Schriften zur Musikwissenschaft, 18. Kassel: Bärenreiter, 1970.

Landmann, Ortrun. "Das Werk Sebastian Knüpfers in Überblick." Diss., Karl-Marx-Universität, Leipzig, 1960.

Lehn, Edgar vom. "The Sacred Cantatas of Philipp Heinrich Erlebach (1657-1714)." Ph.D. diss., University of North Carolina, 1958.

Lindberg, Folke. "Katalog över Dübensamlingen i Uppsala Universitets Bibliothek: Vokalmusik i hansckrift, med en inledning." Unpublished ms., Uppsala Universitetsbibliothek, 1947.

Lobstein, Johann Franz. *Beiträge zur Geschichte der Musik im Elsaß und besonders in Straßburg.* Straßburg: Dannbach, 1840.

Mackey, Elizabeth J. "The Sacred Music of Johann Theile." Ph.D. diss., University of Michigan, 1968.

Mantuani, Joseph, ed. *Tabulae codicum manuscriptorum praeter graecas et orientales in Bibliotheca Palatina Vindobonensi Asservatorum*, vols. 9-10. Vienna: Geroldi, 1897-99.

Maier, Julius J. *Die Musikalischen Handschriften der K. Hof- und Staatsbibliothek in München.* 1. Teil: *Die Handschriften bis zum Ende des XVII. Jahrhunderts.* München: Palmischen Hofbuchhandlung, 1879.

Marx, Hans Joachim. "Johann Mattheson's Bequest." *Early Music* 10/3 (July 1982): 365-67.

_____. "Johann Matthesons Nachlass: Zum Schicksal der Musiksammlung der alten Stadtbibliothek Hamburg." *Acta musicologica* 55/1 (January-June 1983): 108-24.

Masseangeli, Masseangelo. *Catalogo della collezione d'autografi lasciata alla R. Accademia Filarmonica de Bologna.* Bologna: Regia tipgrafia, 1881; reprint, Bologna: Forni, 1969.

Meier, Gabriel. *Catalogus codicum manu scriptorum qui in bibliotheca monasterii Einsidlensis O.S.B. servantur.* Einsiedeln: Sumptibus Monasterii, 1899-.

Melamed, Daniel R. "The Authorship of the Motet *Ich lasse dich nicht*, (BWV Anh. 159)." *Journal of the American Musicological Society* 41/3 (Fall 1988): 491-526.

Mitjana, Rafael, and Ake Davidsson. *Catalogue critique et descriptif des imprimés de musique des XVIe et XVIIe siècles conservés à la Bibliothèque de l'Université Royale d'Upsala.* 3 vols. Uppsala: Almquist & Wiksell, 1911-51.

Morris, Mary Smith. "Four Chorale Cantatas by Johann Schelle: A Modern Edition." M.A. thesis, University of Tennessee, 1971.

Mueller, Harold. "The *Musicalische Gespräche über die Evangelia* of Andreas Hammerschmidt." Ph.D. diss., University of Rochester, 1956.

Müller-Blattau, Joseph Maria. *Georg Friedrich Händel.* Potsdam: Akademische Verlagsgesellschaft Athenaion, 1933.

Murray, Robert A. "The German Church Cantatas of Johann Schelle (1648-1701)." Ph.D. diss., University of Michigan, 1971.

Die Musik in Geschichte und Gegenwart. Kassel: Bärenreiter, 1949-86.

Nausch, Annemarie. *Augustin Pfleger: Leben und Werke, ein Beitrag zur Entwicklungsgeschichte der Kantate in 17. Jahrhundert.* Schriften des Landesinstituts für Musikforschung, Kiel, 14. Kassel: Bärenreiter, 1954.

The New Grove Dictionary of Music and Musicians. Ed. Stanley Sadie. London: Macmillan; New York: Grove's Dictionaries of Music, 1980.

Niemöller, Ursel. *Carl Rosier (1640?-1725), Kölner Dom- und Ratskapellmeister.* Beiträge zur Rheinischen Musikgeschichte, 23. Köln: Arno Volk-Verlag, 1957.

Noack, Elisabeth. "Die Bibliothek der Michaeliskirche zu Erfurt." *Archiv für Musikwissenschaft* 7 (1925): 65-116.

_____. "Georg Christoph Strattner (c. 1645-1704): Ein Beitrag zur Entwicklung der süddeutschen Barockmusik." *Archiv für Musikwissenschaft* 3 (1921): 447-83.

_____. *Wolfgang Carl Briegel: Ein Barockkomponist in seiner Zeit.* Berlin: Merseburger, 1963.

Noack, Friedrich. "W. C. Briegel." *Die Kirchenmusik*, 21 (1920-21).

Osthoff, Helmuth. *Adam Krieger (1634-1666): Neue Beiträge zur Geschichte des deutschen Liedes im 17. Jahrhundert.* Leipzig: Breitkopf & Härtel, 1929, 1970.

Otto, Craig A. "A Checklist of Johann Heinrich Schmelzer's Musical Compositions." Typescript, Philadelphia, 1981.

_____. *Seventeenth-Century Music from Kroměříž, Czechoslovakia: A Catalog of the Liechtenstein Music Collection on Microfilm at Syracuse University.* Syracuse: Syracuse University Library, 1977.

Paulke, Karl. "Die Handschriften und alten Drucke im Archiv von St. Nicolai." In "Musikpflege in Luckau," *Niederlausitzer Mitteilungen* 14 (1918): 129-50.

Rackwitz, Werner, and Helmut Steffens. *Georg Friedrich Händel: Persönlichkeit, Umwelt, Vermächtnis.* Leipzig: Deutscher Verlag für Musik, 1962.

Reich, Wolfgang. *Threnodiae sacrae: Katalog der gedruckten Kompositionen des 16.- 18. Jahrhunderts in Leichenpredigtsammlungen innerhalb der Deutschen Demokratischen Republik.* Veröffentlichungen der Sächsischen Landesbibliothek, 7. Dresden: Sächsische Landesbibliothek, 1966.

Répertoire international des sources musicales. Published by the International Musicological Society and the International Association of Music Libraries. Kassel: Bärenreiter, 1971-.

Riedel, Friedrich W. *Das Musikarchiv im Minoritenkonvent zu Wien: Katalog des älteren Bestandes vor 1784.* Catalogus musicus, 1. Kassel: IAML/IMS, 1963.

_____, ed. *Der Göttweiger thematische Katalog von 1830.* 2 vols. Salzburg: Katzbichler, 1979.

Roth, F. W. E. "Musik-Handschriften der Darmstädter Hofbibliothek." *Monatsheften für Musikgeschichte* 20 (1888): 64-73, 82-93.

Rouland, Carl. *Katalog des Musik-Archives der St. Peters Kirche in Wien.* Augsburg, 1908.

Sametz, Steven Paul. "'Jubilus Bernhardi' of Samuel Capricornus (Bockshorn): A Performing Edition of 10 Sections with Commentary and Critical Notes." D.M.A. thesis, University of Wisconsin-Madison, 1980.

Samuel, Harold E. *The Cantata in Nuremberg during the Seventeenth Century.* Studies in Musicology, 56. Ann Arbor: UMI Research Press, 1982.

Santini, Fortunato. *Catalogo della musica esistente presso Fortunato Santini in Roma.* Rome, 1820.

Sartori, Claudio. *Catalogo del fonds musicale nella biblioteca comunale di Assis.* Milan: Istituto Editoriale Italiano, 1962.

Schaal, Richard. *Quellen zu Johann Kaspar Kerll.* Österreichische Akademie der Wissenschaften Mitteilungen der Kommission für Musikforschung, 13. Vienna: Holzhausen, 1962.

Schanzlin, Hans Peter. "Johann Melchior Gletles Kirchenmusik." Introduction to *Schweizerische Musikdenkmäler*, vol. 2. Kassel: Bärenreiter, 1959.

Schempf, William H. "Polychoral Magnificats from H. Praetorius to H. Schütz." Ph.D. diss., University of Rochester, 1960.

Schletterer, Hans Michael. "Katalog in der Kreis- und Stadt Bibliothek, dem Städtischen Archiv und der Bibliothek des Historischen Vereins zu Augsburg befindlichen Musikwerke." Beilage zu den *Monatsheften für Musikgeschichte* 10 (1878).

Schlichte, Joachim. *Thematischer Katalog der kirchlichen Musikhandschriften des 17. und 18. Jahrhunderts in der Stadt- und Universitätsbibliothek Frankfurt am Main (Signaturengruppe Ms. Ff. Mus).* Kataloge der Stadt- und Universitätsbibliothek Frankfurt am Main, 8. Frankfurt am Main: Klostermann, 1979.

Schmieder, Wolfgang. *Musik alte Drucke bis etwa 1750.* Kataloge der Herzog-August-Bibliothek, Wolfenbüttel, Neue Reihe, Bd. 12. Frankfurt: Vittorio Klostermann, 1967.

Schneider, Max. "Thematisches Verzeichnis den musikalischer Werke der Familie Bach." *Bach Jahrbuch* 4 (1907): 103-77.

Schnitzler, Rudolf. "The Sacred-Dramatic Music of Antonio Draghi." Ph.D. diss., University of North Carolina, 1971.

Seiffert, Max. "Die Chorbibliothek der St. Michaeliskirche zu Lüneburg zu Seb. Bach's Zeit." *Sammelbände der Internationalen Musikgesellschaft* 9 (1907-08): 593-621.

Serauky, Walter. *Musikgeschichte der Stadt Halle.* Beiträge zur Musikforschung, Bd. 1, 6-9. Halle: Buchhandlung des Waisenhauses, 1935-43; reprint, Hildesheim, New York: Olms, 1971.

Sevier, Zay V. David. "The Theoretical Works and Music of Johann Georg Ahle (1651-1706)." Ph.D. diss., University of North Carolina, 1974.

Snyder, Kerala Johnson. *Dieterich Buxtehude: Organist in Lübeck.* New York: Schirmer, 1987.

_____. "Johann Rosenmüller's Music for Solo Voice." Ph.D. diss., Yale University, 1970.

Squire, William Barclay. *Catalogue of Printed Music in the Library of the Royal College of Music, London.* London: Royal College of Music, 1909.

_____. *Catalogue of the King's Music Library.* London: British Museum, 1927-29.

Steude, Wolfram. "Die Markuspassion in der Leipziger Passionen-Handschrift des Johann Zacharias Grundig." *Deutsches Jahrbuch für Musikwissenschaft* 14 (1969): 96-116.

_____. *Die Musiksammelhandschriften des 16. und 17. Jahrhunderts in der Sächsischen Landesbibliothek zu Dresden.* Quellenkataloge zur Musikgeschichte, 6. Wilhelmshaven: Heinrichshofer, 1974.

Streetman, Richard David. "Christoph Bernard." Ph.D. diss., North Texas State University, 1967.

Süss, Karl, and Peter Epstein. *Thematischer Katalog der Kirchlichen Musikhandschriften des 17. und 18. Jahrhunderts in der Stadt und Universitätsbibliothek Frankfurt am Main.* Ed. Joachim Schlichte. Kataloge der Stadt und Universitätsbibliothek Frankfurt am Main, 8. Berlin and Frankfurt: Klostermann, 1979.

Thomas, Günther. *Friedrich Wilhelm Zachow.* Kölner Beiträge zur Musikforschung, 38. Ed. Karl Gustav Fellerer. Regensburg: Gustav Bosse, 1966.

Vogel, Emil. *Die Handschriften nebst den älteren Druckwerken der Musik-Abteilung.* Kataloge der Herzog-August-Bibliothek, Wolfenbüttel, 8. Wolfenbüttel: J. Zwissler, 1890.

Vollhardt, Reinhard. *Bibliographie der Musikwerke in der Ratsschulbibliothek zu Zwickau.* Beilage zu den Monatshefte für Musikgeschichte, 15-16. Leipzig: Breitkopf & Härtel, 1893-96.

Walter, Georg. *Katalog der gedruckten und handschriftlichen Musikalien des 17. bis 19. Jahrhunderts im Besitze der Allgemeinen Musikgesellschaft Zürich.* Zürich: Hug, 1960.

Walter, Horst. *Musikgeschichte der Stadt Lüneburg vom Ende des 16. bis zum Anfang des 18. Jahrhunderts.* Tutzing: Schneider, 1967.

Walther, Alexander Ferdinand. *Die Musikalien der grossherzoglichen Hofbibliothek.* Darmstadt: Wittich, 1874.

Webhofer, Peter. "Giovanni Felice Sances, ca. 1600-1679: Biographisch-bibliographische Untersuchung und Studie über sein Motettenwerk." Diss., Pontificio Istituto di Musica Sacra, Rome, 1964.

Weckerlin, Jean-Baptiste. *Bibliothèque du Conservatoire National de musique et de déclamation: Catalogue Bibliographique.* Paris: Didot, 1885.

Welter, Friedrich. *Katalog der Musikalien der Ratsbücherei Lüneburg.* Lippstadt: Kistner & Siegel, 1950.

Werner, Arno. "Die alte Musikbibliothek und die Instrumentensammlung an St.Wenzel in Naumburg a. d. S." *Archiv für Musikwissenschaft* 8 (1926): 390-415.

Wessely-Kropik, Helen. "Romanus Weichlein." In *Bericht über den Internationalen Musikwissenschaftliche Kongress Wien. Mozartjahr 1956,* ed. Erich Schenk. Graz-Köln: Böhlaus, 1958.

Wetherwax, Todd. "'Herr, Wenn ich nur dich habe' by Matthias Weckmann: Edition and Commentary." M.A. thesis, University of Wisconsin, Madison, 1978.

Wettstein, Hermann. *Dietrich Buxtehude (1637-1707): Eine Bibliographie. Mit einem Anhang über Nicolaus Bruhns.* Schriften der Universitätsbibliothek, Freiburg im Breisgau, 2. Freiburg im Breisgau: Universitätsbibliothek, 1979; 2nd ed., rev. and enl., München: Saur, 1989.

Wollny, Peter. "A Collection of 17th-Century German Vocal Music at the Bodleian Library." Paper presented at the meeting of the American Heinrich Schütz Society, Eastman School of Music, Rochester, N.Y., May 1991.

_____. Letter to the authors, 3 June 1991.

Woodward, Henry. "A Study of the Tenbury Manuscripts of Johann Pachelbel." Ph.D. diss., Harvard University, 1952.

Wotquenne, Alfred. *Catalogue de la Bibliothèque du Conservatoire Royal de Musique de Bruxelles.* Brussels: Coosemans, 1898; reprint, Brussels: Editions Culture et Civilisation, 1980.

Zelle, Friedrich. *Joh. Phil. Fötsch.* Dritter Beitrag zur Geschichte der ältesten deutschen Oper. Wissenschaftliche Beilage zum Jahresvericht der Vierten Städtischen Realschule zu Berlin, Ostern 1893. Berlin: R. Gaertner, 1893.

Ziller, Ernst. *Der Erfurter Organist Johann Heinrich Buttstädt (1667-1727).* Beiträge zur Musikforschung, 3. Halle/Saale, Berlin: Waisenhaus, 1935.

German Sacred Polyphonic Vocal Music Between Schütz and Bach

SOURCES AND CRITICAL EDITIONS

A

ANONYMOUS. *See* pp. 20-29

ABERSBACH, Johann Georg

    A0001   **Hymnodia de Sancto Josepho**
          SATB, 2 vln, 3 vla, 3 tpt, bc
          CS-KRa II, 308 (1674)
          parts
          microfilm: US-SY

    A0002   **Ubiqunque fuerit corpus**
          SSATB, 2 vln, 3 tpt, 2 clar, bc
          CS-KRa II, 212 (1673)
          parts
          microfilm: US-SY

AGRICOLA, Georg Ludwig (1643-1676)

    A0003   **Ach siehe da, mein Zeuge ist im Himmel**
          S solo, SATB, 2 vln, 2 vla, vlne, bc
          D-B Mus. ms. 371 (Erfurt)
          score & parts

    A0004   **Der Herr erhöre dich in der Not**
          ATB, 2 vln, bsn, bc
          D-G0l

    A0005   **Gott, man lobet dich in der Stille**
          SATB, corn, 2 vln, 2 clar, 3 tbn, bc
          D-B Mus. ms. 365 (Erfurt) (1682)
          parts

    A0006   **Ich will schweigen und meinen Mund nicht auftun**
          SATB, 4 gamba, bc
          S-Uu 82:1 (Düben)
          tablature
          DMA 1/1942

    A0007   **Was ist der Mensch, daß du sein gedenkest**
          SSTB, 2 vln, 2 vla, vlne, bc
          D-B Mus. ms. 370
          parts

AGRICOLA, Johann Paul (1638/39-1697)

    A0008   **Miserere mei Deus**
          SATB, 2 vln, vla, vc, bc
          D-Bds Mus. ms. 30094, no. 30 (Bokemeyer)
          score

AGRICOLA, M. J.

    A0009   **Weine nicht**
          SSATB, 5 vla, 2 clar, timp, bc
          D-B Mus. ms. 375 (Erfurt)
          score & parts (parts incomplete)

AGRICOLA, Wolfgang Christoph (1600/10-1659)

COLLECTIONS

        Fasciculus musicales octo missarum (1647)
          RISM A442 (parts)
          DMA 3/1

        Fasciculus musicales variorum cantionum (1648)
          PL-Kj Mus. ant. pract. A110
          (not in RISM) (parts)

        Geistliches Waldvöglein I (1664)
          RISM A443 (choirbook)
          DMA 2/1482

AGRICOLA, Wolfgang Christoph (*continued*)

Geistliches Waldvöglein II (1664)
RISM A444 (choirbook)
DMA 2/1482

Geistliches Waldvöglein III (1664)
RISM A445 (choirbook)
DMA 2/1482

WORKS

A0010 **Aber du, du Teufels Brate**
SATB
Geistliches Waldvöglein I, no. 11/2

A0011 **Accipite spiritum**
SSAATT, bc
Fasciculus musicalis variorum cantionum,
no. 24

A0012 **Ach sieh auf mein frommer Christ**
SATB
Geistliches Waldvöglein III, no. 4

A0013 **Ach Gott im Himmel**
SATB
Geistliches Waldvöglein II, no. 17

A0014 **Ach Jesu liebster Heiland mein**
SATB
Geistliches Waldvöglein II, no. 19

A0015 **Ach könnt ich mein Herz verändern gar**
SATB
Geistliches Waldvöglein II, no. 14

A0016 **Ach mein Gott was für Spott mußt du leiden**
SATB
Geistliches Waldvöglein II, no. 10

A0017 **Ach tu dich auf o Wolke**
SATB
Advent
Geistliches Waldvöglein I, no. 1

A0018 **Anima Christi**
SATB, bc
Fasciculus musicalis variorum cantionum,
no. 22

A0019 **Benedic, anima**
SSAATB, bc
Fasciculus musicalis variorum cantionum,
no. 25

A0020 **Benedicam Dominum**
SATB, SATB, bc
Fasciculus musicalis variorum cantionum,
no. 34

A0021 **Bin ich gefallen in schwere Not**
SATB
Geistliches Waldvöglein I, no. 44/15

A0022 **Das liebe Kindlein acht Tage kaum alt**
SATB
Geistliches Waldvöglein I, no. 44/3

A0023 **Der du sieben Wort gesprochen**
SATB
Geistliches Waldvöglein II, no. 22

A0024 **Die Honig fliessen Berg und Tal**
SATB
Christmas Day
Geistliches Waldvöglein I, no. 6

A0025 **Diligam te Domine**
SATB, SATB, bc
Fasciculus musicalis variorum cantionum,
no. 33

A0026 **Domine Dominus noster**
SATB, bc
Fasciculus musicalis variorum cantionum,
no. 23

A0027 **Domine quid multiplicati**
SATB, SATB, bc
Fasciculus musicalis variorum cantionum,
no. 39

A0028 **Drei König aus Morgenland**
SATB
Epiphany
Geistliches Waldvöglein I, no. 26/2

A0029 **Drei Weisen unbekannte**
SATB
Epiphany
Geistliches Waldvöglein I, no. 14

A0030 **Ehrend ist in allen Landen**
SATB
Easter Sunday
Geistliches Waldvöglein III, no. 11

A0031 **Erbarmt euch mein**
SATB
Geistliches Waldvöglein I, no. 38

A0032 **Es ist nunmehr die Stund und Zeit**
SATB
Advent
Geistliches Waldvöglein I, no. 3/1

A0033 **Fahr hin, o schnöde Welt**
SATB
Geistliches Waldvöglein I, no. 44/9

A0034 **Fahr in die Höhe**
SATB
Assumption of the Virgin Mary
Geistliches Waldvöglein III, no. 14

A0035 **Fracto demum Sacramento**
SATB, SATB, bc
Fasciculus musicalis variorum cantionum,
no. 36

A0036 **Freu dich, mein Seel, nun in Ewigkeit**
SATB
Geistliches Waldvöglein I, no. 37

A0037 **Freu dich von Herzen, o Sünder mein**
SATB
Geistliches Waldvöglein I, no. 44/4

A0038 **Gegrüsset seist du, reine Jungfrau**
SATB
Annunciation
Geistliches Waldvöglein I, no. 44/2

A0039 **Gott, der du dein Kreuz getragen hast**
SATB
Geistliches Waldvöglein II, no. 13

A0040 **Gott im Himmel sei es geklaget**
SATB
Geistliches Waldvöglein II, no. 6

A0041 **Gott in der Höhe**
SATB
Christmas Day
Geistliches Waldvöglein I, no. 4

A0042 **Herr, bist du ganz entblößt**
SATB
Geistliches Waldvöglein II, no. 7

A0043 **Herr Jesu Christe, Gottes Sohn**
SATB
Lent
Geistliches Waldvöglein III, no. 10

A0044 **Himmlischer Vater mein**
SATB
Geistliches Waldvöglein II, no. 23

A0045 **Hostia mystica, Jesu Christe**
SATB
Geistliches Waldvöglein I, no. 23/1

A0046 **Ich hör ein Glöcklein in weitem Feld**
SATB
Geistliches Waldvöglein I, no. 44/1

A0047 **Isti sunt triumphatores**
SATB, SATB, bc
Fasciculus musicalis variorum cantionum,
no. 35

A0048 **Jesu Christe, Gott der Ehren**
SATB
Geistliches Waldvöglein II, no. 4

A0049 **Jesu Christe, Gott der Ehren**
SATB
Lent
Geistliches Waldvöglein III, no. 8

A0050 **Jesu, du höchstes Gott**
SATB
Assumption of the Virgin Mary
Geistliches Waldvöglein I, no. 34/2

A0051 **Jesu Maria, gaudium**
SATB
Geistliches Waldvöglein I, no. 29

A0052 **Jesulein, du bist mein Heiland worden**
SATB
Christmas Day
Geistliches Waldvöglein I, no. 23/2

A0053 **Jesus, Mariae Seelen Freud**
SATB
Geitsliches Waldvöglein I, no. 30/1

A0054 **Jesus, mein Lieb und auch mein Herz**
SATB
Geistliches Waldvöglein II, no. 18

A0055 **Jesus, o süßer Name**
SATB
Christmas, New Year
Geistliches Waldvöglein I, no. 44/7

A0056 **Kein wer ist doch zu finden**
SATB
Geistliches Waldvöglein I, no. 15/2

A0057 **Komm Heiliger Geist**
SATB
Pentecost
Geistliches Waldvöglein III, no. 13

A0058 **Komm her nun, o Sünder mein**
SATB
Christmas Day
Geistliches Waldvöglein III, no. 3

A0059 **Komm nun her, mein liebe Seele**
SATB
Geistliches Waldvöglein I, no. 11/1

A0060 **Kommt her ihr Christen insgemein**
SATB
Geistliches Waldvöglein III, no. 16

A0061 **Maria mater gratiae**
SATB, SATB, bc
Fasciculus musicalis variorum cantionum,
no. 32

AGRICOLA, Wolfgang Christoph (*continued*)

A0062   **Maria tut aufwachen**
SATB
Visitation of the Virgin Mary
Geistliches Waldvöglein III, no. 2

A0063   **Mein Gott und Herr**
SATB
Feast of the Conception
Geistliches Waldvöglein I, no. 3/2

A0064   **Mein Seel ist traurig**
SATB
Geistliches Waldvöglein I, no. 33

A0065   **Michael Archangele**
SATB, SATB, bc
Fasciculus musicalis variorum cantionum,
no. 38

A0066   **Missa super Ave Maria**
SATB, SATB
Fasciculus musicalis octo missarum, no. 6

A0067   **Missa super Factum est silentium**
SATB, SATB
Fasciculus musicalis octo missarum, no. 8

A0068   **Missa super Hodie Beata Virgo**
SATB, SATB
Fasciculus musicalis octo missarum, no. 7

A0069   **Missa super Magnificat**
SATB, SATB
Fasciculus musicalis octo missarum, no. 2

A0070   **Missa super Nativitatis**
SATB, SATB
Fasciculus musicalis octo missarum, no. 3

A0071   **Missa super O quam admirabile**
SATB, SATB
Fasciculus musicalis octo missarum, no. 4

A0072   **Missa super Petite**
SATB, SATB
Fasciculus musicalis octo missarum, no. 5

A0073   **Missa super Veni sponsa pfendneri omnes**
SATB, SATB
Fasciculus musicalis octo missarum, no. 1

A0074   **Missus est angelus**
SATB, SATB, bc
Fasciculus musicalis variorum cantionum,
no. 37

A0075   **Mutter mein**
SATB
Geistliches Waldvöglein II, no. 12

A0076   **Nimm hin deine Thron, o Mutter mein**
SATB
Geistliches Waldvöglein III, no. 15

A0077   **Nun mehr ist die Zeit vorhanden**
SATB
Ascension of Christ
Geistliches Waldvöglein III, no. 12

A0078   **O aeternitas opus**
SATB
Geistliches Waldvöglein I, no. 12

A0079   **O Angst! O schwerer Fall!**
SATB
Lent
Geistliches Waldvöglein I, no. 2/2

A0080   **O Anna, liebste Gemahlin mein**
SATB
Birth of the Virgin Mary
Geistliches Waldvöglein I, no. 42

A0081   **O beata benedicti**
See Redivivo tibi Christe

A0082   **O dilecte Jesu Christe**
SATB
Geistliches Waldvöglein I, no. 16

A0083   **O du honigsüsser Mund**
SATB
Feast of St. Bernard
Geistliches Waldvöglein I, no. 27

A0084   **O du kostbarliches Blute**
SATB
Geistliches Waldvöglein I, no. 17

A0085   **O du liebste Mutter mein**
SATB
Geistliches Waldvöglein I, no. 26/1

A0086   **O du liebstes Jesu Kindelein**
SATB
Christmas Day
Geistliches Waldvöglein I, no. 13

A0087   **O du mein allerliebster Herr**
SATB
Geistliches Waldvöglein II, no. 16

A0088   **O du mein lebendiges Brot**
SATB
Geistliches Waldvöglein I, no. 25

A0089   **O du mein liebstes Jesulein**
SATB
Christmas Day
Geistliches Waldvöglein I, no. 44/8

A0090 **O du Sünder insgemeine . . . Hier bin ich verborgen**
SATB
Good Friday
Geistliches Waldvöglein I, no. 10

A0091 **O du Sünder insgemeine . . . Hier hang ich unschuldig**
SATB
Good Friday
Geistliches Waldvöglein I, no. 9

A0092 **O du Sünder insgemeine . . . Hier lieg ich im Stalle**
SATB
Christmas Day
Geistliches Waldvöglein I, no. 8

A0093 **O du unschuldigen Jesu**
SATB
Geistliches Waldvöglein II, no. 5

A0094 **O dulcissima Virgo**
SATB, SATB, bc
Fasciculus musicalis variorum cantionum, no. 31

A0095 **O Erden, tu dich auf**
SATB
Geistliches Waldvöglein II, no. 8

A0096 **O Francisce, Vater mein**
SATB
Feast of Saint Francis
Geistliches Waldvöglein I, no. 28

A0097 **O Gabriel, du getreuer Knecht**
SATB
Purification
Geistliches Waldvöglein III, no. 1

A0098 **O Gott, der du im Paradies**
SATB
Ascension of Christ
Geistliches Waldvöglein I, no. 21

A0099 **O Gott, der du uns hast gesandt**
SATB
Feast of Saint Kilian
Geistliches Waldvöglein I, no. 30/2

A0100 **O Gott im Himmel mein höchster Trost**
SATB
Geistliches Waldvöglein I, no. 36

A0101 **O Gott mein Heiland**
SATB
Lent
Geistliches Waldvöglein III, no. 7

A0102 **O Gott! O Mensch! O Blut!**
SATB
Geistliches Waldvöglein II, no. 9

A0103 **O Gott von sehr grosser Majestät**
SATB
Feast of Saint Michael the Archangel
Geistliches Waldvöglein I, no. 39/2

A0104 **O honigsüsses Engel-Brot**
SATB
Geistliches Waldvöglein I, no. 19/2

A0105 **O ich elende Kreature**
SATB
Geistliches Waldvöglein II, no. 3

A0106 **O ich elende verdammte Seel**
SATB
Geistliches Waldvöglein I, no. 39/1

A0107 **O Jesu, liebster Heiland wert**
SATB
Geistliches Waldvöglein II, no. 1

A0108 **O Jesu, fons purissime**
SATB
Geistliches Waldvöglein I, no. 19/1

A0109 **O Joseph liebster, Joseph mein**
SATB
Geistliches Waldvöglein I, no. 43

A0110 **O Juda, du Verräter verflucht**
SATB
Geistliches Waldvöglein II, no. 2

A0111 **O Judex inscrutabilis**
SATB
Geistliches Waldvöglein I, no. 31

A0112 **O lieber Vater im höchsten Thron**
SATB
Geistliches Waldvöglein I, no. 44/5

A0113 **O liebste Jungfrau mein**
SATB
Geistliches Waldvöglein I, no. 34/1

A0114 **O liebster Jesu mein**
SATB
Geistliches Waldvöglein III, no. 6

A0115 **O liebster, Jesu wie so heiß**
SATB
Geistliches Waldvöglein II, no. 24/2

A0116 **O liebstes Jesulein**
SATB
Christmas Day
Geistliches Waldvöglein I, no. 5/1

AGRICOLA, Wolfgang Christoph (*continued*)

A0117 **O Maria caeli decus**
See Redivivo tibi Christe

A0118 **O Maria, Morgenstern**
SATB
Geistliches Waldvöglein I, no. 18

A0119 **O mein Seel, fang gar schnell au zu loben**
SATB
Geistliches Waldvöglein I, no. 24

A0120 **O Mensch! O Kreuz! O lieber Gott!**
SATB
Geistliches Waldvöglein II, no. 20

A0121 **O mich betrübtes Weibe**
SATB
Geistliches Waldvöglein III, no. 5

A0122 **O mich elenden Sündern**
SATB
Christmas Day
Geistliches Waldvöglein I, no. 2/1

A0123 **O Michael, du berühmter Held**
SATB
Battle between the Archangel & Lucifer
Geistliches Waldvöglein I, no. 44/14

A0124 **O Mutter der Barmherzigkeit**
SATB
Geistliches Waldvöglein I, no. 20

A0125 **O Mutter Gottes Gebärerin**
SATB
Geistliches Waldvöglein I, no. 44/13

A0126 **O Mutter Maria, mein Herz ist zittern**
SATB
Annunciation
Geistliches Waldvöglein I, no. 32

A0127 **O Pater Augustine**
SATB
Feast of St. Augustine
Geistliches Waldvöglein I, no. 15/1

A0128 **O quam suavis**
SATB, SATB, bc
Fasciculus musicalis variorum cantionum,
no. 29

A0129 **O schöne Morgenröt**
SATB
Birth of the Virgin Mary
Geistliches Waldvöglein I, no. 41

A0130 **O schweres Kreuz**
SATB
Lent
Geistliches Waldvöglein III, no. 9

A0131 **O starker Löw von Juda**
SATB
Easter Sunday
Geistliches Waldvöglein I, no. 44/6

A0132 **O Triumphierer groß**
SATB
Palm Sunday
Geistliches Waldvöglein I, no. 5/2

A0133 **O Unkrafte, o lauter Mattigkeit**
SATB
Geistliches Waldvöglein II, no. 15

A0134 **O Vater, liebster Vater mein**
SATB
Geistliches Waldvöglein I, no. 7

A0135 **O Vater Nicolae**
SATB
Feast of St. Nicolas of Tolentino
Geistliches Waldvöglein I, no. 35

A0136 **O wieviel ohne Ziel**
SATB
Geistliches Waldvöglein II, no. 11

A0137 **Redivivo tibi Christe/O Maria caeli decus/O
beata benedicti**
TTB, bc
Fasciculus musicalis variorum cantionum,
no. 21

A0138 **Regina caeli**
SATB, SATB, bc
Fasciculus musicalis variorum cantionum,
no. 28

A0139 **Sei gesundem Leib auf Erden**
SATB
Geistliches Waldvöglein II, no. 24/1

A0140 **Selig, o Mensch, auf Erden bist**
SATB
Geistliches Waldvöglein I, no. 22

A0141 **Te Deum laudamus**
SATB, SATB, bc
Fasciculus musicalis variorum cantionum,
no. 40

A0142 **Triumph, victoria**
SATB
Easter Sunday
Geistliches Waldvöglein I, no. 44/11

A0143 **Vater, siehe, das ist dein Sohne**
SATB
Geistliches Waldvöglein II, no. 21

A0144 Veni sancte spiritus
SATB, SATB, bc
Fasciculus musicalis variorum cantionum,
no. 27

A0145 Virgo prudentissima
SATB, SATB, bc
Fasciculus musicalis variorum cantionum,
no. 30

A0146 Viri Galilaei
SATB, SATB, bc
Fasciculus musicalis variorum cantionum,
no. 26

A0147 Von Ewigkeit empfangen
SATB
Annunciation
Geistliches Waldvöglein I, no. 40

A0148 Wir loben dich, o höchstes Gut
SATB
Ascension
Geistliches Waldvöglein I, no. 44/12

A0149 Wohlan, mein liebster Mann
SATB
Wedding
Geistliches Waldvöglein I, no. 44/10

AHLE, Johann Georg (1651-1706)

COLLECTIONS

Drei neue vierstimmige Betlieder (1681)
RISM A478 (score)
DMA 2/1484

Unstrutische Melpomene (1678)
RISM A475 (score)
DMA 2/1483

Unstrutische Polyhymnia (1678)
RISM A475 (bound with *Melpomene*, not
mentioned in RISM) (score)
DMA 2/1483

WORKS

A0150 Ach! Ach! Ihr Augen, ach!
SSATB
Funeral
Mühlhausen, 1673
RISM A470, Reich 293 (score)
DMA 57//100

A0151 Ach Gott! du unsers Lebens Licht
SATB, bc
Drei neue Betlieder, no. 1
Ed. Sevier (1974), pp. 222-23

A0152 Ach, wann wird in unsern Landen
SATB, 2 vln, 3 vla, vlne, bc
Installation of city council
Mühlhausen, 1679
RISM A477 (parts)
DMA 2/2

A0153 Ach! Wie lang! Ach Herr! Wie lange
SATB
Unstrutische Melpomene, no. 7

A0154 Ach! Wie lange willst du schlafen
SATB
Unstrutische Melpomene, no. 3

A0155 Auf! Auf ihr Völker aller Zeit
SATB
Unstrutische Polyhymnia, no. 10

A0156 Auf, o Freundin, meine Wonne
SATB
Unstrutische Polyhymnia, no. 8

A0157 Aus diesem tiefen Schlunde ruf' ich
SATB
Unstrutische Melpomene, no. 10
Ed. Sevier (1974), pp. 213-14

A0158 Der du den Personen nach
SATB
Trinity
Unstrutische Polyhymnia, no. 7

A0159 Der Mond hat sich verschlichen
SATB
Unstrutische Melpomene, no. 1

A0160 Erbarm dich mein, o Gott
SATB
Unstrutische Melpomene, no. 8

A0161 Herr des Himmels und der Erde
SATB
Unstrutische Melpomene, no. 6

A0162 Herr nun lässest du deinen Diener
SATB
Unstrutische Melpomene, no. 12

A0163 Herr, vormals hast du Gnad' erwiesen
SATB
Unstrutische Melpomene, no. 9

A0164 Heute soll Freude verjagen das Plagen
SATB
Easter Sunday
Unstrutische Polyhymnia, no. 4

A0165 Ich habe Lust abzuscheiden
SATB
Unstrutische Melpomene, no. 11

AHLE, Johann Georg (*continued*)

A0166 **Komm, Heiliger Geist, erfülle die Herzen**
SATB
Pentecost
Unstrutische Polyhymnia, no. 6

A0167 **Lobet den Herren dort in der Feste**
SATB
Unstrutische Polyhymnia, no. 11

A0168 **Nun so kehr doch ein zu mir**
SATB
Unstrutische Melpomene, no. 4

A0169 **Nun weichet der Sonnen Zier**
SATB
Unstrutische Melpomene, no. 2

A0170 **O Christ, dir dank ich sehr**
SATB
Unstrutische Polyhymnia, no. 9
Ed. Sevier (1974), p. 212

A0171 **O Heiliger Geist du werter Hart**
SATB, bc
Drei neue Betlieder, no. 3
Ed. Sevier (1974), pp. 225-26

A0172 **O Jesu, großer Friedens Held**
SATB, bc
Drei neue Betlieder, no. 2
Ed. Sevier (1974), p. 224

A0173 **O Jesu, heilger Same**
SATB
Unstrutische Polyhymnia, no. 2

A0174 **Singet, ihr Christen, springet vor Lusten**
SATB
Ascension of Christ
Unstrutische Polyhymnia, no. 5

A0175 **Veni sancte spiritus**
SSATB, 2 vln, 3 tbn, bc
D-B Mus. ms. 402 (Erfurt)
score
DMA 2/1689

A0176 **Was glimmert und schimmert so lieblich, so
fern?**
SATB
Christmas Day
Unstrutische Polyhymnia, no. 1

A0177 **Weil der große Tagesstern**
SATB
Unstrutische Polyhymnia, no. 12

A0178 **Wer gnädig wird beschützt**
SATB, 2 vln, 2 vla, vlne, bc
Installation of city council
Mühlhausen, 1682
RISM A480 (parts)
DMA 2/4

A0179 **Wie lange doch, Herr, so ich**
SATB
Unstrutische Melpomene, no. 5

A0180 **Wie soll ich dich immer gnugsam preisen**
SATB
Unstrutische Polyhymnia, no. 3

AHLE, Johann Rudolph (1625-1673)

COLLECTIONS

Geistlicher Dialogen I (1648)
RISM A483 (parts)
DMA 2/1025

Musikalische Frühlings-Lust (1666)
RISM A497 (parts)
DMA 3/5

*Neu-gepflantzten thüringischen Lust-Gartens
Nebengang* (1663)
RISM A488 (parts)
DMA 2/6

Neu-gepflantzter thüringischer Lust-garten I (1657)
RISM A485 (parts)
DMA 1/2

Neu-gepflantzter thüringischer Lust-garten II
(1658)
RISM A486 (parts)
DMA 2/588

Neu-gepflantzter thüringischer Lust-garten III
(1665)
RISM A487 (parts)
DMA 2/1485

Neue geistliche Arien I (1660)
RISM A489 (score)
DMA 1/955

Neue geistliche Arien II (1660)
RISM A490 (score)
DMA 2/5

Neue geistliche Arien III (1662)
RISM A491 (score)
DMA 3/3

Neue geistliche Arien IV (1662)
RISM A492 (score)
DMA 3/4

Neue geistliche Chorstücke (1664)
RISM A495 (parts)
DMA 1/496

Neue geistliche Communion . . . Andachten (1668)
RISM A499 (parts)
DMA 32//148

Neue geistliche . . . Festtage . . . Andachten (1662)
RISM A493 (score)
DMA 3/955

Neue geistliche . . . Sonntage . . . Andachten (1664)
RISM A494 (score)
DMA 3/956

Neuverfasste Chor-Music (1668)
RISM A498 (parts)
DMA 2/1486

WORKS

A0181 Ach du Menschenblum
SATB, 2 vln, vla, vlne, bc
Neue geistliche Arien IV, no. 8
DdT 5, p. 24
Ed. Winterfeld II, no. 134

A0182 Ach Herr mich armen Sünder
SSATTB, bc
Neue geistliche Chorstücke, no. 5
DdT 5, pp. 48-50

A0183 Ach Herr, wo soll ich hin
SATB
22nd Sunday after Trinity
Neue geistliche . . . Sonntage . . . Andachten, no. 47

A0184 Ach Jesu du mein Gnadenthron
SATB
6th Sunday after Trinity
Neue geistliche . . . Sonntage . . . Andachten, no. 31

A0185 Ach Jesu treuer Bürge
SATB
9th Sunday after Trinity
Neue geistliche . . . Sonntage . . . Andachten, no. 34

A0186 Ach lasset uns zu Gott im Glauben treten
SATB
5th Sunday after Easter
Neue geistliche . . . Sonntage . . . Andachten, no. 24

A0187 Ach mein herzliches Jesulein
SSAB, ATTB, bc

Neu-gepflantzter thüringischer Lust-garten I, no. 22

A0188 Ach mein herzliches Jesulein
SSATTB, bc
Neu-gepflantzter thüringischer Lust-garten II, no. 13

A0189 Ach mein herzliches Jesulein
ATB, 2 vln, bc
Neu-gepflantzten thüringischen Lust-Gartens Nebengang, no. 5

A0190 Ach, wie eitel sind die Sachen
SATB, 2 vln, vla, vlne, bc
Neue geistliche Arien I, no. 7

A0191 Alsdann wird der Gerechte stehen
TTB, 2 vln, bc
Neu-gepflantzter thüringischer Lust-garten I, no. 7

A0192 Also hat Gott die Welt geliebet
SSATB, bc
Neuverfasste Chor-Music, no. 1

A0193 An Jesum denken oft und viel
SATB, 2 vln, vla, vlne, bc
Neue geistliche Arien III, no. 2

A0194 Auf, auf mein Herz
SATB, 2 vln, 2 vla, bc
Neue geistliche Communion . . . Andachten, no. 1

A0195 Auf, auf mein Herz und geh dem Herrn
SATB
14th Sunday after Trinity
Neue geistliche . . . Sonntage . . . Andachten, no. 39

A0196 Auf meine Seel erhebe Gott
SATB
D-Dlb Mus. ms. 1751-E-500 (Grimma U 600/L 13)
parts

A0197 Auf meine Seel und lobe Gott
SATB, 2 vln, vla, vlne, bc
Neue geistliche Arien IV, no. 4

A0198 Bedenke, liebe Seele, doch
SATB
10th Sunday after Trinity
Neue geistliche . . . Sonntage . . . Andachten, no. 35
DdT 5, p. 28

A0199 Bekümmer dich nimmer
SATB

AHLE, Johann Rudolph (*continued*)

15th Sunday after Trinity
Neue geistliche . . . Sonntage . . . Andachten,
no. 40

A0200   **Benedicamus**
SATTB, 2 tbtta, 3 tbn, bc
Christmas Day
Neu-gepflantzter thüringischer Lust-garten
III, no. 7

A0201   **Beni omnia fecit**
ATB, 2 vln, bc
Neu-gepflantzter thüringischer Lust-garten I,
no. 8

A0202   **Brich, O Morgensonne, lieblich doch herfür**
SATB, 2 vln, vla, vlne, bc
Neue geistliche Arien IV, no. 1

A0203   **Brot will fehlen in der Wüste**
SATB
4th Sunday of Lent
Neue geistliche . . . Sonntage . . . Andachten,
no. 18

A0204   **Christ lag in Todesbanden**
SATB, 2 vln, bc
Easter
Neu-gepflantzter thüringischer Lust-garten II,
no. 15

A0205   **Confitebor tibi Domine**
TTB, 2 vln, 2 vla, vlne, bc
(n.p., n.d.)
RISM A501 (parts)
DMA 2/1487

A0206   **Das Blut Jesu Christi**
SSATB, bc
Neuverfasste Chor-Music, no. 2

A0207   **Das ist je gewißlich wahr**
SSATTB, bc
Neuverfasste Chor-Music, no. 3

A0208   **Das Jahr ist fortgelaufen**
SATB, 2 vln, vla, vlne, bc
Neue geistliche Arien I, no. 3
DdT 5, p. 16
Antiqua Chorbuch I/5, p. 297

A0209   **Denk an Gott zu aller Zeit**
SATB, 2 vln, vla, vlne, bc
Neue geistliche Arien I, no. 5

A0210   **Der arme, blinde Mann gar wenig kann**
SATB

Quinquagesima
Neue geistliche . . . Sonntage . . . Andachten,
no. 14

A0211   **Der große Drache zürnt**
SATB, 2 vln, vla, vlne, bc
Feast of Saint Michael the Archangel
Neue geistliche . . . Festtage . . . Andachten,
no. 14
DdT 5, pp. 101-02
Ed. Winterfeld II, no. 132

A0212   **Der Mensch muß immer kriegen**
SATB, 2 vln, vla, vlne, bc
Neue geistliche Arien II, no. 7

A0213   **Der Sämann gehet aus**
SATB
Sexagesima
Neue geistliche . . . Sonntage . . . Andachten,
no. 13

A0214   **Der Tag ist hin, erlebet hab ich nun**
SATB, 2 vln, vla, vlne, bc
Neue geistliche Arien I, no. 10
DdT 5, p. 17

A0215   **Der Tag ist nun vergangen**
SATB, 2 vln, vla, vlne, bc
Neue geistliche Arien II, no. 9
DdT 5, p. 21
Antiqua Chorbuch I/5, p. 296

A0216   **Der Weinberg Gottes scheint gering**
SATB
Septuagesima
Neue geistliche . . . Sonntage . . . Andachten,
no. 12

A0217   **Des Trösters Amts Geschäfte**
SATB
Sunday after Ascension
Neue geistliche . . . Sonntage . . . Andachten,
no. 25

A0218   **Die Erde ist des Herren**
SSATB, 2 vln, 2 vla, vlne, bc
Advent
Neu-gepflantzten thüringischen Lust-Gartens
Nebengang, no. 10

A0219   **Die Freude dieser Zeitlichkeit**
SATB, 2 vln, vla, vlne, bc
Neue geistliche Arien IV, no. 7

A0220   **Dies ist das Brot des Lebens**
SA soli, SATTB, 2 vln, 2 vla, vlne, bc

Neu-gepflantzter thüringischer Lust-garten I,
no. 20

A0221 **Du ewig-lebendig-selbständiges Sprechen**
SATB, 2 vln, vla, vlne, bc
Christmas Day
Neue geistliche Arien II, no. 3

A0222 **Du keusche Seele du**
SATB, 2 vln, vla, vlne, bc
Visitation of the Virgin Mary
Neue geistliche . . . Festtage . . . Andachten,
no. 13
Ed. Winterfeld II, no. 124

A0223 **Du sollst in allen Sachen von Gott**
SATB, 2 vln, vla, vlne, bc
Neue geistlichen Arien I, no. 2

A0224 **Du zucken-süsses Himmelbrot**
SATB, 2 vln, 2 vla, bc
Neue geistlichen Communion . . . Andachten,
no. 2

A0225 **Ein Herz voll Reu, voll Glaub und Treu**
SATB
11th Sunday after Trinity
Neue geistliche . . . Sonntage . . . Andachten,
no. 36

A0226 **Ein neues Kindelein**
SATB, 2 vln, 2 vla, bc
Christmas Day
Neue geistliche Communion . . . Andachten,
no. 6

A0227 **Ein sonderlicher Krieg**
SATB
2nd Sunday of Lent
Neue geistliche . . . Sonntage . . . Andachten,
no. 16

A0228 **Erschienen ist der herrliche Tag**
SATB, 2 vln, 3 tbn, bc
Neu-gepflantzter thüringischer Lust-garten II,
no. 29

A0229 **Es ist genug, nun geh ich fort**
SATB, 2 vln, vla, vlne, bc
Purification of the Virgin Mary
Neue geistliche . . . Festtage . . . Andachten,
no. 5
Ed. Winterfeld II, no. 128

A0230 **Es ist genug, so nimm Herr meinen Geist**
SSATTB, bc
Funeral

Neue geistliche Arien III, no. 9
DdT 5, p. 47
Ed. Winterfeld II, no. 123

A0231 **Es kommet dein Jesus, du gläubige Schar**
SATB, 2 vln, vla, vlne, bc
Advent
Neue geistliche . . . Festtage . . . Andachten,
no. 1
Ed. Winterfeld II, no. 125

A0232 **Es soll den Herren loben**
SATB, 2 vln, vla, vlne, bc
Neue geistliche Arien I, no. 9

A0233 **Es spricht der Unweisen Mund wohl**
ATB, 2 vln, bc
Neu-gepflantzter thüringischer Lust-garten I,
no. 10

A0234 **Es zeucht mein Heiland ein**
SATB
1st Sunday of Advent
Neue geistliche . . . Sonntage . . . Andachten,
no. 1

A0235 **Fürchtet euch nicht**
S solo, SSST, ATTB, 4 bsn, bc
Christmas Day
Neu-gepflantzter thüringischer Lust-garten II,
no. 28
DdT 5, pp. 92-99
Ed. L. Lillehaug (Concordia 97-6407, 1964)
Ed. V. Kalisch (Carus CV 40.4520/1, 1981)

A0236 **Fürwahr, er trug unser Krankheit**
SSATTB, bc
Neue geistliche Chorstücke, no. 4

A0237 **Gehst du nun zu deinem Vater**
SATB
4th Sunday after Easter
Neue geistliche . . . Sonntage . . . Andachten,
no. 23

A0238 **Glaub ich doch, der Satan sei ganz ausgelassen**
SATB
3rd Sunday of Lent
Neue geistliche . . . Sonntage . . . Andachten,
no. 17

A0239 **Gleich wie der Adler**
SATB
25th Sunday after Trinity
Neue geistliche . . . Sonntage . . . Andachten,
no. 50

AHLE, Johann Rudolph (*continued*)

A0240 **Gloria in excelsis Deo**
SATB, SATB, SSA, 4 tbn, bc
Christmas Day
Neu-gepflantzter thüringischer Lust-garten III,
no. 10

A0241 **Gott, sei mir gnädig**
SATB, SA(TB, bc)
Neue geistliche Chorstücke, no. 10

A0242 **Halt stille, Bruder, halt**
SATB
4th Sunday after Trinity
Neue geistliche . . . Sonntage . . . Andachten,
no. 29
DdT 5, p. 27

A0243 **Heilige euch, ihr Menschkinder**
SATB, 2 vln, vla, vlne, bc
Trinity
Neue geistliche . . . Festtage . . . Andachten,
no. 11

A0244 **Herr der König freuet sich**
SSTT, 2 vln, bc
Easter and Ascension of Christ
*Neu-gepflantzten thüringischen Lust-Gartens
Nebengang*, no. 6

A0245 **Herr, du erforschest mich**
ATB, bc
Musikalische Frühlings-Lust, no. 7

A0246 **Herr, es sind Heiden in dein Erbe gefallen**
SSATTB, bc
Neuverfasste Chor-Music, no. 4

A0247 **Herr Jesu Christ, ich weiß gar wohl**
SSATTB, bc
Neue geistliche Chorstücke, no. 6

A0248 **Herr, meine Tochter ist gestorben**
SATB
24th Sunday after Trinity
Neue geistliche . . . Sonntage . . . Andachten,
no. 49
DdT 5, p. 28

A0249 **Heute ist der geboren**
SATB, 2 vln, vla, vlne, bc
Feast of Saint John the Baptist
Neue geistliche . . . Festtage . . . Andachten,
no. 12

A0250 **Hier grünt des Aaronis Stab**
SATB, 2 vln, vla, vlne, bc
Christmas Day
Neue geistliche . . . Festtage . . . Andachten,
no. 2
Ed. Winterfeld II, no. 126

A0251 **Hilf mir, Jesu, daß ich übe dir allein**
SATB
1st Sunday after Trinity
Neue geistliche . . . Sonntage . . . Andachten,
no. 26

A0252 **Höre, Gott**
SSATB, 7 tbn, bc
Sunday after Ascension
Neu-gepflantzter thüringischer Lust-garten III,
no. 9

A0253 **Hört doch, wie die Wölfe heulen**
SATB
2nd Sunday after Easter
Neue geistliche . . . Sonntage . . . Andachten,
no. 21

A0254 **Ich armer Sünder, ich**
SATB
17th Sunday after Trinity
Neue geistliche . . . Sonntage . . . Andachten,
no. 42

A0255 **Ich bin nackt von meiner Mutterleib kommen**
SSATB, bc
Neue geistliche Chorstücke, no. 2

A0256 **Ich danke dem Herrn**
SATB, 2 vln, bc
Neu-gepflantzter thüringischer Lust-garten I,
no. 17

A0257 **Ich danke dir, Gott**
TTB, bc
11th Sunday after Trinity
Geistlicher Dialogen I, no. 9
DdT 5, pp. 9-12

A0258 **Ich denke stets daran**
SSAATTB, bc
Funeral
Neue geistliche Arien III, no. 10

A0259 **Ich, ein Fürst der Engelschaar**
SATB, 2 vln, vla, vlne, bc
Annunciation
Neue geistliche . . . Festtage . . . Andachten,
no. 7

A0260 **Ich hab einen guten Kampf gekämpfet**
SSATTB, bc
Neuverfasste Chor-Music, no. 5

A0261   **Ich habe nun geendet den Wandel auf der Welt**
         SATB, SATB, 2 vln, vla, vlne, bc
         Neue geistliche Arien II, no. 10

A0262   **Ich hab's gewagt**
         SATB, 2 vln, vla, vlne, bc
         Neu-gepflantzter thüringischer Lust-garten II,
         no. 27
         DdT 5, pp. 83-91
         Ed. Johnson II, pp. 151-80

A0263   **Ich schreie mit meiner Stimme zu Gott**
         SSATB, bc
         Neue geistliche Chorstücke, no. 1

A0264   **Ich will den Herren loben allezeit**
         SAT, SATB, 2 vln, 2 tbtta, bc
         Neu-gepflantzter thüringischer Lust-garten II,
         no. 12

A0265   **Ich will euch wiedersehen**
         SATB, 2 vln, bc
         3rd Sunday after Easter
         *Neu-gepflantzten thüringischen Lust-Gartens
         Nebengang*, no. 7

A0266   **Ihr meine Seufzer, fahret auf**
         SATB
         5th Sunday after Trinity
         Neue geistliche . . . Sonntage . . . Andachten,
         no. 30

A0267   **Ihr seid nun alle Gottes Kinder**
         SSATB, 2 vln, 2 vla, vlne, bc
         Neu-gepflantzter thüringischer Lust-garten II,
         no. 30

A0268   **Ist auch der Glaube gut**
         SATB
         8th Sunday after Trinity
         Neue geistliche . . . Sonntage . . . Andachten,
         no. 33

A0269   **Ist das Grab auch noch verriegelt?**
         SATB, 2 vln, vla, vlne, bc
         Easter Sunday
         Neue geistliche . . . Festtage . . . Andachten,
         no. 8
         Ed. Winterfeld II, no. 129

A0270   **Ist mein Heiland vor Johannes schon?**
         SATB
         4th Sunday of Advent
         Neue geistliche . . . Sonntage . . . Andachten,
         no. 4

A0271   **Ists nicht ein Lästermund**
         SATB

4th Sunday of Lent
Neue geistliche . . . Sonntage . . . Andachten,
no. 19

A0272   **Ja, er ist das Heil der Welt**
         SATB
         3rd Sunday of Advent
         Neue geistliche . . . Sonntage . . . Andachten,
         no. 3
         Ed. Winterfeld II, no. 133

A0273   **Jesu, Jesu, meine Freude**
         SATB, 2 vln, 2 vla, bc
         Neue geistliche Communion . . . Andachten,
         no. 4

A0274   **Jesu, komm doch selbst zu mir**
         SATB, 2 vln, 2 vla, bc
         Neue geistliche Communion . . . Andachten,
         no. 10

A0275   **Jesu, meine Freude**
         SATB, 2 vln, vla, vlne, bc
         Neue geistliche Arien IV, no. 5

A0276   **Jesu, süsser Ohrenklang**
         SATB
         12th Sunday after Trinity
         Neue geistliche . . . Sonntage . . . Andachten,
         no. 37

A0277   **Jesu wunder-guter Meister**
         SATB
         21st Sunday after Trinity
         Neue geistliche . . . Sonntage . . . Andachten,
         no. 46

A0278   **Jesus Christus unser Heiland**
         SATB, 2 vln, bc
         Neu-gepflantzter thüringischer Lust-garten I,
         no. 16

A0279   **Jesus dulcis memoria**
         SATB, 2 vln, vla, vlne, bc
         Neue geistliche Arien III, no. 3

A0280   **Jesus ist nun von tötlichen Bande fröhlich erstanden**
         SATB
         1st Sunday after Easter
         Neue geistliche . . . Sonntage . . . Andachten,
         no. 20

A0281   **Jetzt will unser Schifflein sinken**
         SATB
         4th Sunday after Epiphany
         Neue geistliche . . . Sonntage . . . Andachten,
         no. 10

AHLE, Johann Rudolph (*continued*)

A0282 **Jubilate Deo**
ATB, 2 vln, bc
Neu-gepflantzter thüringischer Lust-garten I,
no. 11

A0283 **Komm, meine Braut von Libanon**
STB soli, SATB, 5 instr, bc
Wedding
D-B Mus. ms. 40210 (1677)
score & parts
DMA 1/1943

A0284 **Komm, Seele, setze dich**
SATB, 2 vln, vla, vlne, bc
Passion
Neue geistliche . . . Festtage . . . Andachten,
no. 6

A0285 **Komm, werter Pfingstgast**
SATB, 2 vln, 2 vla, bc
Pentecost
Neue geistliche Communion . . . Andachten,
no. 9

A0286 **Kommet, denn es ist alles bereit**
ATTTB, bc
2nd Sunday after Trinity
Geistlicher Dialogen I, no. 4

A0287 **Lasset die Kindelein zu mir kommen**
SSAB, ATTB, bc
Neuverfasste Chor-Music, no. 8

A0288 **Liebet Friede, legt zur Zeiten**
SATB, 2 vln, vla, vlne, bc
Neue geistliche Arien I, no. 4

A0289 **Lieblich und schöne sein ist nichts**
SSSAB, ATTBB, bc
Neuverfasste Chor-Music, no. 11

A0290 **Lobet den Herren, alle Heiden**
SATB, SATB, 2 tbtta, bc
Neuverfasste Chor-Music, no. 14

A0291 **Lobet den Herrn**
SSATB, 2 vln, 2 vla, vlne, bc
Neu-gepflantzter thüringischer Lust-garten III,
no. 8

A0292 **Lobt Gott, lobt alle Gott**
SATB, 2 vln, vla, vlne, bc
Neue geistliche Arien III, no. 1

A0293 **Mag ich Unglück nicht widerstehn**
SSB, bc
Geistlicher Dialogen I, no. 18

A0294 **Magnificat**
SATB, corn/vln, 2 tbn/vla, tbn/vlne, bc
Neu-gepflantzter thüringischer Lust-garten I,
no. 24
DdT 5, pp. 132-46
Ed. Johnson II, pp. 80-134

A0295 **Magnificat**
ATB, 3 tbn/vla, tbn majore, bc
Neu-gepflantzter thüringischer Lust-garten II,
no. 22

A0296 **Magnificat V. toni**
SATB, bc
Neu-gepflantzter thüringischer Lust-garten II,
no. 9

A0297 **Mein Seelchen, Jesu, sehnet sich**
SATTB, bc
Funeral
Neue geistliche Arien III, no. 8

A0298 **Meine Seele erhebet den Herren**
SATB, 2 vln, bc
Neu-gepflantzter thüringischer Lust-garten II,
no. 20

A0299 **Meine Seele erhebet den Herren (Magnificat I. toni)**
SATB, 2 vln, bc
Neu-gepflantzter thüringischer Lust-garten II,
no. 19
Ed. Schempf (1960), vol. 2, pp. 349-74

A0300 **Merk auf, mein Herz und sieh dorthin**
SATB, 2 vln, bc
Neu-gepflantzter thüringischer Lust-garten I,
no. 18
DdT 5, pp. 147-59
Ed. Adrio (Merseburger EM 918; Evangelische
Verlagsanstalt, 1948)
Ed. Johnson II, pp. 1-41

A0301 **Missa**
SATB, 2 vln, 4 tbn, bc
Neu-gepflantzter thüringischer Lust-garten I,
no. 26

A0302 **Missa (brevis)**
SSATTB, bc
Neuverfasste Chor-Music, no. 6
DdT 5, pp. 51-61
Ed. Johnson II, pp. 252-304

A0303 **Mit Sausen, mit Brausen, mit schwingendem Winde**
SATB, 2 vln, vla, vlne, bc
Pentecost
Neue geistliche Arien II, no. 5

A0304 **Nach trüber Zeit**
SATB
2nd Sunday after Epiphany
Neue geistliche . . . Sonntage . . . Andachten,
no. 8

A0305 **Niemand will dich leiden**
SATB
Sunday after New Year
Neue geistliche . . . Sonntage . . . Andachten,
no. 6

A0306 **Nun danket alle Gott**
SATB, 2 vln, bc
Neu-gepflantzter thüringischer Lust-garten II,
no. 17

A0307 **Nun gibet der Höchste den gnädigen Regen**
SATB, 2 vln, vla, vlne, bc
Pentecost
Neue geistliche . . . Festtage . . . Andachten,
no. 10
Ed. Winterfeld II, no. 131

A0308 **Nun hab ich ausgehaucht**
SSATB, bc
Neue geistliche Arien IV, no. 10

A0309 **Nun ist es billig, Jesu Christ**
SATB, 2 vln, 2 vla, bc
Neue geistliche Communion . . . Andachten,
no. 5
DdT 5, pp. 103-104

A0310 **O Domine Jesu Christe**
SATTB, bc
Neu-gepflantzter thüringischer Lust-garten II,
no. 10

A0311 **O Heiliger Geist**
SAB, SSATB, 2 vln, vla, vlne, bc
Neu-gepflantzter thüringischer Lust-garten II,
no. 23

A0312 **O Heiligster Vater**
SATB, 2 vln, vla, vlne, bc
Neue geistliche Arien IV, no. 3

A0313 **O Herr Jesu, mein Heiland**
SATB, bc
Neu-gepflantzter thüringischer Lust-garten II,
no. 7

A0314 **O Himmels-Prinz**
SATB
20th Sunday after Trinity
Neue geistliche . . . Sonntage . . . Andachten,
no. 45

A0315 **O Jesu, Herzenkündiger**
SATB
23rd Sunday after Trinity
Neue geistliche . . . Sonntage . . . Andachten,
no. 48

A0316 **O Leicht geboren aus dem Leichte**
SATB, 2 vln, vla, vlne, bc
Neue geistliche Arien I, no. 1

A0317 **O lux beata Trinitas**
SSATTB, bc
Neu-gepflantzter thüringischer Lust-garten II,
no. 16

A0318 **O Mensch, in ganzen Leben**
SATB, 2 vln, vla, vlne, bc
Neue geistliche Arien III, no. 4
DdT 5, p. 22

A0319 **O sichre Welt, wie lange willst du träumen**
SATB
2nd Sunday of Advent
Neue geistliche . . . Sonntage . . . Andachten,
no. 2

A0320 **O Tod, O Traurigkeit**
SATB
16th Sunday after Trinity
Neue geistliche . . . Sonntage . . . Andachten,
no. 41

A0321 **O wahrer Mensch, O Gottes Knecht**
SATB
2nd Sunday after Trinity
Neue geistliche . . . Sonntage . . . Andachten,
no. 27

A0322 **O Welt! ich muß dich lassen**
SATB, SA (TB, bc)
Neue geistliche Chorstücke, no. 9

A0323 **Salve cordis gaudium**
SATB, 2 vln, vla, vlne, bc
Neue geistliche Arien II, no. 8

A0324 **Seelchen, was ist Schöners wohl**
SATB, 2 vln, vla, vlne, bc
Neue geistliche Arien IV, no. 9
Ed. Winterfeld II, no. 135

A0325 **Sehn wir dich ein kleines nicht**
SATB
3rd Sunday after Easter
Neue geistliche . . . Sonntage . . . Andachten,
no. 22

A0326 **Seht euch vor den falschen Propheten**
SAT, 3 fl, tbn, bc
Neu-gepflantzter thüringischer Lust-garten II,
no. 21

AHLE, Johann Rudolph (*continued*)

A0327 **Sei gegrüßt**
SATB, 2 vln, 2 vla, bc
Christmas Day
Neue geistliche Communion . . . Andachten,
no. 7

A0328 **Selig sind die, Jesu, dich sein und hören**
SATB
13th Sunday after Trinity
Neue geistliche . . . Sonntage . . . Andachten,
no. 38

A0329 **Selig sind die Toten**
SSAB, ATTB, bc
Neue geistliche Chorstücke, no. 8
Handbuch II/1, pp. 375-84

A0330 **Sie ist fest gegründet**
SSATB, 2 vln, bc
Pentecost
*Neu-gepflantzten thüringischen Lust-Gartens
Nebengang*, no. 8

A0331 **Siehe, der Gerechte kommet um**
SSATTB, bc
Funeral of Laurentius Helmsdorff
Mühlhausen, 1669
RISM A500, Reich 291 (score)

A0332 **Siehe, ich verkündige euch**
ATB, 2 vln, (bc)
Musikalische Frühlings-Lust, no. 11

A0333 **Siehe, wie fein und lieblich ists**
SSAB, ATTB, 2 tbtta, bc
Neuverfasste Chor-Music, no. 13

A0334 **Sollt ich leben ohne Wunder**
SATB
Sunday after Christmas
Neue geistliche . . . Sonntage . . . Andachten,
no. 5

A0335 **Sprich nur ein Wort**
SATB
3rd Sunday after Epiphany
Neue geistliche . . . Sonntage . . . Andachten,
no. 9

A0336 **Surge, propera, amica mea**
SATB, SATB, bc
Neu-gepflantzter thüringischer Lust-garten II,
no. 26

A0337 **Teufel, daß du dich erkühnest**
SATB
1st Sunday of Lent

Neue geistliche . . . Sonntage . . . Andachten,
no. 15
DdT 5, p. 26

A0338 **Tota pulchra es**
SATB, 2 vln, bc
Neu-gepflantzter thüringischer Lust-garten I,
no. 12

A0339 **Tota pulchra es**
SATB, 2 vln, bc
Neu-gepflantzter thüringischer Lust-garten II,
no. 18

A0340 **Tritt in dein Kirchenschiffelein**
SATB
19th Sunday after Trinity
Neue geistliche . . . Sonntage . . . Andachten,
no. 44

A0341 **Triumph, ihr Himmel**
SATB, 2 vln, vla, vlne, bc
Ascension of Christ
Neue geistliche . . . Festtage . . . Andachten,
no. 9
Ed. Winterfeld II, no. 130

A0342 **Und als der Tag der Pfingsten erfüllet war**
SAT, SAT(B, bc)
Neue geistliche Chorstücke, no. 7

A0343 **Unser Herr Jesus Christus**
SATB, SATB, bc
Neuverfasste Chor-Music, no. 9

A0344 **Unser keiner lebet ihm selber**
SSAATTB, bc
Neuverfasste Chor-Music, no. 7
DdT 5, pp. 67-71
Ed. Johnson II, pp. 305-31

A0345 **Veni sancte spiritus**
SSATB, ATTBB, bc
Neuverfasste Chor-Music, no. 12

A0346 **Verzücke mich, mein Jesu**
SATB, 2 vln, 2 vla, bc
Neue geistliche Communion . . . Andachten,
no. 3

A0347 **Von Gnad und Recht**
SSATB, 3 vln, bc
19th and 23rd Sundays after Trinity
Neu-gepflantzter thüringischer Lust-garten III,
no. 4
DdT 5, pp. 105-14
Ed. Johnson II, pp. 181-210

A0348 **Vor dir ist nichts verborgen**
SATB, 2 vln, vla, vlne, bc
Neue geistliche Arien II, no. 1

A0349 **Warum läßt die Welt sich schreiben**
SATB, 2 vln, vla, vlne, bc
Neue geistliche Arien I, no. 8

A0350 **Was mag doch diese Welt**
SATB, 2 vln, vla, vlne, bc
Neue geistliche Arien II, no. 6
DdT 5, p. 20

A0351 **Was säumest du dich doch**
SATB
1st Sunday after Epiphany
Neue geistliche . . . Sonntage . . . Andachten,
no. 7
DdT 5, p. 25

A0352 **Was soll ich doch Leide tragen**
SATB, 2 vln, vla, vlne, bc
Neue geistliche Arien II, no. 4
DdT 5, p. 19

A0353 **Was soll ich, liebstes Kind**
SATB, 2 vln, vla, vlne, bc
Epiphany
Neue geistliche . . . Festtage . . . Andachten,
no. 4

A0354 **Was werden wir essen**
SATB, bc
Neu-gepflantzter thüringischer Lust-garten II,
no. 8
Ed. Winterfeld II, no. 122

A0355 **Was wird doch für Freude werden**
SATB, 2 vln, vla, vlne, bc
Neue geistliche Arien IV, no. 6

A0356 **Weg, du lüstre Sünden Welt**
SATB, 2 vln, vla, vlne, bc
Funeral
Neue geistliche Arien III, no. 7

A0357 **Weinet alle, die ihr vorüber gehet**
SSAB, ATTB, bc
Neu-gepflantzter thüringischer Lust-garten II,
no. 25

A0358 **Welch tröstliches Wunder entspringet**
SATB
7th Sunday after Trinity
Neue geistliche . . . Sonntage . . . Andachten,
no. 32

A0359 **Welcher Mensch ist unter euch**
SATB

3rd Sunday after Trinity
Neue geistliche . . . Sonntage . . . Andachten,
no. 28

A0360 **Welt, tobe wie du willst und wüte**
SATB, 2 vln, vla, vlne, bc
Neue geistliche Arien I, no. 6

A0361 **Wenn uns Gott nun einmal**
SATB, 2 vln, vla, vlne, bc
Neue geistliche Arien III, no. 5

A0362 **Wer hier zu etwas kommen will**
SATB, 2 vln, vla, vlne, bc
Neue geistliche Arien II, no. 2
DdT 5, p. 18

A0363 **Wer ist, der so von Edom kommet**
SSAB, ATTB, bc
Neu-gepflantzter thüringischer Lust-garten II,
no. 24
DdT 5, pp. 76-82
Ed. Johnson II, pp. 135-50

A0364 **Wer sollt doch nun nicht fröhlich sein**
SATB, 2 vln, vla, bc
Annunciation
Neu-gepflantzter thüringischer Lust-garten III,
no. 3

A0365 **Wer ungeregt die Sinnen träget**
SATB, 2 vln, vla, vlne, bc
Neue geistliche Arien IV, no. 2

A0366 **Wie bin ich doch so herzlich froh**
ATB, 2 vln, 4 tbn, bc
Epiphany
Neu-gepflantzter thüringischer Lust-garten III,
no. 6

A0367 **Wie bist du Davids Herr**
SATB
18th Sunday after Trinity
Neue geistliche . . . Sonntage . . . Andachten,
no. 43

A0368 **Wie ein lieber Buhle**
SSAB, ATTB, bc
Neu-gepflantzter thüringischer Lust-garten I,
no. 25

A0369 **Wir glauben all an einen Gott**
SATB, SATB, bc
Neu-gepflantzter thüringischer Lust-garten I,
no. 23
DdT 5, pp. 121-31
Ed. Johnson II, pp. 42-79

AHLE, Johann Rudolph (*continued*)

A0370   **Wir haben auch ein Osterlamm**
SATB, 2 vln, 2 vla, bc
Easter Sunday
Neue geistliche Communion . . . Andachten,
no. 8

A0371   **Wir sehen als ein Luchs was andern Übel stehe**
SATB, 2 vln, vla, vlne, bc
Neue geistliche Arien III, no. 6
DdT 5, p. 23

A0372   **Wir sehens in der Welt zu aller Zeit**
SATB
5th Sunday after Epiphany
Neue geistliche . . . Sonntage . . . Andachten,
no. 11

A0373   **Wir sind Kinder der Heiligen**
SSAB, ATTB, bc
Neuverfasste Chor-Music, no. 10

A0374   **Wisset, daß ihr nicht mit verlänglichen Silber**
SSATB, (bc)
Neue geistliche Chorstücke, no. 3
Handbuch II/1, pp. 313-20
Ed. Hellmann, *Die Motette* 92

A0375   **Zerreißet eure Herzen**
ATB, 2 vln, bc
Neu-gepflantzter thüringischer Lust-garten I,
no. 9

A0376   **Zions Fürst aus Davids**
SATB, 2 vln, vla, vlne, bc
Circumcision
Neue geistliche . . . Festtage . . . Andachten,
no. 3
Ed. Winterfeld II, no. 127

A0377   **Zwingt die Saiten in Cithara**
SSATTB, bc
Neu-gepflantzter thüringischer Lust-garten I,
no. 15

A0378   **Zwingt die Saiten in Cithara**
ATB, 2 vln, 4 tbn, bc
Epiphany
Neu-gepflantzter thüringischer Lust-garten III,
no. 5
DdT 5, pp. 160-69
Ed. Johnson II, pp. 211-51

ANONYMOUS

A0379   **Ach das drückt, fast erstickt**
ATB

Funeral of Anna Blandine Reyer
Gotha, 1670
RISM AN1425, Reich 108 (score)
DMA 66//50

A0380   **Ach daß doch mein Jesus käme**
SATB
Funeral of Maria Dietzsch
Coburg, 1673
Reich 203, no. 2 (score)
DMA 70//12

A0381   **Ach du jammervolles Leben**
SATB
Funeral of Maria Dietzsch
Coburg, 1673
Reich 203, no. 4 (score)
DMA 70//12

A0382   **Ach du süße Liebesbrunst**
SSATB, 2 vln, 2 vla, 2 fl, vlne, bc
Pentecost
S-Uu 38:2 (Düben)
parts

A0383   **Ach Herr, laß deine liebe Engelein**
SAB, 2 vln, 2 clar, timp, bsn, bc
D-Bds Mus. ms. autogr. Georg Österreich
5 (Bokemeyer)
score
Kümmerling: No evidence for Österreich's
authorship

A0384   **Ach Jesu, mir ist weh**
SB, SSATB, 2 vln, 2 vla, bc
D-Bds Mus. ms. anon. 1025 (Erfurt)
score and parts

A0385   **Ach mein herzliebes Jesulein**
ATB, 2 vln, gamba, bc
S-Uu 67:2 (Düben)
parts (S lacking)

A0386   **Ach wann kommet doch die Stunde**
SATB
Funeral of Johann Jakob Botsack
Jena, 1672
Reich 161
EdM 79, pp. 6-7

A0387   **Ach, was ist doch unser Leben**
SATB
Funeral of Johann Volckamern
Nürnberg, 1660
RISM AN2834 (score)

A0388   **Ach, was ist doch unser Leben**
SSATB

Funeral of Christoph Bötticher
Sulzbach, 1673
  RISM C2639 (score)
  DMA 52//15
Cataloged under the name of the pastor,
  Tobias Clausnitzer, by US-Cn

A0389 **Ach, wer ist der nicht beklage**
SATB
Funeral of Susanna Hagendorn
Nürnberg, 1663
  RISM AN2860, Reich 327

A0390 **Ach wie flüchtig, ach wie nichtig**
5 vv
Funeral of Johann Feinlern
Jena, 1689
  RISM AN2494

A0391 **Ach wie schmerzlich wir begleiten**
SATB
Funeral of Jakob Lackorn der Älter
Schwäbish Hall, 1655
  Reich 393

A0392 **Adjuro vos**
ATB, bc
D-Bds Mus. ms. anon. 1245 (Erfurt) (1674)
  parts

A0393 **Allein nach dir, mein Herr und Gott**
SATTB
Funeral of Anna Maria, Herzogin zu Sachsen
Halle, 1670
  RISM AN2768, Reich 126 (score)
  DMA 69//151

A0394 **Alleluia, lobet den Herren**
SSAT, ATTB, 2 clar/tbtta, 2 gamba, bc
D-Bds Mus. ms. anon. 1036 (Erfurt) (1679)
  parts

A0395 **Also hat Gott die Welt geliebet**
SSATB, SSATB, 2 vln, 2 vla, ob, 2 taille, bc
D-F Ms. Ff. Mus. 770
Previously attributed to Telemann

A0396 **Amor Jesu**
SAT, bc
D-Bds Mus. ms. anon. 1246 (Erfurt)
  parts

A0397 **Beatus vir qui timet Dominum**
SATB, 2 vln, 3 vla, 2 ob, bc
D-F Ms. Ff. Mus. 3
  parts
Ms.: "A. K."; *New Grove*: probably by G.
  Strattner

A0398 **Bekümmer dich nimmer, o christliches Herz**
SATB, 2 vln, vla, vlne, bc
15th Sunday after Trinity
S-Uu 38:17 (Düben)
  parts

A0399 **Bewein, o vaterloses Land**
SSATB
Funeral of Joachim Ernst, Graf zu Oettingen
n.p., 1659
  RISM AN1420

A0400 **Brunnquell aller Güter, Herrscher der Gemüter
Lebend**
SATB, 3 gamba, bc
S-Uu 24:5 (Düben)
  tablature and parts
Possibly by M. Gletle

A0401 **Chorus ille caelitum/Ich hab dich erhöret**
SSB, 3 vln, 2 vla, bsn, bc
Christmas
D-Dlb Mus. ms. 2-E-568 (Grimma U
  315/N22) (1698)
  parts
German text underlaid below Latin

A0402 **Christo hat mein Leben**
SATB, bc
Funeral of Wilke Berglaß
Jena, 1679
  RISM AN2833, Reich 167

A0403 **Danksaget dem Herrn**
SSATB, 2 corn, 2 clar, 3 tbn, bc
D-Dlb Mus. ms. 2-E-511 (Grimma U
  510/T 48 XXXII)
  parts

A0404 **Danksaget dem Vater**
SSATB, 2 vln, 2 vla, bsn, bc
Epiphany
D-Dlb Mus. ms. 2-E-572 (Grimma U
  320/N 7) (1702)
  parts

A0405 **Das ist meine Freude**
SSATB, 2 vln, 2 clar, 3 tbn, bc
D-Bds Mus. ms. anon. 1039 (Erfurt) (1681)
  score and parts

A0406 **Der Engel sprach zu den Hirten**
SATB, 2 vln, 2 vla, 2 ob, taille, bsn,
  bassone, bc
D-Dlb Mus. ms. 2-E-556 (Grimma U
  377/N 64) (1701)
  parts

ANONYMOUS (*continued*)

A0407 **Der Ruhm der Gottlosen stehet nicht lang**
SATB, 2 vln, bsn, bc
D-F Ms. Ff. Mus. 5
parts (B, vln 2 lacking)

A0408 **Die den Herrn fürchten**
SATB
D-Dlb Mus. ms. 2-E-616, #1 (Grimma R
94/M 30)
parts

A0409 **Die Engel sind allzumal dienstbare Geister**
SATB, 2 vln, vla, 2 corn, bc
Feast of St. Michael the Archangel
D-Dlb Mus. ms. 2-E-601 (Grimma a.5./T 56)
score and parts

A0410 **Die Erlöseten des Herren**
SATB
Funeral of Peter Schreiber
Rudolstadt, 1671
RISM IN235, Reich 386

A0411 **Die Liebe Gotts ist ausgegossen**
SSAATTBB, 2 vln, 3 vla, 2 clar, timp, bsn, bc
D-Dlb Mus. ms. 2-E-557 (Grimma U
385/N 72)
score
Cover indicates "Knüpfer?"

A0412 **Die Menschen sprechen oft den Segen**
ATB, 2 vln, bc
D-Bds Mus. ms. anon. 869 (Bokemeyer)
score

A0413 **Die so ihrem Herrn und Gott**
SATB, 2 vln, vla, vlne, bc
Funeral of Conrad Fabricius
Darmstadt, 1675
RISM AN1566, Reich 48 (parts)
Tentatively attributed to Johann Heinrich
Seip by Reich

A0414 **Dies ist der Tag**
SSATB, 2 vln, 2 fl, corn, 2 tpt, vlne, bc
D-F Ms. Ff. Mus. 6/7
parts
Schlickte: possibly by Herbst

A0415 **Diese sinds, die kommen sind**
SATB, bc
Funeral of Johannes & Brigitte Schödter
Wittenberg, 1663
Reich 427

A0416 **Domine salvum fac regem**
SSATB, 5 vla, bc
S-Uu 81:135, fol. 136r-138r (Düben)
tablature
DMA 2/2298
Attributed to Steingaden by Eitner, MGG, &
New Grove, based on tentative attribution
of A. Lagerberg, S-Uu librarian, ca. 1885

A0417 **Dreieiniger Gott, der du wohnest im Licht**
SSATB, vln, tbn, vlne, theorbo, bc
Trinity
S-Uu 40:16 (Düben)
parts

A0418 **Drei schöne Dinge sind**
SSATB, 2 vln, bc
D-Bds Mus. ms. anon. 1193 (Erfurt) (1677)
score and parts

A0419 **Dulcis Christe, bone Jesu**
ATB, 4 vla, bc
D-Bds Mus. ms. anon. 1041 (Erfurt) (1674)
score and parts

A0420 **Ein Mensch ist in seinem Leben**
SSATB
D-Bds Mus. ms. anon. 26 (Erfurt) (1702)
score and parts

A0421 **Erschrecke, liebste Seele, nicht**
SATTB, 5 instr, bc
S-Uu 18:14 (Düben)
tablature
Parallel Swedish text: "Förfäras icke Min
siäl"

A0422 **Es ist ein elend jämmerlich Ding**
SATB, vln, 3 gamba, bc
D-Dlb Mus. ms. 2-E-544 (Grimma U
424/P 24)
parts

A0423 **Es ist nun aus**
SATB
D-Bds Mus. ms. anon. 876 (Erfurt)
parts

A0424 **Es steh Gott auf, daß seine Feinde zerstreuet
werden**
SSATB, 2 vln, 2 vla, bsn, bc
S-Uu 67:17 (Düben)
parts

A0425 **Es war ein reicher Mann**
SSTTBB, 2 vln, 2 vla, bc

D-Dlb Mus. ms. 2-E-516 (Grimma U
  518/T 39 XLI)
  parts

A0426 **Es wird ein Durchbrecher**
  SSATB, 2 vln, 2 clar, 3 tbn, bc
  Easter
  D-Bds Mus. ms. anon. 1043 (Erfurt) (1679)
  parts

A0427 **Et cum spiritu tuo**
  SATB
  D-Dlb Mus. ms. 2-E-628 (Grimma, without
    number)
  score and parts

A0428 **Fließet meiner Augen Quellen**
  SATB
  Funeral of Maria Dietzsch
  Coburg, 1673
    Reich 203, no. 1 (score)
    DMA 70//12
  Reich: parody of Johann Crüger's "Du
    geballtes Weltgebäude"

A0429 **Freuet euch des Herrn**
  SSATB, 2 vln, vla, 2 fl, 2 tpt, bc
  D-F Ms. Ff. Mus. 11
    score
  Schlickte: possibly by Herbst

A0430 **Fürwahr, er trug unser Krankheit**
  SSB, 2 vln, bc
  S-Uu 41:14 (Düben); 46:22a (Düben)
    parts

A0431 **Gelobet sei der Herr**
  SSATTB, 2 vln, tbtta, timp, bc
  D-Bds Mus. ms. anon. 1044 (Erfurt) (1676)
    parts (timp lacking)

A0432 **Gott, der da reich ist von Barmherzigkeit**
  SATB, 2 vln, 2 vla, vlne, bsn, bc
  D-Dlb Mus. ms. 2-E-666 (Grimma, without
    number)
    parts

A0433 **Gott ist unser Zuversicht**
  SATB, 2 vln, 2 vla, bc
  D-F Ms. Ff. Mus. 59
    parts (B, bc lacking)

A0434 **Gottlob, es geht nun mehr zum Ende**
  SSATB, bc
  Funeral of Johann Geoge II, Kurfürst von
    Sachsen

Dresden & Zittau, 1681
    RISM T846, Reich 58 (score)
    DMA 70//113
  Tentatively attributed to Erhard Titius by
    Reich

A0435 **Gott, sei mir gnädig**
  SATB, 2 vln, 2 vla, vlne, bc
  D-F Ms. Ff. Mus. 12
    score and parts
  Schlickte: possibly by Herbst. *New Grove*:
    probably Strattner

A0436 **Gott, sei mir gnädig nach deiner Güte**
  SATB, vln, 3 vla, bsn, bc
  17th Sunday after Trinity
  D-Dlb Mus. ms. 2-E-558 (Grimma U
    408/P 8) (1711)
    parts

A0437 **Gottlob, es geht nun mehr zu Ende**
  SSATB, bc
  Funeral of Johann Georg II, Kurfürst von
    Sachsen
  Dresden & Zittau, 1681
    Reich 58 (score)
    DMA 70//113

A0438 **Heile mich, Herr**
  SSATB, 2 vln, vla, vlne, bc
  19th Sunday after Trinity
  D-Bds Mus. ms. anon. 1045 (Erfurt) (1680)
    score and parts

A0439 **Herr auf dich traue ich**
  SATB, 2 vln, 2 vla, vlne, bc
  D-F Ms. Ff. Mus. 14
    parts

A0440 **Herr, der König freuet sich**
  SSATB, 2 vln/corn, 3 tbn, bc
  D-Bds Mus. ms. anon. 648 (Erfurt) (1677)
    parts
  Attributed to "M. B." on manuscript

A0441 **Herr, erhöre mein Gebet**
  ATB, 2 vln, bc
  GB-Ob
    parts

A0442 **Herr, lehre uns bedenken**
  SATB, 2 vln, 3 vla, tbn, bc
  D-Dlb Mus. ms. 2-E-566 (Grimma U
    152/V 78) (1682)
    parts
  Attributed to "J. H." on manuscript

ANONYMOUS (*continued*)

A0443 **Herr, wie groß ist meine Sünderschuld**
SATB, 2 vln, 2 vla, vlne, bc
22nd Sunday after Trinity
D-Bds Mus. ms. anon. 1040 (Erfurt) (1670)
score

A0444 **Herzlich tut mich verlangen**
SATB, STB, 2 vln, vla, vlne, bc
16th Sunday after Trinity
D-Bds Mus. ms. anon. 696 (Erfurt) (1688)
score

A0445 **Herzlich tut mich verlangen**
SSATB, 2 vln, 2 vla, ob, 2 tailles, bsn, bc
16th Sunday after Trinity
D-Dlb Mus. ms. 2-E-573 (Grimma U
321/N 26) (1702)
parts
Attributed by Thomas to Zachow

A0446 **Heut triumphieret Gottes Sohn**
SSATB
D-Dlb Mus. ms. 2-E-665 (Grimma U
599/LXI)
parts

A0447 **Historia von dem Leiden und Sterben unsers lieben
Herrn Jesu**
SATB, 3 gamba, bc
S-Uu 86:34 (Düben) (1667)
tablature

A0448 **Historia von der Geburt Christi**
STBBB, SSATB, 2 vln, 2 vla, bsn, bc
D-Dlb Mus. ms. 2-E-560 (Grimma U
372/N 59) (1686)
parts

A0449 **Ich begehre nicht mehr zu leben**
SATB
Funeral
D-Gs Cod. Ms. philos. 84e J.1 (1718)
Composer: "N. G. J."

A0450 **Ich hab dich erhöret**
See Chorus ille caelitum

A0451 **Ich komm, o höchster Gott, zu dir**
SATB, 2 vln, vla, vc, 2 fl, vlne, bc
D-F Ms. Ff. Mus. 17
parts
Schlichte: Telemann; *New Grove*: probably
by Strattner

A0452 **Ich sehe nur auf Gottes Willen**
SATB

Funeral
Leipzig, 1694
RISM AN1312 (score)

A0453 **Ich verlasse mich auf Gottes**
SATB, 2 vln, bc
GB-Ob
parts

A0454 **Ich weiß, daß mein Erlöser lebet**
SSATB, 2 vln/corn, 2 clar, bc
Ascension
D-Bds Mus. ms. anon. 1203 & 1204 (Erfurt)
(1680)
score and parts

A0455 **Ich will den Herren loben**
SSATB, 2 vln, 2 vla, 2 tbn, bc
D-F Ms. Ff. Mus. 18
parts

A0456 **Ihr Hirten in Hürden**
SS, ATTB, 3 vln, bc
Christmas
D-Bds Mus. ms. anon. 666 (Erfurt)
parts

A0457 **In Christi Wunden**
SATB
D-Bds Mus. ms. anon. 882 (Erfurt)
score

A0458 **Jauchzet Gott, alle Land**
SATB, 2 vln, 2 clar, 2 corn, 2 horns, bc
D-F Ms. Ff. Mus. 16
score

A0459 **Jesu, du mein Schatz auf Erden**
SATB
Funeral of Maria Dietzsch
Coburg, 1673
Reich 203, no. 3 (score)
DMA 70//12

A0460 **Jubilate Deo, omnis terra**
ATB, 2 vln, bc
S-Uu 33:17 (Düben)
parts
Attributed to "A. S."

A0461 **Kein Mensch soll darum traurig sein**
SATB, bc
Funeral of Wilke Berglaß
Jena, 1679
RISM AN 2833, Reich 167
EdM 79, p. 7

A0462   **Komm, Heiliger Geist, Herre Gott**
SSATB, 2 vln, 2 vla, bsn, bc
Pentecost
D-Dlb Mus. ms. 2-E-546 (Grimma U
  342/N 37) (1703)
parts

A0463   **Komm, schöner Abend, komm gegangen**
SSB, 2 vln, vlne, bc
S-Uu 42:23 (Düben)
tablature and parts

A0464   **Kommt her, ihr Gesegneten meines Vaters**
SATB, 4 vln, vla, bc
26th Sunday after Trinity
D-Dlb Mus. ms. 2-E-580 (Grimma U
  619/T 51)
score and parts

A0465   **Kommt her zu mir, alle**
SSAB, 2 vln, 2 gamba, vlne, bc
D-Bds Mus. ms. anon. 658 (Erfurt) (1680)
parts

A0466   **Kündlich groß ist das gottseelige Geheimnis**
SSATB, 2 vln, 2 vla, 4 ob, bsn, bc
1st and 3rd Days of Christmas
D-Dlb Mus. ms. 2-E-561 (Grimma U
  379/N 66)
parts

A0467   **Laudate, pueri, Dominum**
ATB, 2 vln, bc
D-B Mus. ms. 40323, no. 3 (Erfurt)
score

A0468   **Lob, Ehr sei Gott**
SSATB, 2 vln, 2 fl, corn, 2 tpt, vlne, bc
D-F Ms. Ff. Mus. 7
parts
Schlickte: possibly by Herbst

A0469   **Lobe den Herrn, meine Seele**
SSB, 2 vln, 2 vla, vlne, bc
D-F Ms. Ff. Mus. 22
score and parts

A0470   **Lobe den Herrn, meine Seele**
SATB, 2 vln, vltta, bc
D-Dlb Mus. ms. 2-E-597 (Grimma a 19/T 69)
score and parts

A0471   **Lobe den Herrn, meine Seele**
SATB
D-Dlb Mus. ms. 2-E-616, no. 2 (Grimma
  R 94/M 30)
parts

A0472   **Lobet den Herren, alle Heiden**
SATB, 2 ob, 2 tpt, timp, bc
D-F Ms. Ff. Mus. 23
parts (bc lacking)

A0473   **Lobt Gott, ihr Christen allzugleich**
SATB, vln, ob, vlne, bc
Christmas Day
D-Dlb Mus. ms. 2-E-625 (Grimma U
  397/N 83) (1721)
score and parts

A0474   **Lobt, ihr Knechte des Herrn**
ATB, 2 vln, bc
D-F Ms. Ff. Mus. 24
score

A0475   **Magnificat à 10** (BuxWV Anh. 1)
SSATB, 2 vln, 2 vla, vlne, bc
S-Uu 86:50 (Düben)
parts
S-Uu 69:17 (Düben)
parts, attr. Buxtehude
Ed. Grusnick (Bärenreiter no. 543)
Ed. Graulich, *SBuxA* 5

A0476   **Magnificat in F**
B solo, SSATB, 2 vln, 2 vla, bsn/vlne, bc
D-Bds Mus. ms. anon. 1250 (Erfurt) (1674
  & 1675)
parts

A0477   **Magnificat in G**
ATB, bc
D-Bds Mus. ms. anon. 1251 (Erfurt) (1674)
parts

A0478   **Man singet mit Freuden vom Sieg** (BuxWV
Anh. 2)
SSATB, 2 vln, 2 vla/tbn, 2 tpt, bsn, bc
D-B Mus. ms. 2680, no. 5
score
Ed. Fedtke, *Die Kantate* 200

A0479   **Meine Seele ist betrübt bis in den Tod**
SSATB, 3 gamba, vlne, bc
D-Dlb Mus. ms. 2-E-543 (Grimma U
  370/N 56)
parts
Ms. cover: "Schelle?"

A0480   **Meister, welches ist das vornehmste Gebot?**
SATB, SATB, 2 vln, bc
18th Sunday after Trinity
D-Bds Mus. ms. anon. 1010 (Erfurt) (1679)
score and parts

ANONYMOUS (*continued*)

A0481 **Mir ist mein Gott nicht unbekannt**
SSATB, bc
Funeral of Johannes Pascovius
Stettin, 1658
RISM AN784, Reich 401

A0482 **Mir ist wohl**
SST
Funeral of Anna Blandine Reyer
Gotha, 1670
RISM AN1425, Reich 108 (score)
DMA 66//50

A0483 **Missa (brevis)**
SATB, 2 vln, bsn, bc
S-Uu 69:8 (Düben)
parts
Attributed to "J. W. F."

A0484 **Missa (brevis)**
SSATB, 2 vln, 2 vla, bsn, bc
S-Uu 69:5 (Düben)
parts

A0485 **Missa ex D**
SSATB, 2 vln, bc
D-Bds Mus. ms. anon. 742 (Erfurt)
score

A0486 **Missa ex F**
SSATTB, 2 vln, 3 vla, 2 fl, 2 corn, tbn/bsn, bc
D-Bds Mus. ms. anon. 1037 (Erfurt)
parts

A0487 **Missa Minutta (brevis)**
SSATB, SATB, 2 vln, 2 vla, 3 tbn, bsn, bc
S-Uu 80:75, fol. 75v-85 (Düben) (1665)
tablature

A0488 **Nun ade, du Jammer-Welt**
SSATB
Funeral of Elisabeth Böttiger
Mühlhausen, 1670
RISM AN1995, Reich 292

A0489 **Nun danket alle Gott**
SATB, 2 vln, 2 tbtta, bc
D-Bds Mus. ms. anon. 1572 (Erfurt) (1674)
parts

A0490 **Nun danket alle Gott**
SSATTB, 2 vln, 3 tbn, bc
D-Bds Mus. ms. anon. 1046 (Erfurt) (1674)
parts

A0491 **Nun Gottlob es ist vollbracht**
SSATB
Funeral of Christoph Bötticher

Sulzbach, 1673
RISM C2639 (score)
DMA 52//15
Cataloged under the name of the pastor,
Tobias Clausnitzer, in US-Cn

A0492 **Nun gute Nacht**
SSATB
Funeral
D-Bds Mus. Ms. anon. 898 (Erfurt)
score and parts

A0493 **Nun gute Nacht, du Jammerwelt**
SATB, 3 vla, bc
S-Uu 44:9 (Düben)
tablature and parts
Same music as S-Uu 18:24 (text: "Sa haff
gud Natt")

A0494 **Nun, Herr wes soll ich mich trösten**
SSAATTBB, bc
D-Dlb Mus. ms. 2-E-610 (Grimma U
383/N 68)
score and parts

A0495 **Nun lab und erquicke mein durstiges Herz**
SSATB, 2 vln, 2 vla, 2 fl, vlne, bc
Pentecost
S-Uu 44:10 (Düben)
parts

A0496 **Nun laßt uns den Leib begraben**
SATB, 2 vln, 2 vla, vlne, bc
Funeral of Jakob Ilgen (pastor of Michaelis-
kirche, Erfurt) (1679)
D-Bds Mus. ms. anon. 899 (Erfurt) (1679)

A0497 **Nun wir denn sind gerecht worden durch den
Glauben**
SATB
Funeral of Magdalena Sibyll, Kurfürstin zu
Sachsen
n.p., 1687
D-HAu
score
DMA 70//195
Composer identified only as "J. E. S." in source

A0498 **O du mein ganz betrübtes Herz**
SATB
Funeral of Joachim Nüzel
Nürnberg, 1671
Reich 346

A0499 **O Ewigkeit, grausame Zeit**
SSATB, 2 vln, 3 vla, bc
S-Uu 44:15 (Düben)
parts

A0500 **O Gott, nun lässest du mich hin**
SATB, bc
Funeral of Johann Schilling
Ansbach, 1672
RISM IN132, Reich 19
Composer identified only as "I. R." in source

A0501 **O immensa bonitas entangit**
SATB, 2 vln, gamba, vlne, bc
Pentecost
S-Uu 33:18 (Düben)
parts
Attributed to "A. S."

A0502 **O süßer Tag, nun wird der Geist**
SATB, 2 vln, 2 vla, vlne, theorbo, bc
Pentecost
S-Uu 45:18 (Düben)
parts

A0503 **Recht ist aller Menschen Leben**
SSATB, SSATB, 3 gamba, bc
Funeral of Christian von Meußbach
Jena, 1684
RISM AN2298, Reich 169 (parts)
DMA 70//137

A0504 **Regnet, ihr Wolken, und treufelt, ihr Himmel**
SATB, 2 vln, 2 vla, 2 clar, vlne, bc
D-F Ms. Ff. Mus. 49
parts

A0505 **Schwinge, liebe Seele, dich**
SATB
Funeral of Hieronymus Rötel
Frankfurt am Main, 1676
RISM AN554, Reich 78 (score)
DMA 69//148

A0506 **Sehet, wir gehen hinauf gen Jerusalem**
SSB, SSB, SATB, 2 vln, bc
Quinquagesima
D-Bds Mus. ms. anon. 1047 (Erfurt) (1680)
parts

A0507 **Seht euch vor, vor den falschen Propheten**
SATTB, 2 vln/corn, 2 vla/tbn, bc
8th Sunday after Trinity
D-Bds Mus. ms. anon. 1011 (Erfurt) (1680)
score (conclusion lacking) and parts

A0508 **Sei willkommen, süsse Ruh**
SATB
Funeral of Christoph Bötticher
Sulzbach, 1673
RISM C2639 (score)
DMA 52//15
Cataloged under the name of the pastor,
Tobias Clausnitzer, in US-Cn

A0509 **Selig ist der Mann**
ATB, bc
D-Bds Mus. ms. anon. 1048 (Erfurt) (1681)
parts

A0510 **Selig sind die Toten**
SSATB, SSATB
D-Bds Mus. ms. anon. 1266 (Erfurt)
parts

A0511 **Selig sind die Toten**
SSAB, 2 vln, vla, vlne, theorbo, bc
S-Uu 45:19 (Düben)
parts

A0512 **Siehe! Wie bös ist des Menschen Leben**
SATB
Funeral of Christoph Bötticher
Sulzbach, 1673
RISM C2639 (score)
DMA 52//15
Cataloged under the name of the pastor,
Tobias Clausnitzer, in US-Cn

A0513 **Siehe, wie fein und lieblich ist**
SATB, 2 vln, 2 cornettino, bc
S-Uu 70:11 (Düben)
parts

A0514 **So spricht der Herr: Bestelle dein Haus**
SATB, 2 vln, 2 vla, bsn, bc
D-Dlb Mus. ms. 2-E-550 (Grimma U 389)
parts

A0515 **Sollt und müßt ihr uns denn meiden**
SSATB, 2 vla, vltta, bc
Funeral of Christian von Meußbach
Jena, 1684
RISM AN2298 (parts)
DMA 70//137

A0516 **Stehe auf, meine Freundin**
SSAATB, 2 vln, 2 vla, 2 piffari, bsn, bc
Visitation of the Virgin Mary
D-Dlb Mus. ms. 2-E-570 (Grimma U
317/N 24)
parts
Formerly attributed to Zachow

A0517 **Still, still, o Mutter-Herz**
SSB
Funeral of Bernhard Erasmus von Brand
Jena, 1672
RISM AN1489, Reich 162 (score)

A0518 **Suchet den Herren**
ATB, 2 vln, bsn, bc
D-Bds Mus. ms. anon. 1269 (Erfurt) (1674)
parts

ANONYMOUS (*continued*)

A0519 **Suchet in der Schrift**
SATB, 2 vln, 2 vla, bsn, bc
D-Dlb Mus. ms. 2-E-552 (Grimma U 537/T 6)
parts

A0520 **Triumph, victoria!**
SATBBB, 2 vln, 2 clar, 2 tbn, timp, bsn, bc
Easter
D-Dlb Mus. ms. 2-E-571 (Grimma U 318/N 6)
parts
Formerly attributed to Zachow

A0521 **Und nach sechs Tagen nahm Jesus zu sich Petrum**
SATB, 2 vln, 2 vla, vlne, bc
6th Sunday after Trinity
D-F Ms. Ff. Mus. 29
score (voices, bc only) and parts

A0522 **Uns ist ein Kind geboren**
SATB, SATB, SATB, B, 2 vln, vla, vlne, bc
D-Bds Mus. ms. anon. 1049 (Erfurt) (1678)
parts

A0523 **Uns ist ein Kind geboren**
SSATB, 2 vln, 2 clar, bc
D-Dlb Mus. ms. 2-E-562 (Grimma U 419/P 19)
score and parts
On ms. cover: "Hammerschmidt?"

A0524 **Unser keiner lebt ihm selber**
SSATB, bc
Funeral of Johann Christoph Zwillingen
Ulm, 1681
RISM AN1483 (parts)

A0525 **Unsere Harfe ist ein Klagen worden**
SATB, vltta, 2 gamba, bc
D-Bds Mus. ms. anon. 1050 (Erfurt) (1678)
parts

A0526 **Veni sancte spiritus**
SSATB, 2 vln, 2 vla, 2 clar, bc
D-Bds Mus. ms. anon. 1051 (Erfurt) (1680)
score and parts

A0527 **Venite ad me, omnes**
SATB, 2 vln, bsn, bc
D-Dlb Mus. ms. 2-E-569 (Grimma U 316/N 23)
parts
Formerly attributed to Zachow

A0528 **Wach auf, schlafe nicht**
SATB, 2 vln, 2 vla, bc
D-F Ms. Ff. Mus. 63
parts (S, bc lacking)

A0529 **Wacht! Euch zum Streit** (BuxWV Anh. 3)
SSATB, 2 vln, 2 vla, bc
S-Uu caps 71 (Düben)
parts
Ed. Grusnick (Bärenreiter no. 1165-1170)

A0530 **Wahrlich, ich sage dir**
SATB, 2 vln, vla, vlne/bsn, bc
4th Sunday of Advent or after Trinity
D-Bds Mus. ms. anon. 1013 (Erfurt) (1680)
score and parts

A0531 **Warum bin ich betrübt**
SSATB, 2 vln, 2 vla, vltta, vlne, bc
D-F Ms. Ff. Mus. 33
score (voices, bc only) and parts

A0532 **Was Angst hab ich erlitten**
SATB, bc
Funeral of Jakob Bosecker
Ansbach, 1666
Reich 16

A0533 **Was der Himmel selber gibt**
S solo, SATB, 2 vln, 2 vla, 2 harps, 2 fl, 2 clar, timp, bsn, bc
D-Dlb Mus. ms. 2-E-559 (Grimma U 341/N 40)
score and parts
D-Dlb catalog: "Samuel Jacobi?"

A0534 **Was erhebet sich die arme Erde**
ATB, 2 vln, bc
D-Bds Mus. ms. anon. 1052 (Erfurt)
parts

A0535 **Was ist dieses Elend Leben**
SSATB, 4 vla, bc
S-Uu 46:13 (Düben)
parts (A lacking)

A0536 **Was ist doch auf dieser Welt**
4 vv
Funeral of Susanna Judith Fermond
n.p., 1667
RISM AN10

A0537 **Welt ade, zu tausend guter Nacht**
SSB, SSSB
Funeral of Anna Susanne Kirchner
Nordhausen, 1679
Reich 295 (score)
DMA 70//167

A0538 **Wenn uns das Verhängnis heißt**
SATB
Funeral of Georg Pezold
Liegnitz, 1676
RISM AN3000, Reich 277 (score)

A0539 **Wer Gott nicht kindlich traut**
SATB, 2 vla, vlne, bc
GB-Ob
parts

A0540 **Wer will uns nun scheiden von der Liebe Gottes**
SATB, 2 vln, 2 vla, vlne, theorbo, bc
Sunday after Ascension
S-Uu 46:21 (Düben)
parts

A0541 **Wie lieblich ist mein Los gefallen**
SATB
Funeral
Leipzig, 1692
RISM AN3023 (score)

A0542 **Wir sind Kinder der Heiligen**
SATB, 5 vla, bc
D-Bds Mus. ms. anon. 1055 (Erfurt) (1679)
parts (T, vla III lacking)

A0543 **Wird das nicht Freude sein**
SSATB, bc
Funeral of Theodora von Schweinitz
Lauban, 1690
Reich 210

A0544 **Wirf dein Anliegen**
SATTB, 3 vla, bc
D-Bds Mus. ms. anon. 1034 (Erfurt) (1680)
score

A0545 **Wo ist jemand, der da lebet**
SATB, 3 vla, bsn, bc
Ascension
D-Bds Mus. ms. anon. 1012 (Erfurt) (1676)
parts

A0546 **Wo ist nun hin mein Leiden?**
SATB, bc
D-Dlb Mus. ms. 2-E-563 (Grimma U
353/N 92)
parts

A0547 **Wohl dem, der den Herrn fürchtet**
SATB, SATB
D-Bds Mus. ms. anon. 1014 (Erfurt) (1682)
parts

A0548 **Wohl dem, der den Herrn fürchtet**
ATB, 2 vln, 2 vla, 2 corn, 2 clar, vlne, bsn,
bc
D-F Ms. Ff. Mus. 34
parts

A0549 **Wohl sind des rauen Herbstes Zeiten**
SATB
Funeral of Regina Elisabeth Faber

n.p., 1664
RISM AN1418 (score)

A0550 **Wünschet Jerusalem Gluck**
SATB, 2 vln, 2 clar, timp, bc
D-Dlb Mus. ms. 2-E-589 (Grimma U
462/P 36)
parts

A0551 **Ziehet hin, ihr Liebsten beide**
SATB, bc
Funeral of Maria Dietzsch
Coburg, 1673
Reich 203, no. 7 (score)
DMA 70//12

ARNOLD, Georg (d. 1676)

COLLECTIONS

Liber primus missarum, psalmorum, et magnificat
(1656)
RISM A2162 (parts)
DMA 2/595

Liber primus sacrarum cantionum (1651)
RISM A2161 (parts)
DMA 2/1505

Liber secundus sacrarum cantionum (1661)
RISM A2164 (parts—some lacking)
DMA 2/1506

Psalmi de Beata Mariae Virgine (1662)
RISM A2165 (parts)
DMA 35//89

Psalmi vespertini (1663)
RISM A2166 (parts)
DMA 2/23

Quatuor missae (1672)
RISM A2168 (parts)
DMA 1/1793

Tres missae pro defunctis (1665)
RISM A2167 (parts)
DMA 2/596

WORKS

A0552 **Alma Redemptoris mater**
SSB, 2 vln, vla, bc
Psalmi de Beata Mariae Virgine, no. 9

A0553 **Audite populi quid loquator Dominus**
SST, 2 vln, bc
S-Uu 77, fol. 78v-82r (Düben) (1663)
tablature
DMA 3/2002

ARNOLD, Georg (*continued*)

A0554   **Ave Maris stella**
      SSATB, 2 vln, gamba, bc
      Psalmi vespertini, no. 15

A0555   **Ave Regina coeli**
      ATB, 2 vln, vla, bc
      Psalmi de Beata Mariae Virgine, no. 8

A0556   **Beatus vir**
      SSATB, 2 vln, 2 corn, vlne, bc
      Liber missarum I, no. 4

A0557   **Beatus vir**
      SSATB, 2 vln, vla, gamba, vltta, bc
      S-Uu 85:15 (Düben)
        tablature
        DMA 3/197
      Psalmi vespertini, no. 3

A0558   **Bellator magne Georgi**
      SSB, 2 vln, bc
      Sacrarum cantionum I, no. 18

A0559   **Benedic Domine**
      SSB, 2 vln, vla, bc
      Sacrarum cantionum II, no. 20
      S-Uu 77, fol. 66v-68r (Düben)
        tablature
        DMA 3/2003
      S-Uu 38:19 (Düben)
        parts
        DMA 3/2003

A0560   **Confitebor tibi**
      SSATB, 2 vln, vla, gamba, vltta, bc
      Psalmi vespertini, no. 2

A0561   **Confitebor tibi Domine**
      SSATB, 2 vln, 2 corn, vlne, bc
      Liber missarum I, no. 3

A0562   **Credidi propter quod locutus sum**
      SSATB, 2 vln, 2 corn, vlne, bc
      Liber missarum I, no. 10

A0563   **Cur mundus militat sub vana Gloria**
      SST, 2 vln, 2 vla, vltta, bc
      S-Uu 77, fol. 73v-75r (Düben) (1663)
        tablature (text lacking)
        DMA 3/2004
      S-Uu 39:13 (Düben) (1663)
        parts (text lacking)
        DMA 3/2004

A0564   **Danket dem Herrn, denn er ist freundlich**
      SAB, 2 vln, bc

      D-DS Mus. ms. 47
        parts
        DMA 2/1711

A0565   **Dixit Dominus**
      SSATB, 2 vln, 2 corn, vlne, bc
      Liber missarum I, no. 2

A0566   **Dixit Dominus**
      SSB, 2 vln, vla, bc
      Psalmi de Beata Mariae Virgine, no. 1

A0567   **Dixit Dominus**
      SSATB, 2 vln, vla, gamba, vltta, bc
      Psalmi vespertini, no. 1

A0568   **Dixit Dominus**
      SSATB, 2 vln, vla, gamba, vltta, bc
      Psalmi vespertini, no. 7

A0569   **Domine ad adjuvandum me festina**
      SSATB, 2 vln, 2 corn, vlne, bc
      Liber missarum I, no. 1

A0570   **Domine probasti me**
      SSATB, 2 vln, 2 corn, vlne, bc
      Liber missarum I, no. 12

A0571   **Dulcis Christe, ad te venio**
      SSAB, bc
      Sacrarum cantionum I, no. 14

A0572   **Dulcis Jesu, quam decorus rutila in patria**
      SSB, 2 vln, vla, vltta, bc
      Easter Sunday
      S-Uu 77, fol. 27v-31r (Düben) (1663)
        tablature
        DMA 3/1574
      S-Uu 40:17 (Düben)
        parts
        DMA 3/1574

A0573   **Ecce hic est ille**
      SSB, bc
      Sacrarum cantionum I, no. 9

A0574   **Estote fortes in bello**
      SSB, 2 vln, vla, bc
      Sacrarum cantionum II, no. 23
      S-Uu 77:70, fol. 70v-72r (Düben)
        tablature (text lacking)
        DMA 3/3005
      S-Uu 41:7 (Düben)
        parts
        DMA 3/3005

A0575   **Gaudete omnes et laetamini**
      SSB, bc
      Sacrarum cantionum I, no. 8

A0576 **In convertendo**
SSATB, 2 vln, 2 corn, vlne, bc
Liber missarum I, no. 11

A0577 **In te Domine speravi**
SSAB, bc
Sacrarum cantionum I, no. 15

A0578 **Jubilent in caeli**
SSB, 2 vln, bc
Sacrarum cantionum I, no. 20

A0579 **Laetatus sum**
SSATB, 2 vln, 2 corn, vlne, bc
Liber missarum I, no. 7

A0580 **Laetatus sum**
SSB, 2 vln, vla, bc
Psalmi de Beata Mariae Virgine, no. 3

A0581 **Laetatus sum**
SSATB, 2 vln, vla, gamba, vltta, bc
Psalmi vespertini, no. 9

A0582 **Laetentur caeli**
SST, 2 vln, vla, bc
Sacrarum cantionum II, no. 21

A0583 **Lauda anima mea**
SSATB, 2 vln, vla, gamba, vltta, bc
Psalmi vespertini, no. 12

A0584 **Lauda Jerusalem**
SSB, 2 vln, vla, bc
Psalmi de Beata Mariae Virgine, no. 5

A0585 **Lauda Jerusalem**
SSATB, 2 vln, vla, gamba, vltta, bc
Psalmi vespertini, no. 11

A0586 **Lauda Jerusalem Dominum**
SSATB, 2 vln, 2 corn, vlne, bc
Liber missarum I, no. 9

A0587 **Laudate Dominum, omnes gentes**
SSATB, 2 vln, vla, gamba, vltta, bc
Psalmi vespertini, no. 5
S-Uu 81, fol. 146v-148r (Düben) (1665)
tablature

A0588 **Laudate Dominum, omnes gentes**
SSATB, 2 vln, 2 corn, vlne, bc
Liber missarum I, no. 6

A0589 **Laudate Dominum, quoniam**
SSATB, 2 vln, vla, gamba, vltta, bc
Psalmi vespertini, no. 13

A0590 **Laudate, pueri**
ATB, 2 vln, vla, bc
Psalmi de Beata Mariae Virgine, no. 2

A0591 **Laudate, pueri**
SSATB, 2 vln, vla, gamba, vltta, bc
Psalmi vespertini, no. 4

A0592 **Laudate, pueri**
SSATB, 2 vln, vla, gamba, vltta, bc
Psalmi vespertini, no. 8

A0593 **Laudate, pueri**
SSATB, 2 vln, 2 corn, vlne, bc
Liber missarum I, no. 5

A0594 **Magnificat**
SSB, 2 vln, vla, bc
Psalmi de Beata Mariae Virgine, no. 6

A0595 **Magnificat**
SSATB, 2 vln, vla, gamba, vltta, bc
Psalmi vespertini, no. 6

A0596 **Magnificat**
SSATB, 2 vln, vla, gamba, vltta, bc
Psalmi vespertini, no. 14

A0597 **Magnificat octavi toni**
SSATB, 2 vln, 2 corn, vlne, bc
Liber missarum I, no. 14

A0598 **Magnificat sexti toni**
SSATB, 2 vln, 2 corn, vlne, bc
Liber missarum I, no. 13

A0599 **Missa**
SATB, 2 vln, 2 vla, vltta, bc
Quatuor missae, no. 4

A0600 **Missa**
SSATB, 2 vln, 2 corn, vlne, bc
Liber missarum I, no. 1

A0601 **Missa**
SSATB, 2 vln, clar/vln, corn, vlne, bc
Liber missarum I, no. 2

A0602 **Missa**
SSATB, 3 vln, tbn, vlne, bc
Liber missarum I, no. 3

A0603 **Missa**
SSATB, 2 vln, 2 corn, vlne, bc
Liber missarum I, no. 4

A0604 **Missa Laudativa à 7**
SSATB, 2 vln, vla, vltta, bc
Missae pro defunctis, no. 4

A0605 **Missa pro defunctis à 4**
SATB, 2 vln, vla, vltta, bc
Missae pro defunctis, no. 1

ARNOLD, Georg (*continued*)

A0606 **Missa pro defunctis à 5**
SSATB, 4 vla, bc
Missae pro defunctis, no. 2

A0607 **Missa pro defunctis à 7**
SSATB, 2 vln, vla, vltta, bc
Missae pro defunctis, no. 3

A0608 **Missa super O beatum virum**
SATB, 2 vln, 2 vla, vltta, bc
Quatuor missae, no. 2

A0609 **Missa super O foelix, o fausta dies**
SATB, 2 vln, 2 vla, vltta, bc
Quatuor missae, no. 1

A0610 **Missa super Vidimus dominum**
SATB, 2 vln, 2 vla, vltta, bc
Quatuor missae, no. 3

A0611 **Nisi Dominus**
SSATB, 2 vln, 2 corn, vlne, bc
Liber missarum I, no. 8

A0612 **Nisi Dominus**
ATB, 2 vln, vla, bc
Psalmi de Beata Mariae Virgine, no. 4

A0613 **Nisi Dominus**
SSATB, 2 vln, vla, gamba, vltta, bc
Psalmi vespertini, no. 10

A0614 **Nulla scientia melior est illa**
SSATB, 2 vln, bc
Sacrarum cantionum II, no. 28
S-Uu 77, fol. 12v-15r (Düben) (1663)
tablature
DMA 1/1950
S-Uu 2:11 (Düben)
parts
DMA 1/1950

A0615 **O Jesu mi dulcissime**
SSAB, bc
Sacrarum cantionum I, no. 13

A0616 **Omnes gentes laeti gaudentes**
ATB, bc
Sacrarum cantionum I, no. 7

A0617 **Pater alme quam decorus**
SSB, 2 vln, 2 vla, bc
Sacrarum cantionum II, no. 27

A0618 **Plaudet, jubilet, exultet, gaudeat, laetetur**
ATB, 2 vln, 2 vla, bc
Easter Sunday

Sacrarum cantionum II, no. 26
S-Uu 77, fol. 24v-27r (Düben)
tablature (text lacking)
DMA 3/1575
S-Uu 45:2 (Düben)
parts (text lacking)
DMA 3/1575

A0619 **Plaudite populi**
SSB, 2 vln, vla, bc
Sacrarum cantionum II, no. 19

A0620 **Potestis bibere calicem**
ATB, 2 vln, bc
Feast of Saint Jacobi [i.e., St. James, Son of Zebedee]
S-Uu 2:15 (Düben) (1665)
parts
DMA 1/1954

A0621 **Propter te mortificamur**
SSB, 2 vln, vltta, vla, vlne, bc
S-Uu 77, fol. 75v-76r (Düben) (1663)
tablature
DMA 1/1955
S-Uu 2:16 (Düben)
parts
DMA 1/1955

A0622 **Quemadmodum desiderat cervus**
SSB, 2 vln, bc
Sacrarum cantionum I, no. 21
S-Uu 77, fol. 97v-101r (Düben) (1663)
tablature
DMA 1/1956
S-Uu 2:17 (Düben)
parts
DMA 1/1956

A0623 **Regina caeli**
ATB, 2 vln, vla, bc
Psalmi de Beata Mariae Virgine, no. 10

A0624 **Rex magne caelitus**
SSB, 2 vln, bc
Sacrarum cantionum I, no. 16

A0625 **Salve, lux mundi**
SSB, 2 vln, vla, bc
Sacrarum cantionum II, no. 22

A0626 **Salve regina**
SSB, 2 vln, vla, bc
Psalmi de Beata Mariae Virgine, no. 7

A0627 **Una es o Maria**
SAT, 2 vln, bc
Sacrarum cantionum I, no. 19

A0628 **Unser keiner lebet ihm selber**
SATB
Funeral of Johann Jakob Weiss(e)
Mühlhausen, 1661
  RISM A2170, Reich 290 (score)
  DMA 57//122

A0629 **Vidimus Dominum**
SATB, 2 vln, bc
S-Uu 77, fol. 30v-33r (Düben) (1663)
  tablature (text lacking)
  DMA 3/200

ASCHENBRENNER, Christian Heinrich (1654-1732)

A0630 **Die Seele Christi heilige mich**
SATB, 3 vla, vlne, bc
S-Uu 47:14 (Düben)
  parts
  DMA 1/1958

A0631 **O Jesu süß, wer dein gedenkt**
SSA, 2 vln, va, bc
D-Bds Mus. ms. 30091, no. 26
  (Bokemeyer)
  score

B

BACH, Georg Christoph (1642-1697)

B0001 **Siehe, wie fein und lieblich ist**
TTB, vln, 3 gamba, vlne, bc
Birthday
D-Berlin Singakademie (lost)
EdM I/2, pp. 22-38.
Ed. Hofmann, *Stuttgarter Bach-Ausgaben*
801

BACH, Heinrich (1615-1692)

B0002 **Ich danke dir, Gott, daß ich wunderbarlich gemacht bin**
SSATB, 2 vln, 2 vla, bc
17th Sunday after Trinity
D-B Mus. ms. Bach St. 342; Mus. ms.
Bach 941 (Erfurt) (1681)
parts
EdM I/2, pp. 3-21
Ed. H. Bergmann, *Stuttgarter Bach-Ausgaben*
402
Ed. Geiringer, *Music of the Bach Family*
(1955), pp. 13-22

BACH, Johann (1604-1673)

B0003 **Sei nun wieder zufrieden**
SSAT, ATTB, bc
D-Berlin Singakademie (lost)
EdM I/1, pp. 3-8
Ed. Graulich, *Stuttgarter Bach-Ausgaben*
132

B0004 **Unser Leben ist ein Schatten**
SSATTB, ATB, bc
D-Berlin Singakademie (lost)
EdM I/1, pp. 9-17
Ed. Graulich, *Stuttgarter Bach-Ausgaben* 131

B0005 **Weint nicht um meinen Tod**
SATB
D-Berlin Singakademie (lost)
EdM I/1, p. 18

BACH, Johann Christoph (1642-1703)

B0006 **Der Gerechte, ob er gleich zu zeitlich stirbt**
SATTB, bc
D-B Mus. ms. Bach P. 3 (1676); Mus. ms.
Bach P. 4/2, no. 4
score
D-Bds Mus. ms. Bach P. 5, no. 1
score
D-B Mus. ms. Bach St. 167; Mus. ms.
Bach St. 344
parts
D-Berlin Singakademie (lost)
EdM I/2, pp. 101-8
Ed. A. Neithardt, *Musica sacra* (Bote &
Bock), vol. 7, pp. 61-67

B0007 **Der Mensch vom Weibe geboren**
SSATB, bc
D-Mbs Mus. ms. 3150
score
D-Berlin, Hochschule (lost)
EdM I/1, pp. 95-97
Ed. Kubik, *Stuttgarter Bach-Ausgaben* 564

B0008 **Die Furcht des Herren**
    SSATB, 2 vln, 2 vla, bsn, bc
    D-Berlin Singakademie (lost)
    EdM I/2, pp. 72-90
    Ed. H. Bergmann, *Stuttgarter Bach-Ausgaben*
      502

B0009 **Es erhub sich ein Streit**
    SATTB, 2 vln, 4 vla, 4 tpt, timp, bsn, bc
    D-B Aut. ms. Bach P. 1; Mus. ms. Bach
      P. 2
      score
    D-B Mus. ms. Bach St. 166
      parts
    D-Bds Amalienbibliothek 91
      score (attr. to J. Michael Bach)
    Ed. Krüger, *Die Kantate* 75
    Ed. Geiringer, *Music of the Bach Family*
      (1955), pp. 36-52

B0010 **Es ist nun aus**
    SATB, bc
    Funeral
    D-Berlin Singakademie (lost)
    EdM I/1, pp. 91-92

B0011 **Fürchte dich nicht**
    SATTB, bc
    D-B Amalienbibliothek 116, no. 1
      score
    Ed. V. Junk (Breitkopf & Härtel no.
      B2544, 1922)
    Ed. G. Graulich, *Stuttgarter Bach-Ausgaben*
      561

B0012 **Herr nun lässest du deinen Diener in Frieden fahren**
    SATB, SATB
    D-B Mus. ms. Bach P. 4/2, no. 6
      score
    Ed. V. Junk (Breitkopf & Härtel no.
      B2544, 1922)
    Ed. G. Graulich, *Stuttgarter Bach-Ausgaben*
      569

B0013 **Herr, wende dich und sei mir gnädig**
    SATB, 2 vln, 2 vla, vlne/bsn, bc
    D-B Mus. ms. Bach St. 337 (Erfurt) (1676)
      parts
    Ed. H. Bergmann, *Stuttgarter Bach-Ausgaben*
      504

B0014 **Ich lasse dich nicht** (BWV Anh. 159)
    SATB, SATB
    D-B Mus. ms. Bach P. 4/1; Mus. ms.
      Bach P. 4/2, no. 2
      score

USSR-KA Ms. 13583 (lost)
    BGA 39, pp. 157-66
    Ed. Ameln (Möseler, 1950)
    Ed. Graulich, *Stuttgarter Bach-Ausgaben*
      568
    Variously attributed to both J. S. and Joh.
      Christoph Bach; currently thought to be an
      early work of J. S. Bach; cf. Melamed

B0015 **Lieber Herr Gott, wecke uns auf**
    SATB, SATB, bc
    D-B Aut. ms. Bach P. 4/2, no. 1 (1672)
      score
    D-Bds Mus. ms. Bach P. 5, no. 2
      score
    D-B Mus. ms. Bach St. 168
      parts
    Ed. V. Junk (Breitkopf & Härtel no.
      B2544, 1922)
    Ed. G. Graulich, *Stuttgarter Bach-Ausgaben*
      566

B0016 **Meine Freundin, du bist schön**
    SATB, vln, 3 vla, vlne, bc
    Wedding
    D-Berlin Singakademie (lost)
    EdM I/2, pp. 91-135
    Ed. H. Bergmann, *Stuttgarter Bach-
      Ausgaben* 503

B0017 **Mit Weinen hebt sichs an**
    SATB, bc
    D-Berlin Singakademie (lost)
    EdM I/1, pp. 93-94

B0018 **Sei getreu bis in den Tod**
    SSATB, bc
    D-Mbs Mus. ms. 3150, p. 4
      score
    D-Berlin, Hochschule (lost)
    EdM I/1, pp. 98-100
    Ed. Kubik, *Stuttgarter Bach-Ausgaben* 563

B0019 **Unsers Herzens Freude**
    SATB, SATB, bc
    D-Bds Mus. ms. Bach P. 5, no. 3
      score
    D-B Mus. ms. Bach P. 4/2, no. 5
      score
    Ed. Steinitz (Oxford University Press,
      1968, 1990)
    Musica sacra 16, no. 18
    Ed. G. Graulich, *Stuttgarter Bach-Ausgaben*
      562
    Ed. Hertzberg, *Musica sacra* (Bote & Bock),
      vol. 14, pp. 91-108

BACH, Johann Michael (1648-1694)

B0020 **Ach bleib bei uns, Herr Jesu Christ**
SATB, 2 vln, 3 vla, bsn, bc
D-B Mus. ms. Bach St. 165
parts
EdM I/2, pp. 61-71
Ed. Bergmann, *Stuttgarter Bach-Ausgaben* 623

B0021 **Benedictus**
SATTB
A-Wgm I/24478
parts

B0022 **Das Blut Jesu Christi**
SATTB, corn, 2 tbn, bc
D-Berlin Singakademie (lost)
D-GOa Sign. B.V 36
EdM I/1, pp. 22-28
Ed. R. Kubik, *Stuttgarter Bach-Ausgaben* 603

B0023 **Dem Menschen ist gesetzt, einmal zu sterben**
SATB, ATTB, bc
D-B Amalienbibliothek 116, no. 12
score
EdM I/1, pp. 75-83
Ed. Kubik, *Stuttgarter Bach-Ausgaben* 610

B0024 **Ehre sei Gott in der Höhe**
SATB, SATB
USSR-KA Ms. 13661, no. 38 (lost)
DdT 49-50, pp. 116-20
Ed. Melamed, *Stuttgarter Bach-Ausgaben* 612
Anon. in ms., attributed by Seiffert (see DdT 49-50, p. VII)

B0025 **Fürchtet euch nicht**
SATB, SATB
D-Bds Amalienbibliothek 90, no. 1
score
D-Berlin Singakademie (lost)
USSR-KA Ms. 13661, no. 39 (lost)
EdM I/1, pp. 62-67
DdT 49-50, pp. 121-24
Ed. R. Kubik, *Stuttgarter Bach-Ausgaben* 605

B0026 **Halt was du hast**
SATB, ATTB, bc
D-Bds Amalienbibliothek 326, no. 34
score
EdM I/1, pp. 53-61
Ed. R. Kubik, *Stuttgarter Bach-Ausgaben* 611

B0027 **Herr, du lässest mich erfahren**
SATB, ATTB

D-B Amalienbibliothek 116, no. 10
score
EdM I/1, pp. 68-74

B0028 **Herr, ich warte auf dein Heil**
SATB, SATB, bc
D-B Amalienbibliothek 116, no. 11
score
EdM I/1, pp. 84-89
Ed. K. Hofmann, *Stuttgarter Bach-Ausgaben* 602
Ed. Geiringer, *Music of the Bach Family* (1955), pp. 59-66

B0029 **Herr, wenn ich nur dich habe**
SATTB, bc
D-Berlin Singakademie (lost)
EdM I/1, pp. 29-35
Ed. R. Kubik, *Stuttgarter Bach-Ausgaben* 608

B0030 **Ich weiß, daß mein Erlöser lebt**
SATTB, vlne, bc
D-Berlin Singakademie (lost)
A-Wgm I/38266
parts
EdM I/1, pp. 36-38
Ed. A. Neithardt, *Musica sacra* (Bote & Bock), vol. 5, pp. 83-84
Ed. R. Kubik, *Stuttgarter-Bach-Ausgaben* 606

B0031 **Liebster Jesu, hör mein Flehen**
SATTB, 2 vln, 2 vla, vlne, bc
2nd Sunday of Lent
D-B Mus. ms. Bach P. 882
score
EdM I/2, pp. 53-59
Ed. Bergmann, *Stuttgarter Bach-Ausgaben* 622

B0032 **Nun hab ich überwunden**
SATB, SATB, bc
D-Berlin Singakademie (lost)
A-Wgm V/47167
parts
EdM I/1, pp. 47-52
Ed. A. Neithardt, *Musica sacra* (Bote & Bock), vol. 7, pp. 74-81

B0033 **Sei, lieber Tag, willkommen**
SSATTB, bc
USSR-KA Ms. 13661, no. 37 (lost)
EdM I/1, pp. 39-46
DdT 49-50, pp. 110-15
Ed. K. Hofmann, *Stuttgarter Bach-Ausgaben* 604

B0034 **Sei nun wieder zufrieden**
SATB, ATTB, bc
source unknown
Ed. Naue (Leipzig, ca. 1828)
J. M. Bach's authorship uncertain

B0035 **Unser Leben ist ein Schatten**
SSATTB, ATB, bc
source unknown
Ed. Naue (Leipzig, ca. 1828)
J. M. Bach's authorship uncertain

B0036 **Unser Leben währet siebenzig Jahr**
SATTB, bc
D-B Mus. ms. Bach P. 890 (Erfurt)
score and parts
EdM I/1, pp. 19-21
Ed. K. Hofmann, *Stuttgarter Bach-Ausgaben*
601

BACHIUS, C.

B0037 **Veni Sancte Spiritus**
SSB, 3 vln, vlne, bc
D-Dbl Mus. ms. 2128-E-500 (Grimma U
11/O 13) (1688)
parts

BADENHAUPT, Herman

COLLECTION

Choragium melicum (1674)
RISM B625 (parts)

WORKS

B0038 **Ach Herr Jesu Christe**
SSB, 2 vln, vlne, bc
Choragium melicum, no. 11

B0039 **Anxia et perterrefacta corda**
SSB, 2 vln, vlne, bc
Choragium melicum, no. 16

B0040 **Danket dem Herren**
SSB, 2 vln, vlne, bc
Choragium melicum, no. 1

B0041 **Der heilige Geist**
SSB, 2 vln, vlne, bc
Pentecost
Choragium melicum, no. 28

B0042 **Der Herr, der große Gott im Himmel**
SSB, 2 vln, bc
Choragium melicum, no. 39

B0043 **Die mit Tränen säen**
SSB, 2 vln, bc
Choragium melicum, no. 31

B0044 **Dies ist der Tag den der Herr machet**
SSB, 2 vln, vlne, bc
Choragium melicum, no. 8

B0045 **Dieser Zeit leiden**
SSB, 2 vln, bc
Choragium melicum, no. 32

B0046 **Ein Kind ist uns geboren**
SSB, 2 vln, vlne, bc
Christmas Day
Choragium melicum, no. 19

B0047 **Ein Tag in deinen Vorhofen**
SSB, 2 vln, bc
Choragium melicum, no. 34

B0048 **Eins bitt ich vom Herren**
SSB, 2 vln, bc
Choragium melicum, no. 35

B0049 **Fürchte dich nicht**
SSB, 2 vln, vlne, bc
Easter
Choragium melicum, no. 25

B0050 **Fürchtet euch nicht**
SSB, 2 vln, bc
Christmas Day
Choragium melicum, no. 20

B0051 **Heilig, heilig, heilig, ist Gott der Allmächtige**
SSB, 2 vln, vlne, bc
Choragium melicum, no. 4

B0052 **Herr, wenn ich nur dich hab**
SSB, 2 vln, bc
Choragium melicum, no. 7

B0053 **Ich ruf zu dir, Herr Jesu Christ**
SSB, 2 vln, bc
Choragium melicum, no. 38

B0054 **Joseph, was ist, daß**
SSB, 2 vln, vlne, bc
Christmas Day
Choragium melicum, no. 21

B0055 **Kommt her zu**
SSB, 2 vln, vlne, bc
Choragium melicum, no. 2

B0056 **Lasset uns Ostern halten**
SSB, 2 vln, vlne, bc
Easter
Choragium melicum, no. 24

BADENHAUPT, Herman (*continued*)

B0057 **O daß ich könnt ein Schloß an meinem Mund legen**
SSB, 2 vln, bc
Choragium melicum, no. 18

B0058 **Quid prosunt lamenta?**
SSB, 2 vln, vlne, bc
Choragium melicum, no. 13

B0059 **Schaff in mir, Gott, ein reines Herz**
TBB, 2 vln, vlne, bc
Pentecost
Choragium melicum, no. 27

B0060 **So oft ihr von diesem Brot esset**
SSB, 2 vln, vlne, bc
Choragium melicum, no. 12

B0061 **Tibi soli peccavi**
SSB, 2 vln, bc
Choragium melicum, no. 15

B0062 **Vespera jam venit**
SSB, 2 vln, vlne, bc
Easter
Choragium melicum, no. 26

B0063 **Viel so unter der Erden schlafen liegen**
SSB, 2 vln, bc
Choragium melicum, no. 36

B0064 **Widerfahret dir Gnad**
SSB, 2 vln, bc
Choragium melicum, no. 40

B0065 **Wohl dem, der barmherzig ist**
SSB, 2 vln, bc
Choragium melicum, no. 33

B0066 **Zweierlei bitt ich von dir**
SSB, 2 vln, bc
Choragium melicum, no. 37

BAUDREXEL, Philipp Jakob (1627-1691)

COLLECTIONS

Pro primitis musicalibus continentibus (1664)
RISM B1326 (parts)
DMA 3/22

Psalmi vespertini (1668)
RISM B 1327 (parts) (several works designated
à 5, but no fifth voice parts exists)
DMA 2/1965

WORKS

B0067 **Alma redemptoris mater**
SATB (5), 2 vln, bc
Psalmi vespertini, Psalms of the Apostles, no. 17

B0068 **Ante oculos tuos**
SSATB, 2 vln, bc
Time of tribulation
Pro primitis musicalibus continentibus, no. 18

B0069 **Ave maris stella**
SATB (5), 2 vln, bc
Psalmi vespertini, Psalms of the Virgin Mary, no. 8

A0070 **Ave Regina caelorum**
SATB (5), 2 vln, bc
Psalmi vespertini, Psalms of the Apostles, no. 18

B0071 **Avete solitudinis**
SATB (5), 2 vln, bc
Feast of Saint Benedict
Psalmi vespertini, Psalms of the Virgin Mary, no. 12

B0072 **Beati omnes qui timent**
SATB, 2 vln, bc
Psalmi vespertini, Psalms for Sundays, no. 12

B0073 **Beatus vir**
SATB, 2 vln, bc
Psalmi vespertini, Psalms for Sundays, no. 5

B0074 **Caelestis Jerusalem**
SATB (5), 2 vln, bc
Dedication of a church
Psalmi vespertini, Psalms of the Virgin Mary, no. 22

B0075 **Confitebor tibi Domine**
SATB, 2 vln, bc
Psalmi vespertini, Psalms for Sundays, no. 4

B0076 **Confitebor tibi Domine quoniam**
SATB, 2 vln, bc
Psalmi vespertini, Psalms for Sundays, no. 13

B0077 **Credidi propter**
SATB, 2 vln, bc
Psalmi vespertini, Psalms of the Apostles, no. 4

B0078 **Cum invocarem**
SATB, 2 vln, bc
Psalmi vespertini, Psalms of the Apostles, no. 10

B0079 **De profundis**
SATB, 2 vln, bc
Psalmi vespertini, Psalms for Sundays, no. 10

B0080 **Deus tuorum militum**
SATB (5), 2 vln, bc
Feast of a Martyr
Psalmi vespertini, Psalms of the Virgin
Mary, no. 17

B0081 **Dixit Dominus**
SATB, 2 vln, bc
Psalmi vespertini, Psalms for Sundays, no. 2

B0082 **Dixit Dominus**
SATB, SATB, 2 vln, bc
Psalmi vespertini, Psalms for Sundays, no. 3

B0083 **Dixit Dominus**
SATB, SATB, 2 vln, bc
Psalmi vespertini, Psalms of the Virgin Mary,
no. 2

B0084 **Dixit Dominus**
SATB, 2 vln, bc
Psalmi vespertini, Psalms of the Apostles,
no. 2

B0085 **Domine ad adiuvandum**
SATB, 2 vln, bc
Psalmi vespertini, Psalms for Sundays, no. 1

B0086 **Domine ad adiuvandum**
SATB, SATB, 2 vln, bc
Psalmi vespertini, Psalms of the Virgin
Mary, no. 1

B0087 **Domine ad adiuvandum**
SATB, 2 vln, bc
Psalmi vespertini, Psalms of the Apostles,
no. 1

B0088 **Domine probasti me**
SATB, 2 vln, bc
Psalmi vespertini, Psalms of the Apostles,
no. 6

B0089 **Ecce nunc benedicite**
SATB, 2 vln, bc
Psalmi vespertini, Psalms of the Apostles,
no. 13

B0090 **Ecce sacerdos magnus**
SATB, SATB, 2 vln, bc
Feast of a Confessor Pope
Pro primitis musicalibus continentibus, no. 13

B0091 **Exultet caelum laudibus**
SATB (5), 2 vln, bc
Psalmi vespertini, Psalms of the Apostles,
no. 7

B0092 **Exurgat Deus**
SATB, SATB, 2 vln, bc
Time of war
Pro primitis musicalibus continentibus, no. 20

B0093 **Factum est praelium**
SATB, SATB, 2 vln, bc
Feast of Angels
Pro primitis musicalibus continentibus, no. 9

B0094 **Fortem virili pectore**
SATB (5), 2 vln, bc
Feast of the Bereaved
Psalmi vespertini, Psalms of the Virgin
Mary, no. 21

B0095 **Gaude mater ecclesia**
SATB (5), 2 vln, bc
Feast of Saint Dominic
Psalmi vespertini, Psalms of the Virgin
Mary, no. 13

B0096 **Gaudeamus omnes**
SSATB, 2 vln, bc
Feast of the Blessed Virgin
Pro primitis musicalibus continentibus, no. 8

B0097 **Hic est vere martyr**
SATB, SATB, 2 vln, bc
Feast of One Martyr
Pro primitis musicalibus continentibus, no. 11

B0098 **In convertendo**
SATB, 2 vln, bc
Psalmi vespertini, Psalms of the Apostles,
no. 5

B0099 **In dedicatione templi**
SSATB, 2 vln, bc
Dedication of a church
Pro primitis musicalibus continentibus, no. 17

B0100 **In exitu Israel**
SATB, 2 vln, bc
Psalmi vespertini, Psalms for Sundays, no. 8

B0101 **In te Domine speravi**
SATB, 2 vln, bc
Psalmi vespertini, Psalms of the Apostles,
no. 11

B0102 **Iste confessor Domini**
SATB (5), 2 vln, bc
Feast of a Confessor
Psalmi vespertini, Psalms of the Virgin
Mary, no. 19

B0103 **Isti sunt triumphatores**
SSATB, 2 vln, bc
Feast of Apostles
Pro primitis musicalibus continentibus, no. 10

BAUDREXEL, Philipp Jakob (*continued*)

B0104 **Jesu, corona virginum**
SATB (5), 2 vln, bc
Feast of Virgins
Psalmi vespertini, Psalms of the Virgin
Mary, no. 20

B0105 **Laetatus sum in his**
SATB, SATB, 2 vln, bc
Psalmi vespertini, Psalms of the Virgin
Mary, no. 4

B0106 **Lauda anima mea Dominum**
SATB, 2 vln, bc
Psalmi vespertini, Psalms for Sundays, no. 15

B0107 **Lauda Jerusalem Dominum**
SATB, 2 vln, bc
Psalmi vespertini, Psalms for Sundays, no. 14

B0108 **Lauda Jerusalem Dominum**
SATB, SATB, 2 vln, bc
Psalmi vespertini, Psalms of the Virgin
Mary, no. 6

B0109 **Laudate Dominum, omnes gentes**
SATB, 2 vln, bc
Psalmi vespertini, Psalms for Sundays, no. 7

B0110 **Laudate Dominum, quoniam bonus**
SATB, 2 vln, bc
Psalmi vespertini, Psalms for Sundays, no. 16

B0111 **Laudate, pueri Dominum**
SATB, 2 vln, bc
Psalmi vespertini, Psalms for Sundays, no. 6

B0112 **Laudate, pueri Dominum**
SATB (5), 2 vln, bc
Psalmi vespertini, Psalms of the Virgin
Mary, no. 3

B0113 **Laudate, pueri Dominum**
SATB, 2 vln, bc
Psalmi vespertini, Psalms of the Apostles,
no. 3

B0114 **Laudibus cives**
SATB (5), 2 vln, bc
Feast of Saint Benedict
Psalmi vespertini, Psalms of the Virgin
Mary, no. 11

B0115 **Lucis Creator Optime**
SATB (5), 2 vln, bc
Psalmi vespertini, Psalms of the Virgin
Mary, no. 9

B0116 **Magne Pater Augustine**
SATB (5), 2 vln, bc
Feast of Saint Augustine
Psalmi vespertini, Psalms of the Virgin
Mary, no. 10

B0117 **Magnificat**
SATB, 2 vln, bc
Psalmi vespertini, Psalms for Sundays, no. 17

B0118 **Magnificat**
SATB, 2 vln, bc
Psalmi vespertini, Psalms for Sundays, no. 9

B0119 **Magnificat**
SATB (5), 2 vln, bc
Psalmi vespertini, Psalms of the Virgin Mary,
no. 7

B0120 **Magnificat**
SATB, SATB, 2 vln, bc
Psalmi vespertini, Psalms of the Apostles,
no. 9

B0121 **Media vita**
SSATB, 2 vln, bc
Time of pestilence
Pro primitis musicalibus continentibus, no. 19

B0122 **Memento Domine, David**
SATB, 2 vln, bc
Psalmi vespertini, Psalms for Sundays, no. 11

B0123 **Militia est vita hominis**
SSATB, 2 vln, bc
Feast of a Confessor not a Pope
Pro primitis musicalibus continentibus, no. 14

B0124 **Missa I**
SATB, SATB, 2 vln, bc
Pro primitis musicalibus continentibus, no. 3

B0125 **Missa II**
SSATB, 2 vln, bc
Pro primitis musicalibus continentibus, no. 4

B0126 **Mulierem fortem**
SSATB, 2 vln, bc
Feast of the Bereaved
Pro primitis musicalibus continentibus, no. 16

B0127 **Nisi Dominus aedificaverit dominum**
SATB (5), 2 vln, bc
Psalmi vespertini, Psalms of the Virgin
Mary, no. 5

B0128 **Nunc dimittis**
SATB, 2 vln, bc
Psalmi vespertini, Psalms of the Apostles,
no. 15

B0129 **Praecinite Domino**
SATB, SATB, 2 vln, bc
Pro primitis musicalibus continentibus, no. 21

B0130 **Proles de caelo**
SATB (5), 2 vln, bc
Feast of Saint Francis
Psalmi vespertini, Psalms of the Virgin Mary, no. 14

B0131 **Qui habitat in adiutorio**
SATB, 2 vln, bc
Psalmi vespertini, Psalms of the Apostles, no. 12

B0132 **Quisquis amas mundum**
SSATB, 2 vln, bc
Pro primitis musicalibus continentibus, no. 22

B0133 **Regina caeli**
SATB (5), 2 vln, bc
Psalmi vespertini, Psalms of the Apostles, no. 19

B0134 **Regis superni nuntia**
SATB (5), 2 vln, bc
Feast of Saint Theresa
Psalmi vespertini, Psalms of the Virgin Mary, no. 15

B0135 **Regnum mundi**
SSATB, 2 vln, bc
Feast of Virgins
Pro primitis musicalibus continentibus, no. 15

B0136 **Requiem I**
SSATB, 2 vln, bc
Pro primitis musicalibus continentibus, no. 5

B0137 **Requiem II**
SATB, 2 vln, bc
Pro primitis musicalibus continentibus, no. 6

B0138 **Rex gloriose martyrum**
SATB (5), 2 vln, bc
Feast of Martyrs during Eastertide
Psalmi vespertini, Psalms of the Virgin Mary, no. 16

B0139 **Salve regina**
SATB (5), 2 vln, bc
Psalmi vespertini, Psalms of the Apostles, no. 16

B0140 **Sanctorum meritis**
SATB (5), 2 vln, bc
Feast of Martyrs

Psalmi vespertini, Psalms of the Virgin Mary, no. 18

B0141 **Stabunt justi**
SSATB, 2 vln, bc
Feast of Martyrs during Eastertide
Pro primitis musicalibus continentibus, no. 12

B0142 **Te Deum**
SSATB, 2 vln, 2 tpt, bc
Pro primitis musicalibus continentibus, no. 2

B0143 **Te Deum**
SATB, SATB, 2 vln, bc
Pro primitis musicalibus continentibus, no. 1

B0144 **Te Deum**
SATB, SATB, 2 vln, bc
Psalmi vespertini, Psalms of the Apostles, no. 20

B0145 **Te lucis ante terminum**
SATB, 2 vln, bc
Psalmi vespertini, Psalms of the Apostles, no. 14
Ed. Gottron, pp. 42-43

B0146 **Tristes erant Apostoli**
SATB (5), 2 vln, bc
Feast of the Apostles during Easter
Psalmi vespertini, Psalms of the Apostles, no. 8

B0147 **Vidi Dominum**
SSATB, 2 vln, bc
Trinity
Pro primitis musicalibus continentibus, no. 7

BAUER, Peter

B0148 **Ach! was für Schmerzen**
SATB
Funeral of Veit Ludwig von Hutten
Koburg, 1655
RISM B1338, Reich 190 (score)

BAUMGARTEN, Georg

B0149 **Was erhebt sich doch für großes Klagen**
SSATB, bc
Funeral of Margaretha von Zabeltitz
Berlin, 1664
RISM B1378, Reich 33 (score)
DMA 57//148

BECK, J. B.

B0150 **Meine Seele ist voll Jammers**
SATB, 2 vln, tbtta, bc
Easter
D-Gs Cod. Ms. philos. 84e Beck 1 (1717)
score and parts

BECK, Paul

B0151 **Mein Jesus bleibet mir im Herzen eingeprägt**
SATB
Funeral of Elisabeth Wegerich
Jena, 1660
RISM B1534 (parts)
DMA 57//121

BECKER, Dietrich (1623-1679)

B0152 **Es ist ein großer Gewinn**
SATB, vln, 3 vla, bsn, bc
Funeral of Johann Helm
Glüchstadt, 1678
RISM B1528 (parts)
DMA 2/1516

BECKER, Jakob

B0153 **Gott, man lobt dich in der Stille**
ATT, SSATB, 2 vln, 2 vla, 2 gamb, timp,
bsn, bc
D-B Mus. ms. 1225 (Erfurt) (1677)
score and parts

BECKER, Paul

B0154 **Wohl dem, der den Herrn fürchtet**
SSATB, 2 vln, 2 vla/tbn, vlne/bsn, bc
D-B Mus. ms. 1227 (Erfurt) (1674)
score and parts

BECKER, Samuel

B0155 **Ach Jesu Christe! wie sind wir betrübet**
SSATB
Funeral of Johann Georg I, Herzog zu
Sachsen
Görlitz, 1657
Reich 89

BEER, Johann (1655-1700)

B0156 **Alleluia, siehe es hat überwunden**
SSATB, 2 vln, 2 vla, 2 piff, timp, bsn, bc
D-Dlb 2187-E-504 (Grimma U 333/N 33)
parts
Anon.; attributed by Steude

BERGEN, Cyriacus

B0157 **Schaffe in mir, Gott, ein reines Herz**
SSATB, 2 vln, 2 vla, bsn, bc
D-Dlb 2103-E-500 (Grimma U 29/O 4)
parts

BERNABEI, Ercole (1622-1687)

COLLECTION

Sacro modulationes (1691)
RISM B2034 (parts)
DMA 41//19

WORKS

B0158 **Ad Dominum cum tribularer**
SATB, bc
Sacro modulationes, no. 20

B0159 **Ad novam Jerusalem**
SSS, 2 vln, bc
Sacro modulationes, no. 11

B0160 **Ad te levavi**
SATB
1st Sunday of Advent
D-Mk Ms. Mk 1053, no. 26
score
D-Mbs Mus. ms. 2755, no. 4
choirbook

B0161 **Alma cum tumidam**
SATB
D-Mbs Mus. ms. 2756, no. 9 (1675)
choirbook
DMA 22//76

B0162 **Beatus vir**
SSB, bc
Sacro modulationes, no. 6

B0163 **Benedicite Dominum**
SATB
D-Mbs Mus. ms. 2755, no. 2
choirbook
D-Mk Ms. Mk 1053, no. 24
score

B0164 **Benedicte gentes**
SATB, bc
Sacro modulationes, no. 15

B0165 **Cantate Domino**
SSB, 2 vln, bc
Sacro modulationes, no. 8

B0166 **Discerne causam meam**
SAT, bc
Sacro modulationes, no. 7

B0167 **Domine probasti me**
SATB, SATB, bc
I-Rsm, Nr. 294
parts
D-Mbs Mus. Mss. App. 2009 (photocopy)

B0168 **Dominus illuminatio mea**
SATB, bc
Sacro modulationes, no. 17

B0169 **Esto mihi**
SATB, bc
Sacro modulationes, no. 18

B0170 **Exaudiat Dominus**
SSB, bc
Sacro modulationes, no. 5

B0171 **Exultate Deo**
SATB, 2 vln, bc
Sacro modulationes, no. 14

B0172 **Favus distillans**
SSB, bc
Sacro modulationes, no. 9

B0173 **Gaudete in Domino**
SATB
3rd Sunday of Advent
D-Mk Ms. Mk 1053, no. 28
score
D-Mbs Mus. ms. 2755, no. 6
choirbook

B0174 **In voluntate tua**
ATB, 2 vln, bc
Sacro modulationes, no. 12

B0175 **Longe a mundo**
SSA, bc
Sacro modulationes, no. 10

B0176 **O Jesu mi dulcissime**
SSATB, bc
Sacro modulationes, no. 21

B0177 **Pange lingua**
SSAT
D-Mbs Mus. ms. 2758 A & B

choirbook
DMA 45//28
D-Mbs Mus. ms. 2756, no. 20 (from "Nobis datus . . .")
choirbook
DMA 22//76

B0178 **Parasti in conspectu meo**
SSATB, bc
Sacro modulationes, no. 22

B0179 **Perfice gressus meus**
SATB, 2 vln, bc
Sacro modulationes, no. 13
GB-Lbl Mss. Add. 5054, no. 15
score

B0180 **Populis Sion**
SATB
2nd Sunday of Advent
D-Mk Ms. Mk 1053, no. 27
score
D-Mbs Mus. ms. 2755, no. 5
choirbook

B0181 **Portas caeli**
SATB, bc
Sacro modulationes, no. 16

B0182 **Regina caeli laetare**
SATB
D-Mbs Mus. ms. 2756, no. 19
choirbook
DMA 22//76

B0183 **Respice in me**
SATB, bc
Sacro modulationes, no. 19

B0184 **Rorate caeli desuper**
SATB
4th Sunday of Advent
D-Mk Ms. Mk 1053, no. 29
score
D-Mbs Mus. ms. 2755, no. 7
choirbook

B0185 **Salve regina**
4 vv
A-Wgm V Verschiedene 30436
score

B0186 **Salve sancta parens**
SATB
D-Mk Ms. Mk 1053, no. 23
score
D-Mbs Mus. ms. 2755, no. 1
choirbook

BERNABEI, Ercole (*continued*)

B0187 **Sperent in te omnes**
SSATB, bc
Sacro modulationes, no. 24

B0188 **Te Deum**
SATB, SATB, bc
D-Mbs Mus. ms. 2955, fol. 30 (1832);
Mus. ms. 3211, pg. 35
score

B0189 **Tribulationes cordis mei**
SSATB, bc
Sacro modulationes, no. 23
GB-Lbl Mss. Add. 31409, no. 1
score
GB-Cfm Ms. 23 F 9, p. 111; Ms. 24 F 3,
section 3, p. 50
score

B0190 **Vultum tuum**
SATB
D-Mk Ms. Mk 1053, no. 25
score
D-Mbs Mus. ms. 2755, no. 3
choirbook

BERNABEI, Giuseppe Antonio (1649[?]-1732)

COLLECTION

Sex missarum brevium (1710)
RISM B2035 (parts)

WORKS

B0191 **Ad regias agni dapes**
SATB, bc
Any Sunday in Eastertide
A-Wn Ms. 16523, no. 22 (1716)
score
D-Mk Ms. Mk 229 (1720)
parts (2 copies)

B0192 **Ad te Domine levavi**
SATB, vc, vlne, bc
1st Sunday of Advent
D-Mk Ms. Mk 230
parts

B0193 **Ad te levavi**
SATB, vc, vlne, bc
3rd Sunday of Lent
D-Mk Ms. Mk 231
parts

B0194 **Adorna thalamum**
SATB
D-Mbs Mus. ms. 13034
score

B0195 **Aestimatus sum**
SATB, bc
Holy Week
D-Mk Ms. Mk 279, no. 26
score and parts

B0196 **Agnus Dei**
4 vv, bc
A-Wgm I/24476
parts
D-Mbs Mus. ms. 688
score
Ed. A. Neithardt, *Musica sacra* (Bote &
Bock), vol. 7, pp. 5-8

B0197 **Alleluia, excita Domine**
SATB, vc, vlne, bc
3rd Sunday of Advent
D-Mk Ms. Mk 252, no. 3
parts (1715)

B0198 **Alleluia, laetatus sum**
SATB, vc, vlne, bc
2nd Sunday of Advent
D-Mk Ms. Mk 252, no. 2
parts (1715)

B0199 **Alleluia, ostende nobis**
SATB, vc, vlne, bc
1st Sunday of Advent
D-Mk Ms. Mk 252, no. 1
parts (1715)

B0200 **Alleluia, veni Domine**
SATB, vc, vlne, bc
4th Sunday of Advent
D-Mk Ms. Mk 252, no. 4
parts (1715)

B0201 **Alma redemptoris mater (I)**
4 vv, bc
D-Mbs Mus. ms. 656, fol. 23
score
Ed. S. Lück, *Sammlung ausgezeichneter
Compositionen II*, pp. 291-93

B0202 **Alma redemptoris mater (II)**
SATB, bc
D-Mbs Mus. ms. 6163, no. 6
score

B0203 **Amicus meus**
SATB, bc

Holy Week
D-Mk Ms. Mk 279, no. 4
score and parts

B0204   **Antiphone ad tumulum**
4 vv, bc
D-Mbs Mus. ms. 4396
score

B0205   **Astiterunt reges**
SATB, bc
Holy Week
D-Mk Ms. Mk 279, no. 25
score and parts

B0206   **Audi benigne conditor**
SATB, bc
Any Sunday in Lent
D-Mk Ms. Mk 233 (1715)
parts (2 sets)
A-Wn Ms. 16523, no. 21 (1716)
score

B0207   **Aurore coelum purpurat**
SATB, bc
Common of Apostles in Eastertide
A-Wn Ms. 16523, no. 23 (1716)
score

B0208   **Ave Maria**
SATB, 3 vla, tbn, bc
D-Mbs Mus. ms. 687, fol. 19
score
I-Bc R280

B0209   **Ave Maria gratia plena**
SATB, vc, vlne, bc
4th Sunday of Advent
D-Mk Ms. Mk 234
parts
D-Mk 1053, no. 35, fol. 103r-105v
score

B0210   **Ave maris stella**
SATB, bc
Feast of the Virgin Mary
D-Mk Ms. Mk 235
parts
A-Wn Ms. 16523, no. 5 (1699)
score

B0211   **Ave regina (I)**
SATB, bc
D-Mbs Mus. ms. 6163, no. 4
score

B0212   **Ave regina (II)**
SATB, bc

D-Mk Ms. Mk 236
parts

B0213   **Ave regina (III)**
SATB, SAB, bc
D-Bds Mus. ms. 30098, no. 2; Mus. ms.
Winterfeld 71
score
D-Mbs Mus. ms. 687, fol. 9; Mus. ms.
113; Mus. ms. Coll. Mus. Max. 77
score
D-MÜs Hs. 1219
I-Bc DD58
A-Wn Ms. 15618
score

B0214   **Benedictus Dominus Deus Israel**
SATB, 3 vla, vc, vlne, bc
Vigil for the Dead
D-Mk Ms. Mk 281, no. 12 (1716)
parts

B0215   **Benedictus Dominus Deus Israel**
SATB, SATB, 3 vltta, bc
D-Mk Ms. Mk 1049, no. 8
score

B0216   **Benedictus Dominus Deus Israel**
SATB, SATB, 3 vla, bc
Holy Saturday
A-Wn Ms. 16253 (1697)
score

B0217   **Benedictus Dominus Deus Israel**
SATB, SATB, 3 vla, vc, vlne, bc
D-Mk Ms. Mk 237
parts (2 copies)
D-Mbs Mus. ms. 13014
score (voices, bc only)

B0218   **Benedixisti Domine**
SATB, vc, vlne, bc
3rd Sunday of Advent
D-Mk Ms. Mk 238
parts

B0219   **Caelestis urbs Jerusalem**
SATB, bc
Dedication of a church
A-Wn Ms. 16523, no. 4 (1699)
score
D-Mk Ms. Mk 239
parts

B0220   **Caligaverunt oculi**
SATB, bc
Holy Week

BERNABEI, Giuseppe Antonio (*continued*)

D-Mk Ms. Mk 279, no. 18
score and parts

B0221   **Christus factus est**
SATB, vc, vlne, bc
D-Mk Ms. Mk 240
parts

B0222   **Confitebor tibi**
SATB, vc, vlne, bc
5th Sunday of Lent
D-Mk Ms. Mk 241
parts

B0223   **Confitemini Domino quoniam**
SATB, vc, vlne, bc
2nd Sunday of Lent
D-Mk Ms. Mk 242
parts

B0224   **Creator alme siderum**
SATB, bc
Sundays in Advent
D-Mk Ms. Mk 243 (1715)
parts
A-Wn Ms. 16523, no. 8 (1715)
score

B0225   **Credidi**
4 vv
I-Af Mss. N. 140/5
score

B0226   **Credidi**
4 vv, bc
D-Rp Mappe Benevoli Nr. 27
I-Bc DD58

B0227   **Credo quod redemptor**
SATB, 3 vla, vc, vlne, bc
Vigil for the Dead
D-Mk Ms. Mk 281, no. 3 (1716)
parts

B0228   **Crudelis Herodes**
SATB, bc
Epiphany
D-Mk Ms. Mk 244
parts

B0229   **Decora lux**
SATB, bc
Feast of Saints Peter & Paul
D-Mk Ms. Mk 245
parts

A-Wn Ms. 16523, no. 17 (1715)
score

B0230   **Dedit contra me**
SATB, bc
Holy Week
D-Mk Ms. Mk 279, no. 15
score and parts

B0231   **Deus tu convertens**
SATB, vc, vlne, bc
2nd Sunday of Advent
D-Mk Ms. Mk 246
parts

B0232   **Deus tuorum militum . . . hic nempe mundi gaudia**
SATB, bc
Common of One Martyr
D-Mk Ms. Mk 247
parts
A-Wn Ms. 16523, no. 2 (1698)
score

B0233   **Deus tuorum militum . . . sors et corona**
SATB, bc
Common of One Martyr in Eastertide
D-Mk Ms. Mk 248 (1716)
parts
A-Wn Ms. 16523, no. 30 (1716)
score
D-Mbs Mus. ms. 13015 (1716)
score

B0234   **Dextera Domini**
SATB, vc, vlne, bc
D-Mk Ms. Mk 249
parts (bc lacking)

B0235   **Domine ad adjuvandum (I)**
SATB
D-Mbs Mus. ms. 6163, no. 2
score

B0236   **Domine ad adjuvandum (II)**
SATB
D-Mbs Mus. ms. 6163, no. 3
score

B0237   **Domine quando veneris**
SATB, 3 vla, vc, vlne, bc
Vigil for the Dead
D-Mk Ms. Mk 281, no. 5 (1716)
parts

B0238   **Domine secundum actum**
SATB, 3 vla, vc, vlne, bc
Vigil for the Dead

D-Mk Ms. Mk 281, no. 10 (1716)
parts

B0239 **Ecce quomodo moritur**
SATB, bc
Holy Week
D-Mk Ms. Mk 279, no. 24
score and parts

B0240 **Ecce videmus eum**
SATB, bc
Holy Week
D-Mk Ms. Mk 279, no. 3
score and parts

B0241 **Eram quasi**
SATB, bc
Holy Week
D-Mk Ms. Mk 279, no. 7
score and parts

B0242 **Exsultet orbis gaudiis**
SATB, bc
Common of Apostles
A-Wn Ms. 16523, no. 6 (1709)
score
D-Mk Ms. Mk 250
parts

B0243 **Fortem virili pectore**
SATB, bc
Feast of Saint Adelaide or any Female Saint
A-Wn Ms. 16523, no. 33 (1697)
score
D-Mk Ms. Mk 251
parts

B0244 **Haec dies quam fecit**
SATB, bc
Easter Sunday
A-Wn Ms. 16523, no. 11 (1715)
score
D-Mbs Mus. ms. 4435/2 (1715)
score
D-Mk Ms. Mk 253
parts (2 sets)

B0245 **Hei mihi Domine**
SATB, 3 vla, vc, vlne, bc
Vigil for the Dead
D-Mk Ms. Mk 281, no. 7 (1716)
parts

B0246 **Hostis Herodes impie**
SATB, bc
Epiphany

A-Wn Ms. 16523, no. 10 (1715)
score

B0247 **Improperium expectavit**
SATB, vc, vlne, bc
Palm Sunday
D-Mk Ms. Mk 254
score and parts

B0248 **In monte Oliveti**
SATB, bc
Holy Week
D-Mk Ms. Mk 279, no. 1
score and parts

B0249 **Iste confessor**
SATB, 2 vla, 3 tbn, bc
Common of a Confessor
A-Wn Ms. 16523, no. 12 (1715)
score
D-Mk Ms. Mk 255
parts
D-Mbs Mus. ms. 13015
score

B0250 **Jam sol recedit**
SATB, bc
Trinity or any Saturday
A-Wn Ms. 16523, no. 25 (1716)
score
D-Mk Ms. Mk 256 (1716)
parts (2 sets)

B0251 **Jerusalem, surge**
SATB, bc
Holy Week
D-Mk Ms. Mk 279, no. 20
score and parts

B0252 **Jesu, corona virginum**
SATB, bc
Common of a Virgin
A-Wn Ms. 16523, no. 19 (1715)
score
D-Mk Ms. Mk 257 (1715)
parts

B0253 **Jesu dulcis memoria**
SATB, bc
Feast of the Blessed Name of Jesus
A-Wn Ms. 16523, no. 32 (1720)
score
D-Mk Ms. Mk 258
parts

B0254 **Jesu, redemptor omnium**
SATB, bc
Christmas and Circumcision

BERNABEI, Giuseppe Antonio (*continued*)

A-Wn Ms. 16523, no. 9 (1715)
score
D-Mk Ms. Mk 259
parts

B0255 **Jesum Nazareth**
SATTB
Good Friday
D-Mk Ms. Mk 278
score and parts

B0256 **Jesum tradidit impius**
SATB, bc
Holy Week
D-Mk Ms. Mk 279, no. 17
score and parts

B0257 **Judas mercator pessimus**
SATB, bc
Holy Week
D-Mk Ms. Mk 279, no. 5
score and parts

B0258 **Justitiae Domini**
SATB, vc, vlne, bc
Sundays during Lent
D-Mk Ms. Mk 260
parts

B0259 **Lauda Sion salvatorem (I)**
SATB, 2 vln, 2 vla, 2 ob, 3 tbn, bc
Corpus Christi
A-Wn Ms. 16642, no. 1
score

B0260 **Lauda Sion salvatorem (II)**
SATB, 2 vln, vla, ob, 3 tbn, bc
Sunday in the Octave of Corpus Christi
A-Wn Ms. 16642, no. 2
score

B0261 **Laudate Dominum, quia**
SATB, vc, vlne, bc
4th Sunday of Lent
D-Mk Ms. Mk 261
parts

B0262 **Libera**
SATB
D-Mbs Mus. ms. 10750
score

B0263 **Libera me, Domine**
SATB, 3 vla, vc, vlne, bc
Vigil for the Dead
D-Mk Ms. Mk 281, no. 11 (1716)
parts

B0264 **Libera me, Domine**
SATB, bc
D-WD B22, Hs. 427
parts
DMA 56//20

B0265 **Lucis Creator optime**
SATB, bc
Any Sunday
A-Wn Ms. 16523, no. 7 (1712)
score
D-Mk Ms. Mk 262
parts

B0266 **Magnificat**
SATB, 3 vla, vc, vlne, bc
Vigil for the Dead
D-Mk Ms. Mk 281, no. 1 (1716)
parts

B0267 **Magnificat primi toni**
SATB
D-Mbs Chorbuch Mus. ms. 2753, no. 1 (1690)
DMA 3/702
D-Mk Ms. Mk 1053, no. 15
score

B0268 **Magnificat secundi toni**
SATB
D-Mbs Chorbuch Mus. ms. 2753, no. 2 (1690)
DMA 3/702
D-Mk Ms. Mk 1053, no. 16
score

B0269 **Magnificat tertii toni**
SATB
D-Mbs Chorbuch Mus. ms. 2753, no. 3 (1690)
DMA 3/702
D-Mk Ms. Mk 1053, no. 17
score

B0270 **Magnificat quarti toni**
SATB
D-Mbs Chorbuch Mus. ms. 2753, no. 4 (1690)
DMA 3/702
D-Mk Ms. Mk 1053, no. 18
score

B0271 **Magnificat quinti toni**
SATB
D-Mbs Chorbuch Mus. ms. 2753, no. 5 (1690)
DMA 3/702
D-Mk Ms. Mk 1053, no. 19
score

B0272 **Magnificat sexti toni**
SATB
D-Mbs Chorbuch Mus. ms. 2753, no. 6 (1690)

DMA 3/702
D-Mk Ms. Mk 1053, no. 20
score

B0273 Magnificat septimi toni
SATB
D-Mbs Chorbuch Mus. ms. 2753, no. 7 (1690)
DMA 3/702
D-Mk Ms. Mk 1053, no. 21
score

B0274 Magnificat octavi toni
SATB
D-Mbs Chorbuch Mus. ms. 2753, no. 8 (1690)
DMA 3/702
D-Mk Ms. Mk 1053, no. 22
score

B0275 Meditabor in mandatis
SATB, vc, vlne, bc
2nd Sunday of Lent
D-Mk Ms. Mk 263
parts

B0276 Memento mei, Deus
SATB, 3 vla, vc, vlne, bc
Vigil for the Dead
D-Mk Ms. Mk 281, no. 6 (1716)
parts

B0277 Miserere mei Deus
SATB, 4 vla, vc, vlne, bc
D-Mbs Mus. ms. 4266/11 (1697)
score
D-Mk Ms. Mk 264 (1697)
score and parts
D-Mk Ms. Mk 1053, no. 32
score
A-Wn Ms. 16617 (1697)
score

B0278 Missa a tre voci (Kyrie, Gloria, Credo)
TTB, bc
D-Bds Mus. ms. T 72, fol. 1r-34r
score
D-MÜs Mus. ms. 452

B0279 Missa Ad regias agni dapes
SATB
D-Mbs Chorbuch Mus. ms. 2754, no. 6
(1715)
DMA 3/703
D-Mk Ms. Mk 1053, no. 6
score
A-Wn Ms. 16522, no. 6
score
A-Wgm I/33529

Ed. H. Bäurle, *Altklassische Messen* (Leipzig,
Breitkopf & Härtel, 1953)

B0280 Missa Custodi nos Domine
SATB
D-Mbs Chorbuch Mus. ms. 2754, no. 5 (1715)
DMA 3/703
D-Mk Ms. Mk 1053, no. 5
score
A-Wn Ms. 16522, no. 5
score
Ed. S. Lück, *Sammlung ausgezeichneter
Kompositionen I*, pp. 106-28

B0281 Missa Da pacem Domine
SATB
D-Mbs Chorbuch Mus. ms. 2754, no. 3 (1715)
DMA 3/703
D-Mk Ms. Mk 1053, no. 3
score
A-Wn Ms. 16522, no. 3
score

B0282 Missa Defunctorum
SATB, 2 vln, 2 vla, bsn/vlne, bc
Sex missarum brevium, no. 7

B0283 Missa Firstenfeldensis
SATB, 2 vln, 2 vla, bsn, bc
D-WD B21 Hs. 425
parts
DMA 56//13

B0284 Missa Gaudent brevitate moderni
SATB, 2 vln, 2 vla, bsn/vlne, bc
Sex missarum brevium, no. 5

B0285 Missa Hyemalis
SATB, 2 vln, 2 vla, bsn/vlne, bc
Sex missarum brevium, no. 6

B0286 Missa In sudore vultus mei vescor pane meo
4 vv, instr
I-Bc DD58

B0287 Missa Jubilate Deo, omnis terra
4 vv
I-Bc DD58

B0288 Missa Laudate cum laetitia
4 vv
I-Bc DD58
Agnus Dei in D-Bds Ms. L331

B0289 Missa Oettingana
SATB, 2 vln, vla, bsn, bc
D-WD B20 Hs. 426
parts
DMA 56//18

BERNABEI, Giuseppe Antonio (*continued*)

B0290   **Missa Servite Domine in timore**
         SATB
         D-Mbs Chorbuch Mus. ms. 2754, no. 4 (1715)
             DMA 3/703
         D-Mk Ms. Mk 1053, no. 4
             score
         A-Wn Ms. 16522, no. 4
             score

B0291   **Missa Sicut fulgur**
         SATB, 2 vln, 2 vla, bsn/vlne, bc
         Sex missarum brevium, no. 3

B0292   **Missa Timete Dominum**
         SATB, 2 vln, 2 vla, bsn/vlne, bc
         Sex missarum brevium, no. 1

B0293   **Missa Velociter currit**
         SATB, 2 vln, 2 vla, bsn/vlne, bc
         Sex missarum brevium, no. 2

B0294   **Missa Venatorum**
         SATB, 2 vln, 2 vla, bsn/vlne, bc
         Sex missarum brevium, no. 4

B0295   **Missa Veni creator spiritus**
         SATB
         D-Mbs Chorbuch Mus. ms. 2754, no. 1 (1715)
             DMA 3/703
         D-Mk Ms. Mk 1053, no. 1
             score
         D-Mk Ms. Mk 265
             parts
         A-Wn Ms. 16522, no. 1
             score
         I-Bc DD58
         Ed. S. Lück, *Sammlung ausgezeichneter
             Kompositionen I*, pp. 218-40
         Ed. H. Bäurle, *Altklassische Messen*
             (Breitkopf & Härtel, PB-3133, CHB-2543)

B0296   **Missa Vias tuas, Domine**
         SATB
         D-Mbs Chorbuch Mus. ms. 2754, no. 2 (1715)
             DMA 3/703
         D-Mk Ms. Mk 1053, no. 2; Ms. Mk 266
             score
         A-Wn Ms. 16522, no. 2
             score
         Ed. S. Lück, *Sammlung ausgezeichneter
             Kompositionen I*, pp. 144-65

B0297   **Ne recorderis peccata**
         SATB, 3 vla, vc, vlne, bc
         Vigil for the Dead

         D-Mk Ms. Mk 281, no. 8 (1716)
             parts

B0298   **Nunc dimittis primi toni**
         SATB
         D-Mk Ms. Mk 1053, no. 7 (1687)
             score
         D-Mbs Chorbuch Mus. ms. 2752, no. 1 (1687)
             DMA 3/704

B0299   **Nunc dimittis secundi toni**
         SATB
         D-Mk Ms. Mk 1053, no. 8 (1687)
             score
         D-Mbs Chorbuch Mus. ms. 2752, no. 2 (1687)
             DMA 3/704

B0300   **Nunc dimittis tertii toni**
         SATB
         D-Mk Ms. Mk 1053, no. 9 (1687)
             score
         D-Mbs Chorbuch Mus. ms. 2752, no. 3 (1687)
             DMA 3/704

B0301   **Nunc dimittis quarti toni**
         SATB
         D-Mk Ms. Mk 1053, no. 10 (1687)
             score
         D-Mbs Chorbuch Mus. ms. 2752, no. 4 (1687)
             DMA 3/704

B0302   **Nunc dimittis quinti toni**
         SATB
         D-Mk Ms. Mk 1053, no. 11 (1687)
             score
         D-Mbs Chorbuch Mus. ms. 2752, no. 5 (1687)
             DMA 3/704

B0303   **Nunc dimittis sexti toni**
         SATB
         D-Mk Ms. Mk 1053, no. 12 (1687)
             score
         D-Mbs Chorbuch Mus. ms. 2752, no. 6 (1687)
             DMA 3/704

B0304   **Nunc dimittis septimi toni**
         SATB
         D-Mk Ms. Mk 1053, no. 13 (1687)
             score
         D-Mbs Chorbuch Mus. ms. 2752, no. 7 (1687)
             DMA 3/704

B0305   **Nunc dimittis octavi toni**
         SATB
         D-Mk Ms. Mk 1053, no. 14 (1687)
             score

D-Mbs Chorbuch Mus. ms. 2752, no. 8 (1687)
DMA 3/704

B0306 O quam suavis est Domine
SATB, bc
A-Wn Ms. 15604, fol. 161-
score
D-Mk Ms. Mk 267
score and parts
D-Mbs Mus. ms. 690
score

B0307 O sacrum convivium
SATB, bc
D-Mbs Mus. ms. 4435/1; Mus. ms. 689,
no. 2
score
A-Wn Ms. 15604, fol. 157v-
score
A-Wgm I Verschiedene 22972
parts
Ed. Proske, *Musica divina* I/2, pp. 204-06

B0308 O vos omnes
SATB, bc
Holy Week
D-Mk Ms. Mk 279, no. 23
score and parts

B0309 Occurrunt turbae
SATB, bc
Palm Sunday
A-Wn Ms. 15604, fol. 141r-142v
score
D-Mk Ms. Mk 268 (1720)
score and parts
D-Mbs Mus. Ms. 691
score

B0310 Omnes amici mei
SATB, bc
Holy Week
D-Mk Ms. Mk 279, no. 10
score and parts

B0311 Pange lingua
SATB, bc
Corpus Christi
D-Mk Ms. Mk 269
parts
A-Wn Ms. 16523, no. 3
score

B0312 Pater superni luminis
SATB, bc
Feast of Saint Mary Magdalene

A-Wn Ms. 16523, no. 15 (1715)
score
D-Mk Ms. Mk 270
parts

B0313 Peccantem me quotidie
SATB, 3 vla, vc, vlne, bc
Vigil for the Dead
D-Mk Ms. Mk 281, no. 9 (1716)
parts

B0314 Placare Christe servulis
SATB, bc
All Saints Day
A-Wn Ms. 16523, no. 31 (1717)
score
D-Mk Ms. Mk 271
parts

B0315 Plange plebs mea
SATB, bc
Holy Week
D-Mk Ms. Mk 279, no. 21
score and parts

B0316 Popule meus (I)
4 vv
A-KR Kasten F, Facs. 34, no. 35

B0317 Popule meus (II)
SATB, SATB
D-Rp
Ed. Proske, *Musica divina* I/4, pp. 298-306

B0318 Popule meus (III)
SATB, SATB
Good Friday
D-Mk Ms. Mk 272
score and parts
D-Mbs Mus. ms. 686
score
D-MÜs Hs. 454

B0319 Popule meus (IV)
SATB, SATB
Good Friday
D-Mk Ms. Mk 273 (1675)
score and parts

B0320 Popule meus (V)
SATB, SATB
Good Friday
D-Bds Mus. ms. 30098, no. 1
score

B0321 Popule meus (VI)
SATB, SATB

BERNABEI, Giuseppe Antonio (*continued*)

A-Wn Ms. 15604, fol. 145-150v
score

B0322 **Qui Lazarum**
SATB, 3 vla, vc, vlne, bc
Vigil for the Dead
D-Mk Ms. Mk 281, no. 4 (1716)
parts

B0323 **Qui confidunt in Domino**
SATB, vc, vlne, bc
4th Sunday of Lent
D-Mk Ms. Mk 274
parts

B0324 **Qui habitat in adjutorio**
SATB, vc, vlne, bc
1st Sunday of Lent
D-Mk Ms. Mk 275
parts

B0325 **Recessit pastor noster**
SATB, bc
Holy Week
D-Mk Ms. Mk 279, no. 22
score and parts

B0326 **Regem cui omnia vivunt**
SATB, 3 vla, vc, vlne, bc
Vigil for the Dead
D-Mk Ms. Mk 281, no. 2 (1716)
parts

B0327 **Regem venturum**
SATB, bc
D-Mk Ms. Mk 232
parts

B0328 **Regina caeli laetare**
SATB, 2 vln, 3 vla, 2 ob, 3 tbn, vlne, bc
A-Wn Ms. 16684, no. 1 (1701)
score

B0329 **Regina caeli laetare**
SATB, bc
A-Wn Ms. 16684, no. 2
score

B0330 **Regina caeli laetare**
SATB, 2 vln, 2 vla, 2 ob, 3 tbn, vc, bc
A-Wn Ms. 16684, no. 3 (1715)
score

B0331 **Regina caeli laetare**
SATB
D-Mbs Mus. ms. 4435/3 (1702)
score

B0332 **Regina caeli laetare**
SATB, vc, vlne, bc
D-Mk Ms. Mk 276 (1702)
parts

B0333 **Regina caeli laetare**
SATB, bc
D-Mbs Mus. ms. 6163, no. 5
score

B0334 **Regina caeli laetare**
SATB
Ed. S. Lück, *Sammlung ausgezeichneter Compositionen II*, pp. 297-99

B0335 **Regis superni nuntia**
SATB, bc
Feast of Saint Theresa
A-Wn Ms. 16523, no. 18 (1715)
score
D-Mk Ms. Mk 277
parts

B0336 **Requiem Mass (I)**
SATB, 2 vln, 2 vla, 2 ob, 2 clar, bc
A-Wn Ms. 16641, no. 1
score

B0337 **Requiem Mass (II)**
SATB, 2 vln, 2 vla, 2 ob, bc
A-Wn Ms. 16641, no. 2
score

B0338 **Requiem Mass (III)**
4 vv
I-Af Mss. N. 140/4
score and parts

B0339 **Requiem Mass (IV)**
SATB, bc
D-Bds Mus. ms. L 194
score

B0340 **Responsoria in Passione Domine Palmarum**
SSATTB
D-Mk Ms. Mk 280
score and parts
Appears to be polyphonic settings of the
crowd portions of the Passion text

B0341 **Saepe expugnaverunt**
SATB, vc, bc
Passion Sunday
D-Mk Ms. Mk 282
parts

B0342 **Salutis humanae sator**
SATB, bc

Ascension
A-Wn Ms. 16523, no. 24 (1716)
score
D-Mk Ms. Mk 283
parts

B0343 **Salve regina (I)**
SATB, bc
A-Wn Ms. 16686, no. 1 (1690)
score

B0344 **Salve regina (II)**
SATB, bc
A-Wn Ms. 16686, no. 2 (1692)
score

B0345 **Salve regina (III)**
SATB, 2 vln, 2 vla, 2 ob, bc
A-Wn Ms. 16686, no. 3 (1702)
score

B0346 **Salve regina (IV)**
SATB, bc
A-Wn Ms. 16686, no. 3 (1728)
score

B0347 **Salve regina (V)**
SATB, vc, vlne, bc
D-Mk Ms. Mk 284
parts

B0348 **Salve regina (VI)**
SATB, vlne, bc
D-Mk Ms. Mk 285
score and parts
D-Bds Mus. ms. 30098, no. 3; Mus. ms.
Winterfeld 71; Mus. ms. Teschner 120,
pp. 16-19
score
Ed. S. Lück, *Sammlung ausgezeichneter
Kompositionen II*, pp. 301-03
Ed. R. von Hertzberg, *Musica sacra* (Bote
& Bock), vol. 14, pp. 22-24

B0349 **Salve regina (VII)**
SATB, bc
D-Mbs Mus. ms. 6163, no. 1
score

B0350 **Salvete flores martyrum**
SATB, bc
Feast of the Holy Innocents
A-Wn Ms. 16523, no. 13 (1715)
score
D-Mk Ms. Mk 286
parts

B0351 **Sanctorum meritis**
SATB, bc
Common of Many Martyrs
A-Wn Ms. 16523, no. 14 (1715)
score
D-Mk Ms. Mk 287 or 288
parts

B0352 **Sanctorum meritis enclyta**
SATB, bc
Common of Many Martyrs
A-Wn Ms. 16523, no. 1 (1738)
score
D-Mk Ms. Mk 287 or 288
parts

B0353 **Scapulis suis**
SATB, vc, vlne, bc
1st Sunday of Lent
D-Mk Ms. Mk 289
parts

B0354 **Seniores populi**
SATB, bc
Holy Week
D-Mk Ms. Mk 279, no. 9
score and parts

B0355 **Sepulto Domino**
SATB, bc
Holy Week
D-Mk Ms. Mk 279, no. 27
score and parts

B0356 **Stabat Mater (I)**
SATB, 2 vln, 2 vla, bc
D-Mk Ms. Mk 291 (1680)
score and parts
D-Mk Ms. Mk 1053, no. 33
score
D-Mbs Mus. ms. 4439 (1680)
score
A-Wn Ms. 16685, no. 1 (1680)
score

B0357 **Stabat Mater (II)**
SATB, 2 vln, 2 vla, 2 tbn, vlne, bsn, bc
D-Mk Ms. Mk 290 (1715)
score and parts
D-Mk Ms. Mk 1053, no. 34
score
D-Mbs Mus. ms. 4422 (1725)
score
A-Wn Ms. 16685, no. 2 (1725)
score

BERNABEI, Giuseppe Antonio (*continued*)

B0358   **Tamquam ad latronem**
SATB, bc
Holy Week
D-Mk Ms. Mk 279, no. 13
score and parts

B0359   **Te Deum laudamus**
SATB, SATB, 2 vln, 2 vla, clar, 3 tromba,
bc
A-Wn Ms. 15999
score
D-MÜs Hs. 453

B0360   **Te Deum laudamus**
SATB, SATB, 2 vln, 2 vla, 2 clar, 3 tbn, bc
D-Mk Ms. Mk 1050, no. 12
score

B0361   **Te Joseph celebrent**
SATB, bc
Feast of Saint Joseph
A-Wn Ms. 16523, no. 29 (1716)
score
D-Mk Ms. Mk 292
parts

B0362   **Te splendor et virtus**
SATB, bc
Feast of Saint Michael the Archangel
A-Wn Ms. 16523, no. 16 (1715)
score
D-Mk Ms. Mk 293 (1715)
parts

B0363   **Tenebrae factae sunt**
SATB, bc
Holy Week
D-Mk Ms. Mk 279, no. 14
score and parts

B0364   **Tenuisti manum dexteram**
SATB, vc, vlne, bc
Palm Sunday
D-Mk Ms. Mk 294
parts

B0365   **Tradiderunt me**
SATB, bc
Holy Week
D-Mk Ms. Mk 279, no. 16
score and parts

B0366   **Tradidit in mortem animam**
SATB, bc
Holy Week
D-Mk Ms. Mk 279, no. 19
score and parts

B0367   **Tristes erant Apostoli**
SATB, bc
Common of Apostles in Eastertide
D-Mk Ms. Mk 295 (1716)
parts

B0368   **Tristis est anima**
SATB, bc
Holy Week
D-Mk Ms. Mk 279, no. 2
score and parts

B0369   **Una hora**
SATB, bc
Holy Week
D-Mk Ms. Mk 279, no. 8
score and parts

B0370   **Unus ex discipulis**
SATB, bc
Holy Week
D-Mk Ms. Mk 279, no. 6
score and parts

B0371   **Ut queant laxis**
SATB, bc
Feast of Saint John the Baptist
A-Wn Ms. 16523, no. 20 (1716)
score
D-Mk Ms. Mk 296 (1716)
parts

B0372   **Velum templi**
SATB, bc
Holy Week
D-Mk Ms. Mk 279, no. 11
score and parts

B0373   **Veni creator spiritus (I)**
SATB, bc
Pentecost
D-Mk Ms. Mk 297 (1716)
parts

B0374   **Veni creator spiritus (II)**
SATB, bc
Pentecost
D-Mk Ms. Mk 298
parts

B0375   **Veni creator spiritus (III)**
SATB, bc
Pentecost
A-Wn Ms. 16523, no. 26 (1716)
score

B0376   **Veni creator spiritus (IV)**
SATB, bc
Pentecost

A-Wn Ms. 16523, no. 27 (1716)
score

B0377 **Verbum caro**
4 vv
D-Rp Mappe Benevoli 24
I-Bc R280

B0378 **Verbum caro panem**
SATB
D-Mk Ms. Mk 299 (1696)
score and parts

B0379 **Vexilla regis**
SATB
A-Wn Ms. 15604, fol. 151r-157r
score

B0380 **Vexilla regis prodeunt (I)**
SATB, bc
Feast of the Discovery of the Cross
A-Wn Ms. 16523, no. 28 (1716)
score
D-Mk Ms. Mk 300
parts

B0381 **Vexilla regis prodeunt (II)**
SATB, bc
Good Friday
D-Mk Ms. Mk 301
parts
D-Mbs Mus. ms. 689; Mus ms. 13034
score

B0382 **Vinea mea electa**
SATB, bc
Holy Week
D-Mk Ms. Mk 279, no. 12
score and parts

BERNABEI, Vincenzo (1660-1732/36)

B0383 **Salve Regina**
S/T solo, SATB, 2 vln, 2 vla, 4 clar, vlne,
bc
D-OB MO 128 (1723)
parts

BERNHARD, Christoph (1628-1692)

COLLECTION

Geistliche Harmonien (1665)
RISM B2078 (parts)
DMA 1/1389

WORKS

B0384 **Ach mein herzliebes Jesulein**
SSB, 2 vln, bc
Geistliche Harmonien, no. 16
S-Uu 79:35v-35r (Düben)
tablature
DMA 2/2135
S-Uu 3:11 (Düben)
parts
DMA 2/2135
EdM 65, pp. 130-41
Ed. Streetman (1967), pp. 256-72

B0385 **Benedic, anima mea**
SSATB, SATB, 2 vln, 2 vla, 2 corn, 4 tbn,
bsn, bc
S-Uu 82:6a (Düben) (1664)
tablature
DMA 3/208
EdM 90, pp. 55-76

B0386 **Da pacem, Domine**
SSATB, 2 vln, 4 vla, bc
S-Uu 79:127v-129 (Düben) (1664);
80:68v-71 (Düben) (1665)
tablature
DMA 3/2008
EdM 90, pp. 35-54

B0387 **Das alte Jahr vergangen ist**
STB, bc
S-Uu 36:14 (Düben)
tablature
S-Uu 4:1 (Düben) (1665)
parts
DMA 2/2137
EdM 90, pp. 165-72

B0388 **Euch ists gegeben zu wissen das Geheimnis**
STB, 2 vln, bsn, bc
Geistliche Harmonien, no. 20
EdM 65, pp. 172-85
Ed. Streetman (1967), pp. 312-36

B0389 **Gott, sei mir gnädig**
SATB, 2 vln, 3 vla, bc
Funeral of Johann Rist
Hamburg, 1667
RISM B2081 (parts)
DMA 3/488

B0390 **Habe deine Lust an dem Herrn**
SATB, bc
Geistliche Harmonien, no. 13
EdM 65, pp. 102-7

BERNHARD, Christoph (*continued*)

Ed. Streetman (1967), pp. 337-49

Ed. Streetman (Schirmer)

B0391 Haec dies quam fecit Dominus
SSB, bc
Easter
S-Uu 80:106v-109r, no. 106 (Düben)
tablature
DMA 3/2009
S-Uu 41:17 (Düben) (1665)
parts
DMA 3/2009
EdM 90, pp. 109-18

B0392 Herr nun läßest du deinen Diener
SSATB, SSATB, 2 vln, 2 vla, vlne/bsn,
2 corn, 3 tbn, bc
D-Bds Mus. ms. 30096, no. 8 (Bokemeyer)
(1693)
score
DMA 2/1259
D-Dlb (lost, WW II)
DdT 6, pp. 142-60

B0393 Ich sahe an alles tun
SATB, 2 vln, 2 vla, vlne, bc
Funeral of Hinrich Langebeck
Hamburg, 1669
RISM B2083 (parts)
DMA 57//46
S-Uu 86:22, fol. 6v-10r (Düben)
tablature and parts
DMA 1/1961
D-Bds Mus. ms. 30096, no. 5 (Bokemeyer)
score
DMA 2/1260
DdT 6, pp. 128-41

B0394 Ich sandte die Propheten nicht
ATB, 2 vln, bc
Geistliche Harmonien, no. 19
EdM 65, pp. 162-71
Ed. Streetman (1967), pp. 381-96

B0395 In unbesternter Nacht
SSATB, 2 vln, 2 vla, vc, bc
D-Bds Mus. ms. 30096, no. 7 (Bokemeyer)
score

B0396 Jam mesta quiesce querela
SATB
Funeral for relatives of R. Capelli

Hamburg, 1669
RISM BB2083a (D-Ha A 710/802, fol.
557) (score)
DMA 78//188

B0397 Jerusalem, die du tötest die Propheten
SSB, 2 vln, bc
S-Uu 78:16, fol. 16v-18 (Düben)
tablature
DMA 3/209
Geistliche Harmonien, no. 18
EdM 65, pp. 153-61
Ed. Streetman (1967), pp. 421-33
Ed. Streetman (Concordia, 1973)

B0398 Jubilate Deo, omnis terra
STB, bc
S-Uu 80:109, fol. 109v-110r (Düben)
tablature
DMA 3/2010
S-Uu 42:19 (Düben) (1665)
parts
DMA 3/2010
EdM 90, pp. 119-26

B0399 Lieber Herre Gott, wecke uns auf
SATB, bc
Geistliche Harmonien, no. 14
EdM 65, pp. 108-14
Ed. Streetman (1967), pp. 434-47
Ed. Streetman (Schirmer, as: Hear our
prayer, O Lord)

B0400 Missa à 5
SATTB, 2 vln, 2 vla, 2 ob, bc
D-Bds Mus. ms. 30167, no. 1
score
DMA 2/2139
D-B Mus. ms. 1610
parts
DMA 2/1716
EdM 90, pp. 173-88

B0401 Missa (brevis) Christ unser Herr zum Jordan kam
SSATB
D-B Mus. ms. 1620, no. 2
score
Das Chorwerk 16 (1932), pp. 23-30

B0402 Missa (brevis) Durch Adams Fall
SATTB
D-B Mus. ms. 1620, no. 1
score
Das Chorwerk 107 (1969), pp. 1-13
Ed. Streetman (G. Schirmer, 1973)

B0403 **Missa Minutta**
9 vv, 9 inst in 3 groups
S-Uu
tablature
Information from Streetman, p. 71; not in
Lindberg catalog

B0404 **O anima mea accipe pennas aurorae**
SSATTB, 5 vla, 3 tbn, vlne, bc
S-Uu 4:5 (Düben) (1671-1672)
parts (bc missing)
DMA 2/2140
EdM 90, pp. 135-60
Ed. Grusnick, *Die Düben-Sammlung* 2 (1979)

B0405 **Prudentia prudentiana**
See Jam mesta quiesce querela

B0406 **Reminiscere miseratiorum tuarum, Domine**
ATB, bc
S-Uu 4:6 (Düben)
parts
DMA 2/2141
EdM 90, pp. 25-34

B0407 **Salvum me fac, Deus**
SSATB, 2 vln, 3 vla, bsn, bc
S-Uu 80:70, fol. 70v-75 (Düben)
tablature
S-Uu 45:16 (Düben)
parts
Anonymous: attributed by Streetman (1967),
p. 72

B0408 **Surgit Christus cum trophaeo**
STB soli, SATB choir, 2 vln, 4 vla, vlne,
theorbo, bc
S-Uu 80:64v-68r (Düben) (1665)
tablature
DMA 3/2011
S-Uu 4:7 & 46:5 (Düben)
parts
DMA 3/2011
EdM 90, pp. 77-100

B0409 **Surrexit Christus spes mea, alleluia**
S solo, SATTB choir, 4 vla, vla 5/bsn, bc
S-Uu 4:8 (Düben) (1664)
tablature and parts
DMA 2/2141
EdM 90, pp. 3-24

B0410 **Tribularer si nescirem misericordias**
SSATB, SSATB, 2 vln, 2 corn, 3 tbn,
2 vltta, bsn, bc
D-Bds Mus. ms. 30096, no. 4 (Bokemeyer)
score

DMA 2/1292
D-Dlb (lost in WW II)
DdT 6, pp. 161-72

B0411 **Unser keiner lebt ihm selber**
ATB, 2 vln, bc
Geistliche Harmonien, no. 17
S-Uu 81:152v-154r (Düben)
tablature
DMA 2/2143
S-Uu 4:9 (Düben) (1665)
parts
DMA 2/2143
EdM 65, pp. 142-52
Ed. Streetman (1967), pp. 498-511

B0412 **Wahrlich, wahrlich, ich sage euch**
B solo, SATB, 2 vln, 2 vla, bsn, bc
S-Uu 70:98v-102r (Düben) (1664)
tablature
DMA 3/212
DdT 6, pp. 111-19
Ed. Freudenthal (Deutscher Verlag für
Musik, 1976)

B0413 **Weine nicht, es hat überwunden der Löwe**
See under Matthias Weckmann

B0414 **Wie der Hirsch schreiet nach frischem Wasser**
SATB, bc
Geistliche Harmonien, no. 12
EdM 65, pp. 89-101
Ed. Streetman (1967), pp. 522-43
Ed. Streetman (Roberton, 1974)

B0415 **Zur selbigen Zeit wird dein Volk erlöset werden**
SAT5B, bc
Funeral of Barthold Müller
Hamburg, 1667
RISM B2082 (parts)
DMA 42//73
S-Uu 4:11 (Düben)
parts
Das Chorwerk 107, pp. 14-20
EdM 79, pp. 69-78

BERTALI, Antonio (1605-1669)

B0416 **Accipite**
SATB, bc
Whit Tuesday and Sunday in the Octave of
Corpus Christi
A-KR Ms. Ser. C, Fasc. 51, no. 3/3
score

BERTALI, Antonio (*continued*)

B0417   **Aqua sapientia**
SATB, bc
Easter Tuesday
A-KR Ms. Ser. C, Fasc. 51, no. 2/3
score

B0418   **Beatus vir**
See Vesperae dominicales

B0419   **Benedicite Dominum**
SATB, bc
Feast of the Holy Angels
A-KR Ms. Ser. C, Fasc. 51, no. 4/6
score

B0420   **Benedicta sit**
SATB, bc
Trinity
A-KR Ms. Ser. C, Fasc. 51, no. 3/4
score

B0421   **Benedictus sit Deus pater**
SSAATTBB, 2 vln, 2 tbn, vlne, bc
Trinity
A-Sd A 182
parts

B0422   **Cibavit eos**
SATB, bc
Whit Monday and Corpus Christi
A-KR Ms. Ser. C, Fasc. 51, no. 3/2
score

B0423   **Confessio et pulchri**
SATB, bc
Feast of Saint Lawrence
A-KR Ms. Ser. C, Fasc. 51, no. 4/5
score

B0424   **Confitebor**
See Vesperae dominicales

B0425   **Confitebor tibi Domine**
SSATTB, 2 vln, vltta, 3 tbn, bc
CS-KRa III, 22 (1666)
parts
microfilm: US-SY

B0426   **De ventre matris meae**
SATB, bc
Feast of Saint John the Baptist
A-KR Ms. Ser. C, Fasc. 51, no. 4/2
score

B0427   **Dilexisti justitiam**
SATB, bc
Common of Virgins
A-KR Ms. Ser. C, Fasc. 51, no. 6/7
score

B0428   **Dixit Dominus**
5 vv, instr., bc
D-DS Mus. ms. 102
parts

B0429   **Dixit Dominus**
See also Vesperae dominicales

B0430   **Ecce advenit dominator Dominus**
SATB, bc
Epiphany
A-KR Ms. Ser. C, Fasc. 51, no. 1/4
score

B0431   **Ecce diem triumphalen**
SSAATTBB, 2 vln, 2 vltta, 3 tbn, bc
S-Uu 47:19 (Düben)
parts
DMA 3/1606

B0432   **Ecce illuxit nobis dies redemptionis**
SSATTB, 3 vla, 3 fl, vlne, bc
Christmas Sunday
CS-KRa II, 145
parts
microfilm: US-SY

B0433   **Exultate et cantate**
SAB
RISM 1649[1]
US-Wc M1490.M88, pp. 46-49
score
US-Wc film 312

B0434   **Gaudeamus**
SATB, bc
Assumption of the Virgin Mary
A-KR Ms. Ser. C, Fasc. 51, no. 5/3
score

B0435   **In deserto iuxta Torrentam**
SATBB, 2 vln, 2 vla, vlne, bc
A-Sd A184
parts

B0436   **In medio ecclesia**
SATB, bc
Feast of Saint John the Evangelist
A-KR Ms. Ser. C, Fasc. 51, no. 1/3
score

B0437   **Intret in conspectu**
SATB, bc
Common of Many Martyrs
A-KR Ms. Ser. C, Fasc. 51, no. 6/4
score

B0438 Introduxit
SATB, bc
Easter Monday
A-KR Ms. Ser. C, Fasc. 51, no. 2/2
score

B0439 Justus germinabit sicut lilium
SSATTB, 6 vla, vlne, bc
CS-KRa II, 183 (1676)
parts
microfilm: US-SY

B0440 Laudate Dominum
See Vesperae dominicales

B0441 Laudate, pueri
See Vesperae dominicales

B0442 Litaniae Beatae Mariae Virginis
SSAATTBB, 2 vln, vlne, bc
CS-KRa III, 56
parts
microfilm: US-SY

B0443 Loquebar de testimonius
SATB, bc
Common of Virgins and Martyrs
A-KR Ms. Ser. C, Fasc. 51, no. 6/6
score

B0444 Magna dies laetitiae
SSAATTBB, 3 vla, 4 tbn, bc
Visitation of the Virgin Mary
CS-KRa II, 159
parts
microfilm: US-SY

B0445 Magnificat
See Vesperae dominicales

B0446 Maria Magdalena
SSTT, vln, 4 vla, 2 corn, tbn, bc
A-Wn Ms. 16010
score

B0447 Me expectave
SATB, bc
Feast of Saint Mary Magdalene
A-KR Ms. Ser. C, Fasc. 51, no. 4/4
score

B0448 Mihi autem nimis
SATB, bc
Common of Apostles and Evangelists
A-KR Ms. Ser. C, Fasc. 51, no. 6/1
score

B0449 Miserere mei Deus
SSATB, 3 vln, vlne, bc
CS-KRa XII, 14

parts
microfilm: US-SY

B0450 Missa Afflictorum
SSAATTBB, 2 vln, 3 vla, vlne, bc
CS-KRa I, 189
parts
microfilm: US-SY

B0451 Missa Angeli custodis
SATB, 3 vla, 3 tbn, bc
CS-KRa I, 18
parts
microfilm: US-SY

B0452 Missa Ante patrum
SATB, 2 vln, 2 vla, vlne, bc
CS-KRa I, 152
parts
microfilm: US-SY

B0453 Missa Archiducalis
SSATTB, 2 vln, 2 vltta, 2 vla, clar, 2 corn,
4 tbn, bc
CS-KRa I, 6 (1669)
parts
microfilm: US-SY

B0454 Missa Cellensis
SSAATTBB, 2 vln, 4 vla, 2 corn, 3 tbn,
vlne, bc
CS-KRa I, 137
parts
microfilm: US-SY

B0455 Missa Consecrationis
SSSAATTTBB, 2 vln, 2 vla, 2 corn, 4 tbn,
5 tbtta, vlne, bc
CS-KRa I, 184
parts
microfilm: US-SY

B0456 Missa in contrapuncto
SATB, vlne, bc
CS-KRa I, 116 (1676)
parts
Lacking in US-SY microfilm collection

B0457 Missa In partu
SATTB, 2 vln, 4 vltta, 4 tbn, vlne, bc
CS-KRa I, 14
parts
microfilm: US-SY

B0458 Missa In periculis
SATB, 2 vln, 4 vltta, 3 tbn, vlne, bc
CS-KRa I, 188
parts (vltta II-IV and all tbn parts lacking)
microfilm: US-SY

BERTALI, Antonio (*continued*)

B0459 **Missa Lachrymarum**
SATB, 2 vln, 3 vla, bc
CS-KRa I, 21 (1676)
score
microfilm: US-SY

B0460 **Missa Minima**
SSATTB, 2 vln, vltta/tbn, vlne, bc
CS-KRa I, 17 (1666); I, 192
parts
microfilm: US-SY

B0461 **Missa Mixta**
SSAATTBB, 2 vln, 4 vla, 4 tbn, vlne, bc
CS-KRa I, 121; I, 228
parts
microfilm: US-SY
A-KR Kasten C, Fasc. 7, no. 654
parts

B0462 **Missa Nec non**
SSATB, 5 vla, vlne, bc
CS-KRa I, 190
score and parts
microfilm: US-SY

B0463 **Missa Nihil**
SATB, 2 vln, 3 vla, 2 corn, 4 tbn, bc
CS-KRa I, 12
parts (vla, corn, & tbn parts lacking)
microfilm: US-SY

B0464 **Missa Novi anni**
SSAATTBB, 2 vln, 4 vla, 4 tbn, bc
CS-KRa I, 225
parts
microfilm: US-SY

B0465 **Missa Novi regis**
SSAATTBB, 2 vln, 2 vltta, 4 tbn, theorbo, bc
CS-KRa I, 7 (1668)
parts
microfilm: US-SY

B0466 **Missa Omnium sanctorum**
SSAATTBB, 2 vln, 2 vla, 3 vla/tbn, 2 corn, bsn/tbn, vlne, bc
CS-KRa I, 46
parts
microfilm: US-SY

B0467 **Missa Pacis (I)**
SATTB, 2 vln, 4 vla/tbn, bc
CS-KRa I, 9
parts
microfilm: US-SY

B0468 **Missa Pacis (II)**
SSAATTBB, 2 vln, 3 tbn, bc
CS-KRa I, 11 (1665)
parts
microfilm: US-SY

B0469 **Missa Post partem**
SATTB, 2 vln, 4 vla, 4 tbn, vlne, bc
CS-KRa I, 191
parts (tbn parts lacking)
microfilm: US-SY

B0470 **Missa Redemptoris**
SSAATTBB, 2 vln, 4 vla, 2 corn, 5 tbn, vlne, bc
A-KR Kasten C, Fasc. 12, no. 688
parts
CS-KRa I, 234 (1677)
score and parts
microfilm: US-SY

B0471 **Missa Reditus**
SSATTB, 2 vln, 4 vla, 2 clar, 4 tbn, vlne, bc
CS-KRa I, 10
parts
microfilm: US-SY

B0472 **Missa Resurrectionis**
SSAATTBB, 2 vln, 4 vltta, 2 corn, 2 clar, 5 tbn, bc
CS-KRa I, 13
parts
microfilm: US-SY

B0473 **Missa Sanctae crucis**
SATB, 2 vln, 3 vla, bc
CS-KRa I, 139
parts
microfilm: US-SY

B0474 **Missa Sancti Francisci Xaverii**
SATTB, 2 vln, 4 tbn/vla, bc
CS-KRa I, 285
parts
microfilm: US-SY

B0475 **Missa Sancti Josephi**
SATB, vlne, bc
CS-KRa I, 131
parts
microfilm: US-SY

B0476 **Missa Sancti Spiritus**
SATB, SATB, 2 vln, 3 vla, 2 corn, 2 clar,
4 tbn, vlne, bc
CS-KRa I, 185
parts
microfilm: US-SY

B0477 **Missa Semiminima**
SATB, SATB, 4 vltta, 4 tbn, bc
A-KR Kasten C, Fasc. 12, no. 690
parts

B0478 **Missa Vivorum**
SSATTB, 2 vln, vltta, 2 vla, vlne, bc
S-Uu 80:94 (Düben) (1665)
tablature
CS-KRa I, 16 (1666)
parts (SSATTB, 6 vla, 4 tbn, bc)
microfilm: US-SY

B0479 **Nos autem gloriari**
SATB, bc
Feast of the Discovery of the Cross
A-KR Ms. Ser. C, Fasc. 51, no. 4/1
score

B0480 **Nunc sciovere**
SATB, bc
Feast of Saints Peter and Paul
A-KR Ms. Ser. C, Fasc. 51, no. 4/3
score

B0481 **O gloriosissima Virgo**
SSATTB, 4 vla ad lib, vlne, bc
CS-KRa II, 279 (1672)
parts
microfilm: US-SY

B0482 **O virginum virgo, corona sanctorum**
SSATTB, 2 vln, 3 tbn, vlne, bc
Feast of the Virgin Mary
A-Sd A 183
parts

B0483 **Oratorio Maria Magdalena**
See Maria Magdalena

B0484 **Os justi medita**
SATB, bc
Common of a Confessor not a Pope
A-KR Ms. Ser. C, Fasc. 51, no. 6/5
score

B0485 **Protexisti me**
SATB, bc
Common of One Martyr in Eastertide
A-KR Ms. Ser. C, Fasc. 51, no. 6/3
score

B0486 **Puer natus est nobis**
SATB, bc
Christmas and Circumcision
A-KR Ms. Ser. C, Fasc. 51, no. 1/1
score

B0487 **Resurrexi**
SATB, bc
Easter Sunday
A-KR Ms. Ser. C, Fasc. 51, no. 2/1
score

B0488 **Salve regina**
SATB, vln, 4 vla, bc
CS-KRa VI, 4
parts
microfilm: US-SY

B0489 **Salve sancta parens**
SATB, bc
Birth of the Virgin Mary
A-KR Ms. Ser. C, Fasc. 51, no. 5/4
score

B0490 **Scio cui credidi**
SATB, bc
Feast of the Conversion of Saint Paul
A-KR Ms. Ser. C, Fasc. 51, no. 1/5
score

B0491 **Sederunt principes**
SATB, bc
Feast of Saint Stephen
A-KR Ms. Ser. C, Fasc. 51, no. 1/2
score

B0492 **Spiritus Domini**
SATB, bc
Pentecost
A-KR Ms. Ser. C, Fasc. 51, no. 3/1
score

B0493 **Statuit ei, Dominus**
SATB, bc
Common of One Martyr or Confessor Pope
A-KR Ms. Ser. C, Fasc. 51, no. 6/2
score

B0494 **Surge fidelis anima**
SAT, vln, bc
F-Ssp

B0495 **Suscepimus Deus**
SATB, bc
Purification of the Virgin Mary
A-KR Ms. Ser. C, Fasc. 51, no. 5/1
score

BERTALI, Antonio (*continued*)

B0496   **Terra triumphans jubila**
       4 vv, 2 vln, vlne, bc
       F-Ssp

B0497   **Terribilis est**
       SATB, bc
       Dedication of a church
       A-KR Ms. Ser. C, Fasc. 51, no. 6/8
          score

B0498   **Veni sancte spiritus**
       SSATTBB, 2 vln, 2 vltta, tbn, bc
       D-Dlb Mus. ms. 1505-E-500 (Grimma U
          25/O 8)
          parts

B0499   **Venite, gentes**
       4 vv, 3 vla, 3 vltta, bc
       F-Ssp

B0500   **Vesperae dominicales**
       SSAATTBB, vlne, bc
       CS-KRa III, 35
          parts
          microfilm: US-SY
          Includes: Dixit Dominus, Confitebor, Beatus
             vir, Laudate pueri, Laudate Dominum,
             Magnificat

B0501   **Vidi luciferum**
       SSAATTBB, 2 vln, 2 gamba, 2 corn, 3 tbn,
          vlne, bc
       "For the dedication of St. Michael"
       CS-KRa II, 282
          parts
          microfilm: US-SY

B0502   **Viri Galilaei**
       SATB, bc
       Ascension
       A-KR Ms. Ser. C, Fasc. 51, no. 2/4
          score

B0503   **Vultum tuum**
       SATB, bc
       Annunciation to the Virgin Mary
       A-KR Ms. Ser. C, Fasc. 51, no. 5/2
          score

BERTOUCH, Georg von (1668-1743)

B0504   **Gott der Herr der Mächtige redet**
       SATB, 3 vln, 3 gambas, bc
       D-Bds 30095, no. 10 (Bokemeyer) (1694)
          score

BIBER, Heinrich Ignaz Franz (1644-1704)

COLLECTION

       Vesperai longiores ac breviores (1693)
       RISM B2613 (parts)
       DMA 3/26

WORKS

B0505   **Beati omnes** (Psalmi per annum necessarii)
       SATB, 2 vln, 2 vla, 3 tbn ad lib., bc
       Vesperae longiores ac breviores, no. 28

B0506   **Beatus vir** (Psalmi breviores)
       SATB, 2 vln, 2 vla, 3 tbn ad lib., bc
       Vesperae longiores ac breviores, no. 15

B0507   **Beatus vir** (Psalmi longiores)
       SATB, 2 vln, 2 vla, 3 tbn ad lib., bc
       Vesperae longiores ac breviores, no. 3

B0508   **Confitebor** (Psalmi breviores)
       SATB, 2 vln, 2 vla, 3 tbn ad lib., bc
       Vesperae longiores ac breviores, no. 14

B0509   **Confitebor** (Psalmi longiores)
       SATB, 2 vln, 2 vla, 3 tbn ad lib., bc
       Vesperae longiores ac breviores, no. 2

B0510   **Credidi** (Psalmi per annum necessarii)
       SATB, 2 vln, 2 vla, 3 tbn ad lib., bc
       Vesperae longiores ac breviores, no. 23

B0511   **De profundis** (Psalmi per annum necessarii)
       SATB, 2 vln, 2 vla, 3 tbn ad lib., bc
       Vesperae longiores ac breviores, no. 26

B0512   **Dixit Dominus**
       SATB, SATB, 2 vln, 2 vla, 4 tpt, timp,
          2 corn, 3 tbn, vlne, bc
       CS-KRa III, 89 (autograph)
          parts
          microfilm: US-SY

B0513   **Dixit Dominus** (Psalm de B. M. Virgine)
       SATB, 2 vln, 2 vla, 3 tbn ad lib., bc
       Vesperae longiores ac breviores, no. 7

B0514   **Dixit Dominus** (Psalmi breviores)
       SATB, 2 vln, 2 vla, 3 tbn ad lib., bc
       Vesperae longiores ac breviores, no. 13

B0515   **Dixit Dominus** (Psalmi longiores)
       SATB, 2 vln, 2 vla, 3 tbn ad lib., bc
       Vesperae longiores ac breviores, no. 1

B0516   **Domine probasti** (Psalmi per annum necessarii)
       SATB, 2 vln, 2 vla, 3 tbn ad lib., bc
       Vesperae longiores ac breviores, no. 25

B0517   **Huc poenitentes**
       SSATB, 2 vln, 2 vla, 3 tbn, bsn, vlne, 3 org

A-Sd A 180
parts

B0518   **In convertendo** (Psalmi per annum necessarii)
SATB, 2 vln, 2 vla, 3 tbn ad lib., bc
Vesperae longiores ac breviores, no. 243

B0519   **In exitu Israel** (Psalmi per annum necessarii)
SATB, 2 vln, 2 vla, 3 tbn ad lib., bc
Vesperae longiores ac breviores, no. 29

B0520   **Laetatus sum** (Psalm de B. M. Virgine)
SATB, 2 vln, 2 vla, 3 tbn ad lib., bc
Vesperae longiores ac breviores, no. 9

B0521   **Laetatus sum** (Psalmi breviores)
SATB, 2 vln, 2 vla, 3 tbn ad lib., bc
Vesperae longiores ac breviores, no. 19

B0522   **Lauda Jerusalem** (Psalm de B. M. Virgine)
SATB, 2 vln, 2 vla, 3 tbn ad lib., bc
Vesperae longiores ac breviores, no. 110

B0523   **Lauda Jerusalem** (Psalmi breviores)
SATB, 2 vln, 2 vla, 3 tbn ad lib., bc
Vesperae longiores ac breviores, no. 21

B0524   **Laudate Dominum** (Psalmi breviores)
SATB, 2 vln, 2 vla, 3 tbn ad lib., bc
Vesperae longiores ac breviores, no. 176

B0525   **Laudate Dominum** (Psalmi longiores)
SATB, 2 vln, 2 vla, 3 tbn ad lib., bc
Vesperae longiores ac breviores, no. 5

B0526   **Laudate, pueri** (Psalm de B. M. Virgine)
SATB, 2 vln, 2 vla, 3 tbn ad lib., bc
Vesperae longiores ac breviores, no. 8

B0527   **Laudate, pueri** (Psalmi breviores)
SATB, 2 vln, 2 vla, 3 tbn ad lib., bc
Vesperae longiores ac breviores, no. 16

B0528   **Laudate, pueri** (Psalmi breviores)
SATB, 2 vln, 2 vla, 3 tbn ad lib., bc
Vesperae longiores ac breviores, no. 18

B0529   **Laudate, pueri** (Psalmi longiores)
SATB, 2 vln, 2 vla, 3 tbn ad lib., bc
Vesperae longiores ac breviores, no. 4

B0530   **Litania de S. Josepho**
SATB, SATB, 2 vln, 5 vla, 2 tpt, 3 tbn, bc
A-Sd A 435
parts

B0531   **Litaniae Lauretanae** (Psalmi per annum necessarii)
SATB, 2 vln, 2 vla, 3 tbn ad lib., bc
Vesperae longiores ac breviores, no. 30

B0532   **Lux perpetua**
SATB, SATB, 2 vln, 2 vla, 3 tbn, vlne, bc
CS-KRa II, 259 (1673)

parts
microfilm: US-SY

B0533   **Magnificat**
SATB, SATB, 2 vln, 2 vla, 4 tpt, timp,
2 corn, 3 tbn, vlne, bc
CS-KRa III, 89 (autograph) and III, 95
parts
microfilm: US-SY

B0534   **Magnificat** (Psalm de B. M. Virgine)
SATB, 2 vln, 2 vla, 3 tbn ad lib., bc
Vesperae longiores ac breviores, no. 12

B0535   **Magnificat** (Psalmi breviores)
SATB, 2 vln, 2 vla, 3 tbn ad lib., bc
Vesperae longiores ac breviores, no. 22

B0536   **Magnificat** (Psalmi longiores)
SATB, 2 vln, 2 vla, 3 tbn ad lib., bc
Vesperae longiores ac breviores, no. 6

B0537   **Memento** (Psalmi per annum necessarii)
SATB, 2 vln, 2 vla, 3 tbn ad lib., bc
Vesperae longiores ac breviores, no. 27

B0538   **Missa Aileluia**
SATB, SATB, 2 vln, 3 vla, 6 tpt, timp,
2 corn, 3 tbn, theorbo, vlne, bc
A-KR Ms. C/8, 661
score and parts
CH-E 438, 8
score

B0539   **Missa Bruxellensis**
SATB, SATB, 2 vln, 3 vla, 4 tpt, 2 corn, 3
tbn, timp, bc
B-Br Ms. II 3862
score
Ed. Feininger, Orazio Benevoli, *Opera
omnia* 7a
Cf. Chafe (1987), pp. 63-66

B0540   **Missa Christi resurgentis**
SATB, SATB, 2 vln, 2 vla, 2 corn, 2 clar,
3 tbn, vlne, bc
CS-KRa I, 103
parts

B0541   **Missa ex B**
SSATBB, bc
A-SEI
parts

B0542   **Missa Quadragemisalis**
SATB, bc
CS-KRa I, 297
parts
microfilm: US-SY

BIBER, Heinrich Ignaz Franz (*continued*)

    A-SEI D III 2a
    parts
    CH-E
    score
    D-Mbs
    score
    Cf. Chafe (1987), p. 234

B0543   **Missa Sancti Alexii**
    SATB, bc
    D-OB MO 130a (1725)
    parts

B0544   **Missa Sancti Henrici**
    SSATB, 2 vln, 3 vla, 2 clar, 3 tpt, timp,
      3 tbn, vlne, bc
    A-KR Ms. C,12,685
    parts
    CH-E
    score
    DTÖ 49, pp. 1-47

B0545   **Missa Salisburgensis**
    SSAATTBB, SSAATTBB, 4 vln, 8 vla, 4 rec,
      2 ob, 2 corn, 2 tpt, 2 clar, 4 tbn, 2 org, bc
    A-Sca Hs. 751
      score
      Facsimile in Orazio Benevoli, *Opera omnia* 7b
    B-Br Ms. I 3864
      score
    DTÖ 20, pp. 1-89
    Cf. Chafe (1987), pp. 63-66

B0546   **Ne cedite mentes**
    SSATB, 2 vln, 2 vla, 3 tbn, org, org/tiorbo,
      org/vla
    A-Sd A 179
    parts

B0547   **Nisi Dominus** (Psalm de B. M. Virgine)
    SATB, 2 vln, 2 vla, 3 tbn ad lib., bc
    Vesperae longiores ac breviores, no. 10

B0548   **Nisi Dominus** (Psalmi breviores)
    SATB, 2 vln, 2 vla, 3 tbn ad lib., bc
    Vesperae longiores ac breviores, no. 20

B0549   **Plaudite tympana**
    SSAATTBB, SSAATTBB, 4 vln, 8 vla, 4 rec,
      2 ob, 2 corn, 2 tpt, 2 clar, 4 tbn, 2 org, bc
    A-Sca Hs. 751
      score
    DTÖ 20, pp. 90-100
    Facsimile in Orazio Benevoli, *Opera omnia* 7a
    Cf. Chafe (1987), pp. 63-66

B0550   **Quo abiit dilectus tuus**
    SATB, 4 vla, 4 org
    A-GÖ Ms. 1009
    parts
    A-Sd A 178
    parts

B0551   **Requiem à 15**
    SSATBB, 4 vltta, 2 trombe basse, 2 ob,
      3 tbn, vlne, bsn, bc
    A-Sd A 181
    parts
    Ed. Jaksch (1977)

B0552   **Requiem ex F**
    SSATB, 2 vln, 3 vla, 3 tbn, bc
    A-Sd A 182
    parts
    A-H Archiv no. 51
    parts
    DtÖ 59, pp. 41-72

B0553   **Stabat Mater**
    SATB, bc
    A-Sd Wachskammer Archiv, Wb. 21
      score
    A-Ssp 1229.55
      parts
    CH-E
      score

BLEYER, Georg (1647-after 1694)

B0554   **Ich danke dir, Herr mein Gott**
    SSATB, 2 vln, 2 vla, bsn, bc
    D-F Ms. Ff. Mus. 141 (1694)
    parts

B0555   **Lobe den Herrn, meine Seele**
    SATB, 2 vln, 3 vla, 4 tpt, timp, bsn, bc
    D-Bds Mus. ms. 30096, no. 14 (Bokemeyer)
    score

B0556   **Nisi dominus aedificaverit**
    SATB, 2 vln, 3 vla, bc
    D-Bds Mus. ms. 30096, no. 15 (Bokemeyer)
    score

BÖDDECKER, Philipp Friedrich (1607-1683)

B0557   **Öffnet euch, ihr Herzensquellen**
    SSB, bc
    Funeral of Maria Agnes Myller
    Stuttgart, 1661
      RISM B3265, Reich 410 (score)
      DMA 57//178

B0558 Te Deum laudamus
    SSATTB, 2 vln, 3 tpt, bsn, bc
    Strassburg, 1655
        RISM B3264 (parts)
        DMA 2/38

BÖHM, Georg (1661-1733)

B0559 Ach Herr, komme hinab
    SSATB, 2 vln, 2 vla, bsn, bc
    21st Sunday after Trinity
    D-Bds Mus. ms. 30242, no. 7 (Bokemeyer)
        score
    Böhm, *Vokalwerke* I, pp. 25-44

B0560 Auf, ihr Völker, danket Gott
    SSATB
    D-WRiv 52:470/AW-1756, no. 15
        score
    Böhm, *Vokalwerke* II, pp. 156-60

B0561 Das Himmelreich ist gleich einem Könige
    SSATB, 2 vln, 2 vla, bsn, bc
    20th Sunday after Trinity
    D-Bds Mus. ms. 30099, no. 2 (Bokemeyer)
        score
    Böhm, *Vokalwerke* I, pp. 1-24
    Hänssler ed. 44/120

B0562 Jauchzet Gott alle Land
    SSATB, 2 vln, 2 vla, 2 corn, 3 tbn, bsn, bc
    D-Bds Mus. ms. 30099, no. 5 (Bokemeyer)
        score
    Böhm, *Vokalwerke* I, pp. 45-68

B0563 Mein Freund ist mein
    SATB, 2 vln, 2 vla, bsn, bc
    2nd Sunday after Epiphany, 20th Sunday
        after Trinity
    D-Bds Mus. ms. 30099, no. 4 (Bokemeyer);
        Mus. ms. 30101, no. 15 (Bokemeyer)
        score
    Böhm, *Vokalwerke* II, pp. 109-34
    Ed. F. Schroeder, *Die Kantate* 42 (1960)

B0564 Nun danket alle Gott
    SSATB
    D-Ell (no shelf number, no. 36 in collection)
        score
    Böhm, *Vokalwerke* II, pp. 161-67

B0565 Nun komm, der Heiden Heiland
    SSATB, 2 vln, 3 tbn, bsn, bc
    D-Bds Mus. ms. 30099, no. 3 (Bokemeyer)
        score
    Böhm, *Vokalwerke* I, pp. 89-108

B0566 Sanctus est Dominus Deus Sabaoth
    SATB, 2 vln, bsn, bc
    D-Bds Mus. ms. 30101, no. 14 (Bokemeyer)
        score
    Böhm, *Vokalwerke* II, pp. 168-81
    New Grove: possibly by Friedrich Nicolaus
        Bruhns

B0567 Satanas und sein Getümmel
    SATB, 2 vln, 2 vla, 2 ob, bsn, bc
    D-Bds Mus. ms. 30101, no. 13 (Bokemeyer)
        score
    Böhm, *Vokalwerke* II, pp. 135-55
    New Grove: possibly by Friedrich Nicolaus
        Bruhns

B0568 Warum toben die Heiden
    SATB, 2 vln, vla, 2 fl, 2 ob, 2 tpt, timp, bc
    D-Bds Mus. ms. 30241, no. 11 (Bokemeyer)
        score
    Böhm, *Vokalwerke* II, pp. 182-215

B0569 Wie lieblich sind deine Wohnungen
    SATB, 2 vln, 2 vla, 2 tpt, bsn, bc
    D-F Ms. Ff. Mus. 163 (1709)
        parts
    Böhm, *Vokalwerke* I, pp. 69-88

BONTEMPI, Giovanni Andrea (ca. 1624-1705)

B0570 Paratum cor meum
    STB, bc
    S-Uu 4:15
        parts

BRANCOVIUS, Simon

B0571 Ach Gott, ich muß in Traurigkeit
    SATB, SSATB, bc
    Funeral of Agnes Elisabeth von Breitenbauch
    Jena, 1651
        RISM B4214 (parts)

BRIEGEL, Wolfgang Carl (1626-1712)

COLLECTIONS

    Braunens . . . Davidische Evangelische Harpfen
        (1685)
        RISM B4486 (parts)
        DMA 2/1053

    Concentus Apostolico-Musicus (1697)
        RISM B4488 (parts)
        DMA 2/1054

BRIEGEL, Wolfgang Carl (*continued*)

Der Psalter Davids, I. Teil (1654)
RISM B4467 (parts)
DMA 2/1537

Des Königs und Propheten Davids 7 Buß-
Psalmen (1692)
RISM B4487 (parts)
DMA 3/500

Evangelische Gespräch I (1660)
RISM B4471 (parts)
DMA 2/1048

Evangelische Gespräch II (1661-1662)
RISM B4472 (parts)
DMA 1/510

Evangelische Gespräch III (1681)
RISM B4473 (parts)
DMA 2/1052

Evangelischer Blumengarten I (1666)
RISM B4474 (parts)
DMA 2/1539

Evangelischer Blumengarten II (1666)
RISM B4475 (parts)
DMA 2/1540

Evangelischer Blumengarten III (1666)
RISM B4476 (parts)
DMA 2/1541

Evangelischer Blumengarten IV (1668)
RISM B4477 (parts)
DMA 3/30

Geistliche Gespräche und Psalmen (1674)
RISM B4480 (parts)
DMA 2/1542

Geistlicher musikalischer Rosengarten I (1658)
RISM B4468 (parts)
DMA 2/1976

Kriegsmanns evangelisches Hosianna (1677)
RISM B4481 (parts)
DMA 2/604

Kriegsmanns evangelisches Hosianna, 2nd ed.
(1690)
RISM B4482 (parts)
DMA 2/1544

Letzter Schwanen-Gesang (1709)
RISM B4489 (parts)
DMA 2/1978

Musicalische Trost-Quelle (1679)
RISM B4483 (parts)
DMA 3/499

Musicalischer Lebens-Brunn (1680)
RISM B4484 (parts)
DMA 2/1977

Rehefelds evangelischer Palmen-Zweig (1684)
RISM B4485 (parts)
DMA 3/31

Zwölf madrigalische Trost-Gesänge (1670-1671)
RISM B4479 (parts)
DMA 2/603

WORKS

B0572　**Ach, ach, wer klaget**
SATB
Funeral of Princess Sophie
D-GOs (1657)
According to E. Noack (1963)

B0573　**Ach daß die Hilfe aus Zion**
SATB, 2 vln, 2 vla, bc
Christmas Day
Musicalische Trost-Quelle, no. 5

B0574　**Ach daß du den Himmel zerrissest**
SSTTB, 2 vln, bc
3rd Sunday of Advent
Evangelische Gespräch I, no. 3
Winterfeld II, no. 140

B0575　**Ach Gott! Ach liebster Gott!**
SATB, 2 vln, bc
22nd Sunday after Trinity
Braunens . . . Davidische Evangelische
Harpfen, no. 63

B0576　**Ach Gott, hilf mir mein Sach recht greifen an**
SATB, 2 vln, vlne, bc
14th Sunday after Trinity
Concentus Apostolico-Musicus, no. 50

B0577　**Ach Gott vom Himmel sieh darein**
SATB, 2 vln, 2 vla, bc
8th Sunday after Trinity
Musicalische Trost-Quelle, no. 43

B0578　**Ach Gott wenn kommt die liebe Zeit**
ATB, 2 vln, vlne, bc
23rd Sunday after Trinity
Concentus Apostolico-Musicus, no. 59

B0579　**Ach Gott wie manches Herzeleid**
SATB, 2 vln, 2 vla, bc
3rd Sunday after Easter
Musicalische Trost-Quelle, no. 28

B0580　**Ach Herr, du Sohn David**
STB, 2 vln, bc

2nd Sunday of Lent
Evangelische Gespräch II, no. 3

B0581 **Ach Herr, du Sohn David**
SATB, 2 vln, 2 vla, bc
2nd Sunday of Lent
Musicalische Trost-Quelle, no. 19

B0582 **Ach Herr, es ist nichts gesundes an meinem Leibe**
SATB, 2 vln, 2 vla, bc
12th Sunday after Trinity
Musicalische Trost-Quelle, no. 47

B0583 **Ach Herr, es ist nichts gesundes an meinem Leibe**
SATB, 2 vln, 2 vla, bc
19th Sunday after Trinity
Musicalischer Lebens-Brunn, no. 58

B0584 **Ach Herr, lehre doch mich**
SSATTB, bc
Zwölf madrigalische Trost-Gesänge, no. 6

B0585 **Ach Herr, lehre doch mich**
SATB, bc
Funeral
Letzter Schwanen-Gesang, no. 7

B0586 **Ach Herr, lehre mich tun**
SATB, 2 vln, 2 vla, bc
4th Sunday after Easter
Musicalische Trost-Quelle, no. 29

B0587 **Ach Herr, lehre mich tun**
SATB, 2 vln, vlne, bc
2nd Sunday of Lent
Concentus Apostolico-Musicus, no. 20

B0588 **Ach Herr mich armen Sünder**
SATB, 2 vln, vlne, bc
Des Königs und Propheten Davids 7 Buß-Psalmen, no. 11

B0589 **Ach Herr, reinige mich wohl**
STB, 2 vln, bc
3rd Sunday after Epiphany
Evangelische Gespräch I, no. 14

B0590 **Ach Herr, strafe mich nicht**
SATB
Der Psalter Davids, I. Teil, pp. 50-56

B0591 **Ach Herr, strafe mich nicht**
SATB, 2 vln, 2 vla, bc
1st Sunday after Easter
Musicalischer Lebens-Brunn, no. 29

B0592 **Ach Herr, strafe mich nicht**
SATB, 2 vln, vlne, bc

Des Königs und Propheten Davids 7 Buß-Psalmen, no. 1

B0593 **Ach Herr, wie ist meiner Feinde**
SATB
Der Psalter Davids, I. Teil, pp. 21-26

B0594 **Ach Herr, wie ist meiner Feinde**
SATB, 2 vln, 2 vla, bc
3rd Sunday of Lent
Musicalische Trost-Quelle, no. 20

B0595 **Ach höret auf zu weinen**
SATB, bc
Funeral
Musicalischer Lebens-Brunn, no. 82

B0596 **Ach Jesu meiner Seelen Wonne**
SATB, 2 vln, bc
Kriegsmanns evangelisches Hosianna, 2nd ed., Anh. no. 1

B0597 **Ach lieben Christen seid getrost**
SSATTB, bc
Zwölf madrigalische Trost-Gesänge, no. 4

B0598 **Ach, was ist unser Leben?**
SSATB, bc
Funeral
Letzter Schwanen-Gesang, no. 13

B0599 **Ach weh mir, sie haben meinen Herrn weggenommen**
STB, 3 vln, bc
Easter Sunday
Evangelische Gespräch II, no. 8

B0600 **Ach, wer hilft mir aus der Not**
STB, 2 instr, bc
Easter Tuesday
Evangelische Gespräch II, no. 12

B0601 **Ach wie elend ist unser Zeit**
SATB, 2 vln, 2 vla, bc
16th Sunday after Trinity
Musicalischer Lebens-Brunn, no. 55

B0602 **Ach wie elend ist unser Zeit**
SATB, bc
Funeral
Letzter Schwanen-Gesang, no. 10

B0603 **Ach wie gar nichts sind doch alle Menschen**
SSATTB
Funeral of Anna Maria Hess
Gotha, 1666
RISM B4497, Reich 103 (score)
DMA 57//44

BRIEGEL, Wolfgang Carl (*continued*)

B0604 **Ach wie gar nichts sind doch alle Menschen**
SSATTB, bc
Zwölf madrigalische Trost-Gesänge, no. 10

B0605 **Ach wie schmerz mich deine Unglücke**
SATB, 2 vln, vlne, bc
Des Königs und Propheten Davids 7 Buß-Psalmen, no. 8

B0606 **Ade verfluchtes Tränental**
SATB, bc
Funeral
Musicalischer Lebens-Brunn, no. 81

B0607 **Alle Augen warten auf dich, Herr**
SAB, 2 vln, gamba, bc
4th Sunday of Lent
Rehefelds evangelischer Palmen-Zweig, no. 15
Ed. F. Noack, *Die Kirchenmusik*, Jg. 1921, p. 85
————, *Vier kleine Kantaten* (Möseler, 1961)
————, "Lose Blätter," no. 250 (Wolfenbüttel: Kallmeyer)

B0608 **Alle die Gottselig leben wollen**
SATB, bc
Feast of Saint James, son of Zebedee
Evangelischer Blumengarten IV, no. 14

B0609 **Alle die Gottselig leben wollen**
SSATB, 2 vln, tbn, bc
3rd Sunday after Easter
Rehefelds evangelischer Palmen-Zweig, no. 23

B0610 **Alle Leibs- und Seelengaben**
SATB, 2 vln, bc
New Year's Day
Braunens . . . Davidische Evangelische Harpfen, no. 9
Cf. Noack (1963)

B0611 **Allein zu dir Herr Jesu Christ**
STB, 2 vln, bc
12th Sunday after Trinity
Evangelische Gespräch III, no. 13

B0612 **Alleluja, der Tag der ist**
SSATTB, 2 vln, bc
Christmas Day
Evangelische Gespräch I, no. 5

B0613 **Alleluja, der Tod ist verschlungen**
SSATTB, 2 vln, bc
Easter Sunday
Evangelische Gespräch II, no. 9

B0614 **Als Jesus Christus in der Nacht, darin er ward verraten**
SATB, 2 vln, 2 vla, bc
Musicalischer Lebens-Brunn, no. 66

B0615 **Also hat Gott die Welt geliebet**
SATB, 2 vln, bc
Whit Monday
Evangelische Gespräch II, no. 21

B0616 **Also hat Gott die Welt geliebet**
SATB, bc
Whit Monday
Evangelischer Blumengarten II, no. 18

B0617 **Also hat Gott die Welt geliebet**
SATB, 2 vln, 2 vla, bc
Whit Monday
Musicalische Trost-Quelle, no. 65

B0618 **Auf den wilden Löwen wirst du gehen**
SATB, 2 vln, bc
3rd Sunday of Lent
Braunens . . . Davidische Evangelische Harpfen, no. 23

B0619 **Auf dich Herr traue ich**
SATB
Der Psalter Davids, I. Teil, pp. 57-74

B0620 **Auf dich Herr traue ich**
SATB, bc
5th Sunday of Lent
Evangelischer Blumengarten II, no. 6

B0621 **Auf dich Herr traue ich**
SATB, 2 vln, 2 vla, bc
5th Sunday of Lent
Musicalische Trost-Quelle, no. 22

B0622 **Auf Seele, auf, auf erwache**
SATB, 2 vln, 2 vla, bc
Septuagesima
Rehefelds evangelischer Palmen-Zweig, no. 9

B0623 **Aus der Tiefen rufe ich Herr**
SATB, 2 vln, vlne, bc
Des Königs und Propheten Davids 7 Buß-Psalmen, no. 6

B0624 **Bedenket doch, ihr Menschenkinder**
SSATB, 2 vln, bc
10th Sunday after Trinity
Kriegsmanns evangelisches Hosianna, no. 46

B0625 **Bei den eitlen Leuten sitz ich nicht**
SATB, 2 vln, bc
4th Sunday after Trinity
Braunens . . . Davidische Evangelische Harpfen, no. 45

B0626 **Bene fecit omnia et surdos fecit audire**
SSATB, 2 vln, tbn, bc
12th Sunday after Trinity
Rehefelds evangelischer Palmen-Zweig, no. 43

B0627 **Betrübtes Herz, O kreuzbelegte Seele**
SATB, 2 vln, bc
3rd Sunday after Easter
Braunens . . . Davidische Evangelische Harpfen, no. 33

B0628 **Bist du Gottes Sohn**
STB, 2 vln, bc
1st Sunday of Lent
Evangelische Gespräch II, no. 2

B0629 **Bringet her dem Herrn ihr Gewaltigen**
SSAB, 2 vln, tbn, bc
Epiphany
Rehefelds evangelischer Palmen-Zweig, no. 2

B0630 **Christum lieb haben ist viel besser denn alles Wissen**
SAB, 2 vln, vlne, bc
16th Sunday after Trinity
Concentus Apostolico-Musicus, no. 52

B0631 **Christus ist mein Leben**
SSATB, bc
Funeral
Letzter Schwanen-Gesang, no. 15

B0632 **Da aber erschien die Freundlichkeit**
SATB, 2 vln, vlne, bc
Sunday after Circumcision
Concentus Apostolico-Musicus, no. 8

B0633 **Da acht Tage um waren, daß das Kind beschnitten würde**
SATB, bc
New Year's Day
Evangelischer Blumengarten I, no. 9

B0634 **Da die Zeit erfüllet war**
SATB, 2 vln, vlne, bc
Sunday after Christmas
Concentus Apostolico-Musicus, no. 6

B0635 **Da Jesus von dem Berge kommt**
SATB, 2 vln, 2 vla, bc
3rd Sunday after Epiphany
Musicalische Trost-Quelle, no. 12

B0636 **Dafür halt uns Jederman**
SSATB, 2 vln, 2 vla, bc
9th Sunday after Trinity
Rehefelds evangelischer Palmen-Zweig, no. 40

B0637 **Dafür halt uns Jederman**
SATB, 2 vln, vlne, bc

3rd Sunday of Advent
Concentus Apostolico-Musicus, no. 3

B0638 **Danket dem Herrn, denn er ist freundlich**
SSATB, bc
7th Sunday after Trinity
Evangelischer Blumengarten III, no. 8

B0639 **Danket dem Herrn, denn er ist freundlich**
SATB, 2 vln, 2 vla, bc
Whit Monday
Musicalischer Lebens-Brunn, no. 37

B0640 **Danket dem Herrn und predigt seinen Namen**
SATB, 2 vln, 2 vla, bc
24th Sunday after Trinity
Musicalischer Lebens-Brunn, no. 63

B0641 **Danket dem Herrn und prediget seinen Namen**
SATB, 2 vln, tbn, bc
2nd Sunday after Epiphany
Rehefelds evangelischer Palmen-Zweig, no. 4

B0642 **Danksaget dem Vater der uns tüchtig**
SSTB, 2 vln, bc
Palm Sunday
Evangelische Gespräch II, no. 7

B0643 **Danksaget dem Vater der uns tüchtig**
SATB, 2 vln, vlne, bc
24th Sunday after Trinity
Concentus Apostolico-Musicus, no. 60

B0644 **Daran ist erschienen die Liebe Gottes**
SSATB, 2 vln, 2 vla, bc
Whit Monday
Rehefelds evangelischer Palmen-Zweig, no. 29

B0645 **Das Blut Jesu Christi des Sohnes Gottes**
SSATB, bc
Good Friday
Evangelischer Blumengarten IV, no. 8

B0646 **Das Ende kommt, es kommt das Ende**
SSATB, 2 vln, bc
27th Sunday after Trinity
Kriegsmanns evangelisches Hosianna, no. 63

B0647 **Das Gebet der Elenden dringet durch**
SSATB, 2 vln, tbn, bc
5th Sunday after Easter
Rehefelds evangelischer Palmen-Zweig, no. 25

B0648 **Das Geschlecht der frommen Seelen**
SATB, 2 vln, bc
2nd Sunday after Epiphany
Braunens . . . Davidische Evangelische Harpfen, no. 13

B0649 **Das große Mahl des Herren**
SATB, 2 vln, bc

BRIEGEL, Wolfgang Carl (*continued*)

Kriegsmanns evangelisches Hosianna, 2nd
ed., Anh. no. 2

B0650 **Das Himmelreich ist gleich einem Menschen**
SATB, bc
5th Sunday after Epiphany
Evangelischer Blumengarten I, no. 1

B0651 **Das Himmelreich ist gleich einem Menschen**
SATB, 2 vln, 2 vla, bc
5th Sunday after Epiphany
Musicalische Trost-Quelle, no. 14

B0652 **Das ist das ewige Leben**
SATB, bc
Feast of Saints Peter and Paul
Evangelischer Blumengarten IV, no. 12

B0653 **Das ist je gewißlich wahr**
SSATB, 2 vln, 2 vla, bc
19th Sunday after Trinity
Rehefelds evangelischer Palmen-Zweig, no. 50

B0654 **Das ist meine Freude**
SSTB, 2 vln, bc
5th Sunday of Lent
Evangelische Gespräch II, no. 6

B0655 **Das ist uns zum Vorbild geschrieben**
SATB, 2 vln, vlne, bc
9th Sunday after Trinity
Concentus Apostolico-Musicus, no. 45

B0656 **Das Reich Gottes ist nicht Essen und Trinken**
SSB, 2 vln, gamba, bc
45th Sunday after Easter
Rehefelds evangelischer Palmen-Zweig, no. 24

B0657 **Das verstockte Jerusalem jauchze du, Tochter Zion**
SATB, 2 vln, vla, bc
10th Sunday after Trinity
Evangelische Gespräch III, no. 11

B0658 **Das Wort ward Fleisch und wohnet unter uns**
SATB, bc
3rd Day of Christmas
Evangelischer Blumengarten I, no. 7

B0659 **Dazu ist erschienen der Sohn Gottes**
SATB, 2 vln, vla, bc
3rd Sunday of Lent
Rehefelds evangelischer Palmen-Zweig, no. 14

B0660 **Dein Blut, Herr Jesu Christ**
SSATB, bc
Funeral of Anna Christina Wild
Gotha, 1664

RISM B4495, Reich 101 (parts)
DMA 57//181

B0661 **Dein Sohn, O Gott, der Trost der Frommen**
SSATB, 2 vln, bc
3rd Sunday of Advent
Kriegsmanns evangelisches Hosianna, no. 3
Ed. F. Noack (Bern: Krompholz)

B0662 **Deine Kirch, Herr Jesu Christ**
SATB, 2 vln, bc
4th Sunday after Epiphany
Kriegsmanns evangelisches Hosianna, no. 14

B0663 **Den frommen Herzen gehet auf**
SATB, 2 vln, bc
Easter Monday
Braunens . . . Davidische Evangelische Harpfen, no. 29

B0664 **Der Bräutgam wird bald rufen**
SATB, 2 vln, bc
20th Sunday after Trinity
Evangelische Gespräch III, no. 21

B0665 **Der Engel des Herrn lagert sich**
SATB, 2 vln, 2 vla, bc
1st Sunday of Lent
Rehefelds evangelischer Palmen-Zweig, no. 12

B0666 **Der Engel sprach: Fürchtet euch nicht**
SATB, bc
Christmas Day
Evangelischer Blumengarten I, no. 5

B0667 **Der Gerechte ob er gleich zu zeitlich stirbt**
SSATTB, bc
Zwölf madrigalische Trost-Gesänge, no. 7

B0668 **Der Herr, der aller Enden regiert**
SATB, 2 vln, 2 vla, bc
Musialischer Lebens-Brunn, no. 70

B0669 **Der Herr der Tode und Leben**
SATB, 2 vln, bc
Easter Tuesday
Braunens . . . Davidische Evangelische Harpfen, no. 30

B0670 **Der Herr erhöre dich**
SSTTB, 2 vln, 2 vla, vlne, bc
D-B Mus. ms. 2435 (Erfurt) (1673)
parts

B0671 **Der Herr erhöre dich**
SATB, 2 vln, bc
Geistliche Gespräche und Psalmen, no. 3

B0672 **Der Herr erhöret mich**
SATB, 2 vln, bc
Sunday after Ascension

Braunens . . . Davidische Evangelische Harpfen, no. 37

B0673 Der Herr hat wohlgefallen
SATB, 2 vln, bc
12th Sunday after Trinity
Braunens . . . Davidische Evangelische Harpfen, no. 53

B0674 Der Herr ist mein Hirt
SSATB, bc
2nd Sunday after Easter
Evangelischer Blumengarten II, no. 12

B0675 Der Herr ist unser Richter, der Herr ist unser Meister
SATB, 2 vln, 2 vla, bc
3rd Sunday of Advent
Musicalischer Lebens-Brunn, no. 3

B0676 Der Herr Jesu in der Nacht
SATB, bc
Maundy Thursday
Evangelischer Blumengarten IV, no. 7

B0677 Der Herr lobet den ungerechten Haushalten
SATB, bc
9th Sunday after Trinity
Evangelischer Blumengarten III, no. 10

B0678 Der Herr schauet vom Himmel
SSATB, 2 vln, bc
11th Sunday after Trinity
Evangelische Gespräch III, no. 12

B0679 Der Herr sprach zu meinem Herren
SATB, bc
18th Sunday after Trinity
Evangelischer Blumengarten III, no. 19

B0680 Der Herr sprach zu meinem Herren
SATB, 2 vln, 2 vla, bc
18th Sunday after Trinity
Musicalischer Lebens-Brunn, no. 57

B0681 Der Mensch vom Weib geboren
SATB, bc
Funeral
Letzter Schwanen-Gesang, no. 8

B0682 Der Speisemeister rufet dem Bräutigam
SATB, bc
2nd Sunday after Epiphany
Evangelischer Blumengarten I, no. 13

B0683 Der starke Himmels-Held
SATB, 2 vln, bc
3rd Sunday after Epiphany
Braunens . . . Davidische Evangelische Harpfen, no. 14

B0684 Der Tod ist verschlungen in den Sieg
SATB, 2 vln, corn, tbn, bc
Easter Sunday
Rehefelds evangelischer Palmen-Zweig, no. 19

B0685 Des Herren Werke, die sind groß
SATB, 2 vln, bc
Palm Sunday
Braunens . . . Davidische Evangelische Harpfen, no. 26

B0686 Die Greuel die können nicht länger bestehen
SATB, 2 vln, bc
25th Sunday after Trinity
Braunens . . . Davidische Evangelische Harpfen, no. 66

B0687 Die Jünger traten zu Jesu, weckten ihn auf
SATB, bc
4th Sunday after Epiphany
Evangelischer Blumengarten I, no. 15

B0688 Die Menschen wollen sich meinen Geist
SATTB, 2 vln, bc
4th Sunday after Easter
Evangelische Gespräch II, no. 17

B0689 Die mit Tränen säen
SATB, 2 vln, bc
5th Sunday after Epiphany
Braunens . . . Davidische Evangelische Harpfen, no. 16

B0690 Die Opfer, so dem höchsten Gott gefallen
SATB, 2 vln, bc
11th Sunday after Trinity
Braunens . . . Davidische Evangelische Harpfen, no. 52

B0691 Die reichen Geizhäls in der Welt
SATB, 2 vln, bc
15th Sunday after Trinity
Braunens . . . Davidische Evangelische Harpfen, no. 56

B0692 Die so ihr den Herrn fürchtet, vertrauet auf ihn
SATB, bc
19th Sunday after Trinity
Evangelischer Blumengarten III, no. 20

B0693 Die Zeichen so der Mond und Stern
SSATB, 2 vln, bc
2nd Sunday of Advent
Kriegsmanns evangelisches Hosianna, no. 2

B0694 Dies ist das Zeugnis Johannis
SATB, bc
4th Sunday of Advent

BRIEGEL, Wolfgang Carl (*continued*)
Evangelischer Blumengarten I, no. 4
Ed. Ameln & Kümmerling, *Chor-Archiv
Spruchmotetten*, vol. 1

B0695 **Dies ist der Tag, den der Herr gemacht hat**
SATB, 2 vln, 2 vla, bc
Easter Sunday
Musicalische Trost-Quelle, no. 25

B0696 **Dies ist der Tag der Fröhlichkeit**
SATB, 2 vln, 2 vla, bc
Annunication
Musicalischer Lebens-Brunn, no. 24

B0697 **Dies ist die Last über die Duma**
SATB, 2 vln, bc
Geistliche Gespräche und Psalmen, no. 10

B0698 **Diese letzten haben nur eine Stunde gearbeitet**
ATB, 2 vln, bc
Septuagesima
Evangelische Gespräch I, no. 19

B0699 **Diese letzten haben nur eine Stunde gearbeitet**
SATB, bc
Septuagesima
Evangelischer Blumengarten I, no. 17

B0700 **Dir, Gott Vater, dir sei Ehre**
SSATB, 2 vln, bc
Easter Sunday
Kriegsmanns evangelisches Hosianna, no. 27
Ed. E. Noack (Merseberger)

B0701 **Drei schöne Dinge sind, die beide**
SATB, 2 vln, 2 vla, bc
6th Sunday after Trinity
Musicalischer Lebens-Brunn, no. 45

B0702 **Drei sind die da zeugen im Himmel**
SATB, 2 vln, bc
7th Sunday after Epiphany
Evangelische Gespräch I, no. 18

B0703 **Drei sind die da zeugen im Himmel**
SSATB, vln, tbn, bc
Trinity
Rehefelds evangelischer Palmen-Zweig, no. 30

B0704 **Dreieinig, ewig, wahrer Gott**
SATB, 2 vln, bc
Trinity
Kriegsmanns evangelisches Hosianna, no. 36

B0705 **Du aber, Daniel, gehe hin**
SATTB, bc
Zwölf madrigalische Trost-Gesänge, no. 1

B0706 **Du bist mein Sohn, heut hab ich dich gezeuget**
SATB, bc
Christmas Day
*Braunens . . . Davidische Evangelische
Harpfen*, no. 5

B0707 **Du Christenmensch, sei guten Muts**
SATB, 2 vln, bc
5th Sunday after Trinity
*Braunens . . . Davidische Evangelische
Harpfen*, no. 46

B0708 **Du Gott des Lebens sei gepriesen**
SSATB, 2 vln, bc
21st Sunday after Trinity
Kriegsmanns evangelisches Hosianna, no. 57

B0709 **Du hast dir unser Herz zum Anker**
SSATB, 2 vln, bc
5th Sunday after Epiphany
Kriegsmanns evangelisches Hosianna, no. 15

B0710 **Du hoch erhabner Gott**
SSATB, 2 vln, bc
17th Sunday after Trinity
Kriegsmanns evangelisches Hosianna, no. 53

B0711 **Du Lebens-Brot, Herr Jesu Christ**
SATB, 2 vln, 2 vla, bc
Musicalischer Lebens-Brunn, no. 69

B0712 **Du Tochter Zion, freue dich sehr**
SATB, 2 vln, 2 vla, bc
Palm Sunday
Musicalische Trost-Quelle, no. 23

B0713 **Du Tochter Zion, freue dich sehr**
SATB, vln, tbn, bc
Palm Sunday
Rehefelds evangelischer Palmen-Zweig, no. 18

B0714 **Du treuer Samariter, Jesu**
SSATB, 2 vln, bc
13th Sunday after Trinity
Kriegsmanns evangelisches Hosianna, no. 49

B0715 **Durch unsres Gottes Gütigkeit**
SATB, 2 vln, vlne, bc
1st Sunday after Epiphany
Concentus Apostolico-Musicus, no. 10

B0716 **Ecce quomodo moritur**
SSATB, bc
Funeral
Letzter Schwanen-Gesang, no. 16

B0717 **Eifer fürchten Gott**
SATB, 2 vln, bc

7th Sunday after Trinity
*Braunens . . . Davidische Evangelische
Harpfen*, no. 48

B0718 **Ein großes ists auf Erden**
SATB, 2 vln, bc
Wedding
Kriegsmanns evangelisches Hosianna, 2nd
ed., Anh. no. 10

B0719 **Ein Hirt der hundert Schafe weidt**
SSATB, 2 vln, bc
3rd Sunday after Trinity
Kriegsmanns evangelisches Hosianna, no. 39

B0720 **Ein Ochse kennet seinen Herrn**
SATB, 2 vln, 2 vla, bc
22nd Sunday after Trinity
Musicalischer Lebens-Brunn, no. 61

B0721 **Ein solch Vertrauen haben wir durch Christum**
SATB, 2 vln, vlne, bc
12th Sunday after Trinity
Concentus Apostolico-Musicus, no. 48

B0722 **Einen guten Kampf**
SSATB
Funeral of Nikolaus Martin Drach
Darmstadt, 1679
    RISM B4504, Reich 50 (score)
    DMA 57//94

B0723 **Einen guten Kampf**
SATB, bc
Funeral
Letzter Schwanen-Gesang, no. 4

B0724 **Eitle Wohllust, packe dich**
SATB, 2 vln, bc
3rd Sunday of Advent
*Braunens . . . Davidische Evangelische
Harpfen*, no. 3

B0725 **Ephraim ist sehr betrübt**
SSTB, 2 vln, vlne, bc
2nd Sunday after Easter
Evangelische Gespräch II, no. 15

B0726 **Er, das versprochne Heil der Welt**
SATB, 2 vln, bc
Easter Sunday
*Braunens . . . Davidische Evangelische
Harpfen*, no. 28

B0727 **Er hat alles wohl gemacht**
SATB, bc
12th Sunday after Trinity
Evangelischer Blumengarten III, no. 13

B0728 **Erhöre mich wenn ich rufe**
SATB
Der Psalter Davids, I. Teil, pp. 27-36

B0729 **Erkennets und nehmets wohl in Acht**
SATB, 2 vln, bc
Whit Tuesday
*Braunens . . . Davidische Evangelische
Harpfen*, no. 40

B0730 **Erschrecklich ist es, daß man nicht der Höllen**
SATB, 2 vln, vlne, bc
27th Sunday after Trinity
Concentus Apostolico-Musicus, no. 63

B0731 **Erwecke dich, Herr, warum schläffest du?**
SATB, 2 vln, 2 vla, bc
Sunday after Ascension
Musicalische Trost-Quelle, no. 32

B0732 **Erwecke dich, Herr, warum schläffst du?**
SATB, 2 vln, vlne, bc
4th Sunday after Trinity
Concentus Apostolico-Musicus, no. 39

B0733 **Es begab sich nach dreien Tagen**
SATB, 2 vln, 2 vla, bc
1st Sunday after Epiphany
Musicalische Trost-Quelle, no. 10

B0734 **Es ging ein Sämann aus zu säen**
SSTB, 2 vln, bc
Sexagesima
Evangelische Gespräch I, no. 20

B0735 **Es ging ein Sämann aus zu säen**
SATB, bc
Sexagesima
Evangelischer Blumengarten I, no. 18

B0736 **Es ging ein Sämann aus zu säen**
SATB, 2 vln, 2 vla, bc
Sexagesima
Musicalische Trost-Quelle, no. 16

B0737 **Es gingen zweien Menschen hinauf in**
SATB, 2 vln, 2 vla, bc
11th Sunday after Trinity
Musicalische Trost-Quelle, no. 46

B0738 **Es ist ein elend jämmerlich Ding**
SSAATB, bc
Zwölf madrigalische Trost-Gesänge, no. 5

B0739 **Es ist ein elend jämmerlich Ding**
SATB, 2 vln, bc
Geistliche Gespräche und Psalmen, no. 9

BRIEGEL, Wolfgang Carl (*continued*)

B0740   **Es ist ein elend jämmerlich Ding**
SATB, bc
Funeral
Letzter Schwanen-Gesang, no. 2

B0741   **Es ist ein elend jämmerliche Ding**
SATB, 2 vln, bc
6th Sunday after Trinity
Evangelische Gespräch III, no. 7

B0742   **Es ist eine Stimme eines Predigers**
SSATB, 2 vln, vla, bc
4th Sunday of Advent
Rehefelds evangelischer Palmen-Zweig, no. 59

B0743   **Es ist erschienen die heilsame Gnade Gottes**
SATB, 2 vln, vlne, bc
Christmas Day
Concentus Apostolico-Musicus, no. 5

B0744   **Es ist genug**
SSATB, bc
Funeral
Letzter Schwanen-Gesang, no. 12

B0745   **Es ist gewißlich an der Zeit**
SATB, 2 vln, 2 vla, bc
25th Sunday after Trinity
Musicalischer Lebens-Brunn, no. 64

B0746   **Es ist gewißlich an der Zeit**
SSATB, 2 vln, bc
25th Sunday after Trinity
Evangelische Gespräch III, no. 26

B0747   **Es ist in keinem andern Heil**
SSATB, 2 vln, vla, bc
New Year's Day
Rehefelds evangelischer Palmen-Zweig, no. 1

B0748   **Es ist mir lieb, Herr**
SATB, 2 vln, bc
2nd Sunday of Lent
Braunens . . . Davidische Evangelische Harpfen, no. 22

B0749   **Es ist nicht gut, daß der Mensch allein sei**
SSTTB, 2 vln, 2 vla, vlne, bc
2nd Sunday after Epiphany
Evangelische Gespräch I, no. 13

B0750   **Es ist nicht gut, daß der Mensch allein sei**
SATB, 2 vln, 2 vla, bc
2nd Sunday after Epiphany
Musicalischer Lebens-Brunn, no. 12

B0751   **Es ist nicht gut, daß der Mensch allein sei**
SATB, 2 vln, bc
Wedding
Kriegsmanns evangelisches Hosianna, 2nd ed., Anh. no. 7

B0752   **Es ist nun aus**
SATB
Funeral of Anna Elisabeth Leuth
Darmstadt, 1678
RISM B4503, Reich 49 (score)
DMA 2/1543

B0753   **Es ist nun aus**
SSATB, bc
Funeral
Letzter Schwanen-Gesang, no. 19

B0754   **Es krankt an uns Leib, Seel, und Sinn**
SSATB, 2 vln, bc
24th Sunday after Trinity
Kriegsmanns evangelisches Hosianna, no. 60

B0755   **Es liegt die werte Christenheit**
SSATB, 2 vln, bc
3rd Sunday after Easter
Kriegsmanns evangelisches Hosianna, no. 30

B0756   **Es saß ein Blinder am Wege und bettelt**
SSATB, bc
Quinquagesima
Evangelischer Blumengarten II, no. 1

B0757   **Es sei denn euer Gerechtigkeit besser denn**
SATB, 2 vln, 2 vla, bc
6th Sunday after Trinity
Musicalische Trost-Quelle, no. 41

B0758   **Es spricht der unweisen Mund wohl**
SATB, 2 vln, 2 vla, bc
8th Sunday after Trinity
Musicalischer Lebens-Brunn, no. 47

B0759   **Es spricht der unweisen Mund wohl**
SATB, 2 vln, vlne, bc
20th Sunday after Trinity
Concentus Apostolico-Musicus, no. 56

B0760   **Es war ein armer Mann, der nur ein Schäfchen**
AB soli, SATB cho, 2 vln, vlne, bc
Des Königs und Propheten Davids 7 Buß-Psalmen, no. 13

B0761   **Es war ein Mensch, der ging von Jerusalem**
SATB, bc
13th Sunday after Trinity
Evangelischer Blumengarten III, no. 14

B0762   **Es war ein Mensch, der machte ein groß Abendmahl**
SATB, bc

2nd Sunday after Trinity
Evangelischer Blumengarten III, no. 3

B0763 **Es war ein reicher Mann**
SATB, 2 vln, 2 vla, bc
9th Sunday after Trinity
Musicalische Trost-Quelle, no. 44

B0764 **Es werden Zeichen geschehen an der Sonnen**
SATB, 2 vln, 2 vla, bc
2nd Sunday of Advent
Musicalische Trost-Quelle, no. 2

B0765 **Es wird eine gute Rute aufgehen**
SATB, 2 vln, vlne, bc
Visitation of the Virgin Mary
Concentus Apostolico-Musicus, no. 40

B0766 **Es wird eine Rute aufgehen**
SAB, 2 vln, tbn, bc
Annunciation
Rehefelds evangelischer Palmen-Zweig, no. 17

B0767 **Fahret auf die Höhe und werfet**
STTB, 2 vln, vla, bc
5th Sunday after Trinity
Evangelische Gespräch III, no. 6
Ed. F. Noack, *Kirchenmusik der Darmstädter Meister des Barock*, vol. 4 (Merseburger, no. 931, 1955)

B0768 **Feget den alten Sauerteig aus**
SATB, 2 vln, vlne, bc
Easter Sunday
Concentus Apostolico-Musicus, no. 26

B0769 **Folgt gute Lehr, ihr lieben Christen**
SATB, 2 vln, vlne, bc
7th Sunday after Trinity
Concentus Apostolico-Musicus, no. 43

B0770 **Freue dich, du Christenschar**
SATB, 2 vln, bc
Easter Sunday
Kriegsmanns evangelisches Hosianna, no. 26

B0771 **Freuet euch, ihr Menschenkinder**
SATB, 2 vln, bc
Christmas Day
Kriegsmanns evangelisches Hosianna, no. 5
Ed. F. Noack, *Vier kleine Kantaten* (Möseler, 1961)
————, *Die Kirchenmusik*, Jg. 1920, p. 41
————, *Lose Blätter*, no. 182 (Wolfenbüttel: Kallmeyer, 1929)

B0772 **Freuet euch in dem Herrn allezeit**
SATB, 2 vln, vlne, bc

4th Sunday of Advent
Concentus Apostolico-Musicus, no. 4
Ed. W. Bodmer (Bern: Krompholz)

B0773 **Freuet euch mit mir, den ich habe**
SSATB, bc
3rd Sunday after Trinity
Evangelischer Blumengarten III, no. 4

B0774 **Freund, wie bist du herein gekommen**
SSATB, 2 vln, vla, bc
20th Sunday after Trinity
Rehefelds evangelischer Palmen-Zweig, no. 51

B0775 **Friede sei mit euch, sehet meine Hände**
SSTB, 2 vln, 2 vla, vlne, bc
1st Sunday after Easter
Evangelische Gespräch II, no. 14

B0776 **Friedens-Stiffter Jesu Christ**
SATB, 2 vln, bc
1st Sunday after Easter
Kriegsmanns evangelisches Hosianna, no. 28

B0777 **Frohlocket mit Freuden ihr menschlichen Kinder**
SATB, 2 vln, bc
Ascension
Braunens . . . Davidische Evangelische Harpfen, no. 36

B0778 **Frohlocket mit Händen**
SSATB, bc
Ascension
Evangelischer Blumengarten IV, no. 10

B0779 **Frohlocket mit Händen**
SATB, 2 vln, 2 vla, bc
Ascension
Musicalischer Lebens-Brunn, no. 34

B0780 **Führ uns Herr in Versuchung nicht**
SATB, 2 vln, 2 vla, bc
1st Sunday of Lent
Musicalischer Lebens-Brunn, no. 20
Winterfeld II, no. 141

B0781 **Fürchte dich nicht Abraham**
SATB, 2 vln, vlne, bc
13th Sunday after Trinity
Concentus Apostolico-Musicus, no. 49

B0782 **Fürchtet den Herrn ihr seine Heiligen**
SATB, 2 vln, 2 vla, bc
5th Sunday after Trinity
Musicalischer Lebens-Brunn, no. 44

B0783 **Fürchtet euch nicht**
STTB, 2 vln, 2 vla, corn, bc
Christmas Day
Evangelische Gespräch I, no. 6

BRIEGEL, Wolfgang Carl (*continued*)

B0784 **Fürchtet euch nicht vor denen, die den Leib**
SSATB, 2 vln, bc
Sunday after Ascension
Rehefelds evangelischer Palmen-Zweig, no. 27

B0785 **Fürchtet euch nicht, siehe**
SSATB, 2 vln, 2 vla, bc
Christmas Day
Rehefelds evangelischer Palmen-Zweig, no. 60

B0786 **Gebet dem Kaiser was des Kaisers ist**
SATB, bc
23rd Sunday after Trinity
Evangelischer Blumengarten III, no. 24

B0787 **Gegrüßet seist du Holdselige**
SATB, bc
Annunciation
Evangelischer Blumengarten IV, no. 6

B0788 **Gegrüßet seist du Holdselig**
SATB, 2 vln, 2 vla, bc
Annunciation
Musicalische Trost-Quelle, no. 24

B0789 **Gehe hin in deine Kammer**
SATB, bc
Funeral
Musicalischer Lebens-Brunn, no. 78

B0790 **Gehe hin, mein Volk, in eine Kammer**
SATB, 2 vln, 2 vla, bc
16th Sunday after Trinity
Musicalische Trost-Quelle, no. 51

B0791 **Gehet hin in alle Welt**
SATB, 2 vln, vlne, bc
6th Sunday after Trinity
Concentus Apostolico-Musicus, no. 42

B0792 **Gelobet sei der Herr, der Gott Israel**
SATB, bc
Feast of Saint John the Baptist
Evangelischer Blumengarten IV, no. 11

B0793 **Gelobet sei der Herr täglich**
SSATB, bc
14th Sunday after Trinity
Evangelischer Blumengarten III, no. 15

B0794 **Gelobet sei der Herr täglich**
SATB, 2 vln, 2 vla, bc
14th Sunday after Trinity
Musicalischer Lebens-Brunn, no. 53

B0795 **Gelobet sei der Herr täglich**
SSATB, 2 vln, bc
14th Sunday after Trinity
Evangelische Gespräch III, no. 15

B0796 **Gelobet sei Gott und der Vater**
SATB, 2 vln, 2 vla, bc
Easter Monday
Musicalischer Lebens-Brunn, no. 28

B0797 **Gelobet sei täglich der mächtige Gott**
SATB, 2 vln, bc
1st Sunday of Lent
*Braunens . . . Davidische Evangelische
Harpfen*, no. 21

B0798 **Gleich wie der Blitz ausgehet von Aufgang**
SATB, 2 vln, 2 vla, bc
25th Sunday after Trinity
Musicalische Trost-Quelle, no. 60

B0799 **Gott alleine kann uns schützen**
SATB, 2 vln, bc
1st Sunday after Easter
*Braunens . . . Davidische Evangelische
Harpfen*, no. 31

B0800 **Gott, der du bist ein reines Wesen**
SATB, 2 vln, bc
Pentecost
*Braunens . . . Davidische Evangelische
Harpfen*, no. 38

B0801 **Gott der Götter, Herr der Herren**
SSATB, 2 vln, bc
23rd Sunday after Trinity
Kriegsmanns evangelisches Hosianna, no. 59

B0802 **Gott der Herr, der mächtige redet**
SATB, 2 vln, 2 vla, bc
2nd Sunday of Advent
Musicalischer Lebens-Brunn, no. 2

B0803 **Gott des Segens, deinen Segen**
SSATB, 2 vln, bc
5th Sunday after Trinity
Kriegsmanns evangelisches Hosianna, no. 41

B0804 **Gott fähret auf mit Jauchzen**
SSATB, 2 vln, tbn, bc
Ascension
Rehefelds evangelischer Palmen-Zweig, no. 26

B0805 **Gott, gib dein Gericht dem Könige**
SATB, 2 vln, 2 vla, bc
Epiphany
Musicalischer Lebens-Brunn, no. 10

B0806 **Gott hat uns nicht gesetzt zum Zorn**
SATB, 2 vln, vlne, bc
4th Sunday of Lent
Concentus Apostolico-Musicus, no. 22

B0807 Gott hilf mir, denn das Wasser gehet
SATB, 2 vln, 2 vla, bc
3rd Sunday after Easter
Musicalischer Lebens-Brunn, no. 31

B0808 Gott, mein Ruhm schweige nicht
SATB, 2 vln, vla, bc
5th Sunday of Lent
Rehefelds evangelischer Palmen-Zweig, no. 16

B0809 Gott, sei mir gnädig
SATB, 2 vln, vlne, bc
*Des Königs und Propheten Davids 7 Buß-
Psalmen,* no. 4

B0810 Gott Vater, dessen Sohn
SSATB, 2 vln, bc
6th Sunday after Trinity
Kriegsmanns evangelisches Hosianna, no. 42

B0811 Gott, warum verstößest du uns so gar
SATB, 2 vln, bc
Geistliche Gespräche und Psalmen, no. 4

B0812 Gott Zebaoth, dich wende doch
SATB, 2 vln, bc
Septuagesima
*Braunens . . . Davidische Evangelische
Harpfen*, no. 18

B0813 Großer Gott du wohnst dort oben
SATB, 2 vln, bc
Dedication of a church
Kriegsmanns evangelisches Hosianna, no. 64

B0814 Grundgütigster Vater
SATB, 2 vln, bc
13th Sunday after Trinity
*Braunens . . . Davidische Evangelische
Harpfen*, no. 54

B0815 Gute Nacht, du eitles Leben
SATB, 2 vln, bc
Funeral
Kriegsmanns evangelisches Hosianna, 2nd
ed., Anh, no. 18

B0816 Gute Nacht, du eitles Leben
SSATB, bc
Funeral
Letzter Schwanen-Gesang, no. 20

B0817 Guter Hirt, der du dein Leben
SSATB, 2 vln, bc
2nd Sunday after Easter
Kriegsmanns evangelisches Hosianna, no. 29

B0818 Gutes Kindlein Jesu, mußt du fliehen
SSATB, 2 vln, bc

Sunday after New Year
Kriegsmanns evangelisches Hosianna, no. 9

B0819 Heilger Geist, sei uns willkommen
SATB, 2 vln, bc
Pentecost
Kriegsmanns evangelisches Hosianna, no. 35

B0820 Herr, auf dich traue ich, mein Gott
SATB, 2 vln, 2 vla, bc
Sunday after New Year
Musicalischer Lebens-Brunn, no. 9

B0821 Herr, der Herren Gott
SSATB, 2 vln, bc
11th Sunday after Trinity
Kriegsmanns evangelisches Hosianna, no. 47

B0822 Herr, du hast mir fünf Zentner getan
SATB, 2 vln, 2 vla, bc
9th Sunday after Trinity
Musicalischer Lebens-Brunn, no. 48

B0823 Herr, du prüfest Herz und Seele
SATB, 2 vln, bc
8th Sunday after Trinity
*Braunens . . . Davidische Evangelische
Harpfen*, no. 49

B0824 Herr, erhöre mein Gebet
SATB, 2 vln, vlne, bc
*Des Königs und Propheten Davids 7 Buß-
Psalmen,* no. 7

B0825 Herr, gehe nicht ins Gericht mit deinem Knecht
ATB, 2 vln, bc
22nd Sunday after Trinity
Evangelische Gespräch III, no. 23

B0826 Herr Gott, barmherzig und gnädig und geduldig
SSATB, 2 vln, 2 vla, bc
22nd Sunday after Trinity
Rehefelds evangelischer Palmen-Zweig, no. 53

B0827 Herr Gott, erscheine doch!
SATB, 2 vln, bc
27th Sunday after Trinity
*Braunens . . . Davidische Evangelische
Harpfen*, no. 68

B0828 Herr Gott, Vater und Herr meines Lebens
SATB, 2 vln, 2 vla, bc
23rd Sunday after Trinity
Musicalischer Lebens-Brunn, no. 62

B0829 Herr, hadere mit meine Haderern
SATB, 2 vln, bc
17th Sunday after Trinity
Evangelische Gespräch III, no. 18

BRIEGEL, Wolfgang Carl (*continued*)

B0830   **Herr hast du nicht guten Samen**
SATBB, 2 vln, bc
5th Sunday after Epiphany
Evangelische Gespräch I, no. 16

B0831   **Herr, heile mich, heile du mich, Herr**
SSATB, 2 vln, vla, bc
14th Sunday after Trinity
Rehefelds evangelischer Palmen-Zweig, no. 45

B0832   **Herr, Herr, lehr uns doch dieses**
SATB, 2 vln, bc
16th Sunday after Trinity
*Braunens . . . Davidische Evangelische
    Harpfen*, no. 57

B0833   **Herr, hilf uns, wir verderben**
SSTTB, 2 vln, bc
4th Sunday after Epiphany
Evangelische Gespräch I, no. 15

B0834   **Herr, hilf uns, wir verderben**
SATB, 2 vln, 2 vla, bc
4th Sunday after Epiphany
Musicalische Trost-Quelle, no. 13

B0835   **Herr, höre mein Gebet**
SATB, 2 vln, vlne, bc
*Des Königs und Propheten Davids 7 Buß-
    Psalmen*, no. 5

B0836   **Herr, höre mein Gebet**
SATB, 2 vln, vlne, bc
Sexagesima
Concentus Apostolico-Musicus, no. 17

B0837   **Herr, höre mein Wort**
SATB
Der Psalter Davids, I. Teil, pp. 37-49

B0838   **Herr, höre meine Stimme, wenn ich rufe**
SATB, 2 vln, 2 vla, bc
19th Sunday after Trinity
Musicalische Trost-Quelle, no. 54

B0839   **Herr, ich bin wie ein verirrtes und verloren
    Schaf**
SSATB, 2 vln, bc
3rd Sunday after Trinity
Evangelische Gespräch III, no. 4

B0840   **Herr, ich warte auf dein Heil**
SSTB, 2 vln, bc
2nd Sunday of Advent
Evangelische Gespräch I, no. 2

B0841   **Herr Jehova, Gott der Götter**
SATB, 2 vln, bc
24th Sunday after Trinity
*Braunens . . . Davidische Evangelische
    Harpfen*, no. 65

B0842   **Herr Jesu Christ, wie sollen wir dich**
SSATB, 2 vln, bc
7th Sunday after Trinity
Kriegsmanns evangelisches Hosianna, no. 43

B0843   **Herr Jesu, grosser Himmels-Fürst**
SSATB, 2 vln, bc
26th Sunday after Trinity
Kriegsmanns evangelisches Hosianna, no. 62

B0844   **Herr Jesus, laß uns in deiner Liebe**
SATB, 2 vln, vlne, bc
18th Sunday after Trinity
Concentus Apostolico-Musicus, no. 54

B0845   **Herr lehre mich tun nach deinem Wohlgefallen**
SSTB, 2 vln, 2 vla, vlne, bc
Pentecost
Evangelische Gespräch II, no. 20

B0846   **Herr, meine Tochter ist jetzt gestorben**
SATB, 2 vln, 2 vla, bc
24th Sunday after Trinity
Musicalische Trost-Quelle, no. 59

B0847   **Herr, meinen Geist befehl ich dir**
SSTB, vln, 2 vla, bc
21st Sunday after Trinity
Evangelische Gespräch III, no. 22

B0848   **Herr, meiner Jugend Sünde**
SATB, 2 vln, bc
Sunday after Christmas
*Braunens . . . Davidische Evangelische
    Harpfen*, no. 8

B0849   **Herr, neige mein Herz zu deinen Zeugnissen**
SATB, 2 vln, bc
15th Sunday after Trinity
Evangelische Gespräch III, no. 16

B0850   **Herr, nun lässest du deinen Diener**
SSATB, bc
Purification of the Virgin Mary
Evangelischer Blumengarten IV, no. 4

B0851   **Herr, nun lässest du deinen Diener**
SATB, bc
Funeral
Letzter Schwanen-Gesang, no. 5

B0852 **Herr, strafe mich nicht**
SATB, 2 vln, vlne, bc
Des Königs und Propheten Davids 7 Buß-Psalmen, no. 3

B0853 **Herr unser Gott, du Schöpfer gross**
SSATB, 2 vln, bc
15th Sunday after Trinity
Kriegsmanns evangelisches Hosianna, no. 51

B0854 **Herr, unser Herrscher**
SATB
Der Psalter Davids, I. Teil, pp. 75-84

B0855 **Herr, unser Herrscher, wie herrlich ist dein Name**
SATB, 2 vln, 2 vla, bc
1st Sunday of Advent
Musicalischer Lebens-Brunn, no. 1

B0856 **Herr, warum trittest du so ferne**
SATB
Der Psalter Davids, I. Teil, pp. 105-25

B0857 **Herr, warum trittest du so ferne**
SATB, 2 vln, 2 vla, bc
Sunday after Ascension
Musicalischer Lebens-Brunn, no. 35

B0858 **Herr, wenn ich dich nur hab**
SATB, 2 vln, bc
Feast of Saint John
Braunens . . . Davidische Evangelische Harpfen, no. 7

B0859 **Herr, wenn ich nur dich habe**
SSATB
Funeral of Johann Veit Wild
Gotha, 1655
RISM B4493, Reich 94 (parts)
DMA 2/1047
Ed. Commer (1870), p. 80

B0860 **Herr, wer wird in deiner Hütte wohnen**
SATB, 2 vln, bc
23rd Sunday after Trinity
Braunens . . . Davidische Evangelische Harpfen, no. 64

B0861 **Herr, wie sind deine Werke so groß**
SATB, 2 vln, bc
Geistliche Gespräche und Psalmen, no. 2

B0862 **Herr, wie sind deine Werke so groß**
SSATB, 2 vln, 2 vla, bc
7th Sunday after Trinity
Rehefelds evangelischer Palmen-Zweig, no. 38

B0863 **Herr, wir haben nicht in deinem Namen**
SSATB, 2 vln, 2 vla, bc
8th Sunday after Trinity
Rehefelds evangelischer Palmen-Zweig, no. 39

B0864 **Herr, wo dein Gesetz**
SSATB, 4 vln, vlne, bc
D-B Mus. ms. 2431 (Erfurt) (1681)
parts

B0865 **Herzlich tut mich verlangen**
SATB, 2 vln, vla, bc
24th Sunday after Trinity
Evangelische Gespräch III, no. 25

B0866 **Hier in der Wüsten argen Welt**
SSATB, 2 vln, bc
1st Sunday of Lent
Kriegsmanns evangelisches Hosianna, no. 20

B0867 **Hilf, Herr die Heiligen haben abgenommen**
ATB, 2 vln, 2 vla, bc
Sexagesima
Musicalischer Lebens-Brunn, no. 18

B0868 **Hilf, Herr die Heiligen haben abgenommen**
SSATB, 2 vln, 2 vla, bc
Sexagesima
Rehefelds evangelischer Palmen-Zweig, no. 10

B0869 **Hilf, höchster Gott, mir deinem Kinde**
SATB, 2 vln, bc
4th Sunday after Epiphany
Braunens . . . Davidische Evangelische Harpfen, no. 15

B0870 **Himmel öffne Tor und Türen**
SATB, 2 vln, bc
Ascension
Kriegsmanns evangelisches Hosianna, no. 33

B0871 **Hinweg, du Jammerleben**
SATB, bc
Funeral of Johann Christoph Ayrer
Ansbach, 1671
Reich 18 (not in RISM)
Noack (1963): Same piece as *Evangelischer Blumengarten II* (1666), no. 13 (Über ein kleines so werdet)

B0872 **Hochgelobter Gottes Sohn**
SSATB, 2 vln, bc
3rd Sunday of Lent
Kriegsmanns evangelisches Hosianna, no. 22

B0873 **Höchster Gott, du Herr der Ehren**
SSB, 2 instr, bc

BRIEGEL, Wolfgang Carl (*continued*)

Trinity
Evangelische Gespräch III, no. 1

B0874 **Höre, Israel, der Herr unser Gott**
SATB, 2 vln, 2 vla, bc
Trinity
Musicalischer Lebens-Brunn, no. 38

B0875 **Höre, Israel, der Herr unser Gott**
SATB, 2 vln, bc
18th Sunday after Trinity
Evangelische Gespräch III, no. 19

B0876 **Höre, Jesus, das Geschrei der Armen**
SSATB, 2 vln, bc
2nd Sunday of Lent
Kriegsmanns evangelisches Hosianna, no. 21

B0877 **Höre nimmer auf zu loben**
SATB, 2 vln, bc
14th Sunday after Trinity
*Braunens . . . Davidische Evangelische
Harpfen*, no. 55

B0878 **Höre, Tochter, schaue drauf**
SATB, 2 vln, bc
20th Sunday after Trinity
*Braunens . . . Davidische Evangelische
Harpfen*, no. 61

B0879 **Höret, ihr Himmel und Erden**
SATB, 2 vln, 2 vla, bc
10th Sunday after Trinity
Musicalischer Lebens-Brunn, no. 49

B0880 **Hört auf mit Trauren und Klagen**
SATB, bc
Funeral
Musicalischer Lebens-Brunn, no. 83

B0881 **Hört was Johannes sagt beim Jordan**
SATB, 2 vln, 2 vla, bc
4th Sunday of Advent
Musicalische Trost-Quelle, no. 4

B0882 **Hosianna dem Sohn David**
SATB, 2 vln, 2 vla, bc
1st Sunday of Advent
Musicalische Trost-Quelle, no. 1

B0883 **Hütet euch, daß eure Herzen nicht beschweret
werden**
SATB, bc
2nd Sunday of Advent
Evangelischer Blumengarten I, no. 2

B0884 **Ich armer Mensch, weiß nicht wohin**
SATB, 2 vln, bc

3rd Sunday after Trinity
*Braunens . . . Davidische Evangelische
Harpfen*, no. 44

B0885 **Ich bin ein guter Hirte**
SATB, 2 vln, 2 vla, bc
2nd Sunday after Easter
Musicalische Trost-Quelle, no. 27

B0886 **Ich bin eine Blume zu Saron**
SATB, 2 vln, 2 vla, bc
Wedding
Musicalischer Lebens-Brunn, no. 77

B0887 **Ich danke dem Herrn**
SATB
Der Psalter Davids, I. Teil, pp. 85-105

B0888 **Ich danke dir, Gott, daß ich nicht bin wie
andere Leute**
SATB, bc
11th Sunday after Trinity
Evangelischer Blumengarten III, no. 12

B0889 **Ich danke dir, Herr**
SATB, 2 vln, bc
Geistlicher musikalischer Rosengarten I, no. 8

B0890 **Ich danke meinem Gott so oft ich**
SATB, 2 vln, vlne, bc
22nd Sunday after Trinity
Concentus Apostolico-Musicus, no. 58

B0891 **Ich eifere mich schier zu tot**
SATB, 2 vln, bc
10th Sunday after Trinity
*Braunens . . . Davidische Evangelische
Harpfen*, no. 51

B0892 **Ich elender Mensch, stricke des Todes**
SSTB, 2 vln, bc
3rd Sunday of Lent
Evangelische Gespräch II, no. 4

B0893 **Ich fahre auf zu meinem Vater**
SATB, 2 vln, 2 vla, bc
Ascension
Musicalische Trost-Quelle, no. 31

B0894 **Ich freue mich**
T solo, SSATB choir, 2 vln, bc
Geistlicher musikalischer Rosengarten I,
no. 11

B0895 **Ich freue mich das, das mir gesagt ist**
SAB, 2 vln, bc
1st Sunday after Epiphany
Evangelische Gespräch I, no. 12

B0896 **Ich hab einen guten Kampf gekämpft**
SATB, bc
Funeral
Letzter Schwanen-Gesang, no. 3

B0897 **Ich habe dich ein klein Augenblick verlassen**
SSATTB, bc
Zwölf madrigalische Trost-Gesänge, no. 12

B0898 **Ich habe mich müde geschrien**
SSATB, bc
21st Sunday after Trinity
Evangelischer Blumengarten III, no. 22

B0899 **Ich habe ritterlich gekämpfet**
SATB
Funeral of Christoph Brunchorst
Gotha, 1665
RISM B4496, Reich 102 (parts)
DMA 57//183

B0900 **Ich hebe meine Augen auf**
SATB, 2 vln, 2 vla, bc
21st Sunday after Trinity
Musicalischer Lebens-Brunn, no. 60

B0901 **Ich hielte mich**
SSATB, 2 vln, bc
Whit Tuesday
Evangelische Gespräch II, no. 22

B0902 **Ich lag in teifstem Höllenleid**
SATB, 2 vln, bc
Whit Monday
Braunens . . . Davidische Evangelische Harpfen, no. 39

B0903 **Ich sage euch, viel werden kommen von Morgen**
SATB, bc
3rd Sunday after Epiphany
Evangelischer Blumengarten I, no. 14

B0904 **Ich sage gut Nacht**
SSATB, bc
Funeral
Letzter Schwanen-Gesang, no. 14

B0905 **Ich weiß, daß mein Erlöser lebt**
SATB, bc
Funeral
Letzter Schwanen-Gesang, no. 6

B0906 **Ich will aufstehen und in der Stadt umgehen**
SATB, 2 vln, bc
4th Sunday of Advent
Evangelische Gespräch I, no. 4

B0907 **Ich will den Erdboden heimsuchen**
SATB, 2 vln, vlne, bc

Des Königs und Propheten Davids 7 Buß-Psalmen, no. 10

B0908 **Ich will des Herren Zorn tragen**
SATB, 2 vln, 2 vla, bc
11th Sunday after Trinity
Musicalischer Lebens-Brunn, no. 50

B0909 **Ich will mich mit dir verloben in Ewigkeit**
SSATB, bc
20th Sunday after Trinity
Evangelischer Blumengarten III, no. 21

B0910 **Ich will singen von der Gnade des Herrn**
SATB, 2 vln, 2 vla, bc
Christmas Day
Musicalischer Lebens-Brunn, no. 5
Ed. Krüger, *Die Kantate* 14 (1957)
Ed. Egidi, *Musikschätze der Vergangenheit* (Vieweg no. 5, 1885, 1930)

B0911 **Ich will Wasser gießen auf die Durstigen**
SSATB, 2 vln, tbn, bc
Pentecost
Rehefelds evangelischer Palmen-Zweig, no. 28

B0912 **Ihr betrübten Sünderseelen**
SATB, 2 vln, bc
1st Sunday of Advent
Braunens . . . Davidische Evangelische Harpfen, no. 1

B0913 **Ihr Christen, frohlocket mit Händen**
SATB, 2 vln, 2 vla, bc
Easter Monday
Musicalische Trost-Quelle, no. 64

B0914 **Ihr Christen, führet zu Gemüte**
SATB, 2 vln, bc
18th Sunday after Trinity
Braunens . . . Davidische Evangelische Harpfen, no. 59

B0915 **Ihr Christen, wendet euren Sinn**
SSATB, 2 vln, bc
Quinquagesima
Kriegsmanns evangelisches Hosianna, no. 19

B0916 **Ihr Heiden nah und fern**
SATB, 2 vln, bc
Epiphany
Braunens . . . Davidische Evangelische Harpfen, no. 11

B0917 **Ihr Lieben, lasset uns untereinander lieb haben**
SATB, 2 vln, vlne, bc
1st Sunday after Trinity
Concentus Apostolico-Musicus, no. 36

BRIEGEL, Wolfgang Carl (*continued*)

B0918   **Ihr Männer von Galiläa**
SATB, 2 vln, vlne, bc
Ascension
Concentus Apostolico-Musicus, no. 32

B0919   **Ihr Menschenkinder, schauet doch**
SATB, 2 vln, bc
Good Friday
*Braunens . . . Davidische Evangelische
Harpfen*, no. 27

B0920   **Ihr seid alle Gottes Kinder**
SSTB, 2 vln, vlne, bc
New Year's Day
Concentus Apostolico-Musicus, no. 7

B0921   **Ihr sollt das Heiligtum**
SATB, 2 vln, bc
Geistliche Gespräche und Psalmen, no. 7

B0922   **Immer Streiten, immer Not**
SATB
Funeral of Martin Hecker
Gotha, 1653
    RISM B4490, Reich 92 (score)
    DMA 57//178

B0923   **Ist nicht Ephraim mein teurer Sohn**
SATB, bc
22nd Sunday after Trinity
Evangelischer Blumengarten III, no. 23

B0924   **Jammer hat mich ganz umgeben**
SATB, 2 vln, 2 vla, bc
2nd Sunday of Lent
Musicalischer Lebens-Brunn, no. 21

B0925   **Jauchzet Gott alle Land**
SSTTB, 2 vln, bc
Geistlicher musikalischer Rosengarten I,
no. 10

B0926   **Jauchzet Gott alle Land**
SATB, 2 vln, 2 vla, 2 tbtta, vlne, bc
Easter
D-B Mus. ms. 2430 (Erfurt) (1677/78)
    score and parts

B0927   **Jauchzet Gott alle Land**
SATB, 2 vln, 2 vla, bc
Sunday after Christmas
Musicalischer Lebens-Brunn, no. 7

B0928   **Jerusalem, die du tötest die Propheten**
SSATTB, 2 vln, bc
2nd Day of Christmas
Evangelische Gespräch I, no. 8

B0929   **Jerusalem, die du tötest die Propheten**
SATB, bc
2nd Day of Christmas
Evangelischer Blumengarten I, no. 6

B0930   **Jerusalem, die du tötest die Propheten**
SATB, 2 vln, 2 vla, bc
2nd Day of Christmas
Musicalische Trost-Quelle, no. 63

B0931   **Jerusalem, du hochgebaute Stadt**
SSATB, bc
Feast of Saints Philip and James
Evangelischer Blumengarten IV, no. 9

B0932   **Jerusalem, wenn du es wüßtest**
SATB, 2 vln, 2 vla, bc
10th Sunday after Trinity
Musicalische Trost-Quelle, no. 45

B0933   **Jesu, der du uns zu gut vom Himmel kommen**
SATB, 2 vln, bc
4th Sunday after Easter
Kriegsmanns evangelisches Hosianna, no. 31
Ed. F. Noack, *Die Kirchenmusik*, Jg.
    1920, p. 21

B0934   **Jesu, Geber guter Gaben**
SATB, 2 vln, bc
3rd Sunday after Epiphany
Kriegsmanns evangelisches Hosianna, no. 13

B0935   **Jesu, Lehrer der Gelehrten**
SSATB, 2 vln, bc
1st Sunday after Epiphany
Kriegsmanns evangelisches Hosianna, no. 11

B0936   **Jesu, Quell gewünschter Freuden**
SATB, 2 vln, 2 vla, bc
Palm Sunday
Musicalischer Lebens-Brunn, no. 26

B0937   **Jesu sprach: Die Starken bedürfen des Artztes
nicht**
SATB, bc
Feast of Saint Matthew
Evangelischer Blumengarten IV, no. 16

B0938   **Jesu, wahrer Lebensgott**
SSATB, 2 vln, bc
16th Sunday after Trinity
Kriegsmanns evangelisches Hosianna, no. 52

B0939   **Jesus fing an zu reden zu dem Volk**
SATB, bc
3rd Sunday of Advent
Evangelischer Blumengarten I, no. 3

B0940   **Jesus, lieber Meister, erbarme dich**
SATB, 2 vln, 2 vla, bc

14th Sunday after Trinity
Musicalische Trost-Quelle, no. 49

B0941 **Jesus, meines Herzens Freund**
SATB, 2 vln, 2 vla, bc
Musicalischer Lebens-Brunn, no. 67

B0942 **Jesus sprach: Ich bin die Auferstehung**
SSATB, bc
Easter Monday
Evangelischer Blumengarten II, no. 9

B0943 **Jesus sprach: Wahrlich ich sage euch . . . Ich bin die Tür**
SATB, bc
Whit Tuesday
Evangelischer Blumengarten II, no. 19

B0944 **Jesus sprach: Wer mir will nachfolgen**
SATB, bc
Feast of Saint Andrew
Evangelischer Blumengarten IV, no. 1

B0945 **Jesus sprach zu seinen Jüngern: Das gebiete ich euch**
SATB, bc
Feast of Simon and Judas
Evangelischer Blumengarten IV, no. 18

B0946 **Jesus sprach zu seinen Jüngern: Die weltlichen Könige**
SATB, bc
Feast of Saint Bartholemew
Evangelischer Blumengarten IV, no. 15

B0947 **Jesus sprach zu seinen Jüngern: Friede sei mit euch**
SATB, bc
1st Sunday after Easter
Evangelischer Blumengarten II, no. 11

B0948 **Jesus sprach zu seinen Jüngern: Gehet hin**
SATB, 2 vln, 2 vla, bc
4th Sunday of Advent
Musicalischer Lebens-Brunn, no. 4

B0949 **Jesus sprach zu seinen Jüngern: Nun geht hin**
SATB, bc
4th Sunday after Easter
Evangelischer Blumengarten II, no. 14

B0950 **Jesus sprach zu seinen Jüngern: Wahrlich ich sage euch**
SATB, bc
5th Sunday after Easter
Evangelischer Blumengarten II, no. 15

B0951 **Jesus sprach zu seinen Jüngern: Wenn aber der Tröster kommen**
SATB, bc

Sunday after Ascension
Evangelischer Blumengarten II, no. 16

B0952 **Jesus sprach zu seinen Jüngern: Wer mich liebet**
SATB, bc
Pentecost
Evangelischer Blumengarten II, no. 17
Ed. Ameln & Kümmerling (Bärenreiter BA 5474 & BA 6329)

B0953 **Jesus sprach zu Simon: Fahre auf die Höhe**
SATB, bc
5th Sunday after Trinity
Evangelischer Blumengarten III, no. 6

B0954 **Kehre wieder, o Sulamith**
STB, 2 vln, bc
3rd Day of Christmas
Evangelische Gespräch I, no. 9

B0955 **Kein Mensche kann dich einer Sünde ziehen**
SSATB, 2 vln, bc
5th Sunday of Lent
Kriegsmanns evangelisches Hosianna, no. 24

B0956 **Komm, meine Braut von Libanon**
SATB, 2 vln, 2 vla, bc
20th Sunday after Trinity
Musicalischer Lebens-Brunn, no. 59

B0957 **Komm, meine Braut von Libanon**
SSATB, 2 vln, bc
26th Sunday after Trinity
Evangelische Gespräch III, no. 27

B0958 **Komm, Mensch, und lern an diesem Tag**
SATB, 2 vln, 2 vla, bc
5th Sunday after Trinity
Musicalische Trost-Quelle, no. 39

B0959 **Kommet her, ihr Gesegneten meines Vaters**
SSATB, bc
26th Sunday after Trinity
Evangelischer Blumengarten III, no. 27

B0960 **Kommet her, ihr Gesegneten meines Vaters**
SATB, 2 vln, 2 vla, bc
26th Sunday after Trinity
Musicalische Trost-Quelle, no. 61

B0961 **Kommet her zu mir alle die ihr mühselig und beiladen ist**
SATB, 2 vln, bc
19th Sunday after Trinity
Evangelische Gespräch III, no. 20

B0962 **Kommet hier und sehet an die Werke Gottes**
SAB, 2 vln, tbn, bc
4th Sunday after Epiphany
Rehefelds evangelischer Palmen-Zweig, no. 6

BRIEGEL, Wolfgang Carl (*continued*)

B0963 **Kommt, denn es ist alles bereit**
SATB, 2 vln, 2 vla, bc
2nd Sunday after Trinity
Musicalische Trost-Quelle, no. 36

B0964 **Kommt her zu mir, alle**
SSATB, bc
Feast of Saint Matthew
Evangelischer Blumengarten IV, no. 5

B0965 **Kommt her zu mir, alle die ihr mühselig**
SATB, 2 vln, 2 vla, bc
17th Sunday after Trinity
Musicalischer Lebens-Brunn, no. 56

B0966 **Kommt herzu, laßt uns dem Herrn**
SATB, 2 vln, 2 vla, bc
2nd Sunday after Easter
Musicalischer Lebens-Brunn, no. 30

B0967 **Kommt, lasset uns zum Herren gehen**
SATB, 2 vln, 2 vla, bc
1st Sunday after Easter
Musicalische Trost-Quelle, no. 26

B0968 **Kommt, laßt uns unsers Gottes Preis**
SATB, 2 vln, 2 vla, bc
Trinity
Musicalische Trost-Quelle, no. 34

B0969 **Kommt zur Hochzeit, siehe meine Mahlzeit**
SATB, 2 vln, 2 vla, bc
20th Sunday after Trinity
Musicalische Trost-Quelle, no. 55

B0970 **Kündlich groß ist das gottseelige Geheimnis**
SSATB, 2 vln, 2 vla, bc
2nd Day of Christmas
Rehefelds evangelischer Palmen-Zweig, no. 61

B0971 **Küsset euren Himmels-König**
SATB, 2 vln, bc
2nd Sunday of Advent
*Braunens . . . Davidische Evangelische
Harpfen*, no. 2

B0972 **Laß, mein Herz, die Sorge fahren**
SATB, 2 vln, 2 vla, bc
13th Sunday after Trinity
Musicalische Trost-Quelle, no. 48

B0973 **Laß rasen immerhin**
SATB, 2 vln, bc
Sunday after New Year
*Braunens . . . Davidische Evangelische
Harpfen*, no. 10

B0974 **Laßt uns das Hochzeit-Fest**
SATB, 2 vln, bc
Wedding
Kriegsmanns evangelisches Hosianna, 2nd
ed., Anh, no. 9

B0975 **Laßt uns jauchzen, laßt uns singen**
SATB, 2 vln, 2 vla, bc
Easter Sunday
Musicalischer Lebens-Brunn, no. 27

B0976 **Leid' unverzagt um Gottes Ehre**
SATB, 2 vln, bc
Feast of Saint Stephen
*Braunens . . . Davidische Evangelische
Harpfen*, no. 6

B0977 **Liebe Seele, nun dich schwinge**
SATB, 2 vln, 2 vla, bc
Musicalischer Lebens-Brunn, no. 68

B0978 **Liebe Seele, nun dich schwinge**
SATB, 2 vln, bc
Kriegsmanns evangelisches Hosianna, 2nd
ed., Anh. no. 3

B0979 **Lieben Brüder alle gute Gabe**
ATB, 2 vln, vlne, bc
4th Sunday after Easter
Concentus Apostolico-Musicus, no. 30

B0980 **Lieben Brüder, ein jeglicher sei gesinnet**
SATB, 2 vln, vlne, bc
Palm Sunday
Concentus Apostolico-Musicus, no. 25

B0981 **Lieben Brüder, ein jeglicher sei schnell**
SSATB, 2 vln, 2 vla, bc
6th Sunday after Trinity
Rehefelds evangelischer Palmen-Zweig, no. 37

B0982 **Lieben Brüder haltet euch nicht selbst**
ATB, 2 vln, vlne, bc
3rd Sunday after Epiphany
Concentus Apostolico-Musicus, no. 12

B0983 **Lieben Brüder, ich erinnere euch des Evangelii**
SATB, 2 vln, vlne, bc
11th Sunday after Trinity
Concentus Apostolico-Musicus, no. 47

B0984 **Lieben Brüder, ich ermahne euch**
SATB, 2 vln, vlne, bc
3rd Sunday after Easter
Concentus Apostolico-Musicus, no. 29

B0985 **Lieben Brüder, seid niemand nichts schuldig**
SATB, 2 vln, vlne, bc
4th Sunday after Epiphany
Concentus Apostolico-Musicus, no. 13

B0986 **Lieben Brüder, seid Täter des Worts**
ATB, 2 vln, vlne, bc
5th Sunday after Easter
Concentus Apostolico-Musicus, no. 31

B0987 **Lieben Brüder so wir im Geist leben**
SATB, 2 vln, vlne, bc
15th Sunday after Trinity
Concentus Apostolico-Musicus, no. 51

B0988 **Lieben Brüder, so ziehet nun**
ATB, 2 vln, vlne, bc
5th Sunday after Epiphany
Concentus Apostolico-Musicus, no. 14

B0989 **Lieben Brüder was vorhin geschrieben ist**
SATB, 2 vln, vlne, bc
2nd Sunday of Advent
Concentus Apostolico-Musicus, no. 2

B0990 **Lieben Brüder weil wir wissen**
SATB, 2 vln, vlne, bc
1st Sunday of Advent
Concentus Apostolico-Musicus, no. 1

B0991 **Lieben Brüder wenn ich mit Menschen**
SATB, 2 vln, vlne, bc
Quinquagesima
Concentus Apostolico-Musicus, no. 18

B0992 **Lieben Brüder wir haben mancherlei Gaben**
SATB, 2 vln, vlne, bc
2nd Sunday after Epiphany
Concentus Apostolico-Musicus, no. 11

B0993 **Lieben Brüder wisset ihr nicht**
SATB, 2 vln, vlne, bc
Septuagesima
Concentus Apostolico-Musicus, no. 16

B0994 **Lieber Herre Gott, wecke uns auf**
SSB, 3 instr, bc
1st Sunday of Advent
Evangelische Gespräch I, no. 1

B0995 **Lieber Herre Gott, wecke uns auf**
SATB, 2 vln, vlne, bc
25th Sunday after Trinity
Concentus Apostolico-Musicus, no. 61

B0996 **Lieber Meister Jesu Christ**
SSATB, 2 vln, bc
14th Sunday after Trinity
Kriegsmanns evangelisches Hosianna, no. 50
Ed. Fr. Noack, *Die Kirchenmusik*, Jg.
1920, p. 25

B0997 **Lieber Vater, dessen Herz in Liebe brennt**
SSATB, 2 vln, bc

18th Sunday after Trinity
Kriegsmanns evangelisches Hosianna, no. 54

B0998 **Lieblich und schöne sein ist nichts**
SATB, 2 vln, 2 vla, bc
Wedding
Musicalischer Lebens-Brunn, no. 76

B0999 **Lobe den Herren meine Seele**
SATB, 2 vln, bc
Geistliche Gespräche und Psalmen, no. 1

B1000 **Lobe den Herren meine Seele**
SATB, 2 vln, tbn, bc
Visitation of the Virgin Mary
Rehefelds evangelischer Palmen-Zweig, no. 34

B1001 **Lobet den Herrn, alle Heiden**
SATB, 2 vln, bc
Geistlicher musikalischer Rosengarten I,
no. 7

B1002 **Lobet den Herren, alle Heiden**
SATB, 2 vln, 2 vla, bc
Epiphany
Musicalische Trost-Quelle, no. 9

B1003 **Lobet, ihr Knechte**
SATB, 2 vln, 2 clar, bc
Geistlicher musikalischer Rosengarten I,
no. 12

B1004 **Lobet ihr Völker unsern Gott**
SATB, 2 vln, 2 vla, bc
4th Sunday after Epiphany
Musicalischer Lebens-Brunn, no. 14

B1005 **Mache dich auf und werde Licht**
SATB, 2 vln, vlne, bc
Epiphany
Concentus Apostolico-Musicus, no. 9
Ed. E. Noack, *Kirchenmusik der Darmstädter
Meister des Barock*, vol. 6 (Merseberger
no. 933, 1962)

B1006 **Machet die Tore weit**
SATB, 2 vln, vla, bc
1st Sunday of Advent
Rehefelds evangelischer Palmen-Zweig, no. 56
Ed. F. Noack, *Die Kirchenmusik*, Jg.
1921, p. 81
————, *Vier kleine Kantaten* (Möseler,
1961)

B1007 **Machet die Tür weit**
SATB, bc
Palm Sunday

BRIEGEL, Wolfgang Carl (*continued*)

Evangelischer Blumengarten II, no. 7
Ed. Ameln & Kümmerling, *Chor-Archiv*,
no. 86 (Bärenreiter no. 6234, 1977)

B1008 **Mein Gott und Schirmer, steh mir bei**
SATB, 2 vln, 2 vla, bc
1st Sunday of Lent
Musicalische Trost-Quelle, no. 18

B1009 **Mein Gott, warum hast du mich verlassen**
SATB, 2 vln, 2 vla, bc
5th Sunday of Lent
Musicalischer Lebens-Brunn, no. 25
Ed. Krüger, *Die Kantate* 15 (1960)

B1010 **Mein Kind, willst du Gottes Diener sein**
SATB, 2 vln, vlne, bc
2nd Sunday after Easter
Concentus Apostolico-Musicus, no. 28

B1011 **Meine Schafe hören meine Stimme**
SSAB, 2 vln, tbn, bc
2nd Sunday after Easter
Rehefelds evangelischer Palmen-Zweig, no. 22

B1012 **Meine Seele erhebet den Herrn**
SATB, bc
Visitation of the Virgin Mary
Evangelischer Blumengarten IV, no. 13

B1013 **Meine Seele erhebt den Herren**
SATB, 2 vln, 2 vla, bc
Visitation of the Virgin Mary
Musicalische Trost-Quelle, no. 40

B1014 **Meister, welches ist das vornehmste Gebot**
SATB, 2 vln, 2 vla, bc
18th Sunday after Trinity
Musicalische Trost-Quelle, no. 53

B1015 **Meister, welches ist das vornehmste Gebot**
SSATB, 2 vln, vla, bc
18th Sunday after Trinity
Rehefelds evangelischer Palmen-Zweig, no. 49

B1016 **Meister, wir wissen, daß du wahrhaftig bist**
SAATB, 2 vln, bc
23rd Sunday after Trinity
Evangelische Gespräch III, no. 24

B1017 **Mensch, laß dichs gar nicht irren**
SATB, 2 vln, bc
1st Sunday after Trinity
*Braunens . . . Davidische Evangelische
Harpfen*, no. 42

B1018 **Mensch, willst du auf der guten Bahn**
SATB, 2 vln, vlne, bc

17th Sunday after Trinity
Concentus Apostolico-Musicus, no. 53

B1019 **Mensch, willst du hinfort selig sein**
SATB, 2 vln, vlne, bc
3rd Sunday of Lent
Concentus Apostolico-Musicus, no. 21

B1020 **Mich jammert des Volks**
SATB, 2 vln, 2 vla, bc
7th Sunday after Trinity
Musicalische Trost-Quelle, no. 42

B1021 **Nach dir, Herr, verlanget mich**
TTB, 2 vln, bc
Geistlicher musikalischer Rosengarten I,
no. 6

B1022 **Nicht uns, Herr, sondern deinem Namen gibt
Ehre**
SATB, 2 vln, 2 vla, bc
12th Sunday after Trinity
Musicalischer Lebens-Brunn, no. 51

B1023 **Niemand fähret gen Himmel**
SSATB, bc
Trinity
Evangelischer Blumengarten III, no. 1

B1024 **Nimm wohl in acht mein Herz**
SATB, 2 vln, bc
Sexagesima
*Braunens . . . Davidische Evangelische
Harpfen*, no. 19

B1025 **Nun ade, du Jammer-Welt**
SATB, 2 vln, bc
Funeral
Kriegsmanns evangelisches Hosianna, 2nd
ed., Anh, no. 17

B1026 **Nun danket alle Gott, dem sich der Himmel**
SATB, 2 vln, bc
New Year's Day
Kriegsmanns evangelisches Hosianna, no. 7

B1027 **Nun danket alle Gott, der große Dinge tut**
SATB, 2 vln, 2 vla, bc
New Year's Day
Musicalische Trost-Quelle, no. 7

B1028 **Nun freu sich, alle Christenheit**
SATB, bc
Easter Tuesday
Evangelischer Blumengarten II, no. 10

B1029 **Nun lob, mein Seele**
SSTB, 2 corn, 3 tbn, bc
Geistlicher musikalischer Rosengarten I,
no. 14

B1030 **Nun, nun hab ich meinen Lauf erfüllt**
SATB
Funeral of Justina Seebach
Gotha, 1658
RISM B4494, Reich 98 (score)
DMA 2/1538

B1031 **Nun ruhe, meine Seele, laß alle Arbeit liegen**
SATB, 2 vln, 2 vla, bc
17th Sunday after Trinity
Musicalische Trost-Quelle, no. 52

B1032 **Nun wir sind gerecht worden durch den Glauben**
SSATB, 2 vln, 2 vla, bc
1st Sunday after Easter
Rehefelds evangelischer Palmen-Zweig, no. 21

B1033 **Nun wohlauf ihr Christen-Sinnen**
SSTB, 2 vln, bc
Easter Monday
Evangelische Gespräch II, no. 10

B1034 **O des Schmerzen, O der Plagen**
SATTB
Funeral of Nicola Krause
Gotha, 1670
RISM B4502, Reich 107 (score)
DMA 57//185

B1035 **O du allersüßester, allerfreundlichster**
SATB, 2 vln, 2 vla, bc
New Year's Day
Musicalischer Lebens-Brunn, no. 8

B1036 **O großer Gott, der du die Welt**
SATB, 2 vln, 2 vla, bc
23rd Sunday after Trinity
Musicalische Trost-Quelle, no. 58

B1037 **O Herr, gerechter Gott**
SSATB, 2 vln, bc
19th Sunday after Trinity
Kriegsmanns evangelisches Hosianna, no. 55

B1038 **O Jesu Christ, du machst es lang mit deinem Jüngsten Tage**
SATB, bc
25th Sunday after Trinity
Evangelischer Blumengarten III, no. 26

B1039 **O Jesu, mein Bräutigam**
SATB, 2 vln, bc
Kriegsmanns evangelisches Hosianna, 2nd ed., Anh. no. 5

B1040 **O tiefster Grund! O Allmachts höchste**
SATB, 2 vln, bc
Trinity

Braunens . . . Davidische Evangelische Harpfen, no. 41

B1041 **O Vater alles Lebens**
SATB, 2 vln, bc
4th Sunday of Advent
Braunens . . . Davidische Evangelische Harpfen, no. 4

B1042 **O Vater, frommer Gott**
SSATB, 2 vln, bc
12th Sunday after Trinity
Kriegsmanns evangelisches Hosianna, no. 48

B1043 **O welch eine Tiefe des Reichtums**
ATB, 2 vln, vlne, bc
Trinity
Concentus Apostolico-Musicus, no. 35

B1044 **O Welt, O arge falsche Welt**
SATB, 2 vln, bc
17th Sunday after Trinity
Braunens . . . Davidische Evangelische Harpfen, no. 58

B1045 **Preise, Jerusalem**
SSAB, 3 vla, vlne, bc
Geistlicher musikalischer Rosengarten I, no. 13

B1046 **Regierer und Führer der Sternen und Jahr**
ATB, 2 vln, bc
New Year's Day
Kriegsmanns evangelisches Hosianna, no. 8

B1047 **Reicher Vater aller Armen**
SSATB, 2 vln, bc
1st Sunday after Trinity
Kriegsmanns evangelisches Hosianna, no. 37

B1048 **Saul, Saul, was verfolgst du mich**
SATB, bc
Conversion of Saint Paul
Evangelischer Blumengarten IV, no. 3

B1049 **Schmecket und sehet wie freundlich**
SSATB, bc
4th Sunday of Lent
Evangelischer Blumengarten II, no. 5

B1050 **Schmecket und sehet wie freundlich**
SATB, 2 vln, 2 vla, bc
2nd Sunday after Trinity
Musicalischer Lebens-Brunn, no. 40

B1051 **Schmecket und sehet wie freundlich**
SSAB, 2 vln, tbn, bc
3rd Sunday after Epiphany
Rehefelds evangelischer Palmen-Zweig, no. 5

BRIEGEL, Wolfgang Carl (*continued*)

B1052   **Seele, willst du selig werden**
ATB, 2 vln, gamba, bc
Easter Monday
Rehefelds evangelischer Palmen-Zweig, no. 20

B1053   **Sehet euch vor den falschen Propheten**
SATB, 2 vln, bc
8th Sunday after Trinity
Evangelische Gespräch III, no. 9

B1054   **Sehet euch vor vor den falschen Propheten**
SATTB, bc
8th Sunday after Trinity
Evangelischer Blumengarten III, no. 9

B1055   **Sehet, wir gehen hinauf gen Jerusalem**
SSTB, 2 vln, bc
Quinquagesima
Evangelische Gespräch II, no. 1

B1056   **Sehet, wir gehen hinauf gen Jerusalem**
SATB, 2 vln, 2 vla, bc
Quinquagesima
Musicalische Trost-Quelle, no. 17

B1057   **Sei hochgelobt, o Gott**
SSATB, 2 vln, bc
Septuagesima
Kriegsmanns evangelisches Hosianna, no. 17

B1058   **Sei, höchster Gott, gepriesen**
SSATB, 2 vln, bc
Sexagesima
Kriegsmanns evangelisches Hosianna, no. 18

B1059   **Sei unser Gast, Herr Jesu Christ**
SSATB, 2 vln, bc
2nd Sunday after Epiphany
Kriegsmanns evangelisches Hosianna, no. 12

B1060   **Sei willfertig deinem Widersacher**
SATB, bc
6th Sunday after Trinity
Evangelischer Blumengarten III, no. 7

B1061   **Sei willkommen, Kind der Freuden**
SATB, 2 vln, bc
Epiphany
Kriegsmanns evangelisches Hosianna, no. 10

B1062   **Seid allesamt gleichgesinnt**
SATB, 2 vln, 2 vla, bc
13th Sunday after Trinity
Musicalischer Lebens-Brunn, no. 52

B1063   **Seid allesamt gleichgesinnt**
SATB, 2 vln, bc
13th Sunday after Trinity
Evangelische Gespräch III, no. 14

B1064   **Seid barmherzig, wie auch euer Vater**
SATB, bc
4th Sunday after Trinity
Evangelischer Blumengarten III, no. 5

B1065   **Seid barmherzig, wie auch euer Vater**
SATB, 2 vln, 2 vla, bc
4th Sunday after Trinity
Musicalische Trost-Quelle, no. 38

B1066   **Seid barmherzig, wie auch euer Vater**
STB, 2 vln, bc
4th Sunday after Trinity
Evangelische Gespräch III, no. 5

B1067   **Seid nüchtern und wachet**
SATB, bc
1st Sunday of Lent
Evangelischer Blumengarten II, no. 2

B1068   **Seid nüchtern und wachet**
SSATB, 2 vln, 2 vla, bc
5th Sunday after Epiphany
Rehefelds evangelischer Palmen-Zweig, no. 8

B1069   **Seid nun mäßig und nüchtern zum Gebet**
SATB, 2 vln, vlne, bc
Sunday after Ascension
Concentus Apostolico-Musicus, no. 33

B1070   **Seid stark in dem Herrn und in der Macht**
ATB, 2 vln, vlne, bc
21st Sunday after Trinity
Concentus Apostolico-Musicus, no. 57

B1071   **Selig sind die Toten**
SSATB, bc
24th Sunday after Trinity
Evangelischer Blumengarten III, no. 25

B1072   **Selig sind die Toten**
SSAB, 2 vln, vla, bc
Purification of the Virgin Mary
Rehefelds evangelischer Palmen-Zweig, no. 7

B1073   **Selig sind die Toten**
SSATB, bc
Funeral
Letzter Schwanen-Gesang, no. 18

B1074   **Si bona suscepimus**
SSATB, bc
Zwölf madrigalische Trost-Gesänge, no. 3

B1075   **Si bona suscepimus**
SSATB, bc
Funeral
Letzter Schwanen-Gesang, no. 17

B1076 **Sieh an, wie der Verwüstungs-Greuel steht**
SSATB, 2 vln, bc
25th Sunday after Trinity
Kriegsmanns evangelisches Hosianna, no. 61

B1077 **Siehe, da erschien der Engel des Herrn dem Joseph in Traum**
SATB, bc
Sunday after New Year
Evangelischer Blumengarten I, no. 10
Ed. Vetter, *Das frühdeutsche Lied*, Bd. 2, Nr. 104

B1078 **Siehe, dein König kommt zu dir**
SATB, bc
1st Sunday of Advent
Evangelischer Blumengarten I, no. 1
Ed. Ameln & Kümmerling, *Chor-Archiv Spruchmotetten*, vol. 1

B1079 **Siehe, der Gerechte kommt um und niemand ist**
SATB, 2 vln, 2 vla, bc
Purification of the Virgin Mary
Musicalischer Lebens-Brunn, no. 15

B1080 **Siehe, dieser wird gesetzt**
SATB, 2 vln, vla, bc
Sunday after Christmas
Rehefelds evangelischer Palmen-Zweig, no. 62

B1081 **Siehe, eine Jungfrau ist schwanger**
SATB, 2 vln, vlne, bc
Annunciation
Concentus Apostolico-Musicus, no. 24

B1082 **Siehe, ich sende zu euch Propheten**
SATB, 2 vln, 2 vla, bc
2nd Day of Christmas
Musicalischer Lebens-Brunn, no. 6
Ed. Egidi, *Musikschätze der Vergangenheit* (Vieweg no. V 1886, 1930)

B1083 **Siehe, ich will meinen Engel senden**
SSATB, 2 vln, vla, bc
3rd Sunday of Advent
Rehefelds evangelischer Palmen-Zweig, no. 58

B1084 **Siehe, ich will meinen Engel senden**
SATB, 2 vln, vlne, bc
Purification of the Virgin Mary
Concentus Apostolico-Musicus, no. 15

B1085 **Siehe, lobet den Herrn, alle Knechte**
ATB, 2 vln, bc
Sunday after Christmas
Evangelische Gespräch I, no. 10

B1086 **Siehe nun, nun ist es Zeit**
SATB, 2 vln, bc
Quinquagesima
Braunens . . . Davidische Evangelische Harpfen, no. 20

B1087 **Siehe, wie fein und lieblich**
ATB, 2 vln, vlne, bc
5th Sunday after Trinity
Concentus Apostolico-Musicus, no. 41

B1088 **Sieht man dich denn so geschwind**
SATB
Funeral of Sabine Elisabeth Aschenbach
Gotha, 1668
RISM B4498, Reich 104 (score)
DMA 57//118

B1089 **Singet dem Herrn ein neues Lied**
SSATB, 2 vln, 2 vla, vlne, bc
Easter Monday
Evangelische Gespräch II, no. 11

B1090 **Singet dem Herrn ein neues Lied**
SSATB, bc
Easter Sunday
Evangelischer Blumengarten II, no. 8

B1091 **Singet dem Herrn ein neues Lied**
SATB, 2 vln, 2 vla, bc
4th Sunday after Easter
Musicalischer Lebens-Brunn, no. 32
Ed. Krüger, *Die Kantate* 13 (1966)

B1092 **Singet fröhlich Gott, der unsere Stärke ist**
SATB, 2 vln, 2 vla, bc
Pentecost
Musicalischer Lebens-Brunn, no. 36

B1093 **Singet umeinander**
ATB, 2 vln, bc
Geistlicher musikalischer Rosengarten I, no. 5

B1094 **Singet umeinander**
SATB, 2 vln, 2 vla, bc
4th Sunday of Lent
Musicalischer Lebens-Brunn, no. 23

B1095 **Singet umeinander**
SATB, 2 vln, 2 vla, bc
7th Sunday after Trinity
Musicalischer Lebens-Brunn, no. 46

B1096 **So demütiget euch nun unter die gewaltige Hand**
ATB, 2 vln, vlne, bc
3rd Sunday after Trinity
Concentus Apostolico-Musicus, no. 38

BRIEGEL, Wolfgang Carl (*continued*)

B1097   **So du willst sein ein rechter Christ**
SATB, 2 vln, bc
6th Sunday after Trinity
Braunens . . . Davidische Evangelische
     Harpfen, no. 47

B1098   **So gebet nun jederman, was ihr schuldig seid**
SSATB, 2 vln, 2 vla, bc
23rd Sunday after Trinity
Rehefelds evangelischer Palmen-Zweig, no. 54

B1099   **So leget nun von euch ab nach dem vorigen**
SATB, 2 vln, vlne, bc
19th Sunday after Trinity
Concentus Apostolico-Musicus, no. 55

B1100   **So seid nun wacker allezeit**
SSATB, 2 vln, vla, bc
2nd Sunday of Advent
Rehefelds evangelischer Palmen-Zweig, no. 57

B1101   **So sind wir nun Schuldner nicht dem Fleische**
SATB, 2 vln, vlne, bc
8th Sunday after Trinity
Concentus Apostolico-Musicus, no. 44

B1102   **So spricht der Herr: Beschicke dein Haus**
SATB, 2 vln, 2 vla, bc
3rd Sunday after Epiphany
Musicalischer Lebens-Brunn, no. 13

B1103   **So spricht der Herr: Haltet meinen Sabbat**
SATB, bc
17th Sunday after Trinity
Evangelischer Blumengarten III, no. 18

B1104   **So spricht der Herr: Ich will mich meiner Herde**
SSATB, 2 vln, 2 vla, bc
3rd Sunday after Trinity
Rehefelds evangelischer Palmen-Zweig, no. 33

B1105   **So spricht der Herr: Ich will Wasser gießen**
SATB, 2 vln, 2 vla, bc
Pentecost
Musicalische Trost-Quelle, no. 33

B1106   **So wahr du unser Heiland bist**
SSATB, 2 vln, bc
4th Sunday of Advent
Kriegsmanns evangelisches Hosianna, no. 4

B1107   **Soll denn, was die Tugend pflanzet**
SATB
Funeral of Friedrich Jobst von Seebach
Gotha, 1670

RISM B4500, Reich 109 (score)
DMA 57//182

B1108   **Spielet dem Herrn**
SSATTB, 2 vln/clar, 3 tbtta/tbn, bc
D-B Mus. ms. 2432 (Erfurt) (1679-1680)
score and parts

B1109   **Steh auf und nimm des Kindlein**
SATB, 2 vln, 2 vla, bc
Sunday after New Year
Musicalische Trost-Quelle, no. 8

B1110   **Stehe auf, Joseph**
SSATB, 2 vln, bc
Sunday after New Year
Evangelische Gespräch I, no. 11

B1111   **Stehe auf, meine Freundin, stehe auf**
SATB, 2 vln, 2 vla, bc
Visitation of the Virgin Mary
Musicalischer Lebens-Brunn, no. 42

B1112   **Stimmet Hosianna an**
SSATB, 2 vln, bc
Palm Sunday
Kriegsmanns evangelisches Hosianna, no. 25
Ed. E. Noack, *Drei kleine Kantaten*
     (Merseberger)

B1113   **Suchet den Herrn, weil er zu finden ist**
SATB, 2 vln, bc
2nd Sunday of Lent
Rehefelds evangelischer Palmen-Zweig, no. 13

B1114   **Süßer Jesu, höchster Hort**
SATB, 2 vln, 2 vla, bc
Musicalischer Lebens-Brunn, no. 71

B1115   **Süßer Jesu, höchster Hort**
SATB, 2 vln, bc
Kriegsmanns evangelisches Hosianna, 2nd
     ed., Anh. no. 4

B1116   **Tochter Zion, sing Psalmen**
SSATB, 2 vln, bc
1st Sunday of Advent
Kriegsmanns evangelisches Hosianna, no. 1

B1117   **Trachtet am ersten nach**
SSATB, 2 vln, vla, bc
15th Sunday after Trinity
Rehefelds evangelischer Palmen-Zweig, no. 46

B1118   **Treuer Vater aller Frommen**
SATB, 2 vln, bc
6th Sunday after Epiphany
Kriegsmanns evangelisches Hosianna, no. 16

B1119 Tröstet mein Volk, spricht euer Gott
SATB, 2 vln, vlne, bc
Feast of Saint John
Concentus Apostolico-Musicus, no. 64

B1120 Tut Buß, O lieben Leut
SATB, 2 vln, 2 vla, bc
3rd Sunday after Trinity
Musicalische Trost-Quelle, no. 37

B1121 Über ein kleines, so werdet ihr mich nicht sehen
SATB, bc
3rd Sunday after Easter
Evangelischer Blumengarten II, no. 13
See also Hinweg du Jammerleben

B1122 Und als der Tag der Pfingsten erfüllet war
SATB, 2 vln, vlne, bc
Pentecost
Concentus Apostolico-Musicus, no. 34

B1123 Und als Jesus nahe hinzukam
SATB, bc
10th Sunday after Trinity
Evangelischer Blumengarten III, no. 11

B1124 Und am dritten Tage war eine Hochzeit
SATB, 2 vln, 2 vla, bc
2nd Sunday after Epiphany
Musicalische Trost-Quelle, no. 11
Ed. Moser, *Die mehrstimmige Vertonung des Evangelium I* (Leipzig, 1931), p. 66

B1125 Und du, Bethlehem Ephrata, die du klein bist
SATB, bc
Epiphany
Evangelischer Blumengarten I, no. 11

B1126 Und es begab sich nach drei Tagen
SATB, bc
1st Sunday after Epiphany
Evangelischer Blumengarten I, no. 12

B1127 Und es erhub sich ein Streit im Himmel
SATB, 2 vln, vlne, bc
Feast of Saint Michael
Concentus Apostolico-Musicus, no. 65
Ed. F. Noack, *Kirchenmusik der Darmstädter Meister des Barock*, vol. 3 (Merseberger no. 930, 1955)

B1128 Und ich, Johannes, sage
SATB, 2 vln, vlne, bc
Dedication of a church
Concentus Apostolico-Musicus, no. 66

B1129 Und Simeon segnete sie und sprach zu Maria
SATB, bc
Sunday after Christmas
Evangelischer Blumengarten I, no. 8

B1130 Uns ist ein Kind geborn, ein Sohn ist uns
SATB, 2 vln, 2 vla, bc
Sunday after Christmas
Musicalische Trost-Quelle, no. 6

B1131 Unser keiner lebet ihm selber
SSATB, 2 vln, vla, bc
24th Sunday after Trinity
Rehefelds evangelischer Palmen-Zweig, no. 55

B1132 Unser Leben währet siebenzig Jahr
SATB, bc
Funeral for the elderly
Letzter Schwanen-Gesang, no. 1

B1133 Unser Wandel ist im Himmel
STB, 2 vln, bc
6th Sunday after Epiphany
Evangelische Gespräch I, no. 17

B1134 Valet will ich dir geben
SSATB, bc
Zwölf madrigalische Trost-Gesänge, no. 2

B1135 Vanitas vanitatum et omnia vanitas
SATB, 2 vln, 2 vla, bc
1st Sunday after Trinity
Musicalischer Lebens-Brunn, no. 39

B1136 Vater Abraham, erbarme dich mein
SATB, bc
1st Sunday after Trinity
Evangelischer Blumengarten III, no. 2

B1137 Vater der Barmherzigkeit
SSATB, 2 vln, bc
4th Sunday after Trinity
Kriegsmanns evangelisches Hosianna, no. 40

B1138 Vater, ich habe gesündiget im Himmel
SATB, 2 vln, bc
3rd Sunday after Trinity
Musicalischer Lebens-Brunn, no. 41

B1139 Vater unser, dankbares Gemüte
SSATB, 2 vln, bc
4th Sunday of Lent
Kriegsmanns evangelisches Hosianna, no. 23

B1140 Vater unser, der du bist im Himmel
SATB, 2 vln, 2 vla, bc
5th Sunday after Easter
Musicalische Trost-Quelle, no. 30

B1141 Verbirge dein Antlitz nicht vor mir
SATB, 2 vln, vla, bc
Quinquagesima
Rehefelds evangelischer Palmen-Zweig, no. 11

BRIEGEL, Wolfgang Carl (*continued*)

B1142 **Verlasset euch gar nicht auf Reichtum**
SATB, 2 vln, bc
9th Sunday after Trinity
*Braunens . . . Davidische Evangelische
Harpfen*, no. 50

B1143 **Vertraue Gott und bleibe in deinem Beruf**
SSATB, 2 vln, tbn, bc
5th Sunday after Trinity
Rehefelds evangelischer Palmen-Zweig, no. 36

B1144 **Verzage nicht, o frommer Christ**
SATB, 2 vln, 2 vla, bc
15th Sunday after Trinity
Musicalische Trost-Quelle, no. 50

B1145 **Viel falsche Lehrer sind jetzunter**
SSATB, 2 vln, bc
8th Sunday after Trinity
Kriegsmanns evangelisches Hosianna, no. 44

B1146 **Vom Himmel hoch**
SATB, vln, corn, bc
Christmas Day
Evangelische Gespräch I, no. 7

B1147 **Von den geistlichen Gaben aber will ich euch**
SATB, 2 vln, vlne, bc
10th Sunday after Trinity
Concentus Apostolico-Musicus, no. 46

B1148 **Wach auf, du sichre Welt, der letzte Tag**
SATB, 2 vln, 2 vla, bc
27th Sunday after Trinity
Musicalische Trost-Quelle, no. 62

B1149 **Wahrlich, ich sage euch, so ihr den Vater**
SSTB, 2 vln, bc
5th Sunday after Easter
Evangelische Gespräch II, no. 18

B1150 **Wahrlich, ich sage euch, wer das Reich Gottes**
SSATTB, bc
Zwölf madrigalische Trost-Gesänge, no. 8

B1151 **Wahrlich, wahrlich, spricht der Sohn**
SSATB, 2 vln, bc
5th Sunday after Easter
Kriegsmanns evangelisches Hosianna, no. 32

B1152 **Wann schon der Fromme**
SATB
Funeral of Georg Heinrich von Miltitz
Gotha, 1653
RISM B4491, Reich 93 (score)
DMA 57//180

B1153 **Warum toben die Heiden**
SATB
Der Psalter Davids, I. Teil, pp. 9-20

B1154 **Was betrübst du dich**
SATB, 2 vln, bc
4th Sunday after Easter
*Braunens . . . Davidische Evangelische
Harpfen*, no. 34

B1155 **Was Gott zusammenfügt**
SATB, 2 vln, bc
Wedding
Kriegsmanns evangelisches Hosianna, 2nd
ed., Anh. no. 11

B1156 **Was ist besser als der Orden**
SATB, 2 vln, bc
Wedding
Kriegsmanns evangelisches Hosianna, 2nd
ed., Anh. no. 12

B1157 **Was ist es doch, was ist der Menschen Leben**
SATB, 2 vln, bc
Funeral
Kriegsmanns evangelisches Hosianna, 2nd
ed., Anh. no. 16

B1158 **Was klagst du, Herz, und wimmerst**
SATB, 2 vln, bc
5th Sunday after Easter
*Braunens . . . Davidische Evangelische
Harpfen*, no. 35

B1159 **Was sind wir doch?**
SATB, 2 vln, bc
26th Sunday after Trinity
*Braunens . . . Davidische Evangelische
Harpfen*, no. 67

B1160 **Was soll ich aus dir machen, Ephraim**
SATB, 2 vln, 2 vla, bc
22nd Sunday after Trinity
Musicalische Trost-Quelle, no. 57

B1161 **Was stehet ihr hier den ganzen Tag**
SATB, 2 vln, 2 vla, bc
Septuagesima
Musicalische Trost-Quelle, no. 15

B1162 **Was trotzest du denn, du Tyrann?**
SSTB, 2 vln, bc
Geistliche Gespräche und Psalmen, no. 5

B1163 **Was um und an uns wird geschaut**
SSATB, 2 vln, bc
9th Sunday after Trinity
Kriegsmanns evangelisches Hosianna, no. 45

B1164   **Was will ich klagen der höchste Herr**
SATB, 2 vln, bc
2nd Sunday after Easter
Braunens . . . Davidische Evangelische
Harpfen, no. 32

B1165   **Weg, weg mit allen Schätzen**
SATB, 2 vln, vlne, bc
1st Sunday of Lent
Concentus Apostolico-Musicus, no. 19

B1166   **Weh denen, die auf Erden wohnen**
SATB, 2 vln, 2 vla, bc
3rd Sunday of Lent
Musicalischer Lebens-Brunn, no. 22

B1167   **Weh denen, die des Morgens früh auf sind**
ATB, 2 vln, vla, bc
1st Sunday after Trinity
Rehefelds evangelischer Palmen-Zweig, no. 31

B1168   **Welt ade, mein Ziel ist kommen**
SSATTB
Funeral of Catharina Ottilie Wachter
Gotha, 1670
   RISM B4501, Reich 110 (score)
   DMA 57//67

B1169   **Wenn der Gerechte Gott gereizt**
SATB
Funeral of Anna Maria Hesse
Gotha, 1666
   RISM B4497, Reich 103 (parts)
   DMA 57//44

B1170   **Wenn der Gerechte Gott gereizt**
SATB, 2 vln, bc
Funeral
Kriegsmanns evangelisches Hosianna, 2nd
   ed., Anh. no. 13

B1171   **Wenn mir Angst ist, so rufe ich dem Herrn an**
SSTB, 2 vln, bc
Geistliche Gespräche und Psalmen, no. 8

B1172   **Wenn werd ich dein Abendmahl**
SATB, 2 vln, bc
Kriegsmanns evangelisches Hosianna, 2nd
   ed., Anh. no. 6

B1173   **Wer Gott vertraut, hat wohl gebaut**
SSATTB, bc
Zwölf madrigalische Trost-Gesänge, no. 11

B1174   **Wer ist, der so von Edom kommt**
SATB, 2 vln, 2 vla, bc
Quinquagesima
Musicalischer Lebens-Brunn, no. 19

B1175   **Wer ist, wie der Herr, der sich so hoch**
SATB, 2 vln, bc
17th Sunday after Trinity
Rehefelds evangelischer Palmen-Zweig, no. 48

B1176   **Wer möchte doch wohl länger leben**
5 vv
Funeral of Princess Johanna
D-GOs (1657)
According to E. Noack (1963)

B1177   **Wer sich nach Gottes Rat gedenket zu vermählen**
SATB, 2 vln, 2 vla, bc
Wedding
Musicalischer Lebens-Brunn, no. 74

B1178   **Wer sind diese mit den weißen Kleidern**
SATB, 2 vln, 2 vla, bc
3rd Sunday of Advent
Musicalische Trost-Quelle, no. 3

B1179   **Wer sind diese mit weißen Kleidern**
SATB, 2 vln, vlne, bc
26th Sunday after Trinity
Concentus Apostolico-Musicus, no. 62

B1180   **Wer sind diese mit weißen Kleidern**
SATB, bc
Funeral
Letzter Schwanen-Gesang, no. 9

B1181   **Wer überwindet, dem will ich zu essen geben**
SATB, 2 vln, vlne, bc
1st Sunday after Easter
Concentus Apostolico-Musicus, no. 27

B1182   **Wer unter dem Schirm des Höchsten sitzt**
SSATB, bc
Feast of Saint Michael
Evangelischer Blumengarten IV, no. 17

B1183   **Wer wird es tun und wer wird hinauf gehen**
SATB, 2 vln, bc
6th Sunday after Epiphany
Braunens . . . Davidische Evangelische
Harpfen, no. 17

B1184   **Werter Bräutgam Jesu Christ**
SSB, 2 vln, bc
20th Sunday after Trinity
Kriegsmanns evangelisches Hosianna, no. 56

B1185   **Werter Tröster der Vetrübten**
SSATB, 2 vln, bc
Sunday after Ascension
Kriegsmanns evangelisches Hosianna, no. 34

B1186   **Wie bald vergehen wir**
SATB, bc

BRIEGEL, Wolfgang Carl (*continued*)

Funeral of a child
Musicalischer Lebens-Brunn, no. 80

B1187 **Wie bald vergehen wir**
SATB, 2 vln, bc
Funeral of a child
Kriegsmanns evangelisches Hosianna, 2nd
ed., Anh. no. 14

B1188 **Wie bald vergehen wir**
SSATB, bc
Funeral
Letzter Schwanen-Gesang, no. 11

B1189 **Wie der Hirsch schreiet nach frischem Wasser**
SATB, 2 vln, 2 vla, bc
26th Sunday after Trinity
Musicalischer Lebens-Brunn, no. 65

B1190 **Wie ein Hirsch, der vor den Hunden**
SSATB
Funeral of Margarete Winter
Gotha, 1669
RISM B4499, Reich 105 (score)
DMA 57//66

B1191 **Wie groß ist Gottes Lieb und Treu**
SATB, 2 vln, 2 vla, bc
Septuagesima
Musicalischer Lebens-Brunn, no. 17

B1192 **Wie ist es doch nur zu verstehen**
SATB, bc
Funeral
Musicalischer Lebens-Brunn, no. 79

B1193 **Wie lieblich sind deine Wohnungen**
SSATB, bc
Dedication of a church
Evangelischer Blumengarten IV, no. 19

B1194 **Wie lieblich sind deine Wohnung**
SATB, 2 vln, 2 vla, bc
1st Sunday after Epiphany
Musicalischer Lebens-Brunn, no. 11

B1195 **Wie murren denn die Leute im Leben also**
SATB, 2 vln, vlne, bc
*Des Königs und Propheten Davids 7 Buß-
Psalmen*, no. 9

B1196 **Wie murren die Leute im Leben also**
SSATB, 2 vln, 2 vla, bc
10th Sunday after Trinity
Rehefelds evangelischer Palmen-Zweig, no. 41

B1197 **Wie sind alle verwelket wie die Blätter**
SSATB, 2 vln, 2 vla, bc
11th Sunday after Trinity
Rehefelds evangelischer Palmen-Zweig, no. 42

B1198 **Wie teuer, großer Gott, ist deine große**
SATB, 2 vln, bc
2nd Sunday after Trinity
*Braunens . . . Davidische Evangelische
Harpfen*, no. 43

B1199 **Wir deine Knechte fallen hier**
SSATB, 2 vln, bc
22nd Sunday after Trinity
Kriegsmanns evangelisches Hosianna, no. 58

B1200 **Wir haben einen Gott, der da hilft**
SSATB, 2 vln, vla, bc
16th Sunday after Trinity
Rehefelds evangelischer Palmen-Zweig, no. 47

B1201 **Wir haben hier keine bleibende Stadt**
SATB, bc
16th Sunday after Trinity
Evangelischer Blumengarten III, no. 17

B1202 **Wir haben hier keine bleibende Stadt**
SATB, vln, vla, bc
16th Sunday after Trinity
Evangelische Gespräch III, no. 17

B1203 **Wir haben nicht mit Fleisch und Blut zu
kämpfen**
SATTB, bc
3rd Sunday of Lent
Evangelischer Blumengarten II, no. 4

B1204 **Wir sind getrost allezeit und wissen**
SSATTB, bc
Zwölf madrigalische Trost-Gesänge, no. 9

B1205 **Wirf dein Anliegen auf den Herren**
SATB, bc
2nd Sunday of Lent
Evangelischer Blumengarten II, no. 3

B1206 **Wisset ihr nicht, daß die Ungerechten werden**
SSTTB, 2 vln, bc
9th Sunday after Trinity
Evangelische Gespräch III, no. 10

B1207 **Wo der Herr nicht das Haus bauet**
SATB, 2 vln, 2 vla, bc
Wedding
Musicalischer Lebens-Brunn, no. 72

B1208 **Wo kaufen wir Brot, daß diese essen**
SATB, 2 vln, 2 vla, bc

4th Sunday of Lent
Musicalische Trost-Quelle, no. 21

B1209 **Wo soll ich fliehen hin**
SATB, 2 vln, vlne, bc
5th Sunday of Lent
Concentus Apostolico-Musicus, no. 23

B1210 **Woher nehmen wir Brot**
SSTB, 2 vln, vla, bc
7th Sunday after Trinity
Evangelische Gespräch III, no. 8

B1211 **Wohl dem, dem die Übertretung vergeben ist**
SATB, 2 vln, vlne, bc
Des Königs und Propheten Davids 7 Buß-Psalmen, no. 2
Ed. E. Noack, *Kirchenmusik der Darmstädter Meister des Barock*, vol. 5 (Merseburger no. 932, 1962)

B1212 **Wohl dem, der barmherzig ist**
SSATB, 2 vln, 2 vla, bc
4th Sunday after Trinity
Rehefelds evangelischer Palmen-Zweig, no. 35

B1213 **Wohl dem, der den Herrn fürchtet**
SATB, 2 vln, 2 vla, bc
5th Sunday after Epiphany
Musicalischer Lebens-Brunn, no. 16

B1214 **Wohl dem, der den Herrn fürchtet**
SATB, 2 vln, 2 vla, bc
4th Sunday after Trinity
Musicalischer Lebens-Brunn, no. 43

B1215 **Wohl dem, der den Herren fürchtet**
SATB, 2 vln, 2 vla, bc
Wedding
Musicalischer Lebens-Brunn, no. 73

B1216 **Wohl dem, der ein tugendsam Weib hat**
SATB, 2 vln, 2 vla, bc
Wedding
Musicalischer Lebens-Brunn, no. 75

B1217 **Wohl dem, der ein tugendsam Weib hat**
SATB, 2 vln, bc
Wedding
Kriegsmanns evangelisches Hosianna, 2nd ed., Anh. no. 8

B1218 **Wohl dem, der nicht wandelt**
SATB
Der Psalter Davids, I. Teil, p. 1-8

B1219 **Wohl dem, der sich des Durstigen annimmt**
SATB, 2 vln, 2 vla, bc

1st Sunday after Trinity
Musicalische Trost-Quelle, no. 35

B1220 **Wohl dem, der sich des Durstigen annimmt**
SSATB, 2 vln, vla, bc
13th Sunday after Trinity
Rehefelds evangelischer Palmen-Zweig, no. 44
Ed. F. Noack, *Die Kirchenmusik*, Jg. 1921, p. 77
_____, *Vier kleine Kantaten* (Möseler, 1961)

B1221 **Wohl dem, der sich des Durstigen annimmt**
SATB, 2 vln, vlne, bc
2nd Sunday after Trinity
Concentus Apostolico-Musicus, no. 37

B1222 **Wohl dem, des Hilfe der Gott Jacobs ist**
SATB, 2 vln, bc
21st Sunday after Trinity
Braunens . . . Davidische Evangelische Harpfen, no. 62
Ed. E. Noack, *Drei kleine Kantaten* (Merseburger no. 937, 1963)

B1223 **Wohl dem hier die Übertretung ist vergeben**
SATB, 2 vln, bc
19th Sunday after Trinity
Braunens . . . Davidische Evangelische Harpfen, no. 60

B1224 **Wohl dem Volk, des der Herr ein Gott ist**
SATB, 2 vln, 2 vla, bc
5th Sunday after Easter
Musicalischer Lebens-Brunn, no. 33

B1225 **Wohl euch, o ihr zarten Seelen**
SATB, 2 vln, bc
Funeral of a child
Kriegsmanns evangelisches Hosianna, 2nd ed., Anh. no. 15

B1226 **Wohlan alle die ihr durstig seid**
SSATB, 2 vln/vla, bc
2nd Sunday after Trinity
Evangelische Gespräch III, no. 3

B1227 **Wohlan alle die ihr durstig seid**
ATB, 2 vln, vla, bc
2nd Sunday after Trinity
Rehefelds evangelischer Palmen-Zweig, no. 32

B1228 **Wohlher und lasset uns wohl leben**
SATB, 2 vln, bc
1st Sunday after Trinity
Evangelische Gespräch III, no. 2

B1229 **Wunderkindlein groß und klein**
SSATB, 2 vln, bc

BRIEGEL, Wolfgang Carl (*continued*)

Sunday after Christmas
Kriegsmanns evangelisches Hosianna, no. 6

B1230   **Zion klaget aus der Maßen**
SSTB, 2 vln, bc
3rd Sunday after Easter
Evangelische Gespräch II, no. 16

B1231   **Zion spricht: Der Herr hat mich verlassen**
SATB, 2 vln, 2 vla, bc
21st Sunday after Trinity
Musicalische Trost-Quelle, no. 56

B1232   **Zion spricht: Der Herr hat mich verlassen**
SSATB, 2 vln, vla, bc
21st Sunday after Trinity
Rehefelds evangelischer Palmen-Zweig,
no. 52

B1233   **Zu deinem grossen Abendmahl**
SSATB, 2 vln, bc
2nd Sunday after Trinity
Kriegsmanns evangelisches Hosianna, no. 38

B1234   **Zum Haus der Herren wallen**
SATB, 2 vln, bc
1st Sunday after Epiphany
*Braunens . . . Davidische Evangelische
Harpfen*, no. 12

B1235   **Zweierlei bitte ich, Herr, von dir**
SSATB, bc
15th Sunday after Trinity
Evangelischer Blumengarten III, no. 16

B1236   **Zweierlei bitte ich, Herr, von dir**
SATB, 2 vln, 2 vla, bc
15th Sunday after Trinity
Musicalischer Lebens-Brunn, no. 54

B1237   **Zweierlei bitte ich von dir**
SSTB, 2 vln, bc
4th Sunday of Lent
Evangelische Gespräch II, no. 5

BRONNER, Georg (1667-1720)

B1238   **Es woll uns Gott genädig sein**
STB, 2 vln, 2 vla, vlne/bsn, bc
D-Bds Mus. ms. 30099, no. 9 (Bokemeyer)
score
D-LUC 302A (1714)
parts
Attributed to N. A. Strunck

B1239   **Nun lob, mein Seel, den Herrn**
SSTB, 2 vln, 2 ob, bc
D-Bds Mus. ms. 30099, no. 7 (Bokemeyer)
score

BRÜCKNER, Heinrich Aloys

B1240   **Litaniae Lauretanae B. M. V.**
SSAATTBB, 2 vln, 3 vla, 2 clar, 3 tbn ad
lib, bc
CS-KRa V, 51
parts (3 vla lacking)
microfilm: US-SY
Attributed to "D. Brückner"

B1241   **Missa Cessat et necessitas**
6 vv, 2 vln, 3 vla, gamba, vlne, bc
CS-KRa I, 72 (1672)
parts
microfilm: US-SY

B1242   **Missa Hilaris**
SATB, 2 vln, 3 vla, 2 clar, vlne, bc
CS-KRa I, 76
parts
microfilm: US-SY

B1243   **Missa In albis**
SSATBB, 2 vln, 2 vla, 2 tpt, 3 tbn, bc
CS-KRa I, 74 (1668)
parts
microfilm: US-SY
Attributed to "H. B."; Chafe (pp. 79-84)
assigns to Brückner

B1244   **Missa Posthuma**
4 vv, 2 vln, 2 vla, 2 clar, vlne, bc
CS-KRa I, 71 (1672)
parts
microfilm: US-SY

B1245   **Missa Sanavit eum Dominus**
SSAATTTTBB, 2 vln, 2 vla, 4 clar, 3 tbn,
vlne, bc
CS-KRa I, 70 (1671)
parts
microfilm: US-SY

B1246   **O grande mysterium**
SSATB, vln, 4 vla, bc
D-Bds Mus. ms. 30099, no. 11 (Bokemeyer)
score

B1247   **Vesperae vernales**
4 vv, 3 vla, vlne, bc
CS-KRa III, 38
parts
microfilm: US-SY

BRÜCKNER, Wolfgang

COLLECTION

Zweifaches Zehen ordentlicher Sonn- und Fest-
Täglicher Evangelien (1656)
RISM B4630 (parts)
DMA 3/1876

WORKS

B1248 **Da aber Johannes**
ATTB, 2 vln, bc
3rd Sunday of Advent
Zweyfaches Zehen ordentlicher . . .
Evangelien, no. 3

B1249 **Da die Tage**
SATB, SATB, bc
Purification of the Virgin Mary
Zweyfaches Zehen ordentlicher . . .
Evangelien, no. 16

B1250 **Da Jesus geboren war**
SSST, TTB, bc
Epiphany
Zweyfaches Zehen ordentlicher . . .
Evangelien, no. 11

B1251 **Da Jesus zwölf Jahre alt war**
SSAT, ATTB, bc
1st Sunday after Epiphany
Zweyfaches Zehen ordentlicher . . .
Evangelien, no. 12

B1252 **Da nun viel Volks**
SSAT, ATTB, bc
Sexagesima
Zweyfaches Zehen ordentlicher . . .
Evangelien, no. 20

B1253 **Da sie nun nahe**
SSATB, TTB, bc
1st Sunday of Advent
Zweyfaches Zehen ordentlicher . . .
Evangelien, no. 1

B1254 **Es begab sich**
SSTB, STTB, bc
Christmas Day
Zweyfaches Zehen ordentlicher . . .
Evangelien, no. 5

B1255 **Herr, diese Letzten**
SSAT, ATTB, bc
Septuagesima
Zweyfaches Zehen ordentlicher . . .
Evangelien, no. 19

B1256 **Herr, hast du nicht guten Samen**
SSA, TTB, bc
5th Sunday after Epiphany
Zweyfaches Zehen ordentlicher . . .
Evangelien, no. 17

B1257 **Herr, so du willst**
SSAT, ATTB, bc
3rd Sunday after Epiphany
Zweyfaches Zehen ordentlicher . . .
Evangelien, no. 14

B1258 **Jesus sprach zu Petro**
SSATTB, bc
3rd Day of Christmas
Zweyfaches Zehen ordentlicher . . .
Evangelien, no. 7

B1259 **Jesus trat in das Schiff**
SSAT, ATTB, bc
4th Sunday after Epiphany
Zweyfaches Zehen ordentlicher . . .
Evangelien, no. 15

B1260 **Siehe, ich sende zu euch**
SSATTB, bc
2nd Day of Christmas
Zweyfaches Zehen ordentlicher . . .
Evangelien, no. 6

B1261 **Und am dritten Tage**
SATTB, bc
2nd Sunday after Epiphany
Zweyfaches Zehen ordentlicher . . .
Evangelien, no. 13

B1262 **Und da acht Tage um waren**
SSAB, ATTB, bc
Circumcision
Zweyfaches Zehen ordentlicher . . .
Evangelien, no. 9

B1263 **Und es werden Zeichen geschehen**
SSAB, ATTB, bc
2nd Sunday of Advent
Zweyfaches Zehen ordentlicher . . .
Evangelien, no. 2

B1264 **Und nach sechs Tagen**
SSAT, ATTB, bc
6th Sunday after Epiphany
Zweyfaches Zehen ordentlicher . . .
Evangelien, no. 18

B1265 **Und sein Vater und Mutter**
SATTB, bc
Sunday after Christmas
Zweyfaches Zehen ordentlicher . . .
Evangelien, no. 8

BRÜCKNER, Wolfgang (*continued*)

B1266 **Wer bist du**
ATTB, 2 vln, vla, bc
4th Sunday of Advent
*Zweyfaches Zehen ordentlicher . . .
Evangelien*, no. 4

BRUHNS, Nicolaus (1665-1697)

B1267 **Alleluja. Paratum cor meum**
TTB, vln, 2 gambas, bc
D-Bds Mus. ms. 30101, no. 4 (Bokemeyer)
score
DMA 15//24
EdM II: Schleswig-Holstein, vol. 1, pp.
99-126
Ed. Stein (Litolff/Peters no. 5832, 1939)

B1268 **Die Zeit meines Abschieds ist vorhanden**
SATB, 2 vln, 2 vla, bsn, bc
D-Bds Mus. ms. 30101, no. 8 (Bokemeyer)
score
DMA 15//24
EdM II: Schleswig-Holstein, vol. 1, pp.
3-20
Ed. Krüger, *Die Kantate* 45 (1960)
Ed. Stein (Litolff/Peters no. 5826, 1939,
1960)

B1269 **Hemmt eure Tränenflut**
SATB, 2 vln, 2 vla, bsn, bc
D-Bds Mus. ms. 30101, no. 3 (Bokemeyer)
score
DMA 15//24
EdM II: Schleswig-Holstein, vol. 2, pp.
115-40
Ed. Stein (Litolff/Peters no. 5836, 1939,
1963)

B1270 **Ich habe Lust abzuscheiden**
See Ich liege und schlafe

B1271 **Ich liege und schlafe**
SATB, 2 vln, 2 vla, bsn, bc
D-Bds Mus. ms. 30101, no. 6 (Bokemeyer)
score
DMA 15//24
EdM II: Schleswig-Holstein, vol. 2, pp.
3-18
Ed. Stein (Breitkopf & Härtel Chorbibl.
no. 2682, 1930)
Ed. Stein (Litolff/Peters no. 5833, 1930,
1960)

Opening chorus appears with text "Ich habe
Lust abzuscheiden" in D-Bds Mus. ms.
30101, no. 7 & EdM II: Schleswig-Holstein,
vol. 2, pp. 19-28

B1272 **Muß nicht der Mensch auf dieser Erden**
SATB, 2 vln, 2 clar, bsn, bc
D-Bds Mus. ms. 30101, no. 1 (Bokemeyer)
score
DMA 15//24
EdM II: Schleswig-Holstein, vol. 2, pp.
27-75
Ed. Stein (Litolff/Peters no. 5834, 1939)

B1273 **O werter Heiliger Geist**
SATB, 2 vln, 2 vla, 2 clar, bsn, bc
D-Bds Mus. ms. 30101, no. 11 (Bokemeyer)
(1693)
score
DMA 15//24
EdM II: Schleswig-Holstein, vol. 2, pp.
77-113
Ed. Stein (Litolff/Peters no. 5835, 1939,
1963)

B1274 **Wohl dem, der den Herren fürchtet**
SSB, 2 vln, 2 vla, bsn, bc
D-Bds Mus. ms. 30101, no. 2 (Bokemeyer)
score
DMA 15//24
EdM II: Schleswig-Holstein, vol. 1, pp.
85-98
Ed. Stein (Litolff/Peters no. 5831, 1939)

BRUNCKHORST, Arnold Matthias (1670-1725)

B1275 **Es begab sich aber zu der Zeit**
SATB, 3 vln, vlne, waldhorn/corn, bc
D-Bds Mus. ms. 30101, no. 16 (Bokemeyer)
score

B1276 **Und da der Sabbat vergangen war**
SATB, 2 vln, vla, tpt, bc
D-Bds 30099, no. 10 (Bokemeyer)
score
Ed. Hellmann, *Die Kantate* 12

BUCHNER, Adam

B1277 **Die hier vergießen ihre Tränen**
SATB
Funeral of Werthold Gottfried Strüven
Jena, 1677
RISM B4861

BUCHNER, Philipp Friedrich (1614-1669)

COLLECTIONS

Concerti ecclesiastici I (1642)
RISM B4862 (parts)

Concerti ecclesiastici II (1644)
RISM B4863 (parts)

Sacrarum cantionum (1656)
RISM B4864 (parts)
DMA 2/43

WORKS

B1278 Accurite
ATB, bc
Sacrarum cantionum, no. 15

B1279 Actiones nostras
ATB, bc
Sacrarum cantionum, no. 14

B1280 Assumpta est Maria
SATB, bc
Concerti ecclesiastici II, no. 17

B1281 Beatus
SAB, bc
Concerti ecclesiastici II, no. 10

B1282 Beatus vir
SATTB, bc
Sacrarum cantionum, no. 24

B1283 Benedicam Dominum
SSATB, bc
Concerti ecclesiastici I, no. 18

B1284 Caro mea
SATB, bc
Concerti ecclesiastici II, no. 18

B1285 Deus misereatur
SATB, bc
Concerti ecclesiastici I, no. 15

B1286 Domine exaudi
ATB, bc
Concerti ecclesiastici I, no. 12

B1287 Domine Jesu Christe
SSATB, bc
Concerti ecclesiastici I, no. 19

B1288 Ecce tu pulchra
SATTB, bc
Sacrarum cantionum, no. 25

B1289 Exultate Deo
SATTB, bc
Sacrarum cantionum, no. 23

B1290 Exurgat Deus
ATB, bc
Sacrarum cantionum, no. 11

B1291 In conspectu angelorum
ATB, bc
Concerti ecclesiastici II, no. 14

B1292 In dedicatione templi
ATB, bc
Concerti ecclesiastici II, no. 12

B1293 In illo tempore
SSATB, bc
Concerti ecclesiastici II, no. 20

B1294 In voluntate tua
SATB, bc
Sacrarum cantionum, no. 20

B1295 Jerusalem, Jerusalem
ATB, bc
Concerti ecclesiastici II, no. 13

B1296 Jubilate Deo
ATB, bc
Concerti ecclesiastici I, no. 10

B1297 Justus ut palma
SSATB, bc
Concerti ecclesiastici I, no. 20

B1298 Lilia convallium
SSB, bc
Sacrarum cantionum, no. 9

B1299 Non omnis
SATB, bc
Sacrarum cantionum, no. 18

B1300 Non timebus
SAB, bc
Sacrarum cantionum, no. 10

B1301 O nova, o rara
ATB, bc
Sacrarum cantionum, no. 12

B1302 O quales flores
ATB, bc
Concerti ecclesiastici II, no. 11

B1303 O quanta in coelis
SSATB, bc
Concerti ecclesiastici I, no. 17

BUCHNER, Philipp Friedrich (*continued*)

B1304 **O sacrum convivium**
AATB, bc
Sacrarum cantionum, no. 21

B1305 **O vita cui omnia vivunt**
TTB, bc
Sacrarum cantionum, no. 16

B1306 **Omnes jubilent**
SATB, bc
Sacrarum cantionum, no. 19

B1307 **Ostende nobis**
SAT, bc
Concerti ecclesiastici I, no. 8
Ed. Gottron, *300 Jahre Mainzer
Kirchenmusik*, pp. 25-31

B1308 **Paratum cor meum**
SSATB, bc
Concerti ecclesiastici I, no. 16

B1309 **Pastores**
SATB, bc
Concerti ecclesiastici II, no. 19

B1310 **Peccantem me quotidie**
SATB, bc
Concerti ecclesiastici I, no. 13

B1311 **Qui diligitis Deum**
SSB, bc
Concerti ecclesiastici I, no. 9

B1312 **Si bona suscepimus**
SSATB, bc
Sacrarum cantionum, no. 22

B1313 **Surgamus, cantemus**
SATB, bc
Sacrarum cantionum, no. 17

B1314 **Surge propera**
ATB, bc
Concerti ecclesiastici I, no. 11

B1315 **Veni Sancte Spiritus**
SATB, 2 vln, 2 vla, bc
D-WÜ Domchorbibliothek

B1316 **Venite, gentes**
SATB, bc
Concerti ecclesiastici I, no. 14
Ed. Gottron, *300 Jahre Mainzer
Kirchenmusik*, pp. 32-41

B1317 **Virgo prudentissima**
ATB, bc
Sacrarum cantionum, no. 13

BÜTNER, Crato (1616-1679)

Note: Titles formerly in PL-GD and listed in Günther with shelf numbers in the series "Ms. Cath. q." are now lost, according to a report from the library in April 1986

B1318 **Allein Gott in der Höh sei Ehr**
See Missa Germanica

B1319 **Anima Christi**
SATB, 2 vln, bc
Danzig, 1661
RISM B4912 (parts)
DMA 2/1722 and 3/33

B1320 **Deus in adjutorium**
5 vv, 2 vln, corn, bc
PL-GD Ms. Joh. 406, no. 5
score

B1321 **Du heilige Brunst süßer Trost**
SATB, 2 vln, 3 vla, 2 fl, vlne, theorbo, bc
Pentecost
S-Uu 5:8 (Düben)
parts
Verse 3 from "Komm heiliger Geist" (S-Uu
5:12)

B1322 **Ei du frommer und getreuer Knecht**
SSAATTBB, 2 vln, 3 vla/tbn, bc
S-Uu 5:16 (Düben)
parts
DMA 2/1723

B1323 **Freuet euch ihr Gerechten**
SATB, SATB, 3 vln, 3 tbn, bc
Christmas Day
S-Uu 5:9 (Düben)
parts
DMA 2/1724

B1324 **Frohlocket mit Händen alle Völker**
SSAB, ATTB, 2 vln, 2 tpt, 3 tbn,
trombone grosso, bc
S-Uu 5:10 (Düben)
parts
DMA 2/1725

B1325 **Gott ist unser Zuversicht und Stärke**
SATTB, 2 vln, 2 corn, bsn, bc
S-Uu 41:16 (Düben)
parts
Anonymous: tentative attribution in
Lindberg catalog, citing Krummacher

B1326 **Komm, Heiliger Geist**
SATB, SATB, 2 vln, vltta/tbn, 3 vla/tbn,
vlne, bc

S-Uu 5:12 (Düben)
    parts
    DMA 2/1727
    Verse 3 copied separately as "Du heilige
      Brunst" (S-Uu 5:8)

B1327   **Missa (brevis) Germanica**
    SATB, vln/corn, 2 vla/tbn, vlne/tbn, bc
    D-B Mus. ms. 2627 (Erfurt) (1677)
      score and parts
    German texts: "O Vater allmächtiger Gott"
      and "Allein Gott in der Höh"

B1328   **Nisi Dominus aedificaverit domum**
    SAB, 2 vln, bc
    S-Uu 5:14 (Düben)
      parts
      DMA 2/1729

B1329   **Nun danket alle Gott**
    SSB, 2 vln, bsn, bc
    In honor of Joachim Dinckler
    Danzig, 1653
      RISM B4909 (parts)
      DMA 57//102

B1330   **O quanta in coelis laetita**
    SSAB, ATTB, 2 vln, 3 tbn, vlne, bc
    D-Bds Breslau Mus. ms. 131 (1654)

B1331   **O Vater, allmächtiger Gott**
    See Missa Germanica

B1332   **Siehe, es hat überwunden**
    SSATTB, 3 vla, 2 corn, vlne, bc
    PL-GD Ms. Joh. 406, no. 22 (1690)
      score

B1333   **Siehe, es hat überwunden**
    12 vv
    D-Dlb Mus. Lüb. 53:190

B1334   **Te Deum laudamus**
    SSAB, SATB, ATTB, 2 vln, vla, 2 corn, 2
      tbtta, timp, 4 tbn, vlne, bc
    Danzig, 1662
      RISM B4915 (parts)
      DMA 2/45

B1335   **Vom Himmel hoch da komm ich her**
    SATB, SATB, 3 vln, 2 tbn, vlne, bc
    S-Uu 5:19 (Düben)
      parts
      DMA 2/1730

B1336   **Wir danken dir, Herr Jesu Christ**
    SATB, SATB, 2 vln, 2 vla, vlne, bc

S-Uu 5:17 (Düben)
    parts
    DMA 2/1731

B1337   **Wo der Herr nicht bei uns wäre**
    SSB, 2 vln, vla, vlne, bc
    Danzig, 1661
      RISM B4914 (parts)
      DMA 3/35

B1338   **Wo ist dein Stachel nun, o Tod**
    SSATB, 2 vln, 3 tbn, bc
    S-Uu 5:18 (Düben)
      parts
      DMA 2/1732

BUTTSTEDT, Johann Heinrich (1666-1727)

B1339   **Die Güte des Herrn ist es**
    SATB, 2 vln, 2 vla, clar, bc
    D-Dlb Mus. ms. 2157-E-500 (Grimma U
      535/T 3)
      parts

B1340   **Kommet her zu mir**
    SATB, 2 vla d'amore, 2 gamba, bc
    D-F Ms. Ff. Mus. 167
      score and parts

B1341   **Missa**
    SATB, 2 vln, bsn, bc
    D-B Mus. ms. 2660
      score
      DMA 1/1544

B1342   **Missa**
    SATB, 2 vln, bc
    D-B Mus. ms. 2661 (1695)
      score and parts
      DMA 1/1543

BUXTEHUDE, Dieterich (ca. 1637-1707)

B1343   **Accedite gentes, accurite populi** (BuxWV 1)
    SSATB, 2 vln, bc
    S-Uu 38:1 (Düben)
      parts
      DMA 2/2149
    S-Uu 82:34, no. 1 (Düben)
      tablature
      DMA 2/2149
    Ed. Sørensen, SDM III, no. 138, pp. 37-50
    Authenticity questionable

BUXTEHUDE, Dieterich (*continued*)

B1344 **Ad ubera portabimini** (BuxWV 75/2)
SSATB, 2 vln, vlne, bc
S-Uu 50:12, no. 2 (Düben)
  tablature (autograph)
  DMA 2/434
S-Uu 6:3 (Düben)
  parts
  DMA 1/1545
Ed. Grusnick (Bärenreiter no. 3457)
Ed. Killian (Merseburger EM 982)
Second piece of cycle "Membra Jesu"

B1345 **Afferte Domino gloriam honorem** (BuxWV 2)
SSB, bc
S-Uu 6:4 (Düben)
  parts
  DMA 1/1546
S-Uu 82:42, no. 2 (Düben)
  tablature
  DMA 2/417
Buxtehudes Werke 5, pp. 10-13

B1346 **All solch dein Güt wir preisen** (BuxWV 3)
SSATB, 2 vln, 2 vla, vlne, bc
S-Uu 50:1 (Düben)
  tablature
  DMA 2/2151
S-Uu 50:1a (Düben)
  parts
  DMA 2/2151
Ed. Grusnick (Bärenreiter no. 3197, 1956)
Ed. Killian (Merseburger no. 956)

B1347 **Alles was ihr tut** (BuxWV 4)
SATB, 2 vln, 2 vla, vlne, bc
S-Uu 13:29 (Düben)
  tablature
  DMA 3/217
S-Uu 50:2 (Düben)
  parts
  DMA 2/2150
D-LÜh Mus. A 373, no. 1 (presently in
  D-Bds)
  tablature
  DMA 3/1607
D-B Mus. ms. 2680, no. 8 (Bokemeyer)
  score
  DMA 1/1985
DdT 14, pp. 39-58
Buxtehudes Werke 9, pp. 3-34
Ed. Graulich, SBuxA 1

B1348 **An filius non est Dei** (BuxWV 6)
ATB, 2 vln, gamba, bc

S-Uu 50:3 (Düben)
  parts
  DMA 2/2152
Buxtehudes Werke 7, pp. 49-55

B1349 **Aperite mihi portas justitiae** (BuxWV 7)
ATB, 2 vln, bc
S-Uu 50:4 (Düben)
  parts
  DMA 2/2153
Buxtehudes Werke 7, pp. 62-68

B1350 **Bedenke, Mensch, das Ende** (BuxWV 9)
SSB, 3 vln, vlne, bc
S-Uu 85:6 (Düben)
  tablature
  DMA 2/2154
D-LÜh Mus. A 373, no. 6 (presently in
  D-Bds)
  tablature
  DMA 3/1607
Buxtehudes Werke 5, pp. 14-20

B1351 **Befiehl dem Engel, daß er komm** (BuxWV 10)
SATB, 2 vln, vlne, bc
S-Uu 50:5 (Düben)
  parts
  DMA 2/2155
Buxtehudes Werke 8, pp. 73-84

B1352 **Benedicam Dominum** (BuxWV 113)
SSATB, SATB, 2 vln, 2 corn, 4 tbtta, 3
  tbn, vlne, bsn, bomb, bc
S-Uu 50:6 (Düben) (1683)
  parts
  DMA 2/2156
Buxtehudes Werke 4, pp. 23-73

B1353 **Canite Jesu nostro** (BuxWV 11)
SSB, 2 vln, vlne, bc
S-Uu 82:43, no. 5 (Düben) (1683)
  tablature
  DMA 1/1987
Buxtehudes Werke 5, pp. 21-28
Ed. Grusnick (Bärenreiter no. 3349, 1974)

B1354 **Cantate Domino** (BuxWV 12)
SSB, bc
S-Uu 67:8 (Düben)
  parts
S-Uu 83:16 (Düben)
  tablature
  DMA 2/418
Buxtehudes Werke 5, pp. 29-34
Ed. Graulich, SBuxA 7
Ed. Steude (Deutscher Verlag für Musik
  no. 7902)

B1355 **Das neugeborne Kindelein** (BuxWV 13)
SATB, 3 vln, vlne/bsn, bc
S-Uu 50:7 (Düben)
    parts
    DMA 2/2157
Buxtehudes Werke 8, pp. 121-40
Ed. Graulich, SBuxA 2

B1356 **Dein edles Herz** (BuxWV 14)
SATB, 2 vln, 2 vla, vlne, bc
S-Uu 82:35, no. 8 (Düben)
    tablature
    DMA 2/419
Buxtehudes Werke 9, pp. 35-59

B1357 **Der Herr erhöre dich**
See Herren vår Gud

B1358 **Der Herr ist mit mir** (BuxWV 15)
SATB, 2 vln, vlne, bc
S-Uu 85:17 (Düben)
    tablature
    DMA 2/2158
Buxtehudes Werke 8, pp. 85-104
SDM 3, no. 89

B1359 **Domine, salvum fac regem** (BuxWV 18)
SSATB, 2 vln, 2 vla, vlne, bc
S-Uu 85:16 (Düben)
    tablature
    DMA 2/2160
Ed. Sørensen, SDM 3, no. 138

B1360 **Du Frieden Fürst, Herr Jesu Christ** (BuxWV 20)
SSATB, 2 vln, vlne, bc
S-Uu 50:10 (Düben)
    parts
    DMA 2/2161
Ed. Grusnick (Bärenreiter, no. 3362)
Ed. Sørensen (Copenhagen: Engstrøm &
    Sødring no. 410)

B1361 **Du Frieden Fürst, Herr Jesu Christ** (BuxWV 21)
SSB, 2 vln, 2 vla, vla/bsn, bc
S-Uu 6:5 (Düben)
    parts
    DMA 1/1547
Buxtehudes Werke 5, pp. 35-43

B1362 **Du Lebensfürst, Herr Jesu Christ** (BuxWV 22)
SATB, 2 vln, 2 vltta, vlne, bc
S-Uu 50:11 (Düben)
    parts
S-Uu 83:43 (Düben)
    tablature
    DMA 2/420
Buxtehudes Werke 9, pp. 61-89

B1363 **Ecce nunc benedicite** (BuxWV 23)
ATTB, 2 vln, bc
S-Uu 6:6 (Düben)
    parts
    DMA 1/1548
S-Uu 82:34, no. 2 (Düben)
    tablature
    DMA 1/1548
Buxtehudes Werke 8, pp. 105-20
Ed. Sørensen, SDM 3, no. 138

B1364 **Ecce super montes** (BuxWV 75/1)
SSATB, 2 vln, vlne, bc
S-Uu 50:12, no. 1 (Düben)
    tablature (autograph)
    DMA 2/434
S-Uu 6:2 (Düben)
    parts
    DMA 1/1549
Ed. Grusnick (Bärenreiter no. 3456)
Ed. Killian (Merseburger no. 981)
First piece of cycle "Membra Jesu"

B1365 **Eins bitte ich vom Herrn** (BuxWV 24)
SSATB, 2 vln, 2 vla, bsn, bc
25th Sunday after Trinity
S-Uu 50:13 (Düben)
    parts
    DMA 2/2162
S-Uu 85:8 (Düben)
    tablature
    DMA 2/2162
DdT 14, pp. 15-38

B1366 **Erfreue dich, Erde** (BuxWV 26)
SSAB, 2 vln, 2 vla, 2 tpt, tbn, vlne, bc
S-Uu 50:15 (Düben)
    tablature and parts
    DMA 1/1566
Ed. Killian (Merseburger no. 976)

B1367 **Erhalt uns, Herr, bei deinem Wort** (BuxWV 27)
SATB, 2 vln, vlne/bomb, bc
S-Uu 50:14 (Düben)
    parts
    DMA 2/2163
S-Uu 85:15 (Düben)
    tablature
    DMA 2/2163
Buxtehudes Werke 8, pp. 47-63

B1368 **Frohlocket mit Händen** (BuxWV 29)
SSATB, 2 vln, 2 vla, 2 tpt, vlne, bc
S-Uu 82:36 (Düben)
    tablature
    DMA 2/422
Ed. Sørensen (Hansen no. 29165)

BUXTEHUDE, Dieterich (*continued*)

B1369 Fürwahr, er trug unsere Krankheit (BuxWV 31)
SSATB, 2 vln, 2 gamba, vlne/bsn, bc
S-Uu 6:9 (Düben)
score (autograph)
DMA 1/1551
Ed. Grusnick (Bärenreiter no. 1093)
Ed. Graulich, SBuxA 4

B1370 Gott fähret auf mit Jauchzen (BuxWV 33)
SSB, 2 vln, 2 vla/tbn, 2 corn, 2 tpt, bsn, bc
S-Uu 82:43, no. 4 (Düben)
tablature
DMA 2/424
Buxtehudes Werke 5, pp. 44-55

B1371 Gott hilf mir (BuxWV 34)
SSATBB, 2 vln, 2 vla, vlne, bc
S-Uu 50:19 (Düben)
parts
DMA 1/1533
DdT 14, pp. 57-84
Ed. Graulich, SBuxA 6

B1372 Herren var Gud/Der Herr erhöre dich (BuxWV 40)
SATB, 2 vln, vlne, bc
S-Uu 85:14 (Düben) (1687)
tablature
DMA 2/2166
Buxtehudes Werke 8, pp. 64-72

B1373 Herzlich lieb hab ich dich, o Herr (BuxWV 41)
SSATB, 2 vln, 2 vla, 2 tpt, vlne/bsn, bc
D-LÜh Mus. A 373, no. 7 (presently in D-Bds)
tablature
DMA 3/1607
Ed. Grusnick (Bärenreiter no. 544)

B1374 Heut triumphieret Gottes Sohn (BuxWV 43)
SSATB, 2 vln, 2 vla, 2 tpt, vlne, bc
D-B Mus. ms. 2680, no. 2 (Bokemeyer)
score
DMA 1/1993
Ed. Grusnick (Bärenreiter no. 1736)
Ed. Killian (Merseburger no. 966)
Alleluia only: DdT 14, pp. 167-77
Alleluia only: *Die Kantate* 4
Authenticity questionable

B1375 Ich habe Lust abzuscheiden (BuxWV 46)
SSB, 2 vln, vlne/bsn, bc
S-Uu 51:4 (Düben)
parts
DMA 2/426, 2/427

S-Uu 82:42, no. 7 (Düben)
tablature
DMA 2/426, 2/427
Buxtehudes Werke 5, pp. 56-61
Early version of BuxWV 47

B1376 Ich habe Lust abzuscheiden (BuxWV 47)
SSB, 2 vln, vlne, bc
D-LÜh Mus. A 373, no. 10 (presently in D-Bds)
tablature
DMA 3/1607
Buxtehudes Werke 5, pp. 62-68
Revised version of BuxWV 46

B1377 Ihr lieben Christen, freut euch (BuxWV 51)
SSATB, 3 vln, 2 vla, 3 corn, 2 tpt, 3 tbn, vlne, bsn, bc
2nd Sunday of Advent
D-LÜh Mus. A 373, no. 2 (presently in D-Bds)
tablature
DMA 3/1607
D-LÜh Mus. A 312a
score
A-Wgm III 30288
DdT 14, pp. 107-38
Ed. Graulich, SBuxA 9
Ed. Seiffert, *Die Kantate* 18

B1378 Illustra faciem tuam (BuxWV 75/7)
SSATB, 2 vln, vlne, bc
S-Uu 50:12, no. 7 (Düben)
tablature (autograph)
DMA 2/434
S-Uu 51:10 (Düben)
parts
DMA 2/2167
Ed. Grusnick (Bärenreiter)
Ed. Killian (Merseburger)
Seventh piece of cycle "Membra Jesu"

B1379 In dulci jubilo (BuxWV 52)
SSB, 2 vln, bc
S-Uu 82:43, no. 8 (Düben)
tablature
DMA 1/1996
D-B Mus. ms. 2680, no. 5 (Bokemeyer)
score
DMA 1/1997
Buxtehudes Werke 5, pp. 69-75
Ed. Graulich, SBuxA 3
Ed. Steude (Deutsche Verlag für Musik no. 7902)

B1380   **In te Domine speravi** (BuxWV 53)
SAB, bc
S-Uu 83:19 (Düben)
tablature
DMA 2/429
Buxtehudes Werke 7, pp. 8-9
Ed. Trubel, *Die Kantate* 36, 37

B1381   **Ist es recht** (BuxWV 54)
SSATB, 2 vln, 2 vla, vlne, bc
S-Uu 51:11 (Düben)
parts
DMA 1/1555
Ed. Grusnick (Bärenreiter no. 1738)

B1382   **Je höher du bist** (BuxWV 55)
SSB, 2 vln, vlne, bc
S-Uu 51:5 (Düben)
parts
DMA 2/430
S-Uu 82:35, no. 5 (Düben) (1684)
tablature
DMA 2/430
Buxtehudes Werke 5, pp. 76-86

B1383   **Jesu dulcis memoria** (BuxWV 57)
ATB, 2 vln, bc
S-Uu 51:8 (Düben)
parts
DMA 2/2169
Buxtehudes Werke 7, pp. 72-80

B1384   **Jesu, komm, mein Trost und Lachen** (BuxWV 58)
ATB, 2 vln, vla, vlne, bc
S-Uu 6:12 (Düben)
parts
DMA 1/1556
Buxtehudes Werke 7, pp. 81-87

B1385   **Jesu, meine Freude** (BuxWV 60)
SSB, 2 vln, bsn, bc
S-Uu 85:7 (Düben)
tablature
DMA 2/2171
D-LÜh Mus. A 373, no. 11 (presently in D-Bds)
tablature
DMA 3/1607
Buxtehudes Werke 5, pp. 87-95
Ed. Graulich, SBuxA 11
Ed. Steude (Deutsche Verlag für Musik no. 7902)

B1386   **Jesu, meiner Freuden Meister** (BuxWV 61)
SATB, 3 vla, vlne, bc
Funeral of Margarita Nieman

Ratzeburg, 1677
RISM B5201 (score)
DMA 2/47
S-Uu 86:36 (Düben)
tablature
Ed. Sørensen (W. Hansen no. 29408, 1977)

B1387   **Jesu, meines Lebens Leben** (BuxWV 62a)
SATB, 2 vln, 2 vla, vlne, bc
S-Uu 82:37, no. 1 (Düben)
tablature
DMA 1/1557
S-Uu 6:13 (Düben)
parts (bc only)
Buxtehudes Werke 9, pp. 247-60
Original version of BuxWV 62b

B1388   **Jesu, meines Lebens Leben** (BuxWV 62b)
SATB, 2 vln, 2 vla, vlne, bc
S-Uu 6:13 (Düben)
parts
S-Uu 82:37, no. 3 (Düben)
tablature
DMA 1/1557
Buxtehudes Werke 9, pp. 91-107
"Corrected" version of BuxWV 62a

B1389   **Jesulein, du Tausendschön** (BuxWV 63)
ATB, 2 vln, vlne/bsn, bc
S-Uu 51:9 (Düben)
parts
DMA 2/2170
Buxtehudes Werke 7, pp. 89-99

B1390   **Klinget mit Freuden** (BuxWV 65)
SSB, 2 vln, 2 tpt, bc
S-Uu 6:14 (Düben)
tablature and parts
DMA 1/1558, 2/2173
Buxtehudes Werke 5, pp. 96-97

B1391   **Kommst du, Licht der Heiden** (BuxWV 66)
SSB, 2 vln, 2 vla, vlne, bc
S-Uu 6:15 (Düben)
parts
S-Uu 82:42, no. 9 (Düben)
tablature
DMA 1/1559
Buxtehudes Werke 6, pp. 14-23
Ed. Horn, *Die Kantate* 5

B1392   **Lauda Sion salvatorem** (BuxWV 68)
SSB, 2 vln, bc
S-Uu 51:14 (Düben)
parts
DMA 1/1560

BUXTEHUDE, Dieterich (*continued*)

S-Uu 82:42, no. 5 (Düben)
tablature
DMA 2/431
D-LÜh Mus. A 373, no. 8 (presently in
D-Bds)
tablature
DMA 3/1607
D-LÜh Mus. A 334
score
Buxtehudes Werke 6, pp. 24-29
Ed. Steude (Deutsche Verlag für Musik no.
7902)

B1393 Magnificat à 10
See under Anonymous

B1394 Man singet mit Freuden vom Sieg
See under Anonymous

B1395 Mein Gemüt erfreuet sich (BuxWV 72)
SAB, 4 vln, 2 fl, 4 corn, 2 tpt, 3 tbn, 3
bsn, bc
S-Uu 85:5 (Düben)
tablature
DMA 2/2178
Buxtehudes Werke 7, pp. 10-19

B1396 Meine Seele, willst du ruhn (BuxWV 74)
SSB, 2 vln, vlne, bc
S-Uu 51:16 (Düben)
parts
DMA 2/2177
D-LÜh Mus. A 373, no. 13 (presently in
D-Bds)
tablature
DMA 3/1607
Buxtehudes Werke 6, pp. 30-38

B1397 Membra Jesu (BuxWV 75)
See Ad ubera, Ecce super montes, Illustra
faciem, Quid sunt plagae, Sicut modo,
Surge amica mea, Vulnerasti cor meum

B1398 Missa Alla brevis (BuxWV 114)
SSATB, bc
S-Uu 6:16 (Düben)
parts
DMA 1/1562
D-LÜh Mus. A 336
score (Kyrie only)
Buxtehudes Werke 4, pp. 12-19

B1399 Nichts soll uns scheiden (BuxWV 77)
SAB, 2 vln, vlne, bc

D-LÜh Mus. A 373, no. 9 (presently in
D-Bds)
tablature
DMA 3/1607
Buxtehudes Werke 7, pp. 20-28
Ed. Trubel, *Die Kantate* 20

B1400 Nimm von uns, Herr, du treuer Gott (BuxWV 78)
SATB, 2 vln, 2 vltta, bsn, bc
S-Uu 82:38 (Düben)
tablature (autograph)
DMA 2/2179
Buxtehudes Werke 9, pp. 109-50

B1401 Nu låt oß Gudh wår Herra
See Nun laßt uns Gott dem Herren

B1402 Nun danket alle Gott (BuxWV 79)
SSATB, 2 vln, 2 corn, 2 tpt, vlne, bsn, bc
S-Uu 82:39 (Düben)
tablature (autograph)
DMA 2/2181
D-LÜh Mus. A 373, no. 3 (presently in
D-Bds)
tablature
DMA 3/1607
Ed. Sørensen (Hansen no. 29307)

**B1403 Nun laßt uns Gott dem Herren/Nu låt oß
Gudh wår Herra** (BuxWV 81)
SATB, 2 vln, bc
S-Uu 51:17 (Düben)
parts (Swedish text only)
DMA 2/2180
S-Uu 85:3 (Düben)
tablature (German and Swedish text)
DMA 2/2180
Buxtehudes Werke 8, pp. 9-21

B1404 O fröhliche Stunden, o herrliche Zeit (BuxWV 85)
SSAB, 2 vln, 2 vla, vlne, bc
S-Uu 51:13a, no. 1 (Düben)
tablature (autograph)
DMA 1/1563
S-Uu 86:61 (Düben)
tablature
DMA 3/219
Buxtehudes Werke 9, pp. 151-82

B1405 O Gott, wir danken deiner Güt (BuxWV 86)
SSATB, 2 vln, vlne, bc
S-Uu 85:10 (Düben)
tablature
DMA 1/1564
Ed. Killian (Merseburger no. 962)
Ed. Sørensen (Hansen no. 29145)

B1406 **O Jesu mi dulcissime** (BuxWV 88)
SSB, 2 vln, vlne, bc
S-Uu 82:40 (Düben)
tablature (autograph)
DMA 1/2004
Buxtehudes Werke 6, pp. 39-45
Fragment

B1407 **Pange lingua** (BuxWV 91)
SSAB, 2 vln, 2 vltta, vlne, bc
S-Uu 51:22 (Düben)
parts
DMA 1/2005
S-Uu 83:42 (Düben) (1684)
tablature
DMA 1/2005
Buxtehudes Werke 9, pp. 183-209
Ed. Sørensen, SDM 3, no. 138

B1408 **Quid sunt plagae istae** (BuxWV 75/3)
SSATB, 2 vln, vlne, bc
S-Uu 50:12, no. 3 (Düben)
tablature (autograph)
DMA 2/434
S-Uu 51:23 (Düben)
parts
DMA 1/1565
Ed. Grusnick (Bärenreiter no. 3458)
Ed. Killian (Merseburger no. 983)
Third piece of cycle "Membra Jesu"

B1409 **Salve, desiderium** (BuxWV 93)
SSB, 2 vln, vlne/bsn, bc
S-Uu 51:24 (Düben)
parts
DMA 2/436, 2/437
S-Uu 82:42, no. 1 (Düben)
tablature (variant ending)
DMA 2/436, 2/437
Buxtehudes Werke 6, pp. 46-50

B1410 **Schwinget euch himmelan** (BuxWV 96)
SSATB, 3 vln, vlne, bc
S-Uu 70:8 (Düben)
parts
S-Uu 85:11 (Düben)
tablature
DMA 1/1567, 2/438
Ed. Grusnick (Bärenreiter no. 3366)

B1411 **Sicut modo geniti** (BuxWV 75/5)
ATB, 2 vln, vlne, bc
S-Uu 50:12, no. 5 (Düben)
tablature (autograph)
DMA 2/434

S-Uu 6:18 (Düben)
parts
DMA 1/1559
Ed. Grusnick (Bärenreiter no. 3460)
Ed. Killian (Merseburger no. 985)
Fifth piece of cycle "Membra Jesu"

B1412 **Surge, amica mea** (BuxWV 75/4)
SSATB, 2 vln, vlne, bc
S-Uu 50:12, no. 4 (Düben)
tablature (autograph)
DMA 2/434
S-Uu 6:1 (Düben)
parts
DMA 1/1570
Ed. Grusnick (Bärenreiter no. 3459)
Ed. Killian (Merseburger no. 984)
Fourth piece of cycle "Membra Jesu"

B1413 **Surrexit Christus hodie** (BuxWV 99)
SSB, 3 vln, bsn, bc
S-Uu 86:23 (Düben)
tablature
DMA 1/2009
Buxtehudes Werke 6, pp. 51-59
Ed. Hellmann, *Die Kantate* 11

B1414 **Vulnerasti cor meum** (BuxWV 75/6)
SSB, 5 gamba, bc
S-Uu 50:12, no. 6 (Düben)
tablature (autograph)
DMA 2/434
S-Uu 46:25 (Düben)
parts
DMA 3/220
Ed. Grusnick (Bärenreiter no. 3461)
Ed. Killian (Merseburger no. 986)
Sixth piece of cycle "Membra Jesu"

B1415 **Wachet auf, ruft uns die Stimme** (BuxWV 100)
SSB, 3 vln, vln/vla, bsn, bc
D-B Mus. ms. 2680, no. 4 (Bokemeyer)
score
DMA 1/2011
Buxtehudes Werke 6, pp. 60-74
Die Kantate 189

B1416 **Wachet auf, ruft uns die Stimme** (BuxWV 101)
ATB, 2 vln, bc
D-B Mus. ms. 2680, no. 3 (Bokemeyer)
score
DMA 1/2010
DdT 14, pp. 139-66
Buxtehudes Werke 7, pp. 100-114
Authenticity questionable

BUXTEHUDE, Dieterich (*continued*)

B1417   **Wacht! Euch zum Streit**
        See under Anonymous

B1418   **Walts Gott, mein Werk ich lasse** (BuxWV 103)
        SATB, 2 vln, vla, bc
        S-Uu 85:13 (Düben)
            tablature
            DMA 2/2186
        Buxtehudes Werke 8, pp. 31-46

B1419   **Wär Gott nicht mit uns diese Zeit** (BuxWV 102)
        SATB, 2 vln, bc
        S-Uu 84:4 (Düben)
            tablature
            DMA 2/2187
        Buxtehudes Werke 8, pp. 22-30

B1420   **Was frag ich nach der Welt** (BuxWV 104)
        SAB, 2 vln, vlne, bc
        D-LÜh Mus. A 373, no. 12 (presently in
            D-Bds)
            tablature
            DMA 3/1607
        Buxtehudes Werke 7, pp. 29-38
        Ed. Trubel, *Die Kantate* 111

B1421   **Welt, packe dich** (BuxWV 106)
        SSB, 2 vln, vlne, bc
        S-Uu 51:28 (Düben)
            parts
            DMA 2/440, 2/441
        S-Uu 82:42, no. 6 (Düben)
            tablature
            DMA 2/440, 2/441
        Buxtehudes Werke 6, pp. 75-83

B1422   **Wie schmeckt es so lieblich und wohl** (BuxWV 108)
        SAB, 2 vln, vlne, bc
        S-Uu 82:43, no. 6 (Düben)
            tablature
            DMA 2/442
        Buxtehudes Werke 7, pp. 39-48

B1423   **Wie soll ich dich empfangen** (BuxWV 109)
        SSB, 2 vln, bsn, bc
        S-Uu 51:29 (Düben)
            parts
            DMA 2/443
        S-Uu 82:35, no. 7 (Düben)
            tablature
            DMA 2/443
        Buxtehudes Werke 6, pp. 84-88
        Ed. Graulich, SBuxA 8

B1424   **Wie wird erneuet, wie wird erfreuet** (BuxWV
        110)
        SSATTB, 3 vln, 3 tpt, 3 tbn, cym, vlne, bc
        D-LÜh Mus. A 373, no. 5 (presently in
            D-Bds)
            tablature
            DMA 3/1607
        Ed. Sørensen (Hansen no. 29406, 1977)

B1425   **Wo soll ich fliehen hin** (BuxWV 112)
        SATB, 2 vln, 2 vla, vlne, bc
        D-LÜh Mus. A 373, no. 4 (presently in
            D-Bds)
            tablature
            DMA 3/1607
        DdT 14, pp. 85-106
        Buxtehudes Werke 9, pp. 211-43

C

CAESAR (Kayser), Johann Melchior (ca. 1648-1692)

COLLECTIONS

Hymni de dominicis (1691-1692)
RISM C20 (parts)
DMA 3/965

Missa breves (1686-1687)
RISM C17 (parts)
DMA 3/40

Psalmi vespertini (1690)
RISM C19 (parts)
DMA 3/41

Trisagion musicum (1682-1683)
RISM C16 (parts)
DMA 3/1879

WORKS

C0001 **Ad coenam agni**
SATB, 2 vln, vla, bc
1st Sunday after Easter
Hymni de dominicis, no. 9

C0002 **Afferentur Regi**
SATB, 2 vln, 3 vla, bsn, bc
Common of Virgins and Martyrs
Trisagion musicum, no. 16

C0003 **Audi benigne**
SATB, 2 vln, vla, bc
Lent
Hymni de dominicis, no. 6

C0004 **Ave Maria**
SATB, 2 vln, 3 vla, bsn, bc
Pentecost

Christmas Day
Trisagion musicum, no. 22 (misnumbered 21)

C0005 **Beata es**
SATB, 2 vln, 3 vla, bsn, bc
Eastertide
Pentecost
Trisagion musicum, no. 21 (misnumbered 22)

C0006 **Beati omnes**
SATB, 2 vln, 2 vla, bsn, bc
Psalmi vespertini, no. 15

C0007 **Beatus vir**
SATB, 2 vln, 2 vla, bsn, bc
Psalmi vespertini, no. 3

C0008 **Caelestis urbs**
SSB, 2 vln, 2 vla, bc
Dedication of a Church
Hymni de dominicis, no. 39

C0009 **Confitebor**
SATB, 2 vln, 2 vla, bsn, bc
Psalmi vespertini, no. 2

C0010 **Confitebor quoniam audisti**
SATB, 2 vln, 2 vla, bsn, bc
Psalmi vespertini, no. 16

C0011 **Confitebuntur coeli**
SATB, 2 vln, 3 vla, bsn, bc
Common of a Martyr in Eastertide
Trisagion musicum, no. 8

C0012 **Constitues eos**
SATB, 2 vln, 3 vla, bsn, bc
Common of Apostles
Trisagion musicum, no. 2

CAESAR (Kayser), Johann Melchior (*continued*)

C0013 **Creator alme**
SAT, bc
Advent
Hymni de dominicis, no. 1

C0014 **Credidi**
SATB, 2 vln, 2 vla, bsn, bc
Psalmi vespertini, no. 10

C0015 **Custodes hominum**
AAT, bc
Feast of the Guardian Angels
Hymni de dominicis, no. 26

C0016 **De profundis**
SATB, 2 vln, 2 vla, bsn, bc
Psalmi vespertini, no. 13

C0017 **Decora lux**
SATB, 2 vln, 2 vla, bc
Feast of Saints Peter and Paul
Hymni de dominicis, no. 20

C0018 **Decus morum**
SSB, 2 vln, bc
Feast of Saint Francis
Hymni de dominicis, no. 29

C0019 **Desiderium animae**
SATB, 2 vln, 3 vla, bsn, bc
Common of an Abbot
Trisagion musicum, no. 15

C0020 **Deus tuorum**
SSB, bc
Common of One Martyr
Hymni de dominicis, no. 34

C0021 **Diffusa est gratia**
SATB, 2 vln, 3 vla, bsn, bc
Common of Virgins
Common of Many Martyrs
Trisagion musicum, no. 17

C0022 **Dixit Dominus**
SATB, 2 vln, 2 vla, bsn, bc
Psalmi vespertini, no. 1

C0023 **Doctor egregie**
SATB, 2 vln, bc
Conversion of Saint Paul
Hymni de dominicis, no. 15

C0024 **Domine ad adjuvandum**
SATB, 2 vln, 2 vla, bsn, bc
Psalmi vespertini, no. 0 [*sic*]

C0025 **Domine Deus**
SATB, 2 vln, 3 vla, bsn, bc
Anniversary of the Dedication of a church
Trisagion musicum, no. 19

C0026 **Domine probasti me**
SATB, 2 vln, 2 vla, bsn, bc
Psalmi vespertini, no. 12

C0027 **Exultabunt**
SATB, 2 vln, 3 vla, bsn, bc
Common of Martyrs outside Eastertide
Trisagion musicum, no. 11

C0028 **Exultet orbis**
SATB, 2 vln, bc
Common of Apostles outside Eastertide
Hymni de dominicis, no. 32

C0029 **Felix namque es**
SATB, 2 vln, 3 vla, bsn, bc
Christmas Day
Eastertide
Trisagion musicum, no. 20

C0030 **Filiae regurti**
SATB, 2 vln, 3 vla, bsn, bc
Common of a Virgin
Trisagion musicum, no. 18

C0031 **Fortem virili**
SATB, bc
Common of a Non-virgin
Hymni de dominicis, no. 38

C0032 **Gaude mater**
SATB, 2 vln, bc
Feast of Saint Dominic
Hymni de dominicis, no. 23

C0033 **Gloria et honore**
SATB, 2 vln, 3 vla, bsn, bc
Common of a Martyr not a Pope
Trisagion musicum, no. 6

C0034 **Haec dies**
SATB, 2 vln, 2 vla, bc
Easter Sunday
Hymni de dominicis, no. 8

C0035 **Hostis Herodes**
SATB, 2 vln, 2 vla, bc
Epiphany
Hymni de dominicis, no. 4

C0036 **In convertendo (I)**
SATB, 2 vln, 2 vla, bsn, bc
Psalmi vespertini, no. 11

C0037 In convertendo (II)
ATB, bc
Psalmi vespertini, no. 26

C0038 In exitu
SATB, 2 vln, 2 vla, bsn, bc
Psalmi vespertini, no. 5

C0039 In omnem terram
SATB, 2 vln, 3 vla, bsn, bc
Common of Apostles
Trisagion musicum, no. 1

C0040 In virtute tua
SATB, 2 vln, 3 vla, bsn, bc
Common of a Confessor not a Pope
Trisagion musicum, no. 14

C0041 Inveni David
SATB, 2 vln, 3 vla, bsn, bc
Common of a Martyr Pope or a Confessor
Pope
Trisagion musicum, no. 5

C0042 Iste confessor
SATB, 2 vln, 2 vla, bc
Common of a Confessor
Hymni de dominicis, no. 36

C0043 Jesu, corona virginum
SSB, bc
Common of Virgins
Hymni de dominicis, no. 37

C0044 Jesu, nostra redemptio
SATB, 2 vln, 2 vla, bc
Ascension
Hymni de dominicis, no. 10

C0045 Jesu, redemptor omnium
SATB, 2 vln, 2 vla, bc
Christmas and Circumcision
Hymni de dominicis, no. 2

C0046 Justorum animae
SATB, 2 vln, 3 vla, bsn, bc
Common of Martyrs outside Eastertide
Trisagion musicum, no. 12

C0047 Justus ut palma
SATB, 2 vln, 3 vla, bsn, bc
Common of a Doctor of the Church
Trisagion musicum, no. 13

C0048 Laetamini in Domino
SATB, 2 vln, 3 vla, bsn, bc
Common of Martyrs in Eastertide
Trisagion musicum, no. 9

C0049 Laetatus sum
SATB, 2 vln, 2 vla, bsn, bc
Psalmi vespertini, no. 7

C0050 Lauda Jerusalem
SATB, 2 vln, 2 vla, bsn, bc
Psalmi vespertini, no. 9

C0051 Laudate Dominum, omnes gentes
SATB, 2 vln, 2 vla, bsn, bc
Psalmi vespertini, no. 6

C0052 Laudate, pueri
SATB, 2 vln, 2 vla, bsn, bc
Psalmi vespertini, no. 4

C0053 Laudate, pueri
SST, bc
Psalmi vespertini, no. 21

C0054 Laudibus cives
SSB, 2 vln, bc
Feast of Saint Benedict
Hymni de dominicis, no. 18

C0055 Lucis Creator
SATB, 2 vln, 2 vla, bc
Hymni de dominicis, no. 5

C0056 Magne Pater Augustine
SSB, 2 vln, bc
Feast of Saint Augustine
Hymni de dominicis, no. 25

C0057 Magnificat (I)
SATB, 2 vln, 2 vla, bsn, bc
Psalmi vespertini, no. 17

C0058 Magnificat (II)
SATB, 2 vln, 2 vla, bsn, bc
Psalmi vespertini, no. 18

C0059 Memento
SATB, 2 vln, 2 vla, bsn, bc
Psalmi vespertini, no. 14

C0060 Mihi autem
SATB, 2 vln, 3 vla, bsn, bc
Common of Apostles
Trisagion musicum, no. 3

C0061 Mirabilis Deus
SATB, 2 vln, 3 vla, bsn, bc
Common of Martyrs outside Eastertide
Trisagion musicum, no. 10

C0062 Missa Amor vincit omnia
SATB, 2 vln, 2 vla, bsn, bc
Feast of Saint Arnold
Missa breves, no. 5

CAESAR (Kayser), Johann Melchior (*continued*)

C0063 **Missa Aut Caesar, aut nihil**
SATB, 2 vln, 2 vla, bsn, bc
Epiphany
Missa breves, no. 1

C0064 **Missa Beneveneritis**
SATB, 2 vln, 2 vla, bsn, bc
Feast of Saints Chilian and Sociorum
Missa breves, no. 3

C0065 **Missa Dulcia non meruit**
SATB, 2 vln, 2 vla, bsn, bc
Immaculate Conception
Missa breves, no. 7

C0066 **Missa Landgraviana**
SATB, 2 vln, 2 vla, bsn, bc
Feast of Saint Frederick
Missa breves, no. 8

C0067 **Missa Nulla falus bello**
SATB, 2 vln, 2 vla, bsn, bc
Feast of Saint Joseph
Missa breves, no. 6

C0068 **Missa Sic transit gloria mundi**
SATB, 2 vln, 2 vla, bsn, bc
Feast of Saint Eleonor
Missa breves, no. 2

C0069 **Missa Tentare licet**
SATB, 2 vln, 2 vla, bsn, bc
Assumption of the Virgin Mary
Missa breves, no. 4

C0070 **Nisi Dominus (I)**
SATB, 2 vln, 2 vla, bsn, bc
Psalmi vespertini, no. 8

C0071 **Nisi Dominus (II)**
ATB, bc
Psalmi vespertini, no. 24

C0072 **O lux beata**
SATB, 2 vln, 2 vla, bc
Trinity
Hymni de dominicis, no. 12

C0073 **Pange lingua**
SATB, 2 vln, 2 vla, bc
Corpus Christi
Hymni de dominicis, no. 13

C0074 **Pater superni**
SSB, bc
Feast of Saint Mary Magdalene
Hymni de dominicis, no. 21

C0075 **Petrus beatus**
SST, 2 vln, bc
Feast of Saint Peter
Hymni de dominicis, no. 22

C0076 **Placare Christe**
SATB, 2 vln, 2 vla, bc
All Saints Day
Hymni de dominicis, no. 31

C0077 **Posuisti Domine**
SATB, 2 vln, 3 vla, bsn, bc
Common of a Martyr not a Pope
Trisagion musicum, no. 7

C0078 **Quicunque Christum quaritis**
SATB, 2 vln, 2 vla, bc
Feast of the Transfiguration
Hymni de dominicis, no. 24

C0079 **Quodcunque vinclis**
ATB, 2 vln, bc
Feast of Saint Peter
Hymni de dominicis, no. 14

C0080 **Regis superni**
SATB, 2 vln, bc
Feast of Saint Theresa
Hymni de dominicis, no. 30

C0081 **Sanctorum meritis**
ATB, bc
Common of Many Martyrs
Hymni de dominicis, no. 35

C0082 **Tantum ergo**
SATB, 2 vln, 2 vla, bc
Hymni de dominicis, no. 40

C0083 **Te Joseph celebrent**
SATB, 2 vln, 2 vla, bc
Feast of Saint Joseph
Hymni de dominicis, no. 17

C0084 **Te splendor et virtus patris**
SATB, 2 vln, 2 vla, bc
Feast of Saint Michael the Archangel
Hymni de dominicis, no. 27

C0085 **Tristes erant**
SSB, bc
Common of Apostles during Eastertide
Hymni de dominicis, no. 33

C0086 **Ut queant laxis**
SATB, 2 vln, 2 vla, bc
Feast of Saint John the Baptist
Hymni de dominicis, no. 19

C0087 Veni creator
SATB, 2 vln, 2 vla, bc
Pentecost
Hymni de dominicis, no. 11

C0088 Veritas mea
SATB, 2 vln, 3 vla, bsn, bc
Common of a Martyr Pope and of a
Confessor Pope
Trisagion musicum, no. 4

C0089 Vexilla regis
SSB, 2 vln, bc
Passion Sunday
Hymni de dominicis, no. 7

CALMBACH, Georg

C0090 Actus musicus in Dominic
SSAATTB, T, SATBBB, 2 vln, 3 vla, 2
gamba, 2 fl, 2 corn, 2 clar, bsn, bc
3rd Sunday after Trinity
D-B Mus. ms. 2796 (Erfurt) (1675-1680)
score and parts

CAPRICORNUS, Samuel Friedrich (1628-1665)

COLLECTIONS

Continuatio theatri musici (1669)
RISM C938 (parts)
DMA 3/1881

Geistliche Concerten I (1658)
RISM C929 (parts)
DMA 2/1981

Geistliche Concerten II (1665)
RISM C936 (parts)
DMA 54//97

Geistliche Harmonien I (1659)
RISM C930 (parts)
DMA 2/1058

Geistliche Harmonien II (1660)
RISM C931 (parts)
DMA 2/1059

Geistliche Harmonien III (1664)
RISM C935 (parts)
DMA 2/1060

Jubilus Bernhardi (1660)
RISM C932 (parts)
DMA 3/1447

Opus aureum missarum (1670)
RISM C940 (parts)
DMA 3/1448

Opus musicum (1655)
RISM C928 (parts)
DMA 3/44
Ed. R. Rybarič (Bratislava: Opus, 1975)

Theatrum musicum (1669)
RISM C937 (parts)
DMA 1/28

WORKS

C0091 A solis ortu
See Judicum Salomonis

C0092 Ach Gott wie manches
SSB, bc
Geistliche Concerten I, no. 10

C0093 Ach lieber Gott
SSB, bc
Geistliche Concerten I, no. 9

C0094 Ach lieber Herr
SST, 2 vln, bc
Geistliche Harmonien III, no. 1

C0095 Ad te suspiro
SAB, 2 vln, 3 vla, bc
Geistliche Harmonien III, no. 17
D-B Mus. ms. 2980, no. 25 (Bokemeyer)
score
DMA 2/2188
S-Uu 54:16 (Düben)
bc part only

C0096 Also hat Gott
ATB, bc
Geistliche Concerten II, no. 1

C0097 Amor Jesu dulcissimus
SSATB, 4 vla, bc
Jubilus Bernhardi, no. 8
S-Uu 83:21, fol. 1v-3 (Düben)
tablature
DMA 3/1139
S-Uu 9:3 (Düben)
parts (5 vla parts)
DMA 3/1139

C0098 Amor tuus continuus
SSATB, 4 vla, bc
Jubilus Bernhardi, no. 14

C0099 Anima mea in aeterna
STB, 2 vln, bc
Geistliche Harmonien III, no. 13

CAPRICORNUS, Samuel Friedrich (*continued*)

S-Uu 84:93, fol. 3v-5 (Düben)
tablature
DMA 1/2013

C0100 **Audi Domine Deus meus**
ATB, 4 vla, bc
Theatrum musicum, no. 4
S-Uu 83:41, fol. 1r-3r (Düben)
tablature
DMA 3/1140
S-Uu 9:4 (Düben)
parts
DMA 3/1140

C0101 **Beati immaculati in via**
SSATTB, 2 vln, 3 vla, 2 gamba, bc
S-Uu 9:5 (Düben)
parts
DMA 3/1141

C0102 **Beati omnes**
SSATB, 2 vln, 2 clar, 4 tbn, bc
S-Uu 83:46 (Düben)
tablature
DMA 3/715

C0103 **Caeli cives occurrite**
SSATB, 4 vla, bc
Jubilus Bernhardi, no. 22
S-Uu 9:17 (Düben)
parts
DMA 3/1142

C0104 **Christum lieb haben**
TTB, 2 vln, bc
Geistliche Harmonien II, no. 8

C0105 **Christus ist erstanden**
SSB, 2 vln, 3 vla, bsn, bc
D-B Mus. ms. 2980, no. 2 (Bokemeyer)
score
DMA 2/2189

C0106 **Clamavi in toto corde meo**
ATB, 2 vln, bc
Geistliche Harmonien III, no. 14
F-Ssp

C0107 **Cor mundum**
AATTBB, 3 vla, 2 bsn, bc
Opus musicum, no. 13

C0108 **Crescite et multiplicate**
SSATB, 2 vln, bc
Opus musicum, no. 11
S-Uu 86:27, fol. 18v-20v (Düben)
tablature

DMA 1/2015
S-Uu 9:8 (Düben)
parts (2 vln, bc only)
DMA 1/2015

C0109 **Cum Maria diluculo**
SSATB, 4 vla, bc
Jubilus Bernhardi, no. 5
S-Uu 9:9 (Düben)
parts
DMA 3/717
Ed. Sametz (1980), pp. 146-75

C0110 **Da mihi, Domine Deus meus**
ATB, 4 vla, bc
Theatrum musicum, no. 8
S-Uu 83:38 fol. 46v-48r (Düben)
tablature
DMA 3/718
S-Uu 9:10 (Düben)
parts
DMA 3/718

C0111 **Danket dem Herrn**
SATB, 2 vln, gamba, bc
D-Dlb Mus. ms. 1-E-770, no. 1 (Grimma
U 17a)
score

C0112 **Daran ist erschienen die Liebe Gottes**
TTB, bc
Geistliche Concerten II, no. 8

C0113 **Der gerechten Seelen sind in Gottes Hand**
SATB, 2 vln, 2 vla, theorbo, bc
S-Uu 53:3 (Düben)
parts
DMA 3/222
Ed. Grusnick (Bärenreiter BA 957, 1953)

C0114 **Der Herr ist gerecht**
ATB, 2 vln, bc
Geistliche Harmonien III, no. 2
D-B Mus. ms. 2980, no. 9 (Bokemeyer)
score
DMA 2/2190

C0115 **Der Herr ist mein Hirte**
SSATTB, 2 vln, 2 corn, 3 tbn/vla,
tbn/bsn, bc
D-B Mus. ms. 2980, no. 3 (Bokemeyer)
score
DMA 2/2191

C0116 **Deus, deus meus, respici in me**
SSATTB, 5 instr, bc
S-Uu 83:47, fol. 1v-5 (Düben)
tablature
DMA 3/1143

C0117 **Deus meus cornu**
ATB, 4 vla, bc
Theatrum musicum, no. 3

C0118 **Die Erlöseten**
SSB/TTB, 2 vln, bc
Geistliche Harmonien I, no. 9

C0119 **Die Gerechten**
SAT, 2 vln, bc
Geistliche Harmonien I, no. 8

C0120 **Dixit Dominus**
SSATTBB, 2 vln, bc
Opus musicum, no. 4
CS-KRa III, 30 (1665)
parts (plus 3 tbn)
microfilm: US-SY

C0121 **Domine ad adjuvandum**
SSATTBB, 2 vln, bc
Opus musicum, no. 3

C0122 **Du grosser König**
ATB, 2 vln, bc
Geistliche Harmonien III, no. 11
D-B Mus. ms. 2979
parts
DMA 3/223
P-Kj Mus. ms. 40129, no. 3
tablature

C0123 **Dulcis amor Jesu dulce bonum**
SSB, 2 vla, bsn, bc
Geistliche Harmonien III, no. 15
S-Uu 83:55 (Düben)
tablature and parts
DMA 1/2016

C0124 **Dulcis Christe, bone Jesu**
ATB, 4 vla, bc
Theatrum musicum, no. 6
D-B Mus. ms. 2980, no. 24 (Bokemeyer)
score
DMA 2/2192

C0125 **Dulcissime, amantissime**
ATB, 4 vla, bc
Theatrum musicum, no. 1
S-Uu 83:45, fol. 12v-14 (Düben)
tablature
DMA 3/1145
S-Uu 9:13 (Düben)
parts
DMA 3/1145
D-B Mus. ms. 2980, no. 23 (Bokemeyer)
score
DMA 2/2193

C0126 **Ecce quam bonum**
SAB, 2 vln, bc
D-B Mus. ms. 2966
parts
DMA 3/721
P-Kj Mus. ms. 40129, no. 2
tablature
Not concordant with the following piece

C0127 **Ecce quam bonum et quam jucundum**
SAB, 2 vln, bc
S-Uu 86:24, fol. 12v-15 (Düben)
tablature
DMA 1/2017
S-Uu 9:14 (Düben)
parts
DMA 1/2017
Not concordant with the preceding piece

C0128 **Ecce quomodo moritur justus**
SSATB, 4 vla, bc
Opus musicum, no. 10
S-Uu 9:15 (Düben) (1664)
parts
DMA 3/1146

C0129 **Egredimini**
SSS, bc
Geistliche Concerten I, no. 4

C0130 **Es hat kein Aug gesehen**
SSB, bc
Geistliche Concerten II, no. 12

C0131 **Es stehe Gott auf**
SSB, 2 vln, bsn, bc
Geistliche Harmonien III, no. 5

C0132 **Fürchtet den Herrn**
SAT, bc
Geistliche Concerten I, no. 6

C0133 **Gott hat uns**
SST, bc
Geistliche Concerten II, no. 9

C0134 **Groß und wundersam sind deine Werke**
ATB, 2 vln, bc
Geistliche Harmonien II, no. 7
D-B Mus. ms. 2980, no. 5 (Bokemeyer)
score
DMA 2/2195

C0135 **Heilig ist Gott der Herr Zebaoth**
SSSATTB, 2 vln, 3 vla, 2 clar, 2 tpt, timp,
bsn, bc
D-B Mus. ms. 2980, no. 1 (Bokemeyer)
score
DMA 2/2196

CAPRICORNUS, Samuel Friedrich (*continued*)

C0136 **Herr Gott Zebaoth**
ATB, bc
Geistliche Concerten I, no. 7

C0137 **Herr Jesu Christ, wahr Mensch und Gott**
SSATTB, 5 vla, bc
D-B Mus. ms. 2980, no. 8 (Bokemeyer)
score
DMA 2/2197

C0138 **Herr, sei mir gnädig**
STB, bc
Geistliche Concerten I, no. 8

C0139 **Herr, warum trittest du so ferne**
SAT, bc
Geistliche Concerten II, no. 6

C0140 **Herr, wenn ich nur dich habe**
TTB, 2 vln, bc
Geistliche Harmonien III, no. 4

C0141 **Ich bin das Brot**
ATB, 2 vln, bc
Geistliche Harmonien III, no. 3

C0142 **Ich bin der Weg**
SAB, bc
Geistliche Concerten II, no. 11

C0143 **Ich bin eine Blume**
SAT, 2 vln, tbn/gamba, bc
Geistliche Harmonien III, no. 7

C0144 **Ich freue mich**
SAT, bc
Geistliche Concerten II, no. 5

C0145 **Ich halte es dafür**
ATB, bc
Geistliche Concerten II, no. 2

C0146 **Ich weiß, daß der Herr**
SSB, 2 vln, bsn, bc
Geistliche Harmonien III, no. 9

C0147 **Ich werde bleiben**
SST, 2 vln, tbn, bc
Geistliche Harmonien III, no. 10

C0148 **Ihr Lieben**
ATB, bc
Geistliche Concerten II, no. 4

C0149 **In dich hab ich gehoffet, Herr**
SATB, 2 vln, 2 vla, bsn, bc
D-B Mus. ms. 2977 (Pölchau)
parts
DMA 3/225

C0150 **Jesu benigne**
SATB, 3 vln, bc
Continuatio theatri musici, no. 1
S-Uu 9:21 (Düben)
parts (SATB, 2 fl, 2 vln, vltta, gamba,
vlne, theorbo, bc)
DMA 3/1148

C0151 **Jesu clemens, pie Deus**
SSATTB, 2 vln, bc
Opus musicum, no. 12
S-Uu 83:56 (Düben)
tablature
DMA 3/723
D-B Mus. ms. 2980, no. 21 (Bokemeyer)
score
DMA 2/2199

C0152 **Jesu, decus angelicum**
SSATB, 4 vla, bc
Jubilus Bernhardi, no. 13

C0153 **Jesu, der du meine Seele**
SSB, 2 vln, bc
Geistliche Harmonien II, no. 10

C0154 **Jesu, du Blum**
SSB, 2 vln, bc
Geistliche Harmonien I, no. 12

C0155 **Jesu, du hast weggenommen**
SSB, 2 vln, bc
Geistliche Harmonien II, no. 11

C0156 **Jesu, du höchste Gütigkeit**
SSB, 2 vln, bc
Geistliche Harmonien I, no. 11

C0157 **Jesu, du höchste Gütigkeit**
SATB, 2 vln, 3 vla, bc
D-B Mus. ms. 2980, no. 6 (Bokemeyer)
score
DMA 2/2200

C0158 **Jesu, du lieber Bräutigam**
SSB, bc
Geistliche Concerten I, no. 12

C0159 **Jesu dulcedo cordium**
SSATB, 4 vla, bc
Jubilus Bernhardi, no. 3
S-Uu 9:22 (Düben)
parts
DMA 29//202
Ed. Sametz (1980), pp. 98-124

C0160 **Jesu dulcis memoria**
SSATB, 4 vla, bc

Jubilus Bernhardi, no. 1
S-Uu 9:23 (Düben)
 parts
 DMA 29//203
Ed. Sametz (1980), pp. 55-74

C0161 **Jesu, flos matris virginis**
SSATB, 4 vla, bc
Jubilus Bernhardi, no. 19

C0162 **Jesu, mein Herr**
SSB, bc
Geistliche Concerten I, no. 11

C0163 **Jesu mi bone sentiam**
SSATB, 4 vla, bc
Jubilus Bernhardi, no. 11
S-Uu 9:24 (Düben)
 parts
 DMA 29//204
Ed. Sametz (1980), pp. 204-26

C0164 **Jesu, rex admirabilis**
SSATB, 4 vla, bc
Jubilus Bernhardi, no. 6
S-Uu 9:25 (Düben)
 parts (SSATB, 2 fl, 4 vla, vlne, org)
 DMA 29//205
Ed. Sametz (1980), pp. 176-203

C0165 **Jesu sole sereniar**
SSATB, 4 vla, bc
Jubilus Bernhardi, no. 20

C0166 **Jesu, spes poenitentibus**
SSATB, 4 vla, bc
Jubilus Bernhardi, no. 2
S-Uu 83:23, fol. 4v-6 (Düben)
 tablature
 DMA 29//206
S-Uu 9:26 (Düben)
 parts
 DMA 29//206
Ed. Sametz (1980), pp. 75-97

C0167 **Jesu, summa benignitas**
SSATB, 4 vla, bc
Jubilus Bernhardi, no. 15

C0168 **Jesu, wer also liebet dich**
SATB, 2 vln, 3 vla, bsn, bc
D-B Mus. ms. 2975 (Erfurt) (1689)
 parts (instrumental parts only)
 DMA 3/226

C0169 **Jesum omnes agnoscite**
SSATB, 4 vla, bc
Jubilus Bernhardi, no. 9

S-Uu 83:22, fol. 2v-4v (Düben)
 tablature
 DMA 29//200
S-Uu 9:20 (Düben)
 parts
 DMA 29//200

C0170 **Jesum quaeram in lectulo**
SSATB, 4 vla, bc
Jubilus Bernhardi, no. 4
Ed. Sametz (1980), pp. 125-45

C0171 **Jesus, auctor clementiae**
SSATB, 4 vla, bc
Jubilus Bernhardi, no. 10
S-Uu 9:17 (Düben)
 parts
 DMA 29//197

C0172 **Jesus cum sic diligitur**
SSATB, 4 vla, bc
Jubilus Bernhardi, no. 17
S-Uu 9:18 (Düben)
 parts
 DMA 29//198

C0173 **Jesus in pace imperat**
SSATB, 4 vla, bc
Jubilus Bernhardi, no. 24
S-Uu 9:19 (Düben)
 parts
 DMA 3/724
Ed. Sametz (1980), pp. 285-309

C0174 **Judicum Salomonis (A solis ortu)**
SSTB, 2 vln, bc
Continuatio theatri musici, no. 4
DT 2

C0175 **Justorum animae**
SSSA, bc
Opus musicum, no. 22
S-Uu 86:42 (Düben)
 tablature
 DMA 3/227

C0176 **Kommet her, ihr Völker**
STB, 2 vln, bc
Geistliche Harmonien III, no. 12

C0177 **Kommet, lasset uns auf den Berg des Herrn gehen**
SST, 2 vln, bc
Geistliche Harmonien I, no. 6
D-B Mus. ms. 2980, no. 7 (Bokemeyer)
 score
 DMA 2/2201

CAPRICORNUS, Samuel Friedrich (*continued*)

C0178 Kommt her zu mir alle
TTB, bc
Geistliche Concerten II, no. 7

C0179 Laudate, pueri, Dominum
ATB, 4 viol, bc
Continuatio theatri musici, no. 8

C0180 Litanie: Kyrie eleison
SS, SATB, 4 gambas, bc
D-B Mus. ms. 2976 (Erfurt) (1678)
parts
DMA 3/229
Ed. Zahn, no. 8651

C0181 Magna est gloria Domini
ATB, 2 vln, bc
S-Uu 53:4 (Düben)
parts

C0182 Magnificat à 5
SSATB, 2 vln, bc
Opus musicum, no. 6

C0183 Magnificat à 5
SSATB, 2 vln, bc
D-B Mus. ms. 2980, no. 16 (Bokemeyer)
score
DMA 2/2203

C0184 Magnificat à 7
SSATTBB, 2 vln, bc
Opus musicum, no. 5
CS-KRa III, 30
parts
microfilm: US-SY

C0185 Mane nobiscum Domine
SSATB, 4 vla, bc
Jubilus Bernhardi, no. 7
S-Uu 10:5, 10:5a (Düben)
parts
DMA 3/1150

C0186 Mein Fleisch ist
SSB, 2 vln, bc
Geistliche Harmonien I, no. 7

C0187 Mein Gott und Herr
SSB, 2 vln, bc
Geistliche Harmonien II, no. 9
S-Uu 83:57, fol. 2v-4r (Düben)
tablature
DMA 1/2022
Ed. E. Selen, *Chor-Archiv* (Bärenreiter BA
6226, 1973)

C0188 Mi dilecte reverte
SSATB, 4 vla, bc
Jubilus Bernhardi, no. 21

C0189 Miserere à 4
SATB, 4 vla, bc
Opus musicum, no. 9
S-Uu 86:53 (Düben)
tablature
DMA 3/1151
S-Uu 10:6 (Düben)
parts
DMA 3/1151

C0190 Miserere à 6
SSATBB, 4 vla, bc
Opus musicum, no. 8
S-Uu 83:58a, fol. 2v-6v (Düben)
tablature
DMA 1/2023
S-Uu 53:5 (Düben)
parts
DMA 1/2023

C0191 Miserere mei
SSAATTBB, 4 vla, bc
D-B Mus. ms. 30315, no. 3
score
PL-Kj Mus. ms. 40129, no. 1
tablature

C0192 Misericordias tuas
SSATB, 2 vln, bc
Opus musicum, no. 14
S-Uu 83:59 (Düben)
tablature
DMA 3/727

C0193 Missa
SATB, 2 vln, 2 vla, bc
D-B Mus. ms. 2980, no. 20 (Bokemeyer)
score
DMA 53//11
Omitted from DMA in-house catalog and
ms. table of contents

C0194 Missa
SATB, 2 vln, 2 corn, 3 tbn, bc
Opus musicum, no. 2
Labeled "Kyrie" in source

C0195 Missa à 9 "per 2 chori"
SATB, SATB, 2 vln, 2 vla, bsn, bc
D-B Mus. ms. 2980, no. 19 (Bokemeyer)
score
DMA 2/2204

C0196 **Missa à 10**
SSAATTBB, 2 vln, bc
D-B Mus. ms. 30291, no. 2
parts

C0197 **Missa brevis quarti toni à 6**
SATB, 2 vln, bc
Opus aureum missarum, no. 4
S-Uu 86:10, fol. 7v-10 (Düben)
tablature
DMA 1/2019

C0198 **Missa brevis tertii toni à 12**
SSAATTBB, 2 vln, 2 corn, bc
Opus aureum missarum, no. 3

C0199 **Missa Nativitatis**
SATTB, 2 vln, 2 clar, 3 tbn, vlne, bc
Opus musicum, no. 1
CS-KRa I, 96 (1665)
parts
microfilm: US-SY

C0200 **Missa primi toni à 6**
SATB, 2 vln, bc
Opus aureum missarum, no. 1
S-Uu 10:2 (Düben)
parts
DMA 1/2020
S-Uu 86:11, fol. 10v-17v (Düben)
tablature
DMA 1/2020
D-B Mus. ms. 30291, no. 1
parts

C0201 **Missa secundi toni à 10**
SSAATTBB, 2 vln, bc
Opus aureum missarum, no. 2

C0202 **O amor qui semper**
ATB, 4 vla, bc
Theatrum musicum, no. 10

C0203 **O beatum incendium**
SSATB, 4 vla, bc
Jubilus Bernhardi, no. 18

C0204 **O bone Jesu**
SSATB, 5 vla, bc
PL-Kj Mus. ms. 40129, no. 4
tablature

C0205 **O felix jucunditas**
ATB, 4 vla, bc
Theatrum musicum, no. 7

C0206 **O guadium super gaudium**
ATB, 4 vla, bc
Theatrum musicum, no. 5

C0207 **O Jesu mi dulcissime**
SSATB, 4 vla, bc
Jubilus Bernhardi, no. 16
S-Uu 10:7 (Düben)
parts
DMA 3/1152
Ed. Sametz (1980), pp. 227-61

C0208 **O Jesu, summa caritas**
SATB, 2 vln, bc
Continuatio theatri musici, no. 3

C0209 **O Jesu süß**
SSB, 2 vln, bc
Geistliche Harmonien I, no. 10

C0210 **O quam gloriosum**
ATB, 4 vla, bc
Theatrum musicum, no. 9
S-Uu 10:4 (Düben)
parts
DMA 28//4

C0211 **O tu vita felicissima**
ATB, 4 vla, bc
Theatrum musicum, no. 2
S-Uu 78:61, fol. 61v-63 (Düben) (1667)
tablature
DMA 46//31
S-Uu 10:8 (Düben)
parts
DMA 46//31

C0212 **Omnis caro foenum**
SATB, 2 vln, 2 vla, bc
Continuatio theatri musici, no. 2

C0213 **Paratum cor meum**
SSB, bc
Geistliche Harmonien III, no. 18
S-Uu 10:9 (Düben) (1665)
parts
DMA 3/728

C0214 **Praeparate**
ATB, vln, corn, tbn, bc
Geistliche Harmonien III, no. 16

C0215 **Protector noster**
ATB, 4 vla, bc
Theatrum musicum, no. 12
S-Uu 10:10 (Düben)
parts
DMA 3/1154

C0216 **Quis dabit capiti meo**
ATB, 4 vla, bc
Theatrum musicum, no. 11

CAPRICORNUS, Samuel Friedrich (*continued*)

S-Uu 83:44, fol. 9v-11 (Düben)
tablature
DMA 3/1156
S-Uu 10:12 (Düben)
parts
DMA 3/1156

C0217 **Rex virtutum, rex gloriae**
SSATB, 4 vla, bc
Jubilus Bernhardi, no. 23
S-Uu 10:13 (Düben)
parts
DMA 3/729
Ed. Sametz (1980), pp. 262-84

C0218 **Selig ist der Mann**
ATB, bc
Geistliche Concerten II, no. 3

C0219 **Singet Gott**
SSB, 2 vln, tbn, bc
Geistliche Harmonien III, no. 6

C0220 **Suchet den Herrn**
SSB, 2 vln, bsn, bc
D-B Mus. ms. 2980, no. 12 (Bokemeyer)
score
DMA 2/2207

C0221 **Te Deum laudamus**
SSAATTBB, 4 vln, 2 clar, bc
Opus musicum, no. 7

C0222 **Tibi, Domine Jesu Christe**
SSATTB, 2 vln, 2 vla, 2 gamba, bc
S-Uu 86:55, fol. 5v-9r (Düben)
tablature
DMA 1/2027
S-Uu 10:15 (Düben)
parts
DMA 1/2027

C0223 **Tua Jesu dilectio**
SSATB, 4 vla, bc
Jubilus Bernhardi, no. 12
S-Uu 10:16 (Düben)
parts
DMA 3/1158

C0224 **Unser Wandel**
SST, bc
Geistliche Concerten II, no. 10

C0225 **Venite ad me, omnes**
SAT, 2 vln, bc
Opus musicum, no. 19

S-Uu 86:15a (Düben)
tablature
DMA 2/2208
D-B Mus. ms. 2980, no. 22 (Bokemeyer)
score
DMA 1/2028

C0226 **Wann ich vors Gericht soll treten**
SSB, 2 vln, bc
Geistliche Harmonien II, no. 12
D-B Mus. ms. 2980, no. 4 (Bokemeyer)
score
DMA 2/2209
Ed. A. F. W. Fischer, DEK II/189:9-12

C0227 **Wie groß ist deine Güte**
ATB, 2 vln, bc
Geistliche Harmonien II, no. 6

C0228 **Willkommen, edles Knäbelein**
SATB, 2 vln, 2 vla, bc
D-B Mus. ms. 2978, no. 4 (Pölchau)
parts
DMA 3/231

CARL, Johann Georg

C0229 **Da Jesus geboren war**
SATB, 2 vln, 3 vla, bsn, bc
D-B Mus. ms. 30305, no. 3 (Bokemeyer)
(1692)
score
DMA 1/2029

C0230 **Gelobet sei Gott mit Freuden**
SSAT, ATTB, bc
D-Bds Mus. ms. 30307, no. 3 (Bokemeyer)
score

C0231 **Lobet den Herren**
SSATB, 2 vln, 2 vla, bsn, bc
D-B Mus. ms. 30305, no. 2 (Bokemeyer)
(1677)
score
DMA 1/2030

CLAUSNITZER, Tobias

See under **Anonymous:**
Ach was ist doch unser Leben
Nun Gott lob es ist vollbracht
Sei willkommen süsse Ruh
Siehe wie bös ist des Menschen Leben

COBERG, Johann Anton

C0232　**Ei du frommer und getreuer Knecht**
SATB, SATB, bc
Funeral of Heinrich Voß
Hamburg, 1683
　RISM C3220, Reich 130 (score)
　DMA 57//72

C0233　**Herr Jesu Christ, meins Lebens Licht**
SSATTB, SSAATTBB, bc
Funeral of Heinrich Voß
Hamburg, 1683
　RISM C3219, Reich 130 (score)
　DMA 57//72

C0234　**Herr, wenn ich nur dich habe**
SATTB, bc
Funeral of Ilse Steding
Hamburg, 1687
　RISM C3221, Reich 131
　DMA 57//73

C0235　**Wo irr' ich um, o Trost und Leben**
SATTB, bc
Funeral of Ilse Steding
Hamburg, 1687
　RISM C3221, Reich 131
　DMA 57//73

CONRADI, Johann Georg (d. 1699)

C0236　**Allein Gott in der Höh sei Ehr**
SSATTB, 2 vln, 2 vla, 2 fl, 2 corn, tbn, bc
D-F Ms. Ff. Mus. 169
　parts

C0237　**Laudate Dominum, omnes gentes**
SATB, 2 vln, 2 vla, vlne, bc
F-Ssp
　parts

C0238　**Lobe den Herren, meine Seele**
ATB, 3 vln, bc
D-B Mus. ms. 4056/1 (1690)
　parts

C0239　**Singet fröhlich, omnes gentes**
SATB, 2 vln, 2 vltta, 2 clar, timp, bsn, bc
F-Pc Sign, Ms. 1708
　parts

C0240　**So tuts, wer hier nach Reichtum strebt**
SAB, 2 vln, vla, bc
1st Sunday after Trinity
D-F Ms. Ff. Mus. 466
　parts

C0241　**Wo soll ich fliehen hin**
S, SATTB, 5 vla, bc
D-B Mus. ms. 4056 (Erfurt)
　parts

CREIL, Johann

C0242　**Est ist ein Geschrei**
TB, SATTB, 3 vla, vlne, bc
D-B Mus. ms. 4271 (Erfurt) (1673)
　parts

C0243　**Herr Jesu, wo sollen wir hingehen**
SSATB, 2 vln, 2 vla, bc
D-B Mus. ms. 4270 (Erfurt)
　parts

CRUSIUS, P.

C0244　**Erhebe dich, mein froher Mund**
SATB, 2 vln, vla, tamb, ob/clarinetti, 2
　corn, 2 tbn, bc
D-Dlb 3347-E-500 (Grimma LSGr 110/T 16)
　score

D

DEDEKIND, Constantin Christian (1628-1715)

COLLECTION

> *König Davids Göldnes Kleinod* (1674)
> RISM D1310 (parts)
> DMA 3/1455

WORKS

D0001 **Dein Wort ist meines Fußes Leuchte**
SSB, SATB, 2 vln, bsn/vlne, bc
König Davids Göldnes Kleinod, no. 14

D0002 **Deine Hand hat mich gemacht**
SSB, SATB, 2 vln, bsn/vlne, bc
König Davids Göldnes Kleinod, no. 10

D0003 **Deine Zeugnisse sind wunderbahrlich**
SSB, SATB, 2 vln, bsn/vlne, bc
König Davids Göldnes Kleinod, no. 17

D0004 **Der Herr ist mein Hirte**
SSB, SATB, 2 vln, bsn/vlne, bc
König Davids Göldnes Kleinod, no. 25

D0005 **Der Welt verkehrter Menschen-Lauf**
SSATTB, bc
Funeral of Christian Findekeller
Dresden, 1675
Reich 57

D0006 **Die Fürsten verfolgen mich ohne Ursach**
SSB, SATB, 2 vln, bsn/vlne, bc
König Davids Göldnes Kleinod, no. 21

D0007 **Du tust Gutes deinem Knecht**
SSB, SATB, 2 vln, bsn/vlne, bc
König Davids Göldnes Kleinod, no. 9

D0008 **Du unser Gott bist freundlich**
SSB, SATB, 2 vln, bsn/vlne, bc
König Davids Göldnes Kleinod, no. 23

D0009 **Gedenke deinem Knecht an dein Wort**
SSB, SATB, 2 vln, bsn/vlne, bc
König Davids Göldnes Kleinod, no. 7

D0010 **Gelobet seist du, Herr Gott Israel**
SSB, SATB, 2 vln, bsn/vlne, bc
König Davids Göldnes Kleinod, no. 24

D0011 **Herr, dein Wort bleibet ewiglich**
SSB, SATB, 2 vln, bsn/vlne, bc
König Davids Göldnes Kleinod, no. 12

D0012 **Herr, du bist gerecht und dein Wort**
SSB, SATB, 2 vln, bsn/vlne, bc
König Davids Göldnes Kleinod, no. 18

D0013 **Herr Jesu! wer dir lebt im Leben**
SSATB, bc
Funeral of Anna Margarethe Metzner
Dresden, 1670
RISM D1307, Reich 56 (score)
DMA 63//109

D0014 **Herr, laß meine Klage vor dich kommen**
SSB, SATB, 2 vln, bsn/vlne, bc
König Davids Göldnes Kleinod, no. 22

D0015 **Herr, laßt mir deine Gnade**
SSB, SATB, 2 vln, bsn/vlne, bc
König Davids Göldnes Kleinod, no. 6

D0016 **Ich habe gesagt, Herr**
SSB, SATB, 2 vln, bsn/vlne, bc
König Davids Göldnes Kleinod, no. 8

D0017   **Ich halte über den Recht**
SSB, SATB, 2 vln, bsn/vlne, bc
König Davids Göldnes Kleinod, no. 16

D0018   **Ich hasse die Flattergeisten**
SSB, SATB, 2 vln, bsn/vlne, bc
König Davids Göldnes Kleinod, no. 15

D0019   **Ich rufe von ganzem Herzen**
SSB, SATB, 2 vln, bsn/vlne, bc
König Davids Göldnes Kleinod, no. 19

D0020   **Meine Seele liegt im Staube**
SSB, SATB, 2 vln, bsn/vlne, bc
König Davids Göldnes Kleinod, no. 4

D0021   **Meine Seele verlanget nach deinem**
SSB, SATB, 2 vln, bsn/vlne, bc
König Davids Göldnes Kleinod, no. 11

D0022   **Nun geh ich aus der Jammer-Welt**
SSATB, bc
Funeral of Wilhelm Abraham von
Trumbschirn
Leipzig, 1661
RISM D1299, Reich 262 (score)
DMA 57//146

D0023   **Nun muß ich nicht mehr sehn**
SSATB, bc
Funeral of Sophie Löbe
Dresden, 1664
RISM D1304, Reich 54 (score)
DMA 57//75

D0024   **Siehe mein Elend und errette mich**
SSB, SATB, 2 vln, bsn/vlne, bc
König Davids Göldnes Kleinod, no. 20

D0025   **Tue wohl deinem Knechte**
SSB, SATB, 2 vln, bsn/vlne, bc
König Davids Göldnes Kleinod, no. 3

D0026   **Was ihr jetzt vertraut der Erden**
SSATB, bc
Funeral of Anna Sibylle Hoffmann
Dresden, 1664
RISM D1303, Reich 53 (score)
DMA 1/1397

D0027   **Wie habe ich dein Gesetz so lieb**
SSB, SATB, 2 vln, bsn/vlne, bc
König Davids Göldnes Kleinod, no. 13

D0028   **Wie wird ein Jüngling seinen Weg**
SSB, SATB, 2 vln, bsn/vlne, bc
König Davids Göldnes Kleinod, no. 2

D0029   **Wo nicht der Herr selbst baut das Haus**
SATB, bc

Wedding
Dresden, 1659
RISM D1298 (score)
DMA 57//142

D0030   **Wohl dem, der sich des Herrn erfreut**
SATB, bc
Wedding
Dresden, 1659
RISM D1298 (score)
DMA 57//142

D0031   **Wohl denen, die ohne Wandel leben**
SSB, SATB, 2 vln, bsn/vlne, bc
König Davids Göldnes Kleinod, no. 1

D0032   **Zeige mir, Herr, den Weg**
SSB, SATB, 2 vln, bsn/vlne, bc
König Davids Göldnes Kleinod, no. 5

DEMELIUS, Christian (1643-1711)

D0033   **Ach, was ist doch unser Leben**
SSATB
D-Gs Cod. Ms. philos. 84e Demelius 1
score and parts

D0034   **Die auf den Herren hoffen**
SSATB, bc
Funeral of Christoff Wiedolt
Nordhausen, 1680
RISM D1610, Reich 296 (score)
DMA 57//144

D0035   **Die Gerechten werden ewiglich leben**
SATB
D-Gs Cod. Ms. philol. 84e Demelius 2
score and parts

D0036   **Die mit Tränen säen**
SSATB
D-Gs Cod. Ms. philos. 84e Demelius 3
(1710)
score and parts

D0037   **Laßt die Kindlein zu mir kommen**
SATB
D-Gs Cod. Ms. philos. 84e Demelius 3a
score

D0038   **Nach dir, Herr, verlanget mich**
ATTB
D-Gs Cod. Ms. philos. 84e Demelius 4
score and parts

D0039   **Sei getreu bis in den Tod**
D-Gs Cod. Ms. philos. 84e Demelius 5
score and parts

DEMELIUS, Christian (*continued*)

D0040   **Wie der Hirsch schreiet nach frischem Wasser**
SSATB
D-Gs Cod. Ms. philos. 84e Demelius 6
score and parts

DIEGELMANN, Georg

D0041   **Warum ist des Menschen Leben**
SATB
Funeral of Georg Otto
Nürnberg, 1674
RISM D2988, Reich 353 (score)
DMA 63//111

DIETBOLD, Johann Caspar

D0042   **Merkur mit Flügeln prangend**
SATB
Funeral
Zürich, 1669
RISM D2990 (choirbook)
DMA 63//145

DIETEL, Johann Caspar

D0043   **Das Verlangen der Elenden hörest du Herr**
SATB, vln, 2 vla, vlne, bc
24th Sunday after Trinity
D-MÜG 359 (1714)
parts

D0044   **Ich hielte mich nicht dafür**
SATB, bc
D-Dlb Mus. ms. 2483-E-500 (Grimma U
415/P 15)
parts

DIETZEL, Johann Sebastian

D0045   **Ach! muß mein Geist nichts tun**
SATB, bc
Funeral of Johann Theodor Schenke
Jena, 1671
RISM D3037, Reich 159 (score)
DMA 57//145

DRAGHI, Antonio (1634/35-1700)

D0046   **Al ingresso di Christo**
SAT, bc
Lent

A-Wn Ms. 16741 (1683)
score

D0047   **Entrata di Christo nel deserto**
SSSAATB, 2 vla, bc
A-Wn Ms. 18883 (1687)
score

D0048   **Epitafii sopra il sepolcro di Christo**
SSSAATB, 2 vln, 2 vla, bc
Maundy Thursday
A-Wn Ms. 16888 (1671)
score (partial)

D0049   **Giuditta**
SSAB, 2 vln, 2 vla, bc
Lent
A-Wn Ms. 16274 (1668)
score

D0050   **Il crocifisso per gratia, overo S[anta] Gaetano**
SSSAATTTBB, SAB, SSA, 2 vln, vltta, bc
Lent
A-Wn Ms. 16844 (1691)
score

D0051   **Il dono della vita eterna**
SSAATTTBB, 2 vln, 3 vla, bc
Good Friday
A-Wn Ms. 16270 (1686)
score

D0052   **Il libro con sette sigilli scritto dentro e fuori**
SAATTBB, 3 vla, 3 tbn, bsn, bc
Good Friday
A-Wn Ms. 18943 (1694)
score

D0053   **Il limbo aperto**
SSAATTB, 2 vln, 4 vla, bc
Maundy Thursday
A-Wn Ms. 16309 (1672)
score (partial)

D0054   **Il sagrificio non impedito**
SSSAAATTB, 4 vla, gamba, bc
Good Friday
A-Wn Ms. 18941 (1692)
score

D0055   **Il segno dell' humana salute**
SSATTB, 4 vla, bc
Good Friday
A-Wn Ms. 18919 (1684)
score (partial)

D0056   **Il sole ecclissato**
SSSATTB, 2 vln, 3 vla, bc
Maundy Thursday

A-Wn Ms. 16878 (1676)
score (partial)

D0057 Il terremoto
SSSATTTBB, vln, 4 vla, bc
Maundy Thursday
A-Wn Ms. 16852 (1682)
score (partial)

D0058 Il titolo posto sù la croce di Christo
SSATTB, 3 vla, bc
Maundy Thursday
A-Wn Ms. 16859 (1679)
score (partial)

D0059 Jephte
SSTTBB, SSATB, SSATB, bc
Lent
A-Wn Ms. 18884 (1687)
score (partial)

D0060 L'Abelle di Boemia
See S[ant] Wenceslao

D0061 La corona di spine
SSSATTB, 3 vla, bc
Maundy Thursday
A-Wn Ms. 16848 (1675)
score

D0062 La pietà contrastata
SSAATTBB, 2 vla, bc
Maundy Thursday
A-Wn Ms. 16541 (1673)
score (partial)

D0063 La sacra lancia
SSSATTBBB, 3 vla, bc
Maundy Thursday
A-Wn Ms. 16273 (1680)
score (partial)

D0064 La virtù della croce
SSAATTB, SSSA, vln, 4 vla, 6 lute, bc
Good Friday
A-Wn Ms. 18886 (1697)
score

D0065 La vita nella morte
SSSAAATTBB, vln, 2 vla, 3 gamba, 2
baryton, bc
Good Friday
A-Wn Ms. 18870 (1688)
score

D0066 Le cinque piaghe di Christo
SSATTB
Maundy Thursday

A-Wn Ms. 18894 (1677)
score (partial; instrumental parts lacking)

D0067 Le cinque vergini prudenti
SSSSSA, bc
Lent
A-Wn Ms. 16007 (1689)
score

**D0068 L'esclamar à gran voce a l'inchinar il capo di
Christo spirando**
SSATTB, 4 vla, bc
Good Friday
A-Wn Ms. 18863 (1689)
score

D0069 L'eternità sogetto al tempo
SSSAAAATTTBB, vln, 4 vla, bc
Good Friday
A-Wn Ms. 18913 (1683)
score (partial)

D0070 L'humanità redenta
SSAATB, 2 vln, 2 vla, bc
Maundy Thursday
A-Wn Ms. 18878 (1669)
score

D0071 Li sette dolori di Maria Vergine
SSSATTB, vln, 2 vla, bc
Maundy Thursday
A-Wn Ms. 16275 (1670)
score (partial)

D0072 Li trè chiodi
SSATTB
Maundy Thursday
A-Wn Ms. 18893 (1678)
score (partial; instrumental parts lacking)

D0073 L'uscita di Christo dal deserto
SSSAT, bc
Lent
A-Wn Ms. 18858 (1688)
score

D0074 Missa à 9
SSATB, 2 vln, 2 vla, vlne, bc
A-KR Ser. C/Fasc. 14, no. 707 (1684)
parts
DTÖ 46 (Jg. 23/1), pp. 1-42

D0075 Missa Assumptionis
SSATB, 2 vln, 4 vla, 2 corn, 4 tbn, vlne, bc
A-KR Ser. C/Fasc. 6, no. 642 (1684)
parts
DTÖ 46 (Jg. 23/1), pp. 43-124

DRAGHI, Antonio (*continued*)

D0076　**Oratorio di Giuditta**
　　　　See Giuditta

D0077　**S[ant'] Agata**
　　　　SSSAB, SATB, bc
　　　　A-Wn Ms. 18949 (1675)
　　　　　　score

D0078　**S[anto] Gaetano**
　　　　See Il crocifisso per gratia

D0079　**S[ant] Wenceslao**
　　　　SSSAATTTBB, bc
　　　　Lent
　　　　A-Wn Ms. 18861 (1680)
　　　　　　score (partial)

D0080　**Stabat Mater**
　　　　SATB
　　　　A-Wn Ms. 18986
　　　　　　score
　　　　　　DTÖ 46 (Jg. 23/1), pp. 125-27

D0081　**Tristes erant Apostoli**
　　　　SAB, vc, vlne, bc
　　　　A-Wn Ms. 16138
　　　　　　parts
　　　　　　DTÖ 46 (Jg. 23/1), pp. 128-29

D0082　**Vexilla regis prodeunt**
　　　　SAB, 2 vln, vlne, theorbo/vlne, bc
　　　　A-Wn Ms. 16139
　　　　　　parts
　　　　　　DTÖ 46 (Jg. 23/1), pp. 130-32

DRESE, Adam (1620-1701)

D0083　**Das Himmelreich ist gleich einen König**
　　　　SSTB, 2 vln, 3 vla, bc
　　　　S-Uu 54:3 (Düben)
　　　　　　parts

D0084　**Herr, höre mein Gebet**
　　　　SATB, 2 vln, 2 vla, bsn, bc
　　　　D-Bds Mus. ms. 30294, no. 2 (Bokemeyer)
　　　　　　score

D0085　**Wie selig sind die Toten**
　　　　SSATTB, bc
　　　　Funeral of Caspar Ermes
　　　　Erfurt, 1648
　　　　　　RISM D3503, Reich 72 (parts)
　　　　　　DMA 54//60

DRESE, Johann Samuel (ca. 1644-1716)

D0086　**Höret auf um mich zu klagen**
　　　　SATB
　　　　Funeral of Adam Gottlieb Struven
　　　　Weimar, 1671
　　　　　　RISM D3504, Reich 421 (score)
　　　　　　DMA 63//45

DRUCKENMÜLLER, Georg Wolfgang

D0087　**Jammer, Elend, Angst und Schmerzen**
　　　　SSATB
　　　　Funeral
　　　　Schwäbisch Hall, 1658
　　　　　　RISM D3585, Reich 391 (score)
　　　　　　DMA 57//140

D0088　**Wie könnt ihr, meine Leiben**
　　　　SATTB
　　　　Funeral
　　　　Schwäbisch Hall, n.d.
　　　　　　RISM D3586, Reich 390 (score)
　　　　　　DMA 63//108

DUBEL, Johann

D0089　**Mein Gott! so wird mir deine Liebe**
　　　　SSATB
　　　　Funeral of Margarethe von Rottenburg
　　　　Krossen/Elster, 1699
　　　　　　RISM D3590, Reich 208 (score)
　　　　　　DMA 63//213

DÜBEN, Gustav

D0090　**Alles Leben dieser Erden**
　　　　SSB, 2 vln, vla, vlne, bc
　　　　S-Uu 19:1 (Düben)
　　　　　　score and parts

D0091　**Fadher was som esti himblom**
　　　　ATTB, 5 vla, bc
　　　　S-Uu 19:5 (Düben) (1663)
　　　　　　tablature and parts

D0092　**Surrexit pastor bonus**
　　　　SATB, 5 vla, bc
　　　　S-Uu 81:92, fol. 92-95v (Düben) (1664)
　　　　　　tablature
　　　　S-Uu 33:8 (Düben)
　　　　　　parts

D0093 **Veni Sancte Spiritus**
SATB, 3 vla, vlne, bc
S-Uu 19:13 (Düben)
(1651)
tablature and parts

D0094 **Wie bistu Davidz soon**
SATB, 4 vla, bc
18th Sunday after Trinity
S-Uu 19:15 (Düben) (1690)
tablature and parts

E

EBART, Samuel (fl. 1609-1683)

E0001   Weg, Welt-Lust
         SSATB
         Funeral of Dorothea Olearius
         Leipzig, 1677
            RISM E31, Reich 271 (score)
            DMA 63//42

EBELING, Johann Georg (1637-1676)

E0002   Ach, befeuchtet nicht die Wangen
         SSATB
         Funeral of Eva Preunelin
         Berlin, 1664
            RISM E41 (score)
            DMA 57//138

E0003   Der Herr erhöre dich in der Noth
         SSATB, 2 vln, 2 vla, vc, bc
         D-Bds Mus. ms. 30294, no. 4 (Bokemeyer)
            score

E0004   Ein Tag in deinen Vorhöfen
         SSATTB, bc
         Funeral of Marie Anne von Löben
         Berlin, 1666
            RISM E42, Reich 34 (parts)
            DMA 64//44

E0005   Laßt uns nun gehen gen Bethlehem
         SATB, 3 vln, 2 trba, timp, bc
         Christmas Day
         D-Gs Cod. Ms. philos. 84e Ebeling 1
            score

EBERLIN, Daniel (1647-1713/15)

E0006   Allmächtiger, heiliger, ewiger Gott
         SATB, 2 vln, 3 vla, bc
         D-Bds Mus. ms. 30294, no. 6 (Bokemeyer)
            score

E0007   Ich kann nicht mehr ertragen diesen Jammer
         SATB, 2 vln, 4 gamba, bc
         S-Uu 54:4
            parts
            DMA 1/747

E0008   Wenn mein Stündlein vorhanden ist
         SATB, 2 fl, vlne, bc
         S-Uu 54:4a
            parts

EBNER, Wolfgang (1612-1665)

E0009   De profundis clamavi ad te Domine
         BBB, bc
         CS-KRa III, 96
            parts
            microfilm: US-SY

E0010   Laudate Dominum, omnes gentes
         SAB, SSS, bc
         CS-KRa III, 21
            parts
            microfilm: US-SY

E0011   Magnificat
         SATB, 3 vla, bc
         CS-KRa III, 33
            parts
            microfilm: US-SY

E0012 **Missa in contrapuncto**
SATB, corn, 3 tbn, vlne, bc
CS-KRa I, 164
parts
microfilm: US-SY

E0013 **Missa Sancti Joannis Baptiste**
SATTB, 5 vla, 4 tbn, vlne, bc
CS-KRa I, 169
parts
microfilm: US-SY

EDELMANN, Moritz (d. 1680)

E0014 **Triumph, denn Jesu lebt**
5 vv
D-Z LXXXIII, 2, no. 42 (1676)
score

EISENHUT, Thomas (Tobias) (1644-1702)

COLLECTIONS

Antiphonarium Marianum (1677)
RISM E591 (parts)
DMA 3/524

Harmonia sacra (1674)
RISM E590 (parts)
DMA 3/61

Hymni ariosi (1680)
RISM E592 (parts)
DMA 3/1460

Offertoria de festis (1694)
RISM E594 (parts)
DMA 3/63

Sacri concentus (1683)
RISM E593 (parts)
DMA 3/62

WORKS

E0015 **Ad cantus**
SSATB, 2 vln, 3 vla, bc
Feast of a Confessor Pope
Offertoria de festis, no. 20

E0016 **Ad te convento**
SSS, bc
Harmonia sacra, no. 5

E0017 **Alma redemptoris (I)**
SSS/TTT, bc
Antiphonarium Marianum, no. 2

E0018 **Alma redemptoris (II)**
SSB, bc
Antiphonarium Marianum, no. 3

E0019 **Alma redemptoris (III)**
SATB, bc
Antiphonarium Marianum, no. 4

E0020 **Alma redemptoris (IV)**
ATB, 2 vln, bc
Antiphonarium Marianum, no. 5

E0021 **Arma et ferrum capite**
SSB, 2 vln, bc
Harmonia sacra, no. 20

E0022 **Ave regina (I)**
SSS/TTT, bc
Antiphonarium Marianum, no. 8

E0023 **Ave regina (II)**
ATB, bc
Antiphonarium Marianum, no. 9

E0024 **Ave regina (III)**
SATB, bc
Antiphonarium Marianum, no. 10

E0025 **Ave regina (IV)**
SSB, 2 vln, bc
Antiphonarium Marianum, no. 11

E0026 **Benedicam**
SSATB, 2 vln, 3 vla, bc
Offertoria de festis, no. 14

E0027 **Cantate virgines**
SATB, bc
Harmonia sacra, no. 12

E0028 **Christe redemptor**
SST, 2 vln, bc
Feast of All Saints
Hymni ariosi, no. 23

E0029 **Christo trophaea**
SSATB, 2 vln, 3 vla, bc
Easter
Offertoria de festis, no. 2

E0030 **Conditor alme**
SATB, 2 vln, bc
Advent
Hymni ariosi, no. 1

E0031 **Congregavit Dominus**
SSATB, 2 vln, 3 vla, bc
Feast of the Blessed Virgin
Offertoria de festis, no. 6

EISENHUT, Thomas (*continued*)

E0032 **Custodes hominum**
SSA, 2 vln, bc
Feast of the Guardian Angels
Hymni ariosi, no. 18

E0033 **Dulce sit vobis**
ATB, 2 vln, vla, bc
Harmonia sacra, no. 28

E0034 **Ego dormio et cor me**
SSA, bc
Harmonia sacra, no. 4

E0035 **Egredimini filiae Sion**
ATB, bc
Harmonia sacra, no. 6

E0036 **Egredimini filiae**
SSATB, 2 vln, 3 vla, bc
Feast of the Seven Sorrows
Offertoria de festis, no. 8

E0037 **Exultate Deo**
SSATB, 2 vln, 3 vla, bc
Offertoria de festis, no. 12

E0038 **Exultet caelum laudibus**
SSB, 2 vln, bc
Feast of the Birth of an Apostle
Hymni ariosi, no. 24

E0039 **Exurge cor meum**
SSATB, 2 vln, 3 vla, bc
Feast of the Blessed Virgin
Offertoria de festis, no. 7

E0040 **Factum est praelium**
SSATB, 2 vln, 3 vla, bc
Feast of Saint Michael
Offertoria de festis, no. 10

E0041 **Fugite**
SSATB, 2 vln, 3 vla, bc
Ascension
Offertoria de festis, no. 3

E0042 **Gloriosum diem**
SSATB, 2 vln, 3 vla, bc
Feast of the Cross
Offertoria de festis, no. 9

E0043 **Haeene est**
SSATB, 2 vln, 3 vla, bc
Offertoria de festis, no. 15

E0044 **Hostis Herodes**
SSS, 2 vln, bc
Feast of the Holy Innocents
Hymni ariosi, no. 3

E0045 **Inspicite fideles**
SSB, 2 vln, bc
Harmonia sacra, no. 19

E0046 **Intonuit de caelo**
SSATB, 2 vln, 3 vla, bc
Pentecost
Offertoria de festis, no. 4

E0047 **Jesu, redemptor**
SAT, 2 vln, bc
Christmas or Circumcision
Hymni ariosi, no. 2

E0048 **Judica**
SSATB, 2 vln, 3 vla, bc
Offertoria de festis, no. 13

E0049 **Laudemus virum**
SSATB, 2 vln, 3 vla, bc
Feast of a Confessor not a Pope
Offertoria de festis, no. 21

E0050 **Laudibus cives**
SST, 2 vln, bc
Feast of Saint Benedict
Hymni ariosi, no. 21

E0051 **Litaniae breves**
SATB, 2 vln, bc
Sacri concentus, no. 27

E0052 **Lucis Creator**
SATB, 2 vln, bc
Hymni ariosi, no. 5

E0053 **Mulierem fortem**
SSATB, 2 vln, 3 vla, bc
Offertoria de festis, no. 23

E0054 **Nihil est quod timeam**
ATB, 2 vln, bc
Harmonia sacra, no. 21

E0055 **O aurora**
SSATB, 2 vln, 3 vla, bc
Feast of a Martyr
Offertoria de festis, no. 17

E0056 **O beata Trinitas**
SATB, 2 vln, bc
Trinity
Hymni ariosi, no. 6

E0057 **O caelis cives**
SSATB, bc
Harmonia sacra, no. 14

E0058 **O felix felicitas**
ATB, bc
Harmonia sacra, no. 8

E0059 **O perfecta caritas**
ATB, bc
Harmonia sacra, no. 7

E0060 **O quam metuendus**
SSATB, 2 vln, 3 vla, bc
Dedication of a church
Offertoria de festis, no. 24

E0061 **O sacrum convivium**
SSATB, 2 vln, 3 vla, bc
Offertoria de festis, no. 5

E0062 **Plaudite cives**
SSATB, 2 vln, 3 vla, bc
Christmas Day
Offertoria de festis, no. 1

E0063 **Quam pretiosa, quam speciosa**
SSB, 2 vln, bc
Harmonia sacra, no. 18

E0064 **Quid superbis**
ATB, bc
Harmonia sacra, no. 10

E0065 **Quis nos separabit**
SSATB, 2 vln, 3 vla, bc
Feast of a Martyr outside Eastertide
Offertoria de festis, no. 19

E0066 **Regina caeli (I)**
SSS/TTT, bc
Antiphonarium Marianum, no. 14

E0067 **Regina caeli (II)**
SST, bc
Antiphonarium Marianum, no. 15

E0068 **Regina caeli (III)**
SATB, bc
Antiphonarium Marianum, no. 16

E0069 **Regina caeli (IV)**
ATB, 2 vln, bc
Antiphonarium Marianum, no. 17

E0070 **Rex magne**
SSB, vln, 3 vla, bc
Harmonia sacra, no. 30

E0071 **Rosa cordis**
SSATB, 2 vln, 3 vla, bc
Offertoria de festis, no. 11

E0072 **Salve regina (I)**
SSS/TTT, bc
Antiphonarium Marianum, no. 20

E0073 **Salve regina (II)**
SSB, bc
Antiphonarium Marianum, no. 21

E0074 **Salve regina (III)**
SATB, bc
Antiphonarium Marianum, no. 22

E0075 **Salve regina (IV)**
BBBB, bc
Antiphonarium Marianum, no. 23

E0076 **Salve regina (V)**
ATB, 2 vln, bc
Antiphonarium Marianum, no. 24

E0077 **Salve regina (VI)**
ATB, 2 vln, 2 clar, bc
Antiphonarium Marianum, no. 26

E0078 **Salvete flores**
SSS, 2 vln, bc
Feast of the Holy Innocents
Hymni ariosi, no. 3

E0079 **Sancti et justi**
SSATB, 2 vln, 3 vla, bc
Feast of a Martyr in Eastertide
Offertoria de festis, no. 18

E0080 **Sanctorum meritis**
SSS, 2 vln, bc
Feast of Martyrs
Hymni ariosi, no. 28

E0081 **Sonuerunt**
SSATB, 2 vln, 3 vla, 2 clar, 3 tbn, bc
Offertoria de festis, no. 25

E0082 **Spargite flores, fundite rosas**
SSB, bc
Harmonia sacra, no. 9

E0083 **Tristes erant apostoli**
AAB, 2 vln, bc
Hymni ariosi, no. 25

E0084 **Urbs Jerusalem**
SAT, 2 vln, vla, bc
Dedication of a church
Hymni ariosi, no. 32

E0085 **Ut queant laxis**
SSA, 2 vln, bc
Nativity of Saint John the Baptist
Hymni ariosi, no. 14

E0086 **Vae dolores in ferni**
SSB, 2 vln, bc
Harmonia sacra, no. 22

E0087 **Veni creator**
SAT, 2 vln, bc
Pentecost
Hymni ariosi, no. 11

EISENHUT, Thomas (*continued*)

E0088   **Veni sponsa**
SSATB, 2 vln, 3 vla, bc
Offertoria de festis, no. 22

E0089   **Vidi conjunctos**
SSATB, 2 vln, 3 vla, bc
Feast of an Apostle
Offertoria de festis, no. 16

ERASMUS, Heinrich

E0090   **Die vielen Unglücks-Winde brausen**
SATB
Funeral of Thomas von dem Knesebeck
Stendal, 1689
D-ALa (score)
DMA 70//146

ERBEN, Johann Balthasar (1626-1686)

E0091   **Audite gentes quae loquor audite**
SAATTB, 2 vln, 3 vltta, bc
S-Uu 80:32, fol. 32v-36 (Düben) (1665)
tablature
DMA 3/1164

E0092   **Confitebor tibi Domine**
ATB, 2 vln, bc
S-Uu 80:53, fol. 53v-59 (Düben) (1665)
tablature
DMA 4/464
S-Uu 20:3 (Düben)
parts
DMA 4/464

E0093   **Dixit Dominus Domino meo**
SSATTB, 2 vln, 3 vltta, gamba, bc
S-Uu 20:4 (Düben)
parts
DMA 3/1165

E0094   **Domine Jesu Christe**
SSATB, bc
S-Uu 20:5 (Düben)
parts
DMA 3/2047

E0095   **Erbarm dich mein, o Herre Gott**
SATTB, 4 vla, bc
D-Bds Mus. ms. 30294, no. 11 (Bokemeyer)
score

E0096   **Es woll uns Gott genädig sein**
SATTB, 4 vla, bc
S-Uu 20:6 (Düben)
parts
DMA 1/2048

E0097   **Gelobet seist du, Jesu Christ**
SAATB, 2 vln, 3 vla, vltta, bsn, bc
S-Uu 81:1, fol. 1v-6v (Düben) (1665)
tablature
DMA 3/745

E0098   **Habe deine Lust an dem Herrn**
SSS, 2 vln, bc
D-Bds Mus. ms. 30294, no. 10 (Bokemeyer)
score

E0099   **Herr Christ der einig Gottes Sohn**
SSATB, 3 vla, vlne, bc
D-Bds Mus. ms. 30294, no. 12 (Bokemeyer)
score
S-Uu 20:7 (Düben)
parts
DMA 1/2049
Ed. F. Keßler, *Danziger Kirchenmusik*, no.
21, pp. 234-61

E0100   **Laudate Dominum, omnes gentes**
SSATTB, 2 vln, 2 gamba, bc
S-Uu 43:8 (Düben)
parts
DMA 3/1166

E0101   **Magnificat anima mea Dominum**
SSATTB, 2 vln, 3 vla, vlne, bc
D-B Mus. ms. 5634
parts

E0102   **Miserere mei Deus**
SSATTB, 4 vla, bc
S-Uu 80:49, fol. 49v-53r (Düben)
tablature
DMA 1/751
S-Uu 44:4 (Düben) (1665)
parts
DMA 1/751

E0103   **O Domine Jesu Christe**
SATB, bc
S-Uu 20:8a (Düben)
parts
DMA 3/1168

E0104   **Peccavi super numerum arenae maris**
SSATTB, 3 vla, vlne, bc
D-Bds Mus. ms. 30294, no. 13 (Bokemeyer)
score

S-Uu 80:26, fol. 26v-32 (Düben) (1665)
 tablature
 DMA 1/2050
S-Uu 20:9 (Düben)
 parts
 DMA 1/752

E0105   **Quam dilecta tabernacula tua Domine**
 SSATB, 2 vln, 2 gamba, bc
 S-Uu 20:10 (Düben)
 parts
 DMA 3/1169

E0106   **Sei getreu bis [in] den Tod**
 SAB, 2 vln, bc
 D-Bds Mus. ms. 30294, no. 9 (Bokemeyer)
 score

E0107   **Solvite jam grates regi**
 SSATTB, 2 vln, 2 vltta, vlne, bc
 S-Uu 80:36, fol. 36v-42r (Düben) (1665)
 tablature
 DMA 3/1171
 S-Uu 20:12 (Düben)
 parts
 DMA 3/1171

E0108   **Sustinuimus pacem et non venit**
 SSATTB, 4 vla, bc
 S-Uu 83:47a, fol. 4v-9r (Düben)
 tablature
 DMA 3/241

ERLEBACH, Philipp Heinrich (1657-1714)

E0109   **Ach daß ich Wassers genug hätte**
 SATB, 2 vln, 2 vla, bsn, bc
 10th Sunday after Trinity
 D-B Mus. ms. 5660, no. 1 (1699)
 parts
 DMA 2/1314
 D-Dlb Mus. ms. 2115-E-522 (Grimma U
 82/O 54)
 parts

E0110   **Ach Herr, strafe mich nicht**
 SATB, 2 vln, 2 vla, bsn, bc
 22nd Sunday after Trinity
 D-Dlb Mus. ms. 2115-E-504 (Grimma U
 73/O 29)
 parts

E0111   **Christus ist mein Leben**
 SATB, 2 vln, 2 vla, bc
 Purification of the Virgin Mary

D-LEm PM 7911 (1720)
 score and parts
 D-WRh (according to *New Grove*)
 D-Gs Cod. Ms. philos. 84e Erlebach 1
 score and parts

E0112   **Da dieser Elende rief**
 SATB, 2 vln, 2 vla, bsn, bc
 Quinquagesima
 D-Dlb Mus. ms. 2115-E-510 (Grimma U
 85/O 57)
 parts

E0113   **Das ist das ewige Leben**
 SATB, 2 vln, 2 vla, bsn, bc
 18th Sunday after Trinity
 F-Ssp Ms. 81
 parts
 DMA 2/465

E0114   **Das ist je gewißlich wahr**
 SSATB
 D-Dlb Mus. ms. 1/D/8, no. 43
 score

E0115   **Das weiß ich fürwahr, wer Gott dient**
 SATB, 2 vln, 3 vla, bsn, bc
 3rd Sunday after Easter
 D-LEm PM 7910
 score and bc part

E0116   **Das Wort ward Fleisch**
 SATB, 2 vln, 2 vla, 2 clar, bsn, bc
 Sunday after Christmas/Christmas Day
 D-F Ms. Ff. Mus. 170
 score and parts
 D-Dlb Mus. ms. 2115-E-525 (Grimma U
 420/P 20)
 score and parts

E0117   **Der Gerechte wird grünen**
 SATB, 2 vln, 2 vla, bc
 D-WRh (according to *New Grove*)

E0118   **Der Herr belohnet die wohl**
 SATB, 2 vln, 2 vla, bsn, bc
 5th Sunday after Trinity
 D-Dlb Mus. ms. 2115-E-519 (Grimma U
 81/O 53)
 parts

E0119   **Der Herr erhöre dich**
 SATB, 2 vln, 3 vla, 2 clar, timp, bc
 D-B Mus. ms. 5659, no. 4 (Bokemeyer)
 score
 DMA 2/1753

ERLEBACH, Philipp Heinrich (*continued*)

E0120   Der Herr hat offenbaret sein Wort
SATB, 2 vln, 2 vla, bsn, bc
D-WRh (according to *New Grove*)

E0121   Der Herr hat offenbaret seinen heiligen Arm
SATB, 2 vln, 2 vla, vlne/bsn, bc
3rd Sunday of Advent/12th Sunday after
Trinity
D-F Ms. Ff. Mus. 171
score and parts
D-Dlb Mus. ms. 2115-E-508 (Grimma U
87/O 59)
parts
Ed. L. Hoffmann-Erbrecht, *Organum I*, 33

E0122   Der Herr ist nahe allen, die ihn anrufen
SATB, 2 vln, 2 vla, bc
3rd Sunday after Epiphany
D-B Mus. ms. 5660, no. 2 (1701)
parts
DMA 2/1315
Ed. O. von Steuben (Stuttgart, 1966)

**E0123   Der Herr weiß die Gottseligen aus der
Versuchung**
SATB, 2 vln, 2 vla, bsn, bc
1st Sunday of Lent
D-Dlb Mus. ms. 2115-E-500 (Grimma U
55/O 32)
parts

E0124   Der Name des Herrn ist ein festes Schloß
SATB, 2 vln, 2 vltta, bc
D-B Mus. ms. 5659, no. 12 (Bokemeyer)
(1709)
score
DMA 2/1754

E0125   Der Ruhm der Gottlosen stehet nicht lange
SATB, 2 vln, 2 vla, bsn, bc
D-Bds Mus. ms. autogr. 1
parts (only vocal parts extant)

E0126   Die Erlöseten des Herrn
SATB
D-Gs Cod. Ms. philos. 84e Erlbach [*sic*] 1
score and parts
Attributed by A. Dürr in *AfM* 25/4, p.
311

E0127   Die Liebe Gottes ist ausgegossen in unser Herz
SSATB, 2 vln, 3 vla, bsn, bc
D-Dlb Mus. ms. 2115-E-512 (Grimma U
90/O 66) (1699)
parts

E0128   Die mit Tränen säen
SATB, 2 vln, 2 vla, bsn, bc
Sexagesima
D-Dlb Mus. ms. 2115-E-509 (Grimma U
84/O 56)
parts
D-Bds Mus. ms. 30282, no. 5 (1701)
score

E0129   Die Welt will nur die Frommen hassen
SATB, 2 vln, bsn, vlne, bc
Sunday after Circumcision
D-F Ms. Ff. Mus. 172 (1700)
parts

**E0130   Die Zeit ist aus, nun mußt du deine Rechnung
führen**
SATB, 2 vln, bsn, bc
D-Dlb Mus. ms. 2115-E-521 (Grimma U
83/O 55)
score and parts

E0131   Dies ist der Tag
SATB
USSR-KA Ms. 13661, no. 84 (lost)
score
DdT 49/50, pp. 258-60
Anthology of Music 47, pp. 98-100

E0132   Er bricht herfür wie die schöne Morgenröte
SATB, 2 vln, 2 vla, 2 clar, bsn, bc
Easter Sunday
D-F Ms. Ff. Mus. 173
score and parts

E0133   Exultemus, gaudeamus, laetemus
SATB, SATB, 2 vln, 2 vla, 2 tpt, bsn,
timp, bc
D-MLHr (1705) (according to *New Grove*)

**E0134   Fürchtet euch nicht: Siehe ich verkündige euch
große Freude**
SATB, 2 vln, 2 vla, 2 clar, bsn, timp, bc
Christmas Day
D-Dlb Mus. ms. 2115-E-527 (Grimma U
395/N 81)
parts
D-F Ms. Ff. Mus. 174
parts
D-LUC (according to *New Grove*)

E0135   Gelobet sei der Herr täglich
SATB, 2 vln, 2 vla, bsn, bc
1st Sunday after Trinity
D-Dlb Mus. ms. 2115-E-515 (Grimma U
79/O 52)
parts

E0136 **Gott, man lobet dich in der Stille**
SATB, 3 vln, 2 vla, 2 clar, bsn, bc
D-B Mus. ms. 5659, no. 5 (Bokemeyer)
score
DMA 2/1755

E0137 **Gott will für alle seine Gaben**
SATB, 2 vln, 2 vla, harp, 3 ob, bsn, db, bc
D-WRh (according to *New Grove*)

E1038 **Gratias agimus**
SSATB, 2 vln, 3 vla, vc, bc
18th Sunday after Trinity
F-Ssp (according to *New Grove* and Lobstein)

E0139 **Held, du hast den Feind gebunden**
SATB, 2 vln, 2 vla, harp, 3 ob, bsn,
bassone, bc
D-Dlb Mus. ms. 2115-E-503 (Grimma U
58/O 28)
parts

E0140 **Herr, ich rufe zu dir**
SATB, 2 vln, 2 vla, bsn, bc
Sunday after Ascension
D-Dlb Mus. ms. 2115-E-514 (Grimma U
86/O 58)
parts

E0141 **Herr unser Herrscher**
SATB, clar, 2 vln, 2 vla, vlne, bc
D-B Mus. ms. 5659, no. 11 (Bokemeyer)
score
DMA 2/1756

E0142 **Herr, wenn Trübsal da ist**
SATB, 2 vln, 2 vla, bsn, bc
21st Sunday after Trinity
D-Dlb Mus. ms. 2115-E-505 (Grimma U
57/O 29) (1699)
parts

E0143 **Herr, wer ist dir gleich?**
SATB, 2 vln, 2 vla, bsn, bc
3rd Sunday of Lent
D-Dlb Mus. ms. 2115-E-501 (Grimma U
56/O 53)
parts
D-Bds Mus. ms. 30282, no. 4
score

E0144 **Hütet euch daß eure Herzen nicht beschweret
werden**
SATB, 2 vln, 2 vla, bsn, bc
2nd Sunday of Advent
D-Dlb Mus. ms. 2115-E-507 (Grimma U
88/O 60)
parts

D-F Ms. Ff. Mus. 175
score and parts

E0145 **Ich bin mit meinem Gott zufrieden**
SATB, 2 vln, 3 vla, bsn, bc
D-Dlb Mus. ms. 2115-E-526 (Grimma U
531/T 10)
parts

E0146 **Ich hebe meine Augen auf**
SATB, 2 vln, 2 vla, bsn, bc
D-B Mus. ms. 5659, no. 7 (Bokemeyer)
score
DMA 2/1757

E0147 **Ich will euch wiedersehen**
SATB, tpt, 2 vln, 2 vla, vlne/bsn, bc
Easter Monday
D-Bds Mus. ms. autogr. Erlebach (See
Krummacher 1965, p. 513)
D-B Mus. ms. 5659, no. 1 (Bokemeyer)
score
DMA 2/1758
D-Dlb Mus. ms. 2115-E-511 (Grimma U
89/O 61)
parts
D-F Ms. Ff. Mus. 176
parts

E0148 **Ich will Ihnen einen einigen Hirten erwecken**
SATB, 2 vln, 2 vla, vlne, bc
2nd Sunday after Easter
D-Bds Mus. ms. 30282, no. 13
score

E0149 **Ich will ihre Speise segnen**
SATB, 2 vln, 2 vla, bsn, bc
4th Sunday of Lent
D-Dlb Mus. ms. 2115-E-502 (Grimma U
72/O 26) (1701)
parts

E0150 **Ich will mit Brandopfer gehen**
SATB, 2 vln, 2 vla, bc
D-B Mus. ms. 5659, no. 3 (Bokemeyer)
score
DMA 2/1759

E0151 **Ich will Wasser gießen auf die Dürstenden**
SATB, 2 vln, 2 vla, bsn, bc
D-B Mus. ms. 5659, no. 6 (Bokemeyer)
score
DMA 2/1760
Ed. O. von Steuber, *Die Kantate* 101

E0152 **Jesu amabilis et summe delectabilis**
SATB, 2 vln, 3 vla, bsn, bc

ERLEBACH, Philipp Heinrich (*continued*)

D-B Mus. ms. 5659, no. 13 (Bokemeyer)
(1697)
score
DMA 2/1762

E0153   **Jesu, segne du dies Jahr**
SATB, 2 vln, bc
D-Bds Mus. ms. 30282, no. 14 (1708)
score

E0154   **Jetzt sind angenehme Zeiten**
SATB, 2 vln, 2 vla, bc
D-B Mus. ms. 5659, no. 9 (Bokemeyer)
score
DMA 2/1761

E0155   **Lobe den Herrn, meine Seele**
SATB, 2 vln, 2 vla, bc
D-Gs Cod. Ms. philos. 84e Erlebach 2
score, 1 part
(Bärenreiter BA 4943): "Sei Lob und Preis
mit Ehren"

E0156   **Lobe den Herrn, meine Seele**
SATB, 2 vln, 2 vltta, bc
D-B Mus. ms. 5659, no. 2 (Bokemeyer)
score
DMA 2/1764
Ed. O. von Steuber (Bärenreiter BA 3453,
1960)

E0157   **Lobe, lobe den Herrn**
SATB, tpt, 2 vln, 2 vla, bc
D-MÜG (according to *New Grove*)

E0158   **Lobt Gott in seinem Heiligtum**
SATB, 2 vln, 2 vla, 2 tpt, bsn, timp, bc
D-UDa (according to *New Grove*)

E0159   **Missa (brevis)**
SATB, 2 vln, 2 vla, bsn, bc
D-B Mus. ms. 5659, no. 14 (Bokemeyer)
score
DMA 2/1763

E0160   **Scrutabor legem tuam**
SSATB, 2 vln, 4 vla, bc
D-B Mus. ms. 5660, no. 5
parts
DMA 2/1316

E0161   **Sei Lob und Preis mit Ehren**
See Lobe den Herrn, meine Seele

E0162   **Seid barmherzig, wie auch euer Vater**
SATB, 2 vln, 2 vla, bsn, bc

D-Dlb Mus. ms. 2115-E-518 (Grimma U
76/O 49)
parts

E0163   **Selig sind die Friedfertigen**
SATB, 2 vln, 2 vla, bsn, bc
6th Sunday after Trinity
D-Dlb Mus. ms. 2115-E-520 (Grimma N 87)
(1699)
parts

E0164   **Siehe, ich verkündige euch große Freude**
SATB, 2 vln, 2 vla, 2 tpt, bsn, bc
Christmas Day
D-B Mus. ms. 5660, no. 3 (1698)
parts
DMA 2/1317
D-Bds Mus. ms. 30378, no. 6
score
Ed. O. von Steuber, *Die Kantate* 19

E0165   **Siehe, lobet den Herrn, alle Knechte**
SSATB, 2 vln, 3 vla, 2 clar, bsn, bc
D-B Mus. ms. 5659, no. 10 (Bokemeyer)
score
DMA 2/1765

E0166   **Siehe, um Trost war mir sehr bange**
SATB, 2 vln, 2 vla, bsn, bc
3rd Sunday after Trinity
D-B Mus. ms. 5660, no. 4 (1699)
parts
DMA 2/1318
D-Dlb Mus. ms. 2115-E-517 (Grimma U
78/O 51)
parts

E0167   **Unsere Missetat drücket uns hart**
SATB, 2 vln, 2 vla, bsn, bc
19th Sunday after Trinity
D-Dlb Mus. ms. 2115-E-506 (Grimma U
74/O 48) (1699)
parts

E0168   **Viderunt omnes fines terrae salutare**
SSATB, ATB, 2 vln, vla, vlne, bsn, bc
D-F Ms. Ff. Mus. 32 (anonymous; attr. in
Schlichte catalog)
parts
D-MÜp (according to *New Grove*)

E0169   **Was erhebet sich die arme Erde**
SATB, 2 vln, 2 vla, bsn, bc
17th Sunday after Trinity

D-Dlb Mus. ms. 2115-E-523 (Grimma U
106/V 1) (1699)
parts

E0170 **Wer bin ich, Herr**
SSATTB
USSR-KA Ms. 13661, no. 36 (lost)
DdT 49/50, pp. 105-09
Antiqua Chorbuch I/5, pp. 304-09

E0171 **Wer sind diese mit weißen Kleidern angetan?**
SATB, 4 vla, bsn, bc
D-Dlb Mus. ms. 2115-E-524 (Grimma U
351/N 1) (1688)
parts

E0172 **Wie lieblich sind deine Wohnungen**
SATB, 3 vln, 2 vla, bc
D-B Mus. ms. 5659, no. 8 (Bokemeyer)
score
DMA 2/1766

E0173 **Wohlan alle, die ihr durstig seid**
SATB, 2 vln, 2 vla, bsn, bc
2nd Sunday after Trinity
D-Dlb Mus. ms. 2115-E-516 (Grimma U
77/O 50) (1699)
parts

E0174 **Zu guter Nacht, du unbeständiges Leben**
SATB
D-Gs Cod. Ms. philos. 84e Erlebach 3
score

EULENHAUPT, Johann Ernst

E0175 **Jauchzet dem Herrn, alle Welt**
SSATTB, 2 vln, 2 vla, 3 tbn, vlne, bsn, bc
D-Dlb Mus. ms. 1812-E-500 (Grimma
XXII U 500/T 19)
parts

F

FABRICIUS, Werner (1633-1679)

Note: Pieces listed in MGG and *New Grove* for D-Lm are now reported lost by the library.

COLLECTION

    Geistliche Arien (1662)
      RISM F35 (parts)
      DMA 3/526

WORKS

F0001 **Ach Gott! Wie gar ein nichtigs Wesen**
      SSATB
      Funeral of Johann Christian Schwertner
      Leipzig, 1657
        RISM F31, Reich 256 (score)
        DMA 63//116

F0002 **Ach höret auf zu weinen**
      SSATB
      Funeral
      Leipzig, 1657
        RISM F33 (score)
        DMA 63//150

F0003 **Du Blut von unserm Blute**
      SSATB
      Funeral of David Bauer
      Leipzig, 1656
        RISM F29, Reich 252 (score)
        DMA 56//210

F0004 **Es erhub sich ein Streit**
      à 6 and 12
      D-NAUw
      Listed in Werner & MGG; unable to verify

F0005 **Herr, Herr wenn ich nur dich habe**
      SSAATTBB, bc
      Funeral of Catharine Pietzsch Schöller
      Leipzig, 1655
        RISM F27, Reich 251 (score)
        DMA 63//220

F0006 **Jauchzet, ihr Himmel**
      SSATB, 2 vln, 2 tpt/corn, bc
      150th anniversary of the Reformation in
        Leipzig
      D-B Mus. ms. 5755 (Erfurt) (1674)
        parts

F0007 **Jesu, liebster Seelen Freund**
      SATB, vln, 2 vla, 3 tbn, bc
      Christmas Day
      Geistliche Arien, no. 2
      Possibly concordant with the following
        entry

F0008 **Jesu, liebster Seelen Freund**
      SATB, vln/corn, 3 tbn, vlne, bc
      Christmas Day
      D-Dlb 1899-E-500 (Grimma U 108/V 2)
        parts
      Possibly concordant with the preceding
        entry

F0009 **Leider, daß von unsern Häuptern**
      SATB
      Funeral of Johann Benedict Carpzov
      Leipzig, 1657
        RISM F32, Reich 254 (score)
        DMA 63//115
      Ed. Schering, Mg. Leipzigs II, pp. 250-52

F0010 **Meine Seele erhebt**
    à 9
    D-NAUw
    Listed in Werner; unable to verify

F0011 **O liebes Kind**
    SATB, vln, 2 vla, 3 tbn, bc
    Christmas Day
    Geistliche Arien, no. 1

F0012 **Schaffe in mir, Gott**
    SATB, 2 corn (schryari), 2 tbn, bc
    Pentecost
    Geistliche Arien, no. 6
    S-Uu 81:128, fol. 128v-132 (Düben)
      tablature
      DMA 3/242

F0013 **Sie haben meinen Herrn**
    SSATTB, 4 vla, 2 tbn, bc
    Easter
    Geistliche Arien, no. 4

F0014 **Siehe, also wird gesegnet**
    à 5
    D-NAUw
    Listed in Werner & MGG; unable to verify

F0015 **Surrexit Christus hodie**
    SSATTTTB, 2 vln, 2 vla, 2 tbtta, 2 corn, 2
      tbn, bc
    Easter
    Geistliche Arien, no. 3

F0016 **Uns ist ein Kind geboren**
    à 8
    D-NAUw
    Listed in Werner; unable to verify

F0017 **Vater, in deine Hände**
    SATB, bc
    Name day of Wentzel Buhlen
    D-Dlb 1899-E-501 (Grimma U 523/T 18)
      parts

F0018 **Veni sancte spiritus**
    SSATB, 2 vln, 2 vla, bc
    Pentecost
    Geistliche Arien, no. 5
    S-Uu 81:125, fol. 125v-128r (Düben);
      77:32, fol. 32v-37r (Düben)
      tablature
      DMA 3/243
    S-Uu 46:16 (Düben) (1663)
      parts
      DMA 3/243

F0019 **Victoria, der Tod ist verschlungen**
    à 7
    D-NAUw
    Listed in Werner & MGG; unable to verify

F0020 **Wann mich Gott von Jugend auf**
    SATB
    Funeral of Margarita Heyland
    Leipzig, 1662
      RISM F36, Reich 264 (score)
      DMA 63//121

F0021 **Wohl dem, der ein tugendsam Weib hat**
    à 5
    D-NAUw
    Listed in Werner & MGG; unable to verify

FALCK, Georg, der Ältere (ca. 1630-1689)

F0022 **Ach! ach mein Herr ist tot**
    SATB, bc
    Funeral
    Rothenburg ob der Tauber, n.d.
      RISM F70, Reich 383 (score)
      DMA 56//217

FEDELI, Ruggiero (1655-1722)

F0023 **Confitebor tibi Domine**
    SATBB, 2 vln, 2 vla, 2 ob, bc
    D-B Mus ms. 6085, no. 9 (Bokemeyer)
      score
    D-B Mus. ms. 6087
      parts

F0024 **Dixit Dominus**
    SATB, 2 vln, vla, bc
    D-B Mus. ms. 6085, no. 7 (Bokemeyer)
      score

F0025 **Gloria in excelsis**
    SSATB, 2 vln, vc, bc
    D-B Mus. ms. 6085, no. 14 (Bokemeyer)
      score

F0026 **Laetatus sum**
    SAB, 2 vln, bc
    D-B Mus. ms. 6085, no. 6 (Bokemeyer)
      score

F0027 **Laetatus sum**
    SAT, 2 vln, 2 vltte, trbtta, bsn, bc
    D-B Mus. ms. 6085, no. 10 (Bokemeyer)
      score

FEDELI, Ruggiero (*continued*)

F0028 **Lauda Jerusalem**
STB, 2 vln, bc
D-B Mus. ms. 6085, no. 4 (Bokemeyer)
score

F0029 **Magnificat**
SATB, 1 treble instr, bc
D-Bds Mus. ms. 30088, no. 6
score

F0030 **Magnificat**
SATB, 3 vln, 2 vltta, bc
D-B Ms. 6086
score

F0031 **Magnificat**
SATB, 3 vln, 2 vla, vlne, bc
D-LUC
parts

F0032 **Magnificat**
4 vv
D-Dlb Mus. ms. 572
score
Written by Francesco Fedeli; revised by
Ruggiero

F0033 **Magnificat**
4 vv, 3 vln, 2 vla, bsn, bc
F-Ssp

F0034 **Missa**
SATB, 2 vln, vla, 2 fl, 2 ob, 2 corn, timp,
bc
D-B Mus. ms. 6080
parts

F0035 **Missa Iste confessor**
SATB, 2 vln, vla, 2 ob, bc
D-B Mus. ms. 6081
parts

F0036 **Nisi Dominus**
SATBB, 3 vln, 2 vla, bsn, bc
D-B Mus. ms. 6085, no. 8 (Bokemeyer)
score

F0037 **O quam vana est**
SSATTBB, 2 vln, vltta, bsn, bc
D-B Mus. ms. 6085, no. 12 (Bokemeyer)
score
BG-Lcm Ms. 1706
score

F0038 **Sanctus**
SATB, 2 vln, vla, 2 ob, bc
D-B 6082, no. 1
parts

F0039 **Sanctus**
SATB, 2 vln, vla, 2 ob, 3 trp, timp, bc
D-B Mus. ms. 6082, no. 2
parts

F0040 **Tandem aliquando**
SATB, SATB, 4 vln, vltta, bsn, bc
D-B Mus. ms. 6085, no. 13 (Bokemeyer)
score

F0041 **Unsers Herzens Freude**
4 vv, 2 vln, vla, bc
F-Ssp

FERDINAND III (1608-1657)

F0042 **Crudelis Herodes**
SATB, 5 vla, bc
Epiphany
D-Lr Mus. ant. pract. K.N. 28, no. 7
(1649)
score

F0043 **Deus misereatur nostri**
SSATTB, bc
D-Lr Mus. ant. pract. K.N. 206, no. 50
score

F0044 **Humanae salutis sator**
SATB, 2 vln, 2 corn, bc
D-Lr Mus. ant. pract. K.N. 28, no. 9
(1650)
score

F0045 **Jesu, redemptor omnium**
SATB, 3 fl, 3 tpt, bc
Christmas Day
D-Lr Mus. ant. pract. K.N. 28, no. 5
(1649)
score
MWKF I, pp. 17-30

F0046 **Jesu, redemptor omnium**
SATB, 2 vla, 2 tbn, bsn, vc, vlne, theorbo,
bc
A-Wn 16042
parts
DMA 3/246

F0047 **Miserere**
SSSAAATTTBBB, bc
A-Wn 18583
score
DMA 3/247
MWKF I, pp. 1-16

F0048 **Pange lingua gloriosi**
SATB, 2 gamba, bc
Corpus Christi
D-Lr Mus. ant. pract. K.N. 28, no. 11
score

F0049 **Veni creator spiritus**
SSATTB, vla, 2 vltta, bc
Pentecost
D-Lr Mus. ant. pract. K.N. 28, no. 10
score

FISCHER, Christoph (1618-1701)

F0050 **Wir danken dir, Herr Jesu Christ**
4 vv
PL-Kj Mus. ms. 40110 and 40112
score and parts

FLIXIUS, Johann Josef

F0051 **Cantate Domino**
SATB, 2 vln, 3 vla, bc
PL-Kj Mus. ms. 40129, no. 7
tablature

F0052 **Magnus Dominus**
SSATBB, 2 vln, corn, 3 tbn, bc
CS-KRa II, 308
parts
microfilm: US-SY

F0053 **So euch die Welt hasset**
STTB, bc
S-Uu St. 21:5
parts
DMA 1/753

FLOR, Christian (1626-1697)

F0054 **Es segne dich der Gott Israel**
SSATB, 2 vln, bc
Wedding
Hamburg, 1656
RISM F1182 (parts)
DMA 61//227

F0055 **Machet die Tore weit**
SATB, 2 vln, 2 vla, bsn, bc
D-B Mus. ms. 30224, no. 10 (Bokemeyer)
score

F0056 **Pastores currite in Bethlehem**
SATB, 5 vla, vlne, bc
S-Uu 21:6 (Düben)
tablature and parts

F0057 **So hast du nun geendigt deine Stunden**
SSATTB, bc
Funeral of Michael Jacobi
1663 (parts)
Listed in *New Grove*; not in RISM, Reich,
or MGG

FÖRCKELRATH, Kaspar

F0058 **Wer überwindet sich**
SB soli, SATB, 4 instr, bc
Funeral of Sibylla Ursula, Herzogin zu
Schleswig-Holstein
Hamburg, 1672
RISM F1375, Reich 129 (score)
Second and third sections entitled **Vollendet
ist der Streit** and **Sei siegende Seele
willkommen**, respectively

FÖRSTER, Kaspar, the younger (1616-1673)
Note: Scores of all Förster polyphonic vocal works are on microfilm
in the Music Library, University of North Carolina, Chapel Hill

F0059 **Ad arma fideles**
SSB, bc
D-Bds Mus. ms. 30298, no. 7 (Bokemeyer)
score (includes 2 vln)
DMA 2/826
S-Uu 78:14, fol. 14v-16v (Düben)
tablature
DMA 46//54
S-Uu 21:7 (Düben)
parts
S-Uu 84:5 (Düben)
tablature (includes 2 vln)
Ed. S. Sørenson (W. Hansen no. 28738)

F0060 **Ah peccatores graves somno delictorum**
SSATTB, 2 vln, 2 vla, vlne, spinetto/gamba,
bc
S-Uu 21:8 (Düben)
parts
DMA 46//49

F0061 **Beatus vir qui timet Dominum**
SAB, 2 vln, bc

FÖRSTER, Kapsar (*continued*)

 S-Uu 21:9 (Düben)
 parts
 DMA 46//58

F0062   Bella movet Israel
 See Congregantes Philistei

F0063   Benedicam Dominum
 SAB, 2 vln, vlne, bc
 S-Uu 84:6a, fol. 1v-4r (Düben)
 tablature
 DMA 46//70
 S-Uu 21:10 (Düben)
 parts

F0064   Confitebor tibi Domine in toto corde meo
 SATB, 2 vln, bc
 S-Uu 83:37a, fol. 42v-46r (Düben)
 tablature
 DMA 24//161
 S-Uu 21:11 (Düben)
 parts

F0065   Confitebor tibi Domine in toto corde meo
 SSATTB, 2 vln, vla/bsn, 4 instr, bc
 S-Uu 21:12 (Düben)
 parts
 DMA 24//97

F0066   Confitebor tibi Domine in toto corde meo
 SATB, 2 vln, vla, bc
 S-Uu 83:37, fol. 38v-42r (Düben)
 tablature
 DMA 28//156
 S-Uu 21:13 (Düben)
 parts

F0067   Congregantes Philistei (Dialogi Davidus cum Philisteo)
 SATB, 2 vln, vltta, vla bassa, bsn, bc
 S-Uu 78:54, fol. 54v-59r (Düben) (1667)
 tablature
 DMA 47//33
 S-Uu 54:7 (Düben)
 parts
 DMA 37//61
 D-Bds Mus. ms. 30298, no. 4 (Bokemeyer)
 score
 DMA 2/468
 D-Bds Mus. ms. 30298, no. 6 (Bokemeyer)
 score (3 clar added by G. Oesterreich)
 DMA 2/469

F0068   Dialogi Davidus cum Philisteo
 See Congregantes Philistei

F0069   Dialogus de Juditha & Holofernes
 See Viri Israelite audite

F0070   Domine Dominus noster, quam admirabile
 SSATB, 5 vla, bc
 S-Uu 79:15, fol. 15v-20r (Düben)
 tablature
 DMA 24//120
 S-Uu 81:104, fol. 104-109 (Düben)
 tablature
 DMA 34//217
 S-Uu 21:16 (Düben)
 parts

F0071   Et cum Jesus ingressus esset
 ATB, bc
 S-Uu 83:18, fol. 33v-35 (Düben)
 tablature
 DMA 27//132

F0072   Exurge Domine sive repleta
 See Repleta est malis

F0073   Gaudeamus exultemus et laetemur
 See Gentes redemptae pascha celebrantes

F0074   Gentes redemptae pascha celebrantes
 ATB, 2 vln, gamba, bc
 S-Uu 85:58, fol. 2v-6 (Düben)
 tablature
 DMA 28//77
 S-Uu 22:3 (Düben)
 parts
 DMA 46//108

F0075   In tribulationibus ad quem clamabimus
 SATB, bc
 S-Uu 85:18, fol. 52v-55 (Düben)
 tablature
 DMA 29//174
 S-Uu 22:5 (Düben)
 parts
 S-Uu 22:5a (Düben)
 parts (includes 2 vln, 2 vla)

F0076   Intenderunt arcum insipientes
 SAB, vlne, bc
 S-Uu 86:9, fol. 5v-7 (Düben)
 tablature
 DMA 24//98
 S-Uu 22:4 (Düben)
 parts

F0077   Laetentur caeli et exultet terra
 SSB, bc
 S-Uu 85:45a, fol. 6v (Düben)
 tablature (incomplete)
 DMA 24//181

S-Uu 22:8a (Düben)
    parts (includes 2 vln, bass vla)
S-Uu 22:8 (Düben)
    parts

F0078 **Lauda Jerusalem Dominum lauda Deum**
    SSATB, 2 vln, 2 vltta, vlne, bc
    S-Uu 22:6 (Düben)
      parts
      DMA 24//144

F0079 **Laudate, pueri Dominum**
    ATB, 2 vln, vlne, bc
    S-Uu 22:7 (Düben)
      parts
      DMA 29//160

F0080 **O bone Jesu, o dulcedo cordis mei**
    SAB, 2 vln, vla, vlne, bc
    S-Uu 84:7 (Düben)
      tablature
      DMA 46//44
    S-Uu 22:9 (Düben)
      parts
      D-Dlb Mus. ms. 1715-E-500 (Grimma U 111/V 5)
      parts (SAB, 2 vln, bc)

F0081 **O plausus orantes jungemus**
    ATB, 2 vln, bc
    S-Uu 22:11 (Düben)
      parts
      DMA 46//67

F0082 **O quam dulcis, quam suavis**
    SAT, 2 vln, vlne, bc
    S-Uu 22:12 (Düben)
      parts
      DMA 46//52

F0083 **O vos omnes qui laboratis**
    SAB, 2 vln, gamba, theorbo, bc
    S-Uu 84:8, fol. 1-3 (Düben)
      tablature
      DMA 34//188
    S-Uu 22:13 (Düben)
      parts

F0084 **Peccavi super numerum**
    SATB, 2 vln, bc
    S-Uu 83:27, fol. 15v-17 (Düben) (1668)
      tablature
      DMA 28//181
    D-Bds Mus. ms. 30298, no. 5 (Bokemeyer)
      score
      DMA 2/828

F0085 **Quanta fecisti, Domine anima mea**
    SATB, 2 vln, gamba, bc

S-Uu 86:46, fol. 8v-12 (Düben) (1684)
    tablature
    DMA 24//144
S-Uu 54:13 (Düben)
    parts

F0086 **Quid faciam misera quo me vertam**
    SSB, 2 vln, bc
    S-Uu 84:9 (Düben)
      tablature
      DMA 46//109
    S-Uu 22:14 (Düben)
      parts

F0087 **Repleta est malis anima nostra**
    ATB, 2 vln, bc
    S-Uu 78:89, fol. 89v-92 (Düben)
      tablature
      DMA 46//45
    S-Uu 22:2 (Düben)
      parts

F0088 **Stillate rores stellae micate**
    ATB, 2 vln, bc
    S-Uu 84:10 (Düben)
      tablature
      DMA 34//189
    S-Uu 22:18 (Düben)
      parts

F0089 **Super numerum arenae**
    See Peccavi super numerum

F0090 **Vanitas vanitatum et omnia vanitas**
    SAB, 2 vln, 3 vla, bc
    1st Sunday after Trinity
    S-Uu 81:77, fol. 78-81 (Düben) (1664)
      tablature
      DMA 34//190
    S-Uu 22:19 (Düben)
      parts

F0091 **Viri Israelite audite (Dialogus de Juditha & Holoferno)**
    SATB, 2 vln, 2 vla, bc
    S-Uu 78:34, fol. 34v-38 (Düben) (1667)
      tablature
      DMA 24//79
    S-Uu 54:11 (Düben)
      parts

F0092 **Vulnerasti cor meum, vulnerasti soror mea**
    SSB, bc
    S-Uu 83:14, fol. 24v-26 (Düben)
      tablature
      DMA 34//191
    S-Uu 22:20 (Düben)
      parts

FÖRTSCH, Johann Philipp (1652-1732)

F0093 **Ach Gott, du bist noch heut so reich**
SATB, 2 vln, 2 vla, vlne, bc
D-B Mus. ms. 6472, no. 6 (Bokemeyer)
score
DMA 3/750

F0094 **Ach, ich elender Mensch, wer wird mich erlösen**
ATB, 3 gamba, bc
D-B Mus. ms. 6471, no. 14 (Bokemeyer)
score
DMA 3/1177

F0095 **Ach, was ist doch dieses Leben**
SSTTB, 2 vln, 2 vla, bc
D-B Mus. ms. 6472, no. 12 (Bokemeyer)
score
DMA 3/751

F0096 **Ad te Domine, ad te clamabo**
SATB, bc
D-B Mus. ms. 6472, no. 27 (Bokemeyer)
score
DMA 3/753

F0097 **Bezahle, was du mir schuldig bist**
SSTTB, 2 vln, 2 vla, bc
D-B Mus. ms. 6470, no. 21 (Bokemeyer)
score
DMA 3/2053

F0098 **Da acht Tage um waren**
SATB, 2 vln, 2 vla, bc
D-B Mus. ms. 6470, no. 29 (Bokemeyer)
score
DMA 3/2054

F0099 **Das dunkle Wesen ist vorbei**
SSTB, 2 vln, 2 vla, bc
D-B Mus. ms. 6472, no. 1 (Bokemeyer)
score
DMA 3/755

F0100 **Das weiß ich fürwahr**
SSB, 2 vln, 2 vla, bc
D-B Mus. ms. 6471, no. 9 (Bokemeyer)
score
DMA 3/1178

F0101 **Der Gottlose lauret wie ein Löwe in der Höhle**
SSATB, 2 vln, bc
D-B Mus. ms. 6470, no. 5 (Bokemeyer)
score
DMA 3/2058

F0102 **Der Herr hat das Recht lieb**
SSB, 2 vln, bc
D-B Mus. ms. 6472, no. 22 (Bokemeyer)
score
DMA 3/763

F0103 **Der Herr hat seinen Engeln befohlen**
SSATB, 2 vln, 2 vla, bc
D-B Mus. ms. 6471, no. 17 (Bokemeyer)
score
DMA 3/1179

F0104 **Die Gnad ist ohne Maß**
SSATB, 2 vln, bc
5th Sunday after Trinity
D-B Mus. ms. 6470, no. 15 (Bokemeyer)
score
DMA 3/2057

F0105 **Die Wunder sind zu groß**
SATTB, 2 vln, bsn, bc
3rd Sunday of Advent
D-B Mus. ms. 6470, no. 26 (Bokemeyer)
score
DMA 3/2082

F0106 **Dies ist das Zeugnis Johannis**
SATTB, 2 vln, bc
D-B Mus. ms. 6472, no. 2 (Bokemeyer)
score
DMA 3/756

F0107 **Du Heiden Trost, du Heil der Welt**
SSATB, 2 vln, 2 vla, bc
Annunciation to the Virgin Mary
D-B Mus. ms. 6471, no. 11 (Bokemeyer)
score
DMA 3/1180

F0108 **Ecce oculi Domini**
TTB, 2 vln, bc
D-B Mus. ms. 6472, no. 31 (Bokemeyer)
score
DMA 3/757

F0109 **Ein Schäflein bin ich matt und schwach**
SATB, 3 vln, bc
D-B Mus. ms. 6472, no. 21 (Bokemeyer)
score
DMA 3/758

F0110 **Er hat alles wohl gemacht**
SSATB, 2 vln, 2 vla, bc
D-B Mus. ms. 6470, no. 2 (Bokemeyer)
score
DMA 3/2056

F0111 **Erschrecklich ist des Satans Macht**
SSATB, 2 vln, 2 vla, bc
3rd Sunday of Lent

D-B Mus. ms. 6471, no. 4 (Bokemeyer)
score
DMA 3/1181

F0112 **Es spricht der Unweisen Mund wohl**
SATB, 2 vln, 2 vla, bc
D-B Mus. ms. 6472, no. 19 (Bokemeyer)
score
DMA 3/759

F0113 **Freue dich, Saba, frohlocket ihr Heiden**
SATTB, 2 vln, bc
D-B Mus. ms. 6471, no. 1 (Bokemeyer)
score
DMA 3/1182

F0114 **Frisch auf mein Geist**
STTB, 2 vln, bc
D-B Mus. ms. 6472, no. 23 (Bokemeyer)
score
DMA 3/760

F0115 **Gelobet seist du, Jesu Christ**
SATB, 2 vln, bc
D-B Mus. ms. 6472, no. 3 (Bokemeyer)
score
DMA 3/761
Zelle (1893), pp. 21-24

F0116 **Gleich wie der Blitz ausgehet**
SSATB, 2 vln, 2 vla, bc
D-B Mus. ms. 6472, no. 20 (Bokemeyer)
score
DMA 3/762

F0117 **Gott wird abwischen alle Tränen**
SSATB, 4 vla, bc
D-B Mus. ms. 6471, no. 6 (Bokemeyer)
score
DMA 3/1183

F0118 **Herr, es wartet alles auf dich**
SSATB, 2 vln, bc
D-B Mus. ms. 6471, no. 13 (Bokemeyer)
score
DMA 3/1184

F0119 **Herr lehre mich tun nach deinem Wohlgefallen**
SSB, 2 vln, 2 vla, bc
D-B Mus. ms. 6471, no. 3 (Bokemeyer)
score
DMA 3/1185

F0120 **Herr, meine Tochter ist jetzt gestorben**
SSTTB, 2 vln, 2 vla, bc
D-B Mus. ms. 6470, no. 7 (Bokemeyer)
score
DMA 3/2059

F0121 **Herr, wer wird wohnen in deiner Hütten**
SATB, 2 vln, 2 vla, bsn, bc
D-B Mus. ms. 6472, no. 4 (Bokemeyer)
score
DMA 3/765

F0122 **Herr, wie muß ein Sündenknecht**
SSATB, 2 vln, bc
D-B Mus. ms. 6472, no. 8 (Bokemeyer)
score
DMA 3/767

F0123 **Heut ist der Mensch schön, jung und lang**
SSATB, 2 vln, 2 vla, bc
D-B Mus. ms. 6470, no. 6 (Bokemeyer)
score
DMA 3/2060

F0124 **Ich sage euch, es sei denn eure Gerechtigkeit**
SSTB, 2 vln, 2 vla, bc
6th Sunday after Trinity
D-B Mus. ms. 6470, no. 1 (Bokemeyer)
score
DMA 3/2061
Kümmerling, p. 62 attributes authorship to
A. Pfleger

F0125 **Ich vergesse was dahinter ist**
SSATB, 2 vln, 2 vla, bc
D-B Mus. ms. 6470, no. 11 (Bokemeyer)
score
DMA 3/2062

F0126 **Ich will den Herren loben allzeit**
ATB, 2 vln, bc
D-B Mus. ms. 6470, no. 18 (Bokemeyer)
score
DMA 3/2063

F0127 **Ihr Sünder tretet bald herzu**
SSATB, 2 vln, bsn, bc
11th Sunday after Trinity
D-B Mus. ms. 6470, no. 27 (Bokemeyer)
score
DMA 3/2064

F0128 **Kommet her zu mir, alle**
STTB, 2 vln, 2 vla, bc
D-B Mus. ms. 6470, no. 3 (Bokemeyer)
score
DMA 3/2065

F0129 **Kommet, ihr Sünder**
SSATB, 2 vln, bc
D-B Mus. ms. 6472, no. 25 (Bokemeyer)
score
DMA 3/771

FÖRTSCH, Johann Philipp (*continued*)

F0130 **Kommt herzu, lasset uns dem Herren frohlocken**
SSATB, 2 vln, 2 vla, bc
D-B Mus. ms. 6470, no. 25 (Bokemeyer)
score
DMA 3/2067

F0131 **Kommt, lasset uns gehen gen Bethlehem**
SATTB, 2 vln, bc
D-B Mus. ms. 6470, no. 28 (Bokemeyer)
score
DMA 3/2066

F0132 **Man wird zu Zion sagen**
SSB, 2 vln, 2 vla, bc
D-B Mus. ms. 6470, no. 10 (Bokemeyer)
score
DMA 3/2068

F0133 **Meine Augen rennen mit Wasserbächen**
SSATB, 2 vln, bc
D-B Mus. ms. 6470, no. 20 (Bokemeyer)
score
DMA 3/2069

F0134 **Mensch, was du tust, bedenk das Ende**
SSATB, 2 vln, 2 vla, bsn, bc
1st Sunday after Trinity
D-B Mus. ms. 6470, no. 23 (Bokemeyer)
score
DMA 3/2070

F0135 **Nun aber geh ich hin zu dem der mich gesandt hat**
SSATB, 2 vln, 2 vla, bc
D-B Mus. ms. 6471, no. 8 (Bokemeyer)
score
DMA 3/1186

F0136 **Nun danket alle Gott**
SATTB, 2 vln, 2 vla, 2 clar, bc
D-B Mus. ms. 6472, no. 5 (Bokemeyer)
score
DMA 3/773

F0137 **Nun ist des Satans Macht gefället**
SSATB, 2 vln, 2 vla, 2 clar, bc
D-B Mus. ms. 6470, no. 14 (Bokemeyer)
score
DMA 3/2071

F0138 **Sage mir an, du, den meine Seele liebet**
SSTB, 2 vln, 2 vla, bc
Whit Tuesday
D-B Mus. ms. 6471, no. 16 (Bokemeyer)
score
DMA 3/1187

F0139 **Saget der Tochter Zion**
SATB, 2 vln, 2 vla, bc
D-B Mus. ms. 6470, no. 17 (Bokemeyer)
score
DMA 3/2072

F0140 **Sanctus**
SATB, 2 vln, 2 vla, bc
US-Wc *case* M2113.A20
score

F0141 **Schaffe in mir, Gott, ein reines Herz**
SSB, 3 vla, bc
D-B Mus. ms. 6471, no. 12 (Bokemeyer)
score
DMA 3/1188

F0142 **Schmecket und sehet wie freundlich der Herr ist**
SSTB, 2 vln, 2 vla, bc
13th Sunday after Trinity
D-B Mus. ms. 6471, no. 19 (Bokemeyer)
score
DMA 3/1189

F0143 **Seht euch vor, vor den falschen Propheten**
SSATB, 2 vln, bc
D-B Mus. ms. 6470, no. 9 (Bokemeyer)
score
DMA 3/2074

F0144 **Selig sind die Toten**
SSATB, 2 vla, 2 gamba, bc
D-B Mus. ms. 6471, no. 2 (Bokemeyer)
score
DMA 3/1190

F0145 **Selig sind die zur Hochzeit des Lammes berufen sind**
SSATB, 2 vln, 2 vla, bc
D-B Mus. ms. 6470, no. 24 (Bokemeyer)
score
DMA 3/2073

F0146 **Siehe, der Herr kommt mit viel tausend**
ATB, 2 vln, 2 vla, bc
D-B Mus. ms. 6470, no. 16 (Bokemeyer)
score
DMA 3/2075

F0147 **Siehe, um Trost war mir sehr bange**
SSB, 2 vln, 2 vla, bc
D-B Mus. ms. 6470, no. 8 (Bokemeyer)
score
DMA 3/2076
Ed. Kümmerling (Merseburger EM 902)

F0148 **Singet dem Herren**
ATB, 3 vln, bc

D-B Mus. ms. 6472, no. 7 (Bokemeyer)
score
DMA 3/775

F0149 Uns ist ein Kind geboren
SSATB, 2 vln, 2 vla, 2 clar, bc
D-B Mus. ms. 6470, no. 30 (Bokemeyer)
score
DMA 3/2077

F0150 Unser Leben wäret siebenzig Jahr
SSATTBB, 4 vln, 2 vla, 4 gamba, bsn, bc
D-B Mus. ms. 6470, no. 19 (Bokemeyer)
score
DMA 3/2078

F0151 Verbum caro factum est
ATB, 2 vln, bc
D-B Mus. ms. 6472, no. 29 (Bokemeyer)
score
DMA 3/778

F0152 Wahrlich, ich sage euch
SSATB, 2 vln, 2 vla, bc
5th Sunday after Easter
D-B Mus. ms. 6471, no. 20 (Bokemeyer)
score
DMA 3/1191

F0153 Was werden wir essen
SSATB, 2 vln, 2 vla, bc
D-B Mus. ms. 6472, no. 9 (Bokemeyer)
score
DMA 3/779

F0154 Weh denen, die auf Erden wohnen
STB, vln, 2 vla, bc
D-B Mus. ms. 6471, no. 18 (Bokemeyer)
score
DMA 3/1192
Zelle (1893), pp. 13-20

F0155 Weichet, Kummer, Angst, und Not
SATB, 2 vln, bc
Easter Tuesday
D-B Mus. ms. 6470, no. 13 (Bokemeyer)
score
DMA 3/2080

F0156 Wer Jesum liebt
SATTB, 2 vln, 2 vla, bc
2nd Day of Christmas
D-B Mus. ms. 6470, no. 12 (Bokemeyer)
score
DMA 3/2081

F0157 Wer mich liebet, der wird mein Wort halten
SSTB, 2 vln, 2 vla, 2 clar, bc
Pentecost

D-B Mus. ms. 6471, no. 15 (Bokemeyer)
score
DMA 3/1193

F0158 Wer wird, o Gott, der dir vertraut
SSTB, 2 vln, 2 vla, bc
D-B Mus. ms. 6470, no. 4 (Bokemeyer)
score
DMA 3/2079

F0159 Wie hör ich das von dir
SSATB, 2 vln, bc
D-B Mus. ms. 6471, no. 10 (Bokemeyer)
score
DMA 3/1194

F0160 Willkommen, höchstes Heil der Welt
SATB, 2 vln, 2 vla, bsn, bc
Christmas Day
D-B Mus. ms. 6472, no. 26 (Bokemeyer)
score
DMA 3/780

F0161 Wohl dem, der den Herren fürchtet
ATB, 2 vln, bsn, bc
D-B Mus. ms. 6471, no. 7 (Bokemeyer)
score
DMA 3/1195

F0162 Wohl dem, der nicht wandelt im Rat der Gottlosen
SSATB, 2 vln, 2 vla, bsn, bc
D-B Mus. ms. 6471, no. 5 (Bokemeyer)
score
DMA 3/1196

FRANCK, Johann Wolfgang (1644-ca. 1710)

F0163 Conturbatae sunt gentes
SSATBB, 2 vln, 2 vla, 2 corn, 4 clar, timp, bc
D-Bds Mus. ms. 30298, no. 12 (Bokemeyer)
score
DMA 2/471

F0164 Ich habe Lust abzuscheiden
SATB, 2 vln, 2 vla, bc
D-Bds Mus. ms. 30298, no. 11 (Bokemeyer)
score
DMA 2/473

F0165 Te Deum laudamus
SSATB, 2 vln, 2 vla, 2 corn, 2 clar, bc
D-Bds Mus. ms. 30298, no. 9 (Bokemeyer)
score
DMA 2/474

FRANCK, Michael (1609-1667)

F0166   **Auf, jauchzet Gott**
     See Wie lange wilt du mein O Herr

F0167   **Freud über alle Freude**
     SATB
     Funeral
     Coburg, 1653
       RISM F1782 (parts)

F0168   **Ist nicht der Menschen Leben**
     SATB
     Funeral of Johann Caspar Scherer
     Coburg, 1652
       RISM F1781, Reich 189 (score)
       DMA 63//216

F0169   **Siehe, wie fein und lieblich**
     5 vv
     Funeral
     Coburg, 1650
       RISM F1778 (score)

F0170   **Was hängst du, Erden-Mensch**
     SATB
     Funeral
     Coburg, 1666
       RISM F1783 (score)

F0171   **Wie lange willst du mein, O Herr**
     TTB
     Funeral
     Coburg, 1649
       RISM F1777 (score)

FRANCK, Peter (b. 1616)

F0172   **Bei vollem Kreuz in allen Nöten**
     SATB
     Funeral of Margarethe Styrtzel
     Coburg, n.d.
       RISM F1788, Reich 171 (score)
       DMA 56//216

F0173   **Christus, Christus, Christus ist mein Leben**
     SATB
     Funeral of Johannes Schulthesius
     Coburg, 1657
       RISM F1787, Reich 191 (score)
       DMA 63//124

F0174   **In Christo will ich sterben**
     SATB
     Funeral of Barbara Franck
     Coburg, 1649

       RISM F1785, Reich 186 (parts)
       DMA 63//218

F0175   **Wer will, mag immer hin zu leben lieben**
     SATB
     Funeral of Elisabeth Reimann
     Coburg, 1651
       RISM F1786, Reich 188 (score)
       DMA 61//111
     EdM 79, p. 4

FRANCK, Sebastian (1606-1668)

F0176   **O wie so gar selig ist doch der Christ**
     SSATB
     Wedding of Elias and Margarethe Barbara
     Schmidt
     n.p., 1659
       RISM F1791 (choirbook)
       DMA 56//218

FRITZIUS, Andreas

F0177   **Was prangst du, armer Madensack**
     SATB
     Funeral of Elisabeth Fabricius
     Stettin, 1656
       Reich 399

FROBERGER, Johann Jacob (1616-1667)

F0178   **Alleluia! Absorpta est mors in victoria**
     STB, 2 vln, bc
     S-Uu 83:49, fol. 6v-9 (Düben)
     tablature
     S-Uu 23:12 (Düben)
     parts

F0179   **Apparuerunt apostolis**
     STB, 2 vln, bc
     S-Uu 83:50, fol. 8v-11 (Düben)
     tablature
     S-Uu 23:13 (Düben)
     parts

FUNCKE, Friedrich (1644-1699)

F0180   **Ach! Herr, ich warte auf dein Heil**
     5vv
     Funeral
     Lüneburg, 1665
     According to *New Grove*; not listed in RISM

F0181 Ach Herzeleid! ja dies lebenlose Leben
SSATTB, bc
Funeral of Leonhard von Dassel
Lüneburg, 1665
RISM F2098, Reich 279 (score)
DMA 63//120

F0182 Ach! was ist doch unser Leben
SSATTB, bc
Funeral of Johannes Lutterloh
Lüneburg, 1664
RISM F2097, Reich 278 (score)
DMA 63//114

F0183 Gelobet sei der Herr aus Zion
SATB, SATB, 2 vln/corn, 2 vla/tbn, bsn, bc
In thanksgiving for the survival of the
tower of St. Johannes, Lüneburg,
through a lightning strike
Hamburg, 1666
RISM F2100 (parts)
DMA 1/998

F0184 Herr Gott, Vater im Himmel
SATB, SATB, bc
D-Lr Mus. ant. pract. K.N. 207/9
score and parts
DMA 1/1140

F0185 Hier kurze Zeit, ach Leid
SSATTB
Funeral for Heinrich Krolow
Lüneburg, 1666
RISM F2099, Reich 280 (score)
DMA 63//113

F0186 Ist Gott für uns
SATB, 2 vln, tbn, bc
Hamburg, 1682
RISM F2102 (parts)
DMA 56//213

F0187 Matthäus Passion
SATB, 3 vla, vlne, bc
D-Lr Mus. ant. pract. K.N. 201
score and parts
DMA 1/1229
Das Chorwerk 78-79 (1961)
Attributed by Birke (1958)

F0188 Was ist doch diese Welt
SSATB, bc
Funeral of Richel Dorothea Lafferdt
Lüneburg, 1669
RISM F2101, Reich 281 (parts)
DMA 69//5

FURCHHEIM, Johann Wilhelm (1635/40-1682)

F0189 Lobe den Herren, meine Seele
SATB, 2 corn, 2 clar, bsn, bc
D-Bds Mus. ms. 30298, no. 15
(Bokemeyer)
score

FUX, Vincent

F0190 Egredimini filiae Sion
SSATTB, 2 vln, 4 vla, 4 tbn, bc
CS-KRa II, 180
parts
microfilm: US-SY

F0191 Missa Ad littora
SSATBB, 2 vln, 2 vla, vlne, bc
CS-KRa I, 53
parts
microfilm: US-SY

F0192 Missa Beatae Mariae Virginis
STTB, 2 vln, 2 vla, gamba, bc
CS-KRa I, 47
parts
microfilm: US-SY

F0193 Missa Corta Sancti Matthaei
SATB, 2 vln, 2 vla, 4 tbn, bc
A-KR Kasten C, Fasc., 25, no. 784
parts

F0194 Missa in honorem Sanctae Barbarae
SSATB, 2 corn, bc
S-Uu 54:14
parts

F0195 Missa Sanctae Caeciliae
SSATB, 4 vla, bc
CS-KRa I, 54
parts
microfilm: US-SY

F0196 Missa Sanctae Catharinae
SATB, 2 vln, vla, 3 tbn, bc
CS-KRa I, 49
parts
microfilm: US-SY

F0197 Missa Sanctae Monicae
SATTB, 2 vln, 3 vla, bc
CS-KRa I, 50
parts
microfilm: US-SY

FUX, Vincent (*continued*)

F0198 **Missa Sancti Ignatii**
SSAATTBB, 2 vln, 4 vla, gamba, 2 corn,
2 clar, 4 tbn, vlne, bc
CS-KRa I, 45
parts
microfilm: US-SY

F0199 **Missa Xaveriana**
SATB, 3 vln, 3 vla, 3 tbtta, 4 tbn, bc

CS-KRa I, 52
parts
microfilm: US-SY
A-KR Ms. Kasten C, Fasc. 25, no. 783
parts

F0200 **Nisi Dominus**
SATB, bc
D-B Mus. ms. 6818 (Bokemeyer)
score

G

GARTHOFF, Heinrich David (fl. 1698-1708)

G0001   **Alleluia, lobt mit Freuden**
        SATB, 2 vln, corn, bc
        S-L M48 (Wenster collection)
        parts

G0002   **An welchem Tage werden die meisten Sünden begangen?**
        SATB, 2 vln, 2 vla, bc
        17th Sunday after Trinity
        D-Gs Cod. Ms. philos. 84e Garthoff 1
        score and parts

G0003   **Bei wem soll man in Angst und Not Hilfe suchen?**
        SATB, 2 vln, 2 vla, bc
        4th Sunday after Epiphany
        D-Gs Cod. Ms. philos. 84e Garthoff 2
        score and parts

G0004   **Das Verlangen der Elenden**
        SATB, 2 vln, 2 vla, bsn/vlne, bc
        D-F Ms. Ff. Mus. 189
        parts

G0005   **Du tust mir kund**
        SATB, 2 vln, 2 vla, 2 clar, bsn, bc
        Easter Sunday
        D-LUC (1714)
        parts

G0006   **Herr allmächtiger Gott**
        SATB, 2 vln, 2 vla, bc
        D-Gs Cod. Ms. philos. 84e Garthoff 4
        score and parts

G0007   **Ich habe Lust abzuscheiden**
        SSATB
        D-Gs Cod. Ms. philos. 84e Garthoff 5
        score and parts

G0008   **In deine Hände befehl ich meinen Geist**
        SATB, 2 vln, 3 vla, bc
        D-F Ms. Ff. Mus. 198
        parts

G0009   **Missa (brevis)**
        SATB, 2 vln, 2 vla, bc
        D-Gs Cod. Ms. philos. 84e Garthoff 6
        score and parts

G0010   **Über welche Große hat man sich sonderlich zu verwundern?**
        SATB, 2 vln, 2 vla, bc
        9th Sunday after Trinity
        D-Gs Cod. Ms. philos. 84e Garthoff 7
        score and parts

G0011   **Von welchem Gespräch hat man den größten Nutzen?**
        SATB, 2 vln, 2 vla, bc
        D-Gs Cod. Ms. philos. 84e Garthoff 9
        score and parts

G0012   **Was führen die Gläubigen vor einen Namen?**
        SATB, 2 vln, 2 vla, bc
        D-Gs Cod. Ms. philos. 84e Garthoff 10
        score and parts

G0013   **Was macht allen Trost der Christen?**
        SATB, 2 vln, 2 vla, bc
        Easter Monday
        D-Gs Cod. Ms. philos. 84e Garthoff 11
        score

GARTHOFF, Heinrich David – (*continued*)

G0014 **Was macht den Himmelsweg den Meisten so unangenehm?**
SATB, 2 vln/tpt, 2 vla, 2 ob, bc
Ascension
D-Gs Cod. Ms. philos. 84e Garthoff 12
score and parts

G0015 **Was scheint böse und ist doch immer gut?**
SATB, 2 vln, 2 vla, bc
Sunday after Ascension
D-Gs Cod. Ms. philos. 84e Garthoff 13
score and parts

G0016 **Was wird am jüngsten Tage erschrecklich zu hören sein?**
SATB, 2 vln, 2 vla, bc
D-Gs Cod. Ms. philos. 84e Garthoff 14
score and parts

G0017 **Welch Gebet ist vergeblich?**
SATB, 2 vln, 2 vla, bc
11th Sunday after Trinity
D-Gs Cod. Ms. philos. 84e Garthoff 30
score and parts

G0018 **Welche Kunst wird in der Welt am wenigsten?**
SATB, 2 vln, 2 vla, bc
3rd Sunday after Trinity
D-Gs Cod. Ms. philos. 84e Garthoff 15
score and parts

G0019 **Welcher Mensch ist recht glückselig zu schätzen?**
SATB, 2 vln, 2 vla, bc
1st Sunday of Lent
D-Gs Cod. Ms. philos. 84e Garthoff 16
score
D-Gs Cod. Ms. philos. 84e Garthoff 17
score and parts

G0020 **Welcher Schade ist der größte?**
SATB, 2 vln, 2 vla, bc
D-Gs Cod. Ms. philos. 84e Garthoff 18
score and parts

G0021 **Welches ist das beste an einem Christen?**
SATB, 2 vln, 2 vla, bc
7th Sunday after Trinity
D-Gs Cod. Ms. philos. 84e Garthoff 19
score and parts

G0022 **Welches ist das größte Unglück?**
SATB, 2 vln, 2 vla, bc
Septuagesima
D-Gs Cod. Ms. philos. 84e Garthoff 20
score and parts

G0023 **Welches ist das lieblichste Bild?**
SATB, 2 vln, 2 vla, bc
D-Gs Cod. Ms. philos. 84e Garthoff 21
score and parts

G0024 **Welches ist der beste Nutz?**
SATB, 2 vln, 2 vla, bc
Quinquagesima
D-Gs Cod. Ms. philos. 84e Garthoff 22
score and parts

G0025 **Welches ist der beste Zeitvertrieb?**
SATB, 2 vln, 2 vla, bc
Visitation of the Virgin Mary
D-Gs Cod. Ms. philos. 84e Garthoff 23
score and parts

G0026 **Welches ist die allergrößte Untreu?**
SATB, 2 vln, 2 vla, bc
Pentecost
D-Gs Cod. Ms. philos. 84e Garthoff 24
score and parts

G0027 **Welches ist die beste und seligste Versammlung?**
SATB, 2 vln, 2 vla, bc
D-Gs Cod. Ms. philos. 84e Garthoff 25
score

G0028 **Welches ist die fröhlichste Botschaft?**
SATB, 2 vln, 2 vla, bc
Whit Monday
D-Gs Cod. Ms. philos. 84e Garthoff 26
score and parts

G0029 **Welches ist die schwerste Arbeit?**
SATB, 2 vln, 2 vla, bc
5th Sunday after Easter
D-Gs Cod. Ms. philos. 84e Garthoff 27
score and parts

G0030 **Welches ist die schwerste und doch sehr vergebliche Arbeit?**
SATB, 2 vln, 2 vla, bc
Purification of the Virgin Mary
D-Gs Cod. Ms. philos. 84e Garthoff 28
score and parts

G0031 **Welches ist für das köstlichste und wunderbarste Wasser?**
SATB, 2 vln, 2 vla, bc
3rd Sunday after Easter
D-Gs Cod. Ms. philos. 84e Garthoff 29
score and parts

G0032 **Wer hat die wenigsten Freunde?**
SATB, 2 vln, 2 vla, bc
2nd Sunday of Lent

D-Gs Cod. Ms. philos. 84e Garthoff 31
   parts
D-Gs Cod. Ms. philos. 84e Garthoff 32
   score

G0033   **Wer hat in der Welt die größte Anfechtung erduldet?**
SATB, 2 vln, 2 vla, bc
Sexagesima
D-Gs Cod. Ms. philos. 84e Garthoff 33
   score and parts

G0034   **Wer hat sich jemals am elendigsten entschuldiget?**
SATB, 2 vln, 2 vla, bc
2nd Sunday after Trinity
D-Gs Cod. Ms. philos. 84e Garthoff 34
   score

G0035   **Wer ist der allergelehrteste Mensch?**
SATB, 2 vln, 2 vla, bc
3rd Day of Christmas
D-Gs Cod. Ms. philos. 84e Garthoff 35
   score and parts

G0036   **Wer kann uns in unserem Beruf den größten Trost geben?**
SATB, 2 vln, 2 vla, bc
D-Gs Cod. Ms. philos. 84e Garthoff 36
   score and parts

G0037   **Wie kann man Gott kurz und am besten rühmen?**
SATB, 2 vln, 2 vla, bc
12th Sunday after Trinity
D-Gs Cod. Ms. philos. 84e Garthoff 37 and 38
   score and parts

G0038   **Wo ist jemals ein unendlicher Einzug vorgangen?**
SATB, 2 vln, 2 vla, tpt, bc
Palm Sunday
D-Gs Cod. Ms. philos. 84e Garthoff 42
   score

G0039   **Wo ließet man in der Schrift von einem fröhlichen?**
SATB, 2 vln/tpt, 2 vla, bc
Easter Sunday
D-Gs Cod. Ms. philos. 84e Garthoff 43 (1721)
   score and parts

G0040   **Wodurch bringet der Satan viel Menschen ins Verderben?**
SATB, 2 vln, 2 vla, bc
5th Sunday after Epiphany
D-Gs Cod. Ms. philos. 84e Garthoff 39
   score and parts

G0041   **Wodurch wird Gotte seine Ehre geraubt?**
SATB, 2 vln, 2 vla, bc
6th Sunday after Trinity

D-Gs Cod. Ms. philos. 84e Garthoff 40
   score and parts

G0042   **Wofür danken die Menschen Gott am wenigsten?**
SATB, 2 vln, 2 vla, tpt, bc
Christmas Day
D-Gs Cod. Ms. philos. 84e Garthoff 41
   score and parts

G0043   **Womit erfreuet Gott die Menschen am allermeisten?**
SATB, 2 vln, 2 vla, bc
4th Sunday of Lent
D-Gs Cod. Ms. philos. 84e Garthoff 44
   score and parts

G0044   **Womit kann ein Mensch im Himmel Freude anrichten?**
SATB, 2 vln, 2 vla, bc
3rd Sunday after Trinity
D-Gs Cod. Ms. philos. 84e Garthoff 45
   score and parts

G0045   **Womit kann man sich in Not und Tod recht kräftig trösten?**
SATB, 2 vln, 2 vla, bc
24th Sunday after Trinity
D-Gs Cod. Ms. philos. 84e Garthoff 46
   score and parts

GARTNER, Christian

G0046   **Ach! Ihr Lieben und Bekannten, lasset ab von Traurigkeit**
SSATTB
Funeral of Jochin Wilchen von Weihe
Lüneburg, 1653
   RISM G445 (choirbook)
   DMA 61//225

G0047   **Es ist allhier auf Erden**
SSATTB
Funeral of Catharina Getrude von Weyhe
Hamburg, 1654
   RISM G446 (choirbook)
   DMA 61//196

GASTORIUS, Severus (1646-1682)

G0048   **Die Gerechten werden ewiglich leben**
SSATB, bc
Funeral of Johann Jacob Botsack
Jena, 1672
   RISM G560, Reich 160 (parts)
   DMA 63//122

GASTORIUS, Severus (*continued*)

G0049 **Du aber gehe hin**
SSATB, bc
Funeral of Johann Arnold Friderici
Jena, 1672
RISM G561, Reich 163 (parts)
DMA 63//127
Funeral of Christoph Philipp Richter
Jena, 1674
RISM G563 (parts)
DMA 56//227

G0050 **Es ist genug, so nimm**
SSATB, bc
Funeral of Christoph Philipp Richter
Jena, 1674
RISM G562, Reich 164 (parts)
DMA 63//117
D-Dlb Mus. ms. 2239-E-500 (Grimma U
419/P 16)
parts

G0051 **O Trauer-Fall! Der mich fast ganz entseelet**
SATB, bc
Funeral of Wilken von Berglasen
Jena, 1679
RISM G564, Reich 168 (parts)
DMA 56//227

GAYERSBACH

G0052 **Dies ist der Tag den der Herr gemacht hat**
SSATB, 2 vln, 2 vla, 2 tbtta, vlne, bc
Easter
D-F Ms. Ff. Mus. 205
score and parts

GEIST, Christian (1640-1711)

G0053 **Adjuro vos o filiae Jerusalem**
SSSB, 2 vln, vlne, bc
S-Uu 82:2:1, fol. 1v-3 (Düben)
tablature
DMA 3/250
S-Uu 54:15 (Düben)
parts (SSS & vlne only)
DMA 3/250

G0054 **Alleluia. Absorpta est mors**
SSB, 2 vln, vlne, bc
S-Uu 84:68, fol. 7v-9 (Düben) (1676)
tablature

S-Uu 25:2 (Düben)
parts
EdM ser. 1, vol. 48, pp. 41-49

G0055 **Alleluia. Surrexit pastor bonus qui animam**
SSTTB, 2 vln, bc
S-Uu 84:67, fol. 6v-8 (Düben)
tablature
DMA 3/2086

G0056 **Alleluia. Virgo Deum genuit quem divina voluit**
SSB, 2 vln, gamba, bc
S-Uu 84:53, fol. 13v-15 (Düben)
tablature
S-Uu 25:3 (Düben) (1672)
parts

G0057 **Altitudo quid hic jaces**
SSB, 2 vln, bc
S-Uu 84:56, fol. 17v-20 (Düben)
tablature
S-Uu 25:4 (Düben) (1670)
parts
EdM ser. 1, vol. 48, pp. 50-60

G0058 **Die mit Tränen säen**
SSATB, 2 fl, 3 gamba, bc
S-Uu 84:14 (Düben)
tablature
S-Uu 25:7 (Düben)
parts
EdM ser. 1, vol. 48, pp. 105-20

G0059 **Dieses ist der Tag der Wonne**
SAB, 2 vln, vlne/gamba, bc
S-Uu 25:6 (Düben) (1680)
parts

G0060 **Dixit Dominus Domino meo**
SATB, 2 vln, bc
S-Uu 25:8 (Düben) (1673)
parts
EdM ser. 1, vol. 48, pp. 72-87

G0061 **Domine in virtute tua laetabiter Rex**
SSATB, 2 vln, 2 vla, 2 clar, gamba, vlne, bc
S-Uu 84:16, fol. 4v-8 (Düben)
tablature
DMA 3/251
S-Uu 54:16 (Düben) (1672)
parts
DMA 3/251

G0062 **Domine ne secundum peccata**
SSTB, 2 vln, bc
S-Uu 84:33, fol. 6v-8 (Düben)
tablature

S-Uu 25:9 (Düben)
parts
EdM ser. 1, vol. 48, pp. 88-97

G0063 Domine quidas salutem (I)
SSATB, 2 vln, vla, gamba, vlne, org
S-Uu 84:19, fol. 1v-7v (Düben)
tablature
DMA 3/1200
S-Uu 54:18 (Düben) (1670)
parts
DMA 3/1200

G0064 Domine quidas salutem (II)
SSTTB, 2 vln, 2 vla, 2 clar, vlne, bsn, bc
S-Uu 84:15, fol. 1v-5 (Düben)
tablature
DMA 3/252
S-Uu 54:17 (Düben) (1672)
parts
DMA 3/252

G0065 Domine quidas salutem (III)
SSATB, 3 vln, vla, vlne, bc
S-Uu 84:65, fol. 1v-4 (Düben) (1676)
tablature
S-Uu 25:10 (Düben) (1675)
parts

G0066 Emendemus in melius quae ignoranter peccavimus
SSTB, 2 vln, vlne, bc
S-Uu 86:19, fol. 2-3 (Düben) (1676)
tablature
S-Uu 25:11 (Düben) (1676)
parts

G0067 Exaudi Deus orationem meam
SSATB, 2 vln, 3 vla, 2 clar, vlne, bc
S-Uu 84:17, fol. 8v-12 (Düben)
tablature
S-Uu 25:12 (Düben)
parts

G0068 Festiva laeta canticis festa jucunda plausibus
SSB, 2 vln, gamba, bc
S-Uu 84:47, fol. 7v-9 (Düben)
tablature
S-Uu 25:13 (Düben)
parts

G0069 Haec est dies quam fecit Dominus
SSB, 2 vln, theorbo, bc
S-Uu 84:49, fol. 9v-10 (Düben)
tablature
S-Uu 25:14 (Düben)
parts

G0070 In te Domine speravi (I)
SSB, 2 vln, gamba, bc
S-Uu 84:29, fol. 2v-4 (Düben)
tablature
S-Uu 25:17 (Düben)
parts

G0071 In te Domine speravi (II)
SATB, 4 instr, bc
S-Uu 84:66, fol. 3v-7 (Düben)
tablature
DMA 3/2087

G0072 Invocavit me et ego exaudiam
SSTB, 2 vln, 2 vla, vlne, theorbo, bc
S-Uu 84:32, fol. 5v-7 (Düben)
tablature
S-Uu 25:18 (Düben)
parts

G0073 Jesu, delitium vultus
SATB, 2 vln, bc
S-Uu 84:20, fol. 10v-13 (Düben) (1671)
tablature
DMA 3/253
S-Uu 25:15 (Düben) (1679)
parts
DMA 3/253
D-F Ms. Ff. Mus. 204 (1689)
parts

G0074 Laudate, pueri, Dominum
SSB, 3 vln, vlne, org
S-Uu 84:30, fol. 3v-5 (Düben) (1674)
tablature
S-Uu 43:13 (Düben)
parts

G0075 Laudet Deum mea gloria laudent eum mea
SSB, 2 vln, gamba, bc
S-Uu 84:41, fol. 24v-27 (Düben)
tablature
S-Uu 26:2 (Düben) (1675)
parts
Ed. Bo Lundgren (Stockholm, Gehrmans no. 4743, 1953)

G0076 Media vita in morta sumus
SSB, 4 vla, vlne, bc
S-Uu 26:3 (Düben); 54:19 (Düben) (1671)
parts

G0077 O caeli sapientia, Jesu, spes mentis unica
SSB, bc
S-Uu 26:4 (Düben) (1670)
parts

GEIST, Christian (*continued*)

G0078   **O immensa bonitas entangit divinitas**
SSB, 2 vln, gamba, bc
S-Uu 84:27, fol. 23v-26 (Düben) (1671)
tablature
DMA 3/2089

G0079   **O Jesu amantissime, quem animam desiderat**
SSB, 2 vln, bc
S-Uu 84:36, fol. 14v-17 (Düben)
tablature

G0080   **O Jesu, dulcis dilectio**
SST, 2 vln, gamba, bc
S-Uu 84:40, fol. 23v-25 (Düben) (1675)
tablature
S-Uu 26:5 (Düben)
parts

G0081   **O jucunda dies, o fortunata dies**
SSB, 2 vln, theorbo, bc
S-Uu 84:48, fol. 8v-10 (Düben)
tablature
S-Uu 26:6 (Düben)
parts

G0082   **O piissime Jesu, ad te o solus mea**
SATB, 3 vla, bc
S-Uu 85:47 (Düben) (1674)
tablature and bc part
DMA 3/2090

G0083   **Pastores dicite quidnam vidistis**
STTB, 2 vln, bc
S-Uu 84:54, fol. 14v-15 (Düben)
tablature (incomplete)
S-Uu 26:9 (Düben) (1672)
parts
EdM ser. 1, vol. 48, pp. 98-104

G0084   **Qui habitat in adjutorio**
SATB, 2 vln, vla, gamba, vlne, bc
S-Uu 84:31, fol. 4v-6 (Düben)
tablature
S-Uu 26:11 (Düben)
parts

G0085   **Qui hostis in caelis accurre**
SSATB, 2 vln, 2 vla, 2 clar, vlne, bc
S-Uu 84:18, fol. 12v-16 (Düben)
tablature
DMA 3/1201
S-Uu 54:20 (Düben) (1672)
parts
DMA 3/1201

G0086   **Resonet in laudibus cum jucundis plausibus**
SSB, 2 vln, vlne, bc
S-Uu 84:43, fol. 3v-5 (Düben)

tablature
S-Uu 26:12 (Düben)
parts
Ed. Grusnick, *Die Düben-Sammlung* 1

G0087   **Schapa i migh, Gudh**
SSB, 2 vln, vla, bc
S-Uu 85:34b, fol. 7v-10 (Düben)
tablature
DMA 3/255
EdM ser. 1, vol. 48, pp. 61-71

G0088   **Schöpfe Hoffnung, meine Seele**
SSATB, 2 vln, bc
S-Uu 54:21 (Düben)
tablature
DMA 3/256
S-Uu 26:14 (Düben)
parts
DMA 3/256
EdM ser. 1, vol. 48, pp. 121-38

G0089   **Se univit Deus coeno factus homo homini**
SSB, 2 vln, vlne, bc
Christmas Day
S-Uu 84:55, fol. 16v-18 (Düben)
tablature
S-Uu 26:16 (Düben) (1670)
parts

G0090   **Selig, ja selig, wer willig erträget**
SSTB, 2 vln, gamba, bc
S-Uu 26:15 (Düben)
parts
DMA 3/257

G0091   **Tristis anima cur langues**
SATB, 2 vln, bc
D-B Mus. ms. 7310, no. 1 (Bokemeyer)
score

G0092   **Veni Sancte Spiritus repletuorum corda fidelium**
SSB, 2 vln, vla, theorbo, bc
S-Uu 85:34a, fol. 6v-8 (Düben)
tablature
DMA 3/262
S-Uu 26:21 (Düben)
parts
DMA 3/262

G0093   **Vide, pater, mi vide dolores**
SST, 2 vln, bsn, bc
D-B Mus. ms. 7310, no. 2 (Bokemeyer)
score
S-Uu 46:23 (Düben)
parts
S-Uu 84:35, fol. 12v-15 and 84:62 (Düben)
tablature

GERSTENBÜTTEL, Joachim (ca. 1650-1721)

G0094   **Ach Herr, laß deine liebe Engelein**
    SAB, 2 vla, 2 clar, timp, bsn, bc
    D-Bds Mus. ms. autogr. G. Oesterreich 5
    (Bokemeyer) (1694)
    score
    Attributed by Krummacher. *See*
    Krummacher 1965, p. 517

G0095   **Ach Herr, wie ist meiner Feinde**
    SSATB, 2 vln, 2 vla, bsn, bc
    D-Bds Mus. ms. 7310, no. 26 (Bokemeyer)
    (1686)
    score

G0096   **Da die Zeit erfüllet war**
    SAB, 2 vln, bsn, bc
    D-Bds Mus. ms. 7310, no. 15 (Bokemeyer)
    score

G0097   **Dazu ist erschienen der Sohn Gottes**
    SSATB, 2 vln, 2 vla, bsn, bc
    D-Bds Mus. ms. 7310, no. 19 (Bokemeyer)
    score

G0098   **Der Gerechte wird grünen**
    SATB, 2 vln, bsn, bc
    D-Bds Mus. ms. 7310, no. 28 (Bokemeyer)
    score

G0099   **Der Herr ist mein Hirte**
    SSB, 2 vln, bsn, bc
    D-Bds Mus. ms. 7310, no. 23 (Bokemeyer)
    score

G0100   **Der Herr sprach zu meinem Herren**
    SSATTB, 2 vln, 3 vla, bsn, bc
    D-Bds Mus. ms. 7310, no. 11 (Bokemeyer)
    score

G0101   **Die Güte des Herrn ists**
    ATB, 2 vln, 2 vla, bc
    D-Bds Mus. ms. 7310, no. 18 (Bokemeyer)
    score

G0102   **Erhalt uns, Herr, bei deinem Wort**
    SSATB, 2 vln, 2 vla, bsn, bc
    D-Bds Mus. ms. 7310, no. 7 (Bokemeyer)
    (1695)
    score

G0103   **Gelobet sei der Herr täglich**
    SAT, 2 vln, bc
    D-Bds Mus. ms. 7310, no. 4 (Bokemeyer)
    score

G0104   **Gelobet sei Gott**
    SATB, 2 vln, bsn, bc
    D-Bds Mus. ms. 7310, no. 14 (Bokemeyer)
    score

G0105   **Habe deine Lust an dem Herrn**
    SATB, 2 vln, 2 vla, bsn, bc
    D-Bds Mus. ms. 7310, no. 27 (Bokemeyer)
    score

G0106   **Herr, erhöre mein Gebet**
    SSATB, 2 vln, 2 vla, bsn, bc
    D-Bds Mus. ms. 7310, no. 30 (Bokemeyer)
    score

G0107   **Heut triumphieret Gottes Sohn**
    STB, 2 clar, timp, bc
    D-Bds Mus. ms. 30242, no. 14 (Bokemeyer)
    score
    Attributed by Krummacher. *See*
    Krummacher 1967, p. 517

G0108   **Ich bin ein verwirret und verloren Schaf**
    SATB, 2 vln, vltta, bsn, bc
    D-Bds Mus. ms. 7310, no. 31 (Bokemeyer)
    score

G0109   **Ich schreie zu dem Herrn**
    SSATB, 2 vln, 2 vla, bsn, bc
    D-Bds Mus. ms. 7310, no. 16 (Bokemeyer)
    score

G0110   **In dich hab ich gehoffet**
    SSATB, 2 vln, 2 vla, bc
    D-Bds Mus. ms. 7310, no. 6 (Bokemeyer)
    score

G0111   **Lieber Herre Gott, weck uns auf**
    SATB, 2 vln, bc
    D-Bds Mus. ms. 7310, no. 17 (Bokemeyer)
    score

G0112   **Lobet den Herrn, ihr seine Engel**
    SATB, 2 ob/vltta, 2 clar/ob, bsn, bc
    D-Bds Mus. ms. 7310, no. 25 (Bokemeyer)
    score

G0113   **O Vater aller Frommen**
    SSATB, 2 vln, 2 vla, bc
    D-Bds Mus. ms. 7310, no. 8 (Bokemeyer)
    score

G0114   **O welche eine Tiefe des Reichtums**
    SSAATB, 2 vln, 2 vla, bsn, bc
    Trinity
    D-Bds Mus. ms. 7310, no. 13 (Bokemeyer)
    score

G0115   **Sammelt euch Schätze**
    SSATB, 2 vln, 2 vla, bsn, bc
    D-Bds Mus. ms. 7310, no. 3 (Bokemeyer)
    score

G0116   **Träufelt, ihr Himmel, von oben**
    SSATB, 2 vln, bsn, bc
    D-Bds Mus. ms. 7310, no. 33 (Bokemeyer)
    score

GERSTENBÜTTEL, Joachim (*continued*)

G0117   **Waschet, reiniget euch**
SSTB, 2 vln, bsn, bc
D-Bds Mus. ms. 7310, no. 5 (Bokemeyer)
score

G0118   **Wenn wir in höchsten Nöten sein**
SSATB, 2 vln, 2 vla, bc
D-Bds Mus. ms. 7310, no. 29 (Bokemeyer)
score

G0119   **Wer sich rächet, an dem wird sich der Herr**
S solo, SSATB, 2 vln, 2 vla, bsn, bc
D-Bds Mus. ms. 7310, no. 22 (Bokemeyer)
score

G0120   **Wo der Herr nicht das Haus bauet**
SAB, 2 vln, bc
D-Bds Mus. ms. 7310, no. 32 (Bokemeyer)
score

G0121   **Wo Gott der Herr nicht bei uns hält**
SSATB, 2 vln, 2 vla, bsn, bc
D-Bds Mus. ms. 7310, no. 24 (Bokemeyer)
(1691)
score

G0122   **Wo soll ich fliehen hin**
SSATB, 2 vln, 2 vla, bsn, bc
D-Bds Mus. ms. 7310, no. 12 (Bokemeyer)
score

G0123   **Wohl dem der in Gottes Furcht steht**
SSATB, 2 vln, 2 vla, bsn, bc
D-Bds Mus. ms. 7310, no. 9 (Bokemeyer)
score

G0124   **Zweierlei bitt ich von dir**
SSATB, 2 vln, 2 vla, bsn, bc
D-Bds Mus. ms. 7310, no. 20 (Bokemeyer)
score

GIBELIUS, Otto

G0125   **Es ist alles ganz eitel**
SSATB, 3 vla, bc
Funeral of Christoph von Kannenberg
Minden, 1673
RISM G2005, Reich 288 (parts)
DMA 61//226

G0126   **Ich hab dich je und je geliebet**
SATB, 2 vln, vlne, bc
Funeral of Maria von Kannenberg
Minden, 1673
RISM G2006, Reich 289 (parts)
DMA 42//116

GLEICH, Andreas

G0127   **Selig sind die Toten**
SSAATTBB, bc
Funeral of Johann Stockelmann
Leipzig, 1651
RISM G2591, Reich 239

GLEITSMANN, Paul (d. 1710)

G0128   **Der Name des Herrn**
SATB, 2 vln, 2 vla, vlne, bc
D-B Mus. ms. 7686 (Erfurt)
parts (lacking vlne)

G0129   **Des Vaters Wort mein höchster Hort**
SATB, 2 vln, 2 vla, bsn, calizon, vc, vlne, bc
Christmas Day
D-LUC
score and parts

G0130   **Herr, nun lässest du deinen Diener**
SATB, 2 vln, 2 vla, vlne, bc
Purification of the Virgin
D-B Mus. ms. 7687 (Erfurt)
parts (lacking vlne)

G0131   **Lieblich und schön sein ist nichts**
SATB, 2 vln, 2 clar, bc
D-Gs Cod. Ms. philos. 84e Gleitsmann 1
score and parts

G0132   **Muß nicht der Mensch immer im Streit sein**
SATB, 2 vln, 2 vla, bc
F-Ssp

GLETLE, Johann Melchior (1626-1683)

COLLECTIONS

Expeditionis musicae classis I (1667)
RISM G2616 (parts)
DMA 2/1589

Expeditionis musicae classis II (1668)
RISM G2617 (parts)
DMA 3/545

Expeditionis musicae classis V (1681)
RISM G2621 (parts)
DMA 3/1473

WORKS

G0133   **Ave Maria (VII)**
ATB
Expeditionis musicae classis V, part 2, no. 7

G0134 **Ave Maria (VIII)**
ATB
Expeditionis musicae classis V, part 2, no. 8

G0135 **Ave Maria (IX)**
BBB
Expeditionis musicae classis V, part 2, no. 9

G0136 **Ave Maria (X)**
SSAT
Expeditionis musicae classis V, part 2, no. 10

G0137 **Ave Maria (XI)**
SATB, bc
Expeditionis musicae classis V, part 2, no. 11
SMd II, pp. 150-52

G0138 **Ave Maria (XIII)**
SSATB, 2 vln, 3 tbn, vlne, bc
Expeditionis musicae classis V, part 2, no. 13

G0139 **Beati omnes**
SSATB, 2 vln/cornettino, 3 vla/tbn, vlne, bc
Expeditionis musicae classis II, no. 15

G0140 **Beatus vir (I)**
SSATB, 2 vln/cornettino, 3 vla/tbn, vlne, bc
Expeditionis musicae classis II, no. 4

G0141 **Beatus vir (II)**
SSATB, 2 vln/cornettino, 3 vla/tbn, vlne, bc
Expeditionis musicae classis II, no. 21

G0142 **Beatus vir (III)**
SSATB, 2 vln/cornettino, 3 vla/tbn, vlne, bc
Expeditionis musicae classis II, no. 32

G0143 **Confitebor (I)**
SSATB, 2 vln/cornettino, 3 vla/tbn, vlne, bc
Expeditionis musicae classis II, no. 3

G0144 **Confitebor (II)**
SSATB, 2 vln/cornettino, 3 vla/tbn, vlne, bc
Expeditionis musicae classis II, no. 20

G0145 **Confitebor (III)**
SSATB, 2 vln/cornettino, 3 vla/tbn, vlne, bc
Expeditionis musicae classis II, no. 31

G0146 **Confitebor . . . quoniam audisti**
SSATB, 2 vln/cornettino, 3 vla/tbn, vlne, bc
Expeditionis musicae classis II, no. 16

G0147 **Credidi (I)**
SSATB, 2 vln/cornettino, 3 vla/tbn, vlne, bc
Expeditionis musicae classis II, no. 10

G0148 **Credidi (II)**
SSATB, 2 vln/cornettino, 3 vla/tbn, vlne, bc
Expeditionis musicae classis II, no. 27

G0149 **Cum jucunditate**
ATB, 2 vln, bsn/vla, bc
Expeditionis musicae classis I, no. 25

G0150 **De profundis**
SSATB, 2 vln/cornettino, 3 vla/tbn, vlne, bc
Expeditionis musicae classis II, no. 13

G0151 **Dixit Dominus (I)**
SSATB, 2 vln/cornettino, 3 vla/tbn, vlne, bc
Expeditionis musicae classis II, no. 2

G0152 **Dixit Dominus (II)**
SSATB, 2 vln/cornettino, 3 vla/tbn, vlne, bc
Expeditionis musicae classis II, no. 19

G0153 **Dixit Dominus (III)**
SSATB, 2 vln/cornettino, 3 vla/tbn, vlne, bc
Expeditionis musicae classis II, no. 30

G0154 **Domine ad adjuvandum (I)**
SSATB, 2 vln/cornettino, 3 vla/tbn, vlne, bc
Expeditionis musicae classis II, no. 1

G0155 **Domine ad adjuvandum (II)**
SSATB, 2 vln/cornettino, 3 vla/tbn, vlne, bc
Expeditionis musicae classis II, no. 18

G0156 **Domine ad adjuvandum (III)**
SSATB, 2 vln/cornettino, 3 vla/tbn, vlne, bc
Expeditionis musicae classis II, no. 29

G0157 **Domine probasti me**
SSATB, 2 vln/cornettino, 3 vla/tbn, vlne, bc
Expeditionis musicae classis II, no. 12

G0158 **Domus mea**
ATB, bc
Expeditionis musicae classis I, no. 13

G0159 **In convertendo**
SSATB, 2 vln/cornettino, 3 vla/tbn, vlne, bc
Expeditionis musicae classis II, no. 11

G0160 **In exitu**
SSATB, 2 vln/cornettino, 3 vla/tbn, vlne, bc
Expeditionis musicae classis II, no. 38

G0161 **Laetatus sum (I)**
SSATB, 2 vln/cornettino, 3 vla/tbn, vlne, bc
Expeditionis musicae classis II, no. 7

G0162 **Laetatus sum (II)**
SSATB, 2 vln/cornettino, 3 vla/tbn, vlne, bc
Expeditionis musicae classis II, no. 24

G0163 **Laetatus sum (III)**
SSATB, 2 vln/cornettino, 3 vla/tbn, vlne, bc
Expeditionis musicae classis II, no. 35

G0164 **Lauda Jerusalem (I)**
SSATB, 2 vln/cornettino, 3 vla/tbn, vlne, bc
Expeditionis musicae classis II, no. 9

G0165 **Lauda Jerusalem (II)**
SSATB, 2 vln/cornettino, 3 vla/tbn, vlne, bc
Expeditionis musicae classis II, no. 26

GLETLE, Johann Melchior (*continued*)

G0166 **Lauda Jerusalem (III)**
SSATB, 2 vln/cornettino, 3 vla/tbn, vlne, bc
Expeditionis musicae classis II, no. 37

G0167 **Laudate Dominum, omnes gentes (I)**
SSATB, 2 vln/cornettino, 3 vla/tbn, vlne, bc
Expeditionis musicae classis II, no. 6

G0168 **Laudate Dominum, omnes gentes (II)**
SSATB, 2 vln/cornettino, 3 vla/tbn, vlne, bc
Expeditionis musicae classis II, no. 23

G0169 **Laudate Dominum, omnes gentes (III)**
SSATB, 2 vln/cornettino, 3 vla/tbn, vlne, bc
Expeditionis musicae classis II, no. 34

G0170 **Laudate, pueri (I)**
SSATB, 2 vln/cornettino, 3 vla/tbn, vlne, bc
Expeditionis musicae classis II, no. 5

G0171 **Laudate, pueri (II)**
SSATB, 2 vln/cornettino, 3 vla/tbn, vlne, bc
Expeditionis musicae classis II, no. 22

G0172 **Laudate, pueri (III)**
SSATB, 2 vln/cornettino, 3 vla/tbn, vlne, bc
Expeditionis musicae classis II, no. 33

G0173 **Litaniae Lauretanae (I)**
SSATB, 2 vln/cornettino, 2 tbn/vla,
tbn/bsn, vlne, bc
Expeditionis musicae classis V, no. 1

G0174 **Litaniae Lauretanae (II)**
SSATB, 2 vln, 3 tbn, vlne, bc
Expeditionis musicae classis V, no. 2

G0175 **Litaniae Lauretanae (III)**
SSATB, 2 vln, 2 tbn/vla, tbn/bsn, vlne, bc
Expeditionis musicae classis V, no. 3

G0176 **Litaniae Lauretanae (IV)**
SSATB, 2 vln/corn, 2 vla/tbn, bsn/tbn,
vlne, bc
Expeditionis musicae classis V, no. 4

G0177 **Litaniae Lauretanae (V)**
SSATB, 2 vln, 2 vla/tbn, bsn/tbn, vlne, bc
Expeditionis musicae classis V, no. 5

G0178 **Litaniae Lauretanae (VI)**
SSATB, 2 vln, 2 vla/tbn, bsn/tbn, vlne, bc
Expeditionis musicae classis V, no. 6

G0179 **Litaniae Lauretanae (VII)**
SSATB, 2 vln, 2 vla/tbn, bsn/tbn, vlne, bc
Expeditionis musicae classis V, no. 7

G0180 **Litaniae Lauretanae (VIII)**
SSATB, 2 vln, 2 vla/tbn, bsn/tbn, vlne, bc
Expeditionis musicae classis V, no. 8

G0181 **Litaniae Lauretanae (IX)**
SSATB, 2 vln/corn, vlne, bc
Expeditionis musicae classis V, no. 9

G0182 **Litaniae Lauretanae (X)**
SSATB, vlne, bc
Expeditionis musicae classis V, no. 10

G0183 **Litaniae Lauretanae (XI)**
SSATB, 2 vln/corn, 2 vla/tbn, bsn/tbn,
vlne, bc
Expeditionis musicae classis V, no. 11

G0184 **Litaniae Lauretanae (XII)**
SSATB, 2 vln, 2 vla/tbn, vla/bsn, vlne, bc
Expeditionis musicae classis V, no. 12

G0185 **Litaniae Lauretanae (XIII)**
SSATB, 2 vln, 2 clar/cornettino, 2
vla/tbn, bsn/tbn, vlne, bc
Expeditionis musicae classis V, no. 13
SMd 2, pp. 101-44

G0186 **Litaniae Lauretanae (XIV)**
SSATB, 2 vln, clar, clar/cornettino, 2
vla/tbn, vlne, bc
Expeditionis musicae classis V, no. 14

G0187 **Litaniae Lauretanae (XV)**
SATB, 2 vln/corn, 2 vla/tbn, bsn/tbn,
vlne, bc
Expeditionis musicae classis V, no. 15

G0188 **Magnificat (I)**
SSATB, 2 vln/cornettino, 3 vla/tbn, vlne, bc
Expeditionis musicae classis II, no. 17
SMd II, pp. 45-54

G0189 **Magnificat (II)**
SSATB, 2 vln/cornettino, 3 vla/tbn, vlne, bc
Expeditionis musicae classis II, no. 28

G0190 **Magnificat (III)**
SSATB, 2 vln/cornettino, 3 vla/tbn, vlne, bc
Expeditionis musicae classis II, no. 39

G0191 **Memento**
SSATB, 2 vln/cornettino, 3 vla/tbn, vlne, bc
Expeditionis musicae classis II, no. 14

G0192 **Minentur turbines**
SSATB, bc
Expeditionis musicae classis I, no. 24

G0193 **Nisi Dominus (I)**
SSATB, 2 vln/cornettino, 3 vla/tbn, vlne, bc
Expeditionis musicae classis II, no. 8

G0194 **Nisi Dominus (II)**
SSATB, 2 vln/cornettino, 3 vla/tbn, vlne, bc
Expeditionis musicae classis II, no. 25

G0195 **Nisi Dominus (III)**
SSATB, 2 vln/cornettino, 3 vla/tbn, vlne, bc
Expeditionis musicae classis II, no. 36

G0196 **O aeternitas**
SSB, bc
Expeditionis musicae classis I, no. 16

G0197 **O Domine Dominator**
SSATBB, 2 vln, bc
Expeditionis musicae classis I, no. 36
A & T partbooks lack this piece, although
it is listed in the index of each

G0198 **O dulcissime Domine**
TTT/SSS/ATB, bc
Expeditionis musicae classis I, no. 8

G0199 **Omne quod habeo**
ATB, bc
Expeditionis musicae classis I, no. 10

G0200 **Qui sperat pascitur**
ATB, bc
Expeditionis musicae classis I, no. 11

G0201 **Quotiescunque diem**
SATB, bc
Expeditionis musicae classis I, no. 17

G0202 **Salve regina (I)**
ATB, bc
Expeditionis musicae classis I, no. 14
SMd II, pp. 12-18

G0203 **Salve regina (II)**
SSS/TTT, bc
Expeditionis musicae classis I, no. 15

G0204 **Salve Rex Christe**
ATB, bc
D-Dlb Mus. ms. 2242-E-500 (Grimma U
113/V 7)
parts

G0205 **Sicut petrum**
ATB, bc
Expeditionis musicae classis I, no. 12

G0206 **Supra dorsum meum**
ATB, bc
Expeditionis musicae classis I, no. 9

GNÜGE, Johann Christoph

G0207 **Nun empfind ich, daß es will**
SATB
Funeral of Georg Hoffmann
Coburg, 1670
RISM G2912, Reich 201 (score)
DMA 63//125

G0208 **Süßer Bräutgam meiner Seele**
SATB
Funeral of Anna Katharina Rauschardt
Coburg, 1666
RISM G2910, Reich 198 (choirbook)
DMA 63//126

G0209 **Wo soll ich mich hinkehren**
SATB
Funeral of Anna Hoffmann
Coburg, 1667
RISM G2911, Reich 197 (choirbook)
DMA 63//119

GÖLDEL, Johann

G0210 **Das ist gewißlich wahr**
SATB
Funeral of Johann Breithaupt
Gotha, 1682
RISM G2926, Reich 113 (score)
DMA 63//126

GRAETERUS, Georg Friderich

G0211 **Ach! wie schmerzlich wir begleiten**
SATB
Funeral of Jacob Lackorn
Schwäbisch Hall, 1655
RISM G3305 (score)
DMA 63//227

GROH, Heinrich

COLLECTION

Kleiner Andachts-Wecker (1662)
RISM G4649 (parts)
DMA 3/547

WORKS

G0212 **Ach, was soll ich armen machen**
SATB, bc
Kleiner Andachts-Wecker, no. 12

G0213 **Als Jesus schon am Kreuze stund**
SATB, bc
Lent
Kleiner Andachts-Wecker, no. 7

G0214 **Auf und jubiliert mit Herzen Matt und Sinn**
SATB, bc
Easter Sunday
Kleiner Andachts-Wecker, no. 8

GROH, Heinrich (*continued*)

G0215　**Das höchste Wort ward Fleisch**
　　　　SATB, bc
　　　　Christmas Day
　　　　Kleiner Andachts-Wecker, no. 6

G0216　**Daß mein Gemüt in eitel Freuden schwebet**
　　　　SATB, bc
　　　　Kleiner Andachts-Wecker, no. 14

G0217　**Dich meinen Schöpfer soll ich billig preisen**
　　　　SATB, bc
　　　　Kleiner Andachts-Wecker, no. 2

G0218　**Dir, mein Jesu, muß ich nun mit betrübten Herzen klagen**
　　　　SATB, bc
　　　　Kleiner Andachts-Wecker, no. 10

G0219　**Heiliger Geist, du Trost der Blöden**
　　　　SATB, bc
　　　　Pentecost
　　　　Kleiner Andachts-Wecker, no. 9

G0220　**In dieser Morgenstund, Jesus, laß mich singen**
　　　　SATB, bc
　　　　Kleiner Andachts-Wecker, no. 1

G0221　**Mein Gott, mein Fels und mein Stärk**
　　　　SATB, bc
　　　　Kleiner Andachts-Wecker, no. 5

G0222　**O blind-verstocktes Menschen Kind**
　　　　SATB, bc
　　　　Kleiner Andachts-Wecker, no. 11

G0223　**O Jesu, allmächtiger Held**
　　　　SATB, bc
　　　　Kleiner Andachts-Wecker, no. 15

G0224　**O sancta Trinitas**
　　　　SATTB, 4 vla, vlne, bsn, bc
　　　　S-Uu 54:31 (Düben)
　　　　　parts
　　　　DMA 1/2054

G0225　**O Vater, dein Versorgen hilfe mich**
　　　　SATB, bc
　　　　Kleiner Andachts-Wecker, no. 4

G0226　**Rorate caeli de super**
　　　　SATTB, 2 vln, 2 tbn, bomb, bc
　　　　D-Dlb Mus. ms. 1879-E-500 (Grimma U 143/V 30)
　　　　　parts

G0227　**Treuer Jesu, kein Gemüte**
　　　　SATB, bc
　　　　Kleiner Andachts-Wecker, no. 13

G0228　**Was ist dir, du betrübtes Herz**
　　　　SATB, bc
　　　　Kleiner Andachts-Wecker, no. 16

G0229　**Was mein schwacher Geist wird denken**
　　　　SATB, bc
　　　　Kleiner Andachts-Wecker, no. 3

G0230　**Weil uns dieses Jammer-Leben**
　　　　SATB, bc
　　　　Kleiner Andachts-Wecker, no. 18

G0231　**Wie kannst du doch, o Gott, so lange schauen**
　　　　SATB, bc
　　　　Kleiner Andachts-Wecker, no. 17

H

HAHN, Michael

H0001   **Herr, ich habe gesündiget im Himmel**
SATB, 2 vln, bc
S-Uu 27:2b (Düben)
parts

H0002   **O welch eine Tiefe**
TTB, 2 vln, bc
S-Uu 84:97 (Düben)
tablature

HAINLEIN, Paul (1626-1686)

H0003   **Ach liebster Gott! heut müssen wir anbinden**
(Samuel no. 16a)
SATB
Funeral of Sophia Müller
Nürnberg, 1660
RISM H1869 (score)
DMA 71//39

H0004   **Die sichre Welt läuft zum Verderben** (Samuel
no. 16b)
SATB
Funeral of Sophia Müller
Nürnberg, 1660
RISM H1869 (score)
DMA 71//39

H0005   **Es ist genug, mein Geist ist matt** (Samuel no. 20b)
SATB
Funeral of Johann Michael Dilherr
Nürnberg, 1669
RISM H1872, Reich 337 (parts)
DMA 1/755, 2/649

Funeral of Sigismund Abesser
Gotha, 1676
RISM AN2828, Reich 112 (parts)

H0006   **Hodie Christus natus est** (Samuel no. 42)
SSATTBB, SATB, 2 vln, vlne, bc
D-B Mus. ms. 10367
parts
DMA 3/275
PL-Kj Mus. ms. 40129, no. 12 (1658)
tablature
DTB 10 (Jg. 6/1), pp. 1-27

H0007   **Hör, liebe Seele, dir ruft der Herz** (Samuel no. 20a)
SSATB, 2 vln, 2 vla, bc
Funeral of Johann Michael Dilherr
Nürnberg, 1669
RISM H1873, Reich 337 (parts)
DMA 1/755, 2/649

H0008   **Ich hab ein guten Kampf gekämpft** (Samuel no. 5)
SATB
Funeral of Maria Endter
Nürnberg, 1657
RISM H1859, Reich 311 (score)
DMA 66//52

H0009   **Ich hab einen guten Kampf gekämpfet** (Samuel
no. 19)
SSATB, 2 vln, 2 vla, bc
Funeral of Leonhard Grundherr
Nürnberg, 1665
RISM H1871 (parts)
DMA 69//134, 70//160

H0010   **Ich halte es dafür, daß dieser Zeit Leiden**
(Samuel no. 12)
STB, vln, 2 vla, bc

HAINLEIN, Paul (*continued*)

Funeral of Daniel Schnabel
Nürnberg, 1659
  RISM H1866 (score)
  DMA 71//39
S-Uu 84:98 (Düben)
  tablature
  DMA 1/1582
S-Uu 27:4 (Düben)
  parts
  DMA 1/1582

H0011 **Ich laß ihn nicht, der sich gelassen** (Samuel no. 26b)
SATB
Funeral of Christoph Endter
Nürnberg, 1672
  RISM H1880, Reich 349 (score)
  DMA 66//52

H0012 **Meine Seele, sei zufrieden** (Samuel no. 24a)
SATB
Funeral of Anna Susanna Endter
Nürnberg, 1672
  RISM H1878, Reich 348 (score)
  DMA 75//40

H0013 **Miserere mei, Deus** (Samuel no. 45)
SATTB, 3 gamba, bc
D-Bds Mus. ms. 30210, no. 12 (Bokemeyer)
  score
  DMA 2/837

H0014 **Mit Dank leb' ich dir, Herr, verpflichtet**
(Samuel no. 24b)
SATB
Funeral of Anna Susanna Endter
Nürnberg, 1672
  RISM H1877, Reich 348 (score)
  DMA 75//40

H0015 **Nur immer selig so geendet** (Samuel no. 26a)
SATB
Funeral of Christoph Endter
Nürnberg, 1672
  RISM H1881, Reich 349 (score)
  DMA 66//52

H0016 **O altitudo** (Samuel no. 46)
SSATTB, 2 vln, 2 gamba, 2 vltta, bc
D-B Mus. ms. 10367/2
  parts
  DMA 3/276
PL-Kj Mus. ms. 40262
  tablature

H0017 **O harter Spalt! wenn Leib und Seel sich scheiden** (Samuel no. 8a)
STB, vln, vla, bc
Funeral of Wolfgang Frank
Nürnberg, 1658
  RISM H1861, Reich 313 (score)
  DMA 66//52

H0018 **So geht ein alter Ehren-Greise** (Samuel no. 38a)
SATB
Funeral of Georg Kamb
Nürnberg, 1686
  RISM H1891 (score)
  DMA 75//34

H0019 **Vater-Herz! so geh nun schlafen** (Samuel no. 38b)
SATB
Funeral of Georg Kamb
Nürnberg, 1686
  RISM H1891 (score)
  DMA 75//34

H0020 **Wie ein Hirsch, der sich erhitzet** (Samuel no. 11)
SATB
Funeral of Wolfgang Endter
Nürnberg, 1659
  RISM H1865, Reich 317 (score)
  DMA 70//173

H0021 **Wo willst du dann nun hin, o blosser Leichnam**
(Samuel no. 8b)
STB, vln, vla, bc
Funeral of Wolfgang Frank
Nürnberg, 1658
  RISM H1861, Reich 313 (score)
  DMA 66//52

HAMMERSCHMIDT, Andreas (1611-1675)

COLLECTIONS

Chor-Music . . . auf Madrigal Manier (1653)
  RISM H1934 (parts)
  DMA 1/1001

Dialogi oder Gespräch I (1645)
  RISM H1940-H1943 (parts)
  DMA 40//85

Fest- Buß- und Danklieder (1658-1659)
  RISM H1951 (parts)
  DMA 2/1094

Geistlicher Gespräche II (1656)
  RISM H1949 (parts)
  DMA 3/1480

Kirchen- und Tafelmusic (1662)
RISM H1952 (parts)
DMA 2/1095

Missae (1663)
RISM H1953 (parts)
DMA 2/653

Musicalische Gespräche (1655)
RISM H1948 (parts)
DMA 3/1479

Musicalischer Andacht I (1638)
RISM H1922-H1925 (parts)
DMA 3/551

Musicalischer Andacht II (1641)
RISM H1926-H1928 (parts)
DMA 3/107

Musicalischer Andacht IV (1646)
RISM H1931-H1933 (parts)
DMA 3/1909

VI-stimmige Fest- und Zeit-Andachten (1671)
RISM H1954 (parts)
DMA 2/1096

WORKS

H0022 **Ach daß ich hören sollte**
SST, bc
Dialogi oder Gespräch I, no. 2
DTÖ 16, pp. 9-15

H0023 **Ach Gott, warum hast du mein vergessen**
SSTB, tbn, bc
Dialogi oder Gespräch I, no. 21
DTÖ 16, pp. 137-48

H0024 **Ach Herr, du Schöpfer**
SATB, bc
Musicalischer Andacht II, no. 10

H0025 **Ach Herr, du Sohn David**
SATB, bc
2nd Sunday of Lent
Musicalische Gespräche, no. 18

H0026 **Ach Herr, gedenke nicht der Sünden meiner Jugend**
SSATTB, bc
VI-stimmige Fest- und Zeit-Andachten, no. 9
Ed. F. Commer, *Musica sacra*, vol. 27, pp. 65-69

H0027 **Ach Herr, wie sind meiner Feinde so viel**
SSATTB, bc
Musicalischer Andacht IV, no. 8

H0028 **Ach Jesu meiner Seelen Freude**
SSATB, 2 vln, vlne, bc

Ascension
Fest- Buß- und Danklieder, no. 23

H0029 **Ach, Jesus stirbt**
SSATTB, bc
VI-stimmige Fest- und Zeit-Andachten, no. 8
Ed. F. Commer, *Musica sacra*, vol. 25, pp. 73-79

H0030 **Ach mein herzliebes Jesulein**
SATB, bc
Musicalischer Andacht II, no. 11

H0031 **Ach was erhebst du dich doch**
SSATB, bc
Chor-Music . . . auf Madrigal Manier, no. 20

H0032 **Ach weh, mir armen Sünder**
SSATB, 2 vln, vlne, bc
Fest- Buß- und Danklieder, no. 27

H0033 **Ach wie gar nichts sind alle Menschen**
SSB, tbn, bc
Dialogi oder Gespräch I, no. 7
DTÖ 16, pp. 40-45

H0034 **Ach wie gar nichts sind alle Menschen**
SSATTB, bc
Musicalischer Andacht IV, no. 10

H0035 **Ach wie gern wollt ich dich preisen**
SSATB, 2 vln, vlne, bc
Fest- Buß- und Danklieder, no. 29

H0036 **Ach wie nichtig, ach wie flüchtig**
SSATB, 2 vln, vlne, bc
Fest- Buß- und Danklieder, no. 9
Ed. Winterfeld II, no. 118

H0037 **Allein zu dir Herr Jesu Christ**
SSATTB, bc
VI-stimmige Fest- und Zeit-Andachten, no. 30
Ed. F. Commer, *Musica sacra*, vol. 26, pp. 31-38

H0038 **Alleluja, freuet euch, ihr Christen alle**
See Freuet euch, ihr Christen alle

H0039 **Alleluja, ich will dem Herren singen**
SSATB, bc
Chor-Music . . . auf Madrigal Manier, no. 29

H0040 **Alleluja, lobet den Herrn in seinem Heiligtum**
TT, SSATB, 2 vln/corn, 3 tbn, bc
Musicalischer Andacht IV, no. 38

H0041 **Alleluja, merk auf, mein Herz**
SSATTB, bc
Musicalischer Andacht II, no. 33
Ed. Nitsche, *Die Motette* 78

HAMMERSCHMIDT, Andreas (*continued*)

H0042   **Alles, was dir widerfährt, das leide**
SSATB, bc
Musicalischer Andacht II, no. 17

H0043   **Also hat Gott die Welt geliebet**
SSATTB, bc
VI-stimmige Fest- und Zeit-Andachten, no. 20
Ed. Kraner, *Die Motette* 595

H0044   **Benedicam Dominum in omni tempore**
SSTB, tbn, bc
Dialogi oder Gespräch I, no. 22
DTÖ 16, pp. 149-60

H0045   **Bis hier an des Kreuzes Stamm**
SSATB, 2 vln, vlne, bc
Lent
Fest- Buß- und Danklieder, no. 21
Ed. D. Hellmann, *Das Chorwerk alter Meister*
    6, pp. 34-44
Ed. D. Hellmann, *Das geistliche Konzert* 76
Ed. Winterfeld II, no. 119

H0046   **Bis willkommen**
SATB, bc
Musicalischer Andacht II, no. 9

H0047   **Bist du Gottes Sohn**
SSAB, bc
1st Sunday of Lent
Musicalische Gespräche, no. 17

H0048   **Bringet her dem Herren**
TBB, bc
Musicalischer Andacht I, no. 19

H0049   **Bringet her dem Herren ihr Gewaltigen**
ST soli, SSATB, 2 vln, 2 vla, vlne, bc
Musicalischer Andacht IV, no. 16

H0050   **Christ lag in Todesbanden**
SST, 3 tbn, vlne, bc
Kirchen- und Tafel-Music, no. 5
Ed. W. Ehmann and J. Haug (Möseler
    M68.019, 1983)

H0051   **Christen Christum zu betrachten**
SSATB, 2 vln, vlne, bc
Lent
Fest- Buß- und Danklieder, no. 20

H0052   **Da aber Johannes die Werk Christi hörete**
SSATB, bc
3rd Sunday of Advent
Musicalische Gespräche, no. 3

H0053   **Danket dem Herrn, denn er ist**
SSATTB, bc
Musicalischer Andacht II, no. 31
Ed. Nitsche, *Die Motette* 76

H0054   **Darum wachet, denn ihr wisset weder**
SSATB, 2 vln, bc
27th Sunday after Trinity
Geistlicher Gespräche II, no. 31
Ed. Mueller 1956, vol. 2, pp. 377-93
Ed. H. Mueller (Concordia 97-6316, 1960)

H0055   **Das ist ein grosser Gewinn**
SSATB, bc
Chor-Music . . . auf Madrigal Manier, no. 17

H0056   **Das ist je gewißlich war**
SSATTB, bc
Musicalischer Andacht IV, no. 12
Ed. Mönkemeyer, *Antiqua Chorbuch I/5*,
    pp. 290-95
Handbuch der deutschen evangelischen
    Kirchenmusik, II/1, pp. 332-36
Ed. D. Hellmann, *Das Chorwerk alter Meister*
    6, pp. 82-89
_____, *Die Motette* 320
Ed. J. Schabasser (Doblinger)
Ed. R. Granville (Fox, 1967)

H0057   **Das Wort ward Fleisch**
SSATTB, bc
VI-stimmige Fest- und Zeit-Andachten, no. 3
Ed. Kraner, *Die Motette* 593

H0058   **Der Herr erhöre dich in der Not**
SSATB, bc
Musicalischer Andacht II, no. 22

H0059   **Der Herr ist König**
SSATTB, bc
Musicalischer Andacht II, no. 32

H0060   **Der Herr ist mein Hirt**
SSB/TTB, bc
Musicalischer Andacht I, no. 18
Ed. Kraner, *Die Motette* 590

H0061   **Der Herr ist mein Hirte**
SSAT, ATBB, bc
Musicalischer Andacht IV, no. 18

H0062   **Der Tod ist verschlungen**
SATB, SATB, 2 vln, bc
Musicalischer Andacht IV, no. 36
Ed. L. Lillehaug (Concordia, 1963)

H0063   **Die antwortet Laban**
SSATB, bc
Chor-Music . . . auf Madrigal Manier, no. 8

H0064   **Die mit Tränen säen**
SSATB, bc
Chor-Music . . . auf Madrigal Manier, no. 27

H0065 **Dies ist der Tag**
SSATB, bc
Chor-Music . . . auf Madrigal Manier, no. 19

H0066 **Du König der Ehren Jesu Christ**
SSATTB, bc
VI-stimmige Fest- und Zeit-Andachten, no. 17

H0067 **Ehre sei Gott in der Höhe**
SSATB, TTB, bc
Musicalischer Andacht IV, no. 23
DdT 40, pp. 91-98
Ed. O. Richter (Bertelsmann, 1928)
Ed. G. Wolters (Möseler, 1970)
Ed. D. Hellmann (Peters 66305, 1970)
Ed. Hellmann, *Die Motette* 318
_____, *Das Chorwerk alter Meister* 6,
   pp. 24-33
(Concordia 98-1811)

H0068 **Ei du frommer und getreuer Knecht**
SSATTB, bc
VI-stimmige Fest- und Zeit-Andachten, no. 24

H0069 **Erbarm dich mein, o Herre Gott**
SSATB, bc
Musicalischer Andacht II, no. 19
DdT 40, pp. 43-50
Ed. Winterfeld II, no. 111

H0070 **Erbarm dich mein, o Herre Gott**
SSATTB, bc
VI-stimmige Fest- und Zeit-Andachten, no. 37
Ed. F. Commer, *Musica sacra*, vol. 27, pp.
   77-82

H0071 **Ermuntert euch, ihr münden Seelen**
SSATB, 2 vln, vlne, bc
Pentecost
Fest- Buß- und Danklieder, no. 25

H0072 **Es segne dich der Gott Israel**
SSATTB, bc
VI-stimmige Fest- und Zeit-Andachten, no. 34

H0073 **Es wird eine große Trübsal sein**
SSB, 2 fl, 2 tbn, bc
25th Sunday after Trinity
Geistlicher Gespräche II, no. 29
Ed. Mueller 1956, vol. 2, pp. 319-37

H0074 **Freude, grosse Freude**
SSATTB, bc
Chor-Music . . . auf Madrigal Manier, no. 28
Ed. Kraner, *Die Motette* 592

H0075 **Freue dich des Weibes deiner Jugend**
TT soli, SSATB, bc
Musicalischer Andacht IV, no. 13

H0076 **Freue dich, du Tochter Zion**
SSTB, 2 corn/vln, bc
1st Sunday of Advent
Musicalische Gespräche, no. 1
Ed. Mueller 1956, vol. 2, pp. 1-13
Ed. Hildebrandt, *Das geistliche Konzert* 166

H0077 **Freue dich sehr, du Tochter Zion**
SSATTB, bc
VI-stimmige Fest- und Zeit-Andachten, no. 38
Ed. F. Commer, *Musica sacra*, vol. 28, pp.
   71-76

H0078 **Freuet euch, ihr Christen alle**
SSATB, TTB, bc
Musicalischer Andacht IV, no. 24
Ed. Winterfeld II, no. 114
Ed. D. Hellmann (Peters 66306, 1970)
Ed. Hellmann, *Die Motette* 308
_____, *Das Chorwerk alter Meister* 6,
   pp. 14-23
*Handbuch der deutschen evangelischen
   Kirchenmusik* III/2
Ed. Ameln (Vandenhoeck & Ruprecht)

H0079 **Freuet euch mit mir**
STB, 2 vln, 2 vla, vlne, bc
3rd Sunday after Trinity
Geistlicher Gespräche II, no. 4
Ed. Mueller 1956, vol. 2, pp. 184-209

H0080 **Freundlicher, lieblicher, süßester Jesu**
SSATTB, bc
VI-stimmige Fest- und Zeit-Andachten, no. 14
Ed. F. Commer, *Musica sacra*, vol. 27, pp.
   70-76

H0081 **Friede sei mit euch**
SSTB, 2 vln, bc
1st Sunday after Easter
Musicalische Gespräche, no. 23

H0082 **Frisch auf und laßt uns singen**
SSATB, 2 vln, vlne, bc
Fest- Buß- und Danklieder, no. 7

H0083 **Gehet hin, ihr Verfluchten**
SSABB, ATBB, bc
Musicalischer Andacht IV, no. 35

H0084 **Gelobet sei der Herr**
SSATB, 2 corn, bc
Feast of Saint John
Geistlicher Gespräche II, no. 6

H0085 **Gelobet sei der Herr aus Zion**
SSATTB, bc
VI-stimmige Fest- und Zeit-Andachten, no. 35

HAMMERSCHMIDT, Andreas (*continued*)

H0086   **Gelobet sei der Herre täglich**
SST, bc
Dialogi oder Gespräch I, no. 4
DTÖ 16, pp. 22-27

H0087   **Gelobt sei Gott der Herr**
SSATB, bc
Musicalischer Andacht II, no. 18

H0088   **Getreuer Gott und Vater**
SSATB, 2 vln, vlne, bc
Fest- Buß- und Danklieder, no. 14

H0089   **Gott, dein Weg ist heilig**
SSATB, bc
Chor-Music . . . auf Madrigal Manier, no. 12

H0090   **Gott, du Gott Israel**
SSATB, bc
Chor-Music . . . auf Madrigal Manier, no. 3
PL-Kj Mus. ms. 40040, no. 34 (1680)
parts

H0091   **Gott hat uns nicht gesetzt zum Zorn**
SSATB, bc
Chor-Music . . . auf Madrigal Manier, no. 10

H0092   **Gott ist die Liebe**
SSATTB, bc
VI-stimmige Fest- und Zeit-Andachten, no. 28
Ed. F. Commer, *Musica sacra*, vol. 28, pp. 65-70

H0093   **Gott mein Herz ist bereit**
SSATTB, bc
Musicalischer Andacht II, no. 34

H0094   **Habe deine Lust an dem Herrn**
SSATB, bc
Musicalischer Andacht II, no. 21
DdT 40, pp. 68-77

H0095   **Haus und Güter erben die Eltern**
SSATTB, bc
Musicalischer Andacht IV, no. 5

H0096   **Heilig ist der Herr**
SSATB, 2 corn, bc
Trinity
Geistlicher Gespräche II, no. 1
Ed. Mueller 1956, vol. 2, pp. 168-83
Ed. H. Mueller (Concordia 97-6314, 1960)

H0097   **Heilig ist unser Gott**
SSATTB, bc
VI-stimmige Fest- und Zeit-Andachten, no. 21

H0098   **Helft mir Gottes Güte preisen**
SSATTB, bc
VI-stimmige Fest- und Zeit-Andachten, no. 5

H0099   **Herr, der du bist vormals**
SSATTB, bc
Musicalischer Andacht IV, no. 6

H0100   **Herr diese Letzten haben nur eine Stunde gearbeitet**
SSB, 2 vln, bc
Septuagesima
Musicalische Gespräche, no. 14

H0101   **Herr, du weißest alle Dinge**
SSATB, 2 vln, bc
Pentecost
Musicalische Gespräche, no. 30
Ed. Mueller 1956, vol. 2, pp. 147-67
Ed. H. Mueller (Concordia, 1971)

H0102   **Herr, hast du nicht guten Samen**
SSB, 2 vln, bc
5th Sunday after Epiphany
Musicalische Gespräche, no. 13

H0103   **Herr, höre mein Wort**
SSAT, ATBB, bc
Musicalischer Andacht IV, no. 19

H0104   **Herr, ich bin nicht wert**
SSTB, 2 tbn, bc
3rd Sunday after Epiphany
Musicalische Gespräche, no. 11

H0105   **Herr, ich trau auf dich**
SSATB, bc
Musicalischer Andacht II, no. 13

H0106   **Herr Jesu aus Barmherzigkeit**
SSATB, 2 vln, vlne, bc
Fest- Buß- und Danklieder, no. 3

H0107   **Herr, kehre dich doch wieder zu uns**
SSB, tbn, bc
Dialogi oder Gespräch I, no. 3
DTÖ 16, pp. 16-21

H0108   **Herr, komm hinab**
SSTB, 2 vln, bc
21st Sunday after Trinity
Geistlicher Gespräche II, no. 24

H0109   **Herr mein Gott, groß sind deine Wunder**
SATB, bc
Musicalischer Andacht II, no. 2
Ed. Nitsche, *Die Motette* 130

H0110   **Herr mein König und mein Gott**
SSATB, bc
Chor-Music . . . auf Madrigal Manier, no. 6

H0111 **Herr nun lässt du deinen Diener**
SSATTB, bc
VI-stimmige Fest- und Zeit-Andachten, no. 6
Ed. F. Commer, *Musica sacra*, vol. 27, pp. 61-64

H0112 **Herr, sie haben nicht Wein**
SSTB, 2 vln, bc
2nd Sunday after Epiphany
Musicalische Gespräche, no. 10

H0113 **Herr, wer wird wohnen in deiner Hütten**
SSB, tbn, bc
Dialogi oder Gespräch I, no. 8
DTÖ 16, pp. 46-52

H0114 **Herr, wie lange willst du mein so gar vergessen**
SSATB, bc
Musicalischer Andacht II, no. 20
DdT 40, pp. 57-67

H0115 **Herr, wo soll ich hingehen für deinen Geist**
SATB, SATB, bc
Musicalischer Andacht IV, no. 27

H0116 **Herzlich lieb hab ich dich, Herr, meine Stärke**
ATB, 2 vln, vla, vlne, bc
Kirchen- und Tafel-Music, no. 14
Ed. D. Hellmann, *Das Chorwerk alter Meister 6*, pp. 65-75

H0117 **Herzlich lieb hab ich dich, o Herr**
SSATTB, bc
VI-stimmige Fest- und Zeit-Andachten, no. 31
Ed. F. Commer, *Musica sacra*, vol. 26, pp. 39-43

H0118 **Himmel und Erden vergehen**
SSATB, bc
2nd Sunday of Advent
Musicalische Gespräche, no. 2
Ed. Mueller 1956, vol. 2, pp. 14-27
Ed. Hildebrandt, *Die Motette 597*

H0119 **Höret zu, es ging ein Sämann aus**
SSATB, 2 vln, bc
Sexagesima
Musicalische Gespräche, no. 15

H0120 **Hosianna Davids Sohne**
SSATB, 2 vln, vlne, bc
Advent
Fest- Buß- und Danklieder, no. 15

H0121 **Hosianna dem Sohne David**
SSATB, bc
Musicalischer Andacht IV, no. 1

H0122 **Ich beschwöre euch ihr Töchter**
SSATTB, bc
VI-stimmige Fest- und Zeit-Andachten, no. 33

H0123 **Ich bin die Wurzel des Geschlechtes David**
SSB, bc
Dialogi oder Gespräch I, no. 1
DTÖ 16, pp. 5-8

H0124 **Ich bin ein guter Hirte**
SSB, 2 tbn, bc
2nd Sunday after Easter
Musicalische Gespräche, no. 24

H0125 **Ich bin eine Stimme eines Predigers**
SSATTB, bc
VI-stimmige Fest- und Zeit-Andachten, no. 26

H0126 **Ich bin gewiß, daß weder Tod**
SSATB, bc
Chor-Music . . . auf Madrigal Manier, no. 15
Ed. F. Commer, *Musica sacra*, vol. 26, pp. 19-24

H0127 **Ich bin gewiß, daß weder Tod noch Leben**
SSATB, bc
Funeral of Michael Theophil Lehmann
Freiburg in Sachsen, 1650
  RISM H1955, Reich 83 (parts)
  DMA 70//129

H0128 **Ich bleib, o Jesu, ganz der deine**
SSATB, 2 vln, vlne, bc
Fest- Buß- und Danklieder, no. 11

H0129 **Ich danke dir, Gott**
ATB, 2 corn, bc
11th Sunday after Trinity
Geistlicher Gespräche II, no. 14

H0130 **Ich danke dir, Herr mein Gott**
SSATB, bc
Chor-Music . . . auf Madrigal Manier, no. 4

H0131 **Ich, der Herr, das ist mein Name**
SSB, bc
Dialogi oder Gespräch I, no. 15
DTÖ 16, pp. 96-103

H0132 **Ich fahre auf zu meinem Vater**
SSATTB, bc
VI-stimmige Fest- und Zeit-Andachten, no. 16

H0133 **Ich hab mein Sach Gott heimgestellt**
SATB, SATB, bc
Musicalischer Andacht IV, no. 21

H0134 **Ich habe den Herren allezeit vor Augen**
SSATB, bc
Musicalischer Andacht II, no. 28

HAMMERSCHMIDT, Andreas (*continued*)

H0135 **Ich hebe meine Augen auf**
TTB, bc
Musicalischer Andacht I, no. 17

H0136 **Ich hebe meine Augen auf**
T solo, SSATB, bc
Musicalischer Andacht IV, no. 11

H0137 **Ich lieg im Streit und Widerstreb**
SSATB, bc
Chor-Music . . . auf Madrigal Manier, no. 30

H0138 **Ich lieg und schlafe und erwache**
SSATTB, bc
Musicalischer Andacht IV, no. 9

H0139 **Ich weiß an welchen ich glaube**
SSATB, bc
Chor-Music . . . auf Madrigal Manier, no. 18

H0140 **Ich will den Herren loben alle Zeit**
SSB, 2 vln, 2 tbn, vlne, bc
Kirchen- und Tafel-Music, no. 19

H0141 **Ich will den Herren loben allezeit**
SSATB, bc
Musicalischer Andacht II, no. 25

H0142 **Ihr Jungen und ihr Alten, hört**
SSB
"für einen Christlichen Gesänglein"
Coburg, 1658
RISM H1957 (parts)
DMA 72//22

H0143 **In te Domine speravi**
SATB, SATB, bc
Musicalischer Andacht IV, no. 30

H0144 **Ist nicht Ephraim**
SSATB, bc
Chor-Music . . . auf Madrigal Manier, no. 11
Ed. F. Commer, *Musica sacra*, vol. 24, pp.
65-69

H0145 **Jauchzet dem Herren, alle Welt**
SSATTB, bc
Chor-Music . . . auf Madrigal Manier, no. 31
Ed. Kraner, *Die Motette* 594

H0146 **Jauchzet Gott, alle Land**
SSST, ATBB, bc
Musicalischer Andacht IV, no. 25

H0147 **Jauchzet, ihr Himmel**
SSATB, 2 vln, vlne, bc
Fest- Buß- und Danklieder, no. 12
Ed. J. M. Bonhôte (Bärenreiter BA 2743,
1952)

H0148 **Jesu, dein will ich sein**
SSATB, 2 vln, vlne, bc
Fest- Buß- und Danklieder, no. 10

H0149 **Jesu, du mein liebstes Leben**
SSATB, 2 vln, vlne, bc
Fest- Buß- und Danklieder, no. 2

H0150 **Jesu hilf, daß ich mit Schmerzen**
SSATB, 2 vln, vlne, bc
Fest- Buß- und Danklieder, no. 13

H0151 **Jesu, Jesu, du mein Hirt**
SSATB, 2 vln, vlne, bc
Fest- Buß- und Danklieder, no. 5

H0152 **Jesu, lieber Meister**
SSATB, 2 vln, bc
14th Sunday after Trinity
Geistlicher Gespräche II, no. 17

H0153 **Jesu, mein Jesu**
SSATTB, bc
VI-stimmige Fest- und Zeit-Andachten, no. 25
Ed. F. Commer, *Musica sacra*, vol. 25, pp.
60-66

H0154 **Jesu, meine Freud und Wonne**
SSATB, 2 vln, vlne, bc
New Year's Day
Fest- Buß- und Danklieder, no. 17

H0155 **Jesu, meine Freude**
SSATB, 2 vln, vlne, bc
Fest- Buß- und Danklieder, no. 1
Ed. J. M. Bonhôte (Bärenreiter BA 2742,
1951)

H0156 **Jesu, o du Lebens Quell**
SSATB, 2 vln, vlne, bc
Fest- Buß- und Danklieder, no. 8

H0157 **Jünglich ich sage dir**
SSAB, 3 tbn, bc
16th Sunday after Trinity
Geistlicher Gespräche II, no. 19

H0158 **Komm, Heiliger Geist**
SSATTB, bc
VI-stimmige Fest- und Zeit-Andachten, no. 18
Ed. F. Commer, *Musica sacra*, vol. 28, pp.
60-64

H0159 **Kommet, denn es ist alles bereit**
SSATB, 2 vln, bc
2nd Sunday after Trinity
Geistlicher Gespräche II, no. 3

H0160 **Kommet her, ihr Gesegneten**
SSATB, 2 vln, 2 vla, vlne, bc

26th Sunday after Trinity
Geistlicher Gespräche II, no. 30
Ed. Mueller 1956, vol. 2, pp. 338-76

H0161 **Kommet her und schauet an die Werk Gottes**
TT soli, SSATB, bc
Musicalischer Andacht IV, no. 14

H0162 **Kommet her zu mir, alle die ihr mühselig**
SSATTB, bc
VI-stimmige Fest- und Zeit-Andachten, no. 15

H0163 **Kommt herzu, laßt uns dem Herren**
SSATB, bc
Musicalischer Andacht II, no. 30

H0164 **Laudate, servi Domini**
STB, SSATB, vln, vla, 3 tbn, bc
Musicalischer Andacht IV, no. 28

H0165 **Liebster Jesu**
SSATB, bc
Chor-Music . . . auf Madrigal Manier, no. 23

H0166 **Lob, Ehr sei Gott im höchsten Thron**
SATB, bc
Musicalischer Andacht II, no. 12

H0167 **Lobe den Herrn, meine Seele**
SSATTB, bc
VI-stimmige Fest- und Zeit-Andachten, no. 11

H0168 **Lobet den Herrn, ihr seine Engel**
SSATTB, bc
VI-stimmige Fest- und Zeit-Andachten, no. 29

H0169 **Machet die Tore weit**
SSATTB, bc
VI-stimmige Fest- und Zeit-Andachten, no. 2
Ed. F. Commer, *Musica sacra*, vol. 25, pp. 52-59
Ed. Wilhelm, *Die Motette* 7
Ed. K. Thiel (Sulzbach)
Ed. M. N. Lundquist (Willis Music 5486-8, 1934)
(Concordia 98-2279)

H0170 **Maria, gegrüsset seist du**
SSATTB, bc
VI-stimmige Fest- und Zeit-Andachten, no. 12

H0171 **Mein Erlöser**
SATB, bc
Musicalischer Andacht II, no. 4

H0172 **Mein Haus ist ein Bethaus**
SSATB, 2 corn, bc
10th Sunday after Trinity
Geistlicher Gespräche II, no. 13

H0173 **Mein Herr Jesu, dir lieb ich**
SSATB, bc
Chor-Music . . . auf Madrigal Manier, no. 2
Ed. F. Commer, *Musica sacra*, vol. 24, pp. 50-54

H0174 **Mein Herr Jesu, höchster Gott**
SSATB, 2 vln, vlne, bc
Fest- Buß- und Danklieder, no. 6

H0175 **Mein Herz ist dir, mein Gott, allzeit**
SSATB, 2 vln, vlne, bc
Fest- Buß- und Danklieder, no. 18

H0176 **Mein Sohn, warum hast du uns das getan**
SAT, 2 vln, 2 vla, bc
1st Sunday after Epiphany
Musicalische Gespräche, no. 9

H0177 **Meine Seele erhebet**
SSATB, 2 corn, bc
Visitation of the Virgin Mary
Geistlicher Gespräche II, no. 7
Ed. Mueller 1956, vol. 2, pp. 226-45

H0178 **Meine Seele erhebet den Herrn**
SSATTB, bc
VI-stimmige Fest- und Zeit-Andachten, no. 27
Ed. Kraner, *Die Motette* 596

H0179 **Meine Seele Gott erhebt**
SSATB, 2 vln, vlne, bc
Fest- Buß- und Danklieder, no. 19
Ed. Winterfeld II, no. 117
Ed. D. Hellmann, *Das Chorwerk alter Meister* 6, pp. 9-13; *Das geistliche Konzert* 75

H0180 **Meinen Jesum laß ich nicht**
SSATB, 2 vln, vlne, bc
Fest- Buß- und Danklieder, no. 4
Ed. Winterfeld II, no. 116
Ed. Hellmann, *Das geistliche Konzert* 49

H0181 **Meister, was muß ich tun**
SSATB, 2 vln, bc
13th and 18th Sundays after Trinity
Geistlicher Gespräche II, nos. 16 and 21

H0182 **Merk auf, mein Herz**
SATB, bc
Musicalischer Andacht II, no. 8

H0183 **Mir hast du Arbeit gemacht**
SSATB, bc
Musicalischer Andacht IV, no. 2
Ed. Winterfeld II, no. 113

H0184 **Miserere mei, Deus**
SST, bc

HAMMERSCHMIDT, Andreas (*continued*)

Dialogi oder Gespräch I, no. 12
DTÖ 16, pp. 74-78

H0185 **Missa (brevis) à 5**
SSATB, bc
Missae, no. 1

H0186 **Missa (brevis) à 6**
SSATTB, bc
Missae, no. 2

H0187 **Missa (brevis) à 6**
SSATTB, bc
Missae, no. 3

H0188 **Missa (brevis) à 6**
SSATTB, bc
Missae, no. 4

H0189 **Missa (brevis) à 6**
SSATTB, bc
Missae, no. 5

H0190 **Missa (brevis) à 7**
SSATB, 2 vln, bc
Missae, no. 6

H0191 **Missa (brevis) à 7**
SSATB, 2 vln, bc
Missae, no. 7

H0192 **Missa (brevis) à 7**
SSSATTB, bc
Missae, no. 8

H0193 **Missa (brevis) à 7**
SSATB, 2 vln, bc
Missae, no. 9

H0194 **Missa (brevis) à 8**
SSATTB, 2 vln, bc
Missae, no. 10

H0195 **Missa (brevis) à 8**
SSATTB, 2 vln, bc
Missae, no. 11

H0196 **Missa (brevis) à 9**
SSATB, 2 vln, 2 tbn, bc
Missae, no. 12

H0197 **Missa (brevis) à 10**
SSATB, 2 vln, 3 tbn, bc
Missae, no. 13

H0198 **Missa (brevis) à 11**
SSATTB, 2 vln, 3 tbn, bc
Missae, no. 14

H0199 **Missa (brevis) à 12**
SSATTB, 2 vln, 4 tbn, bc
Missae, no. 16

H0200 **Missa (Kyrie, Gloria, Sanctus) à 12**
SSATB, 2 vln, 2 corn, timp, 3 tbn, bc
Missae, no. 15
Sanctus: SSATTB, 2 trombetta, 3 tbn, bc

H0201 **Nach dir, Herr, verlanget mich**
SSST, ATBB, bc
Musicalischer Andacht IV, no. 29

H0202 **Nehmet hin und esset, dies ist mein Leib**
SSB, tbn, bc
Dialogi oder Gespräch I, no. 16
DTÖ 16, pp. 104-11

H0203 **Nun aber gehe ich hin**
SSAB, 2 vln, bc
4th Sunday after Easter
Musicalische Gespräche, no. 26

H0204 **Nun komm, der Heiden Heiland**
SSATTB, bc
VI-stimmige Fest- und Zeit-Andachten, no. 1

H0205 **O barmherziger Vater**
SATB, bc
Musicalischer Andacht II, no. 6
DdT 40, pp. 32-35
Ed. M. Martens (Walton 2098)
Ed. D. Hellmann, *Die Motette* 107
Ed. Mönkemeyer, *Antiqua Chorbuch* I/5,
pp. 286-89

H0206 **O Domine Jesu Christe**
SSATB, bc
Chor-Music . . . auf Madrigal Manier, no. 14
Ed. F. Commer, *Musica sacra*, vol. 3, pp.
23-25
Ed. L. Spengler (Oltersdorf)
Ed. V. Söderholm (Nordiska no. 4416, 1955)

H0207 **O dulcissime Jesu**
SSATB, bc
Chor-Music . . . auf Madrigal Manier, no. 13

H0208 **O freundlicher**
SSATB, bc
Chor-Music . . . auf Madrigal Manier, no. 25

H0209 **O Herr, hilf, wir verderben**
SSATBB, bc
4th Sunday after Epiphany
Musicalische Gespräche, no. 12

H0210 **O Herr Jesu Christ**
SATB, bc

Musicalischer Andacht II, no.7
Ed. Nitsche, *Die Motette* 129

H0211 **O ich elender Sünder**
SATB, bc
Musicalischer Andacht II, no. 1

H0212 **O ihr lieben Hirten, fürchtet euch nicht**
SATB, 2 vln/corn, bc
Christmas Day
Musicalische Gespräche, no. 5
Ed. Mueller 1956, vol. 2, pp. 28-44
Ed. H. Mueller (Concordia 97-6332, 1960)
Ed. W. Ehret (Presser, 1979)
Ed. J. M. Bonhôte (Bärenreiter BA 2741, 1952)

H0213 **O Jesu, du allersüßester Heiland**
SST, tbn, bc
Dialogi oder Gespräch I, no. 11
DTÖ 16, pp. 65-73

H0214 **O Jesu, mein Erlöser**
SSATB, bc
Chor-Music . . . auf Madrigal Manier, no. 5
Ed. F. Commer, *Musica sacra*, vol. 24, pp. 55-64

H0215 **O Jesu, mein Heiland**
SSATB, bc
Musicalischer Andacht II, no. 24

H0216 **O Jesu, mein Jesu**
SAB, 2 tbn, bc
3rd Sunday of Lent
Musicalische Gespräche, no. 19

H0217 **O Jesu, wir wissen, daß du**
SSATB, 2 vln, bc
23rd Sunday after Trinity
Geistlicher Gespräche II, no. 27

H0218 **O komm, lieber Herr Jesu**
SSATB, bc
Musicalischer Andacht II, no. 27

H0219 **O süßer, o freundlicher, o gütiger Herr Jesu Christe**
SATB, bc
Musicalischer Andacht II, no. 3
DdT 40, pp. 36-42
Ed. R. Fricke, *Meisterwerke alter Kirchenmusik* III/1
Ed. Grischkat, *Die Motette* 46

H0220 **O Vater, aller Augen warten auf dich**
SSB, 2 tbn, bc
4th Sunday of Lent
Musicalische Gespräche, no. 20

H0221 **O Vater aller Frommen**
SSATB, bc
Chor-Music . . . auf Madrigal Manier, no. 24
Ed. Winterfeld II, no. 115
Ed. G. Grote, *Geistliche Chorlied* (Merseburger, 1950)
Ed. Grischkat, *Die Motette* 45

H0222 **O welch eine Tiefe des Reichtums**
SSATTB, bc
VI-stimmige Fest- und Zeit-Andachten, no. 22

H0223 **Peccavi, Domine, peccavi**
SATB, SATB, bc
Musicalischer Andacht IV, no. 31

H0224 **Schaffe in mir, Gott, ein reines Herz**
SSATTB, bc
VI-stimmige Fest- und Zeit-Andachten, no. 19
Ed. F. Commer, *Musica sacra*, vol. 3, pp. 36-42
Ed. A. Neithardt, *Musica sacra* (Bote & Bock), vol. 5, pp. 53-59
Ed. Hermann, *Die Kantate* 4

H0225 **Schaue, Jesu, schau vom Himmel**
SSATB, 2 vln, vlne, bc
Feast of Saint Michael
Fest- Buß- und Danklieder, no. 26

H0226 **Schläfest du doch, o du sichere verdammliche Seele**
SSATB, bc
Musicalischer Andacht II, no. 14

H0227 **Schmecket und sehet wie freundlich**
SSATB, bc
Musicalischer Andacht II, no. 23

H0228 **Schmücket das Fest mit Maien**
SSATB, 2 vln, vlne, bc
Pentecost
Fest- Buß- und Danklieder, no. 24
Ed. Winterfeld II, no. 120
In *Handbuch der deutschen evangelischen Kirchenmusik* III/2
Ed. J. M. Bonhôte (Bärenreiter BA 2745)
Ed. D. Hellmann, *Das Chorwerk alter Meister* 6, pp. 57-60; *Das geistliche Konzert* 77 (Göttingen: Vandenhoeck & Ruprecht)

H0229 **Seht euch vor den falschen Propheten**
SSATB, 2 vln, bc
8th Sunday after Trinity
Geistlicher Gespräche II, no. 11

HAMMERSCHMIDT, Andreas (*continued*)

H0230 **Sei gegrüßet, Jesu**
SSATB, bc
Chor-Music . . . auf Madrigal Manier, no. 1
Ed. F. Commer, *Musica sacra*, vol. 24, pp. 44-49

H0231 **Sei nun wieder zufrieden meine Seele**
SSATB, bc
Musicalischer Andacht IV, no. 4

H0232 **Sei willkommen, Jesulein**
SSATB, 2 vln, vlne, bc
Christmas Day
Fest- Buß- und Danklieder, no. 16

H0233 **Sei willkommen, Jesulein**
SSATTB, bc
VI-stimmige Fest- und Zeit-Andachten, no. 4

H0234 **Seid barmherzig**
SST, 3 tbn, bc
4th Sunday after Trinity
Geistlicher Gespräche II, no. 5
Ed. Mueller 1956, vol. 2, pp. 210-25

H0235 **Siehe, der Gerechte kommt um**
SSATB, bc
Chor-Music . . . auf Madrigal Manier, no. 16

H0236 **Siehe, der Gerechte kommt um**
SSATTB, bc
VI-stimmige Fest- und Zeit-Andachten, no. 7
Ed. F. Commer, *Musica sacra*, vol. 25, pp. 67-72

H0237 **Siehe des Herren Auge, siehet auf die**
SSATB, bc
Musicalischer Andacht II, no. 26

H0238 **Siehe, eine Jungfrau ist schwanger**
SSATB, bc
Musicalischer Andacht IV, no. 3

H0239 **Siehe, es hat überwunden der Löwe**
SSATTB, bc
VI-stimmige Fest- und Zeit-Andachten, no. 13

H0240 **Siehe, Herr, hier bin ich Elender**
SSATB, bc
Musicalischer Andacht II, no. 29

H0241 **Siehe, wie fein und lieblich**
SATB, SATB, SATB, bc
Musicalischer Andacht IV, no. 40
DdT 40, pp. 99-122

H0242 **Simon fahre auf die Höhe**
ATB, 2 vln, bc

5th Sunday after Trinity
Geistlicher Gespräche II, no. 8

H0243 **Singet dem Herrn ein neues Lied**
STTB, bc
Musicalischer Andacht I, no. 21
Ed. Nitsche, *Die Motette* 75

H0244 **Singet dem Herrn ein neues Lied**
SSAT, STBB, 2 tbtta, 2 tbn, bc
Musicalischer Andacht IV, no. 39

H0245 **So euch die Welt hasset**
SSATB, 2 fl, bc
Sunday after Ascension
Musicalische Gespräche, no. 29
Ed. Mueller 1956, vol. 2, pp. 128-46

H0246 **Steh auf, Herr Gott**
SATB, SATB, bc
Musicalischer Andacht IV, no. 20

H0247 **Süßer Jesu**
SSATB, bc
Chor-Music . . . auf Madrigal Manier, no. 22

H0248 **Triumph, triumph, victoria**
SSATB, 2 vln, vlne, bc
Easter Sunday
Fest- Buß- und Danklieder, no. 22
Ed. J. M. Bonhôte (Bärenreiter BA 2744)

H0249 **Und da acht Tage um waren**
SSATB, 2 vln, bc
New Year's Day
Musicalische Gespräche, no. 7

H0250 **Und dies ist das Zeugnis Johannes**
SSATB, 2 vln, bc
4th Sunday of Advent
Musicalische Gespräche, no. 4

H0251 **Und es erhub sich ein Streit**
SATB, 2 clar, 2 corn, bc
Feast of Saint Michael
Geistlicher Gespräche II, no. 26
Ed. Mueller 1956, vol. 2, pp. 277-99

H0252 **Uns ist ein Kind geboren**
See under Anonymous

H0253 **Unser Herr Jesus Christus**
SSATTB, bc
VI-stimmige Fest- und Zeit-Andachten, no. 10

H0254 **Vater unser, der du bist**
SSATB, ATTB, bc
Musicalischer Andacht IV, no. 33
DdT 40, pp. 78-90

H0255 Veni sancte spiritus
SSATB, ATB, 2 corn/tbtta, bc
Musicalischer Andacht IV, no. 37

H0256 Verleih uns Friede genädiglich
STB, SSATTB, 2 corn, 2 tbn, bc
Musicalischer Andacht IV, no. 34

H0257 Verleih uns Frieden gnädiglich
SSAT, 3 tbn, vlne, bc
Kirchen- und Tafel-Music, no. 6
Ed. Ehmann and Haug (Möseler M 68.012, 1988), with added B vocal part derived from bc line in source

H0258 Viel sind berufen
SSATB, 2 vln, bc
20th Sunday after Trinity
Geistlicher Gespräche II, no. 23

H0259 Vom Himmel hoch
SSATB, 2 vln, vlne, bc
Kirchen- und Tafel-Music, no. 18

H0260 Wahrlich, ich sage euch
SSB, 2 vln, bc
3rd Sunday after Easter
Musicalische Gespräche, no. 25

H0261 Wahrlich, ich sage euch, so ihr
SSSTB, 2 vln, bc
5th Sunday after Easter
Musicalische Gespräche, no. 27
Ed. Mueller 1956, vol. 2, pp. 107-27
Ed. H. Mueller (Concordia 97-5164, 1974)

H0262 Warum betrübst du dich, mein Herz
SSATB, bc
Musicalischer Andacht II, no. 16

H0263 Warum betrübst du dich, mein Herz
SSATTB, bc
VI-stimmige Fest- und Zeit-Andachten, no. 36

H0264 Was betrübst du dich meine Seele
SATB, SATB, bc
Musicalischer Andacht IV, no. 32

H0265 Was betrübst du dich meine Seele
ATB, 4 vla, vlne, bc
Kirchen- und Tafel-Music, no. 17

H0266 Was mein Gott will, das gescheh allzeit
SSATTB, bc
VI-stimmige Fest- und Zeit-Andachten, no. 23

H0267 Was meinest du will aus dem Kindlein werden
ATB, 2 vln/corn, bc
Sunday after Christmas

Musicalische Gespräche, no. 6
Ed. Mueller 1956, vol. 2, pp. 45-57

H0268 Wer mit seinem Bruder zürnet
SST, 3 tbn, bc
6th Sunday after Trinity
Geistlicher Gespräche II, no. 9

H0269 Wer sich selbst erhöhet
ATB, 2 vln, bc
17th Sunday after Trinity
Geistlicher Gespräche II, no. 20

H0270 Wer von Gott ist
SSB, 2 tbn, bc
5th Sunday of Lent
Musicalische Gespräche, no. 21

H0271 Wer wälzet uns den Stein
SSATTB, 2 clar, 3 tbn, bc
Musicalischer Andacht IV, no. 7
Ed. D. Hellmann (Peters 66307, 1970)
Ed. Hellmann, *Das Chorwerk alter Meister* 6, pp. 45-56
Ed. Hellmann, *Das geistliche Konzert* 80

H0272 Wer wälzet uns den Stein
SSATB, 2 vln, bc
Easter Sunday
Musicalische Gespräche, no. 22
Ed. Mueller 1956, vol. 2, pp. 91-106
Ed. H. Mueller (Concordia 97-5166, 1973)
Ed. Hildebrandt, *Das geistliche Konzert* 74

H0273 Wie bin ich doch so herzlich froh
SSTB, ATBB, bc
Musicalischer Andacht IV, no. 22
Ed. Kraner, *Die Motette* 591

H0274 Wie der Hirsch schreiet
SSB/TTB, bc
Musicalischer Andacht I, no. 20
DdT 40, pp. 17-22

H0275 Wie hör' ich das von dir
SSTB, 2 vla, bc
9th Sunday after Trinity
Geistlicher Gespräche II, no. 12

H0276 Wie kann und soll ich dich, Herr Jesu
SSATB, bc
Chor-Music . . . auf Madrigal Manier, no. 21
Ed. F. Commer, *Musica sacra*, vol. 26, pp. 25-30

H0277 Wie lieblich sind deine Wohnungen
SSATB, bc
Musicalischer Andacht II, no. 15
DdT 40, pp. 51-56
Ed. Grischkat, *Die Motette* 47

HAMMERSCHMIDT, Andreas (*continued*)

H0278   **Wie lieblich sind deine Wohnungen**
SATB, SSATB, bc
Freiburg in Sachsen, 1652
RISM H1956 (parts)
DMA 2/2037
Suggestions for instrumental doubling
given in parts

H0279   **Wie schön sind deine Brüste**
SSATTB, bc
VI-stimmige Fest- und Zeit-Andachten, no. 32

H0280   **Wo ist der neugeborne König der Juden**
SSATB, 2 vln, bc
Epiphany
Musicalische Gespräche, no. 8
Ed. H. Mueller (Concordia 97-5038, 1972)
Ed. Hildebrandt, *Das geistliche Konzert* 165

H0281   **Woher nehmen wir Brot**
SSATB, 2 vln, bc
7th & 15th Sundays after Trinity
Geistlicher Gespräche II, nos. 10 and 18
Ed. Mueller 1956, vol. 2, pp. 246-62
Ed. H. Mueller (Concordia 97-6315, 1960)

H0282   **Wohl dem, den die Übertretung vergeben sind**
SATB, SATB, bc
Musicalischer Andacht IV, no. 26

H0283   **Wohl dem, den du, Herr, züchtigest**
ST soli, SSATB, 2 vln, 2 tbn, vlne, bc
Musicalischer Andacht IV, no. 17

H0284   **Wohl dem, der den Herren fürchtet**
SSATB, bc
Chor-Music . . . auf Madrigal Manier, no. 26

H0285   **Wohl dem, der ein tugendsames Weib hat**
SATB, bc
Musicalischer Andacht II, no. 5

H0286   **Zion spricht: Der Herr hat mich verlassen**
SSATB, bc
Chor-Music . . . auf Madrigal Manier, no. 7
Ed. Hertzberg, *Musica sacra*, vol. 14, pp. 84-90
Ed. Wilhelm, *Die Motette* 6

H0287   **Zweierlei bitt ich von dir**
SSATB, bc
Chor-Music . . . auf Madrigal Manier, no. 9
Ed. F. Jöde, *Chorbuch II* (Kallmeyer, 1931), pp. 85-91
Ed. D. Hellmann, *Die Motette* 319
Ed. Hellmann, *Das Chorwerk alter Meister* 6, pp. 76-81

HANFF, Johann Nikolaus (1665-1711/12)

H0288   **Alleluia, der Tod ist verschlungen**
SSB, 2 vln, bsn, bc
D-Bds Mus. ms. 30210, no. 4 (Bokemeyer)
score
DMA 2/838
Ed. Grote (Merseburger EM 1002)

H0289   **Gott sei uns gnädig und segne uns**
SATB, 2 vln, 2 vla, bc
D-Bds Mus. ms. 30210, no. 5
score
DMA 2/839
Ed. Grote (Merseburger EM 1001)

HÄNISCH, Zacharias

H0290   **Blumen, die des Schöpfers Hände**
SSATB
Funeral of Eulalia and Barbara Anna von Bülow
Halle, 1665
RISM H1572 (parts)
DMA 69//126
Reich: parody of Knüpfer's "Asche, die des Schöpfers Hände"

HASSE, Nicolaus (1617-1672)

H0291   **Also hat Gott die Welt geliebet**
SSATB, bc
Funeral of Joachim Stephan
Rostock, 1652
RISM H2317, Reich 380

H0292   **Herr, wenn ich nur dich habe**
SSATB, bc
Funeral of Jakob Fabricius
Rostock, 1652
RISM H2316, Reich 379 (parts)
DMA 68//226

H0293   **Ich habe einen guten Kampf gekämpfet**
SSATB, bc
Funeral of Caspar Poley
Rostock, 1655
RISM H2319, Reich 381 (parts)
DMA 78//155

HÄßLER, Adam

H0294   **Nun hat sich über uns**
SATB, 3 vla, bc
Funeral of Johanna Barbara Marschall von Bieberstein

Merseburg, 1684
RISM H1574, Reich 287 (score)
DMA 72//198

HEERWAGEN, Nicolaus

H0295 Jesus geb, daß unser Kind
6 vv
Funeral of Sophia Amalia
Leipzig, 1657
RISM H4938 (score)
DMA 72//160

HEGENDORF

H0296 Komm, Gott, Heiliger Geist
SSATB, 2 vln, 2 clar, bc
D-B Mus. ms. 10340 (Erfurt) (1682)
parts

HEIDER, Jobst (fl. 1654)

H0297 Frisch fröhlich wolln wir singen
SSTB, 2 vln, bc
D-Kl Mus. ms. 2° 58^n
parts
DMA 3/806

H0298 Herr, wer wird wohnen in deinen Hütten
SSB, 2 vln, bc
D-Kl Mus. ms. 2° 26, no. 2
parts
DMA 1/338

H0299 Jauchzet dem Herrn, alle Welt
STB, 2 vln, bc
D-Kl Mus. ms. 2° 26, no. 4
parts
DMA 1/338

H0300 Lobet den Herrn, alle Heiden
SSB, bc
D-Kl Mus. ms. 2° 52W
parts
DMA 3/274

H0301 Lobet den Herrn in seinem Heiligtum
STB, 2 vln, bc
D-Kl Mus. ms. 2° 26, no. 5
parts
DMA 1/338

H0302 Lobt den Herrn, meine Seele
SSTB, 2 vln, bc

D-Kl Mus. ms. 2° 26, no. 6
parts
DMA 1/338

H0303 Nun danket alle Gott
SSTB, 2 vln, bsn, bc
D-Kl Mus. ms. 2° 52W
parts
DMA 2/486

H0304 Siehe, wie fein und lieblich ist
STB, 2 vln, bc
D-Kl Mus. ms. 2° 26, no. 1
parts
DMA 1/338

H0305 Singet dem Herrn ein neues Lied
SSTB, 2 vln, bc
D-Kl Mus. ms. 2° 52Q
parts
DMA 2/487

HEINRICI, Martin

H0306 Justus florebit sicut palma
SATB, 2 vln, bsn, bc
D-Dlb Mus. ms. 1729-E-500 (Grimma U 582/L 26 XXXV)
parts

HEI[N]ZENRÖDER [Heüzerröder, Hasenrots], Sebastian

H0307 Alleluia! Ich weiß, daß mein Erlöser lebt
SATB, 2 vln, gamba, bc
D-Dlb Mus. ms. 2064-E-500 (Grimma U 150/V [*sic*])
parts

H0308 Missa à 6
SSB, 2 vln, bc
D-B Mus. ms. 30291, no. 7
parts (bc lacking)

H0309 Missa à 7
ATTB, 2 vln, bc
D-B Mus. ms. 30291, no. 5
parts

HELLER, Johann Kilian (1633?-1674)

COLLECTION

Sacer concentus musicus (1671)
RISM H5003 (parts)
DMA 3/116

HELLER, Johann Kilian (*continued*)

WORKS

H0310   **Beatus vir**
       SATB, 2 vln, 2 vla, bc
       Sacer concentus musicus, no. 18

H0311   **Confitebor tibi**
       SATB, 2 vln, 2 vla, bc
       Sacer concentus musicus, no. 17

H0312   **Dixit Dominus**
       SATB, 2 vln, 2 vla, bc
       Sacer concentus musicus, no. 16

H0313   **Domine ad adjuvandum**
       SATB, 2 vln, 2 vla, bc
       Sacer concentus musicus, no. 15

H0314   **Domine probasti me**
       SATB, 2 vln, bc
       Sacer concentus musicus, no. 24

H0315   **In exitu Israel**
       SATB, 2 vla, bc
       Sacer concentus musicus, no. 22

H0316   **Justum deduxit Dominus**
       SATB, 2 vln, 2 vla, bc
       Sacer concentus musicus, no. 10

H0317   **Lauda Jerusalem**
       SATB, 2 vln, 2 vla, bc
       Sacer concentus musicus, no. 21

H0318   **Laudate Dominum, omnes gentes**
       SATB, 2 vln, 2 vla, bc
       Sacer concentus musicus, no. 20

H0319   **Laudate pueri Dominum**
       SATB, 2 vln, 2 vla, bc
       Sacer concentus musicus, no. 19

H0320   **Magnificat (I)**
       SATB, 2 vln, 2 vla, bc
       Sacer concentus musicus, no. 25

H0321   **Magnificat (II)**
       SSAB, 2 vln, 2 vla, bc
       Sacer concentus musicus, no. 26
       S-Uu 85:73, fol. 8v-11 (Düben)
         tablature

H0322   **Memento Domine, David**
       SATB, 2 vln, 2 vla, bc
       Sacer concentus musicus, no. 23

H0323   **Miserere mei**
       SATB, 2 vln, 2 vla, bc
       Lent
       Sacer concentus musicus, no. 14

H0324   **Missa Funebris**
       SATB, 2 vln, 2 vla, bc
       Sacer concentus musicus, no. 6

H0325   **Missa Immaculatissimae Virginis Mariae**
       SATB, 2 vln, 2 vla, bc
       Sacer concentus musicus, no. 2

H0326   **Missa Omnium sanctorum**
       SATB, 2 vln, 2 vla, bc
       Sacer concentus musicus, no. 5

H0327   **Missa Sanctae crucis**
       SATB, 2 vln, bsn, bc
       Sacer concentus musicus, no. 1

H0328   **Missa Sanctae Joannis Baptistae**
       SATB, 2 vln, bsn, bc
       Sacer concentus musicus, no. 3

H0329   **Missa Sanctorum Chiliani, Colonati, atque Totnani**
       SATB, 2 vln, 2 vla, bc
       Sacer concentus musicus, no. 4

H0330   **Missus est angelus**
       SATB, 2 vln, 2 vla, bc
       Sacer concentus musicus, no. 9

HERMANN, Martin

H0331   **Jesu, meine höchste Freude**
       SSATB
       Funeral of Martha Tesch
       Leipzig, 1661
         RISM CC4573a, K2826, Reich 261 (score)
       DMA 70//193
       Reich: parody of Johann Crüger's "Du geballtes
         Weltgebäude"

HEYE, Joh.

H0332   **Die auf den Herren hoffen**
       SATB, 2 vln, bc
       D-B Mus. ms. 10570 (Erfurt) (1681)
       score and parts

HICKMANN, Esaias

H0333   **O tempus amatum**
       SSATB, 2 vln, 2 vla, vlne/bsn, bc
       D-Dlb Mus. ms. 1849-E-502 (Grimma U
         151/V 79)
       parts

H0334 **Wie lieblich sind deine Wohnungen**
SSATB, 2 vln, bomb, 3 tbn, bc
D-Dlb Mus. ms. 1849-E-501 (Grimma U
591-L 34)
parts

HILDEBRAND

H0335 **Wie lieblich sind deine Wohnungen**
SSATB, 2 vln, 3 vla, 2 corn, 3 clar, vlne, bc
D-Gs Cod. Ms. philos. 84e Hildebrand 1
parts (inc.) and score

HILDEBRAND, Johann (1614-1684)

H0336 **Viel tausend gute Nacht**
SATB, bc
Funeral of Magdalena Ruhende
Dresden, 1648
RISM H5242 (score)
DMA 72//90

HILDEBRAND, Johann Heinrich

H0337 **Ach was erhebet sich**
ATB, 2 vln, bc
D-Dlb Mus. ms. 1866-E-500 (Grimma U
594/T 12 LIII)
parts
S-Uu 81:149, fol. 149v-152 (Düben)
tablature (anonymous)
S-Uu 38:5 (Düben)
parts (anonymous)

H0338 **Höre, Tochter, schaue drauf**
SATB, 2 vln, vla, bc
D-B Mus. ms. 10590 (Erfurt) (1677)
parts

H0339 **Jauchzet dem Herren**
SSATTB, 2 vln, 2 clar, 3 tbn, bc
D-B Mus. ms. 10591 (Erfurt) (1683)
parts

HINTZE, Jacob (1622-1702)

COLLECTION

Martini Opitzes . . . Epistolische Lieder (1695)
RISM H5640 (parts)
first published as appendix to Johann Crüger's
Praxis pietatis melica, editio XII (1666)—
RISM B/VIII/1 1666[11] [II], DMA 3/557

WORKS

H0340 **Als durch das schöne Licht der Sonnen**
SATB, 2 vln, bc
Pentecost
Epistolische Lieder, no. 36

H0341 **Auf, auf die rechte Zeit**
SATB, 2 vln, bc
1st Sunday of Advent
Epistolische Lieder, no. 1

H0342 **Bedenkt, ihr Brüder, jederzeit**
SATB, 2 vln, bc
2nd Sunday after Easter
Epistolische Lieder, no. 30

H0343 **Bemühet euch, ihr Brüder**
SATB, 2 vln, bc
21st Sunday after Trinity
Epistolische Lieder, no. 59

H0344 **Brich auf und werde Licht**
SATB, 2 vln, bc
Epiphany
Epistolische Lieder, no. 9

H0345 **Christ lag in Todesbanden**
STB, 2 vln, vla, vlne, bc
Epistolische Lieder, Zugabe no. 3

H0346 **Christus ist auf Erden kommen**
SATB, 2 vln, bc
5th Sunday of Lent
Epistolische Lieder, no. 22

H0347 **Dafür mag uns ein Jederman erkennen**
SATB, 2 vln, bc
3rd Sunday of Advent
Epistolische Lieder, no. 3

H0348 **Das blinde Volk der Heiden**
SATB, 2 vln, bc
25th Sunday after Trinity
Epistolische Lieder, no. 63

H0349 **Das Gnadenlicht des Herren**
SATB, 2 vln, bc
Christmas Day
Epistolische Lieder, no. 5

H0350 **Das, was ihr sollt einander**
SATB, 2 vln, bc
4th Sunday after Epiphany
Epistolische Lieder, no. 13

H0351 **Denkt und erwägt, o Brüder, jederzeit**
SATB, 2 vln, bc
5th Sunday after Epiphany
Epistolische Lieder, no. 14

HINTZE, Jacob (*continued*)

H0352 Die du Christus hast erkauft
SATB, 2 vln, bc
6th Sunday after Trinity
Epistolische Lieder, no. 43

H0353 Dieweil ihr schwaches Fleisches seid
SATB, 2 vln, bc
7th Sunday after Trinity
Epistolische Lieder, no. 44

H0354 Dieweil man ja der Menschen Testament
SATB, 2 vln, bc
13th Sunday after Trinity
Epistolische Lieder, no. 50

H0355 Durch unsers Gottes Gütigkeit
SATB, 2 vln, bc
1st Sunday after Epiphany
Epistolische Lieder, no. 10

H0356 Ein jeder soll wie Christus Sinnes werden
SATB, 2 vln, bc
Palm Sunday
Epistolische Lieder, no. 23

H0357 Ein jedes Ding und Tun
SATB, 2 vln, bc
1st Sunday after Easter
Epistolische Lieder, no. 29

H0358 Erzählet mir ihr deren Rede gehet
SATB, 2 vln, bc
4th Sunday of Lent
Epistolische Lieder, no. 21

H0359 Es ist zu wenig das Wort hören
SATB, 2 vln, bc
5th Sunday after Easter
Epistolische Lieder, no. 33

H0360 Es sind unterschiedene Gaben
SATB, 2 vln, bc
2nd Sunday after Epiphany
Epistolische Lieder, no. 11

H0361 Fegt ab von euch den Sauerteig
SATB, 2 vln, bc
Easter
Epistolische Lieder, no. 26

H0362 Gott ist die Lieb
SATB, 2 vln, bc
1st Sunday after Trinity
Epistolische Lieder, no. 38

H0363 Gott unser Heiland
SATB, 2 vln, bc
New Year's Day
Epistolische Lieder, no. 7

H0364 Hätt ich Beredsamkeit
SATB, 2 vln, bc
Quinquagesima
Epistolische Lieder, no. 17

H0365 Ich ermahn euch jetzt und wieder
SATB, 2 vln, bc
2nd Sunday of Lent
Epistolische Lieder, no. 19

H0366 Ich glaube recht und wohl
SATB, 2 vln, bc
4th Sunday after Trinity
Epistolische Lieder, no. 41

H0367 Ich hof, ihr liebet noch und ehrt
SATB, 2 vln, bc
11th Sunday after Trinity
Epistolische Lieder, no. 48

H0368 Ich muß mit Danke Gott erheben
SATB, 2 vln, bc
18th Sunday after Trinity
Epistolische Lieder, no. 56

H0369 Ich zwar Gefangner Gottes wegen
SATB, 2 vln, bc
17th Sunday after Trinity
Epistolische Lieder, no. 54

H0370 Ihr allesamt sollt haben gleiche Sinnen
SATB, 2 vln, bc
5th Sunday after Trinity
Epistolische Lieder, no. 42

H0371 Ihr Brüder dürft euch nicht betrüben
SATB, 2 vln, bc
2nd Sunday after Trinity
Epistolische Lieder, no. 39

H0372 Ihr Brüder, weil ihr hier
SATB, 2 vln, bc
20th Sunday after Trinity
Epistolische Lieder, no. 58

H0373 Ihr Männer Abrahams Geschlecht
SATB, 2 vln, bc
Easter Tuesday
Epistolische Lieder, no. 28

H0374 Ihr müsset Gott euch rein
SATB, 2 vln, bc
Sunday after Ascension
Epistolische Lieder, no. 35

H0375 Ihr müsset nach dem Fleische sterben
SATB, 2 vln, bc
8th Sunday after Trinity
Epistolische Lieder, no. 45

H0376 **Ihr wisset, daß zwar ihrer viel**
SATB, 2 vln, bc
Septuagesima
Epistolische Lieder, no. 15

H0377 **Im Hause der Unsterblichkeit**
SATB, 2 vln, bc
Feast of Saint Michael
Epistolische Lieder, no. 55

H0378 **Lasst drum nicht ab, ihr Brüder**
SATB, 2 vln, bc
16th Sunday after Trinity
Epistolische Lieder, no. 53

H0379 **Meint nicht, ihr habt die Klugheit**
SATB, 2 vln, bc
3rd Sunday after Epiphany
Epistolische Lieder, no. 12

H0380 **Merk auf, mein Knecht wird**
SATB, 2 vln, bc
Good Friday
Epistolische Lieder, no. 25

H0381 **Nun freuet euch**
SATB, 2 vln, bc
4th Sunday of Advent
Epistolische Lieder, no. 4

H0382 **O Corinth, du Zier der Welt**
SATB, 2 vln, bc
9th Sunday after Trinity
Epistolische Lieder, no. 46

H0383 **O liebste Schar, denkt nach**
SATB, 2 vln, bc
10th Sunday after Trinity
Epistolische Lieder, no. 47

H0384 **O selig ist ein solcher Mann**
SATB, 2 vln, bc
Trinity
Epistolische Lieder, no. 37

H0385 **Petrus Gottes treuer Knecht**
SATB, 2 vln, bc
Easter Monday
Epistolische Lieder, no. 27

H0386 **Schaut, daß ihr von euch legen**
SATB, 2 vln, bc
19th Sunday after Trinity
Epistolische Lieder, no. 57

H0387 **Schaut über euch und auf den Geist**
SATB, 2 vln, bc
14th Sunday after Trinity
Epistolische Lieder, no. 51

H0388 **Seid jetzt und allezeit**
SATB, 2 vln, bc
27th Sunday after Trinity
Epistolische Lieder, no. 65

H0389 **Seit wir in Erfahrung kommen**
SATB, 2 vln, bc
24th Sunday after Trinity
Epistolische Lieder, no. 62

H0390 **Sinnt nach ihr**
SATB, 2 vln, bc
1st Sunday of Lent
Epistolische Lieder, no. 18

H0391 **So lange Zeit ein Erbe bleibt**
SATB, 2 vln, bc
Sunday after Christmas
Epistolische Lieder, no. 6

H0392 **So oft ich an euch denken können**
SATB, 2 vln, bc
22nd Sunday after Trinity
Epistolische Lieder, no. 60

H0393 **So tut nun, was das höchste Gut**
SATB, 2 vln, bc
3rd Sunday of Lent
Epistolische Lieder, no. 20

H0394 **Stellet Gott heim eure Sachen**
SATB, 2 vln, bc
3rd Sunday after Trinity
Epistolische Lieder, no. 40

H0395 **Vom Herren hab ich es bekommen**
SATB, 2 vln, bc
Maundy Thursday
Epistolische Lieder, no. 24

H0396 **Was das Gesetz heißt**
SATB, 2 vln, bc
Sunday after New Year
Epistolische Lieder, no. 8

H0397 **Was unser Glaube gutes tut**
SATB, 2 vln, bc
4th Sunday after Easter
Epistolische Lieder, no. 32

H0398 **Was vor diesen meine Lieben**
SATB, 2 vln, bc
2nd Sunday of Advent
Epistolische Lieder, no. 2

H0399 **Weil ihr seid klug**
SATB, 2 vln, bc
Sexagesima
Epistolische Lieder, no. 16

HINTZE, Jacob (*continued*)

H0400 **Weil unser Gott den Geist**
SATB, 2 vln, bc
15th Sunday after Trinity
Epistolische Lieder, no. 52

H0401 **Wer recht tun will**
SATB, 2 vln, bc
26th Sunday after Trinity
Epistolische Lieder, no. 64

H0402 **Wie Christus auferstanden**
SATB, 2 vln, bc
Ascension
Epistolische Lieder, no. 34

H0403 **Wir sind allhier nur Pilger**
SATB, 2 vln, bc
3rd Sunday after Easter
Epistolische Lieder, no. 31

H0404 **Wollt ihr die gute Straße reisen**
SATB, 2 vln, bc
23rd Sunday after Trinity
Epistolische Lieder, no. 61

H0405 **Zu Gott wir setzen ein Vertrauen**
SATB, 2 vln, bc
12th Sunday after Trinity
Epistolische Lieder, no. 49

HINZ, Ewaldt (d. after ca. 1666)

H0406 **Dulcis amor Jesu**
SSATB, bc
S-Uu 27:1 (Düben)
parts

HIPP, Berthold

COLLECTION

Heliotropium mysticum (1671)
RISM H5641 (parts)
DMA 60//49

WORKS

H0407 **Anima mea**
SATB, bc
Heliotropium mysticum, no. 25

H0408 **Anima nostra**
ATTB, bc
Heliotropium mysticum, no. 26

H0409 **Ave Regina**
SATB, bc
Heliotropium mysticum, no. 29

H0410 **Daniel serve Dei**
SATB, bc
Heliotropium mysticum, no. 24

H0411 **Exaudiat**
SATB, bc
Heliotropium mysticum, no. 33

H0412 **Litaniae de Venerabili Sacramento**
SATB, bc
Heliotropium mysticum, no. 34

H0413 **Litaniae Lauretanea Beatae Mariae Virginis**
SATB, bc
Heliotropium mysticum, no. 35

H0414 **Ne reminiscaris**
ATB, bc
Heliotropium mysticum, no. 13

H0415 **O Beate Pater Francisce**
SAT, bc
Heliotropium mysticum, no. 11

H0416 **O felicissima dies**
SATB, 2 vln, vla, bc
Heliotropium mysticum, no. 31

H0417 **Qui sequitur me**
SATB, bc
Heliotropium mysticum, no. 27

H0418 **Regina caeli**
SAB, bc
Heliotropium mysticum, no. 14

H0419 **Regina caeli**
SATB, bc
Heliotropium mysticum, no. 30

H0420 **Si quaris miracula**
SATB, 2 vln, 2 vla, bc
Heliotropium mysticum, no. 32

H0421 **Sic in suo cinere**
SSB, 2 vln, bc
Heliotropium mysticum, no. 28

H0422 **Tristis est**
SSB, bc
Heliotropium mysticum, no. 12

HOELZEL, J.

H0423 **Du Tochter Zion, freue dich**
SATB, 4 treble instrs, bc
1st Sunday of Advent

D-Bds Mus. ms. 30282 (old no. 198), no. 18
   score
   Attribution questionable

H0424   **Erbarm dich mein, o Herre Gott**
   SATB, 2 vln, vla, bc
   9th Sunday after Trinity
   D-Bds Mus. ms. 30282 (old no. 198), no. 19
      score
      Attribution questionable

H0425   **Magnificat**
   SSAATTBB, 2 vln, 2 vla, clar, 3 tbn, bc
   Pentecost
   D-B Mus. ms. 10696/5 (Bokemeyer) (1685)
      score

H0426   **Missa (brevis)**
   SATB, 2 vln, vla, bc
   D-B Mus. ms. 10696
      score and bc part

HOEZL [Hoelzl], Ludwig

COLLECTIONS

   Missae brevissimae (1695)
      RISM H5734 (parts)

   Musica vespertina tripartita (1688)
      RISM H5733 (parts)
      DMA 1/559

WORKS

H0427   **Beatus vir (I)**
   SATB, 2 vln, 2 vla, bc
   Musica vespertina tripartita, no. 3

H0428   **Beatus vir (II)**
   SATB, vln, 3 vla, bc
   Musica vespertina tripartita, no. 27

H0429   **Confitebor tibi Domine (I)**
   SAT, bc
   Musica vespertina tripartita, no. 2

H0430   **Confitebor tibi Domine (II)**
   SATB, 2 vln, 2 vla, bc
   Musica vespertina tripartita, no. 25

H0431   **Credidi (I)**
   SATB, vln, 3 vla, bc
   Musica vespertina tripartita, no. 33

H0432   **Credidi (II)**
   SATB, vln, 3 vla, bc
   Musica vespertina tripartita, no. 34

H0433   **Dixit Dominus (I)**
   SATB, 2 vln, 2 vla, bc
   Musica vespertina tripartita, no. 1

H0434   **Dixit Dominus (II)**
   SATB, 2 vln, 2 vla, bc
   Musica vespertina tripartita, no. 9

H0435   **Dixit Dominus (III)**
   SATB, vln, 3 vla, bc
   Musica vespertina tripartita, no. 10

H0436   **Dixit Dominus (IV)**
   SATB, 2 vln, 2 vla, bc
   Musica vespertina tripartita, no. 22

H0437   **Dixit Dominus (V)**
   SATB, 2 vln, 2 vla, bc
   Musica vespertina tripartita, no. 23

H0438   **In convertendo**
   SAT, bc
   Musica vespertina tripartita, no. 35

H0439   **In exitu**
   SATB, 2 vln, 2 vla, bc
   Musica vespertina tripartita, no. 6

H0440   **Laetatus sum (I)**
   SATB, vln, 3 vla, bc
   Musica vespertina tripartita, no. 14

H0441   **Laetatus sum (II)**
   SATB, vln, 3 vla, bc
   Musica vespertina tripartita, no. 15

H0442   **Lauda Jerusalem (I)**
   SATB, 2 vln, 2 vla, bc
   Musica vespertina tripartita, no. 18

H0443   **Lauda Jerusalem (II)**
   SATB, vln, 3 vla, bc
   Musica vespertina tripartita, no. 19

H0444   **Laudate Dominum (I)**
   SATB, 4 vla, bc
   Musica vespertina tripartita, no. 30

H0445   **Laudate Dominum (II)**
   SATB, 4 vla, bc
   Musica vespertina tripartita, no. 31

H0446   **Laudate, pueri (I)**
   SSA, bc
   Musica vespertina tripartita, no. 11

H0447   **Laudate, pueri (II)**
   SAT, bc
   Musica vespertina tripartita, no. 13

H0448   **Laudate, pueri (III)**
   SSB, bc
   Musica vespertina tripartita, no. 29

HOEZL [Hoelzl], Ludwig (*continued*)

H0449　**Magnificat (I)**
SATB, 2 vln, 2 vla, bc
Musica vespertina tripartita, no. 7

H0450　**Magnificat (II)**
SATB, 2 vln, 2 vla, bc
Musica vespertina tripartita, no. 8

H0451　**Magnificat (III)**
SATB, 2 vln, 2 vla, bc
Musica vespertina tripartita, no. 20

H0452　**Magnificat (IV)**
SATB, 2 vln, 2 vla, bc
Musica vespertina tripartita, no. 21

H0453　**Magnificat (V)**
SATB, 2 vln, 2 vla, bc
Musica vespertina tripartita, no. 37

H0454　**Magnificat (VI)**
SATB, vln, 3 vla, bc
Musica vespertina tripartita, no. 38

H0455　**Memento**
SATB, 4 vla, bc
Musica vespertina tripartita, no. 32

H0456　**Missa (III)**
SAT
Musica vespertina tripartita, no. 3

H0457　**Missa (V)**
SSA
Missae brevissimae, no. 5

H0458　**Missa (VI)**
ATB
Missae brevissimae, no. 6

H0459　**Missa (VIII)**
SSB/TTB
Missae brevissimae, no. 8

H0460　**Nisi Dominus**
SSB, 2 vla, 3 tbn, bc
Musica vespertina tripartita, no. 17

H0461　**Requiem**
TTB
Missae brevissimae, no. 9

HOFER, Andreas (1629-1684)

Note: Hofer's works list cannot be considered definitive until the manuscripts in the Salzburg cathedral archive are again available and a thorough stylistic and source study of all works thought to have been written by Hofer is undertaken. The titles of a number of the pieces discovered by Gross in D-Mb (see Gross, 1975) concord with works listed as "previously attributed" but now thought by Barndt-Webb (pp. 258-67) to be spurious. The manuscripts in D-Mb are apparently all 19th-century copies of unnamed sources; none of the titles appear among the works known to be by Hofer. A list of spurious compositions is given at the end of this entry

COLLECTIONS

Salmi con una voce (1654)
RISM H5735, 1654[4] (parts)
DMA 3/118

Ver sacrum seu flores musici (1677)
RISM H5736 (parts)
DMA 65//47

WORKS

H0462　**Ad cunas Jesuli**
SSATB, 2 vln, 2 vla, bsn, bc
Circumcision
Ver sacrum seu flores musici, no. 5

H0463　**Ad festum virginis**
SATB, SATB, 2 vln, tbn, bc
Feast of a Virgin Martyr
Ver sacrum seu flores musici, no. 18

H0464　**Ad sereni caeli**
SSATB, 2 vln, 2 vla, bsn, bc
Feast of a Confessor
Ver sacrum seu flores musici, no. 17

H0465　**Adeste fideles**
SSATB, 2 vln, 2 vla, bsn, bc
Feast of Saint Stephen
Ver sacrum seu flores musici, no. 2

H0466　**Ascendens Christus**
SSB
Salmi con una voce, no. 11

H0467　**Audite insulae**
SATB, SATB, 2 vln, 3 vla, bc
Feast of John the Baptist
CS-KRa II, 143
parts
microfilm: US-SY

H0468　**Audite insulae**
SATTB, 2 vln, 3 tbn, bc
Feast of Saint John the Baptist
Ver sacrum seu flores musici, no. 13

H0469　**Beatus vir**
SSATB, 2 vln, 3 vla, bc
CS-KRa III, 69, no. 4
parts
microfilm: US-SY
Accademia musicale, 31

H0470 **Caeli cives**
SSATB, 2 vln, 2 vla, bsn, bc
Ascension
Ver sacrum seu flores musici, no. 10

H0471 **Confitebor**
SSATB, 2 vln, 3 vla, bc
CS-KRa III, 69, no. 3
parts
microfilm: US-SY
Accademia musicale, 31

H0472 **Consurgite fortes**
SSATB, 2 vln, 3 tbn, bc
Purification of the Virgin Mary
Ver sacrum seu flores musici, no. 6

H0473 **Dextera Domini**
SATB, SATB, 4 vla, 2 corn, 3 tbn, org
CS-KRa II, 34
parts
microfilm: US-SY

H0474 **Dixit Dominus**
SATB, SATB, 2 vln/corn, 3 vla/tbn, bc
CS-KRa III, 77
parts
microfilm: US-SY

H0475 **Dixit Dominus**
SSATB, 2 vln, 3 vla, bc
CS-KRa III, 69, no. 2
parts
microfilm: US-SY
Accademia musicale, 31

H0476 **Dum medium**
SSATB, 2 vln, 3 tbn, bc
Christmas Day
Ver sacrum seu flores musici, no. 1

H0477 **Ecce crucem Domini**
SSATB, 2 vln, 3 tbn, bc
Feast of the Discovery of the Cross
Ver sacrum seu flores musici, no. 9

H0478 **Ego flos campi**
SST
Salmi con una voce, no. 13

H0479 **Egredimini**
SSATB, 2 vln, 2 vla, bsn, bc
Feast of the Blessed Virgin
Ver sacrum seu flores musici, no. 14

H0480 **Estote fortes**
SSATB, 2 vln, 3 tbn, bc
Feast of the Apostles
Ver sacrum seu flores musici, no. 15

H0481 **Estote fortes**
SATB, SATB, 2 vln, 2 corn, 3 tbn, bc
Feast of the Apostles
CS-KRa II, 292
parts
microfilm: US-SY

H0482 **Et conventum**
3 vv
CH-E TH 497.2 (Ms. 3970)

H0483 **Et ego exaudium eum**
4 vv, instr
CH-E TH 498.6 (Ms. 3980)

H0484 **Exurge Domini**
ATB
Salmi con una voce, no. 14

H0485 **Fundata est domus**
SSATTB, 2 vln, 2 vla, 2 corn, bc
Dedication of a church
CS-KRa II, 36
parts
microfilm: US-SY

H0486 **Gaudeamus exultemus**
SATB, SATB, 2 vln, 2 corn, 3 tbn, bc
CS-KRa II, 198
parts
microfilm: US-SY

H0487 **Gaudent caeli**
SSATB, 2 vln, 3 tbn, bc
Feast of Saint John the Evangelist
Ver sacrum seu flores musici, no. 3

H0488 **Gaudia fideles**
SSAT
Salmi con una voce, no. 12

H0489 **Hymnus cantate**
SSS
Salmi con una voce, no. 9

H0490 **Lauda Jerusalem**
SSB, bc
CS-KRa III, 65
parts
microfilm: US-SY

H0491 **Laudate Dominum**
SSATB, 2 vln, 3 vla, bc
CS-KRa III, 69, no. 6
parts
microfilm: US-SY
Accademia musicale, 31

H0492 **Laudate, pueri**
SSATB, 2 vln, 3 vla, bc

HOFER, Andreas (*continued*)

CS-KRa III, 69, no. 5
parts
microfilm: US-SY
Accademia musicale, 31

H0493 **Litaniae Beatae Mariae Virginis**
SSATB, 2 vla, 3 tbn, bc
CS-KRa V, 65
parts
microfilm: US-SY

H0494 **Litaniae de Venerabili Sacramento**
SATB, SATB, bc
CS-KRa V, 81
score
microfilm: US-SY

H0495 **Litaniae Lauretanae**
SSATB, bc
CS-KRa V, 67
parts
microfilm: US-SY

H0496 **Magnificat**
SSATB, 2 vln, 2 vla, bc
CS-KRa III, 82
parts
microfilm: US-SY

H0497 **Magnificat**
SATB, SATB, 4 vla, 2 corn, 3 tbn, bc
CS-KRa III, 81
parts
microfilm: US-SY
Ed. C. Sherman, *Accademia musicale*, 10

H0498 **Magnificat**
SSATB, 2 vln, 3 vla, bc
CS-KRa III, 69, no. 7
parts
microfilm: US-SY
Accademia musicale, 31

H0499 **Missa Archiepiscopalis**
SATB, SATB, 2 vln, 2 vla, 2 corn, 2 clar,
3 tbn, bc
A-KR C/7/653 (1699)
parts
CH-E Ms. 498.1
score

H0500 **Missa Quid vobis videtur**
SSATB, 2 vln, 3 vla, 3 tbn, bc
CS-KRa I, 119 (1670)
score and parts
microfilm: US-SY

H0501 **Missa Valete**
SSATB, 2 vla, vltta, corn, bc
A-KR C/7/651
parts
CH-E Ms. 285.4
score
D-Bds Mus. ms. 10698
score

H0502 **O quam metuendus est**
SSATTB, 2 vln, 4 tbn, bc
Dedication of a church
CS-KRa II, 93
parts
microfilm: US-SY

H0503 **O quam metuendus est**
SSATTB, 6 instr, bc
A-Sd
parts
Barndt-Webb indicates that this and the
previous setting are not identical

H0504 **O suavis aura**
SATTB, 2 vln, 3 tbn, bc
Pentecost
Ver sacrum seu flores musici, no. 11

H0505 **Panis candidissime**
SSATB, 2 vln, 3 vla, bc
Corpus Christi
Ver sacrum seu flores musici, no. 12

H0506 **Quam splendita**
SATTB, 2 vln, 2 vla, bsn, bc
Feast of a Martyr
Ver sacrum seu flores musici, no. 16

H0507 **Quia veniet**
8 vv, org
CH-E TH 497.12 (Ms. 3976)

H0508 **Quo progrederis**
5 vv, 2 vln, 3 vla, bc
A-Sd
parts

H0509 **Requiem**
SATB, 3 vla, bc
CS-KRa XIII, 2
score
microfilm: US-SY
CS-KRa XIII, 9
parts
microfilm: US-SY

H0510 **Requiem**
SSATTB, 3 vla, 3 tbn, bc

CS-KRa XIII, 18
parts
microfilm: US-SY

H0511 **Responsoria pro Matutino in coena Domini**
SATB, 3 vla, bc
Maundy Thursday
CS-KRa XVI, 4
parts
microfilm: US-SY
See also Tenebrae

H0512 **Resurgenti Deo**
SSATB, 2 vln, 3 tbn, bc
Easter Sunday
Ver sacrum seu flores musici, no. 7

H0513 **Stabunt justi**
SSATTB, 3 vla, 3 tbn, bc
Feast of a Martyr
CS-KRa II, 162
parts
microfilm: US-SY

H0514 **Te Deum laudamus**
SATB, SATB, 2 vln, 2 vla, 2 corn, 4 tpt, 3
tbn, timp, bc
CS-KRa XI, 1 and XI, 5
parts
microfilm: US-SY
Ed. C. Sherman, *Accademia musicale*, 1

H0515 **Te Deum laudamus**
SATB, SATB, 3 vla, 2 clar, 3 tbtta, 4 tbn,
vlne, bc
CS-KRa XI, 4 and XI, 6
parts
microfilm: US-SY

H0516 **Tenebrae factae sunt** (from Responsoria pro
matutino)
SATB, 3 vla, bc
A-Sn III, 3
parts
D-Bds Mus. ms. 10698, no. 10
parts
CH-E 296.5, p. 36
score

H0517 **Ubi duo aut tres**
SSB
Salmi con una voce, no. 10

H0518 **Veni de Libano**
5 vv, 2 vln, 3 vla, bc
A-Sd
parts

H0519 **Venite, gentes**
SSATTB, 3 vla, 3 tbn, vlne, bc
Feast of the Blessed Virgin
CS-KRa II, 15 and II, 232
parts
microfilm: US-SY

H0520 **Vidi conjunctos**
SSATB, 2 vln, 2 vla, bsn, bc
Feast of Apostles Phillip and Jacob
Ver sacrum seu flores musici, no. 8

H0521 **Vidi conjunctos vivos**
SSATB, 2 vln, 3 vla/tbn, bc
CS-KRa II, 228
parts (vln parts lacking)
microfilm: US-SY

H0522 **Virgo prudentissima**
SATB, SATB, 2 vla, 4 tbn, bc
Feast of Saint Caecilia
CS-KRa II, 35
parts
microfilm: US-SY

H0523 **Vox in Rama**
SSSAT, 2 vln, 3 vla, bc
Feast of the Holy Innocents
Ver sacrum seu flores musici, no. 4

SPURIOUS WORKS

H0524 **Caritas Pater est**
SATB, SATB, bc
D-Mb Gross no. 37 (1871)
score

H0525 **Confitebor**
SATB, SATB
5th Sunday of Lent
D-Mb Gross no. 42
score and parts

H0526 **Dicite pusillamines confortamini**
SATTB, bc
3rd Sunday of Advent
D-Mb Gross no. 38-IV
score
See Barndt-Webb, p. 259

H0527 **Dominus dabit**
SATTB, bc
1st Sunday of Advent
D-Mb Gross no. 38-II
score
See Barndt-Webb, p. 258

H0528 **Ecce virgo**
SATTB, bc

HOFER, Andreas (*continued*)

    4th Sunday of Advent
    D-Mb Gross no. 38-I
    score

H0529 **Gloria et honore**
    SATB, SATB, bc
    Feast of Saint Andrew
    D-Mb Gross no. 40 and 40a (1877)
    score and parts

H0530 **Hoc corpus**
    SATTB, bc
    5th Sunday of Lent
    D-Mb Gross no. 39-I
    score
    Probable composer: Pietro Bonamico; cf.
      Barndt-Webb, p. 264

H0531 **Jerusalem, surge**
    SATTB, bc
    2nd Sunday of Advent
    D-Mb Gross no. 38-III
    score

H0532 **Justitiae Domini rectae**
    SSAT, ATTB
    3rd Sunday of Lent
    D-Mb Gross no. 41 (1877)
    score and parts
    D-Mb Gross no. 45-III
    score
    Probable composer: Pietro Bonamico; cf.
      Barndt-Webb, p. 263

H0533 **Laudate Dominum**
    SATB, SATB, bc
    4th Sunday of Lent
    D-Mb Gross no. 45-I
    score
    Probable composer: Pietro Bonamico; cf.
      Barndt-Webb, p. 263

H0534 **Missa**
    SSATB
    D-Mb Gross no. 44
    parts

H0535 **Pater, si non potest**
    SATTB, bc
    5th Sunday of Lent
    D-Mb Gross no. 39-II
    score
    Probable composer: Pietro Bonamico; cf.
      Barndt-Webb, p. 264

H0536 **Tenuisti manum dexteram**
    SATTB
    Palm Sunday
    D-Mb Gross no. 43
    parts
    Probable composer: Pietro Bonamico; cf.
      Barndt-Webb, p. 264

H0537 **Tollite principes**
    SATB, SATB, bc
    Christmas Day
    D-Mb Gross no. 45-II
    score
    See Barndt-Webb, p. 260

HOFFMANN, Basilius

H0538 **Ach! was für Angst!**
    SSTB, bc
    Funeral of Konrad Steinmann
    Magdeburg, 1668
      RISM H5737, Reich 285 (score)

H0539 **Nun gute Nacht! Ihr Allerliebsten mein**
    AATB, bc
    Funeral of Konrad Steinmann
    Magdeburg, 1668
      RISM H5737, Reich 285 (score)
    DMA 70//176

HOFFMANN, Georg

H0540 **Elend, Jammer, Angst, und Schmerzen**
    SSATTB
    Funeral of Eleanora Magdalena, Gräfin
      von Hohenlohe and Gleich
    Schwäbisch Hall, 1658?
      RISM H5744, Reich 391 (score)
    DMA 66//52

H0541 **Mein Wallfahrt ist vollendet**
    4 vv, 5 vln, bc
    Funeral of Graf Ernst Eberhardt Friderich
      von Hohenlohe and Gleich
    Rothenburg ob der Tauber, 1671
      RISM H5745

HOINECH, Boras

H0542 **Nun danket alle Gott, der große Dinge tut**
    SSB, 2 vln, 2 corn/fl, 3 tpt, bc
    D-F Ms. Ff. Mus. 290
    parts

HORN, Johann Caspar (ca. 1630-1685)

COLLECTIONS

Geistliche Harmonien, Sommerteil (1680-1681)
RISM H7419 (parts)
DMA 3/1000

Geistliche Harmonien, Winterteil (1680)
RISM H7418 (parts)
DMA 3/999

WORKS

H0543 **A solus ortus cardine**
SATB, 2 vln, 2 vla, bc
D-Bds Mus. ms. 30210, no. 13 (Bokemeyer)
score
DMA 2/841

H0544 **Am Abend der desselbigen Sabbats**
SATB, 2 vln, 2 vla, bc
1st Sunday after Easter
Geistliche Harmonien, Winterteil, no. 32

H0545 **Da aber die Pharisäer hörten**
SATB, 2 vln, 2 vla, bc
18th Sunday of Trinity
Geistliche Harmonien, Sommerteil, no. 28

H0546 **Da aber Johannes im Gefängnis**
SATB, 2 vln, 2 vla, bc
3rd Sunday of Advent
Geistliche Harmonien, Winterteil, no. 3

H0547 **Da der Herr wieder ausging vor den Grenzen Tyri**
SATB, 2 vln, 2 vla, bc
12th Sunday after Trinity
Geistliche Harmonien, Sommerteil, no. 20

H0548 **Da der Tag der Pfingsten erfüllet war**
SATB, 2 vln, 2 vla, bc
Pentecost
Geistliche Harmonien, Sommerteil, no. 2

H0549 **Da die Tage ihrer Reinigung**
SATB, 2 vln, 2 vla, bc
Feast of the Purification
Geistliche Harmonien, Winterteil, no. 22

H0550 **Da die Weisen aus Morgenland**
SATB, 2 vln, 2 vla, bc
Sunday after Circumcision
Geistliche Harmonien, Winterteil, no. 11

H0551 **Da gingen die Pharisäer hin**
SATB, 2 vln, 2 vla, bc
23rd Sunday after Trinity
Geistliche Harmonien, Sommerteil, no. 33

H0552 **Da Jesus geboren war**
SATB, 2 vln, 2 vla, bc
Epiphany
Geistliche Harmonien, Winterteil, no. 12

H0553 **Da Jesus solches mit ihnen redet**
SATB, 2 vln, 2 vla, bc
24th Sunday after Trinity
Geistliche Harmonien, Sommerteil, no. 34

H0554 **Da Jesus vom Berge herab ging**
SATB, 2 vln, 2 vla, bc
3rd Sunday after Epiphany
Geistliche Harmonien, Winterteil, no. 15

H0555 **Da Jesus zwölf Jahr alt war**
SATB, 2 vln, 2 vla, bc
1st Sunday after Epiphany
Geistliche Harmonien, Winterteil, no. 13

H0556 **Da nun viel Volks bei einander**
SATB, 2 vln, 2 vla, bc
Sexagesima
Geistliche Harmonien, Winterteil, no. 20

H0557 **Da sie aber davon redeten**
SATB, 2 vln, 2 vla, bc
Easter Tuesday
Geistliche Harmonien, Winterteil, no. 31

H0558 **Da sie nun das Nachtmahl gehalten hatten**
SATB, 2 vln, 2 vla, bc
3rd Day of Christmas
Geistliche Harmonien, Winterteil, no. 7

H0559 **Da sie nun nahe den Jerusalem kamen**
SATB, 2 vln, 2 vla, bc
1st Sunday of Advent
Geistliche Harmonien, Winterteil, no. 1

H0560 **Da war Jesus vom Geist**
SATB, 2 vln, 2 vla, bc
1st Sunday of Lent
Geistliche Harmonien, Winterteil, no. 23

H0561 **Das ist meine Freude**
ATB, SATB, 2 vln, 2 vla, vlne, bc
D-B Mus. ms. 10862 (Erfurt) (1680)
parts
D-Dlb Mus. ms. 1811-E-501 (Grimma U 499/P 72)
parts (voice parts lacking)

H0562 **Der Herr sagete zu etlichen, die sich selbst vermaßen**
SATB, 2 vln, 2 vla, bc
11th Sunday after Trinity
Geistliche Harmonien, Sommerteil, no. 19

HORN, Johann Caspar (*continued*)

H0563   **Der Herr sprach zu den Pharisäen**
SATB, 2 vln, 2 vla, bc
2nd Day of Christmas
Geistliche Harmonien, Winterteil, no. 6

H0564   **Der Herr trat in ein Schiff**
SATB, 2 vln, 2 vla, bc
19th Sunday after Trinity
Geistliche Harmonien, Sommerteil, no. 29

H0565   **Es bat Jesum der Pharisäer einer, daß er mit ihm esse**
SATB, 2 vln, 2 vla, bc
Feast of Mary Magdalene
Geistliche Harmonien, Sommerteil, no. 13

H0566   **Es begab sich aber, da sich das Volk**
SATB, 2 vln, 2 vla, bc
5th Sunday after Trinity
Geistliche Harmonien, Sommerteil, no. 11

H0567   **Es begab sich aber zu der Zeit**
SATB, 2 vln, 2 vla, bc
Christmas Day
Geistliche Harmonien, Winterteil, no. 5

H0568   **Es naheten aber zu Jesus allerlei Zöllner**
SATB, 2 vln, 2 vla, bc
3rd Sunday after Trinity
Geistliche Harmonien, Sommerteil, no. 9

H0569   **Es war ein Mensch**
SATB, 2 vln, 2 vla, bc
Trinity
Geistliche Harmonien, Sommerteil, no. 5

H0570   **Für Elisabeth kam ihre Zeit**
SATB, 2 vln, 2 vla, bc
Feast of John the Baptist
Geistliche Harmonien, Sommerteil, no. 8

H0571   **Gott, es ist mein rechter Ernst**
SSATTB, 2 vln, 2 vla, vlne, bc
D-B Mus. ms. 10863 (Erfurt)
score

H0572   **Im Anfang war das Wort**
SATB, 2 vln, 2 vla, bc
3rd Day of Christmas
Geistliche Harmonien, Winterteil, no. 8

H0573   **Jesus fuhr über das Meer**
SATB, 2 vln, 2 vla, bc
4th Sunday of Lent
Geistliche Harmonien, Winterteil, no. 26

H0574   **Jesus liegt ihnen einander Gleichnis vor**
SATB, 2 vln, 2 vla, bc
5th Sunday after Epiphany
Geistliche Harmonien, Winterteil, no. 17

H0575   **Jesus nahm zu sich die Zwölf**
SATB, 2 vln, 2 vla, bc
Quinquagesima
Geistliche Harmonien, Winterteil, no. 21

H0576   **Jesus sprach zu den Jüden: Welcher unter euch kann mich**
SATB, 2 vln, 2 vla, bc
5th Sunday of Lent
Geistliche Harmonien, Winterteil, no. 27

H0577   **Jesus sprach zu den Jüngern: Wahrlich ich sage euch**
SATB, 2 vln, 2 vla, bc
Whit Tuesday
Geistliche Harmonien, Sommerteil, no. 4

H0578   **Jesus sprach zu den Pharisäern: Es war ein Mensch, der machte**
SATB, 2 vln, 2 vla, bc
2nd Sunday after Trinity
Geistliche Harmonien, Sommerteil, no. 7

H0579   **Jesus sprach zu Nicodemo: Also hat Gott die Welt geliebet**
SATB, 2 vln, 2 vla, bc
Whit Monday
Geistliche Harmonien, Sommerteil, no. 3

H0580   **Jesus sprach zu Petro: Das Himmelreich ist gleich einem König**
SATB, 2 vln, 2 vla, bc
22nd Sunday after Trinity
Geistliche Harmonien, Sommerteil, no. 32

H0581   **Jesus sprach zu seinen Jüngern: Dann wird das Himmelreich**
SATB, 2 vln, 2 vla, bc
27th Sunday after Trinity
Geistliche Harmonien, Sommerteil, no. 37

H0582   **Jesus sprach zu seinen Jüngern: Das Himmelreich ist gleich**
SATB, 2 vln, 2 vla, bc
Septuagesima
Geistliche Harmonien, Winterteil, no. 19

H0583   **Jesus sprach zu seinen Jüngern: Es war ein reicher Mann der hatte einen**
SATB, 2 vln, 2 vla, bc
9th Sunday after Trinity
Geistliche Harmonien, Sommerteil, no. 17

H0584   **Jesus sprach zu seinen Jüngern: Es war ein reicher Mann der kleidete sich**
SATB, 2 vln, 2 vla, bc

1st Sunday after Trinity
Geistliche Harmonien, Sommerteil, no. 6

H0585 **Jesus sprach zu seinen Jüngern: Es werden Zeichen**
SATB, 2 vln, 2 vla, bc
2nd Sunday of Advent
Geistliche Harmonien, Winterteil, no. 2

H0586 **Jesus sprach zu seinen Jüngern: Ich bin der gute Hirte**
SATB, 2 vln, 2 vla, bc
2nd Sunday after Easter
Geistliche Harmonien, Winterteil, no. 33

H0587 **Jesus sprach zu seinen Jüngern: Ich sage euch, es sei denn**
SATB, 2 vln, 2 vla, bc
6th Sunday after Trinity
Geistliche Harmonien, Sommerteil, no. 14

H0588 **Jesus sprach zu seinen Jüngern: Niemand kann zwei Herren**
SATB, 2 vln, 2 vla, bc
15th Sunday after Trinity
Geistliche Harmonien, Sommerteil, no. 23

H0589 **Jesus sprach zu seinen Jüngern: Nun aber gehe ich hin zu dem**
SATB, 2 vln, 2 vla, bc
4th Sunday after Easter
Geistliche Harmonien, Winterteil, no. 35

H0590 **Jesus sprach zu seinen Jüngern: Sehet euch vor den falschen Propheten**
SATB, 2 vln, 2 vla, bc
8th Sunday after Trinity
Geistliche Harmonien, Sommerteil, no. 16

H0591 **Jesus sprach zu seinen Jüngern: Seid barmherzig**
SATB, 2 vln, 2 vla, bc
4th Sunday after Trinity
Geistliche Harmonien, Sommerteil, no. 10

H0592 **Jesus sprach zu seinen Jüngern: Über ein kleines so werdet**
SATB, 2 vln, 2 vla, bc
3rd Sunday after Easter
Geistliche Harmonien, Winterteil, no. 34

H0593 **Jesus sprach zu seinen Jüngern: Wahrlich, wahrlich ich sage**
SATB, 2 vln, 2 vla, bc
5th Sunday after Easter
Geistliche Harmonien, Winterteil, no. 36

H0594 **Jesus sprach zu seinen Jüngern: Wenn aber der Tröster**
SATB, 2 vln, 2 vla, bc

6th Sunday after Easter
Geistliche Harmonien, Winterteil, no. 38

H0595 **Jesus sprach zu seinen Jüngern: Wenn des Menschen Sohn**
SATB, 2 vln, 2 vla, bc
26th Sunday after Trinity
Geistliche Harmonien, Sommerteil, no. 36

H0596 **Jesus sprach zu seinen Jüngern: Wenn ihr nun sehen werdet**
SATB, 2 vln, 2 vla, bc
25th Sunday after Trinity
Geistliche Harmonien, Sommerteil, no. 35

H0597 **Jesus sprach zu seinen Jüngern: Wer mich liebet, der wird**
SATB, 2 vln, 2 vla, bc
Pentecost
Geistliche Harmonien, Sommerteil, no. 1

H0598 **Jesus trat in ein Schiff**
SATB, 2 vln, 2 vla, bc
4th Sunday after Epiphany
Geistliche Harmonien, Winterteil, no. 16

H0599 **Jesus wandte sich zu seinen Jüngern**
SATB, 2 vln, 2 vla, bc
13th Sunday after Trinity
Geistliche Harmonien, Sommerteil, no. 21

H0600 **Maria aber stand auf in den Tagen**
SATB, 2 vln, 2 vla, bc
Feast of the Visitation
Geistliche Harmonien, Sommerteil, no. 12

H0601 **Sein Vater und Mutter wunderten sich**
SATB, 2 vln, 2 vla, bc
Sunday after Christmas
Geistliche Harmonien, Winterteil, no. 9

H0602 **Und als er nahe an Jerusalem kam**
SATB, 2 vln, 2 vla, bc
10th Sunday after Trinity
Geistliche Harmonien, Sommerteil, no. 18

H0603 **Und am dritten Tage war ein Hochzeit**
SATB, 2 vln, 2 vla, bc
2nd Sunday after Epiphany
Geistliche Harmonien, Winterteil, no. 14

H0604 **Und da acht Tage um waren**
SATB, 2 vln, 2 vla, bc
Circumcision
Geistliche Harmonien, Winterteil, no. 10

H0605 **Und da der Sabbat vergangen war**
SATB, 2 vln, 2 vla, bc
Easter Day
Geistliche Harmonien, Winterteil, no. 29

HORN, Johann Caspar (*continued*)

H0606 **Und dies ist das Zeugnis Johannes**
SATB, 2 vln, 2 vla, bc
4th Sunday of Advent
Geistliche Harmonien, Winterteil, no. 4

H0607 **Und er trieb einen Teufel aus**
SATB, 2 vln, 2 vla, bc
3rd Sunday of Lent
Geistliche Harmonien, Winterteil, no. 25

H0608 **Und es begab sich, da Jesus reisete gen Jerusalem**
SATB, 2 vln, 2 vla, bc
14th Sunday after Trinity
Geistliche Harmonien, Sommerteil, no. 22

H0609 **Und es begab sich, daß er kam in ein Haus eines Obersten**
SATB, 2 vln, 2 vla, bc
17th Sunday after Trinity
Geistliche Harmonien, Sommerteil, no. 27

H0610 **Und es begab sich, daß Jesus in eine Stadt mit Namen Nain**
SATB, 2 vln, 2 vla, bc
16th Sunday after Trinity
Geistliche Harmonien, Sommerteil, no. 26

H0611 **Und es erhub sich ein Streit**
SATB, 2 vln, 2 vla, bc
Feast of Saint Michael
Geistliche Harmonien, Sommerteil, no. 25

H0612 **Und es war ein Königischer**
SATB, 2 vln, 2 vla, bc
21st Sunday after Trinity
Geistliche Harmonien, Sommerteil, no. 31

H0613 **Und im sechsten Monat**
SATB, 2 vln, 2 vla, bc
Feast of the Annunciation
Geistliche Harmonien, Winterteil, no. 28

H0614 **Und Jesus antwortet und redet abermals durch ein Gleichnis**
SATB, 2 vln, 2 vla, bc
20th Sunday after Trinity
Geistliche Harmonien, Sommerteil, no. 30

H0615 **Und Jesus ging aus von dannen**
SATB, 2 vln, 2 vla, bc
2nd Sunday of Lent
Geistliche Harmonien, Winterteil, no. 24

H0616 **Und Jesus zog hinein nach Jericho**
SATB, 2 vln, 2 vla, bc
Dedication of a church
Geistliche Harmonien, Sommerteil, no. 38

H0617 **Und nach sechs Tagen**
SATB, 2 vln, 2 vla, bc
6th Sunday after Epiphany
Geistliche Harmonien, Winterteil, no. 18

H0618 **Und siehe, zwei aus ihnen gingen an denselbigen Tage**
SATB, 2 vln, 2 vla, bc
Easter Monday
Geistliche Harmonien, Winterteil, no. 30

H0619 **Zu der Zeit da wieder viel Volks da war**
SATB, 2 vln, 2 vla, bc
7th Sunday after Trinity
Geistliche Harmonien, Sommerteil, no. 15

H0620 **Zu derselbigen Stunde**
SATB, 2 vln, 2 vla, bc
Feast of Saint Michael
Geistliche Harmonien, Sommerteil, no. 24

H0621 **Zuletzt da die Elfe**
SATB, 2 vln, 2 vla, bc
Ascension
Geistliche Harmonien, Winterteil, no. 37

H[UCKE?], G[eorg]

H0622 **Herr, wende deine Plage von mir**
SATB, ATTB, 4 instr, bc
S-Uu 84:96 (Düben)
tablature

HUEBER, Wendelin

COLLECTION

Cantiones sacrae, op. 2 (1650)
RISM H7765 (parts)
DMA 3/1001

WORKS

H0623 **Litaniae**
SATTB, bc
CS-KRa V, 33
parts
microfilm: US-SY

H0624 **Litaniae Lauretanae**
SATB, 2 vln, 3 tbn, bc
CS-KRa V, 57
parts (S missing)
microfilm: US-SY
Attributed by Otto from initials V. H. in ms.

H0625 **Litaniae Lauretanae Beatae Mariae Virginis**
SATB, SATB, vlne, bc
CS-KRa V, 35 (1676)
parts
microfilm: US-SY

H0626 **Missa**
SATB, SATB, bc
CS-KRa I, 64
parts
microfilm: US-SY

H0627 **Missa pleno**
SATB, SATB, 2 vln, 2 corn, 2 clar, 3 tbn,
vlne, bc
CS-KRa I, 69
parts
microfilm: US-SY

H0628 **Nunc dimittis**
TTB, bc
Cantiones sacrae, Op. 2, no. 16

H0629 **Requiem**
SATB, SATB, 4 vla, 3 tbn, vlne, bc
CS-KRa XIII, 8 (1668)
parts (tbn parts lacking)

H0630 **Salve caput cruentatum**
SSB, bc
Cantiones sacrae, Op. 2, no. 15

H0631 **Salve, Jesu, pastor bone**
SSB, bc
Cantiones sacrae, Op. 2, no. 11

H0632 **Salve, Jesu, rex sanctorum**
SSB, bc
Cantiones sacrae, Op. 2, no. 10

H0633 **Salve, Jesu, summe bonus**
SSB, bc
Cantiones sacrae, Op. 2, no. 12

H0634 **Salve mundi salutare**
ATB, bc
Cantiones sacrae, Op. 2, no. 9

H0635 **Salve salus mea Deus**
SSB, bc
Cantiones sacrae, Op. 2, no. 13

H0636 **Stephanus plenus gratia**
SATB, 2 vln, 3 vla, 3 tbn ad lib, vlne, bc
CS-KRa II, 260
parts
microfilm: US-SY

H0637 **Summi regis cor aveto**
SSB, bc
Cantiones sacrae, Op. 2, no. 14

HUNOLD, Georg

H0638 **Klagt nicht, ihr meine Lieben**
SATB
Funeral of Gese Erberfeld
Helmstedt, 1676
RISM H7939, Reich 133 (choirbook)
DMA 70//19

J

JACOBI, Daniel

J0001   **Pax aeterna ab aeterno**
        SSATB, 2 vln, 2 vla, vlne, bc
        S-Uu 81:85, fol. 86r-91r (Düben)
          tablature
          DMA 23//98
        S-Uu 45:1
          parts
          DMA 23//98

J0002   **Preise, Jerusalem, den Herrn**
        SSATTB, 2 vln, 4 tbn, bsn, bc
        D-Bds Mus. ms. 30210, 14
          score
          Ed. Kessler, *Danziger Kirchenmusik*, pp. 106-45

JACOBI, Michael (1618-1663)

J0003   **Ach, es bringt zu große Schmerzen**
        ??
        Funeral of Sebastian Gottfried Stark
        Lüneburg, 1653
          RISM J207 (score)

J0004   **Auf meine Seel und lobe Gott**
        SSATB, bc
        New Year
        Hamburg, 1655
          RISM J211 (score)

J0005   **Gelobet sei der Herr**
        SSATB, 2 vln, bc
        New Year

        Hamburg, 1655
          RISM J210 (parts)
          DMA 64//107

J0006   **Ist uns unser Stark entrissen**
        ??
        Funeral of Sebastian Gottfried Stark
        Lüneburg, 1653
          RISM J207 (score)

J0007   **Timor Domini**
        SSATB, 2 vln, 2 vla, vlne/bsn, bc
        Lüneburg, 1663
          RISM J230 (parts)

J0008   **Und da Jacob vollendet hatte**
        SSATB, bc
        Funeral of Johann Stern
        n.p., 1656
          RISM J215 (parts)
          DMA 70//21

J0009   **Was macht traurige Gebärden**
        ??
        Funeral of Sebastian Gottfried Stark
        Lüneburg, 1653
          RISM J207 (score)

JACOBI, Samuel (1652-1721)

J0010   **Das ist mir lieb, daß der Herr meine Stimme**
        SATB, SATB, bc
        D-Dlb Mus. ms. 1891-E-500 (Grimma U 525/T 37)
          parts (autograph)

J0011   **Der Gerechte, ob er gleich zu zeitlich**
SATB, SATB, bc
D-Dlb Mus. ms. 1891-E-501 (Grimma U 382/N 69)
  score (autograph) and parts
Anonymous; attributed by D-Dlb

J0012   **Du machsts mit mir ein Ende**
SATB
D-Dlb Mus. ms. 1891-E-502 (Grimma U 524/T 36)
  parts (autograph)
Anonymous; attributed by D-Dlb

J0013   **Was der Himmel selber gibt**
See under Anonymous

JACOBI, Tobias

COLLECTION

Scala coeli musicales (1674)
RISM J231 (parts)

WORKS

J0014   **Also hat Gott die Welt geliebt**
SATB, SATB, bc
Scala coeli musicales, no. 16

J0015   **Das ist der Wille des der mich gesandt hat**
SSATB, SAATB, bc
Scala coeli musicales, no. 20

J0016   **Das ist je gewißlich wahr**
SATB, SATB, bc
Scala coeli musicales, no. 12

J0017   **Deine Toten werden leben**
SATB, SATB, bc
Scala coeli musicales, no. 17

J0018   **Der Gerechte kommt um**
SATBB, bc
Scala coeli musicales, no. 9

J0019   **Der Gerechten Seelen sind in Gottes Hand**
SSATB, SATTB, bc
Scala coeli musicales, no. 19

J0020   **Die Gerechten werden ewiglich leben**
SATB, bc
Scala coeli musicales, no. 3

J0021   **Dir sind Kinder der Heiligen**
SSATB, bc
Scala coeli musicales, no. 5

J0022   **Haben wir das Gute empfangen**
SATB, SATB, bc
Scala coeli musicales, no. 13

J0023   **Herr wenn ich nur dich habe**
SSATTTB, bc
Scala coeli musicales, no. 11

J0024   **Ich bin die Auferstehung**
SATB, bc
Scala coeli musicales, no. 2

J0025   **Ich bin gewiß, daß weder Tod**
SATB, SATB, bc
Scala coeli musicales, no. 14

J0026   **Ich weiß, daß mein Erlöser lebet**
SATB, bc
Scala coeli musicales, no. 1

J0027   **Ich will des Herren Zorn tragen**
SSATB, bc
Scala coeli musicales, no. 7

J0028   **Selig sind die Toten, die in dem Herren sterben**
SSATTB, bc
Scala coeli musicales, no. 10

J0029   **Unser keiner lebet ihm selber**
SATTB, bc
Scala coeli musicales, no. 8

J0030   **Unser Wandel ist im Himmel**
SATB, bc
Scala coeli musicales, no. 4

J0031   **Viel so unter der Erden schlafen**
SATB, SATB, bc
Scala coeli musicales, no. 15

J0032   **Wahrlich, wahrlich, ich sage euch**
SSATB, bc
Scala coeli musicales, no. 6

J0033   **Wir wollen euch aber, lieben Brüder**
SATB, SATTB, bc
Scala coeli musicales, no. 18

JOHANN Georg II, Elector of Saxony

J0034   **Laudate Dominum, omnes gentes**
ATB, 2 vln, bc
D-Bds Mus. ms. 30210, no. 15 (Bokemeyer)
  score
DMA 17//58

K

KALDENBACH, Christoph (1613-1698)

COLLECTION

> *Deutsche Sappho* (1687)
> RISM K21, 1687¹³ (parts)
> DMA 3/122

WORKS

K0001 **Ach, wer wird meines Herzens Haus**
SST
Deutsche Sappho, no. 34

K0002 **Also flieht der Zeiten Drang**
SSATB
Funeral of Magdalena Sibylla, Herzogin zu
   Sachsen
Altenburg, 1668
   RISM K19, Reich 12 (score)
   DMA 69//151

K0003 **Andre mögen Lust und Geld**
SST
Deutsche Sappho, no. 16

K0004 **Auch das edle Pfand ist kommen**
SST
Deutsche Sappho, no. 6

K0005 **Auf der Wallfahrt dieses Lebens**
SST
Deutsche Sappho, no. 38

K0006 **Das wunderbare Kind**
SAT
Deutsche Sappho, no. 2

K0007 **Daß auf ein keusches Lied**
SST
Deutsche Sappho, no. 31

K0008 **Den Ruhm, Herr, find ich gänzlich nicht**
SSB
Deutsche Sappho, no. 23

K0009 **Der Herr ist mein Hirt**
5 vv
Wedding of Adam Kaldenbach and Regina
   Sommerfelde
Königsberg, 1645
   RISM K14 (score)

K0010 **Des Lebens Dürftigkeit**
SSA
Deutsche Sappho, no. 25

K0011 **Dich hat selbst Christus ihm zur Braut**
SSA
Deutsche Sappho, no. 32

K0012 **Die größte Klugheit auf der Erden**
SST
Deutsche Sappho, no. 47

K0013 **Die Zeit und ihre Macht vergeht**
SSB, 2 vln, bc
Funeral of Magdalena Sibylla, Herzogin zu
   Sachsen
Altenburg, 1668
   RISM K19, Reich 12 (score)
   DMA 69//151

K0014 **Du habest mich verlassen**
SST
Deutsche Sappho, no. 22

K0015 **Du hast mit väterlicher Zucht**
SST
Deutsche Sappho, no. 21

K0016 **Du reicher Haus-Vogt dieser Erden**
SST
Deutsche Sappho, no. 35

K0017 **Du siehst den Wechsel dieser Zeit**
SSA
Deutsche Sappho, no. 24

K0018 **Gott, du Herrscher aller Dinge**
SST
Deutsche Sappho, no. 7

K0019 **Gott, du wahrer Amens**
SST
Deutsche Sappho, no. 18

K0020 **Herr, dir selber ist bewußt**
SSA
Deutsche Sappho, no. 14

K0021 **Herr, ich liege ganz darnieder**
SSB
Deutsche Sappho, no. 45

K0022 **Herz, du hast dort aufgeschlagen**
SAT
Deutsche Sappho, no. 43

K0023 **Herz, ich komme her zu beten**
SSB
Deutsche Sappho, no. 37

K0024 **Ich fühle ja**
SST
Deutsche Sappho, no. 11

K0025 **Ich habe dir, o grosser Gott**
SAT
Deutsche Sappho, no. 30

K0026 **Irr ich, oder seh ich schon meiner Wunsch den Himmel offen?**
SST
Deutsche Sappho, no. 46

K0027 **Jesu, o mein süßer Hort**
SSB
Deutsche Sappho, no. 20

K0028 **Kommt, schaut den großen Bürgern**
SST
Deutsche Sappho, no. 3

K0029 **Lasst dann Furcht und Zagen weichen**
SSA
Deutsche Sappho, no. 42

K0030 **Meiner Feinde Macht erlieget**
SST
Deutsche Sappho, no. 4

K0031 **Meiner Hoffnung Grund steht fest**
SATTB
Funeral of Karl Leonhard von Rohr
Tübingen, 1657
RISM K16, Reich 415 (choirbook)
DMA 70//191

K0032 **Meiner Hoffnung Grund steht fest**
TTB
Deutsche Sappho, no. 48

K0033 **Mit erneutem Licht und Tage**
SSA
Deutsche Sappho, no. 26

K0034 **Mit so gehäußter Sünden-Last**
SAT
Deutsche Sappho, no. 13

K0035 **Muß gleich ein Gerechter wo eine Weil im Dunkeln liegen**
SST
Deutsche Sappho, no. 39

K0036 **Nicht nur eines Todes Schrecken**
SST
Deutsche Sappho, no. 28

K0037 **O Christe, trautster Seelen Hort**
SSA
Deutsche Sappho, no. 12

K0038 **O du König aller Erden**
SAT
Deutsche Sappho, no. 19

K0039 **O du Stifter aller Zeit**
SST
Deutsche Sappho, no. 27

K0040 **Ob der Satan grimme Wunden**
SST
Deutsche Sappho, no. 29

K0041 **Red, O Herr, zu deinen Füssen**
SST
Deutsche Sappho, no. 10

K0042 **Schickt nun Gott zu Herz und Mut**
SAB
Deutsche Sappho, no. 41

K0043 **Selig Ewigkeit, Lohn der Himmelserben**
SATTB
Funeral of Sophie Schimmelpfennig
Königsberg, 1656
source lost
EdM, 2nd ser., Ostpreussen & Danzig, vol. 1,
p. 14

KALDENBACH, Christoph (*continued*)

K0044   **Sie steht noch fest und wohl gegründet**
SST
Deutsche Sappho, no. 8

K0045   **So beginnt dann Gott zu preisen**
SST
Deutsche Sappho, no. 36

K0046   **So oft ein Wetter steigt empor**
SST
Deutsche Sappho, no. 40

K0047   **Starker Gott der starken Scharen**
SST
Deutsche Sappho, no. 9

K0048   **Unser Haupt geht vor uns hin**
SAT
Deutsche Sappho, no. 5

K0049   **Vater des, der Segen ist**
SSA
Deutsche Sappho, no. 17

K0050   **Von Gott, der mich ging an so nah**
SST
Deutsche Sappho, no. 1

K0051   **Wann die Nacht das Chor der Stern**
SSB
Deutsche Sappho, no. 44

K0052   **Wann meine Sach ich überlege**
SST
Deutsche Sappho, no. 15

K0053   **Wohin ich außer dir, mein Gott**
SST
Deutsche Sappho, no. 33

KEGEL, Emanuel (1655-1724)

K0054   **Christ lag in Todesbanden**
SATB, 2 vln, 2 vla, 4 ob, vlne, bc
D-Dlb Mus. ms. 1920-E-500 (Grimma U
     168/V 61) (1710)
     parts

K0055   **Ich will den Herrn loben allezeit**
SATB, 2 vln, 2 vla, vlne, bc
D-Gs Cod. Ms. philos. 84e Kegel 1 (1732)
     score and parts

K0056   **Meinen Jesum laß ich nicht**
SATB, 2 vln, 2 vla, vlne, bc
F-Ssp
     parts

KERLL, Johann Caspar (1627-1693)

COLLECTIONS

Delectus sacrarum cantionum (1669)
     RISM K456 (parts)

Missa sex (1689)
     RISM K458 (parts)
     DMA 2/672

WORKS

K0057   **Age plaude**
SATB, bc
Delectus sacrarum cantionum, no. 14

K0058   **Alma Redemptoris Mater**
SSATB, bc
Delectus sacrarum cantionum, no. 23

K0059   **Angelorum esca**
SATB, 2 vln, 3 vla, 3 tbn, bc
D-B Mus. ms. 11564
     parts
     DMA 28//140
D-B Mus. ms. 11564/1
     tablature
D-B Mus. ms. 30315, no. 2
     score
D-Bds 11563
     score

K0060   **Ave Regina**
SSBB, bc
Delectus sacrarum cantionum, no. 17
D-Mbs Mus. ms. 6192
     score

K0061   **Ave Regina**
SAATB, bc
Delectus sacrarum cantionum, no. 24

K0062   **Cantate laudes Mariae**
SSATB, bc
Delectus sacrarum cantionum, no. 22

K0063   **Dic mihi imprudens anima**
ATB, bc
Delectus sacrarum cantionum, no. 10

K0064   **Dignare me**
SAB, bc
Delectus sacrarum cantionum, no. 9
DTB III (Jg. II/2), pp. 120-25

K0065   **Dominus regnavit**
BBBB, bc
Delectus sacrarum cantionum, no. 18

D-Bds Mus. ms. Kerll 11558 (1690)
score
DMA 2/1346
Ed. Commer, *Musica sacra* II

K0066 Estote fortes in bello
BBB, 2 vln, bc
Delectus sacrarum cantionum, no. 21

K0067 Exultant justi
SSATB, 2 vln, 2 vla, bc
A-Sd ms. A-211
parts

K0068 Exultate corda devota
SST, bc
Delectus sacrarum cantionum, no. 7
DTB III (Jg. II/2), pp. 110-11

K0069 Gaudete, pastores
SATB, 3 vltta, bc
D-Bds Mus. ms. 30215, no. 3 (Bokemeyer)
score

K0070 Jesu gratias
ATB, bc
Delectus sacrarum cantionum, no. 12

K0071 Justus ut palma
SSATB, 2 vln, 2 vla, 2 corn, bc
A-Sd ms. A-209
parts

K0072 Laetabundus
SSB, 2 vln, bc
Delectus sacrarum cantionum, no. 19

K0073 Laudate, pueri, Dominum
SSB, 2 vln, 2 vla, bc
S-Uu 10:4 (Düben)
parts
DMA 3/1227

K0074 Laudate, pueri, Dominum
SSATB, SATB, 2 vln, bc
D-B Mus. ms. 11557
parts

K0075 Laudate, pueri, Dominum
SSAATTBB, 2 vln, bc
PL-Kj Mus. ms. 40129, fol. 27r-34r (1665)
tablature

K0076 Magnificat (A)
SATB, 2 vln, bc
D-Bds Mus. ms. 30215, no. 4 (Bokemeyer)
score

K0077 Magnificat (G)
SSATTB, 2 vln, bc

D-Bds Mus. ms. 30215, no. 5 (Bokemeyer)
score

K0078 Missa à 12
CS-KRa Ms. I, 223
Lacking in Syracuse film collection

K0079 Missa à 2 chori (D)
SATB, SATB, instr, bc
D-Bds Mus. ms. 30179
score
Not available for verification, 2/83. D-Bds
cat.: score and instr. by Harrer

K0080 Missa à 3 chori
SATB, SATB, SATB, 2 vln, 3 vla, 2 corn,
3 clar, 3 tbn, vlne, bc
A-KR Ms. Ser. C, Fasc. 14, Nr. 702
parts
DTÖ 49 (Jg. 25/1), pp. 106-63

K0081 Missa brevis
SSATB, 2 vln, bc
D-Bds Mus. ms. 30215, no. 2 (Bokemeyer)
score

K0082 Missa brevis
SSATB, 2 vln, 2 vla, bc
D-B Mus. ms. 11555
score
DMA 28//147
Instrumentation thought by Giebler to be
by Harrer
D-B Mus. ms. 11555/1
vocal parts only

K0083 Missa brevis
SATB, 2 vln, 2 vla, 2 ob, bsn, bc
D-Bds Mus. ms. 30167, no. 11
score
DMA 2/2241
Instrumentation by Harrer
D-B Mus. ms. 11555/5
vocal parts only
DMA 2/1347

K0084 Missa Corona virginum
SSATB, 2 vln, 2 vla, bass viol/bsn, bc
Missae sex, no. 4
D-Mbs Mus. Pr. 1751, no. 4
score

K0085 Missa Cujus toni
SATB, 2 vln, 3 tbn, vlne, bass viol/bsn, bc
A-KR Ms. Ser. C, Fasc. 14, Nr. 704
parts
DTÖ 49 (Jg. 25/1), pp. 74-105

KERLL, Johann Caspar (*continued*)

K0086   Missa In fletu solatium
SATTB, 2 vln, 3 vla, vlne/bsn, bc
Missae sex, no. 5
D-Mbs Mus. Pr. 1751, no. 5
score
Ed. Giebler (1956), vol. 2, pp. 1-118

K0087   Missa Nigra
SSATTB, 2 vln, 2 vla, bc
A-KR Ms. Ser. C, Fasc. 14, Nr. 706
parts
CS-KRa Ms. I-108
includes 3 tbn
lacking in Syracuse film collection

K0088   Missa Non sine quare
SATB, 2 vln, bc
Missae sex, no. 1
D-Mbs Mus. Pr. 1751, no. 1
score
Ed. W. Fürlinger, *Süddeutsche Kirchenmusik des Barock*, vol. 6

K0089   Missa Patientiae et spei
SATB, 2 vln, 3 vla, bass viol/bsn, bc
Missae sex, no. 2
D-Mbs Mus. Pr. 1751, no. 2
score

K0090   Missa pro defunctis
SATTB, 3 vla, vlne/bsn, bc
Missae sex, no. 7
D-Mbs Mus. Pr. 1751, no. 7
score
DTÖ 59 (Jg. 30/1), pp. 73-99
See also Requiem

K0091   Missa Quasi modo genita
SATB, 2 vln, 4 vla, 3 tbn, vlne, bc
CS-KRa Ms. I, 107
parts
microfilm: US-SY

K0092   Missa Quid vobis videtur
See under Hofer

K0093   Missa Renovationis
SSATTB, 2 vln, bc
Missae sex, no. 6
D-Mbs. Mus. Pr. 1751, no. 6
score

K0094   Missa Sanctorum innocentium
SSSSA or SSTTB, 2 vln, tbn/bsn, bc
Missae sex, no. 3
D-Mbs. Mus. Pr. 1751, no. 3
score

K0095   Missa Superba
SSAATTBB, 2 vln, 2 vla, 4 tbn, vlne, bc
A-KR Ms. Ser. C, Fasc. 14, Nr. 705
parts
CS-KRa Ms. I, 118
score
microfilm: US-SY
Ed. Giebler (1956), vol. 2, pp. 118-231
Ed. Giebler, RRMBE 3

K0096   Missa Volante
SATB, 2 vln, 3 vla, bsn, bc
D-Bds Mus. ms. 30215, no. 1 (Bokemeyer)
score

K0097   O Jesu, cor meum
ATB, bc
D-B Mus. ms. 11562
parts
DMA 28//11

K0098   O mortales
ATB, bc
Delectus sacrarum cantionum, no. 11

K0099   O panis mellifluus
AAB, 2 vln, bc
Delectus sacrarum cantionum, no. 20

K0100   Plaudentes, virgini
SATB, bc
Delectus sacrarum cantionum, no. 15
DTB III (Jg. II/2), pp. 126-34

K0101   Plorate
SATB, bc
Delectus sacrarum cantionum, no. 13

K0102   Quemadmodum desiderat cervus
SSATB, 3 vla, 3 tbn, bc
D-B Mus. ms. 11559
parts

K0103   Qui sperat pascitur
SSB, bc
Delectus sacrarum cantionum, no. 8

K0104   Regina caeli
SATTB, bc
Delectus sacrarum cantionum, no. 25
DTB III (Jg. II/2), pp. 148-55

K0105   Requiem
SATTB, 5 vla, bc
D-B Mus. ms. 11556/1
score
DMA 28//107
D-B Mus. ms. 11556
parts
D-Mbs Mus. Pr. 587, Mus. Pr. 866

score
DMA 2/1345
See also Missa pro defunctis

K0106 **Responsoria**
SATB, bc
Maundy Thursday
A-Wm ms. XII/617
score
DMA 51/150
No. XII/618 in Riedel catalog of
Minoritenkonvent

K0107 **Salve regina**
SATBB, bc
Delectus sacrarum cantionum, no. 26

K0108 **Sanctus**
SATB, SATB, 2 vln, 3 vla, 2 ob, 4 tbn, bc
F-Pc ms. D 11.33g, no. 2
score

K0109 **Tantum ergo**
SATB, bc
A-Gö ms. Kerl 1
score
DMA 69//51

K0110 **Tota pulchra es**
SSATB, 2 vln, 2 vla, bass vla/bsn, bc
A-Sd ms. A-212
parts

K0111 **Triumphate sidera**
SSATTB, 2 vln, 3 vla, 2 corn, 4 tbn, vlne,
bass vla/bsn, bc
A-Sd ms. A-210
parts

KERN, Andreas

K0112 **Caelestes volucres de Sancta Catherina**
SATB, 2 vln, 2 vla, 2 clar, vlne, bc
CS-KRa II, 51
parts
microfilm: US-SY

K0113 **Missa Ariosa**
SATB, 2 vln, 3 vla, vlne, bc
CS-KRa I, 113 (1676)
parts (vla parts lacking)
microfilm: US-SY

K0114 **Missa Boni pastoris**
SATB, 2 vln, 3 tbn ad lib, vlne, bc
CS-KRa I, 82; CS-KRa I, 259
parts
microfilm: US-SY

K0115 **Missa Sancti Georgii**
SATB, 2 vln, 3 tbn, vlne, bc
CS-KRa I, 111 (1676)
parts
microfilm: US-SY

K0116 **Missa Sancti Joannis**
SATB, 2 vln, 3 vla, vlne, bc
CS-KRa I, 112 (1676)
parts
microfilm: US-SY
Not concordant with following piece

K0117 **Missa Sancti Joannis**
SATB, 2 vln, 2 vla, 2 clar, vlne, bc
CS-KRa I, 133
parts
microfilm: US-SY
Not concordant with preceding piece

KERZINGER, Pater August

K0118 **Caelesti salve librium**
SSATB, 2 vln, vltta, tbn, vlne, bc
CS-KRa II, 17 (1676)
parts
microfilm: US-SY

K0119 **Dixit Dominus**
SATB, 2 vln, 2 vla, vlne, bc
CS-KRa III, 45
parts
microfilm: US-SY

K0120 **Magnificat**
SATB, 2 vln, vlne, bc
CS-KRa III, 46
parts
microfilm: US-SY

K0121 **Missa Sancti Augustin**
SSATB, 2 vln, 2 vla, 3 clar, 3 tbn, bc
CS-KRa I, 138
score
microfilm: US-SY

K0122 **Vesperae dominicales**
SATB, SATB, 2 vln, 2 vla, vlne, bc
CS-KRa III, 47
parts
microfilm: US-SY

K0123 **Vesperae dominicales**
SSATB, ATB, 2 vln, vltta, 3 tbn, bc
CS-KRa III, 71
parts
microfilm: US-SY

KESSEL, Johann (fl. 1657-1670)

K0124   **Dir klag ich, frommer Gott**
SAAB
D-Dlb Mus. Löb 53, no. 108
parts
DMA 2/538

K0125   **Ich habe Lust abzuscheiden**
SSATTB, bc
Funeral of Christian Scheffrichen
Breslau, 1657
RISM K485 (parts)
DMA 72//48

K0126   **Ich will mir eine Kirche bauen**
SATB
D-Dlb Mus. Löb 53, no. 102
parts
DMA 2/538

K0127   **Siehe, wie fein und lieblich ists**
SSATB, 2 vla/tbn, vlne/tbn, bc
Brieg, 1663
RISM K486 (parts)
DMA 52//101

K0128   **Weg, Satan, du besiegst mich nicht**
SATB
D-Dlb Mus. Löb 53, no. 111
parts
DMA 2/538

KLINGENBERG, Martin

K0129   **Also werden die Erlöseten**
SSATB, bc
Funeral of Luise Hedwig von Löben
Berlin, 1669
RISM K914, Reich 37 (parts)
DMA 66//138

KNÜPFER, Sebastian (1633-1676)

K0130   **Ach Herr, laß deine lieben Engelein**
SSATB, 2 vln, bc
D-B Mus. ms. 11780, no. 2 (Bokemeyer)
score
DMA 3/814

K0131   **Ach Herr, strafe mich nicht in deinem Zorn**
SSATB, 2 vln, 2 vltta, 2 fl, 2 clar, timp,
bsn, bc
D-B Mus. ms. 11780, no. 1 (Bokemeyer)
score
DMA 3/815

D-Dlb Mus. ms. 1825-E-501 (Grimma U
180/V 38)
score and parts
DdT 58-59, pp. 60-90

K0132   **Ach mein herzliebes Jesulein**
SSATB, 2 vln, 2 vla, 2 ob, 2 corn, 3 tbn,
2 taille, vlne, bsn, bc
Christmas Day
D-Dlb Mus. ms. 1825-E-502 (Grimma U
181/V 40)
parts
DMA 2/2245
D-Dlb Mus. ms. 1825-E-503, no. 2 (Grimma
U 179/V 39)
score

K0133   **Alleluia, man singet mit Freuden**
D-Dlb (Grimma N 70/V 42)
Missing from D-Dlb Grimma collection

K0134   **Asche die des Schöpfers Hände**
SSATB
Original lost; extant only in parody version
by Z. Hänisch. See Reich

K0135   **Christ lag in Todesbanden**
SSATB, vln piccolo, vln, 3 vla, cornettino,
3 bombarde, bc
D-Dlb Mus. ms. 1825-E-525 (Grimma U
335/N 34)
parts
Anonymous; attributed by Krummacher,
Mf 16 (1963): 346

K0136   **De profundis**
SSATB, 4 vla, vlne, bsn, bc
GB-Ob Ms. Mus. Sch. C. 31, fol. 104-22
parts
Cited in Crum (1985)

K0137   **Der Gerechte wird grünen**
SSATB, 2 vln, 2 vla, vltta, 2 corn, 3 tbn,
vlne, bc
3rd Sunday of Advent/Feast of John the
Baptist
D-B Mus. ms. 11782 (1681) (Erfurt)
score and parts
DMA 28//115

K0138   **Der Herr ist König**
SSAATTBB, 2 vln, 5 vla, 7 tbn, bc
D-B Mus. ms. 11780, no. 3 (Bokemeyer)
(1677)
score
DMA 3/816

K0139   **Der Herr schaffet deinen Grenzen Friede**
ATB, 2 vln, tbn, bc

4th Sunday of Lent/7th Sunday after
Trinity
D-B Mus. ms. 11784 (Erfurt) (1682)
score and parts
DMA 28//117

K0140 **Der Segen des Herrn machet reich**
SAATB, 2 vln, 3 vla, bc
5th Sunday after Trinity
D-B Mus. ms. 11783 (Erfurt) (1682)
score and parts
DMA 28//116

K0141 **Die Liebe Gotts ist ausgegossen**
See under Anonymous

K0142 **Die Turteltaube läßt sich hören**
SSATB, 2 vln, 2 vla, 4 clar, timp, bsn, bc
D-Dlb Mus. ms. 1825-E-518 (Grimma U
183/V 41)
parts
D-Dlb Mus. ms. 1825-E-519 (Grimma)
score

K0143 **Dies est laetitiae**
SSATTB, 2 vln, 3 vla, 3 tpt, 2 clar, 4
bomb (3 piff, bsn), timp, bc
Christmas Day
D-Dlb Mus. ms. 1825-E-503 (Grimma U
179/V 39)
parts
DMA 2/2246
D-Dlb Mus. ms. 1825-E-503, no. 1 (Grimma
U 179/V 39)
score

K0144 **Dies ist der Tag den der Herr macht**
SSATB, 2 vln, 2 vla, 2 clar, 2 tbn, bsn, bc
D-B Mus. ms. 11780, no. 4 (Bokemeyer)
(1679)
score
DMA 3/817

K0145 **Dies ist der Tag des Herrn**
SSATB, 2 vln, 2 vla, 2 clar, timp, 3 tbn,
bsn, bc
D-Dlb Mus. ms. 1739-E-510, no. 1 (Grimma
U 251/U 52)
score
Instrumental lines blank after first page

K0146 **Ecce quam bonum/Siehe, wie fein und lieblich**
SATTB, 2 vln, 3 vla, bsn, bc
D-Dlb Mus. ms. 1825-E-504 (Grimma U
173/V 37)
parts
Includes both Latin and German text

K0147 **Erforsche mich, Gott**
SATB, SATB, bc
Funeral of Johanna Lorentz
Leipzig, 1674
RISM K1005, Reich 269 (choirbook)
DMA 1/1021
D-B Mus. ms. autogr. 11788
score and parts (includes instrumental parts)
DMA 1/1584, 28//121
D-B Mus. ms. Bach P4/2, no. 3 (1660)
score
EdM 79, pp. 46-54

K0148 **Erheb dich, meine Seele**
SATB
Funeral of Anna Dorothea Feller
Leipzig, 1676
RISM K1006, 1007, Reich 270 (score)
DMA 72//92, 75//35

K0149 **Erstanden ist der heilige Christ**
SSATB, 2 vln, 4 vla, 2 tpt, 2 clar, bomb,
timp, bsn, bc
D-B Mus. ms. 11780, no. 5 (Bokemeyer)
score
DMA 3/818
D-Dlb Mus. ms. 1825-E-505 (Grimma U
184/V 42)
parts
DMA 2/2247

K0150 **Es haben mir die Hoffärtigen**
SATB, 2 vln, 3 vla, bsn, bc
D-B Mus. ms. 11780, no. 8 (Bokemeyer)
score
DMA 3/819

K0151 **Es ist eine Stimme eines Predigers**
SATB, 2 vln, 3 vla, bsn, bc
D-B Mus. ms. 11780, no. 6 (Bokemeyer)
score
DMA 3/820

K0152 **Es spricht der Unweisen Mund wohl**
SSAATTBB, 2 vln, 3 vla, 2 corn, 3 tbn,
bsn, bc
D-B Mus. ms. 11780, no. 7 (Bokemeyer)
score
DMA 3/821
DdT 58-59, pp. 30-59

K0153 **Gelobet sei Gott**
SSATB, instr, bc
D-Dlb (Grimma)
Missing from D-Dlb Grimma collection

KNÜPFER, Sebastian (*continued*)

K0154 **Gen Himmel zu dem Vater mein**
SSATTB, 2 vln, 2 clar, timp, 2 tbn, bsn, bc
D-Dlb (Grimma N 70/V 50, U 192)
score and parts
Missing from D-Dlb Grimma collection

K0155 **Gott sei mir gnädig nach deiner Güte**
SSATB, 4 vla, vlne, bsn, bc
D-Dlb Mus. ms. 1825-E-506 (Grimma U 185/V 43)
parts

K0156 **Herr Christ, der einig Gottes Sohn**
SSATB, 2 vln, 3 vla, 2 corn, 3 tbn, bsn, bc
D-B Mus. ms. 11780, no. 10 (Bokemeyer)
score
DMA 3/822

K0157 **Herr, hilf uns, wir verderben**
SATB, 2 vln, 2 vla, bsn, bc
D-B Mus. ms. 11780, no. 9 (Bokemeyer)
score
DMA 3/823

K0158 **Herr, ich habe lieb die Stätte**
ATB, 2 vln/corn, vla/tbn, bc
1st Sunday after Epiphany
D-B Mus. ms. 11780, no. 13 (Bokemeyer)
score
DMA 3/824
D-B Mus. ms. 11785 (Erfurt) (1682)
score and parts
DMA 28//118

K0159 **Herr Jesu Christ, wahr Mensch und Gott**
SSTTB, 2 vln, vlne, bc
S-Uu 57:4
parts
DMA 1/2065

K0160 **Herr, lehre mich tun nach deinem Wohlgefallen**
SATTB, 2 vln, 2 vla, bsn, bc
D-Dlb Mus. ms. 1825-E-507 (Grimma U 538/T 11)
parts

K0161 **Herr, lehre uns bedenken**
SSATTB, 2 vln, 3 vla, bsn, bc
D-B Mus. ms. 11780, no. 12 (Bokemeyer)
score
DMA 3/825

K0162 **Herr, strafe mich nicht in deinem Zorn**
SATB, 3 vla, vlne/bsn, bc
D-Dlb Mus. ms. 1825-E-508 (Grimma U 186/V 44)
parts

K0163 **Herr, wer wird wohnen in deinen Hütten**
SAB, 3 vla, 2 corn, bc
D-B Mus. ms. 11780, no. 11 (Bokemeyer)
score
DMA 3/826

K0164 **Ich freue mich in dir**
SSATB, 2 vln, 2 vla, 2 fl, 3 tbn, vlne, bc
D-B Mus. ms. 11780, no. 14 (Bokemeyer)
score
DMA 3/827

K0165 **Ich habe dich zum Licht**
SATTB, 2 vln, 3 vla, 2 cornettini, 3 tbn, bsn, bc
Feast of the Purification
D-Dlb Mus. ms. 1825-E-509 (Grimma U 188/V 46)
parts

K0166 **Ich will singen von der Gnade**
SATB, 2 vln, 3 vla, bsn, bc
D-Dlb (Grimma U 189/V 47)
parts
Missing from D-Dlb Grimma collection
Ed. Krüger, *Die Kantate* 81

K0167 **Jauchzet dem Herrn, alle Welt**
SATB, SATB, 2 vln, 3 vla, 2 cornettini, tpt, 2 clar, 2 tbn, bsn, bc
D-Dlb Mus. ms. 1825-E-510 (Grimma U 187/V 45)
parts

K0168 **Jesu, meine Freud und Wonne**
5 vv, 5 instr
D-RUl

K0169 **Jesus Christus, unser Heiland, der den Tod überwand**
SSATB, 2 vln, 3 vla, bsn, bc
D-Dlb Mus. ms. 1825-E-511 (Grimma U 190/V 48)
parts
DMA 2/2248

K0170 **Justus ut palma florebit**
SATB, bc
D-B Mus. ms. 11780, no. 22 (Bokemeyer)
score
DMA 3/828

K0171 **Komm, du schöne Freudenkrone**
SSATB, 2 vln, 3 vltta, 2 clar, timp, 3 tbn,
vltta/bsn, bc
D-Dlb Mus. ms. 1-E-771, no. 2 (Grimma
L 55a)
score

K0172 **Komm, Heiliger Geist**
SATB, 3 vla, 3 tbn, vlne, bc
Pentecost
D-Bds Mus. ms. 11787 (Erfurt)
score and parts
DMA 28//120

K0173 **Kommet herzu, laßet uns den Herzen frohlocken**
SSATB, 2 vln, vla, bc
D-B Mus. ms. 11786
parts
DMA 28//119

K0174 **Laßt uns den fürnen Wein**
SATB, 2 vln, bc
S-Uu 57:3
parts
DMA 2/2249

K0175 **Lauda Jerusalem**
SATB, 2 vln, vlne, bsn, bc
GB-Ob Ms. Mus. Sch. C. 30, fol. 33-56
parts
Cited by Crum (1985)

K0176 **Machet die Tore weit**
SSATB, 2 vln, 4 vla, 2 corn/bomb, 3 tbn, bc
D-Dlb Mus. ms. 1825-E-512 (Grimma U
191/V 49)
parts
DdT 58-59, pp. 91-121

K0177 **Mein Gott, betrübt ist meine Seele**
SSATTB, bc
Funeral of Samuel Lange
Leipzig, 1667
RISM K1003, Reich 265 (parts)
DMA 1/1019

K0178 **Mein Herz hält dir für dein Wort**
SAT, 2 vln, bsn, bc
5th Sunday after Easter
D-B Mus. ms. 11780, no. 15 (Bokemeyer)
score
DMA 3/829

K0179 **Missa (brevis) super Freu dich selig**
SSAATTB, 2 vln, 5 vla, bc
D-Bds Mus. ms. 30171, no. 8
score

K0180 **Missa (brevis) super Herr Jesu Christ, wahr Mensch und Gott**
SSATTB, 2 vln, 5 vla, bc
D-Bds Mus. ms. 30167, no. 12
score
DMA 2/2250

K0181 **Missa (brevis) super O Welt ich muß dich lassen**
SSAATTB, 2 vln, 5 vla, bc
D-Bds Mus. ms. 30171, no. 7
score

K0182 **Nun danket alle Gott**
SSATTB, 2 vln, 3 vla, bc
D-B Mus. ms. 11780, no. 16 (Bokemeyer)
score
DMA 3/830

K0183 **Nun freut euch, lieben Christen gmein**
SSTTB, 2 vln, 2 vla, bsn, bc
D-B Mus. ms. 11780, no. 17 (Bokemeyer)
score
DMA 3/831

K0184 **O benignissime Jesu**
ATB, 2 vln/cornettini, gamba/bomb, bc
D-Dlb Mus. ms. 1825-E-513 (Grimma U
174/V 36)
parts

K0185 **Quare fremuerunt gentes**
SSATTB, 2 vln, 3 vla, 2 cornettini, 4 tbn,
bsn, bc
D-Dlb Mus. ms. 1825-E-514 (Grimma U
175/V 35) (1672)
parts

K0186 **Sende dein Licht**
SATB, 2 vln, 2 vla, bsn, bc
D-Dlb Mus. ms. 1825-E-515 (Grimma U
192/V 50)
parts
Ed. Krüger, *Die Kantate* 199

K0187 **Siehe, wie fein und lieblich**
See Ecce quam bonum

K0188 **Super flumina Babylonis**
SATB, 2 vln, 3 vla, 2 cornettini, 3 tbn,
bsn, bc
D-Dlb Mus. ms. 1825-E-516 (Grimma U
176/V 34)
score and parts

K0189 **Surgite, populi**
SATB, SATB, 2 vln, 3 vla, 2 cornettini,
corn, 5 tpt, timp, 3 tbn, bc

KNÜPFER, Sebastian (*continued*)

D-Dlb Mus. ms. 1825-E-517 (Grimma U
177/V 33)
score and parts

K0190   **Veni Sancte Spiritus**
SSATB, 2 vln, 2 vla, 2 cornettini, 4 clar,
timp, 3 tbn, bsn, bc
D-Dlb Mus. ms. 1825-E-519 (Grimma U
178/V 32)
score and parts

K0191   **Victoria, die Fürsten sind geschlagen**
SSATB, 2 vln, 2 vla, 3 tbn, bsn, bc
S-Uu 57:5
parts
DMA 1/2066
3 tbn parts missing

K0192   **Vom Himmel hoch da komm ich her**
chorus angelorum: SSS 3 vln; SSS, 3 vln rip
choro dei pastori: ATB, 3 bomb
choro pieno: SATB, 2 clar, timp, harp, bc
D-Dlb Mus. ms. 1825-E-520 (Grimma U
193/V 51)
score and parts
DMA 2/2251

K0193   **Was mein Gott will, das gescheh allzeit**
SSATTB, 2 vln, 3 vla, 2 corn, 3 tbn, bsn, bc
D-B Mus. ms. 11780, no. 19 (Bokemeyer)
score
DMA 3/832
DdT 58-59, pp. 1-29

K0194   **Was werden wir essen**
SATB, 4 vla, bc
15th Sunday after Trinity
D-B Mus. ms. 11781 (Erfurt) (1678)
score and parts
DMA 28//114

K0195   **Weichet von mir, ihr Boshaftigen**
SSATTB, bc
Funeral of Johann Hülsemann
Leipzig, 1661
RISM K1001, Reich 260 (parts)
DMA 66//138, 70//169

K0196   **Wenn mein Stündlein vorhanden ist**
SATB, 2 vln, 2 vla, vlne, bc
D-Dlb Mus. ms. 1825-E-522 (Grimma U
194/V 72)
parts
DMA 2/2252

K0197   **Wer ist, der so von Edom kommt**
SAB, 4 vla, bc
D-B Mus. ms. 11780, no. 21 (Bokemeyer)
score
DMA 3/834

K0198   **Wer ist, der so von Edom kommt**
SSATB, 2 vln, 2 vla, 4 tbtta, timp, bsn, bc
D-B Mus. ms. 11780, no. 20 (Bokemeyer)
score
DMA 3/833
D-Dlb Mus. ms. 1825-E-523 (Grimma U
195/V 53)
score and parts
D-Dlb parts include 2 clar & 2 trombe

K0199   **Wohl dem, der in der Gottesfurcht steht**
SSATB, 2 vln, 3 vla, 2 corn, 3 tbn,
bombard, bsn, bc
D-B Mus. ms. 11780, no. 18 (Bokemeyer)
score
DMA 3/825

KOCH, Jeremias (1637-1693)

K0200   **Gehabt euch wohl, habt gute Nacht**
ATB
Funeral of Anthon Günther, Graf zu
Schwarzburg
Arnstadt, 1666
RISM K1061 (score)
DMA 72//27

K0201   **Höchst traurig kommet uns euer Fall**
SSATB
Funeral of Anthon Günther, Graf zu
Schwarzburg
Arnstadt, 1666
RISM K1061 (score)
DMA 72//27

K0202   **Nun gute Nacht, o weltlich Wesen**
SSATB
Funeral of Hans Ernst von Heringen
Arnstadt, 1672
RISM K1062, Reich 23 (score)
DMA 70//139, 66//138

K0203   **O Jammer, Elend, Angst, und Not**
SSATB
Funeral of Anthon Günther, Graf zu
Schwarzburg
Arnstadt, 1666
RISM K1061, Reich 22 (score)
DMA 70//183, 72//27

KOCH, Johann Georg

> **K0204** **Ist noch jemand, dem die Schmerzen Rahels**
> SATB
> Funeral of Ursula Catharina Elisabeth
> Schlosser
> Giessen, 1688
> RISM K1065 (score)
> DMA 72//92

KÖLER, Martin (ca. 1620-ca. 1703)

> **K0205** **Alleluia, lobet den Herren**
> SSATB, 2 vln, 2 vla, 2 corn, 3 tbn, bc
> D-B Mus. ms. 3840, no. 11 (Bokemeyer)
> score
> DMA 2/844

> **K0206** **Das Himmelreich ist gleich einem Hausvater**
> SSATTB, 2 vln, 2 vla, bsn, bc
> Septuagesima
> D-B Mus. ms. 3840, no. 14 (Bokemeyer)
> score
> DMA 2/846

> **K0207** **Der Herr hat seinem Engel befohlen**
> SSB, 2 vln, bsn, bc
> S-Uu 53:13 (Düben)
> parts
> DMA 1/2033

> **K0208** **Der Tod ist verschlungen**
> SATTB, 2 vln, 2 vla, vlne, bc
> D-B Mus. ms. 3840, no. 13 (Bokemeyer)
> score
> DMA 2/847

> **K0209** **Er nahm aber zu sich die Zwölfe**
> SSTTB, 2 vln, 2 vla, bsn, bc
> Quinquagesima
> D-B Mus. ms. 3840, no. 3 (Bokemeyer)
> score
> DMA 2/850

> **K0210** **Es ist ein köstlich Ding**
> ATB, 2 vln, bsn, bc
> D-B Mus. ms. 3840, no. 8 (Bokemeyer)
> score
> DMA 2/851

> **K0211** **Lobet, ihr Knechte des Herrn**
> SSB, 2 vln, 2 gamba, bc
> D-W Vogel 44
> parts
> DMA 1/334

> **K0212** **Meine Seele erhebet den Herrn**
> SSATTB, 2 vln, 4 tbn, bc
> Visitation of the Virgin Mary
> D-B Mus. ms. 3840, no. 10 (Bokemeyer)
> score
> DMA 2/855

> **K0213** **Übe dich selbst aber an der Gottseligkeit**
> SSB, 2 vln, bsn, bc
> D-B Mus. ms. 3840, no. 4 (Bokemeyer)
> score
> DMA 2/856

> **K0214** **Unser Herr Jesus Christus in der Nacht**
> SSB, 2 vln, 2 vla, bsn, bc
> D-B Mus. ms. 3840, no. 2 (Bokemeyer)
> score
> DMA 2/857
> Ed. Haacke (Bärenreiter BA 956, 1953)

KONWALYNKA, Paul

> **K0215** **Wer Gott geliebt, hat wohl geliebt**
> SATB
> Funeral of Gottlieb Ernst Schildbach
> Jena, 1673
> RISM K1335 (choirbook)
> DMA 78//81

KOPPE

> **K0216** **Fürchtet euch nicht, siehe, ich verkündige euch
> große Freude**
> SATB, 2 vln/ob, bc
> Christmas Day
> D-Gs Cod. Ms. philos. 84e Koppe 1
> score and parts

KREICHEL, Christoph

> **K0217** **Cantate Domino**
> SATTB, 2 vln, 2 vla, bsn, bc
> Christmas Day
> S-Uu 67:7 (Düben)
> parts
> DMA 23//56

> **K0218** **Herr, kehre dich doch wieder**
> ATB, 2 vln, bsn, bc
> D-Bds Mus. ms. 30215, no. 7 (Bokemeyer)
> score

KREICHEL, Christoph (*continued*)

K0219   **Missa [brevis]**
SSATB, 4 vla, bsn, bc
D-Bds Mus. ms. 30215, no. 8 (Bokemeyer)
score

K0220   **Si bona suscepimus de manu Domini**
SSATB, 4 vln, vlne, bc
S-Uu 86:20 (Düben)
tablature
S-Uu 5:4 (Düben)
parts

KREMBERG, Jacob

K0221   **Ade o Weltlichkeit**
SATB, bc
Funeral of Anna Maria Bose
Dresden, 1687
RISM K2008, Reich 60 (score)
DMA 70//205
EdM 79, pp. 9-10

KRESS (Cress), Johann Albrecht (1644-1684)

COLLECTIONS

Der süße Nahme Jesu (1681)
RISM K2011 (parts)
DMA 74//152

Musicalische Seelen-Belustigung (1681)
RISM K2012 (parts)
DMA 2/85

WORKS

K0222   **Cantabo Domino in vita mea**
SATB, 2 vln, 3 vla, bc
Musicalische Seelen-Belustigung, no. 11
D-B Mus. ms. 4320, no. 3 (Bokemeyer)
score

K0223   **Christum ducem qui per crucem redemit nos**
SATB, 2 vln, 3 vla, bc
Musicalische Seelen-Belustigung, no. 13
D-B Mus. ms. 4320, no. 4 (Bokemeyer)
score

K0224   **Das ist meine Freude**
SATB, 2 vln, 3 vla, bc
Musicalische Seelen-Belustigung, no. 5
D-B Mus. ms. 4320, no. 20 (Bokemeyer)
score

K0225   **Dein Liebe, Jesu, mich entzückt**
ATB, bc
Der süße Nahme Jesu, no. 8

K0226   **Delectare in Domino**
SATB, 2 vln, 3 vla, bc
Musicalische Seelen-Belustigung, no. 8
D-B Mus. ms. 4320, no. 1 (Bokemeyer)
score

K0227   **Der Gnaden Jesus Stifter ist**
SST, bc
Der süße Nahme Jesu, no. 7

K0228   **Die allersüßest Lieb du bist**
SSA, bc
Der süße Nahme Jesu, no. 5

K0229   **Du Jesu bist der Engel-Wonn**
SST, bc
Der süße Nahme Jesu, no. 9

K0230   **Dulcis Jesu, pie Deus**
SATB, 2 vln, 3 vla, bc
Musicalische Seelen-Belustigung, no. 9
D-B Mus. ms. 4320, no. 6 (Bokemeyer)
score
S-Uu 85:12, fol. 37v-40 (Düben)
tablature
DMA 1/759
S-Uu 57:6
parts

K0231   **Ermuntre dich, mein ganzes**
SATB, 2 vln, 3 vla, bc
Musicalische Seelen-Belustigung, no. 1
D-B Mus. ms. 4320, no. 13 (Bokemeyer)
score

K0232   **Es stehe Gott auf**
SSATB, 2 vln, 3 vla, 4 clar, timp, bc
D-B Mus. ms. 4320, no. 14 (Bokemeyer)
(1688)
score
D-F Ms. Ff. mus. 418 (1688)
parts

K0233   **Et quando Domine**
ATB, 2 vln, bc
D-B Mus. ms. 4320, no. 9 (Bokemeyer)
score

K0234   **Herr, est ist ein köstlich Ding**
SATB, 2 vln, 3 vla, bc
Musicalische Seelen-Belustigung, no. 2
D-B Mus. ms. 4320, no. 19 (Bokemeyer)
score

K0235 **Herr, warum trittest du so ferne**
SATB, 2 vln, 3 vla, bc
Musicalische Seelen-Belustigung, no. 6
D-B Mus. ms. 4320, no. 18 (Bokemeyer)
score

K0236 **Huc me sidereo**
SATB, 2 vln, 3 vla, bc
Musicalische Seelen-Belustigung, no. 12
D-B Mus. ms. 4320, no. 8 (Bokemeyer)
score

K0237 **Ich ruf zu dir, Herr Jesu Christ**
SSATB, 4 vla, bsn, bc
13th Sunday after Trinity
D-B Mus. ms. 4320, no. 17 (Bokemeyer)
score
D-F Ms. Ff. mus. 419
score and parts

K0238 **Ich suche Jesum in dem Bett**
ATB, bc
Der süße Nahme Jesu, no. 3

K0239 **Jesu, dein Angedenken macht**
SAT, bc
Der süße Nahme Jesu, no. 1

K0240 **Komm, König, komm, ach frömmster Herr**
SAT, bc
Der süße Nahme Jesu, no. 12

K0241 **Magnificat**
SATB, 2 vln, 3 vla, bc
Musicalische Seelen-Belustigung, no. 14
D-B Mus. ms. 4320, no. 7 (Bokemeyer)
score

K0242 **Mein Jesus herrscht, hat Fried gestifft**
SST, bc
Der süße Nahme Jesu, no. 15

K0243 **Mein Lieber, kehre wieder um**
SSB, bc
Der süße Nahme Jesu, no. 13

K0244 **O cor meum**
SATB, 2 vln, 3 vla, bc
D-B Mus. ms. 4320, no. 5 (Bokemeyer)
score

K0245 **O Jesu, höchste Gütigkeit**
SAB, bc
Der süße Nahme Jesu, no. 10

K0246 **O Jesu, Hoffnung wahrer Reu**
SSB, bc
Der süße Nahme Jesu, no. 2

K0247 **O Jesu, Wunder-König du**
SAB, bc
Der süße Nahme Jesu, no. 4

K0248 **O König grosser Kraft und Ehr**
ATB, bc
Der süße Nahme Jesu, no. 14

K0249 **O mein Heiland, wie süß**
SATB, 2 vln, 3 vla, bc
Musicalische Seelen-Belustigung, no. 3
D-B Mus. ms. 4320, no. 16 (Bokemeyer)
score

K0250 **Schaut, daß ihr Jesum kennt und ehrt**
BBB, bc
Der süße Nahme Jesu, no. 6

K0251 **Sei gegrüßet, Preis der Erden**
SATB, 2 vln, 3 vla, bc
Musicalische Seelen-Belustigung, no. 7
D-B Mus. ms. 4320, no. 11 (Bokemeyer)
score

K0252 **Selig ist der Mensch**
SATB, 2 vln, 3 vla, bc
Musicalische Seelen-Belustigung, no. 4
D-B Mus. ms. 4320, no. 15 (Bokemeyer)
score

K0253 **Summi regis cor aveto**
SATB, 2 vln, 3 vla, bc
Musicalische Seelen-Belustigung, no. 10
D-B Mus. ms. 4320, no. 2 (Bokemeyer)
score

K0254 **Wie der Hirsch schreiet nach frischem Wasser**
SATB, 2 vln, bc
F-Ssp (1678)

K0255 **Wo Jesus so beliebet wird**
ATB, bc
Der süße Nahme Jesu, no. 11

K0256 **Wohl dem, der die Gottseligkeit und Furcht des Höchsten übet**
SATB, 2 vln, 3 vla, bc
D-F Ms. Ff. mus. 420 (1692)
parts

KRIEGER, Adam (1634-1666)

K0257 **Ach meine Eltern, meine Lieben**
SATB
Funeral of Ursula Katharina Dietzsch
Coburg, 1667
RISM K2445, Reich 199
Parody of the composer's "Kommt, meine Freunde, meine Lieben"

K0258 **An den Wassern zu Babel saßen wir und weineten**
STB, 2 vln, bc

KRIEGER, Adam (*continued*)

D-Bds Mus. ms. 30215, no. 9 (Bokemeyer)
score
Ed. Osthoff (Bärenreiter no. 448, 1948)
Partially ed. in Osthoff, *Adam Krieger*,
pp. 3-4

K0259 **Ich preise dich, Herr**
SATB, 2 vln, 2 vla, bsn, bc
D-Bds Mus. ms. 30215, no. 10 (Bokemeyer)
score
Partially ed. in Osthoff, *Adam Krieger*,
pp. 6-8

K0260 **Kommt, meine Freunde, meine Leben**
SATB
Funeral of Regina Bose
Leipzig, 1654
RISM K2439, Reich 244
RISM K2440, Reich 245 (choirbook)
DMA 72//92, 75//231
Funeral of Daniel Schleicher
Coburg, 1661
RISM K2444, Reich 193
DMA 72//41
Ed. in Osthoff, *Adam Krieger*, pp.
84-85

K0261 **Kommt nun und scharrt mich in die Erde**
SATB
Funeral of Maria Dietzsch
Coburg, 1673
Reich 203, no. 5 (score)
Reich: identical to "Legt ein und scharrt
mich in die Erde"

K0262 **Legt ein und scharrt mich in die Erde**
SATB
Funeral of Sebastian Otte
Leipzig, 1656
RISM K2441, Reich 253
DMA 70//136
Ed. Osthoff, *Adam Krieger*, pp. 86-87
Reich: identical to "Kommt nun und
scharrt mich in die Erde"

K0263 **O ihr schnöden Eitelkeiten**
SATB
Funeral of Valtin Braun
Leipzig, 1659
RISM 2443, Reich 258
DMA 70//136
Ed. Osthoff, *Adam Krieger*, pp.
88-89

KRIEGER, Johann (1652-1735)

COLLECTION

Neue musicalische Ergetzlichkeit (1684)
RISM K2448 (parts)

WORKS

K0264 **Ach Gott, du bist mein rechtes Licht** (Samuel
no. 9)
SATB
Funeral of Zacharia Seligmann
Zittau, 1687
RISM K2449, Reich 433 (score)
DMA 65//51

K0265 **Also hat Gott die Welt geliebet** (Samuel no. 25)
SATB, SATB, 2 vln, 2 vla, vc, bc
D-B Mus. ms. 12153, no. 1 (Bokemeyer)
score
DMA 30//67

K0266 **Confitebor tibi Domine** (Samuel no. 29)
SATB, 2 vln, 3 vla, bsn, bc
D-B Mus. ms. 12153, no. 14 (Bokemeyer)
score
DMA 30//67
GB-Lbl R.M. 24.a.1. (10)
score

K0267 **Da kommt der kleine Sohn**
SATB
Neue musicalische Ergetzlichkeit, no. 22

K0268 **Danket dem Herrn, denn er ist freundlich**
(Samuel no. 30)
SATB, 2 vln, 2 vla, vc, bc
D-B Mus. ms. 12153, no. 2 (Bokemeyer)
score
DMA 30//67
DTB 6/1, pp. 166-86

K0269 **Danksaget dem Vater** (Samuel no. 31)
SATB, 2 vln, 3 vla, bc
D-B Mus. ms. 12153, no. 5 (Bokemeyer)
score
DMA 30//67

K0270 **Delectare in Domino** (Samuel no. 32)
SATB, 2 vln, 3 vla, bsn, bc
GB-Lbl R.M. 24.a.1. (8)
score

K0271 **Die Kinder ziehen hin**
SATB
Neue musicalische Ergetzlichkeit, no. 23

K0272 **Dies ist der Tag, den der Herr gemacht hat**
(Samuel no. 33)
SATB, 3 vln, 2 vla, vc, bc
D-B Mus. ms. 12153, no. 3 (Bokemeyer)
score
DMA 30//67

K0273 **Dixit Dominus Domino meo sede a dextris meis**
SSATB, 2 vln, 3 vla, vlne, bc
S-Uu 40:9 (Düben)
parts
Anonymous in manuscript, with tentative
attribution by S-Uu, citing Krummacher

K0274 **Frohlocket Gott in allen Landen** (Samuel no. 39)
SATB, 2 vln, 2 clar, bc
D-ZI B22
score
DMA 3/1718

K0275 **Gelobet sei der Herr** (Samuel no. 41)
SATB, 2 vln, 3 vla, bc
D-B Mus. ms. 12152, no. 5 (Bokemeyer)
score
DMA 3/1234
DTB 6/1, pp. 146-65

K0276 **Gott ist unser Zuversicht** (Samuel no. 42)
SATB, 2 vln, vla, bsn, bc
D-ZI B22
parts
DMA 3/1711

K0277 **Gott liebet dieses Kind** (Samuel no. 13)
SATB
Funeral of Christiane Gottlieb Seligmann
Zittau, 1689
RISM KK2449d (score)
DMA 65//51

K0278 **Gott, wende dich von deinem Grimme**
SATB
Neue musicalische Ergetzlichkeit, no. 29

K0279 **Halleluja! Lobet den Herren in seinem Heiligtum**
(Samuel no. 43)
SATB, SATB, 2 vln, 2 vla, vc, 2 fl, 2 corn,
2 tpt, timp, 3 tbn, harp, cymbals, bsn, bc
D-ZI B140c (1685)
parts
DMA 3/2136

K0280 **Herr, straf mich nicht in deinem Grimme**
SATB
Neue musicalische Ergetzlichkeit, no. 25

K0281 **Ich sehe nur auf Gottes Willen** (Samuel no. 20)
SATB

Memorial service for Johann Georg IV
Zittau, 1694
RISM KK2450g (score)
DMA 65//51

K0282 **Ihr Feinde, weichet weg** (Samuel no. 23b)
SATB, 2 vln, bc
D-ZI B22
score
DMA 3/1716

K0283 **Laudate Dominum, omnes gentes** (Samuel
no. 46)
SSATB, bc
D-Bds Mus. ms. 30309
score
D-B Mus. ms. 12147
parts
DMA 28//124

K0284 **Laudate, pueri, Dominum** (Samuel no. 47)
ATB, 2 vln, 2 vla, vlne, bc
D-Dlb Mus. ms. 2102-E-500 (Grimma U
608/T 14 LXX)
parts
S-Uu 86:48 (Düben)
tablature
S-Uu 43:16 (Düben)
parts

K0285 **Magnificat** (Samuel no. 49)
SATB, 2 vln, 3 vla, vc, bc
D-B Mus. ms. 12149
parts
DMA 28//128

K0286 **Magnificat** (Samuel no. 48)
SATB, bc
D-Bds Mus. ms. 30088, no. 9
score

K0287 **Mein Gott, ich habe dich** (Samuel no. 5)
SATB
Funeral of Christian Möller
Zittau, 1684
score
DMA 1/1435

K0288 **Mein Kind, du beugest mich** (Samuel no. 8)
SATB
Funeral of Anna Christiane Girisch
Zittau, 1687
RISM KK2449a (score)
DMA 65//51

K0289 **Meine Seele, willst du klagen**
SATB
Neue musicalische Ergetzlichkeit, no. 26

KRIEGER, Johann (*continued*)

K0290 **Nun danket alle Gott** (Samuel no. 50)
SATB, SATB, 2 vln, vla, timp, 3 tbn, bc
D-ZI B22
parts
DMA 3/1709

K0291 **Rühmet den Herrn, die ihr ihm fürchtet** (Samuel no. 52)
SATB, 2 vln, 2 vla, vc, bc
D-B Mus. ms. 12153, no. 4 (Bokemeyer)
score
DMA 30//67

K0292 **Sanctus** (Samuel no. 54)
SATB, 2 vln, vla, bc
D-B Mus. ms. 12148, no. 1 (1699)
parts
DMA 28//125

K0293 **Sanctus** (Samuel no. 55)
SATB, 2 vln, vla, vc, bc
D-Bds Mus. ms. 30221, no. 4b
score
D-B Mus. ms. 12145
parts
DMA 28//122

K0294 **Sanctus** (Samuel no. 57)
SATB, 2 vln, 3 vla, vc, bc
D-B Mus. ms. 12146
score and parts
DMA 28//123

K0295 **Sanctus** (Samuel no. 58)
SATB, 2 vln, 3 vla, bsn, bc
D-B Mus. ms. 12148, no. 3
score and parts
DMA 28//127

K0296 **So zeuch wohin dich Gott begleitet** (Samuel no. 22)
SATB
Graduation ceremony
Zittau, 1697
score
DMA 1/1442

K0297 **Sulamith, auf, auf zum Waffen** (Samuel no. 59)
SSATB, 2 vln, vla, tbn, bsn, bc
Reformation
D-ZI B22
parts
DMA 3/1712

K0298 **Was sind wir doch in unsern Leben** (Samuel no. 15)
SATB
Funeral of Anna Maria Noack
Zittau, 1691
RISM K2450, Reich 434 (score)
DMA 1/1440

K0299 **Wie kann sich unsre Seele grämen** (Samuel no. 10)
SATB
Funeral of an unbaptised child
Zittau, 1688
RISM KK2449c (score)
DMA 65//51

K0300 **Wie lieblich ist mein Los gefallen** (Samuel no. 16)
SATB
Memorial service for Johann Georg III
Zittau, 1691
RISM KK2450a (score)
DMA 65//51

K0301 **Wohl dem, der am Gebirge wohnet** (Samuel no. 17)
SATB
Wedding of Johann Christian Kübel and Rosine Elisabeth Vogel
Zittau, 1692
RISM KK2450b (score)
DMA 65//51

KRIEGER, Johann Philipp (1649-1725)

K0302 **Ad cantus, ad sonos venite** (Samuel no. 8)
SST, 3 vln, bc
D-Bds Mus. ms. 30378, no. 7
score

K0303 **Attendite verbum Domini** (Samuel no. 10)
SSB, 2 vln, bc
D-Dlb Mus. ms. 1862-E-500 (Grimma U 166/V 64)
parts

K0304 **Beati omnes qui timent Dominum** (Samuel no. 11)
SST, bc
S-Uu 83:20, fol. 35v-38r (Düben)
tablature
DMA 24//63
S-Uu 57:7
parts
GB-Ob Mss. Mus. Sch. 30
parts
cited by Wollny

K0305 **Cantate Domino canticum novum** (Samuel no. 12)
SATB, 2 vln, 2 vla, tpt/corn, bsn, bc
D-B Mus. ms. 30224, no. 2 (Bokemeyer)
score

S-Uu 84:100, fol. 1v-7r (Düben)
tablature
DMA 24//64
S-Uu 57:8 (Düben)
parts
GB-Lbl R.M. 24.a.1. (7)
score
Die Kantate, no. 50

K0306 **Christus hat ausgezogen**
SATB, 2 vln, 2 vla, tbn, bsn, bc
D-Dlb Mus. ms. 1862-E-505 (Grimma U
328/N 38)
parts
Instrumental parts missing

K0307 **Confitebor tibi Domine**
SAB, 2 vln, bc
D-Dlb Mus. ms. 1862-E-507 (Grimma U
407/P 7)
parts
Anonymous. Attributed by D-Dlb, based
on DdT 53/54, p. xvi

K0308 **Cor meum atque omnia** (Samuel no. 14)
SSATB, 3 vln, 2 vla, bc
GB-Lbl R.M. 24.a.1 (9)
score
D-B Mus. ms. 12153, no. 11 (Bokemeyer)
score
DMA 30//67

K0309 **Crudelis infernus inimicus armavit** (Samuel no. 15)
SAB, 2 vln, bc
D-B Mus. ms. 30224, no. 1 (Bokemeyer)
score
D-Dlb Mus. ms. 1862-E-501 (Grimma U
160/V 70)
parts

K0310 **Das ist meine Freude, daß ich mich zu Gott
halte** (Samuel no. 16)
ATB, 2 vln, 3 vla, bc
D-F Ms. Ff. Mus. 421
score

K0311 **Die Gerechten werden weggerafft** (Samuel no. 21)
SATB, 2 gamba, vltta, bsn, bc
D-B Mus. ms. 12152, no. 2 (Bokemeyer)
score
DMA 3/1230
Organum I/6
DTB 6/1, pp. 118-24

K0312 **Die Welt kann den Geist der Wahrheit nicht**
(Samuel no. 67)
SAB, bc

D-B Mus. ms. 12152, no.1 (Bokemeyer)
score
DMA 3/1231
DdT 53-54, pp. 99-110

K0313 **Diligam te domine** (Samuel no. 17)
SAB, 2 vln, vlne, bc
S-Uu 85:24, fol. 14v-16r (Düben)
tablature
DMA 27//207
S-Uu 27:12 (Düben)
parts

K0314 **Ecce quomodo moritur justus** (Samuel no. 89)
SATB, 2 vln, 3 vla, vlne, bc
D-Dlb Mus. ms. 1862-E-502 (Grimma U
329/N 39)
parts

K0315 **Ein feste Burg ist unser Gott** (Samuel no. 20)
SATB, 2 vln, 3 vla, bsn, bc
D-B Mus. ms. 12152, no. 3 (Bokemeyer)
(1691-1693)
score
DMA 3/1232
D-F Ms. Ff. Mus. 422 (1692)
parts
DdT 53-54, pp. 111-28

K0316 **Gloria in excelsis deo** (Samuel no. 22)
SATB, 2 vln, 2 vltta, tromba, bsn, bc
D-B Mus. ms. 12153, no. 13 (Bokemeyer)
score
DMA 30//67

K0317 **Gott, du Brunnquell aller Güte** (Samuel no. 23)
SATB, 2 vln, 2 vla, bc
D-Bds Mus. ms. 30378
score (string parts omitted)
D-B Mus. ms. 12157/4
parts
DMA 28//132

K0318 **Haurietis aquas in gaudio** (Samuel no. 24)
SSATB, 2 vln, 2 vla, vlne, bsn, bc
S-Uu 85:44, fol. 17v-20v (Düben) (1681)
tablature
DMA 24//68
S-Uu 57:12 (Düben)
parts

K0319 **Heilig, heilig, heilig ist der Herr Zebaoth** (Samuel
no. 25)
SATB, 2 vln, 2 vla, vc, ob, bsn, bc
D-B Mus. ms. 12155/5
score and parts
DMA 12//213

KRIEGER, Johann Philipp (*continued*)

    DdT 53-54, pp. 309-11
    Die Kantate, no. 2

K0320 **Ich freue mich, daß mir geredt ist** (Samuel no. 29)
    SSATB, 3 vln, 2 vla, bc
    D-B Mus. ms. 12153, no. 8 (Bokemeyer)
      score
      DMA 30//67
    DdT 53-54, pp. 84-98

K0321 **Ich freue mich in dem Herrn** (Samuel no. 30)
    SSATB, 2 vln, 2 vla, vc, bc
    D-B Mus. ms. 12152, no. 7
      score
      DMA 3/1237

K0322 **Ich habe Lust abzuscheiden** (Samuel no. 31)
    SATB, 2 vln, vla, vc, ob, bsn, bc
    Purification of the Virgin Mary
    D-Dlb Mus. ms. 1862-E-506 (Grimma U 220/U 1)
      parts
    Also attributed to Kuhnau in manuscript

K0323 **Ich verlasse mich auf Gottes Güte** (Samuel no. 33)
    SAB, 2 vln, vc, bc
    D-Bds Mus. ms. 30282
      score
    D-B Mus. ms. 12157/8
      parts
      DMA 28//134
    D-B Mus. ms. 12152, no. 8 (Bokemeyer)
      score
      DMA 1/1238
    GB-Ob Mss. Mus. Sch. C.43

K0324 **In aeternum Domine verbum tuum** (Samuel no. 35)
    SSATB, 2 vln, 3 vla, bc
    D-B Mus. ms. 30224, no. 4 (Bokemeyer)
      score

K0325 **Laudate Dominum, omnes gentes** (Samuel no. 38)
    STB, 2 vln, bc
    D-B Mus. ms. 30224, no. 5 (Bokemeyer)
      score

K0326 **Laudate Dominum, omnes gentes** (Samuel no. 39)
    SSATB, 2 vln, 2 vla, bc
    F-Ssp
      parts

K0327 **Laudate, pueri, Dominum**
    SSB, 2 vln, 2 vla, vlne, bc

    S-Uu 83:17, fol. 30v-34 (Düben)
      tablature
      DMA 28//171

K0328 **Laudate, pueri, Dominum** (Samuel no. 40)
    SSATB, 2 vln, 2 vla, vc, bsn, bc
    F-Ssp
      parts

K0329 **Liebster Jesu, willst du scheiden** (Samuel no. 41)
    SATB, 2 vln, 3 vla, bc
    D-B Mus. ms. 12152, no. 10 (Bokemeyer)
      score
      DMA 3/1239
    DdT 53-54, pp. 37-50

K0330 **Magnificat** (Samuel no. 42)
    SATB, 2 vln, 3 vla, 2 clar, timp, bsn, bc
    D-B Mus. ms. 12156
      parts
    DdT 53-54, pp. 1-23

K0331 **Mein Gott, dein ist doch alles** (Samuel no. 43)
    SSB, 2 vln, bc
    D-Mbs Mus. ms. 5477
      parts and tablature

K0332 **Mein Herz dichtet ein feines Lied** (Samuel no. 44)
    SATB, SATB, 2 vln, 6 vltta, bsn, bc
    D-B Mus. ms. 12152, no. 11 (Bokemeyer)
      score
      DMA 3/1240
    DdT 53-54, pp. 137-80

K0333 **Mein Vater, nicht wie ich will** (Samuel no. 45)
    SATTB, 2 vln, 3 vla, bc
    D-B Mus. ms. 12158/1 (Erfurt)
      score
      DMA 28//135

K0334 **Missa (brevis)** (Samuel no. 46)
    SATB, 2 vln, 3 vla, vc, bc
    D-B Mus. ms. 12155 (Erfurt)
      score and parts
      DMA 28//129
    DdT 53-54, pp. 312-20

K0335 **Nun danket alle Gott, der grosse Dinge tut** (Samuel no. 47)
    STB, 2 vln, bc
    S-Uu 85:1, fol. 1r-3r (Düben)
      tablature
      DMA 24//71
    S-Uu 57:16 (Düben)
      tablature and parts

K0336 **Perfunde me gratia coelesti** (Samuel no. 50)
    SAB, 2 vln, vlne, bc

S-Uu 86:8, fol. 2v-5r (Düben) (1670)
tablature
DMA 24//9
S-Uu 27:16 (Düben)
parts

K0337 Preise, Jerusalem, den Herrn (Samuel no. 51)
SATB, 2 vln, 2 vla, 2 corn, 2 tpt, timp, 3
tbn, bsn, bc
D-B Mus. ms. 12153, no. 9 (Bokemeyer)
score
DMA 30//67
DdT 53-54, pp. 221-48

K0338 Quis me territat, quis me devorat (Samuel no. 52)
SAB, 2 vln, vc, bsn, bc
F-Pn Vm¹ 1213
score
S-Uu 85:43, fol. 14v-18r (Düben) (1681)
tablature
DMA 24//205
S-Uu 70:5 (Düben)
parts
D-B Mus. ms. 12153, no. 12 (Bokemeyer)
score
DMA 30//67

K0339 Rufet nicht die Weisheit (Samuel no. 54)
SATB, 2 vln, gamba, bc
D-B Mus. ms. 12157/2
parts
DMA 12//213
DdT 53-54, pp. 275-90
Organum I/10

K0340 Schaffe in mir, Gott, ein reines Herz (Samuel no. 56)
SATB, 2 vln, 2 vla, vc, bc
D-B Mus. ms. 12157/6
parts
DMA 28//133
Bärenreiter BA 3682

K0341 Singet dem Herrn ein neues Lied (Samuel no. 57)
SATB, 2 vln, 3 vla, bsn, bc
D-B Mus. ms. 12152, no. 13 (Bokemeyer)
score
DMA 3/1243
D-F Ms. Ff. Mus. 424
parts
DdT 53-54, pp. 24-36
Die Kantate, no. 188

K0342 Sit laus piena sit sonora (Samuel no. 58)
SSTB, 2 vln, bc
D-B Mus. ms. 30224, no. 6 (Bokemeyer)
score

K0343 Trauriges Leben, betrübte Zeit (Samuel no. 63)
SATB, 2 vln, 3 vla, bc
D-B Mus. ms. 12152, no. 15 (Bokemeyer)
score
DMA 3/1244

K0344 Uns ist ein Kind geboren (Samuel no. 64)
SAB, 2 vln, bsn, bc
D-B Mus. ms. 12152, no. 16 (Bokemeyer)
score
DMA 3/1245
D-Mbs Mus. ms. 5675
score
DdT 53-54, pp. 202-20
Ed. Samuel (Concordia 97-4692)

K0345 Wachet auf, ihr Christen alle (Samuel no. 65)
SATB, 2 vln, 2 vla, bsn, bc
D-B Mus. ms. 12153, no. 10 (Bokemeyer)
score
DMA 30//67
DdT 53-54, pp. 258-74

K0346 Was ist doch das Menschen Leben (Samuel no. 66)
SATB, 2 vln, bsn, bc
D-B Mus. ms. 12152, no. 18 (Bokemeyer)
score
DMA 3/1241

K0347 Wenn du gegessen hast und satt bist (Samuel no. 68)
SATB, 2 vln, gamba, bc
D-B Mus. ms. 12152, no. 17 (Bokemeyer)
score
DMA 3/1247

KÜHNHAUSEN, Johann Georg (d. 1714)

K0348 Passio Christi secundum Matthäum
STTB soli, SATB, bc
D-Bds Mus. ms. 30092
score
Das Chorwerk 50

KÜNSTEL, Georg Friedrich (fl. 1670-1680)

K0349 Bezahle mir, was du mir schuldig bist
SATB, 2 vln, 2 vla, vlne, bsn, bc
D-F Ms. Ff. Mus. 425
parts

K0350 Herr Gott, wie steck ich doch in Not
SATB, 3 vla, vlne, bsn, bc
D-F Ms. Ff. Mus. 426
parts

KÜNSTEL, Georg Friedrich (*continued*)

K0351   **Hilf, Herr, die Heiligen haben abgenommen**
         SSATB, 2 vln, 2 vla, vlne, bsn, bc
         D-F Ms. Ff. Mus. 427
         parts

K0352   **Jesus gibt sich in den Tod**
         ATB, 2 vln, vlne, bc
         D-F Ms. Ff. Mus. 428
         parts

K0353   **Lobet, ihr Knechte des Herrn**
         SATB, 2 vln, vla, bsn, bc
         D-F Ms. Ff. Mus. 429
         parts (vla, bsn, bc lacking)

K0354   **Nun hat das heilig Gottes Lamm**
         SSATB, 3 vln, 2 vla, vlne, 2 bsn, bc

D-F Ms. Ff. Mus. 431
2 conducting scores and parts

KUSSER, Johann (1626-1692)

K0355   **In te Domine speravi**
         ATB, 3 vln, bc
         D-Dlb Mus. ms. 1754-E-500 (Grimma U
         581/L 25 XXXIII)
         parts

K0356   **Magnificat**
         SSATB, 2 vln, 3 tbn, bc
         D-B Mus. ms. 12370
         parts
         DMA 28//139
         Possibly by Johann Sigismund Kusser

L

LANG, Kaspar

COLLECTION

Musae sacrae seu sacrae cantiones binis (1660)
RISM L544 (parts)
DMA 71//34

WORKS

L0001 **Anni recurso**
SSS/TTT, 2 vln, bc
Musae sacrae, no. 26-8

L0002 **Beatus vir**
SSB
Musae sacrae, no. 14

L0003 **Caelestis urbs**
SSS/TTT, 2 vln, bc
Musae sacrae, no. 26-11

L0004 **Desiderium animae**
SSS/TTT, 2 vln, bc
Musae sacrae, no. 22

L0005 **Exultet orbis**
SSS/TTT, 2 vln, bc
Musae sacrae, no. 26-4

L0006 **Fortem virili**
SSS/TTT, 2 vln, bc
Musae sacrae, no. 26-10

L0007 **Gaude Maria**
SSS/TTT, 2 vln, bc
Musae sacrae, no. 19

L0008 **Gustate**
SSS/TTT, 2 vln, bc
Musae sacrae, no. 17

L0009 **Hoc est praeceptum**
SSS/TTT, 2 vln, bc
Musae sacrae, no. 21

L0010 **In caelistibus regnis**
SSS/TTT, 2 vln, bc
Musae sacrae, no. 23

L0011 **In conspectu**
SSS/TTT, 2 vln, bc
Musae sacrae, no. 20

L0012 **Invicte martyr**
SSS/TTT, 2 vln, bc
Musae sacrae, no. 26-5

L0013 **Jesu, corona**
SSS/TTT, 2 vln, bc
Musae sacrae, no. 26-9

L0014 **Jesu dulcedo**
SSS/TTT, 2 vln, bc
Musae sacrae, no. 26-2

L0015 **Jesu, redemptor**
SSS/TTT, 2 vln, bc
Musae sacrae, no. 26-7

L0016 **Laetare**
SSTB
Musae sacrae, no. 15

L0017 **Laudate mecum**
SSS/TTT, 2 vln, bc
Musae sacrae, no. 26-1

L0018 **Maria gustum**
SSS/TTT, 2 vln, bc
Musae sacrae, no. 26-3

LANG, Kaspar (*continued*)

L0019 **Non sunt condig**
ATB
Musae sacrae, no. 13

L0020 **O amantissime**
ATB
Musae sacrae, no. 11

L0021 **O gravem dexteram**
SSS/TTT, 2 vln, bc
Musae sacrae, no. 26-12

L0022 **O Jesu**
SSS/TTT, 2 vln, bc
Musae sacrae, no. 18

L0023 **O quam pulchra**
ATB
Musae sacrae, no. 12

L0024 **Paratum**
SSB
Musae sacrae, no. 10

L0025 **Prudentes virgines**
SSS/TTT, 2 vln, bc
Musae sacrae, no. 24

L0026 **Regnum mundi**
SSS/TTT, 2 vln, bc
Musae sacrae, no. 25

L0027 **Rex gloriose**
SSS/TTT, 2 vln, bc
Musae sacrae, no. 26-6

L0028 **Veni electa**
ATB
Musae sacrae, no. 16

LANGWEIL, Duario

L0029 **Miserere**
SATTB, 4 vla, bc
CS-KRa XII, 18
parts
microfilm: US-SY

LAUER, Wolfgang

L0030 **Wohl sind des rauen Herbstes Zeiten**
SATB
Funeral of Regina Elisabeth Faber
Nürnberg, 1664
RISM L1089, Reich 330 (score)
DMA 75//35

LEIBNITZ, Johann Georg

L0031 **Weg mit dir, du falsche Welt**
SATB
Funeral of the composer
Nürnberg, 1671
RISM L1650, Reich 345

LEOPOLD I (1640-1705)

L0032 **Ave maris stella** (Brosche no. 12)
SATB soli, SATB, 4 vla, bass viol, corn, 3
tbn, vlne, theorbo, bc
A-Wn Ms. 16049
parts

L0033 **Beatus vir** (Brosche no. 14)
A solo, SATB, 2 vla, vltta, vc, corn, clar,
2 tbn, vlne, bsn, bc
A-Wn Ms. 16045
parts

L0034 **Caelestis urbs Jerusalem** (Brosche no. 22)
SSATTB soli, SSATTB, 2 vln, vla, vltta,
vc, corn, 2 clar, 2 tbn, vlne, bsn, bc
Dedication of a church
A-Wn Ms. 16064
parts
Ed. Adler I, pp. 129-52

L0035 **Confitebor** (Brosche no. 15)
T solo, SATB, 2 vln, vc, corn, clar, 3 tbn,
vlne, bc
A-Wn Ms. 16050
parts

L0036 **Custodes hominum, psallimus Angelos** (Brosche
no. 19)
SSAA, 2 vln, vc, vlne, bc
A-Wn Ms. 16048
parts

L0037 **Decora lux** (Brosche no. 23)
SATB soli, SATB, 2 vln, vc, corn, 2 tbn,
vlne, bsn, bc
Feast of Saints Peter and Paul
A-Wn Ms. 16057
parts

L0038 **Dies irae** (Brosche no. 16)
SATB soli, SATB, 2 vln, vla/corn, 2
vla/tbn, bass viol/bsn, 2 clar, vlne, bc
Requiem
A-Wn Ms. 16055 (1673)
parts

L0039   **Dixit Dominus** (Brosche no. 17)
S solo, SATB, 2 vla, vltta, vc, corn, clar,
2 tbn, vlne, bsn, bc
A-Wn Ms. 16044
parts

L0040   **Domine Jesu Christe** (Brosche no. 18)
SSATTB soli, SSATTB, gamba, 3 vltta, 2
corn, 2 tbn, vlne, bsn, bc
A-Wn Ms. 16041 (1662)
parts

L0041   **Fortem virili pectore** (Brosche no. 20)
SATB soli, SATB, 2 vln, corn, 2 tbn, vlne,
theorbo, bc
Feast of a Saint neither Virgin nor Martyr
A-Wn Ms. 16757
score
A-Wgm I/17.563
parts
Ed. Adler I, pp. 167-80

L0042   **Heu! heu! peccatores** (Brosche no. 41)
SATB soli, SATB, 3 vla, bass viol, 3
gamba, corn, 3 tbn, vlne, theorbo, bc
A-Wn Ms. 15844
score
A-Wn Ms. 16053
parts

L0043   **Il transito di San Giuseppe** (Brosche no. 7)
SATTBB soli, SSA, bc
A-Wn Ms. 18899
score

L0044   **Iste confessor Domini** (Brosche no. 21)
SSATTB soli, SSATTB, 2 vln, 2 vltta, vc,
2 corn, 2 clar, 2 tbn, vlne, bsn, bc
Feast of a Confessor Pope
A-Wn Ms. 16062
parts

L0045   **Laudate Dominum, omnes gentes** (Brosche
no. 31)
S solo, SATB, 2 vln, vltta, vc, corn, clar,
2 tbn, vlne, bsn, bc
A-Wn Ms. 16047
parts
S-Uu 57:20
parts (only voices, clarino, and organ)
DMA 3/852

L0046   **Laudate, pueri** (Brosche no. 32)
B solo, SSSAB, 2 vln, vc, 2 corn, clar,
vlne, bsn, bc

A-Wn Ms. 16051
parts
Ed. Adler I, pp. 239-56

L0047   **Litaniae Lauretanae** (Brosche no. 35)
SSATB, bc
A-Wn Ms. 18831 (1655)
score

L0048   **Litaniae Lauretanae** (Brosche no. 36)
SATB soli, SATB, 2 vln, vc, corn, 2 tbn,
vlne, bsn, bc
A-Wn Ms. 16052
parts

L0049   **Magnificat** (Brosche no. 37)
SSATB soli, SSATB, 2 vln, 2 vla, vc, 2
corn, 2 clar, 2 tbn, vlne, bsn, bc
A-Wn Ms. 16046
parts

L0050   **Miserere** (Brosche no. 38)
SATB soli, SATB, 4 vla, 2 vltta, 3 tbn,
bsn, bc
A-Wn Ms. 15640
score
A-Wn Ms. 18946
score (autograph with corrections)
A-Wgm A 187, Carl VI
score
D-Mb Mus. ms. 311
score
Ed. Adler I, pp. 257-98

L0051   **Miserere per la Settimana Santa** (Brosche no. 39)
SATB soli, SATB, bass viol, 2 gamba, 5
vltta, vlne, lyra, 2 baritoni, bc
A-Wn Ms. 16263
score
A-Wgm I 17561
parts

L0052   **Missa Angeli custodis** (Brosche no. 10)
SATB soli, SATB, 2 vln, 3 vltta, 3 tbn,
vlne, theorbo, bc
A-Wn Ms. 16067
parts
Ed. Adler I, pp. 55-104

L0053   **Missa pro defunctis** (Brosche no. 11)
SSATB soli, SSATB, 4 vla, 2 corn, 3 tbn,
vlne, bc
A-Wn Ms. 16054 (1673)
parts
Ed. M. Dietz (Hofbauer, ca. 1891)

LEOPOLD I (*continued*)

L0054 **Oratorio di San Antonio di Padova** (Brosche
no. 2)
SATB soli, SATB, bc
A-Wn Ms. 16847 (1684)
score
Ed. Adler II, pp. 40-54 (excerpts)

L0055 **Oratorio di San Giuseppe** (Brosche no. 4)
SSSAT soli, SSAT, 2 vln, vla, vlne, bc
A-Wn Ms. 16585
score

L0056 **Parce mihi** (Brosche no. 33)
SSATB soli, SSATB, 4 vla, 2 corn, 2 tbn,
vlne, bsn, bc
Funeral
A-Wn Ms. 15642 (1676)
parts
Ed. Adler I, pp. 181-230

L0057 **Pater superni** (Brosche no. 27)
SST, 2 vln, vc, tbn, vlne, bc
Feast of Saint Mary Magdalene
A-Wn Ms. 16059
parts

L0058 **Salve decus Bohemiae** (Brosche no. 43)
SATB soli, SATB, 2 vln, vc, corn, 2 tbn,
vlne, bsn, bc
A-Wn Ms. 16066
parts

L0059 **Salve regina** (Brosche no. 45)
S solo, SATB, 2 vla, vltta, vc, corn, 2 tbn,
vlne, bsn, bc
A-Wn Ms. 16043
parts
A-Wn Ms. 15848
score (voices and organ only)

L0060 **Sancte Ladislae** (Brosche no. 26)
SSATB
A-Wn Ms. 16056
parts

L0061 **Sancte Wenceslae** (Brosche no. 30)
SATB, vla, vltta, vc, corn, 2 tbn, vlne,
bsn, bc
A-Wn Ms. 16056
parts

L0062 **Stabat Mater** (Brosche no. 47)
SATB soli, SATB, 2 vla, vltta, vc, corn, 2
tbn, vlne, bsn, bc
A-Wn Ms. 15731
score

A-Wgm I 17562 (1678)
parts
Ed. M. Dietz (Hofbauer, ca. 1891)

L0063 **Sub tuum praesidium** (Brosche no. 48)
S solo, SATB, vla, vltta, vc, corn, 2 tbn,
vlne, bsn, bc
A-Wn Ms. 16052
parts
Ed. Adler I, pp. 231-38

L0064 **Sub tuum praesidium** (Brosche no. 49)
SSATB, bc
A-Wn Ms. 18831 (1654)
score

L0065 **Te Josephi** (Brosche no. 25)
SATB soli, SATB, 2 vln, vc, corn, 2 tbn,
vlne, bsn, bc
Feast of Saint Joseph
A-Wn Ms. 16058
parts
Ed. Adler I, pp. 153-66

L0066 **Te splendor** (Brosche no. 28)
SATB soli, SATB, 2 vln, vc, corn, 2 tbn,
vlne, bsn, bc
Feast of Saint Michael the Archangel
A-Wn Ms. 16060
parts

L0067 **Ut queant laxis** (Brosche no. 24)
SATB soli, SATB, 2 vln, vc, corn, 2 tbn,
vlne, bsn, bc
Feast of Saint John the Baptist
A-Wn Ms. 16061
parts

L0068 **Vertatur in luctum** (Brosche no. 40)
SSATB soli, SSATB, 4 vla, vc, corn, 3
tbn, vlne, theorbo, bc
Feast of the Seven Sorrows
A-Wn Ms. 16070
parts
A-Wn Ms. 16069
parts (opening section of piece missing)
Ed. Adler I, pp. 105-28

LEUTNER, Georg Christoph (1644-1703)

L0069 **Domine ad adjuvandum** (2 settings)
SSATB, 2 vln, vlne, bc
D-OB M0602 (1706)
parts

LIEBE, Christian (1654-1708)

L0070 Ach liebster Jesu komm herein
SSATB, 2 vln, 2 vla, bsn, bc
New Year
D-Dlb Mus. ms. 1896-E-502 (Grimma U
528/L 16)
parts

L0071 Alle Bitterkeit und Grimm und Zorn
SATB, 2 vln, 2 vla, vlne, bc
6th Sunday after Trinity
F-Ssp
parts
DMA 2/2259

L0072 Als der Tag der Pfingsten
SATB, 2 vln, 2 ob, taille, bsn, bc
Pentecost
D-Dlb Mus. ms. 1896-E-500 (Grimma U
368/N 55)
parts

L0073 Aus der Tiefe rufe ich Herr zu dir
SATB, 2 vln, 2 vla, bsn, bc
D-Dlb Mus. ms. 1896-E-503 (Grimma U
539/T 6)
score and parts

L0074 Darum seid barmherzig
SATB, 2 vln, 2 vla, vlne, bc
4th Sunday after Trinity
F-Ssp Ms. 229
parts
DMA 2/2260

L0075 Das neugeborne Kindelein
SSATB, 2 vln, 2 vla, 2 clar, timp, bsn, bc
D-Dlb Mus. ms. 1896-E-506 (Grimma U
323/N 28)
parts

L0076 Das Wort ward Fleisch
SSATB, bc
D-Dlb Mus. ms. 1896-E-505 (Grimma U
544/L 20)
score and parts

L0077 Der Engel des Herrn
SATB, 2 vln, 2 vla, 2 clar, vlne/bsn, bc
F-Ssp Ms. 243
parts
DMA 2/866

L0078 Der Herr ist Gott
SATB, 2 vln, 2 clar, bsn, bc
Pentecost

D-Dlb Mus. ms. 1896-E-504 (Grimma L
14/L 14)
parts

L0079 Der Mensch vom Weibe geboren
SATB, 2 vln, 4 ob, bc
16th Sunday after Trinity
F-Ssp Ms. 251
parts
DMA 2/867

L0080 Es ist umsonst
SATB, 2 vln, 2 vla, bsn, bc
5th Sunday after Trinity
F-Ssp Ms. 230
parts
DMA 2/868

L0081 Gloria in excelsis Deo
SSATTB, 2 vln, 3 vla, 2 clar, timp, vlne, bc
D-Bds Mus. ms. 30222, no. 15 (Bokemeyer)
score

L0082 Gnade, Gnade, Jesu, Gnade
SSATB, 2 vln, 2 vla, bsn, bc
F-Ssp

L0083 Herr, höre und sei mir gnädig
SATB, 2 vln, 2 vla, bsn, bc
14th Sunday after Trinity
F-Ssp
parts
DMA 2/2261

L0084 Ich danke dir, Gott
SATB, vln, 3 vla, bc
11th Sunday after Trinity
F-Ssp
parts
DMA 2/869

L0085 Ich habe einen guten Kampf gekämpfet
SSATB, 2 vln, 2 vla, bc
D-Bds Mus. ms. 30222, no. 11 (Bokemeyer)
(1695)
score
F-Ssp
parts
DMA 2/2262

L0086 Ich halte es dafür
SATTB, bc
D-Dlb Mus. ms. 1896-E-501 (Grimma U
543/L 45)
parts

L0087 Ihr wisset die Gnade unsers Herrn Jesu Christi
SATB, vln, 2 vla, 4 ob, 4 harps, vlne, bc

LIEBE, Christian (*continued*)

D-Dlb Mus. ms. 1896-E-509 (Grimma U
326/N 32 and U 374/N 62)
score and parts

L0088   **Komm an, du sanftes Brausen**
SATTB, vln, 4 vla, bsn, bc
Pentecost
D-Dlb Mus. ms. 1896-E-510 (Grimma U
327/N 32)
parts

L0089   **Liebet eure Feinde**
SATB, 2 vln, vla/tbn, clar, bc
13th Sunday after Trinity
F-Ssp
parts
DMA 2/2263

L0090   **Machet die Tore weit**
SATB, 2 vln, 2 clar, bsn, bc
D-Dlb Mus. ms. 1896-E-507 (Grimma U
324/N 29)
parts

L0091   **Machet euch Freunde**
SATB, 2 vln, 4 ob, bc
9th Sunday after Trinity
F-Ssp Ms. 246
parts
DMA 2/870

L0092   **Mein Freund, ich tue dir nicht unrecht**
SATB, 2 ob, taille, bsn, bc
F-Ssp
parts

L0093   **Meine Seele erhebet den Herrn**
SATB, 2 vln, vla, clar, timp, vlne, bc
Visitation of the Virgin Mary
F-Ssp Ms. 235
parts
DMA 2/871

L0094   **Missa à 5**
??
F-Ssp
Listed in Lobstein (1840); presumed extant

L0095   **O Heiland aller Welt**
SATB, 2 vln, bc
Christmas Day
D-Dlb Mus. ms. 1896-E-508 (Grimma U
325/N 30)
parts

L0096   **Sehet euch vor vor den falschen Propheten**
SATB, 2 vln, 2 ob, taille, bsn, bc

8th Sunday after Trinity
F-Ssp
parts
DMA 2/872

L0097   **Sei nun wieder zufrieden**
5 vv, 2 vln, 2 shawms, 2 corn, bsn, bc
F-Ssp

L0098   **Siehe! des Herrn Auge siehet auf die**
SATB, 2 vln, 2 vla, bsn, bc
7th Sunday after Trinity
F-Ssp Ms. 233
parts
DMA 2/873

L0099   **Trachtet am ersten nach dem Reich Gottes**
SATB, vln, 2 vla, bsn, bc
15th Sunday after Trinity
F-Ssp
parts
DMA 2/874

L0100   **Und du, Bethlehem, in jüdischen Lande**
SATB, 2 vln, vc, 2 fl, bc
D-Bds Mus. ms. 30222, no. 14 (Bokemeyer)
(1695)
score

L0101   **Und du, Kindlein**
SATB, 2 ob, taille, bsn, bc
Feast of John the Baptist
F-Ssp Ms. 234
parts
DMA 2/875

L0102   **Wenn du es wüßtest**
SATB, 2 vln, 2 ob, taille, bsn, bc
F-Ssp
parts
DMA 2/876

L0103   **Wohl dem, der ein tugendsam Weib**
SATB, 2 vln, 2 vla, bsn, bc
Wedding
F-Ssp

LOEW, Daniel

L0104   **Erde die du mir gegeben**
SATB
Funeral of M. Philipp Bostar
Gotha, 1660
RISM L2738 (score)
DMA 72//92

LÖHNER, Johann (1645-1705)

L0105   **Sei willkommen, süße Ruh**
SATB
Funeral of Margareta Magdalena Birken
Bayreuth, 1670
RISM L2694 (score)
DMA 3/1016

L0106   **So pflegt es Gott mit uns zu machen**
SATB
Funeral of Margareta Magdalena Birken
Bayreuth, 1670
RISM L2694 (score)
DMA 3/1016

LÖSER, Hans

L0107   **Ehstands-Licht, der Liebe Sonne**
SSATB
Funeral of Eva Dorothea von Löser
Chemnitz, 1685
RISM L2734, Reich 45 (score)
DMA 75//66

L0108   **Mein Kind, wie sehe ich**
SSATB, bc
Funeral of Ursula Elisabeth von Löser
Altenburg, 1689
RISM L2735, Reich 13 (score)
DMA 75//212, 70//162, & 75//66

L0109   **Mein Seufzen ist doch ganz vergebens**
SSATB, bc
Funeral of Magnus Wilhelm, Kurt, and
Rudolph August von Löser
Altenburg, 1696
RISM L2736, Reich 14 (score)
DMA 75//66

L0110   **Unglück hat sich recht verschworen**
SSATB, bc
Funeral of Ursula Elisabeth von Löser
Altenburg, 1689
RISM L2735, Reich 13 (score)
DMA 75//66

LÖWE VON EISENACH, Johann Jakob (1629-1703)

L0111   **Gustate et videte**
SSB, 2 vln, bc
Neue geistliche Concerten (1660)
RISM L2751 (parts incomplete)
DMA 1/141

S-Uu 85:26a, fol. 1v-3 (Düben)
tablature

LÜBECK, Vincent (1654-1740)

L0112   **Es ist ein großer Gewinn**
ATB, SATB, 2 vln, 2 gamba, 2 ob, bsn, bc
Funeral of Queen Eleonora Ulrica of Sweden
D-Stade, Niedersächsisches Staatsarchiv,
Rep. 5a, F 108, Nr. 34 (1693)
parts
Ed. W. Syré (Möseler M68.020, 1987)

L0113   **Gott, wie dein Name, so ist auch dein Ruhm**
ATB, 3 vln, bc
D-B Mus. ms. 30300, no. 9 (Bokemeyer)
score
DMA 2/508
Ed. F. Stein (Merseberger EM 909; Bärenreiter
BA 5436, 1946); reprint (Kalmus A6330)

L0114   **Hilf deinen Volk**
SATB, 2 vln, 2 vla, bsn, bc
D-B Mus. ms. 30300, no. 11
score
DMA 2/509
Ed. F. Stein (Merseberger EM 907; Bärenreiter
BA 5437, 1946); reprint (Kalmus A6331)

L0115   **Ich hab hie wenig guter Tag**
??
Funeral of Queen Eleonora Ulrica of
Sweden
D-Stade, Niedersächsisches Staatsarchiv,
Rep. 5a, F 108
parts
Ed. W. Syré (Möseler M68.021)

LUNSDÖRFFER, Albrecht Martin (d. 1690)

L0116   **Selig ist der Mensch**
SSATB, 5 vla, bc
Funeral of Sophia Margaretha, Markgräfin
zu Brandenburg
Ansbach, 1664
Reich 15 (parts)
DMA 70//171

L0117   **Unser Leben währet siebenzig Jahr**
SSB, bc
Funeral of Matthäus Lundsdörffer
Nürnberg, 1647
Reich 301

M

MAGER, Joachim (1607-1678)

M0001   **Der Ehstand ist in Gottes Wort**
SSAT, ATTB, bc
Gosslar, 1645
    parts (apparently no longer extant)
Ed. Jacobs (1894)

MATTHAEI, Conrad (1619-1678)

M0002   **Herr Jesu, Trost in aller Not**
SATTB
D-Bds Mus. ms. Winterfeld 107, pp.
    103-04 and 129
    score
Ed. Winterfeld II, no. 70

M0003   **Neue Herzens-Freude**
??
Birthday (?) of Friedrich Stegemann
Königsberg, 1650
    RISM M1387

M0004   **Wer seinem Sinn auf Gott nicht eilig stellt**
SATTB, bc
Funeral of M. Martin Wolder
Königsberg, 1657
    RISM M1389 (parts)
    DMA 52//22

MAYER, Johann Wilhelm

M0005   **Angst und Klagen**
SSA, bc
Funeral of Georg Lomer

Augsburg, 1682
    RISM M1483 (score)
    DMA 70//170

MAYER, Martin (d. 1707)

M0006   **Alle die gottselig leben wollen**
SSATB, 2 vln, 3 tbn, vlne, bc
Sunday after Ascension
D-Bds Mus. ms. CLXXI, no. 32 (1676)
    parts

M0007   **Alles was ihr tut mit Worten**
SSATB, 2 vln, 3 tbn, bsn, bc
Circumcision
D-Bds Mus. ms. CLXXI, no. 7 (1675)
    parts

M0008   **Aus Gnaden seid ihr selig worden**
SATB, 2 vln, 3 tbn, vlne, bc
Septuagesima
D-Bds Mus. ms. CLXXI, no. 16 (1677)
    parts

M0009   **Christus hat gelitten für uns**
SSATB, 2 vln, 3 tbn, vlne, bc
Quinquagesima
D-Bds Mus. ms. CLXXI, no. 18 (1676)
    parts (lacking bc)

M0010   **Da Jesus geboren war zu Bethlehem**
SATTBB, 2 vln, bc
Epiphany
D-Bds Mus. ms. CLXXI, no. 9 (1677)
    parts

M0011 **Das ist je gewißlich wahr**
SSATB, 2 vln, 3 tbn, vlne, bc
3rd Sunday after Trinity
D-Bds Mus. ms. CLXXI, no. 37 (1676)
parts

M0012 **Das ist sein Gebot, daß wir glauben**
SSATB, 2 vln, 2 tbn/vla, tbn, vlne, bc
13th Sunday after Trinity
D-Bds Mus. ms. CLXXI, no. 47 (1674)
parts

M0013 **Der Geist des Herren ist über mir**
SSATB, 2 vln, 3 tbn, bsn, bc
3rd Sunday of Advent
D-Bds Mus. ms. CLXXI, no. 3 (1675)
parts

M0014 **Der Herr bringet die Lügner um**
SATB, 2 vln, 3 tbn, bc
23rd Sunday after Trinity
D-Bds Mus. ms. CLXXI, no. 57
parts

M0015 **Der Segen des Herren machet reich**
SSATB, 2 vln, 2 corn, 2 clar, 2 prin, timp,
2 tbn, tbn/bsn, vlne, bc
5th Sunday after Trinity
D-Bds Mus. ms. CLXXI, no. 39 (1675)
parts

M0016 **Der Teufel ist ein Mörder**
SATB, 2 vln, 3 tbn, bc
5th Sunday of Lent
D-Bds Mus. ms. CLXXI, no. 23 (1678)
parts

M0017 **Dienet einander ein jeglicher mit der Gabe**
SSATB, 2 vln, 3 tbn, vlne, bc
9th Sunday after Trinity
D-Bds Mus. ms. CLXXI, no. 43 (1676)
parts

M0018 **Es ist dir gesagt, Mensch, was gut ist**
SSATB, 2 vln, 3 tbn, vlne, bc
3rd Sunday of Lent
D-Bds Mus. ms. CLXXI, no. 21 (1676)
parts

M0019 **Es ist ein großer Gewinn**
SSATB, 2 vln, 3 tbn, vlne, bc
15th Sunday after Trinity
D-Bds Mus. ms. CLXXI, no. 49 (1674)
parts

M0020 **Es ist mir ein geringes**
SSATB, 2 vln, 2 vla, vlne, bc
Purification of the Virgin Mary

D-Bds Mus. ms. CLXXI, no. 14 (1675)
parts (lacking bc)

M0021 **Es kommt die Zeit**
SATB, 2 vln, 3 tbn, vlne, bc
5th Sunday after Easter
D-Bds Mus. ms. CLXXI, no. 31 (1676)
parts

M0022 **Es wird das Szepter von Juda**
SSATB, 2 vln, 2 corn, 3 clar, 2 timp, 3
tbn, vlne, bc
Christmas Day
D-Bds Mus. ms. CLXXI, no. 5 (1676)
parts (lacking 1st soprano and vlne parts)

M0023 **Es wird geschehen, daß des Menschen Sohn**
SSATB, 2 vln, 2 vla, bsn, vlne, bc
2nd Sunday of Advent
D-Bds Mus. ms. CLXXI, no. 2 (1675)
parts

M0024 **Freude! Jesus ist erstanden**
SSATB, 2 vln, 2 corn, 2 clar, 3 tbn, vlne, bc
Easter Sunday
D-Bds Mus. ms. CLXXI, no. 26 (1677)
parts

M0025 **Gott hat den Menschen geschaffen**
SATB, 2 vln, 3 tbn, vlne, bc
24th Sunday after Trinity
D-Bds Mus. ms. CLXXI, no. 58 (1676)
parts (lacking vlne)

M0026 **Gott ist die Liebe, und wer in der Liebe**
SATB, 2 vln, 3 tbn, vlne, bc
18th Sunday after Trinity
D-Bds Mus. ms. CLXXI, no. 52 (1676)
parts

M0027 **Gott ist unser Zuversicht und Stärke**
SATB, 2 vln, 2 corn, 3 tbn, vlne, bc
4th Sunday after Epiphany
D-Bds Mus. ms. CLXXI, no. 13 (1677)
parts

M0028 **Gott lieben ist die allerschönste Weisheit**
SSATB, 2 vln, 3 tbn, vlne, bc
1st Sunday after Epiphany
D-Bds Mus. ms. CLXXI, no. 10 (1675)
parts

M0029 **Gottes Name wird ewiglich bleiben**
SSATB, 2 vln, 2 vla, vlne, bsn, bc
14th Sunday after Trinity
D-Bds Mus. ms. CLXXI, no. 48 (1674)
parts

MAYER, Martin (*continued*)

M0030 **Heilig ist der Herre Zebaoth**
SSATBB, 2 vln, 2 corn, 2 clar, 2 tbn/vla,
tbn, vlne, bc
Trinity
D-Bds Mus. ms. CLXXI, no. 34 (1676)
parts

M0031 **Heiliget den Herren Zebaoth**
SATB, 2 vln, 3 tbn, vlne, bc
Sunday after Christmas
D-Bds Mus. ms. CLXXI, no. 6 (1675)
parts

M0032 **Herr, Herr Gott, barmherzig und gnädig**
SATB, 2 vln, 3 tbn, bc
22nd Sunday after Trinity
D-Bds Mus. ms. CLXXI, no. 56 (1676)
parts

M0033 **Herr, wir liegen vor dir**
SSATB, 2 vln, 3 tbn, vlne, bc
11th Sunday after Trinity
D-Bds Mus. ms. CLXXI, no. 45 (1674)
parts

M0034 **Hosianna dem Sohne David**
SSATB, 2 vln, 2 clar/corn, 3 tbn, 2 vlne, bc
1st Sunday of Advent
D-Bds Mus. ms. CLXXI, no. 1 (1674)
parts

M0035 **Ich will mich mit dir verloben**
SATB, 2 vln, 2 clar, 3 tbn, bc
20th Sunday after Trinity
D-Bds Mus. ms. CLXXI, no. 54 (1676)
parts

M0036 **Ihr Lieben, gläubet nicht**
SSATB, 2 vln, 2 corn ad lib, 2 clar, 3 tbn,
vlne, bc
8th Sunday after Trinity
D-Bds Mus. ms. CLXXI, no. 42 (1677)
parts

M0037 **Ihr Lieben, lasset euch die Hitze**
SSATB, 2 vln, 2 tbn, tbn/bsn, vlne, bc
Sexagesima
D-Bds Mus. ms. CLXXI, no. 17 (1676)
parts

M0038 **Jesus Christus, ob er wohl in göttlicher Gestalt war**
SSATB, 2 vln, 3 tbn, vlne, bc
Palm Sunday
D-Bds Mus. ms. CLXXI, no. 24 (1678)
parts (lacking vlne)

M0039 **Kommet her zu mir, alle**
SATB, 2 vln, 2 corn/fl, 2 tbn, tbn/bsn,
vlne, bc
2nd Sunday after Trinity
D-Bds Mus. ms. CLXXI, no. 36 (1676)
parts

M0040 **Lasset das Wort Gottes reichlich**
SSATB, 2 vln, 3 tbn, bc
17th Sunday after Trinity
D-Bds Mus. ms. CLXXI, no. 51 (1676)
parts

M0041 **Liebet eure Feinde, segnet die euch fluchen**
SSATB, 2 vln, 3 tbn, vlne, bc
6th Sunday after Trinity
D-Bds Mus. ms. CLXXI, no. 40 (1676)
parts

M0042 **Mein Herz hält dir für dein Wort**
SSATB, 2 vln, 2 tbn, tbn/bsn, vlne, bc
2nd Sunday of Lent
D-Bds Mus. ms. CLXXI, no. 20 (1676)
parts

M0043 **Mein Kind, verwirf die Zucht des Herrn nicht**
SSATB, 2 vln, 3 tbn, vlne, bc
21st Sunday after Trinity
D-Bds Mus. ms. CLXXI, no. 55 (1677)
parts (lacking vlne)

M0044 **Meine Schafe hören meine Stimme**
SATB, 2 vln, 2 tbn, tbn/bsn, vlne, bc
2nd Sunday after Easter
D-Bds Mus. ms. CLXXI, no. 28 (1676)
parts

M0045 **Mir ist gegeben alle Gewalt im Himmel**
SSATB, 2 vln, 2 tbn/vla, tbn, bc
19th Sunday after Trinity
D-Bds Mus. ms. CLXXI, no. 53 (1676)
parts

M0046 **Niemand sage, wenn er versucht wird**
SATB, 2 vln, 2 tbn, tbn/bsn, vlne, bc
1st Sunday of Lent
D-Bds Mus. ms. CLXXI, no. 19 (1676)
parts

M0047 **Schaffe in mir, Gott, ein reines Herz**
SSATB, 2 vln, 2 corn, 2 clar, 2 prin, 3
tbn, vlne, bc
Pentecost
D-Bds Mus. ms. CLXXI, no. 33 (1679)
parts

M0048 **Schmecket und sehet wie freundlich**
SATB, 2 vln, 2 corn, 3 tbn/vla, vlne, bc

2nd Sunday after Epiphany
D-Bds Mus. ms. CLXXI, no. 11 (1676)
parts

M0049 **Sei nicht stolz sondern fürchte dich**
SSATB, 2 vln, 3 tbn, vlne, bc
10th Sunday after Trinity
D-Bds Mus. ms. CLXXI, no. 44 (1674)
parts

M0050 **Siehe, es kommt die Zeit, daß ich dem David**
SSATB, 2 vln, 2 corn, 2 clar, 3 tbn, bc
Annunciation
D-Bds Mus. ms. CLXXI, no. 25 (1679)
parts

M0051 **So spricht der Herr, dein Erlöser**
SATB, 2 vln, 2 tbn, tbn/bsn, vlne, bc
3rd Sunday after Easter
D-Bds Mus. ms. CLXXI, no. 29 (1676)
parts

M0052 **Tue deinen Mund auf für die Stummen**
SSATB, 2 vln, 3 tbn, 2 vlne, bc
12th Sunday after Trinity
D-Bds Mus. ms. CLXXI, no. 46 (1674)
parts

M0053 **Unser Wandel ist im Himmel**
SSATB, 2 vln, 2 tbn, vlne, bsn, bc
1st Sunday after Easter
D-Bds Mus. ms. CLXXI, no. 27 (1676)
parts

M0054 **Vertraue Gott und bleibe in deinem Beruf**
SATB, 2 vln, 3 tbn, vlne, bc
7th Sunday after Trinity
D-Bds Mus. ms. CLXXI, no. 41 (1676)
parts

M0055 **Wachet und betet, daß ihr nicht**
SSATB, 2 vln, 3 tbn, vlne, bc
5th Sunday after Epiphany
D-Bds Mus. ms. CLXXI, no. 15 (1677)
parts

M0056 **Was du tust, so bedenke das Ende**
SSATB, 3 vla, 2 vltta, vlne, bc
16th Sunday after Trinity
D-Bds Mus. ms. CLXXI, no. 50 (1674)
parts

M0057 **Was ihr wollt, daß euch die Leute tun sollen**
SSATB, 2 vln, 3 tbn, vlne, bc
4th Sunday after Trinity
D-Bds Mus. ms. CLXXI, no. 38 (1677)
parts

M0058 **Welche der Geist Gottes treibet**
SSATB, 2 vln, 3 tbn, vlne, bc
4th Sunday after Easter
D-Bds Mus. ms. CLXXI, no. 30 (1676)
parts

M0059 **Weltlich Ehr und zeitlich Gut**
SATB, 2 vln, 2 tbn, tbn/vlne, vlne, bc
1st Sunday after Trinity
D-Bds Mus. ms. CLXXI, no. 35 (1676)
parts

M0060 **Wer beharret bis ans Ende**
SSATB, 2 vln, 3 tbn, vlne, bc
25th Sunday after Trinity
D-Bds Mus. ms. CLXXI, no. 59 (1676)
parts (lacking vlne)

M0061 **Wer mich bekennt vor den Menschen**
SATB, 2 vln, 3 tbn, vlne, bc
4th Sunday of Advent
D-Bds Mus. ms. CLXXI, no. 4 (1675)
parts

M0062 **Wie teuer ist deine Güte, Gott**
SSATB, 2 vln, 3 tbn, bsn, bc
Sunday after Circumcision
D-Bds Mus. ms. CLXXI, no. 8 (1675)
parts

M0063 **Wir haben einen Gott, der da hilft**
SATB, 2 vln, 3 tbn, vlne, bc
3rd Sunday after Epiphany
D-Bds Mus. ms. CLXXI, no. 12 (1676)
parts

M0064 **Zweierlei bitte ich von dir, Herr**
SSATB, 2 vln, 3 tbn, vlne, bc
4th Sunday of Lent
D-Bds Mus. ms. CLXXI, no. 22 (1676)
parts

MAYR, Rupert Ignaz (1646-1712)

COLLECTIONS

Gazophylacium musico-sacrum (1702)
RISM M1498 (parts)

Psalmodia brevis ad Vesperas totius anni (1706)
RISM M1499 (parts)

WORKS

M0065 **Ad te Domine**
SATB, 2 vln, 3 tbn/vla, bc
1st Sunday of Advent
Gazophylacium musico-sacrum, no. 1

MAYR, Rupert Ignaz (*continued*)

M0066   **Angelus Domini**
       SATB, 2 vln, 3 tbn/vla, bc
       1st Sunday after Easter
       Gazophylacium musico-sacrum, no. 19

M0067   **Ascendit Deus in jubilatione**
       SATB, 2 vln, 2 vla, vc, bc
       Ascension and Sunday after Ascension
       Gazophylacium musico-sacrum, no. 23
       EdM, Bayern, vol. 1, pp. 96-107

M0068   **Ave Maria**
       SATB, 4 vla, bc
       4th Sunday of Advent
       Gazophylacium musico-sacrum, no. 4

M0069   **Beati omnes**
       SATB, 2 vln, 2 vla/tbn, vla/bsn, vlne, bc
       Psalmodia brevis, no. 17

M0070   **Beatus vir**
       SATB, 2 vln, 2 vla/tbn, vla/bsn, vlne, bc
       Psalmodia brevis, no. 4

M0071   **Benedicite**
       SATB, 2 vln, 3 tbn/vla, bc
       5th Sunday after Easter
       Gazophylacium musico-sacrum, no. 22

M0072   **Benedictus**
       SATB, 2 vln, 3 tbn/vla, bc
       Quinquagesima
       Gazophylacium musico-sacrum, no. 11

M0073   **Benedictus**
       SATB, 2 vln, 3 tbn/vla, bc
       Trinity
       Gazophylacium musico-sacrum, no. 25

M0074   **Benedixisti**
       SATTB, 2 vln, 3 tbn/vla, bc
       3rd Sunday of Advent
       Gazophylacium musico-sacrum, no. 3

M0075   **Bonum est**
       SATB, 2 vln, 3 tbn/vla, bc
       Septuagesima
       Gazophylacium musico-sacrum, no. 9

M0076   **Confirma**
       SATB, 2 vln, 2 clar, 3 tbn/vla, bc
       Pentecost
       Gazophylacium musico-sacrum, no. 24

M0077   **Confitebor tibi Domine**
       SATTB, bc
       5th Sunday of Lent

       Gazophylacium musico-sacrum, no. 16
       EdM, Bayern, vol. 1, pp. 93-95

M0078   **Confitebor tibi Domine**
       SATB, 2 vln, 2 vla/tbn, vla/bsn, vlne, bc
       Psalmodia brevis, no. 3
       EdM, Bayern, vol. 1, pp. 113-19

M0079   **Credidi propter**
       SATB, 2 vln, 2 vla/tbn, vla/bsn, vlne, bc
       Psalmodia brevis, no. 12
       EdM, Bayern, vol. 1, pp. 136-40

M0080   **De profundis**
       SATB, 2 vln, 2 vla/tbn, vla/bsn, vlne, bc
       Psalmodia brevis, no. 16

M0081   **Deus meus**
       SATB, 2 vln, 3 tbn/vla, bc
       2nd Sunday after Easter
       Gazophylacium musico-sacrum, no. 20

M0082   **Deus tu conversus**
       SATB, 2 vln, 3 tbn/vla, bc
       2nd Sunday of Advent
       Gazophylacium musico-sacrum, no. 2

M0083   **Dextera Domini**
       SATB, 2 vln, 3 tbn/vla, bc
       3rd Sunday after Epiphany
       Gazophylacium musico-sacrum, no. 8

M0084   **Dixit Dominus Domino meo**
       SATB, 2 vln, 2 vla/tbn, vla/bsn, vlne, bc
       Psalmodia brevis, no. 2

M0085   **Domine ad adjuvandum**
       SATB, 2 vln, 2 vla/tbn, vla/bsn, vlne, bc
       Psalmodia brevis, no. 1
       EdM, Bayern, vol. 1, pp. 111-12

M0086   **Domine probasti me**
       SATB, 2 vln, 2 vla/tbn, vla/bsn, vlne, bc
       Psalmodia brevis, no. 14

M0087   **Dominus regnavit**
       SATB, 2 vln, 2 vla, vc, bc
       Christmas Day
       Gazophylacium musico-sacrum, no. 5
       EdM, Bayern, vol. 1, pp. 67-74

M0088   **Improperium**
       SATB, bc
       Palm Sunday
       Gazophylacium musico-sacrum, no. 17

M0089   **In convertendo**
       SATB, 2 vln, 2 vla/tbn, vla/bsn, vlne, bc
       Psalmodia brevis, no. 13

M0090 **In exitu Israel**
SATB, 2 vln, 2 vla/tbn, vla/bsn, vlne, bc
Psalmodia brevis, no. 7

M0091 **Jubilate Deo**
SATB, 2 vln, 3 tbn/vla, bc
1st Sunday after Epiphany
Gazophylacium musico-sacrum, no. 6

M0092 **Jubilate Deo, inversa terra**
SATB, 2 vln, 2 vla, vc, bc
2nd Sunday after Epiphany and 4th Sunday
after Easter
Gazophylacium musico-sacrum, no. 7
EdM, Bayern, vol. 1, pp. 75-82

M0093 **Laetatus sum**
SATB, 2 vln, 2 vla/tbn, vla/bsn, vlne, bc
Psalmodia brevis, no. 9

M0094 **Lauda animae**
SATB, 2 vln, 3 tbn/vla, bc
3rd Sunday after Easter
Gazophylacium musico-sacrum, no. 21

M0095 **Lauda Jerusalem**
SATB, 2 vln, 2 vla/tbn, vla/bsn, vlne, bc
Psalmodia brevis, no. 11

M0096 **Laudate**
SSATB, 2 vln, 3 tbn/vla, bc
4th Sunday of Lent
Gazophylacium musico-sacrum, no. 15

M0097 **Laudate Dominum, omnes gentes**
SATB, 2 vln, 2 vla/tbn, vla/bsn, vlne, bc
Psalmodia brevis, no. 6
EdM, Bayern, vol. 1, pp. 124-25

M0098 **Laudate, pueri, Dominum**
SATB, 2 vln, 2 vla/tbn, vla/bsn, vlne, bc
Psalmodia brevis, no. 5
EdM, Bayern, vol. 1, pp. 120-23

M0099 **Magnificat**
SATB, 2 vln, 2 vla/tbn, vla/bsn, vlne, bc
Psalmodia brevis, no. 8
EdM, Bayern, vol. 1, pp. 126-31

M0100 **Meditabor in mandatis tuis**
SATB, bc
2nd Sunday of Lent
Gazophylacium musico-sacrum, no. 13
EdM, Bayern, vol. 1, pp. 87-89

M0101 **Memento**
SATB, 2 vln, 2 vla/tbn, vla/bsn, vlne, bc
Psalmodia brevis, no. 15

M0102 **Nisi Dominus aedificaverit**
SATB, 2 vln, 2 vla/tbn, vla/bsn, vlne, bc
Psalmodia brevis, no. 10
EdM, Bayern, vol. 1, pp. 132-35

M0103 **Passer invenit sibi domum et turtur nidum**
SATB, bc
3rd Sunday of Lent
Gazophylacium musico-sacrum, no. 14
EdM, Bayern, vol. 1, pp. 90-92

M0104 **Perfice**
SATB, 2 vln, 3 tbn/vla, bc
Sexagesima
Gazophylacium musico-sacrum, no. 10

M0105 **Scapulis suis obum brabit tibi**
SATB, bc
1st Sunday of Lent
Gazophylacium musico-sacrum, no. 12
EdM, Bayern, vol. 1, pp. 83-86

M0106 **Terra tremuit**
SATB, 2 vln, 2 clar, 3 tbn/vla, bc
Easter Sunday
Gazophylacium musico-sacrum, no. 18

MAZAK, Alberik (1609-1661)

COLLECTIONS

Cultus harmonicus, op. 1 (1649)
RISM M1500 (parts)
DMA 1/148

Cultus harmonicus, op. 2 (1650)
RISM M1501 (parts)
DMA 1/1037

WORKS

M0107 **Amavit Leopoldum**
TTB, vln, bc
Cultus harmonicus, op. 1

M0108 **Ave Maria**
SSATB, bc
Cultus harmonicus, op. 1

M0109 **Ave Maria gratia plena**
SATB, bc
Cultus harmonicus, op. 2, no. 3

M0110 **Ave maris stella**
SSATB, 2 vln, bc
Cultus harmonicus, op. 2, no. 32

M0111 **Beata es Virgo Maria**
SATB, bc
Cultus harmonicus, op. 2, no. 5

MAZAK, Alberik (*continued*)

M0112 **Beatus vir qui timet**
STB, bc
Cultus harmonicus, op. 1

M0113 **Benedicite omnia opera**
SATB, bc
Cultus harmonicus, op. 2, no. 2

M0114 **Cantate Domino**
SSSS, bc
Cultus harmonicus, op. 2, no. 57

M0115 **Cantemus**
SATB, 2 vln, bc
Cultus harmonicus, op. 2, no. 24

M0116 **Christ ist erstanden**
SSB, bc
Cultus harmonicus, op. 1

M0117 **Confitebor tibi**
SSB, bc
Cultus harmonicus, op. 1

M0118 **Confitemini Domino**
SSB, bc
Cultus harmonicus, op. 1

M0119 **Crux fidelis inter omnes**
SATB, SATB, bc
Cultus harmonicus, op. 2, no. 42

M0120 **Cum sancto sanctus**
STB, vln, bc
Cultus harmonicus, op. 1

M0121 **Deus in adjutorium**
SATB, bc
Cultus harmonicus, op. 2, no. 1

M0122 **Dignare me laudarate**
SSATB, 2 vln, bc
Cultus harmonicus, op. 2, no. 29

M0123 **Dignare me laudare**
SATB, bc
Cultus harmonicus, op. 1

M0124 **Dixit Dominus**
SSATB, bc
Cultus harmonicus, op. 1

M0125 **Dixit Maria**
SATB, bc
Cultus harmonicus, op. 2, no. 4

M0126 **Domine non nos reliquas orphanos**
SATB, STTB, 2 vln, bc
Cultus harmonicus, op. 2, no. 47

M0127 **Domine secundum actum**
ATB, bc
Cultus harmonicus, op. 1

M0128 **Dulcis Jesu, dulce nomen**
SATTB, bc
Cultus harmonicus, op. 2, no. 64

M0129 **Ecce nunc**
SATB, SATB, 2 vln, vla, bc
Cultus harmonicus, op. 2, no. 52

M0130 **Ecce quam bonum**
SATB, bc
Cultus harmonicus, op. 1

M0131 **Ein Kind geboren zu Bethlehem**
SSATB, bc
Cultus harmonicus, op. 2, no. 63

M0132 **Ein Kind geboren zu Bethlehem**
SATB, 2 vln, tbn, bc
Cultus harmonicus, op. 2, no. 65

M0133 **Ein kleines Kindelein ist uns heute geboren**
SSATB, 2 clar/vln, 3 vla, vlne, bc
Cultus harmonicus, op. 2, no. 66

M0134 **Euge serve bone**
SATB, bc
Cultus harmonicus, op. 1

M0135 **Exaudiat te Dominus**
STB, 2 vln, bc
Cultus harmonicus, op. 1

M0136 **Exultabo te**
SATB, SATTB, 2 vln, vla, bc
Cultus harmonicus, op. 2, no. 53

M0137 **Exurgat Deus**
SATB, SATB, 2 vln, bc
Cultus harmonicus, op. 2, no. 48

M0138 **Felix namque es sacra Virgo Maria**
SSATB, bc
Cultus harmonicus, op. 2, no. 13

M0139 **Filii audite**
STTB, bc
Cultus harmonicus, op. 2, no. 56

M0140 **Gaudeamus omnes in Domino**
SATTB, 2 vln, bc
Cultus harmonicus, op. 2, no. 28

M0141 **Gaudent in caelis**
SATB, SATB, bc
Cultus harmonicus, op. 2, no. 41

M0142 **Hic est vere martyr**
SATB, bc
Cultus harmonicus, op. 1

M0143 **Hodie Christus natus**
SATB, bc
Cultus harmonicus, op. 1

M0144 **Hymnum dicamus**
SATB, bc
Cultus harmonicus, op. 1

M0145 **Illumina oculos meos**
SATB, SATB, vln, bc
Cultus harmonicus, op. 2, no. 46

M0146 **In te Domine speravi**
SSATB, bc
Cultus harmonicus, op. 2, no. 18

M0147 **Invocavi Dominum**
SSB, bc
Cultus harmonicus, op. 1

M0148 **Jam non estis**
SAATB, bc
Cultus harmonicus, op. 1

M0149 **Jesu dulcis memoria**
SATB, bc
Cultus harmonicus, op. 2, no. 73

M0150 **Jesu, summa benignitas**
SAATB, 3 vla, bc
Cultus harmonicus, op. 2, no. 74

M0151 **Jesus Christus nascitur**
SATB, SATB, 2 vln, bc
Cultus harmonicus, op. 2, no. 49

M0152 **Laetamini in Domino**
SSATB, bc
Cultus harmonicus, op. 2, no. 19

M0153 **Lauda anima mea**
SST, bc
Cultus harmonicus, op. 1

M0154 **Laudate Dominum de coelis**
SSATB, bc
Cultus harmonicus, op. 1

M0155 **Laudate Dominum de coelis**
SATTB, 2 vln, bc
Cultus harmonicus, op. 2, no. 27

M0156 **Laudate Dominum in sanctis ejus**
SATB, SATB, bc
Cultus harmonicus, op. 2, no. 38

M0157 **Laudate Dominum, omnes**
TTB, bc
Cultus harmonicus, op. 1

M0158 **Laudate Dominum, omnes gentes**
SAATB, bc
Cultus harmonicus, op. 1

M0159 **Laudate, pueri**
SSSS, bc
Cultus harmonicus, op. 1

M0160 **Laudate Virgine Mariam**
SSSAATTB, bc
Cultus harmonicus, op. 2, no. 44

M0161 **Laus et benediciti**
SSATB, bc
Cultus harmonicus, op. 2, no. 12

M0162 **Litaniae Lauretanae**
SATB, bc
Cultus harmonicus, op. 1

M0163 **Litaniae Lauretanae**
SATB, 2 vln, bc
Cultus harmonicus, op. 2, no. 60

M0164 **Litaniae Lauretanae**
STTB, bc
Cultus harmonicus, op. 2, no. 59

M0165 **Litaniae Lauretanae**
SATTB, bc
Cultus harmonicus, op. 1

M0166 **Litaniae Lauretanae**
SAB, bc
Cultus harmonicus, op. 1

M0167 **Magnificat**
SATB, bc
Cultus harmonicus, op. 1

M0168 **Magnificat**
SATB, 2 vln, 3 vla, bc
CS-KRa III, 25
parts
microfilm: US-SY

M0169 **Miserere**
SATB, bc
Cultus harmonicus, op. 2, no.10

M0170 **Miserere**
SATB, SATB, 2 vln, bc
Cultus harmonicus, op. 2, no. 51

M0171 **Missa**
SSATB, bc
Cultus harmonicus, op. 2, no. 22

M0172 **Missa**
SATB, 2 vln, bc
Cultus harmonicus, op. 2, no. 26
Ed. R. Walter (Augsburg: Anton Böhm,
no. 11921, 1980)

M0173 **Missa**
SATB, SATB, 2 vln, bc
Cultus harmonicus, op. 2, no. 50

MAZAK, Alberik (*continued*)

M0174 **Missa super Jam non estis**
SAATB, bc
Cultus harmonicus, op. 2, no. 21

M0175 **Multi collaudabunt**
SSBB, bc
Cultus harmonicus, op. 1

M0176 **Nos misereros peccatores**
SATB, bc
Cultus harmonicus, op. 2, no. 7

M0177 **O Maria, mater Dei**
SATB, 2 vln, vla, bc
Cultus harmonicus, op. 2, no. 33

M0178 **O salutaris hostia**
SSA, bc
Cultus harmonicus, op. 1

M0179 **O vos omnes qui transitis per viam**
STB, bc
Cultus harmonicus, op. 2, no. 54

M0180 **Omnes fitientes**
SST, bc
Cultus harmonicus, op. 1

M0181 **Omni die dic Mariae**
SATTB, bc
Cultus harmonicus, op. 2, no. 75

M0182 **Omni die Mariae mea laudes anima**
SSATB, bc
Cultus harmonicus, op. 2, no. 76

M0183 **Ora pro nobis**
SATB, bc
Cultus harmonicus, op. 2, no. 9

M0184 **Peto Domine mi Jesu Christe**
SSATTTB, bc
Cultus harmonicus, op. 2, no. 35

M0185 **Popule meus**
SSATB, bc
Cultus harmonicus, op. 2, no. 20

M0186 **Puellulo tenello infantulo**
SSATB, bc
Cultus harmonicus, op. 2, no. 61

M0187 **Puer natus**
SATTB, bc
Cultus harmonicus, op. 2, no. 62

M0188 **Quasi modo geniti**
SSSSS, bc
Cultus harmonicus, op. 2, no. 58

M0189 **Qui habitat in adjutoris**
STB, bc
Cultus harmonicus, op. 2, no. 55

M0190 **Regem sempiternum**
SATB, bc
Cultus harmonicus, op. 1

M0191 **Regina caeli I**
SSATB, bc
Cultus harmonicus, op. 1

M0192 **Regina caeli II**
SAATB, bc
Cultus harmonicus, op. 1

M0193 **Regina caeli III**
SSATB, bc
Cultus harmonicus, op. 2, no. 15

M0194 **Regina caeli IV**
SSATB, 2 vln, bc
Cultus harmonicus, op. 2, no. 31

M0195 **Regina caeli V**
SSATB, bc
Cultus harmonicus, op. 2, no. 17

M0196 **Salve regina**
TTB, bc
Cultus harmonicus, op. 1

M0197 **Salve regina**
SATB, bc
Cultus harmonicus, op. 1

M0198 **Sancta et immaculata virginitas**
SATB, 2 vln, bc
Cultus harmonicus, op. 2, no. 23

M0199 **Sancta Maria**
SSATB, bc
Cultus harmonicus, op. 2, no. 14

M0200 **Sancta Maria, ora pro nobis**
SATBB, 2 vln, bc
Cultus harmonicus, op. 2, no. 30

M0201 **Sanctissime confessor**
TTT, bc
Cultus harmonicus, op. 1

M0202 **Sancto cantate**
SATB, bc
Cultus harmonicus, op. 2, no. 8

M0203 **Sit laus Deo patris**
SATB, SATB, bc
Cultus harmonicus, op. 2, no. 43

M0204 **Sub tuum praesidium**
SATB, SATB, bc
Cultus harmonicus, op. 2, no. 16

M0205   **Sub tuum praesidium**
SATB, SATB, bc
Cultus harmonicus, op. 2, no. 40

M0206   **Surrexit Christus I**
SSA, bc
Cultus harmonicus, op. 2, no. 67

M0207   **Surrexit Christus II**
SSATB, bc
Cultus harmonicus, op. 2, no. 68

M0208   **Surrexit Christus III**
SSATB, bc
Cultus harmonicus, op. 2, no. 69

M0209   **Surrexit Christus IV**
SSATB, bc
Cultus harmonicus, op. 2, no. 70

M0210   **Surrexit Christus V**
SSATB, bc
Cultus harmonicus, op. 2, no. 71

M0211   **Surrexit Christus**
SATB, 2 vln, bc
Cultus harmonicus, op. 2, no. 72

M0212   **Surrexit Christus hodie**
SATB, 2 vln, bc
Cultus harmonicus, op. 2, no. 25

M0213   **Te Deum laudamus**
SSSAATTB, bc
Cultus harmonicus, op. 2, no. 45

M0214   **Te Domine corneli**
SATB, bc
Cultus harmonicus, op. 1

M0215   **Tota pulchra es**
SSATB, bc
Cultus harmonicus, op. 2, no. 11

M0216   **Tota pulchra es**
SATB, 2 vln, 2 vla, vlne, bc
CS-KRa II, 205
     parts
     microfilm: US-SY

M0217   **Vanitas vanitatum**
SSATB, 2 vln, bc
Cultus harmonicus, op. 2, no. 36

M0218   **Veni Sancte Spiritus**
SSATB, 2 vln, bc
Cultus harmonicus, op. 2, no. 34

M0219   **Virgo gloriosissima Maria**
SATTB, 2 vln, bc
Cultus harmonicus, op. 2, no. 37

M0220   **Virgo prudentis**
SSATTB, 2 vln, bc
Cultus harmonicus, op. 2, no. 39

M0221   **Virgo prudentissima quo progrederis**
SATB, bc
Cultus harmonicus, op. 2, no. 6

MEDER, Johann Valentin (1649-1719)

M0222   **Ach Herr mich armen Sünder**
SATB, vln, 2 vla, vlne, bc
PL-GD Bibl. Joh. Ms. 191
     parts
     DMA 2/511

M0223   **Die höllische Schlange darf nimmer uns beißen**
SSTB, 2 vln, 2 vla, vlne, bc
Annunciation
S-Uu 28:4 (Düben)
     parts
     DMA 1/1586

M0224   **Gott, du bist derselbst mein König**
STB, 2 vln, vla, vc, 2 clar, timp, bc
S-Uu 28:6 (Düben)
     parts
     DMA 1/1587

M0225   **Gott, mein Herz ist bereit**
SSB, 2 vln, vla, bass vla, 2 ob ad lib, bsn
ad lib, bc
S-Uu 28:7 (Düben)
     parts
     DMA 1/1588

M0226   **Herzlich tut mich verlangen**
SATB, vln, 2 vla, 2 fl, 2 ob, vlne, bsn, bc
PL-GD Bibl. Joh. Ms. 194
     parts (only string parts extant)

M0227   **Höret das Leiden und Sterben**
SSATB, 2 vln, 2 fl, 2 ob, bsn, bc
D-Bds Mus. ms. autogr. Meder 1 (1700)
     score
     DMA 1/1591
     Ed. B. Smallmann, *Das Chorwerk* 133

M0228   **Leben wir, so leben wir dem Herrn**
See Unser keiner lebt ihm selber

M0229   **Meine Seele seufzt und stöhnet**
4 vv, 5 gamba, 2 ob, bsn, bc
PL-GD Bibl. Joh. Ms. 193 (1714)
     parts

M0230   **Passions-Oratorium nach Matthäus**
See Höret das Leiden und Sterben

MEDER, Johann Valentin (*continued*)

M0231 Quid est hoc, quod sentio
SAB, 2 vln, gamba, bc
S-Uu 61:7 (Düben)
parts
DMA 3/1256

M0232 Singet, lobsinget mit Herzen und Zungen
SATB soli, SATB, 2 vln, vla, vc, 2 ob,
bsn, bc
PL-GD Bibl. Joh. Ms. 192
parts

M0233 Trauen und Leiden soll heute verschwunden
SSATB, 2 vla, 2 ob/vln, 2 corn, vlne, bc
D-LUC Ms. 221A
parts
DMA 2/512

M0234 Unser keiner lebt ihm selber
S solo, SATB, vln, 2 gamba, vc, bc
S-Uu 61:6 (Düben)
parts
DMA 1/1255

M0235 Vox mitte clamorem, cor redde ardorem
SST, 3 vln, bc
S-Uu 61:9 (Düben)
parts (2 complete sets)
DMA 3/1258

MEGERLE, Abraham (1607-1680)

Note: Manuscript works by Megerle in A-Sd were unavailable for examination in 1983. They are omitted from this list until such time as a complete inventory can be taken.

COLLECTIONS

Ara musica solemni concertu (1647)
RISM M1749 (parts)

Psalmodia Jesu et Mariae sacra (1657)
RISM M1750 (parts)
DMA 81//81

WORKS

M0236 Ad usque terrae limitem
4 vv
CH-E Th 546.12 (Ms. 4139)

M0237 Adjuvabit eam
SATB, bc
Feast of Virgin Martyrs
Ara musica, no. 80

M0238 Aeternitatis auream diem
3 vv
CH-E Th 546.14 (Ms. 4141)

M0239 Afferentur regi
SSATTB, SSATTB, vla, bc
Feast of Virgin Martyrs
Ara musica, no. 86

M0240 Afferentur regi virgines
SATB, SATB, SSATTB, 2 corn, 3 clar, 5
tbtta, 4 tbn, bc
Feast of Virgin Martyrs
Ara musica, no. 87

M0241 Alleluia Amavit
TTT, bc
Feast of a Confessor Pope
Ara musica, no. 52

M0242 Alleluia Beatus vir qui suffert
SSB, vla, bc
Feast of a Confessor not a Pope
Ara musica, no. 66

M0243 Alleluia. Haec est vera
ATTB, bc
Feast of a Martyr outside Eastertide
Ara musica, no. 38

M0244 Alleluia. Haec est virgo sapiens
STB, bc
Feast of Virgin Martyrs
Ara musica, no. 83

M0245 Alleluia. Juravit Dominus
SSATB, bc
Feast of a Confessor Pope
Ara musica, no. 51

M0246 Alleluia. Justus ut palma
ATT, bc
Feast of an Abbot
Ara musica, no. 75

M0247 Alleluia Sancti tui Domine
TTB, bc
Feast of a Martyr in Eastertide
Ara musica, no. 23

M0248 Alleluia tu es sacerdos
SST, bc
Feast of a Confessor Pope
Ara musica, no. 49

M0249 Anima nostra
SSSAATT, bc
Feast of the Holy Innocents
Ara musica, no. 43

M0250 **Auctor beate saeculi**
SATB, bc
Feast of the Sacred Heart
D-Mbs Mus. ms. 599, no. 1, fol. 1b-4
score
Same music as for "Exite Sion filiae"

M0251 **Aurora coelum rutilat**
4 vv, bc
Easter Sunday
D-Mbs Mus. ms. 3141 (1649)
score

M0252 **Beatus vir qui inventus est**
SSATTB, 2 corn/vln, 4 tbn, bc
Feast of a Confessor not a Pope
Ara musica, no. 71

M0253 **Bene fundata est**
TTTTB, 2 vln, 2 tbn, bc
Anniversary of the Dedication of a church
Ara musica, no. 102

M0254 **Cantate populi**
SATTB, 2 corn/vln, bc
Feast of a Confessor not a Pope
Ara musica, no. 72

M0255 **Confitebor**
STB, 2 vln/vla, bass vla, bc
Psalmodia Jesu et Mariae sacra, no. 10

M0256 **Confitebuntur coeli**
SSATTB, SSATTB, 6 instr, 4 tbtta, bc
Feast of a Martyr in Eastertide
Ara musica, no. 22

M0257 **Corpora sanctorum**
TTB, bc
Feast of a Martyr outside Eastertide
Ara musica, no. 33

M0258 **Desiderium animae ejus**
SATB, SATB, bc
Feast of an Abbot
Ara musica, no. 77

M0259 **Diffusa est gratia**
TB soli, 10 vv, 3 corn/vln, 3 tbn, bc
Feast of Virgin Martyrs
Ara musica, no. 88

M0260 **Dixit Dominus (I)**
SSB, 2 clar/tromba marina, 2 vla, bc
Psalmodia Jesu et Mariae sacra, no. 2

M0261 **Dixit Dominus (II)**
SSATB, 3 vla/tbn, bc
Psalmodia Jesu et Mariae sacra, no. 9

M0262 **Domine ad adjuvandum (I)**
SSB, 2 vla, 2 clar/tromba marina, bc
Psalmodia Jesu et Mariae sacra, no. 1

M0263 **Domine ad adjuvandum (II)**
SSATB, vln, 2 vla, bc
Psalmodia Jesu et Mariae sacra, no. 8

M0264 **Domine Deus**
SATB, 2 vln/corn, 3 tbn, bc
Anniversary of the Dedication of a Church
Ara musica, no. 104

M0265 **Domine Deus**
SSATB, 2 corn/vln, 2 clar, 4 tbtta, 3 tbn, bc
Anniversary of the Dedication of a Church
Ara musica, no. 105

M0266 **Domus mea**
SSATTB, SSATTB, 2 corn/vln, 4 tbn, bc
Anniversary of the Dedication of a Church
Ara musica, no. 106

M0267 **Ecce sacerdos**
SSB/TTB, 3 vla, bc
Feast of a Confessor Pope
Ara musica, no. 45

M0268 **Exite Sion filiae**
SATB, bc
Feast of the Crown of Thorns
D-Mbs Mus. ms. 12286
parts
D-Mbs Mus. ms. 13007
score
Same music as for "Auctor beate saeculi"

M0269 **Exultabunt sancti**
SSATTB, SSATTB, bc
Feast of Many Martyrs outside Eastertide
Ara musica, no. 41

M0270 **Fidelis servus**
SSB, bc
Feast of a Confessor Pope
Ara musica, no. 53

M0271 **Filiae regum**
SSATTB, SSATTB, 2 vln/corn, 4 tbn, bc
Feast of a Virgin
Ara musica, no. 95

M0272 **Gloria et divitiae**
SATB, SATB, bc
Feast of a Martyr Pope
Ara musica, no. 9

M0273 **Gloria et honore**
SATB, SATB, bc
Feast of an Apostle
Ara musica, no. 2

MEGERLE, Abraham (*continued*)

M0274   **Gloria et honore**
SATB, SATB, SATB, bc
Feast of a Martyr not a Pope
Ara musica, no. 17

M0275   **Gloriabuntur in te**
SSATTB, SSATTB, bc
Feast of Many Martyrs outside Eastertide
Ara musica, no. 44

M0276   **Hodie sponsa**
SATTB, 3 vln, 5 vla, bc
Feast of Virgin Martyrs
Ara musica, no. 89

M0277   **Homo quidam**
SATTB soli, SATTB, 6 vla, 2 corn, 4 tbn, bc
Feast of a Confessor Pope
Ara musica, no. 57

M0278   **In virtute tua**
SSATTB, bc
Feast of a Confessor not a Pope
Ara musica, no. 70

M0279   **Inveni David**
SSAT, SATB, bc
Feast of a Martyr Pope
Ara musica, no. 8

M0280   **Juravit Dominus**
ATB, bc
Feast of a Confessor Pope
Ara musica, no. 48

M0281   **Justi epulentur**
SSS, bc
Feast of a Martyr outside Eastertide
Ara musica, no. 34

M0282   **Justorum animae**
SATB, SATB, SSATTB, 2 corn, 4 tbn, bc
Feast of Many Martyrs outside Eastertide
Ara musica, no. 42

M0283   **Justus ut palma (I)**
SATB, bc
Feast of an Apostle
Ara musica, no. 1

M0284   **Justus ut palma (II)**
SSATTB, SSATTB, SATB, corn, clar, 4
tbtta, 8 tbn, bc
Feast of a Doctor
Ara musica, no. 65

M0285   **Laetabitur justus**
SSS/TTT, bc
Feast of a Martyr in Eastertide
Ara musica, no. 21

M0286   **Laetamini in Domino**
SATB, SATB, SATB, SATB, SATB, bc
Feast of a Martyr in Eastertide
Ara musica, no. 26

M0287   **Laetatus sum**
SAB, 2 clar, bass viol, bc
Psalmodia Jesu et Mariae sacra, no. 4

M0288   **Lauda Jerusalem**
ATB, 2 vla, 2 clar/tromba marina, bc
Psalmodia Jesu et Mariae sacra, no. 6

M0289   **Laudate Dominum**
SSB, 2 vln, bc
Psalmodia Jesu et Mariae sacra, no. 13

M0290   **Laudate, pueri (I)**
ATTB, clar/tromba marina, bass viola, bc
Psalmodia Jesu et Mariae sacra, no. 3

M0291   **Laudate, pueri (II)**
ATB, 2 vln, bass vla, bc
Psalmodia Jesu et Mariae sacra, no. 12

M0292   **Laudemus Deum nostrum**
SSATB, 2 vln/corn, 3 tbn, bc
Feast of a Martyr not a Virgin, or neither
Ara musica, no. 98

M0293   **Lauream certaminis**
See Pange lingua gloriosi lauream certaminis

M0294   **Magnificat (I)**
SSB, SATB, 2 vla, 2 clar/tromba marina, bc
Psalmodia Jesu et Mariae sacra, no. 7

M0295   **Magnificat (II)**
SSATB, vln, 2 vla, bc
Psalmodia Jesu et Mariae sacra, no. 14

M0296   **Magnificate Dominum mecum**
SSATB, 2 corn/vln, 2 clar, 3 tbn, bc
Feast of a Confessor not a Pope
Ara musica, no. 73

M0297   **Mirabilis Deus**
SSATTB, bc
Feast of many Martyrs outside Eastertide
Ara musica, no. 40

M0298   **Non est inventus**
SATB, bc
Feast of a Confessor Pope
Ara musica, no. 47

M0299   **O beatum virum**
SATB, 2 vln/corn, 3 vla, 5 tbn/vla, 5
bsn/tbn, bc

Feast of a Confessor Pope
Ara musica, no. 58

M0300   O vere felix
SSATTB, SSATTB, SSATTB, 2 vln/corn,
4 tbn, bc
Feast of a Confessor Pope
Ara musica, no. 59

M0301   Pange lingua gloriosi lauream certaminis
SATB
Feast of the Five Wounds
D-Mbs Mus. ms. 12283
score
D-Mbs Mus. ms. 12284
parts
CH-E Th 546.13 (Ms. 4140)

M0302   Posuisti Domine
SATB, SATB, bc
Feast of a Martyr not a Pope
Ara musica, no. 18

M0303   Qui sequitur me
ATB, vla, 2 corn, bc
Feast of a Martyr not a Pope
Ara musica, no. 14

M0304   Sacerdotes ejus
ATTB, bc
Feast of a Confessor Pope
Ara musica, no. 46

M0305   Simile est regnum
SSATB, 5 instr, bc
Feast of Virgin Martyrs
Ara musica, no. 90

M0306   Tollite portas
SSATB, 2 vln, bc
Anniversary of the Dedication of a church
Ara musica, no. 107

M0307   Veni creator spiritus
SATB, bc
Pentecost
D-Mbs Mus. ms. 599, no. 2, fol. 5
score

M0308   Veritas mea
SATB, SATB, bc
Feast of a Martyr Pope
Ara musica, no. 7

M0309   Vox caelestis
SSATTB, SSATTB, 2 corn, 4 tbn, 6 bsn, bc
Feast of an Abbot
Ara musica, no. 78

MEINONG, Paul

M0310   Missa à 6
SATB, 2 vln
D-B Mus. ms. 30291
parts

MEISTER, Johann Friedrich (before 1638-1697)

M0311   Ach, es ist ein elend, jämmerlich Ding
SSTTB, 4 vla, bc
D-Bds Mus. ms. 30236, no. 1 (Bokemeyer)
(1695)
score
DMA 3/302

M0312   Habe deine Lust an dem Herrn
TTB, 2 vln, gamba, bc
D-Bds Mus. ms. 30236, no. 5 (Bokemeyer)
score
DMA 3/306

M0313   Ich bin das Brot des Lebens
ATB, 2 vln, bc
D-Bds Mus. ms. 30236, no. 6 (Bokemeyer)
score
DMA 3/307

M0314   Unser Wandel ist im Himmel
SSB, 2 vln, bsn, bc
D-Bds Mus. ms. 30236, no. 13 (Bokemeyer)
(1694)
score
DMA 3/309

M0315   Was mein Gott will, das muß geschehen
SATB, 2 vln, bsn, bc
D-Bds Mus. ms. 30236, no. 8 (Bokemeyer)
score
DMA 3/310

M0316   Welt ist Welt, drum mein Gemüt
SATB, 2 vln, 3 vla, bsn, bc
D-Bds Mus. ms. 30236, no. 12 (Bokemeyer)
score
DMA 3/311

M0317   Wie schön leuchtet der Morgenstern
B solo, SATB, 4 vln, bc
D-Bds Mus. ms. 30236, no. 9 and 10
(Bokemeyer)
score
DMA 3/312

M0318   Wo soll ich fliehen hin
SSB, 2 vln, bsn, bc

MEISTER, Johann Friedrich (*continued*)

    D-Bds Mus. ms. 30236, no. 11 (Bokemeyer)
    (1693)
    score
    DMA 3/313

M0319   **Zum Frieden und zur Ruh**
    SATB, vln, 2 vla, bsn, bc
    D-Bds Mus. ms. 30236, no. 14 (Bokemeyer)
    score
    DMA 3/314

MENGES, Nicolaus

M0320   **Herr Jesu Christ, mein Herr und Gott**
    SATB
    Funeral of Anna Wincklemann
    Arnstadt, 1657
    RISM M2251, Reich 21

MEYER, Bernhard

M0321   **O harter Schlag**
    SSATB, bc
    Funeral of Elisabeth, Princess of Anhalt
    Cöthen, 1677
    RISM M2485, Reich 207 (score)
    DMA 75//230

M0322   **O teuerer Fürsten-Geist**
    SSATB, bc
    Funeral of Sophia Augusta, Princess of
    Anhalt
    Wittenberg, 1681
    RISM M2486, Reich 428 (choirbook)
    DMA 75//230 & 70//3

MEYERHOFF, G. C.

M0323   **Ein feste Burg ist unser Gott**
    SSATB, 2 vln, 4 vla, bsn, bc
    D-Bds Mus. ms. 30236, no. 17 (Bokemeyer)
    score

MEYERHOFFER, Johann Georg (d. 1688)

M0324   **Quam horribilis, quam miserabilis**
    5 vv, 2 vln, 2 vla, bsn, bc
    F-Ssp

MIHL, Erasmus van der (fl. ca. 1675)

COLLECTION

    Psalmodia Davidica (1674)
    RISM M2723 (parts)

WORKS

M0325   **Beatus vir qui timet**
    SSATB, 2 vln, 3 vla, bc
    Psalmodia Davidica, no. 4
    S-Uu 29:1 (Düben)
    parts
    DMA 1/1592
    S-Uu 84:83, fol. 22v-25r (Düben)
    tablature
    DMA 1/1592

M0326   **Confitebor tibi Domine**
    SSATB, 2 vln, 3 vla, bc
    Psalmodia Davidica, no. 3
    S-Uu 61:10 (Düben)
    parts
    S-Uu 84:84, fol. 24v-28r (Düben)
    tablature

M0327   **Dixit Dominus Domino meo**
    SSATB, 2 vln, 3 vla, bc
    Psalmodia Davidica, no. 2

M0328   **Domine ad adjuvandum**
    SSATB, 2 vln, 3 vla, bc
    Psalmodia Davidica, no. 1

M0329   **Laudate Dominum**
    SSATB, 2 vln, 3 vla, bc
    Psalmodia Davidica, no. 6
    S-Uu 29:2 (Düben)
    parts
    DMA 1/1593
    S-Uu 84:85, fol. 29v-30v (Düben)
    tablature
    DMA 1/1593

M0330   **Laudate, pueri**
    SSATB, 2 vln, 3 vla, bc
    Psalmodia Davidica, no. 5

M0331   **Magnificat**
    SSATB, 2 vln, 3 vla, bc
    Psalmodia Davidica, no. 7

MITTERNACHT, Johann Sebastian

M0332   **Ach die güldne Landeskrone**
    SATB, bc

Funeral of Sophie Elisabeth, Duchess of
Saxony and Brandenburg
Altenburg, 1650
RISM M2904, Reich 10 (score)
DMA 70//134

MOLITOR, Fidel (1627-1685)

COLLECTION

Mensa musicalis (1668)
RISM M2954 (parts)

WORKS

M0333   **Audite mortales**
SATB, 2 vln, 2 vla, vlne, bc
Mensa musicalis, no. 9

M0334   **Beatus vir**
SATB, 2 vln, 2 vla, vlne, bc
Mensa musicalis, no. 12

M0335   **Cantate Domino (I)**
SATB, 2 vln, 2 vla, vlne, bc
Mensa musicalis, no. 1

M0336   **Cantate Domino (II)**
SATB, 2 vln, 2 vla, vlne, bc
Mensa musicalis, no. 17

M0337   **Congregati sunt inimici nostri**
SATB, 2 vln, 2 vla, vlne, bc
Mensa musicalis, no. 4

M0338   **Dominus illuminatio**
SATB, 2 vln, 2 vla, vlne, bc
Mensa musicalis, no. 3

M0339   **Exurgat Deus**
SATB, 2 vln, 2 vla, vlne, bc
Mensa musicalis, no. 14

M0340   **Gaudeamus omnes**
SATB, 2 vln, 2 vla, vlne, bc
Mensa musicalis, no. 13

M0341   **Gaudete et exultate**
SATB, 2 vln, 2 vla, vlne, bc
Mensa musicalis, no. 10

M0342   **Isti sunt triumphatores**
SATB, 2 vln, 2 vla, vlne, bc
Mensa musicalis, no. 11

M0343   **Laetentur caeli**
SATB, 2 vln, 2 vla, vlne, bc
Mensa musicalis, no. 15

M0344   **O bone Jesu**
SATB, 2 vln, 2 vla, vlne, bc
Mensa musicalis, no. 5

M0345   **O salvator Jesu dulcissime**
SATB, 2 vln, 2 vla, vlne, bc
Mensa musicalis, no. 8

M0346   **Ornate anima**
SATB, 2 vln, 2 vla, vlne, bc
Mensa musicalis, no. 16

M0347   **Sicut stella matutina**
SATB, 2 vln, 2 vla, vlne, bc
Mensa musicalis, no. 6

M0348   **Sit nomen eius**
SATB, 2 vln, 2 vla, vlne, bc
Mensa musicalis, no. 7

M0349   **Vivit Dominus**
SATB, 2 vln, 2 vla, vlne, bc
Mensa musicalis, no. 2

MOLITOR, Valentin (1637-1713)

COLLECTIONS

Epinicion Marianum (1683)
RISM M2963 (parts)
DMA 41//21

Missa una cum tribus motettis (1681)
RISM M2962 (parts)
DMA 41//21

Odae genethliacae ad Christi (1668)
RISM M2960 (parts)
DMA 3/1944

WORKS

M0350   **A solis ortus cardine**
SSB, 2 vln, bc
S-Uu 29:6 (Düben)
tablature and parts

M0351   **Beata es Virgo Mariae**
SSATB, 2 vln, vlne, bc
Birth of the Virgin Mary
Epinicion Marianum, no. 13

M0352   **Beatissimae Virginis Mariae nativitatem**
SSATB, 2 vln, vlne, bc
Birth of the Virgin Mary
Epinicion Marianum, no. 15

M0353   **Canite caelites**
SSATB, 2 vln, 3 vla, bc
Odae genethliacae, no. 7

MOLITOR, Valentin (*continued*)

M0354 **Congratulamini mihi omnes**
SSATB, 2 vln, vlne, bc
Annunciation
Epinicion Marianum, no. 9

M0355 **Corpora sanctorum in pace**
SATB, SATB, 2 vln, vla/bsn, 2 clar, bc
Missa una cum tribus motettis, no. 3

M0356 **Currite, pastores**
SSATB, 2 vln, 3 vla, bc
Odae genethliacae, no. 9

M0357 **Ecce folis**
SSATB, 2 vln, 3 vla, bc
Odae genethliacae, no. 10

M0358 **Gloriosus Deus in sanctis suis**
SATB, SATB, 2 vln, vla/bsn, 2 clar, bc
Missa una cum tribus motettis, no. 2

M0359 **Io mortalis tartaro**
SSATB, 2 vln, 3 vla, bc
Odae genethliacae, no. 11

M0360 **Jacet in praesepio**
SSATB, 2 vln, 3 vla, bc
Odae genethliacae, no. 13

M0361 **Jam liquescit anima mea**
SSATB, 2 vln, 3 vla, bc
Odae genethliacae, no. 14

M0362 **Jucundare et laetare**
SSATB, 2 vln, vlne, bc
Assumption of the Virgin Mary
Epinicion Marianum, no. 12

M0363 **Magnus Dominus**
SSATB, 2 vln, vlne, bc
Purification of the Virgin Mary
Epinicion Marianum, no. 4

M0364 **Missa**
SATB, SATB, 2 vln, vla/bsn, 2 clar, bc
Missa una cum tribus motettis, no. 1

M0365 **O amor, o timor**
SSATB, 2 vln, 3 vla, bc
Odae genethliacae, no. 12

M0366 **Orbis amans**
SSATB, 2 vln, 3 vla, bc
Odae genethliacae, no. 15

M0367 **Plangite mortales**
SSATB, 2 vln, vlne, bc
Immaculate Conception
Epinicion Marianum, no. 16

M0368 **Puer nudus**
SSATB, 2 vln, 3 vla, bc
Odae genethliacae, no. 8

M0369 **Sancta et immaculata**
SSATB, 2 vln, vlne, bc
Circumcision
Epinicion Marianum, no. 3

M0370 **Suscepimus Deus**
SSATB, 2 vln, vlne, bc
Purification of the Virgin Mary
Epinicion Marianum, no. 6

M0371 **Suscipe verbum Virgo**
SSATB, 2 vln, vlne, bc
Annunciation
Epinicion Marianum, no. 7

M0372 **Tota pulchra es**
SSATB, 2 vln, vlne, bc
Immaculate Conception
Epinicion Marianum, no. 18

M0373 **Viderunt omnes fines terra**
SSATB, 2 vln, vlne, bc
Circumcision
Epinicion Marianum, no. 1

M0374 **Virgo prudentissima**
SSATB, 2 vln, vlne, bc
Assumption of the Virgin Mary
Epinicion Marianum, no. 10

M0375 **Viri sancti**
SATB, SATB, 2 vln, vla/bsn, 2 clar, bc
Missa una cum tribus motettis, no. 4

MÜLLER, Johann (fl. 1656-1682)

M0376 **Dein Wort ist meines Fußes Leuchte**
SSB, 2 vln, bc
D-Bds Mus. ms. 30184, no. 12 (Bokemeyer)
score

M0377 **O Jesu Christe, Gottes Sohn**
SSATB, 2 vln, 2 vla, bsn, bc
D-Bds Mus. ms. 30184, no. 11 (Bokemeyer)
score

MÜLLER, Johann Nicolaus

M0378 **Schaffe in mir, Gott, ein reines Herz**
SSATTB, SSATTB, 2 vln, 2 vla, bc
D-B Mus. ms. 15708 (Erfurt) (1677)
parts

MURSCHHAUSER, Franz Xaver (1663-1738)

COLLECTION

Vespertinus latriae (1700)
RISM M8203 (parts)
DMA 3/1027

WORKS

M0379 **Beatus vir**
SATB, 2 vln, vlne, bc
Vespertinus latriae, no. 3

M0380 **Confitebor**
SATB, 2 vln, vlne, bc
Vespertinus latriae, no. 2

M0381 **Dixit Dominus**
SATB, 2 vln, vlne, bc
Vespertinus latriae, no. 1

M0382 **In exitu Israel**
SATB, 2 vln, vlne, bc
Vespertinus latriae, no. 6

M0383 **Laetatus sum**
SATB, 2 vln, vlne, bc
Vespertinus latriae, no. 7

M0384 **Lauda Jerusalem**
SATB, 2 vln, vlne, bc
Vespertinus latriae, no. 9

M0385 **Laudate Dominum, omnes gentes**
SATB, 2 vln, vlne, bc
Vespertinus latriae, no. 5

M0386 **Laudate, pueri**
SATB, 2 vln, vlne, bc
Vespertinus latriae, no. 4

M0387 **Magnificat octavi toni**
SATB, 2 vln, vlne, bc
Vespertinus latriae, no. 10

M0388 **Nisi Dominus**
SATB, 2 vln, vlne, bc
Vespertinus latriae, no. 8

MYLIUS, Wolfgang Michael (1636-ca. 1712)

M0389 **Eitles Wesen, gute Nacht**
SATB, bc
Funeral of Sibylle Reichardt
Gotha, 1697
RISM 1697[1], Reich 117 (score)
DMA 74//117

M0390 **Maria, gegrüsset seist du**
SA soli, SATB, 2 vln, 2 vla, vlne/bsn, bc
D-Dlb Mus. 1646-E-500 (Grimma U 361/N 48)
score and parts

N

NACHTENHÖFER, C. F.

N0001 **Ach! Prinz Christian, du Held**
SSATB
Funeral of Christian, Prince of Saxony
Coburg, 1663
  Reich 196 (score)
  DMA 70//191
  Reich: parody of Rosenmüller's "Nun Gottlob,
  es ist vollbracht"

NEHRING, Joachim

N0002 **Jesus ist mit seinem Leiden**
SSATB, bc
Funeral of Johann Cyriacus Nehring
Gotha, 1688
  RISM N372, Reich 115 (score)
  DMA 70//200

NICOLAI, Johann Michael (1629-1685)

Note: The additional titles "Allein zu dir" and "Herr wenn ich nur dich habe," both listed in *New Grove*, as well as "Herzlich lieb," survive only in a basso continuo partbook, D-B Mus. ms. 40075 (DMA 2/1891)

COLLECTIONS

Evangelische Harmonien (manuscript)
  D-Sl Mus. ms. II fol. 7
  score
  DMA 25//51

Geistliche Harmonien (1669)
  RISM N587 (parts)
  DMA 3/1948

N0003 **Ach Jesu komm, eh ich verschmachte**
SST, 4 vla, vlne, bc
F-Ssp
Composer identified only as "Nicolai"

N0004 **Als das zarte Jesus Kind**
SATB, 2 vln, 2 vla, bc
Sunday after Circumcision
Evangelische Harmonien, no. 15

N0005 **Als Jesus, nach der Nacht, sah an der Jünger Zahl**
SATB, 2 vln, 2 vla, bc
Feast of Saint John the Evangelist
Evangelische Harmonien, no. 23

N0006 **Auf, auf ihr Christen, laßt uns treten**
SATB, 2 vln, 2 vla, bc
Circumcision
Evangelische Harmonien, no. 13

N0007 **Aus der Tiefe**
ATB, 2 vln, bc
Geistliche Harmonien, no. 10

N0008 **Blöder Mensch, was fürchtst du dich**
SATB, 2 vln, 2 vla, bc
4th Sunday of Advent
Evangelische Harmonien, no. 6

N0009 **Das ist meine Freude**
ATB, 2 vln, bc
Geistliche Harmonien, no. 7

N0010 **Dein Jesus ist, o lieber Gott**
SATB, 2 vln, 2 vla, bc
1st Sunday after Epiphany
Evangelische Harmonien, no. 18

N0011 Der Tod seiner Heiligen ist wert gehalten
ATB, 2 vln, 2 vla, vlne, bsn, bc
S-Uu 29:24 (Düben)
parts
DMA 46//61

N0012 Eile, Gott, mich zu erretten
ATB, 2 vln, bc
Geistliche Harmonien, no. 5

N0013 Erwecke dich, Herr
ATB, 2 vln, bc
Geistliche Harmonien, no. 9

N0014 Freuet euch des Herrn
ATB, 2 vln, bc
Geistliche Harmonien, no. 8

N0015 Gottlob, es läuft uns schier zu Ende
SATB, 2 vln, 2 vla, bc
2nd Sunday of Advent
Evangelische Harmonien, no. 4

N0016 Herr, der du bist vormals
ATB, 2 vln, bc
Geistliche Harmonien, no. 4
D-F Ms. Ff. mus. 447 (1669)
score and parts

N0017 Herr, neige deine Himmel und fahre herab
ATB, 2 vln, bc
Geistliche Harmonien, no. 2

N0018 Herr, wann nur dein Wille
SATB, 2 vln, 2 vla, bc
Purification of the Virgin Mary
Evangelische Harmonien, no. 24

N0019 Hilf Jesu, hilf, du treuer Gott
SATB, 2 vln, 2 vla, bc
2nd Sunday after Epiphany
Evangelische Harmonien, no. 19

N0020 Ist dann mein Jesus jetzt ein Kind
SATB, 2 vln, 2 vla, bc
Christmas Day
Evangelische Harmonien, no. 10

N0021 Jubilate Deo
ATB, 2 vln, bc
Geistliche Harmonien, no. 11

N0022 Komm, König, komm, du Davids Sohn
SATB, 2 vln, 2 vla, bc
1st Sunday of Advent
Evangelische Harmonien, no. 1

N0023 Komm, Thomas, freue dich
SATB, 2 vln, 2 vla, bc
Feast of Saint Thomas
Evangelische Harmonien, no. 8

N0024 Laudate Dominum
ATB, 2 vln, bc
Geistliche Harmonien, no. 12

N0025 Lobet, ihr Knechte
ATB, 2 vln, bc
Geistliche Harmonien, no. 6

N0026 Lobsinget, lobklinget, lobbringet dem Herrn
SATB, 2 vln, 2 vla, bc
Christmas Day
Evangelische Harmonien, no. 9

N0027 Nach dir, Herr, verlanget mich
ATB, 2 vln, bc
Geistliche Harmonien, no. 3

N0028 O Jesu, o König
SATB, 2 vln, 2 vla, bc
1st Sunday of Advent
Evangelische Harmonien, no. 2

N0029 O Jesulein
SATB, 2 vln, 2 vla, bc
Circumcision
Evangelische Harmonien, no. 14
Portion of opening sonata missing

N0030 O Wundertat
SATB, 2 vln, 2 vla, bc
Sunday after Christmas
Evangelische Harmonien, no. 12

N0031 Schaut, ihr Völker
SATB, 2 vln, 2 vla, bc
2nd Sunday of Advent
Evangelische Harmonien, no. 3

N0032 Sei nun wieder zufrieden
3 vv, 2 vln, vla, vlne, bc
F-Ssp
Composer identified only as "Nicolai"

N0033 Singet dem Herrn ein neues Lied
ATB, 2 vln, bc
Geistliche Harmonien, no. 1

N0034 Wann die Flut ganz stille ist
SATB, 2 vln, 2 vla, bc
4th Sunday after Epiphany
Evangelische Harmonien, no. 21

N0035 Wann die schwarze Sünden Nacht
SATB, 2 vln, 2 vla, bc
5th Sunday after Epiphany
Evangelische Harmonien, no. 22

NICOLAI, Johann Michael (*continued*)

N0036   **Was Angst für die Welt**
SATB, 2 vln, 2 vla, bc
3rd Sunday of Advent
Evangelische Harmonien, no. 5

N0037   **Was wimmert, was schimmert**
SATB, 2 vln, 2 vla, bc
Epiphany
Evangelische Harmonien, no. 16

N0038   **Wer will folgen, muß zuschauen**
SATB, 2 vln, 2 vla, bc
Feast of Saint Andrew
Evangelische Harmonien, no. 7

N0039   **Wie selig ist der Geist**
SATB, 2 vln, 2 vla, bc
3rd Sunday after Epiphany
Evangelische Harmonien, no. 20

N0040   **Will ein Jesus Ritter kämpfen**
SATB, 2 vln, 2 vla, bc
Feast of Saint Stephen
Evangelische Harmonien, no. 11

N0041   **Wo werd ich dich, mein Licht**
SATB, 2 vln, 2 vla, bc
Epiphany
Evangelische Harmonien, no. 17

NIEDT, Friedrich Erhard (1674-1708)

N0042   **Es müssen sich freuen und fröhlich sein**
SATB
Christmas Day
USSR-KA Ms. 13661, no. 21 (lost)
DdT 49/50, pp. 64-66

N0043   **Ich will aufstehen und suchen**
SATB
Christmas Day
USSR-KA Ms. 13661, no. 34 (lost)
DdT 49/50, pp. 100-103

NIEDT, Nicolaus (d. 1700)

COLLECTION

Musikalische Sonn- und Fest-Tags Lust (1698)
RISM N683 (parts)
DMA 2/144

WORKS

N0044   **Ach wie gar nichts**
SSATB, 2 vln, 2 vla, vlne, bc
16th Sunday after Trinity

Musikalische Sonn- und Fest-Tags Lust,
no. 60

N0045   **Alle die gottselig leben wollen**
SSATB, 2 vln, 2 vla, vlne, bc
3rd Sunday of Advent
Musikalische Sonn- und Fest-Tags Lust,
no. 3

N0046   **Alleluia . . . denn der allmächtige Gott**
SSATB, 2 vln, 2 vla, vlne, bc
Feast of Saint Michael the Archangel
Musikalische Sonn- und Fest-Tags Lust,
no. 62

N0047   **Also hat Gott die Welt**
SSATB, 2 vln, 2 vla, vlne, bc
Whit Monday
Musikalische Sonn- und Fest-Tags Lust,
no. 40

N0048   **Auf, auf zu Gott**
SSATB
New Year
USSR-KA Ms. 13661, no. 15 (lost)
DdT 49/50, p. 49

N0049   **Bleib bei uns, Herr**
SSATB, 2 vln, 2 vla, vlne, bc
Easter Monday
Musikalische Sonn- und Fest-Tags Lust,
no. 30

N0050   **Christus hat uns geliebet**
SSATB, 2 vln, 2 vla, vlne, bc
Quinquagesima
Musikalische Sonn- und Fest-Tags Lust,
no. 21

N0051   **Christus ist des Gesetzes Ende**
SSATB, 2 vln, 2 vla, vlne, bc
6th Sunday after Trinity
Musikalische Sonn- und Fest-Tags Lust,
no. 50

N0052   **Christus ist uns gemacht von Gott**
SSATB, 2 vln, 2 vla, vlne, bc
Palm Sunday
Musikalische Sonn- und Fest-Tags Lust,
no. 28

N0053   **Das Blut Jesu Christi**
SSATB, 2 vln, 2 vla, vlne, bc
14th Sunday after Trinity
Musikalische Sonn- und Fest-Tags Lust,
no. 58

N0054   **Das Evangelium ist eine Kraft**
SSATB, 2 vln, 2 vla, vlne, bc

Sexagesima
Musikalische Sonn- und Fest-Tags Lust,
no. 20

N0055   **Das ist die Freudigkeit**
SSATB, 2 vln, 2 vla, vlne, bc
5th Sunday after Easter
Musikalische Sonn- und Fest-Tags Lust,
no. 36

N0056   **Das Wort ward Fleisch**
SSATB, 2 vln, 2 vla, vlne, bc
3rd Day of Christmas
Musikalische Sonn- und Fest-Tags Lust,
no. 7

N0057   **Dazu ist erschienen**
SSATB, 2 vln, 2 vla, vlne, bc
3rd Sunday of Lent
Musikalische Sonn- und Fest-Tags Lust,
no. 24

N0058   **Der Herr ist geduldig**
SSATB, 2 vln, 2 vla, vlne, bc
4th Sunday after Trinity
Musikalische Sonn- und Fest-Tags Lust,
no. 46

N0059   **Der Herr ist mein Hirte**
SSATB, 2 vln, 2 vla, vlne, bc
2nd Sunday after Easter
Musikalische Sonn- und Fest-Tags Lust,
no. 33

N0060   **Der Herr ist nahe**
SSATB, 2 vln, 2 vla, vlne, bc
2nd Sunday after Epiphany
Musikalische Sonn- und Fest-Tags Lust,
no. 13

N0061   **Der Herr verstößet nicht**
SSATB, 2 vln, 2 vla, vlne, bc
2nd Sunday of Lent
Musikalische Sonn- und Fest-Tags Lust,
no. 23

N0062   **Der Herr wird euch**
SSATB, 2 vln, 2 vla, vlne, bc
4th Sunday of Lent
Musikalische Sonn- und Fest-Tags Lust,
no. 25

N0063   **Der Mensch vom Weibe**
SSATB, 2 vln, 2 vla, vlne, bc
24th Sunday after Trinity
Musikalische Sonn- und Fest-Tags Lust,
no. 69

N0064   **Der Segen des Herrn**
SSATB, 2 vln, 2 vla, vlne, bc
5th Sunday after Trinity
Musikalische Sonn- und Fest-Tags Lust,
no. 48

N0065   **Der Tod ist verschlungen**
SSATB, 2 vln, 2 vla, vlne, bc
Easter Sunday
Musikalische Sonn- und Fest-Tags Lust,
no. 29

N0066   **Des Menschen Sohn**
SSATB, 2 vln, 2 vla, vlne, bc
3rd Sunday after Trinity
Musikalische Sonn- und Fest-Tags Lust,
no. 45

N0067   **Dieser Jesus, welcher von euch**
SSATB, 2 vln, 2 vla, vlne, bc
Ascension
Musikalische Sonn- und Fest-Tags Lust,
no. 37

N0068   **Eins bitte ich vom Herrn**
SSATB, 2 vln, 2 vla, vlne, bc
Sunday after Christmas
Musikalische Sonn- und Fest-Tags Lust,
no. 8

N0069   **Es ist dir gesagt, Mensch**
SSATB, 2 vln, 2 vla, vlne, bc
18th Sunday after Trinity
Musikalische Sonn- und Fest-Tags Lust,
no. 63

N0070   **Es ist ein großer Gewinn**
SSATB, 2 vln, 2 vla, vlne, bc
15th Sunday after Trinity
Musikalische Sonn- und Fest-Tags Lust,
no. 59

N0071   **Es springen und singen**
SSATTB
Christmas Day
USSR-KA Ms. 13661, no. 24 (lost)
DdT 49/50, pp. 69-70

N0072   **Freue dich und sei fröhlich**
SSATB, 2 vln, 2 vla, vlne, bc
1st Sunday of Advent
Musikalische Sonn- und Fest-Tags Lust,
no. 1

N0073   **Frisch auf, ihr Menschenkinder**
SSATTB
Christmas Day
USSR-KA Ms. 13661, no. 17 (lost)
DdT 49/50, pp. 52-53

NIEDT, Nicolaus (*continued*)

N0074 **Fürchte dich nicht**
SSATB, 2 vln, 2 vla, vlne, bc
Sunday after Circumcision
Musikalische Sonn- und Fest-Tags Lust,
no. 10

N0075 **Gelobet sei der Herr, der Gott Israel**
SSATB, 2 vln, 2 vla, vlne, bc
Feast of Saint John the Baptist
Musikalische Sonn- und Fest-Tags Lust,
no. 47

N0076 **Gott einen Tag gesetzet**
SSATB, 2 vln, 2 vla, vlne, bc
2nd Sunday of Advent
Musikalische Sonn- und Fest-Tags Lust,
no. 2

N0077 **Gott hat den, der von keiner Sünde**
SSATB, 2 vln, 2 vla, vlne, bc
5th Sunday of Lent
Musikalische Sonn- und Fest-Tags Lust,
no. 27

N0078 **Gott ist unser Zuversicht**
SSATB, 2 vln, 2 vla, vlne, bc
25th Sunday after Trinity
Musikalische Sonn- und Fest-Tags Lust,
no. 70

N0079 **Gott, sei mir gnädig**
SSATB, 2 vln, 2 vla, vlne, bc
11th Sunday after Trinity
Musikalische Sonn- und Fest-Tags Lust,
no. 55

N0080 **Haltet fest an der**
SSATB, 2 vln, 2 vla, vlne, bc
17th Sunday after Trinity
Musikalische Sonn- und Fest-Tags Lust,
no. 61

N0081 **Herr, lehre mich tun**
SSATB, 2 vln, 2 vla, vlne, bc
Septuagesima
Musikalische Sonn- und Fest-Tags Lust,
no. 19

N0082 **Herr, nun läßest du**
SSATB, 2 vln, 2 vla, vlne, bc
Purification of the Virgin Mary
Musikalische Sonn- und Fest-Tags Lust,
no. 16

N0083 **Hilf, Herr, die Heiligen**
SSATB, 2 vln, 2 vla, vlne, bc
8th Sunday after Trinity
Musikalische Sonn- und Fest-Tags Lust,
no. 52

N0084 **Ich bin arm**
SSATB, 2 vln, 2 vla, vlne, bc
1st Sunday after Trinity
Musikalische Sonn- und Fest-Tags Lust,
no. 43

N0085 **Ich bin der Weg**
SSATB, 2 vln, 2 vla, vlne, bc
Whit Tuesday
Musikalische Sonn- und Fest-Tags Lust,
no. 41

N0086 **Ich freue mich im Herrn**
SSATB, 2 vln, 2 vla, vlne, bc
Visitation of the Virgin Mary
Musikalische Sonn- und Fest-Tags Lust,
no. 49

N0087 **Ich lebe und ihr sollt auch leben**
SSATB, 2 vln, 2 vla, vlne, bc
Easter Tuesday
Musikalische Sonn- und Fest-Tags Lust,
no. 31

N0088 **Ihr seid alle Gottes Kinder**
SSATB, 2 vln, 2 vla, vlne, bc
Trinity
Musikalische Sonn- und Fest-Tags Lust,
no. 42

N0089 **Kommet her, ihr Gesegneten**
SSATB, 2 vln, 2 vla, vlne, bc
26th Sunday after Trinity
Musikalische Sonn- und Fest-Tags Lust,
no. 71

N0090 **Kommt her zu mir, alle**
SSATB, 2 vln, 2 vla, vlne, bc
2nd Sunday after Trinity
Musikalische Sonn- und Fest-Tags Lust,
no. 44

N0091 **Lasset das Wort Christi**
SSATB, 2 vln, 2 vla, vlne, bc
5th Sunday after Epiphany
Musikalische Sonn- und Fest-Tags Lust,
no. 17

N0092 **Lobe den Herrn, meine Seele**
SSATB, 2 vln, 2 vla, vlne, bc
12th Sunday after Trinity
Musikalische Sonn- und Fest-Tags Lust,
no. 56

N0093   **Lobet den Herrn, der zu Zion wohnet**
SSATB, 2 vln, 2 vla, vlne, bc
13th Sunday after Trinity
Musikalische Sonn- und Fest-Tags Lust,
no. 57

N0094   **Maria wird einen Sohn**
SSATB, 2 vln, 2 vla, vlne, bc
Annunciation to the Virgin Mary
Musikalische Sonn- und Fest-Tags Lust,
no. 26

N0095   **Mein Herz dichtet ein feines Lied**
SSATB, 2 vln, 2 vla, vlne, bc
2nd Day of Christmas
Musikalische Sonn- und Fest-Tags Lust,
no. 6

N0096   **Niemand kann Jesum einen Herrn**
SSATB, 2 vln, 2 vla, vlne, bc
4th Sunday after Easter
Musikalische Sonn- und Fest-Tags Lust,
no. 35

N0097   **Nun aber gibst du, Gott**
SSATB, 2 vln, 2 vla, vlne, bc
Pentecost
Musikalische Sonn- und Fest-Tags Lust,
no. 39

N0098   **Nun danket alle Gott**
SSATB, 2 vln, 2 vla, vlne, bc
Circumcision
Musikalische Sonn- und Fest-Tags Lust,
no. 9

N0099   **Nun erfahre ich mit der Wahrheit**
SSATB, 2 vln, 2 vla, vlne, bc
23rd Sunday after Trinity
Musikalische Sonn- und Fest-Tags Lust,
no. 68

N0100   **Nun, Herr, wes soll ich mich trösten**
SSATB, 2 vln, 2 vla, vlne, bc
21st Sunday after Trinity
Musikalische Sonn- und Fest-Tags Lust,
no. 66

N0101   **O sichre Welt**
SSATTB
Christmas Day
USSR-KA Ms. 13661, no. 13 (lost)
DdT 49/50, pp. 43-44

N0102   **Schläfst du noch, schönste und herrliche Braut**
SSATTB
Christmas Day

USSR-KA Ms. 13661, no. 35 (lost)
DdT 49/50, pp. 103-05

N0103   **Sei getreu bis in den Tod**
SSATB, 2 vln, 2 vla, vlne, bc
9th Sunday after Trinity
Musikalische Sonn- und Fest-Tags Lust,
no. 53

N0104   **Selig sind die zum**
SSATB, 2 vln, 2 vla, vlne, bc
20th Sunday after Trinity
Musikalische Sonn- und Fest-Tags Lust,
no. 65

N0105   **Siehe, das ist Gottes Lamm**
SSATB, 2 vln, 2 vla, vlne, bc
4th Sunday of Advent
Musikalische Sonn- und Fest-Tags Lust,
no. 4

N0106   **Siehe, der Hüter Israel**
SSATB, 2 vln, 2 vla, vlne, bc
4th Sunday after Epiphany
Musikalische Sonn- und Fest-Tags Lust,
no. 15

N0107   **Siehe des Herrn Auge**
SSATB, 2 vln, 2 vla, vlne, bc
7th Sunday after Trinity
Musikalische Sonn- und Fest-Tags Lust,
no. 51

N0108   **Suchet den Herrn, weil er zu finden ist**
SSATB, 2 vln, 2 vla, vlne, bc
3rd Sunday after Epiphany
Musikalische Sonn- und Fest-Tags Lust,
no. 14

N0109   **Und Jesus zug hinein**
SSATB, 2 vln, 2 vla, vlne, bc
"In die Encaeniorum"
Musikalische Sonn- und Fest-Tags Lust,
no. 73

N0110   **Unerträglich ist dein Zorn**
SSATB, 2 vln, 2 vla, vlne, bc
22nd Sunday after Trinity
Musikalische Sonn- und Fest-Tags Lust,
no. 67

N0111   **Uns ist ein Kind geboren**
SSATB, 2 vln, 2 vla, vlne, bc
Christmas Day
Musikalische Sonn- und Fest-Tags Lust,
no. 5

NIEDT, Nicolaus (*continued*)

N0112   **Unser Trübsal**
SSATB, 2 vln, 2 vla, vlne, bc
3rd Sunday after Easter
Musikalische Sonn- und Fest-Tags Lust,
no. 34

N0113   **Vater, ich will, daß wo ich bin**
SSATB, 2 vln, 2 vla, vlne, bc
6th Sunday after Epiphany
Musikalische Sonn- und Fest-Tags Lust,
no. 18

N0114   **Wache dich auf**
SSATB, 2 vln, 2 vla, vlne, bc
Epiphany
Musikalische Sonn- und Fest-Tags Lust,
no. 11

N0115   **Wenn du es wüßtest**
SSATB, 2 vln, 2 vla, vlne, bc
10th Sunday after Trinity
Musikalische Sonn- und Fest-Tags Lust,
no. 54

N0116   **Widerstehet dem Teufel**
SSATB, 2 vln, 2 vla, vlne, bc
1st Sunday of Lent
Musikalische Sonn- und Fest-Tags Lust,
no. 22

N0117   **Wie der Hirsch schreiet**
SSATB, 2 vln, 2 vla, vlne, bc
27th Sunday after Trinity
Musikalische Sonn- und Fest-Tags Lust,
no. 72

N0118   **Wie lieblich sind deine Wohnungen**
SSATB, 2 vln, 2 vla, vlne, bc
1st Sunday after Epiphany
Musikalische Sonn- und Fest-Tags Lust,
no. 12

N0119   **Wir müssen durch viel**
SSATB, 2 vln, 2 vla, vlne, bc
Sunday after Ascension
Musikalische Sonn- und Fest-Tags Lust,
no. 38

N0120   **Wo ist solch ein Gott**
SSATB, 2 vln, 2 vla, vlne, bc
19th Sunday after Trinity
Musikalische Sonn- und Fest-Tags Lust,
no. 64

N0121   **Wo zween oder drei**
SSATB, 2 vln, 2 vla, vlne, bc
1st Sunday after Easter
Musikalische Sonn- und Fest-Tags Lust,
no. 32

O

ÖSTERREICH, Georg (1664-1735)

O0001 **Ach Herr, laß deine liebe Engelein**
See under Anonymous

O0002 **Alle Menschen müssen sterben**
SATBB, 2 vla, 2 vltta, 3 ob, 2 bsn, bc
D-Bds Mus. ms. autogr. G. Österreich 2
(Mus. ms. 16321), no. 6 (Bokemeyer)
(1701)
score

O0003 **Aller Augen warten auf dich**
SATB, 2 vln, 2 vla, bc
D-Bds Mus. ms. autogr. G. Österreich 2
(Mus. ms. 16321), no. 5 (Bokemeyer)
score

O0004 **Der Gerechten Seelen sind in Gottes Hand**
SSATB, 2 vln, 2 vla, bc
D-Bds Mus. ms. autogr. G. Österreich 3
(Mus. ms. 16322), no. 2 (Bokemeyer)
score

O0005 **Dixit Dominus**
STB, 2 vln, vc, bc
D-Bds Mus. ms. autogr. G. Österreich 1
(Mus. ms. 16320), no. 12 (Bokemeyer)
score

O0006 **Du Tochter Zion, freue dich**
SATB, 2 vln, 2 vla, vc, bc
D-Bds Mus. ms. autogr. G. Österreich 2
(Mus. ms. 16321), no. 7 (Bokemeyer)
(1689)
score

O0007 **Durch die Welt erschall und gehe**
SSATB

D-Bds Mus. ms. 30236, no. 3 (Bokemeyer)
score

O0008 **Fahr hin, o Welt**
SATB, vln, 3 gamba, bc
D-Bds Mus. ms. autogr. G. Österreich 2
(Mus. ms. 16321), no. 8 (Bokemeyer)
score

O0009 **Freu dich sehr o meine Seele**
SATB, 2 vln, 2 vltta, bsn, bc
D-Bds Mus. ms. autogr. G. Österreich 2
(Mus. ms. 16321), no. 9 (Bokemeyer)
(1697)
score

O0010 **Herr Jesu Christ, meins Lebens Licht**
SATBB, 2 vln, 2 vltta, bsn, bc
D-Bds Mus. ms. autogr. G. Österreich 2
(Mus. ms. 16321), no. 11 (Bokemeyer)
(1698)
score

O0011 **Herr Jesu Christ, wahr Mensch und Gott**
SATB, 2 vln, 2 vltta, bsn, bc
D-Bds Mus. ms. autogr. G. Österreich 2
(Mus. ms. 16321), no. 10 (Bokemeyer)
(1704)
score

O0012 **Ich bin die Auferstehung**
SSATTBB, 2 vln, 2 vltta, 2 ob/fl, bsn, bc
D-Bds Mus. ms. autogr. G. Österreich 1
(Mus. ms. 16320), no. 3 (Bokemeyer)
(1704)
score

ÖSTERREICH, Georg (*continued*)

O0013 Ich habe einen guten Kampf gekämpfet
SATB, 2 vln, vla, bsn, bc
D-Bds Mus. ms. autogr. G. Österreich 1
(Mus. ms. 16320), no. 4 (Bokemeyer)
score

O0014 Ich will den Herren loben
SATB, 2 vln, 2 vltta, bc
D-Bds Mus. ms. autogr. G. Österreich 2
(Mus. ms. 16321), no. 12 (Bokemeyer)
(1688)
score

O0015 Laetatus sum in his
ATB, 2 vln, 2 vla, bsn, bc
D-Bds Mus. ms. autogr. G. Österreich 1
(Mus. ms. 16320), no. 13 (Bokemeyer)
(1687)
score

O0016 Levavi oculos meos
SATB, 2 vln, 2 vla, vc, bc
D-Bds Mus. ms. autogr. G. Österreich 1
(Mus. ms. 16320), no. 14 (Bokemeyer)
(1688)
score

O0017 O du hochdurchleuchtges Paar
SSATB, 2 vln, 2 vla, bc
D-Bds Mus. ms. autogr. G. Österreich 3
(Mus. ms. 16322), no. 7 (Bokemeyer)
(1693)
score

O0018 Plötzlich müssen die Leute sterben
SSATBB, 2 vln, 2 vltta, ob, vlne, bc
Funeral service
D-Bds Mus. ms. autogr. G. Österreich 3
(Mus. ms. 16322), no. 11 (Bokemeyer)
(1702)
score

O0019 Ruhe sanft in Gottes Hand
SATB, 2 vln, vla, bc
D-Bds Mus. ms. autogr. G. Österreich 1
(Mus. ms. 16320), no. 16 (Bokemeyer)
(1701)
score

O0020 Sei willkommen, werte Nacht
SATB, 2 vln, 2 vla, bc
D-Bds Mus. ms. anon. 637 (Bokemeyer)
score
Attributed by Kümmerling

O0021 Sel'ge Fürstin, ruhe wohl
SATB, 3 gamba, bc
D-Bds Mus. ms. autogr. G. Österreich 3
(Mus. ms. 16322), no. 12 (Bokemeyer)
score

O0022 Selig sind die Toten
SSATB, 2 vln, 2 vla, bc
D-Bds Mus. ms. autogr. G. Österreich 1
(Mus. ms. 16320), no. 5 (Bokemeyer)
score

O0023 Sie ist fest gegründet
SSATB, 2 vln, 2 vltta, vla basso, bc
D-Bds Mus. ms. autogr. G. Österreich 1
(Mus. ms. 16320), no. 6 (Bokemeyer)
(1691)
score

O0024 Und Jesus ging aus von dannen
SSATB, 2 vln, 2 vltta, bsn, bc
D-Bds Mus. ms. autogr. G. Österreich 1
(Mus. ms. 16320), no. 7 (Bokemeyer)
(1693)
score

O0025 Unser keiner lebet ihm selber
SSATB, 2 vln, 2 vla, bsn, bc
D-Bds Mus. ms. autogr. G. Österreich 1
(Mus. ms. 16320), no. 8 (Bokemeyer)
score

O0026 Valet will ich dir geben
SATB, 3 vla, bsn, bc
D-Bds Mus. ms. autogr. G. Österreich 1
(Mus. ms. 16320), no. 11 (Bokemeyer)
(1697)
score

O0027 Verlaß mich nicht
SATB, 2 vln, 2 vla, bc
D-B Mus. ms. 30300, no. 12 (Bokemeyer)
(1693)
score
Attributed by Kümmerling

O0028 Wann ich betracht mein sündliches Wesen
SSATB, 4 vln, 2 vla, vlne, bsn, bc
D-Bds Mus. ms. autogr. G. Österreich 6
(Bokemeyer) (1694)
score

O0029 Weise mir, Herr, deinen Weg
SATB, 2 ob/vln, 2 vltta, vc, bc
D-Bds Mus. ms. autogr. G. Österreich 1
(Mus. ms. 16320), no. 10 (Bokemeyer)
(1695)
score

O0030 **Weise mir, Herr, deinen Weg**
SATB, 2 vln, 2 vla, vc, bc
D-Bds Mus. ms. autogr. G. Österreich 4
(Bokemeyer)
score

O0031 **Wie eilst du, edler Geist**
SSATB, 2 vln, 2 vla, bc
D-Bds Mus. ms. autogr. G. Österreich 3
(Mus. ms. 16322), no. 1 (Bokemeyer)
score

O0032 **Wie kommt es doch, daß Phoebus
goldglänzende Strahlen**
SATB, 2 vln, 2 vla, bsn, bc
D-Bds Mus. ms. autogr. G. Österreich 3
(Mus. ms. 16322), no. 4 (Bokemeyer)
(1695)
score

O0033 **Willkommen, hohe Gäst**
SSATB, 2 vln, 2 vla, bc
D-Bds Mus. ms. anon. 715 (Bokemeyer)
score
Attributed by Kümmerling

O0034 **Wir haben nicht einen Hohen Priester**
SSATTBB, 3 vln, 3 vltta, bsn, bc
D-Bds Mus. ms. autogr. G. Österreich 1
(Mus. ms. 16320), no. 9 (Bokemeyer)
(1695)
score

ÖSTERREICH, Michael

O0035 **Ach bleib bei uns Herr Jesu Christ**
ATB, 2 vln, vltta, bsn, bc
D-Bds Mus. ms. autogr. M. Österreich
(Mus. ms. 16325), no. 1 (Bokemeyer)
(1693)
score
DMA 2/1371

O0036 **Das Wort ward Fleisch**
SATB, 2 vln, 2 vla, bsn, bc
D-Bds Mus. ms. autogr. M. Österreich
(Mus. ms. 16325), no. 2 (Bokemeyer)
(1694)
score
DMA 2/1372

O0037 **Des Menschen Sohn wird seine Engel senden**
SATB, 2 vln, 2 vla, bsn, bc
D-Bds Mus. ms. autogr. M. Österreich
(Mus. ms. 16325), no. 3 (Bokemeyer)
(1693)
score
DMA 2/1373

O0038 **Es ist hier kein Unterschied**
ATB, 2 vln, vltta, bsn, bc
D-Bds Mus. ms. autogr. M. Österreich
(Mus. ms. 16325), no. 4 (Bokemeyer)
(1693)
score
DMA 2/1374

O0039 **Ich habe einen guten Kampf gekämpfet**
ATB, vln, 2 gamba, vlne, bc
D-Bds Mus. ms. autogr. M. Österreich
(Mus. ms. 16325), no. 5 (Bokemeyer)
score
DMA 2/1376

O0040 **Sanctus**
SATB, 2 vln, 2 vla, bsn, bc
D-Bds Mus. ms. autogr. M. Österreich
(Mus. ms. 16325), no. 10 (Bokemeyer)
(1691)
score
DMA 2/1377

O0041 **Sanctus**
SATB, 2 vln, 2 vla, bsn, bc
D-Bds Mus. ms. autogr. M. Österreich
(Mus. ms. 16325), no. 11 (Bokemeyer)
(1692)
score
DMA 2/1378

O0042 **Sanctus**
SSATB, 2 vln, 2 vla, 2 clar, bsn, bc
D-Bds Mus. ms. autogr. M. Österreich
(Mus. ms. 16325), no. 12 (Bokemeyer)
(1693)
score
DMA 2/1379

O0043 **Sanctus**
SSATB, 2 vln, 2 vla, 2 clar, bsn, bc
D-Bds Mus. ms. autogr. M. Österreich
(Mus. ms. 16325), no. 14 (Bokemeyer)
(1694)
score
DMA 2/1380

O0044 **Sende dein Licht und deine Wahrheit**
TTB, 2 vln, gamba, bsn, bc
D-Bds Mus. ms. autogr. M. Österreich
(Mus. ms. 16325), no. 6 (Bokemeyer)
(1690)
score
DMA 2/1381

ÖSTERREICH, Michael (*continued*)

O0045   **Vater unser, der du bist im Himmel**
SSAT, 2 vln, 2 vla, bsn, bc
D-Bds Mus. ms. autogr. M. Österreich
(Mus. ms. 16325), no. 7 (Bokemeyer)
(1693)
score
DMA 2/1382

O0046   **Zweierlei bitt ich von dir**
SSB, 2 vln, 2 vla, bc
9th Sunday after Trinity
D-Bds Mus. ms. autogr. M. Österreich
(Mus. ms. 16325), no. 8 (Bokemeyer)
(1690)
score
DMA 2/1383

P

PACHELBEL, Johann (1653-1706)

P0001 **Christ lag in Todesbanden** (Eggebrecht no. 27)
SATB, 2 vln, 3 vla, bsn, bc
Easter
D-B Mus. ms. 16476/2
parts
DMA 1/2070
Ed. Eggebrecht (Bärenreiter no. 2875)

P0002 **Der Herr ist König, darum toben die Völker**
(Eggebrecht no. 1)
SATB, SATB, bc
D-B Mus. ms. 16475/3
parts
DMA 3/1265
Ed. Krüger, *Die Motette* 135
Ed. Eggebrecht (Bärenreiter no. 2871)

P0003 **Der Herr ist König und herrlich geschmückt**
(Eggebrecht no. 2)
SATB, SATB, bc
D-B Mus. ms. 16475/6
parts
DMA 37//25
Ed. Krüger, *Die Motette* 132

P0004 **Der Herr ist König und herrlich geschmückt,
Alleluia** (Eggebrecht no. 3)
SSATB
D-B Mus. ms. 16475/9
parts
DMA 37//23
Ed. Krüger, *Die Motette* 137

P0005 **Der Name des Herrn sei gelobet** (Eggebrecht
no. 28)
SAB, 2 vln, bc

D-B Mus. ms. 16475/12
parts
DMA 2/516

P0006 **Deus in adjutorium meum** (Ingressus in A,
Eggebrecht no. 8)
SSATB, 2 vln, 3 vla, bsn, bc
GB-Ob Ms. Tenbury 1209, no. 1, fol. 1-14
score
DMA 2/886

P0007 **Deus in adjutorium meum** (Ingressus in a,
Eggebrecht no. 10)
SSATB, 2 vln, 3 vla, bsn, bc
GB-Ob Ms. Tenbury 1209, no. 6, fol.
54-69
score
DMA 2/886

P0008 **Deus in adjutorium meum** (Ingressus in C,
Eggebrecht no. 4)
SATB, 2 vln, vla, bc
D-Bds Mus. ms. 30189, no. 8; Mus. ms.
Commer 123, no. 2
score

P0009 **Deus in adjutorium meum** (Ingressus in C,
Eggebrecht no. 6)
SATB, 2 vln, 3 vla, bsn, bc
GB-Ob Ms. Tenbury 1208, no. 3, fol.
41-45
score
DMA 33//8
Woodward 1952, vol. 2, pp. 1-14

P0010 **Deus in adjutorium meum** (Ingressus in C,
Eggebrecht no. 13)
SSATB, 2 vln, 3 vla, 4 tpt, timp, bsn, bc

PACHELBEL, Johann (*continued*)

GB-Ob Ms. Tenbury 1209, no. 9, fol.
92-109
score
DMA 2/886

P0011 Deus in adjutorium meum (Ingressus in D,
Eggebrecht no. 7)
SSATB, 2 vln, 3 vla, bsn, bc
GB-Ob Ms. Tenbury 1208, no. 5, fol.
73-84
score
DMA 33//8
Ed. Woodward (Marks, Piedmont, 1969)

P0012 Deus in adjutorium meum (Ingressus in D,
Eggebrecht no. 5)
SATB, 2 vln, vla, bc
D-Bds Mus. ms. Commer 123, no. 1
score

P0013 Deus in adjutorium meum (Ingressus in D,
Eggebrecht no. 14)
SATB, 2 vln, 3 vla, bsn, bc
GB-Ob Ms. Tenbury 1209, no. 10, fol.
110-27
score
DMA 2/886

P0014 Deus in adjutorium meum (Ingressus in F,
Eggebrecht no. 9)
SSATB, 2 vln, 4 vla, bsn, bc
GB-Ob Ms. Tenbury 1209, no. 4, fol.
28-43
score
DMA 2/886
Ed. Woodward 1952, vol. 2, pp. 15-46

P0015 Deus in adjutorium meum (Ingressus in g,
Eggebrecht no. 11)
SATB, 2 vln, bsn, bc
GB-Ob Ms. Tenbury 1209, no. 7, fol.
70-73
score
DMA 2/886

P0016 Deus in adjutorium meum (Ingressus in g,
Eggebrecht no. 12)
SSATB, 2 vln, vla, 2 gamba, bsn, bc
GB-Ob Ms. Tenbury 1209, no. 8, fol.
74-91
score
DMA 2/886

P0017 Domine ad adjuvandum me (Ingressus in G,
Eggebrecht no. 15)
SATB, 2 vln, 3 vla, bsn, bc

D-Bds Mus. ms. 30088, no. 12 (old 444)
score (SATB, bc only)
GB-Ob Ms. Tenbury 1209, no. 2, fol.
15-21
score
DMA 2/886

P0018 Exsurgat Deus (Eggebrecht no. 16)
SATB, SATB, bc
D-B Mus. ms. 16475/3
parts
DMA 3/1266
Ed. Krüger, *Die Motette* 134

P0019 Gott, du Gott Israel
SSATB, 4 vln, bc
D-Bds Mus. ms. 30282 (formerly 198)
score
Cf. Krummacher (1967): 369-70

P0020 Gott ist unser Zuversicht (Eggebrecht no. 18)
SATB, 2 vln, 3 vla, bsn, bc
GB-Ob Ms. Tenbury 1208, no. 9, fol.
119-40
score
DMA 33//8

P0021 Gott ist unser Zuversicht (Eggebrecht no. 17)
SATB, SATB, bc
D-B Mus. ms. 16475/20
parts
DMA 3/1267
Ed. Krüger, *Die Motette* 133
Ed. Eggebrecht (Bärenreiter no. 2872)

P0022 Gott sei uns gnädig (Eggebrecht no. 19)
SSATB, 2 vln, 4 vla, timp, bsn, bc
GB-Ob Ms. Tenbury 1208, no. 1, fol. 1-26
score
DMA 33//8
Woodward 1952, vol. 2, pp. 171-220

P0023 Ingressus
See Deus in adjutorium meum; Domine ad
adjuvandum me

P0024 Jauchzet dem Herrn (Eggebrecht no. 20)
SATB, SATB, bc
D-B Mus. ms. 16475/25
score
DMA 3/1268
parts
DMA 3/872
Ed. Eggebrecht (Bärenreiter no. 2874)

P0025 Jauchzet dem Herrn, alle Welt (Eggebrecht no. 30)
SSATB, 2 vln, 3 vla, 4 tpt, timp, bsn, bc

GB-Ob Ms. Tenbury 1208, no. 7, fol.
  105-13
  score
  DMA 33//8

P0026   **Jauchzet dem Herrn, alle Welt** (Eggebrecht no. 29)
  SSATB, 2 vln, 3 vla, 2 ob, bsn, bc
  D-B Mus. ms. 16476/5
  parts
  DMA 1/2071
  Ed. Krüger, *Die Kantate* 157

P0027   **Jauchzet Gott, alle Lande** (Eggebrecht no. 22)
  SATB, SATB, bc
  D-B Mus. ms. 16475, no. 23
  parts
  DMA 37//29

P0028   **Kommt her zu mir** (Eggebrecht no. 31)
  SATB, 2 vln, 2 corn, bc
  GB-Ob Ms. Tenbury 1209, no. 5, fol.
  44r-53v
  score
  DMA 2/886
  Woodward 1952, vol. 2, pp. 221-40
  Ed. Eggebrecht (Bärenreiter)

P0029   **Lobet den Herrn in seinem Heiligtum** (Eggebrecht
  no. 22)
  SSATB, 2 vln, 3 vla, 2 fl, harp, 5 tpt,
  timp, tbn, bc
  GB-Ob Ms. Tenbury 1208, no. 6, fol.
  85-104
  score
  DMA 33//8
  Ed. Eggebrecht (Bärenreiter)

P0030   **Magnificat** (B-flat, Eggebrecht no. 46)
  SSATB, 2 vln, 3 vla, 2 ob, bsn, bc
  GB-Ob Ms. Tenbury 1209, no. 13, fol.
  162-87
  score
  DMA 2/886

P0031   **Magnificat** (C, Eggebrecht no. 48)
  SSATB, 2 vln, vla, 2 gamba, 4 tpt, timp, bc
  GB-Ob Ms. Tenbury 1311
  score
  DMA 2/887
  Ed. Woodward (Boston: Birchard, 1951)

P0032   **Magnificat** (C, Eggebrecht no. 45)
  SATB, 2 vln, 2 vla, 2 tpt, bc
  GB-Ob Ms. Tenbury 1209, no. 12, fol.
  138-61
  score
  DMA 2/886

P0033   **Magnificat** (C, Eggebrecht no. 43)
  SSATB, 2 vln, vla, 2 gamba, 4 tpt, timp,
  bsn, bc
  GB-Ob Ms. Tenbury 1208, no. 12, fol.
  181-208
  score
  DMA 33//8
  Woodward 1952, vol. 2, pp. 99-170

P0034   **Magnificat** (C, Eggebrecht no. 41)
  SSATB, 2 vln, 3 vla, 2 ob, bsn, bc
  GB-Ob Ms. Tenbury 1208, no. 10, fol.
  141-64
  score
  DMA 33//8

P0035   **Magnificat** (D, Eggebrecht no. 37)
  SATB, 4 vla, bc
  D-Bds Mus. ms. 30088, no. 11 (old 444)
  score
  Ed. Eggebrecht (Bärenreiter no. 2877)
  Ed. W. Rodby (Somerset Press no. 403,
  1975)

P0036   **Magnificat** (D, Eggebrecht no. 47)
  SSATB, SSATB, 2 vln, 3 vla, bsn, bc
  GB-Ob Ms. Tenbury 1356
  score
  DMA 2/888

P0037   **Magnificat** (D, Eggebrecht no. 42)
  SSATB, 2 vln, 3 vla, 2 corn/ob, bsn, bc
  GB-Ob Ms. Tenbury 1208, no. 11, fol.
  165-80
  score
  DMA 33//12

P0038   **Magnificat** (E-flat, Eggebrecht no. 40)
  SATB, 2 vln, 3 vla, bsn, bc
  GB-Ob Ms. Tenbury 1208, no. 4, fol.
  46-72
  score
  DMA 33//8
  Woodward 1952, vol. 2, pp. 47-98

P0039   **Magnificat** (F, Eggebrecht no. 39)
  SATB, 2 vln, bsn, bc
  GB-Ob Ms. Tenbury 1208, no. 2, fol.
  27-40
  score
  DMA 33//8

P0040   **Magnificat** (F, Eggebrecht no. 44)
  SSATB, 2 vln, bc
  GB-Ob Ms. Tenbury 1209, no. 11, fol.
  128-37
  score
  DMA 2/886

PACHELBEL, Johann (*continued*)

P0041   **Magnificat** (G, Eggebrecht no. 38)
SATB, 2 vln, bc
GB-Ob Ms. Tenbury 1209, no. 3, fol.
22-27
score
DMA 2/886
D-Bds Mus. ms. 30088, no. 13 (old 444)
score

P0042   **Magnificat** (g, Eggebrecht no. 36)
SATB, bc
D-B Mus. ms. 16474/5 (1705)
parts
DMA 52//60

P0043   **Mein Herr Jesu, dir lieb ich** (Eggebrecht no. 32b)
SATB, 3 vla, bc
D-B Mus. ms. 16476/8
parts
Parody of "Meine Sünde betrüben mich"

P0044   **Meine Sünde betrüben mich** (Eggebrecht no. 32a)
SATB, 4 gamba, bsn, bc
D-Dlb Mus. ms. 2106-E-500 (Grimma U
357/N 88)
parts (anonymous)
D-B Mus. ms. 16476/10
incipits only
DMA 1/2073
The copy formerly in F-Ssp is lost
(Krummacher 1965, p. 288)

P0045   **Missa** (C, Eggebrecht no. 35)
SATB, 2 vln, clar, bc
GB-Ob Ms. Tenbury 1209, no. 14, fol.
188-205
score
DMA 2/886

P0046   **Missa (brevis)** (D, Eggebrecht no. 34)
SATB, bc
D-B Mus. ms. 16472 (1704)
parts
DMA 52//51
(Peters no. HU 1601)

P0047   **Nun danket alle Gott** (Eggebrecht no. 23)
SATB, SATB, bc
D-B Mus. ms. 16475/28 (1705)
parts
DMA 3/1269
Ed. Krüger, *Die Motette* 131
Ed. Eggebrecht (Bärenreiter no. 2873)
Ed. Ehret (Elkan-Vogel no. 362-1290)
Ed. Granville (Fox no. CM13)

P0048   **Paratum cor meum** (Eggebrecht no. 24)
SATB, SATB, bc
D-B Mus. ms. 11474/8
parts
DMA 52//61

P0049   **Singet dem Herrn** (Eggebrecht no. 25)
SATB, SATB, bc
D-B Mus. ms. 16475/30
parts
D-Bds Mus. ms. 30177, no. 9; Mus. ms.
Commer 123, no. 4
score
Ed. Commer, *Musica sacra* III (1843), pp.
72-77
Ed. Burger, *Die Motette* 8
Zehntes Kantate-Chorheft (Leipzig:
Landeskirchen-Chorverband Sachsen,
1937)

P0050   **Tröste uns, Gott unser Heiland** (Eggebrecht no. 26)
SATB, SATB, bc
D-Bds Mus. ms. 16475/32
parts
D-Bds Mus. ms. Commer 123, no. 3
score
DTB X (Jg. VI/I)
Ed. Hermann, *Die Motette* 2
Ed. Trotschel (Müller no. K34)
Ed. Commer, *Musica sacra* III (1843), pp.
65-71
Evangelische Kirchenmusik in Baden 21,
insert

P0051   **Was Gott tut, das ist wohlgetan** (Eggebrecht
no. 33)
SATB, 2 vln, 2 vla, vlne, bc
F-Ssp
parts
DMA 2/517
D-Bds Mus. ms. Commer 123, no. 13
score
DTB X (Jg. VI/1), pp. 100-117
Winterfeld II, no. 219
Ed. Metzler (Merseburger no. EM905)
Ed. Eggebrecht (Bärenreiter no. 2876)
Ed. Keunig (Harmonia no. 1313, 1958)

PERANDA, Marco Giuseppe (ca. 1625-1675)

P0052   **Accurrite gentes, venite**
ATB, 2 corn, bsn, bc
Easter or Christmas

D-Dlb Mus. ms. 1738-E-510 (Grimma U
233/O 63)
parts
S-Uu 85:26b, fol. 2v-6r (Düben)
tablature
DMA 3/1747
S-Uu 30:3 (Düben)
parts
DMA 3/1747

P0053 Ad cantus, ad sonos
SST, 3 vln, bsn, bc
D-Dlb Mus. ms. 1738-E-517 (Grimma U
204/U 6)
parts
D-B Mus. ms. 17081, no. 9 (Bokemeyer)
score
DMA 22//37
D-Dlb Mus. ms. 1738-D-1, no. 9, pp. 169-82
score

P0054 Cantemus Domino
SSS, bc
D-Dlb Mus. ms. 1738-E-511 (Grimma U
229/U 30)
parts
D-B Mus. ms. 17081, no. 2 (Bokemeyer)
score
DMA 22//37
D-Dlb Mus. ms. 1738-D-1, no. 2, pp. 37-47
score
Ed. B. Beyerle (Heinrichshofen, 1935)

P0055 Cogita, o homo
SATB, 2 vln, bc
D-Dlb Mus. ms. 1738-E-515 (Grimma U
211/U 12)
parts

P0056 Credidi, propter quod locutus sum
STB, SATB, 2 vln, 2 vla, bsn, bc
D-Dlb Mus. ms. 1738-E-506 (Grimma U
210/U 11)
parts
D-Dlb Mus. ms. 1857-E-511, no. 2 (pp. 18-43)
score

P0057 Da pacem Domine
SSB, 2 vln, vla, bc
D-B Mus. ms. 17081, no. 10 (Bokemeyer)
score
DMA 22//37
D-Dlb Mus. ms. 1738-D-1, no. 10, pp. 183-98
score

P0058 Dedit abyssus vocem suam
SSBB, bc

D-Dlb Mus. ms. 1738-E-527 (Grimma U
230/U 31)
parts
S-Uu 78:51, fol. 51v-54r (Düben) (1667)
tablature
DMA 3/1749
S-Uu 30:4 (Düben)
parts
DMA 3/1749

P0059 Dic nobis Maria
SSB, 2 vln, bsn, bc
D-B Mus. ms. 17081, no. 3 (Bokemeyer)
score
DMA 22//37
D-Dlb Mus. ms. 1738-D-1, no. 3, pp. 49-62
score
Ed. B. Beyerle (Heinrichshofen, 1935)

P0060 Diligam te, Domine
SSB, 2 vln, bsn, bc
D-Dlb Mus. ms. 1738-E-503 (Grimma U
216/U 17)
parts
D-Dlb Mus. ms. 1-E-770, no. 5, pp. 26-33
score

P0061 Ecce ego mittam piscatores
SSB, 2 vln, vlne, bc
S-Uu 78:47, fol. 47v-49r (Düben)
tablature
DMA 3/1750
S-Uu 30:5 (Düben)
parts
DMA 3/1750

P0062 Factum est praelium magnum
SSATTB, 2 vln, 2 vla, 2 cornettini, 2
tbn/vla, bc
Feast of Saint Michael the Archangel
D-B Mus. ms. 17081, no. 1 (Bokemeyer)
score
DMA 22//37
D-Dlb Mus. ms. 1738-D-1, no. 1, pp. 1-36
score
S-Uu 61:14 (Düben)
parts
DMA 3/1751
S-Uu 61:16 (Düben)
parts
DMA 3/1751

P0063 Fasciculus myrrhae est dilectus meus
SSATB, 2 vln, 2 vla, 2 cornettini, 3 tbn,
bsn, bc

PERANDA, Marco Giuseppe (*continued*)

D-Dlb Mus. ms. 1738-E-509 (Grimma U 235/U 35)
score and parts

P0064 Florete fragrantibus liliis
SST, 2 vln, gamba/bombard, bc
D-Dlb Mus. ms. 1738-E-525 (Grimma U 234/U 33)
parts

P0065 Freuet euch, ihr Himmel
See Laetentur coeli

P0066 Gaudete, cantate
SSB, 2 vln, bc
D-Dlb Mus. ms. 1738-E-523 (Grimma U 214/U 15)
parts

P0067 Herr wenn ich nur dich habe
ATB, 2 vln, bsn, bc
D-B Mus. ms. 17081, no. 19 (Bokemeyer)
score
DMA 22//37
D-Dlb Mus. ms. 1738-D-1, no. 19, pp. 305-19
score

P0068 Historia des Leidens und Sterbens unsers Herrn
See Marcus-Passion

P0069 Hoc luce cunctos assere
ATB, 2 vln, 2 vla, bsn, bc
D-Dlb Mus. ms. 1738-E-514 (Grimma U 213/U 14)
parts

P0070 Jesu dulcis, Jesu pie
SAT, 2 vla, bsn, bc
D-Dlb Mus. ms. 1738-E-522 (Grimma U 220/U 21)
parts

P0071 Kyrie
SSATB, 2 vln, 2 vla, 2 clar, vlne, bc
D-B Mus. ms. 17079/10 (Bokemeyer)
parts

P0072 Laetentur caeli
SSATB, 2 vln, 2 clar, 3 tbn, bc
D-Dlb Mus. ms. 1738-E-531 (Grimma U 371/N 58)
parts
With text underlay: "Freuet euch, ihr Himmel"

P0073 Languet cor meum
SAT, 2 vla, bsn, bc
D-Dlb Mus. ms. 1738-E-508 (Grimma U 209/U 10)
parts

P0074 Laudate Dominum, omnes gentes
SSSATB, 2 vln, 2 vla, bsn, bc
S-Uu 61:17 (Düben)
tablature and parts
DMA 3/1753

P0075 Laudate, pueri, Dominum
SSSB, bc
D-Dlb Mus. ms. 1-E-770, no. 4, pp. 22-27
score

P0076 Marcus-Passion
SATB soli, SATB
D-LEm, Mus. ms. II 2, 15
score
Ed. in H. Schütz, *Sämtliche Werke* (1885), vol. 1, pp. 73-96
Ed. Steude (Deutsche Verlag für Musik DVfM 7671, 1978)

P0077 Miserere mei, Deus
SSSATB, 2 vln, 3 vla, 2 clar, timp, 3 tbn, bsn, bc
D-Dlb Mus. ms. 1738-E-512 (Grimma U 228/U 29)
score and parts
D-Dlb Mus. ms. 1738-D-2
score
D-B Mus. ms. 17080
score
DMA 34//104
D-B Mus. ms. 17081, no. 5 (Bokemeyer)
score
DMA 22//37
D-Dlb Mus. ms. 1738-D-1, no. 5, pp. 77-137
score
S-Uu 61:18 (Düben)
parts
DMA 3/1754

P0078 Missa
SSATB, 2 vln, 2 vla, 2 corn, 2 clar, 3 tbn, vlne, bc
CS-KRa I, 43 (1672)
parts

P0079 Missa
SSATTB, 2 vln, 3 vla, bc
D-B Mus. ms. 30098, no. 6
score

P0080 Missa
SATB, SATB, 2 vln, 2 vla, bsn, bc
D-B Mus. ms. 17079 (Bokemeyer)
score

P0081 **Missa (brevis)**
SATB, 2 vln, 2 vla, bc
D-B Mus. ms. 30088, no. 14
score

P0082 **Missa (brevis)**
SSATTB, 2 vln, 3 vla, bsn, bc
D-B Mus. ms. 17019/11; Mus. ms. 17019/12
parts

P0083 **Missa Beatae Agnetis**
SSATTB, 2 vln, 2 vla, 2 corn, 3 tbn, vlne, bc
CS-KRa I, 44 (1671)
parts

P0084 **Missus est angelus Gabriel**
SSB soli, SSATB, 3 gamba, 2 vltta, bc
D-Dlb Mus. ms. 1738-E-502 (Grimma U 215/U 16)
score and parts

P0085 **O fideles, modicum sustinete tempus**
SATB, 2 vln, bsn, bc
D-Dlb Mus. ms. 1738-E-518 (Grimma U 231/U 32)
score (incomplete) and parts

P0086 **O Jesu mi dulcissime, spes suspiratis animae**
SSA, 2 vln/vltta, 2 gamba, vlne, theorbo, bc
S-Uu 30:6 (Düben)
parts
DMA 3/1757
S-Uu 84:51, fol. 10v-12r (Düben)
tablature
DMA 3/1757

P0087 **Peccavi, o Domine**
SAB, 2 vln, bc
D-Dlb Mus. ms. 1738-E-524 (Grimma U 212/U 13)
score and parts

P0088 **Plange anima suspira**
ATB, bc
S-Uu 30:7 (Düben)
parts
DMA 3/1759

P0089 **Propitiare Domine**
SSATB, 2 vln, 2 vla, bsn, bc
D-Dlb Mus. ms. 1738-E-500 (Grimma U 226/U 27)
score and parts

P0090 **Quis dabit capiti meo aquas**
ATB, 2 vln, bc
D-B Mus. ms. 17081, no. 18 (Bokemeyer)
score
DMA 22//37

D-Dlb Mus. ms. 1738-D-1, no. 18, pp. 291-304
score
D-B Mus. ms. 17019/20
parts

P0091 **Quo tendimus mortales**
SSB, bc
D-Dlb Mus. ms. 1738-E-519 (Grimma U 208/U 9)
parts

P0092 **Repleti sunt omnes spirito sancto**
ATB, 2 vln, 2 corn, bc
D-B Mus. ms. 17081, no. 4 (Bokemeyer)
score
DMA 22//37
D-Dlb Mus. ms. 1738-D-1, no. 4, pp. 65-76
score

P0093 **Rorate cherubim**
SSA, 2 vln, bc
CS-KRa II, 179
parts

P0094 **Seguace d'amore non cerco pieta**
SSB, 2 vln, bc
S-Uu 30:9 (Düben)
tablature

P0095 **Si Dominus mecum**
SATB, 2 vln, bsn, bc
D-Dlb Mus. ms. 1738-E-516 (Grimma U 218/U 19)
parts
D-B Mus. ms. 17081, no. 8 (Bokemeyer)
score
DMA 22//37
D-Dlb Mus. ms. 1738-D-1, no. 8, pp. 157-67
score
S-Uu 78:39, fol. 39v-41v (Düben)
tablature
DMA 3/1761

P0096 **Si vivo, mi Jesu, sic vivam in te**
SST, 3 vln, bc
D-Dlb Mus. ms. 1738-E-504 (Grimma U 217/U 18)
score and parts

P0097 **Sive vivimus, sive morimur**
SAB, 2 vln, bc
D-B Mus. ms. 17081, no. 7 (Bokemeyer)
score
DMA 22//37
D-Dlb Mus. ms. 1738-D-1, no. 7, pp. 149-55
score

PERANDA, Marco Giuseppe (*continued*)

P0098　**Sursum deorsum**
　　　SSS, 3 vln, bc
　　　D-Dlb Mus. ms. 1738-E-530 (Grimma U
　　　　222/U 23)
　　　　parts

P0099　**Te solum aestuat**
　　　SSB, 2 vln, bsn, bc
　　　D-Dlb Mus. ms. 1738-E-521 (Grimma U
　　　　223/U 24)
　　　　parts
　　　D-B Mus. ms. 17081, no. 6 (Bokemeyer)
　　　　score
　　　　DMA 22//37
　　　D-Dlb Mus. ms. 1738-D-1, no. 6, pp. 135-48
　　　　score
　　　S-Uu 78:73, fol. 73v-75r (Düben)
　　　　tablature
　　　　DMA 3/1764
　　　S-Uu 30:12 (Düben)
　　　　tablature and parts
　　　　DMA 3/1764

P0100　**Timor et tremor venerunt super nos**
　　　SATB, 2 vln, bc
　　　D-Dlb Mus. ms. 1738-E-520 (Grimma U
　　　　225/U 26)
　　　　score and parts

P0101　**Tu es cor meum**
　　　SSB, 2 vln, bsn, bc
　　　D-B Mus. ms. 17081, no. 17 (Bokemeyer)
　　　　score
　　　　DMA 22//37
　　　D-Dlb Mus. ms. 1738-D-1, no. 17, pp. 279-90
　　　　score

P0102　**Veni sancte spiritus**
　　　SATB, 2 vln, 2 vla, 2 corn, 3 tbn, bsn, bc
　　　D-Dlb Mus. ms. 1738-E-526 (Grimma U
　　　　206/U 7)
　　　　parts (tbn 3 lacking)

P0103　**Verleih uns Frieden gnädiglich**
　　　SSB, 2 vln, bc
　　　D-B Mus. ms. 17081, no. 20 (Bokemeyer)
　　　　(1693)
　　　　score
　　　　DMA 22//37
　　　D-Dlb Mus. ms. 1738-D-1, no. 20, pp. 321-38
　　　　score

P0104　**Vocibus resonent jubilis reboent**
　　　SAB, 2 vln, gamba, vlne, bc
　　　S-Uu 78:43, fol. 43r-47r (Düben) (1667)

　　　　tablature
　　　　DMA 3/1765
　　　S-Uu 30:13 (Düben)
　　　　parts
　　　　DMA 3/1765

PETER, Christoph (1626-1669)

P0105　**Er Küsse mich mit dem Kusse seines Mundes**
　　　SSAB, ATTB, bc
　　　Wedding of Jacob Klinckebel and Maria Sedlig
　　　Frankfurt an der Oder, 1661
　　　　RISM P1568 (parts)
　　　　DMA 1/1841

P0106　**Ich will den Herren loben jetzund und allezeit**
　　　SSATB
　　　Frankfurt an der Oder, 1658
　　　　RISM P1567 (score)
　　　　DMA 78//102

P0107　**Ihr Kinder Zion freuet euch**
　　　SSTB, bc
　　　Ordination of Zacharias Brescius
　　　Guben, 1667
　　　　RISM P1571 (parts)
　　　　DMA 75//106 & 75//230

P0108　**Ihr lieben Eltern, trauret nicht**
　　　SSATB
　　　Funeral of Johannes Lorentz
　　　Frankfurt an der Oder, 1655
　　　　RISM P1566 (score)
　　　　DMA 72//129

PETZOLD, Abraham

P0109　**Verleih uns Frieden gnädiglich/Gib userm
　　　Fürsten**
　　　SSATB, 2 vln, 2 vla, 2 clar, bsn, bc
　　　D-Dlb Mus. ms. 1870-E-500 (Grimma U
　　　　237/U 37)
　　　　parts
　　　　DMA 34//29

PETZOLDUS, Gottlieb August

P0110　**Lobet den Herrn, alle Heiden**
　　　SATB, 2 vln, 2 vla, vlne, bsn, bc
　　　D-Dlb Mus. ms. 1814-E-500 (Grimma 68/T
　　　　114)
　　　　parts
　　　Composer indicated simply as "G. Petzold"
　　　　on manuscript

PETRITZ, Basilius

P0111   **Die Herrlichkeit des Herrn**
SATB, 2 vln, 2 vla, bsn, bc
3rd Sunday of Advent or Christmas Day
D-Dlb Mus. ms. 1868-E-500 (Grimma U 236)
(1695)
parts
Composer given as "B. P." on manuscript
Attribution by D-Dlb

PEZEL, Johann Christoph (1639-1694)

P0112   **Des Abends, Morgens, und Mittags**
ATB, vla d'amore, 2 vla, bass vla, vlne, bc
D-F Ms. Ff. Mus. 449 (1690)
parts

P0113   **Missa (brevis) ex A**
SSATB, 2 corn/vln, 3 tbn, bc
D-Bds Mus. ms. 30171, no. 9
score

P0114   **Singet dem Herren ein neues Lied**
SSATB, 2 vln, 2 vla, bsn, bc
D-Bds Mus. ms. 30257, no. 8 (Bokemeyer)
score

PFEFFERKORN, Christoph Heinrich

P0115   **Hört, wie ein Schwester Paar**
S solo, SATB, bc
Funeral of Sabine Elisabeth von Brandenstein
Langensalza, 1702
RISM P1706, Reich 209 (score)
DMA 70//167

P0116   **Was ist der Christen Zeit**
SSATB, SSATB, SSATB (echo choirs)
Funeral of Melchior Philipp Trott
Gotha, 1662
RISM P1707, Reich 100 (score)
DMA 70//135

PFLEGER, Augustin (1635-1686)

COLLECTION

Psalmi, dialoghi et motettae (1661)
RISM P1759 (parts)
DMA 3/1953

WORKS

P0117   **Ach daß die Hilfe aus Zion**
See Es wird das Scepter

P0118   **Ach, daß ich Wassers genug hätte**
SSTTB, 2 vla, vlne, bc
5th Sunday of Lent
S-Uu 72:25 (Düben)
tablature and parts
Ed. F. Stein, *Das Chorwerk* 52

P0119   **Ach, die Menschen sind umgeben**
SSTTB, 3 vla, vlne, bc
24th Sunday after Trinity
S-Uu 74:13 (Düben)
parts

P0120   **Ach Herr, du Sohn Davids**
STTB, 2 vla, vlne, bc
2nd Sunday of Lent
S-Uu 72:19 (Düben)
parts
S-Uu 85:32, fol. 45v-48r (Düben)
tablature
EdM 64, pp. 140-49

P0121   **Ach, wenn Christus sich ließ finden**
SSTTB, 3 vla, vlne, bc
3rd Sunday of Advent
S-Uu 72:3 (Düben)
parts
EdM 50, pp. 34-46

P0122   **Christen haben gleiche Freud**
SSTBB, 2 vln, vlne, bc
4th Sunday of Advent
S-Uu 72:4 (Düben)
parts
EdM 50, pp. 47-54

P0123   **Confitebor tibi Domine in toto corde meo**
SATB, 2 vln, vla, vlne, bc
S-Uu 85:40, fol. 6v-9r (Düben)
tablature
S-Uu 31:3 (Düben)
parts

P0124   **Cum complerentur dies pentecostes**
SSTTB, 2 vln, 2 gamba, bc
S-Uu 85:33, fol. 1v-4r (Düben)
tablature
DMA 28//55
S-Uu 31:4 (Düben)
parts
DMA 12//85

P0125   **Der Herr ist ein Heiland der Juden und Heiden**
SSTB, 3 vla, vlne, bc
Purification of the Virgin Mary
S-Uu 74:16 (Düben)
tablature (incomplete) and parts

PFLEGER, Augustin (*continued*)

P0126 **Der Herr ist groß von Wundertat**
SSTTB, 2 vln, vlne, bc
3rd Sunday after Epiphany
S-Uu 72:14 (Düben)
parts
EdM 64, pp. 30-40

P0127 **Der Mensch ist nicht geschaffen**
SSTB, 2 vln, 2 vla, vlne, bc
5th Sunday after Trinity
S-Uu 73:19 (Düben)
parts
D-Bds Mus. ms. 30257, no. 12 (Bokemeyer)
score

P0128 **Die Ernte ist groß, aber wenig sind**
SSTTB, 2 vln, gamba, vlne, bc
Septuagesima
S-Uu 72:21 (Düben)
parts
S-Uu 85:32, fol. 29v-33r (Düben)
tablature
EdM 64, pp. 88-104

P0129 **Diligam te, Domine fortitudo mea**
SSTTB, bc
S-Uu 85:33, fol. 16v-19r (Düben)
tablature
S-Uu 31:5 (Düben)
parts

P0130 **Dominus virtutum nobiscum susceptor noster Deus Jacob**
SST soli, SSTTB, 2 vln, vla, gamba, vlne, bc
S-Uu 85:23, fol. 10v-13r (Düben)
tablature
DMA 29//177
S-Uu 31:6 (Düben)
parts
DMA 12//85

P0131 **Eheu! mortalis quot pro te malis**
SSTB, 3 vla, vlne, bc
S-Uu 85:35 (Düben) (1674)
tablature
S-Uu 31:7 (Düben)
parts

P0132 **Erbarm dich mein, o Herre Gott**
SSTTB, 2 vln, 2 vla, vlne, bc
4th Sunday after Trinity
S-Uu 73:18 (Düben)
parts
D-Bds Mus. ms. 30257, no. 10 (Bokemeyer)
score

P0133 **Es wird das Zepter von Juda nicht entwendet werden**
SSTTB, 2 vln, 2 vla, bc
Christmas Day
S-Uu 31:1 (Düben); 67:19 (= 72:5) (Düben)
parts
EdM 50, pp. 55-66

P0134 **Exurge Domine**
ATB, bc
Psalmi, dialoghi et motettae, no. 7

P0135 **Fratres, ego enim accepi a Domino**
SST, 3 vla, vlne, bc
S-Uu 31:8 (Düben)
parts
DMA 23//40

P0136 **Friede sei mit euch**
SSTB, vln/gamba, 2 gamba, vlne, bc
1st Sunday after Easter
S-Uu 73:4 (Düben)
parts

P0137 **Fürchtet den Herrn, ihr seine Heiligen**
SSTTB, 2 vln, 2 vla, vlne, bc
15th Sunday after Trinity
S-Uu 74:4 (Düben)
parts
S-Uu 85:32, fol. 49bisv-52r (Düben)
tablature

P0138 **Gestern ist mir zugesaget**
SSTB, 2 vln, vlne, bc
2nd Day of Christmas
S-Uu 72:6 (Düben)
parts
EdM 50, pp. 67-76

P0139 **Gott bauet selbst sein Himmelreich**
SSB, 2 vln, bc
5th Sunday after Epiphany
S-Uu 72:16 (Düben)
parts
EdM 64, pp. 57-67

P0140 **Gott ist einem König gleich**
STTB, 2 vla, vlne, bc
22nd Sunday after Trinity
S-Uu 74:11 (Düben)
parts
S-Uu 85:32, fol. 27v-30r (Düben)
tablature

P0141 **Gottes Geist bemüht sich sehr**
SSTB, 2 vln, 2 vla, vlne, bc
Whit Tuesday
S-Uu 73:13 (Düben)
parts

P0142 **Herr, haben wir nicht in deinem Namen geweissaget**
STTB, 3 vla, vlne, bc
8th Sunday after Trinity
S-Uu 73:22 (Düben)
parts
S-Uu 85:32, fol. 36v-39r (Düben)
tablature

P0143 **Herr, wann willst du mich bekehren**
SSB, 4 vla, vlne, bc
12th Sunday after Trinity
S-Uu 74:1 (Düben)
parts
S-Uu 85:32, fol. 11v-14r (Düben)
tablature

P0144 **Herr, wer wird wohnen in deinen Hütten**
SSTB, 3 vla, vlne, bc
Feast of All Saints
S-Uu 74:22 (Düben)
parts
S-Uu 85:32, fol. 54v-58r (Düben)
tablature

P0145 **Herr, wir können uns nicht nähren**
SSTTB, 2 vla, vlne, bc
4th Sunday of Lent
S-Uu 73:11 (Düben)
parts

P0146 **Heut freue dich, Christenheit, rühmet ihr Frommen**
SSTB, 2 vln, 2 vla, vlne, bc
1st Sunday of Advent
S-Uu 85:32, fol. 19v-23r (Düben)
tablature
S-Uu 72:1 (Düben)
parts
EdM 50, pp. 1-15

P0147 **Heut freue dich, Christenheit, weil Christus vom Himmel**
SSTB, 3 vla, vlne, bc
2nd Sunday of Advent
S-Uu 72:2 (Düben)
parts
EdM 50, pp. 16-33

P0148 **Heut ist Gottes Himmelreich einer Königshochzeit gleich**
SSTTB, 2 vln, 2 vla, vlne, bc
20th Sunday after Trinity
S-Uu 74:9 (Düben)
parts
S-Uu 85:32, fol. 38v-42r (Düben)
tablature

P0149 **Heute kann man recht verstehen**
SSTB, 2 vln, 2 vla, vlne, bc

Pentecost
S-Uu 73:10 (Düben)
parts

P0150 **Hilf, Herr Jesu, laß gelingen**
SSTB, 3 vla, vlne, bc
New Year
S-Uu 72:9 (Düben)
parts
EdM 50, pp. 102-11

P0151 **Ich bin das Licht der Welt**
SSTTB, 3 vla, vlne, bc
5th Sunday of Lent
S-Uu 73:9 (Düben)
parts

P0152 **Ich bin ein guter Hirte**
STB, 2 vln, 2 vla, vlne, bc
2nd Sunday after Easter
S-Uu 73:5 (Düben)
parts
S-Uu 85:32, fol. 34v-37r (Düben)
tablature

P0153 **Ich bin wie ein verwirret und verloren Schaf**
SSTB, 2 vln, vlne, bc
3rd Sunday after Trinity
S-Uu 73:17 (Düben)
parts
S-Uu 85:32, fol. 41v-44r (Düben)
tablature
D-Bds Mus. ms. 30257, no. 11 (Bokemeyer)
score

P0154 **Ich danke dir, Gott, daß ich nicht bin**
SSTTB, 4 vla, vlne, bc
11th Sunday after Trinity
S-Uu 73:25 (Düben)
tablature and parts

P0155 **Ich gehe hin zu dem, der mich gesandt hat**
SSTTB, 2 vln, 2 vla, vlne, bc
4th Sunday after Easter
S-Uu 73:7 (Düben)
parts

P0156 **Ich sage euch, es sei denn eure Gerechtigkeit**
SSTB, 2 vln, 2 vla, vlne, bc
6th Sunday after Trinity
S-Uu 73:20 (Düben)
parts
S-Uu 85:32, fol. 1v-6r (Düben)
tablature
See also under Förtsch

P0157 **Ich suchte des Nachts in meinem Bette**
SSTB, 2 vln, 2 vla, vlne, bc

PFLEGER, Augustin (*continued*)

21st Sunday after Trinity
S-Uu 74:10 (Düben)
tablature (voices and bc only) and parts

P0158 **Ich will meinen Mund auftun in Gleichnissen**
SSTB, 2 vln, vlne, bc
Sexagesima
S-Uu 72:22 (Düben)
parts
EdM 64, pp. 105-23

P0159 **Im Anfang war das Wort**
SSTB, 3 vla, vlne, bc
3rd Day of Christmas
S-Uu 72:7 (Düben)
parts
EdM 50, pp. 77-88

P0160 **In tribulatione invocamus Dominum**
SSTT, 3 vla, bc
S-Uu 79:133, fol. 133v-136v (Düben)
tablature
DMA 34//198
S-Uu 31:11 (Düben) (1665)
parts
DMA 14//12

P0161 **Inclina Domine aurem tuam et exaudi me**
SSTB, 4 vla, theorbo, bc
S-Uu 85:36 (Düben)
tablature
S-Uu 31:10 (Düben)
parts

P0162 **Jesu, lieber Meister, erbarme dich unser**
STTB, 4 vla, vlne, bc
14th Sunday after Trinity
S-Uu 74:3 (Düben)
parts
S-Uu 85:32, fol. 48v-50r (Düben)
tablature

P0163 **Jesus trieb ein Teufel aus**
SSTTB, 2 vla, vlne, bc
3rd Sunday of Lent
S-Uu 72:20 (Düben)
parts
EdM 64, pp. 150-64

P0164 **Jetzt gehet an die neue Zeit**
SSTTB, 2 vla, vlne, bc
Annunciation of the Virgin Mary
S-Uu 74:17 (Düben)
parts

P0165 **Kommt, denn es ist alles bereit**
SSTT, 3 vla, vlne, bc

2nd Sunday after Trinity
S-Uu 73:16 (Düben)
parts

P0166 **Kommt her, ihr Christenleut**
SSTTB, 2 vla, vlne, bc
Sunday after Christmas
S-Uu 72:8 (Düben)
parts
EdM 50, pp. 89-101

P0167 **Laetabundus et jucundus exultat fidelis chorus**
SSTT, 2 vln, vlne, bc
S-Uu 78:59, fol. 59v-61r (Düben) (1667)
tablature
S-Uu 63:4 (Düben)
parts

P0168 **Laetatus sum in his quae dicta sunt mihi**
SATB, 2 vln, 3 vla, bc
S-Uu 85:39, fol. 4v-7r (Düben)
tablature
DMA 28//60
S-Uu 31:12 (Düben)
parts
DMA 14//12

P0169 **Lauda Jerusalem Dominum**
SATB, 2 vln, 2 vla, vlne, bc
S-Uu 85:37, fol. 1r-3r (Düben)
tablature (SATB, 4 vla, bc)
DMA 28//58
S-Uu 31:13 (Düben)
parts
DMA 14//12

P0170 **Laudate Dominum, omnes gentes (I)**
SSTB, 2 vln, 2 vla, vlne, bc
S-Uu 85:22, fol. 8v-10r (Düben)
tablature
DMA 29//176
S-Uu 31:15 (Düben)
parts
DMA 14//12

P0171 **Laudate Dominum, omnes gentes (II)**
SATB, 2 vln, 2 vla, vlne, bc
S-Uu 85:38, fol. 3r-5r (Düben)
tablature
DMA 28//59
S-Uu 31:14 (Düben)
parts
DMA 14//12

P0172 **Laudate, pueri, Dominum (I)**
SSSB, bc
Psalmi, dialoghi et motettae, no. 16

P0173 **Laudate, pueri Dominum (II)**
SST, 3 gamba, vlne, bc
S-Uu 85:45 (Düben)
tablature
DMA 28//62
S-Uu 31:16 (Düben)
parts
DMA 14//12

P0174 **Lernet von mir, denn ich bin sanftmütig**
SSTB, 3 vla, vlne, bc
17th Sunday after Trinity
S-Uu 74:6 (Düben)
parts
S-Uu 85:32, fol. 15v-17r (Düben)
tablature

P0175 **Mache dich auf, werde Licht**
SSTB, 2 vln, vlne, bc
Epiphany
S-Uu 72:11 (Düben)
parts
EdM 50, pp. 120-38

P0176 **Mein Sohn, wollt Gott, ich müßte vor dir sterben**
SSB, 3 vla, vlne, bc
16th Sunday after Trinity
S-Uu 74:5 (Düben)
parts
S-Uu 85:32, fol. 13v-16r (Düben)
tablature

P0177 **Meine Tränen sind meine Speise**
STTB, 2 vln, 2 vla, vlne, bc
3rd Sunday after Easter
S-Uu 73:6 (Düben)
parts

P0178 **Meister, was soll ich tun**
SSTTB, 4 vla, vlne, bc
13th Sunday after Trinity
S-Uu 74:2 (Düben)
parts
S-Uu 85:32, fol. 33v-35r (Düben)
tablature

P0179 **Meister, welches ist das vornehmste Gebot**
SSTTB, 3 vla, vlne, bc
18th Sunday after Trinity
S-Uu 74:7 (Düben)
parts
S-Uu 85:32, fol. 51v-54r (Düben)
tablature

P0180 **Meister, wir wissen, daß du wahrhaftig bist**
SSTTB, 3 vla, vlne, bc
23rd Sunday after Trinity

S-Uu 74:12 (Düben)
parts

P0181 **Mensch, lebe fromm und sei getreu**
SSB, 2 vln, vlne, bc
9th Sunday after Trinity
S-Uu 73:23 (Düben)
parts

P0182 **Merket, wie der Herr uns liebet**
STTB, 3 vla, vlne, bc
Easter Monday
S-Uu 73:2 (Düben)
parts
S-Uu 85:32, fol. 25v-28r (Düben)
tablature

P0183 **Mich jammert des Volkes**
SSTTB, 2 vln, vlne, bc
7th Sunday after Trinity
S-Uu 73:21 (Düben)
parts
S-Uu 85:32, fol. 5v-8r (Düben)
tablature

P0184 **Missus est angelus Gabriel**
SAB, 2 vla, bc
Annunciation to the Virgin Mary
Psalmi, dialoghi et motettae, no. 17
S-Uu 77:119, fol. 119v-122r (Düben) (1664)
tablature
S-Uu 31:17 (Düben)
parts

P0185 **Nisi Dominus aedificaveret**
SSS, bc
Psalmi, dialoghi et motettae, no. 11

P0186 **Nun gehe ich hin zu dem, der mich gesandt hat**
SSTTB, 2 vln, vlne, bc
Ascension
S-Uu 74:18 (Düben)
parts

P0187 **O altitudo divitiarum sapientiam et scientiam Dei**
SSTTB, 4 vla, bc
S-Uu 85:46, fol. 1v-4r (Düben)
tablature

P0188 **O anima mea**
SSB, bc
Psalmi, dialoghi et motettae, no. 10

P0189 **O Freude und dennoch Leid**
STTB, 2 vln, 2 vla, vlne, bc
Easter Tuesday
S-Uu 73:3 (Düben)
parts

PFLEGER, Augustin (*continued*)

P0190 **O pulcherrima mulier**
SSATB, bc
Psalmi, dialoghi et motettae, no. 18

P0191 **O Tod, wie bitter bist du**
SSTB, 2 vla, vlne, bc
1st Sunday after Trinity
S-Uu 73:15 (Düben)
parts

P0192 **Pater noster**
SATB, bc
Psalmi, dialoghi et motettae, no. 14

P0193 **Preiset, ihr Christen, mit Herzen und Munde**
SSTTB, 2 vln, 2 vla, vlne, bc
Feast of John the Baptist
S-Uu 74:20 (Düben)
parts

P0194 **Saepe expugnaverunt**
SSS, bc
Psalmi, dialoghi et motettae, no. 12

P0195 **Saget der Tochter Zion: Siehe dein König**
SSTB, 2 vln, 2 vla, vlne, bc
Palm Sunday or 1st Sunday of Advent
S-Uu 72:24 (Düben)
parts

P0196 **Schauet an den Liebesgeist, der uns ist geschenkt**
SSTB, 2 vln, vlne, bc
Whit Monday
S-Uu 73:12 (Düben)
parts

P0197 **Siehe, dein Vater und ich haben dich mit Schmerzen**
SSATB, 3 vla, vlne, bc
1st Sunday after Epiphany
S-Uu 72:12 (Düben)
parts
EdM 64, pp. 1-16

P0198 **So spricht der Herr: Bekehret euch zu mir**
SSTB, 3 vla, vlne, bc
1st Sunday of Lent
S-Uu 72:18 (Düben)
parts
EdM 64, pp. 131-39

P0199 **Sollt nicht das liebe Jesulein**
SSTB, 2 vla, vlne, bc
Sunday after New Year
S-Uu 72:10 (Düben)
parts
EdM 50, pp. 112-19

P0200 **Super flumina Babylonis**
SATB, bc
Psalmi, dialoghi et motettae, no. 15

P0201 **Triumph! Jubilieret, frohlocket**
SSSTTB, 2 vln, 2 vla, vlne, bc
Easter Sunday
S-Uu 73:1 (Düben)
parts
S-Uu 85:32, fol. 23v-26r (Düben)
tablature

P0202 **Und er trat in das Schiff**
SSSTB, 3 vla, vlne, bc
4th Sunday after Epiphany
S-Uu 72:15 (Düben)
parts
EdM 64, pp. 41-56

P0203 **Und es war eine Hochzeit zu Kana**
SSATB, 2 vln, 2 vla, vlne, bc
2nd Sunday after Epiphany
S-Uu 72:13 (Düben)
parts
EdM 64, pp. 17-29

P0204 **Und Jesus ward verkläret**
SSATBB, 2 vln, 2 vla, vlne, bc
6th Sunday after Epiphany
S-Uu 72:17 (Düben)
parts
EdM 64, pp. 68-87

P0205 **Vanitas vanitatum**
ATB, bc
Psalmi, dialoghi et motettae, no. 9

P0206 **Veni sancte spiritus**
SATB, SATB, 2 vln, 3 vla, 2 corn, 2 tbn,
vlne, bsn, bc
S-Uu 86:71a, fol. 3v-6r (Düben)
tablature
S-Uu 31:22 (Düben)
parts

P0207 **Veni sancte spiritus**
SATB, 2 vla, 2 fl, vlne, theorbo, bc
S-Uu 31:23 (Düben)
parts

P0208 **Wahrlich, ich sage dir, es sei denn**
SSTB, 2 vln, 2 vla, vlne, bc
Trinity
S-Uu 73:14 (Düben)
parts

P0209 **Wahrlich, wahrlich, ich sage euch, so ihr den
Vater**
SSTB, 3 vla, vlne, bc

5th Sunday after Easter
S-Uu 73:8 (Düben)
   tablature (S, bc only) and parts

P0210 **Weg mit aller Lust und Lachen**
SSB, 2 vla, vlne, bc
Quinquagesima
S-Uu 72:23 (Düben)
   parts
S-Uu 85:32, fol. 44v-46r (Düben)
   tablature
EdM 64, pp. 124-30

P0211 **Wenn aber der Tröster kommen wird**
SSTTB, 2 vln, 2 vla, vlne, bc
Sunday after Ascension
S-Uu 74:19 (Düben)
   parts

P0212 **Wenn die Christen sind vermessen**
SSTB, 3 vla, vlne, bc
25th Sunday after Trinity
S-Uu 74:14 (Düben)
   parts

P0213 **Wenn du es wüßtest, so würdest auch du bedenken**
SSTB, 4 vla, vlne, bc
10th Sunday after Trinity
S-Uu 73:24 (Düben)
   parts
S-Uu 85:32, fol. 8v-12r (Düben)
   tablature

P0214 **Wer ist der Herr unser Gott**
SSTB, 3 vla, vlne, bc
Feast of Saint Michael the Archangel
S-Uu 74:21 (Düben)
   parts

P0215 **Wir müssen alle offenbar werden**
SSTTB, 3 vla, vlne, bc
26th Sunday after Trinity
S-Uu 74:15 (Düben)
   parts

P0216 **Zwar ich bin des Herren Statt**
SSTB, 3 vla, vlne, bc
19th Sunday after Trinity
S-Uu 74:8 (Düben)
   parts (vla 3 missing)

PLAWENN, Leopold von (d. 1682)

COLLECTIONS

Sacrae nymphae I (1659)
RISM P2603 (parts)
DMA 74//104

Sacrae nymphae II (1669)
RISM P2604 (parts)
DMA 15//7

Sacrae nymphae III (1672)
RISM P2605 (parts)

Sacrae nymphae IV (1679)
RISM P2606 (parts)
DMA 3/1040

WORKS

P0217 **Absterger Deus**
SSB, 2 vln, bc
Sacrae nymphae IV, no. 17

P0218 **Age homo numeremus**
SST, 2 vln, bc
Sacrae nymphae II, no. 17

P0219 **Anima Christi**
SAT, 2 vln, bc
Sacrae nymphae IV, no. 14

P0220 **Asperges me**
SSATB, 2 vln, 2 vla, vlne, bc
Sacrae nymphae III, no. 1

P0221 **Audite populi**
SST, 2 vln, bc
Sacrae nymphae I, no. 24

P0222 **Ave maris stella**
SATB, 2 vln, bc
Sacrae nymphae I, no. 34

P0223 **Ave, o Jesu rex benedicte**
SSB, 2 vln, bc
S-Uu 32:2 (Düben)
   parts
DMA 2/1384

P0224 **Benedicam Dominum**
SATB, 2 vln, bc
Sacrae nymphae II, no. 23

P0225 **Cantabo Domino**
SATB, 2 vln, bc
Sacrae nymphae IV, no. 24

P0226 **Congregavit Dominus aquas**
SAB, 2 vln, bc
Sacrae nymphae II, no. 13

P0227 **Cur mundus militat**
SST, 2 vln, bc
Sacrae nymphae I, no. 20

P0228 **Deus tuorum**
SATB, 2 vln, bc
Sacrae nymphae I, no. 36

PLAWENN, Leopold von (*continued*)

P0229 **Domine ostende nobis patrem**
SSB, 2 vln, bc
Sacrae nymphae I, no. 21

P0230 **Ecce nos relinquimus**
SSB, 2 vln, bc
Sacrae nymphae IV, no. 16

P0231 **Ecce sacerdos magnus**
SATB, 2 vln, bc
Sacrae nymphae IV, no. 26

P0232 **Exultate Deo**
SATB, 2 vln, bc
Sacrae nymphae II, no. 22

P0233 **Exurge psalterium**
SST, 2 vln, bc
Sacrae nymphae II, no. 15

P0234 **Gaudeamus omnes in Domino**
SSB, 2 vln, bc
Sacrae nymphae I, no. 23

P0235 **Hic est vere martyr**
SATB, 2 vln, bc
Sacrae nymphae IV, no. 25

P0236 **Homo Dei creatura**
ATB, 2 vln, bc
Sacrae nymphae II, no. 18
F-Ssp
parts

P0237 **Iste confessor**
SATB, 2 vln, bc
Sacrae nymphae I, no. 35

P0238 **Isti sunt triumphatores**
ATB, 2 vln, bc
Sacrae nymphae IV, no. 20

P0239 **Laudetur sanctissimus sacrum**
ATB, 2 vln, bc
Sacrae nymphae IV, no. 19

P0240 **Litaniae Beatae Mariae Virginis**
SATB, 2 vln, bc
Sacrae nymphae II, no. 26

P0241 **Litaniae Beatae Mariae Virginis**
SATB, 2 vln, bc
Sacrae nymphae IV, no. 35

P0242 **Litaniae Beatae Mariae Virginis**
SSATB, 2 vln, bc
Sacrae nymphae IV, no. 36

P0243 **Litaniae Lauretanae**
SATB, 2 vln, bc
Sacrae nymphae I, no. 38

P0244 **Missa I**
SATB, 2 vln, 2 vla, vlne, bc
Sacrae nymphae III, no. 2

P0245 **Missa II**
SATB, 2 vln, 2 vla, vlne, bc
Sacrae nymphae III, no. 3

P0246 **Missa III**
SSATB, 2 vln, bc
Sacrae nymphae III, no. 4

P0247 **Missa IV**
SSAATTBB, 2 vln, 2 vla, vlne, bc
Sacrae nymphae III, no. 5

P0248 **O beatum virum**
SATB, 2 vln, bc
Sacrae nymphae II, no. 20

P0249 **O dulcissima Virgo**
SSB, 2 vln, bc
Sacrae nymphae IV, no. 15

P0250 **O felix martyris triumphus**
ATB, 2 vln, bc
Sacrae nymphae I, no. 22

P0251 **O felix, o fausta dies**
SATB, 2 vln, bc
Sacrae nymphae I, no. 28
S-Uu 77:123, fol. 123v-127r (Düben) (1664)
tablature
S-Uu 32:3 (Düben)
parts

P0252 **O patroni singulares**
SATB, 2 vln, bc
Sacrae nymphae II, no. 21

P0253 **O quam metuendus est**
SATB, 2 vln, bc
Sacrae nymphae II, no. 24

P0254 **Potestis bibere calicem**
ATB, 2 vln, bc
Sacrae nymphae I, no. 18

P0255 **Propter te mortificamur**
SSB, 2 vln, bc
Sacrae nymphae I, no. 19

P0256 **Quis nos separabit**
SSB, 2 vln, bc
Sacrae nymphae II, no. 14

P0257 **Requiem I**
SATB, 2 vln, 2 vla ad lib, vlne, bc
Sacrae nymphae III, no. 6

P0258 **Requiem II**
SATB, 2 vln, 2 vla ad lib, bc
Sacrae nymphae III, no. 7

P0259 **Requiem III**
SSATB, 2 vln, 2 vla ad lib, bc
Sacrae nymphae III, no. 8

P0260 **Requiem IV**
SSATB, 2 vln, 2 vla ad lib, bc
Sacrae nymphae III, no. 9

P0261 **Sanctum benedictum**
SATB, 2 vln, bc
Sacrae nymphae IV, no. 27

P0262 **Si criminus immanitate turbatus es**
SATB, 2 vln, bc
Sacrae nymphae II, no. 19

P0263 **Stabunt justi**
SSAB, 2 vln, bc
Sacrae nymphae II, no. 25

P0264 **Terra audi sermonem**
ATB, 2 vln, bc
Sacrae nymphae II, no. 16
F-Ssp
parts

P0265 **Valete, mundi delitiae**
SATB, 2 vln, bc
Sacrae nymphae I, no. 30

P0266 **Vidimus Dominum**
SATB, 2 vln, bc
Sacrae nymphae I, no. 32

POGLIETTI, Alessandro (d. 1683)

P0267 **Ave Regina caelorum**
SSATB, bc
CS-KRa VIII, 4
parts and score
microfilm: US-SY

P0268 **Dum sederes beatus Carolus**
SSATB, 2 vln, 3 vla, bc
Feast of Saint Carolus
CS-KRa II, 265
parts
CS-KRa II, 115
score and parts (parts listed under "Justus germinabit" in MGG)
microfilm: US-SY

P0269 **Justus germinabit sicut lilium**
See Dum sederes beatus Carolus

P0270 **Litaniae Lauretanae**
SATB, 2 vln, bc
CS-KRa V, 17
parts
microfilm: US-SY

P0271 **Magnificat**
SST, vln, bc
CS-KRa III, 111
parts
microfilm: US-SY

P0272 **Missa à 3**
SSB, vln, bc
CS-KRa I, 273a (1680)
score
microfilm: US-SY

P0273 **Missa à 4**
4 vv
CS-KRa I, 123

P0274 **Missa à 5**
SSATB, 2 vln, 2 vla, bass vla, gamba, vlne, bc
CS-KRa I, 241
parts
microfilm: US-SY

P0275 **Requiem**
CS-KRa XIII, 5

POHLE, David (1624-1695)

P0276 **Amo te Deus meus amore magno**
SAB, 2 vln, bc
D-Dlb Mus. ms. 1791-E-500 (Grimma U 238/U 38)
parts
S-Uu 82:35, fol. 15r-18r (Düben) (1684)
tablature
DMA 2/518

P0277 **Bonum est confiteri Domino**
ATB, bc
S-Uu 32:5 (Düben)
parts
DMA 2/521

P0278 **Der Engel des Herrn lagert sich**
SATB, vln, corn, tbn, bsn, bc
S-Uu 82:37, fol. 3v-6r (Düben)
tablature
DMA 3/1273

POHLE, David (*continued*)

P0279 **Domine ostende mihi**
SSATB, 2 vln, 2 vla, vlne, bsn, bc
S-Uu 84:19a (Düben) (1672)
tablature
DMA 2/522
S-Uu 32:6 (Düben)
parts
DMA 2/522
Ed. Grusnick, *Die Kantate* 331

P0280 **Domine quis habitabit in tabernaculo tuo**
SATB, 5 instruments (unspecified), bc
S-Uu 83:26, fol. 11v-15r (Düben)
tablature
DMA 28//180
S-Uu 32:7 (Düben)
parts
DMA 28//180

P0281 **Es wird ein Stern aus Jacob aufgehen**
SATB, 2 vln, bsn, bc
D-B Mus. ms. 30260, no. 1 (Bokemeyer)
score
DMA 1/2111

P0282 **Herr wenn ich nur dich habe**
SSB, 2 vln, bsn, bc
S-Uu 32:8 (Düben)
parts
DMA 1/762
Ed. Moser, *Die Kantate* 198

P0283 **Ihr Völker, bringet her**
SAB, 2 vln, bsn, bc
D-B Mus. ms. 30260, no. 3 (Bokemeyer)
score
DMA 1/2113

P0284 **In te Domine speravi**
SAT, 2 vln, bsn, bc
S-Uu 63:5 (Düben)
parts
DMA 46//184

P0285 **Jesu, meine Freude**
SATB, 3 vla, bc
D-B Mus. ms. 30260, no. 2 (Bokemeyer)
score
DMA 1/2114

P0286 **Jesus, auctor clementiae totius spes laetitiae**
ATB, 2 vln, vlne, bc
S-Uu 63:7 (Düben)
parts

DMA 46//186
Also includes German text: Jesus Ursprung
der ewgen Güt

P0287 **Jesus, Ursprung der ewgen Güt**
See Jesus auctor clementiae

P0288 **Miserere mei, Deus**
SSATB, 4 vla, vlne/bsn, bc
D-Kl 2° Mus. 52E
parts
DMA 1/347

P0289 **Nascitur Immanuel**
SSATB, 4 vln, bsn, bc
D-Dlb Mus. ms. 1791-E-501 (Grimma U
239/U 39)
parts

P0290 **Nur in meines Jesu Wunden**
SSATTB, 6 vla, bc
S-Uu 84:42, fol. 20v-24v (Düben)
tablature
DMA 3/1274
S-Uu 32:11 and 63:8 (Düben)
parts
DMA 3/1274

P0291 **Oculi mei semper ad Dominum**
SAB, 2 vln, bc
S-Uu 85:2, fol. 3v-5r (Düben)
tablature
DMA 24//193

P0292 **Siehe, es hat überwunden der Löwe**
SSATB, 2 vln, 2 vla, gamba/bsn, 2 clar, bc
D-B Mus. ms. 30260, no. 4 (Bokemeyer)
score
DMA 1/2115

P0293 **Te sanctum Dominum in excelsis**
SATTB, 2 vln, 2 vla, 2 tbtta, bsn, bc
Trinity
S-Uu 85:54a, fol. 1r-3r (Düben)
tablature
DMA 28//91
S-Uu 63:10 (Düben)
parts
DMA 28//91

P0294 **Tulerunt Dominum de monumento**
SSATTB, 2 vln, 3 vla, bsn, bc
Easter Day
S-Uu 63:11 (Düben)
parts
DMA 29//172

P0295 **Verbum caro factum est**
SSB, 2 vln, bc
S-Uu 46:22 (Düben)
parts
DMA 29//172

PRENTZ, Kaspar (fl. 1673-1695)

P0296 **Hodie natus est Christus**
SSATTB, 3 vla, 2 vltta, bsn, bc
D-B Mus. ms. 30260, no. 13 (Bokemeyer)
score

DMA 2/896
Note: Not the same as Wolfgang Caspar
Printz

PRUCHNER, Sigfried

P0297 **Laudate, pueri, Dominum**
SATB, 2 vln, 2 vla, vlne, bsn, bc
S-Uu 85:34, fol. 4v-6v (Düben)
tablature
S-Uu 32:13 (Düben)
parts

R

RAUCH, Johann Georg (d. 1710)

COLLECTIONS

Harmonicus missarum concentus (1692)
RISM R349 (parts)

Novae sirenes sacrae harmoniae, op. 1 (1687)
RISM R347 (parts)
(unavailable for examination)

Novae sirenes sacrae harmoniae, op. 2 (1690)
RISM R348 (parts)

WORKS

R0001 **Cantate Domino**
SATB, 2 vln, 2 vla, bsn, bc
Harmonicus missarum concentus, no. 4

R0002 **Cantemus Domino**
SATB, 2 vln, bsn, bc
Novae sirenes sacrae harmoniae, op. 2, no. 11

R0003 **Domine Deus**
SATB, 2 vln, bsn, bc
Novae sirenes sacrae harmoniae, op. 2, no. 10

R0004 **Domine salvum fac regum**
SSATB, 2 vln, 2 vla, bsn, bc
Harmonicus missarum concentus, no. 5

R0005 **Missa Beatae Mariae Virginis**
SSATB, 2 vln, 2 vla, bsn, bc
Harmonicus missarum concentus, no. 2

R0006 **Missa Omnium sanctorum**
SATB, SATB, 2 vln, 2 vla, bsn, bc
Harmonicus missarum concentus, no. 3

R0007 **Missa Sanctissimae Trinitatis**
SATB, 2 vln, 2 vla, bsn, bc
Harmonicus missarum concentus, no. 1

R0008 **O caeli beati**
SSB, bc
Novae sirenes sacrae harmoniae, op. 2, no. 1

REICHER, Ferdinand

R0009 **Missa Sancti Caroli**
SSATB, 2 vln, 2 vla/tbn, 4 clar, timp, bc
CS-KRa I, 215
parts
microfilm: US-SY

REIMANN, Johann Georg

R0010 **Ach! wie jammerts mich ins Herzen**
SATB
Funeral of Georg Frantzke
Gotha, 1659
RISM R1008, Reich 99 (score)
DMA 70//183

R0011 **Gehab dich wohl, du Trauer-Welt**
SATB
Funeral of Johann Pfnörs
Gotha, 1657
RISM R1007 (score)

R0012 **Ich hab einen guten Kampf gekämpfet**
SSATB
Funeral of Euphrosyna Tressel

Gotha, 1672
RISM R1010, Reich 111 (score)
DMA 70//177

R0013 **Mein Gott, wie bin ich so betrübt**
SATB
Funeral of Balthasar Christian Bechmann
Gotha, 1670
RISM R1009, Reich 106 (score)

REINCKEN, Johann Adam (1623-1722)

R0014 **Und es erhub sich ein Streit**
SATB, 2 vln, vla, 2 tpt, timp, bc
D-B Mus. ms. 18254
score

RIESSIG

R0015 **Heut triumphieret Gottes Sohn**
SSATB, 2 vln, 2 vla, 2 clar, timp, bsn, bc
D-Dlb Mus. ms. 2184-E-500 (Grimma U 256/U 57)
score and parts

RICHTER, Ferdinand Tobias (1651-1711)

R0016 **Miserere**
4 vv, 2 vln, vltta, bc
A-GÖ no. 2570
parts (vltta lacking)
Manuscript indicates only "Richter"

R0017 **Poi di sue glorie**
SATB, 3 instr, bc
A-Wn Cod. 18597, fol. 30v
score

R0018 **Questa è l'Alba di mia luce**
SSAT, 4 vla, bc
A-Wn Cod. 18597, fol. 53v
score

R0019 **Requiem I**
SATB, vln, 3 vla, bc
A-GÖ no. 444 (1723)
parts

R0020 **Requiem II**
SATB, vln
A-GÖ no. 445 (1704)
parts

R0021 **Sant Ermenegildo**
SSAT, 3 instr, bc
A-Wn Cod. 16012 (1694)
score

R0022 **Santa Teresa**
Anonymous except for 2 choruses by Richter;
see Poi di sue glorie and Questa è l'Alba di mia luce

R0023 **Tenebrae**
SSATB, bc
A-GÖ no. 2528
score and parts
Manuscript indicates only "Richter"

R0024 **Vanitas vanitatum**
SATB, 2 vln, 2 vltta, ob, bsn, bc
D-B Mus. ms. 30260, no. 14 (Bokemeyer)
score
DMA 2/897
Manuscript indicates only "Richter"

R0025 **Vesperae de Beatae Mariae Virginis**
SSATB, 2 vln, 2 vla, 2 clar, bc
A-GÖ no. 2083
parts

RIEGRAF, Johann Georg

R0026 **O trauervolle Eitelkeit**
SATB
Funeral of Christoph Hentschel
Augsburg, 1686
RISM R1400, Reich 29

RITTER, Christian (1645/50-after 1717)

R0027 **Alles was ist auf dieser Welt**
SATB, bc
S-Uu 63:14a (Düben)
parts (2 copies)
DMA 3/2170

R0028 **Also ist's geschrieben und also mußte Christus leiden**
SSB, 2 vln, gamba, bc
S-Uu 85:57, fol. 1r-3r (Düben)
tablature

R0029 **Diese sinds, die da kommen sind**
SATB, 2 vln, gamba, 2 fl, 2 ob, bsn, bc
D-B Mus. ms. 30260, no. 15 (Bokemeyer) (1704)
score
DMA 2/898

RITTER, Christian (*continued*)

R0030   **Einen guten Kampf hab ich gekämpfet**
SATB, 2 vln, 2 vla, vla d'amore, 2 recorder, bc
S-Uu 32:17 (Düben)
    parts
    DMA 1/2117

R0031   **Gelobet sei der Name des Herrn**
SATB, SATB, 2 vln, 2 vla, 2 corn, 4 tpt,
    timp, 3 tbn, bsn, bc
D-B Mus. ms. 30260, no. 16 (Bokemeyer)
    (1672)
    score
    DMA 2/900

R0032   **Gott hat Jesum erwecket**
SATB, 2 vln, bsn, bc
D-Lr Mus. ant. pract. K.N. 207/13 (1706)
    parts
    DMA 1/1181
    Ed. M. Seiffert, *Organum* I/9

R0033   **Herr, wer wird wohnen in deinen Hütten**
ATB, bc
S-Uu 32:19 (Düben) (1666)
    score (autograph)
    DMA 27//164

R0034   **Ich beschwöre euch, ihr Töchter Jerusalems**
SATB, 2 vln, vla, vlne, bc
Wedding
S-Uu 63:15 (Düben) (1669)
    parts (autograph)
    DMA 3/2171

R0035   **Laudate, pueri, Dominum**
SSB, bc
S-Uu 63:16 (Düben)
    parts (bass part missing)
    DMA 23//177

R0036   **Miserere Christi mei**
SATB, 4 vla, bc
S-Uu 86:44, fol. 5v-8r (Düben)
    tablature
    DMA 24//141
S-Uu 63:17 (Düben)
    tablature and parts

R0037   **Nun freut euch, lieben Christen gmein**
SATB, bc
S-Uu 63:18 (Düben) (1684)
    parts
    DMA 3/892

R0038   **Was nimmt der eitle Mensch sich für/Wie dank
ich gnugsam dir, mein Gott**
SAB, 4 vla, fl, theorbo, bc

Funeral of Herr Rehnschildt
S-Uu 86:45, fol. 7v-9 (Düben)
    tablature
    DMA 24//145
S-Uu 63:22 (Düben) (1681)
    parts (two sets)
    DMA 27//149

R0039   **Wie dank ich gnugsam dir, mein Gott**
See Was nimmt der eitle Mensch sich für

R0040   **Wie lieblich sind deine Wohnungen**
SSATB, 2 vln, 2 vla, 2 tpt, vlne, bc
S-Uu 84:102, fol. 9v-13r (Düben)
    tablature
    DMA 3/895
S-Uu 63:21 (Düben)
    parts
    DMA 3/895
    Ed. E. Selen (Bärenreiter 3464, 1967)

RITTLER, Philipp Jakob (ca. 1637-1690)

R0041   **Alma redemptoris mater**
SSB
CS-KRa VII, 14
    score
    microfilm: US-SY

R0042   **Ave regina**
SATB, 2 vln, bc
CS-KRa VIII, 5
    score
    microfilm: US-SY

R0043   **Cum complerentur dies pentecostes**
SSATTB, 2 vln, 3 vla, 4 tbn, bc
CS-KRa II, 219 (1677)
    parts
    microfilm: US-SY

R0044   **Ecce sacerdos magnus**
SSATB, 2 vln, 2 vla, vlne, bc
Feast of a Confessor Pope
CS-KRa II, 29
    parts
    microfilm: US-SY

R0045   **Isti sunt triumphatores**
SSATB, 2 vln, 2 vla, vlne, bc
CS-KRa II, 220
    parts
    microfilm: US-SY

R0046   **Justus germinabit**
SSATB, 2 vln, 2 vla, vlne, bc
Feast of a Confessor not a Pope

CS-KRa II, 222
parts
microfilm: US-SY

R0047 Missa Carolina (I)
SSATTB, 2 vln, 3 vla, 2 clar, 3 tbn, vlne, bc
CS-KRa I, 230 (1675)
parts
microfilm: US-SY
Not concordant with next item

R0048 Missa Carolina (II)
SSATB, 2 vln, 3 vla, 2 clar, 3 tbn, vlne, bc
CS-KRa I, 178 (1677)
parts
microfilm: US-SY
Not concordant with the preceding

R0049 Missa Dominus tecum
SSATTB, 2 vln, 5 vla, 2 clar, 4 tbn, vlne, bc
CS-KRa I, 233 (1675)
parts
microfilm: US-SY

R0050 Missa Harmonia genethliaca
SSATTB, 2 vln, 3 vla, 2 clar, 3 tbn, vlne, bc
CS-KRa I, 232
parts
microfilm: US-SY

R0051 Missa Nativitatis
SSATTBB, 2 vln, 3 vla, 2 clar, 4 tbn, vlne, bc
CS-KRa I, 194
parts
microfilm: US-SY
CS-KRa I, 193 is incomplete and does not concord

R0052 O quam suavis est Domine
SSATB, 2 vln, 2 vla, bc
Corpus Christi
CS-KRa II, 125
parts
microfilm: US-SY

R0053 Prudentes virgines
SATB, 2 vln, 2 vla, vlne, bc
Feast for the Common of Virgins and
Martyrs
CS-KRa II, 25
parts
microfilm: US-SY

R0054 Puer natus
SSATB, 2 vln, 3 vla, 4 tpt, 2 clar, timp, 3
tbn, vlne, bc
CS-KRa II, 224
parts
microfilm: US-SY

R0055 Qui sunt isti
SSATB, 2 vln, 2 vla, vlne, bc
Feast of All Saints
CS-KRa II, 127
parts
microfilm: US-SY

R0056 Regina caeli
SATBB, bc
CS-KRa IX, 17
score
microfilm: US-SY

R0057 Requiem claudiae imperatricis
5 vv, 4 vla, 4 tbn, vlne, bc
CS-KRa XIII, 14
parts (incomplete) and score
microfilm: US-SY

R0058 Salve regina
SATB, 2 vln, 3 tbn, vlne, bc
CS-KRa VI, 38
parts
microfilm: US-SY

R0059 Stella caeli extirpavit
SATTB, 2 vln, 2 vla, bc
CS-KRa II, 28 (1679)
score
microfilm: US-SY

R0060 Te Deum laudamus
SSATTB, 2 vln, 3 vla, 2 clar, vlne, bc
CS-KRa XI, 3
parts
microfilm: US-SY

RITTLINUS, Paul

R0061 Ad mensam dulcissimi convivii tui
ATB, bc
S-Uu 32:21 (Düben)
parts

ROSENMÜLLER, Johann (1619-1684)

COLLECTIONS

Andere Kern-Sprüche (1653)
RISM R2549 (parts)
DMA 2/709

Kern-Sprüche (1648)
RISM R2548 (parts)
DMA 1/189

ROSENMÜLLER, Johann (*continued*)

WORKS

R0062 **Ach, daß Gott erbarm**
T solo, SSATB, 2 vln, 2 clar, bc
D-B Mus. ms. 18899 (Erfurt) (1673)
parts
DMA 42//37

R0063 **Ach Herr, es ist nichts gesundes an meinem Leibe**
(Snyder IV/2)
SATB, 2 vln, 2 vla, bsn, bc
14th and 19th Sundays after Trinity
D-Dlb Mus. ms. 1739-E-508 (Grimma U
511/T 47)
parts
D-Dlb Mus. ms. 1739-E-509 (Grimma U
254/U 55)
parts
DMA 3/1276

R0064 **Ach weh mir, ich kann nun nicht mehr hoffen**
(Snyder IV/1)
See Ach, daß Gott erbarm

R0065 **Ad Dominum cum tribularer** (Snyder IV/3)
SATB, 2 vln, 2 vla, bsn, bc
D-B Mus. ms. 18881, no. 2 (Bokemeyer)
score
DMA 3/896

R0066 **Afferte Domino filii Dei** (Snyder IV/4)
SATB, 2 vln, bc
D-B Mus. ms. 18881, no. 1 (Bokemeyer)
score
DMA 3/897

R0067 **Alle Menschen müssen sterben** (Snyder III/1)
SSATB
Funeral of Paul von Henßberg
Leipzig, 1652
Reich 241, 242
DMA 70//134
Ed. F. Hamel, *Acht Begräbnisgesänge zu fünf
Stimmen* (Wolfenbüttel, 1930), no. 4

R0068 **Als der Tag der Pfingsten erfüllet** (Snyder IV/5)
SSATTBB, 2 vln/corn, 2 vla, 5 tbn, vlne, bc
Pentecost
D-B Mus. ms. 18898 (Erfurt) (1678)
score and parts
DMA 42//33

R0069 **Also hat Gott die Welt geliebet** (Snyder IV/6)
SSATB, 5 str, bc
Andere Kern-Sprüche, no. 19
Ed. Tunger, *Die Kantate* 64

R0070 **Beati omnes qui timent Dominum** (Snyder IV/7)
SATB, 2 vln, 2 vla, bsn, bc
D-B Mus. ms. 18881, no. 4 (Bokemeyer)
score
DMA 3/898

R0071 **Beatus vir qui timet** (Snyder II/2)
ATB, bc
D-B Mus. ms. 18887, no. 1 (Bokemeyer)
score
DMA 44//138
D-Dlb Mus. ms. 1739-E-522 (Grimma U
388/N 76)
parts

R0072 **Beatus vir qui timet** (Snyder IV/9)
SATB, 2 vln/corn, 2 vltta/tbn, bc
D-B Mus. ms. 18887, no. 3 (Bokemeyer)
score
DMA 44//138

R0073 **Beatus vir qui timet** (Snyder IV/10)
SATB, 2 vln, 2 vla, bsn, bc
D-B Mus. ms. 18887, no. 5 (Bokemeyer)
score
DMA 44//138

R0074 **Beatus vir qui timet** (Snyder IV/13)
SATB, SATB, 4 vln, vla, 4 vltta, bc
D-B Mus. ms. 18887, no. 6 (Bokemeyer)
score
DMA 44//138

R0075 **Beatus vir qui timet** (Snyder IV/8)
SATB, tromba, 2 vln, 2 vltta, bassono, bc
D-B Mus. ms. 18887, no. 2 (Bokemeyer)
score
DMA 44//138
GB-Lbl Mus. ms. R.M. 24.a.1, no. 1
score

R0076 **Beatus vir qui timet** (Snyder IV/11)
SATB, 2 vln, 3 vla, bsn, bc
D-B Mus. ms. 18887, no. 4 (Bokemeyer)
score
DMA 44//138
GB-Cfm 32-G-21, no. 4
score
DMA 77//82

R0077 **Beatus vir qui timet** (Snyder IV/12)
SSATB, 2 vln, 3 vla, bsn, bc
D-B Mus. ms. 18887, no. 4a (Bokemeyer)
score
DMA 44//138
D-Dlb Mus. ms. 1739-E-516 (Grimma U
246/U 46)

score
DMA 54//140, 3/1279
GB-Lbl Mus. ms. R.M. 24.a.1, no. 2
score
A 5-voice version of Snyder IV/11, S2
added in the Gloria

R0078 **Benedicam Dominum** (Snyder II/3)
SSB/TTB, bc
D-B Mus. ms. 18881, no. 3 (Bokemeyer)
score
DMA 3/899

R0079 **Bleibe bei uns, Herr Jesu Christ** (Snyder IV/14)
SSATB, 2 vln, 2 corn, 3 tbn, bc
D-B Mus. ms. 18884, no. 1 (Bokemeyer)
score
DMA 44//144

R0080 **Caeli enarrent gloriam Dei** (Snyder II/5)
ATB, 2 vln, bc
Kern-Sprüche, no. 12
S-Uu 85:60, fol. 1r-3r (Düben)
tablature

R0081 **Christum lieb haben** (Snyder II/4)
TTB, 2 vln, bc
Kern-Sprüche, no. 13

R0082 **Christus ist mein Leben** (Snyder IV/15)
SSATB, 2 vln, 2 vla, vlne, bc
2nd day of Christmas
D-B Mus. ms. 18906 (Erfurt) (1683); Mus.
ms. 18906/1 (Bokemeyer)
parts
DMA 37//146

R0083 **Classica tympana, tuba per auras** (Snyder IV/16)
SS soli, SATB, SATB, 2 vln, vla, 6 vltta,
bsn, bc
D-B Mus. ms. 18881, no. 5 (Bokemeyer)
score
DMA 3/900
GB-Lbl Mus. ms. R.M. 24.a.4, no. 2
score

R0084 **Confitebor tibi Domine**
SSATB, 2 vln, 3 vla, bassone, bsn, bc
D-Dlb Mus. ms. 1739-E-523 (Grimma U
392/N 78)
parts
Anonymous; attribution from library
catalogue

R0085 **Confitebor tibi Domine** (Snyder IV/17)
SATB, 2 vln, 2 vla, bc
D-B Mus. ms. 18886, no. 4 (Bokemeyer)

score
DMA 44//145

R0086 **Confitebor tibi Domine** (Snyder IV/18)
SATB, 2 vln, 2 vla, bc
D-B Mus. ms. 18886, no. 6 (Bokemeyer)
score
DMA 44//145
GB-Cfm Mus. ms. 32-G-21, no. 3
score
DMA 77//82

R0087 **Confitebor tibi Domine** (Snyder IV/19)
SATB, 2 vln, 2 vla, bsn, bc
D-B Mus. ms. 18886, no. 7 (Bokemeyer)
score
DMA 44//145

R0088 **Confitebor tibi Domine** (Snyder IV/20)
SATB, 2 vln, 4 vla, bc
D-B Mus. ms. 18886, no. 8 (Bokemeyer)
score
DMA 44//145

R0089 **Confitebor tibi Domine** (Snyder IV/21)
SATB, SATB, 2 corn, bc
D-B Mus. ms. 18886, no. 9 (Bokemeyer)
score
DMA 44//145

R0090 **Confitebor tibi Domine** (Snyder II/7)
ATB, bc
D-B Mus. ms. 18886, no. 3 (Bokemeyer)
score
DMA 44//145

R0091 **Confitebor tibi . . . quoniam** (Snyder IV/22)
SATB, 2 vln, bsn, bc
D-B Mus. ms. 18886, no. 5 (Bokemeyer)
score
DMA 44//145
Ed. F. Hamel, *Nagels Archiv* 59 (1930)

R0092 **Credo in unum Deum** (Snyder IV/23)
SATB, SATB, 2 vln, bc
GB-Lbl Mus. ms. R.M. 24.a.3, no. 6
score
DMA 54//72

R0093 **Danksaget dem Vater** (Snyder IV/24)
SSATB, 2 vln, bc
Kern-Sprüche, no. 20
Ed. Krüger, *Die Kantate* 21

R0094 **Daran ist erschienen die Liebe Gottes** (Snyder IV/25)
SSATB, 2 vln, bc
Kern-Sprüche, no. 19
Ed. Krüger, *Die Kantate* 24

ROSENMÜLLER, Johann (*continued*)

R0095 **Das Blut Jesu Christi** (Snyder IV/26)
SATB, bc
D-SWl Ms. 4598
score and parts
DMA 3/1784

R0096 **Das ist das ewige Leben** (Snyder II/11)
SAT, bc
Kern-Sprüche, no. 3
Ed. Krüger & Hellman, *Die Kantate* 23

R0097 **Das Wort ward Fleisch**
See Gloria in excelsis Deo (Snyder IV/44)

R0098 **De profundis clamavi ad te** (Snyder IV/27)
SATB, 2 vln, 2 vltta, bsn, bc
D-B Mus. ms. 18881, no. 9 (Bokemeyer)
score
DMA 3/903

R0099 **Delectare in Dominum** (Snyder IV/D1. Doubtful)
SATB, 2 vln, 3 vla, bc
GB-Cfm Mus. ms. 32-G-21, no.6
score
DMA 77//82

R0100 **Der Herr ist mein Hirte** (Snyder II/13)
ATB, 2 vln, 2 vltta, vla/bsn, bc
D-B Mus. ms. 18884, no. 2 (Bokemeyer)
score
DMA 44//144

R0101 **Der Name des Herren** (Snyder IV/28)
SSATB, 2 vln, bc
Andere Kern-Sprüche, no. 18

R0102 **Die Augen des Herren** (Snyder IV/29)
SATB, 2 vln, bc
Kern-Sprüche, no. 15
Ed. Krüger, *Die Kantate* 22

R0103 **Die Gnade unseres Herren Jesu Christi** (Snyder IV/30)
SATB, bc
Andere Kern-Sprüche, no. 5
Ed. Tunger, *Die Motette* 128

R0104 **Dies irae** (Snyder IV/31)
SATB, 2 vln, 3 vla, bsn, bc
D-B Mus. ms. 18881, no. 8 (Bokemeyer)
score
DMA 3/904

R0105 **Dilexit quoniam exaudiet Dominus** (Snyder IV/32)
SATB, SATB, 2 vln, vla, 2 vltta, 2 corn, 3 tbn, bc
D-B Mus. ms. 18881, no. 10 (Bokemeyer)
score
DMA 3/905
GB-Lbl Mus. ms. R.M. 24.a.4, no. 1
score

R0106 **Dixit Dominus** (Snyder IV/33)
SATB, 2 vln, 2 vla, bsn, bc
D-B Mus. ms. 18888, no. 1 (Bokemeyer)
score
DMA 44//137

R0107 **Dixit Dominus** (Snyder IV/34)
SATB, 3 vln, vla, 2 vltta, tbtta, bc
D-B Mus. ms. 18888, no. 2 (Bokemeyer)
score
DMA 44//137

R0108 **Dixit Dominus** (Snyder IV/35)
SATB, 2 vln, vla, 2 vltta, bc
D-B Mus. ms. 18888, no. 3 (Bokemeyer)
score
DMA 44//137

R0109 **Dixit Dominus** (Snyder IV/36)
SATB, SATB, 2 vln, 2 vla, 2 corn, 3 tbn, bsn, bc
D-B Mus. ms. 18888, no. 4 (Bokemeyer)
score
DMA 44//137

R0110 **Domine probasti me** (Snyder IV/37)
SATB, SATB, vln, corn, bc
D-B Mus. ms. 18881, no. 11 (Bokemeyer)
score
DMA 3/906
GB-Lbl Mus. ms. R.M. 24.a.5, no. 4
score

R0111 **Ego te laudo** (Snyder II/15)
SSB, bc
D-B Mus. ms. 18881, no. 13 (Bokemeyer)
score
DMA 3/907

R0112 **Ein Tag in deinen Vorhöfen** (Snyder II/16)
STB, 2 vln, bc
Kern-Sprüche, no. 10
Ed. Krüger, *Die Kantate* 109

R0113 **Entsetze dich, Natur** (Snyder IV/38)
SSATTB, 2 vln, 2 corn, 3 tbn, bc
Christmas Day
D-B Mus. ms. 18902 (Erfurt) (1677)
parts
DMA 42//41

R0114 **Es gingen zwei Menschen** (Snyder IV/39)
TTB soli, SSATB, 2 vln, 2 vla, bc
11th Sunday after Trinity
D-B Mus. ms. 18907 (Erfurt)
score and parts
DMA 37//145

R0115 **Fürchte dich nicht, denn ich hab dich erlöst**
(Snyder IV/40)
SSATB, 2 vln, 2 vla, bc
D-B Mus. ms. 18884, no. 3 (Bokemeyer)
score
DMA 44//144
S-Uu 66:1 (Düben)
parts
DMA 23//113

R0116 **Gelobet sei der Herr** (Snyder IV/41)
SSATB, 2 vln, 2 vla, vlne, bc
12th Sunday after Trinity
D-B Mus. ms. 18897 (Erfurt) (1678)
score and parts
DMA 42//32

R0117 **Gloria in excelsis Deo** (Snyder IV/42)
SATB, 2 vln, 2 vltta/tbn, tromba, bsn, bc
D-B Mus. ms. 18880, no. 4 (Bokemeyer)
score
DMA 44//142

R0118 **Gloria in excelsis Deo** (Snyder IV/43)
SATB, SATB, 2 vln, vltta, 2 corn, bc
D-B Mus. ms. 18880, no. 6 (Bokemeyer)
score
DMA 44//142

R0119 **Gloria in excelsis Deo/Das Wort ward Fleisch**
(Snyder IV/44)
SSATTB, 2 vln, 2 corn, 4 tbn, bc
Christmas Day
D-B Mus. ms. 18880, no. 3 (Bokemeyer)
score
DMA 44//142
D-B Mus. ms. 18901 (Erfurt) (1683)
parts
DMA 42//39

R0120 **Herr mein Gott, ich danke dir** (Snyder II/19)
TTB, 2 vln, bc
Andere Kern-Sprüche, no. 12
Ed. Tunger, *Die Kantate* 164

R0121 **Herr mein Gott, wende dich** (Snyder IV/45)
SATB, 2 vln, bc
D-Dlb Mus. ms. 1739-E-501 (Grimma U
577/L 21)

parts
DMA 34//34

R0122 **Ich bin das Brot des Lebens** (Snyder II/20)
ATB, 2 vln, bc
Andere Kern-Sprüche, no. 10
Ed. Tunger, *Die Kantate* 163

R0123 **Ich hielte mich nicht dafür** (Snyder IV/46)
SATB, bc
Andere Kern-Sprüche, no. 6
Ed. Tunger, *Die Motette* 184

R0124 **In hac misera valle** (Snyder II/22)
SSB, bc
source lost
Ed. M. Seiffert, *Organum* I/24

R0125 **In te Domine speravi** (Snyder IV/47)
SSTT, 2 vln, bc
Kern-Sprüche, no. 16

R0126 **In te Domine speravi** (Snyder IV/48)
SATB, SATB, 2 vln, vla, vltta, 2 corn, 3
tbn, bc
D-B Mus. ms. 18889, no. 7 (Bokemeyer)
score
DMA 59//53

R0127 **Jauchzet dem Herrn, alle Welt** (Snyder IV/49)
ATB soli, SSATB, 2 vln, bombard,
bsn/vlne, bc
Christmas Day
D-B Mus. ms. 18903 (Erfurt)
parts
DMA 32//38

R0128 **Jauchzet dem Herrn, denn uns ist ein Kind
geboren** (Snyder IV/50)
SSATB, 2 vln, 2 vla, bc
Christmas Day
D-B Mus. ms. 18900 (Erfurt)
parts
DMA 42//40

R0129 **Jesu mi amor, spes dulcedo** (Snyder II/25)
SSS, bc
D-B Mus. ms. 18882, no. 13 (Bokemeyer)
score
DMA 2/1799
D-B Mus. ms. 18908/1
score

R0130 **Jube Domine** (Snyder IV/51)
SATB, SATB, 2 vln, bc
D-B Mus. ms. 18882, no. 14 (Bokemeyer)
score
DMA 2/1800

ROSENMÜLLER, Johann (*continued*)

  D-Bds Mus. ms. 30309, no. 1
   score
  GB-Lbl Mus. ms. R.M. 24.a.3, no. 1
   score
  US-Bp M222.48, no. 1
   score

R0131 **Kündlich groß ist das gottseelige Geheimnis**
  (Snyder II/26)
  ATB, bc
  Andere Kern-Sprüche, no. 4
  Ed. Hellman, *Die Motette* 89 (SAB)
  Ed. Tunger, *Die Motette* 185 (ATB, TTB)

R0132 **Laetatus sum in his** (Snyder II/27)
  STB, 2 vln, vla, bc
  D-B Mus. ms. 18882, no. 1 (Bokemeyer)
   score
   DMA 2/1801

R0133 **Laetatus sum in his** (Snyder IV/52)
  SATB, SATB, 2 vln, 2 vla, 2 corn, 3 tbn,
   bsn, bc
  D-B Mus. ms. 18882, no. 2 (Bokemeyer)
   score
   DMA 2/1802

R0134 **Lauda Jerusalem Dominum** (Snyder IV/53)
  SATB, 2 vln, 3 vla, bc
  S-Uu 86:47 (Düben)
   tablature
   DMA 1/766
  S-Uu 66:2, fol. 12v-18r
   parts
  GB-Lbl Mus. ms. R.M. 24.a.3, no. 2
   score

R0135 **Lauda Jerusalem Dominum** (Snyder IV/54)
  SATB, SATB, 2 vln, 2 vla, 2 corn, clar, 3
   tbn, bsn, bc
  D-Dlb Mus. ms. 1739-E-519 (Grimma U
   250/U 50) (1704)
   tablature and parts
   DMA 3/1285
  GB-Lbl Mus. ms. R.M. 24.a.3, no. 4
   score

R0136 **Lauda Sion** (Snyder II/28)
  ATB, 2 vln, bc
  D-B Mus. ms. 18882, no. 3 (Bokemeyer)
   score
   DMA 2/1803

R0137 **Laudate Dominum, omnes gentes** (Snyder IV/56)
  SATB, SATB, 2 vln, vla, 2 vltta, 2 corn, 3
   tbn, bc

  D-B Mus. ms. 18882, no. 4 (Bokemeyer)
   score
   DMA 2/1804

R0138 **Laudate Dominum, omnes gentes** (Snyder
  IV/55)
  SSATTB, 2 vln, 3 vla, tromba, bc
  D-B Mus. ms. 18882, no. 5 (Bokemeyer)
   score
   DMA 2/1805

R0139 **Laudate, pueri, Dominum** (Snyder II/29)
  SAB, 2 vln, 3 vla, 2 corn, bsn, bc
  D-B Mus. ms. 18890, no. 1 (Bokemeyer)
   score
   DMA 38//74

R0140 **Laudate, pueri, Dominum** (Snyder II/30)
  SSB, 2 vln, 2 vltta, corn, tbtta/corn, bc
  D-B Mus. ms. 18890, no. 2 (Bokemeyer)
   score
   DMA 38//74

R0141 **Laudate, pueri, Dominum** (Snyder IV/57)
  SATB, 2 vln, 2 vltta, bsn, bc
  D-B Mus. ms. 18890, no. 3 (Bokemeyer)
   score
   DMA 38//74

R0142 **Laudate, pueri, Dominum** (Snyder IV/58)
  SATB, 2 vln, 3 vla, bc
  D-B Mus. ms. 18890, no. 4
   score
   DMA 38//74
  GB-Lbl Mus. ms. R.M. 24.a.1, no. 3
   score
  GB-Cfm Mus. ms. 32-G-21, no. 7
   score
   DMA 77//82

R0143 **Laudate, pueri, Dominum** (Snyder IV/59)
  SSATB, 4 vla, bsn, bc
  D-B Mus. ms. 18890, no. 5 (Bokemeyer)
   score
   DMA 38//74

R0144 **Laudate, pueri, Dominum** (Snyder IV/60)
  SSATB, 2 vln, vla, 2 vltta, bc
  D-B Mus. ms. 18890, no. 6 (Bokemeyer)
   score
   DMA 38//74

R0145 **Laudate, pueri, Dominum** (Snyder IV/61)
  SAT, SAT, 2 vln, 2 vla, bc
  D-B Mus. ms. 18890, no. 7 (Bokemeyer)
   score
   DMA 38//74

R0146 **Laudate, pueri, Dominum** (Snyder IV/61)
SSAATTBB, 2 vln, 2 vla, bsn, bc
D-B 18890, no. 8
score
DMA 38//74
GB-Lbl Mus. ms. R.M. 24.a.5, no. 2
score

R0147 **Laudate, pueri, Dominum** (Snyder IV/62)
SATB, SATB, 2 vln, 2 vltta, tbtta, violoncino,
bc
D-B Mus. ms. 18890, no. 9 (Bokemeyer)
score
DMA 38//74

R0148 **Laudate, pueri, Dominum** (Snyder IV/63)
SSSSAATTBB, 2 vln, 2 vltta bassono, 2
corn, 3 tbn, tromba, bc
D-B Mus. ms. 18890, no. 10 (Bokemeyer)
score
DMA 38//74
GB-Lbl Mus. ms. R.M. 24.a.3, no. 3
score

R0149 **Levavi oculos** (Snyder IV/64)
SATB, SATB, 2 vln, vla, 2 vltta, 2 corn, 3
tbn, bc
D-B Mus. ms. 18882, no. 6 (Bokemeyer)
score
DMA 2/1806

R0150 **Lobt Gott, lobt alle Gott** (Snyder IV/D2. Doubtful)
SATB, 2 vln, 2 clar, 2 tbn, bc
D-B Mus. ms. 18892 (Erfurt) (1680)
score and parts
DMA 42//27

R0151 **Magnificat** (Snyder IV/65)
SSATB, 2 vln, 3 vla, bc
GB-Lbl Mus. ms. R.M. 24.a.5, no. 1
score
DMA 54//73

R0152 **Magnificat** (Snyder IV/66)
SATB, SATB, 2 vln, vla, 2 vltta, 2 corn, 3
tbn, bc
D-B Mus. ms. 18882, no. 15 (Bokemeyer)
score
DMA 2/1807

R0153 **Mater Jerusalem** (Snyder II/32)
ATB, bc
D-B Mus. ms. 18882, no. 16 (Bokemeyer)
score
DMA 2/1808

R0154 **Mein Gott, ich danke dir** (Snyder IV/67)
TT soli, SSATB, 2 vln, vlne, bc
D-B Mus. ms. 18905 (Erfurt) (1681)
score and parts
DMA 37//148

R0155 **Meine Seele harret nur auf Gott** (Snyder II/33)
ATB, 2 vln, bc
Kern-Sprüche, no. 11
Ed. Krüger, *Die Kantate* 40

R0156 **Meine Sünde betrüben mich** (Snyder IV/D3.
Doubtful)
SSATTB, 3 vln, 2 vla, vlne, bc
D-B Mus. ms. 18884, no. 5 (Bokemeyer)
score
DMA 44//144

R0157 **Meines Lebens letzte Zeit** (Snyder III/2)
SSATB
Funeral of Klara Becker
Leipzig, 1654
Reich 249 (score)
DMA 70//136
Ed. F. Hamel, *Acht Begräbnisgesänge zu fünf
Stimmen* (Wolfenbüttel, 1930), no. 8

R0158 **Miserere mei, Deus** (Snyder II/34)
ATB, 2 vln, bc
D-Dlb Mus. ms. 1739-E-520 (Grimma U
253/U 54)
score
DMA 3/1286

R0159 **Missa** (Snyder IV/68)
SATB
source lost
Ed. F. Commer, *Musica sacra*, vol. 24
(1863), pp. 19-39

R0160 **Missa (Kyrie, Gloria, Credo)** (Snyder IV/69)
SATB, bc
D-B Mus. ms. 18880, no. 6 (Bokemeyer)
score and parts
DMA 44//142
D-Bds Mus. ms. 30308, no. 2 (1660)
score

R0161 **Missa brevis** (Snyder IV/70)
SATB, SATB, 2 vln, 2 vla, 2 corn, tbtta, 3
tbn, bsn, bc
D-B Mus. ms. 18880, nos. 1-2 (Bokemeyer)
score
DMA 44//142

R0162 **Nihil novum sub sole** (Snyder IV/71)
SSATB, 2 vln/corn, 3 tbn/vla, bc

ROSENMÜLLER, Johann (*continued*)

    D-B Mus. ms. 18882, no. 7 (Bokemeyer)
        score
        DMA 2/1809
    D-Dlb Mus. ms. 1739-E-511 (Grimma U
        242/U 42)
        parts
        DMA 3/1287

R0163   **Nisi Dominus aedificaverit** (Snyder IV/73)
    SATB, SATB, 2 vln, 2 vla, bc
    D-B Mus. ms. 18889, no. 11 (Bokemeyer)
        score
        DMA 59//53, 77//82

R0164   **Nisi Dominus aedificaverit** (Snyder II/35)
    ATB, 2 vln, bc
    D-B Mus. ms. 18889, no. 9 (Bokemeyer)
        score
        DMA 59//53
    D-Dlb Mus. ms. 1739-E-512 (Grimma U
        243/U 43)
        parts
        DMA 3/1288

R0165   **Nisi Dominus aedificaverit** (Snyder IV/72)
    SATB, 2 vln, 3 vla, bc
    D-B Mus. ms. 18889, no. 10 (Bokemeyer)
        score
        DMA 59//53
    D-Dlb Mus. ms. 1739-E-513 (Grimma U
        244/U 44)
        score and parts
        DMA 3/1289
    GB-Cfm 32-G-21, no. 5
        score
        DMA 77//82
    GB-Ob MS. Mus. Sch. C. 31, fols. 28-33
        score and parts

R0166   **Nun gibst du, Gott, einen gnädigen Regen**
    (Snyder IV/75)
    SSTTBB, 2 vln, 2 vla, 2 corn, 5 tbn,
        spinett/theorbo, vlne, bsn, bc
    D-B Mus. ms. 18893 (Erfurt)
        parts
        DMA 42//28

R0167   **Nun Gottlob, es ist vollbracht** (Snyder III/3)
    SSATB
    Funeral of Magdalena von der Burgk
    Leipzig, 1652
        Reich 240 (score)
        DMA 70//193

    Ed. F. Hamel, *Acht Begräbnisgesänge zu fünf
    Stimmen* (Wolfenbüttel, 1930), no. 3

R0168   **Nunc dimittis** (Snyder IV/74)
    SATB, 2 vln, 2 vla, bsn, bc
    D-B Mus. ms. 18882, no. 17 (Bokemeyer)
        score
        DMA 2/1810

R0169   **Nur Kreuz und Not** (Snyder III/4)
    SSATB
    Funeral of Friedrich Conradt
    Leipzig, 1654
        Reich 247 (score)
        DMA 70//136
    Ed. F. Hamel, *Acht Begräbnisgesänge zu fünf
    Stimmen* (Wolfenbüttel, 1930), no. 7

R0170   **O Domine Jesu Christe, adoro te** (Snyder II/38)
    ATB, bc
    Kern-Sprüche, no. 4

R0171   **O lux beata Trinitas** (Snyder IV/76)
    SATB, 2 vln, 3 vla, vlne, bc
    D-B Mus. ms. 18908/5
        parts
        DMA 37//142

R0172   **O nomen Jesu, nomen dulce** (Snyder IV/77)
    SATB, bc
    Kern-Sprüche, no. 8

R0173   **O welche eine Tiefe des Reichtums** (Snyder IV/78)
    SATB, 5 vla, bc
    D-B Mus. ms. 18884, no. 6 (Bokemeyer)
        score
        DMA 44//144

R0174   **Puer natus est nobis** (Snyder IV/79)
    SATB, 2 vln, 2 vla, clar, corn, bc
    D-Dlb Mus. ms. 1739-E-521 (Grimma U
        255/U 56)
        parts
        DMA 3/1290

R0175   **Qui habitat in adjutorio altissimi** (Snyder IV/80)
    SATB, SATB, 2 vln, vla, 2 vltta, bc
    D-B Mus. ms. 18882, no. 8 (Bokemeyer)
        score
        DMA 2/1813

R0176   **Resonent organa** (Snyder IV/D4. Doubtful)
    SSATB, 2 vln, 2 vla, bsn, bc
    D-B Mus. ms. 18908/3 (Bokemeyer)
        parts
        DMA 37//143

R0177 **Salve mi, Jesus, pater misericordiae** (Snyder II/42)
SAB, 2 vln, 2 vltta, bc
D-B Mus. ms. 18882, no. 9 (Bokemeyer)
score
DMA 2/1815

R0178 **Seine Jünger kamen** (Snyder IV/81)
SSATB, 2 vln, 2 vla, 2 corn, 3 tbn, vlne, bc
D-Dlb Mus. ms. 1739-E-507 (Grimma U 512/T 46)
parts
DMA 61//154

R0179 **Selig sind die Augen** (Snyder IV/82)
TB, SSATB, 3 gamba, bc
13th Sunday after Trinity
D-B Mus. ms. 18894 (Erfurt) (1680)
score and parts
DMA 42//29

R0180 **Siehe an die Werke Gottes** (Snyder IV/83)
SSATB, 2 vln, 3 tbn, bc
Andere Kern-Sprüche, no. 20
D-B Mus. ms. 18891 (Erfurt) (1679)
parts
DMA 42//26

R0181 **Siehe des Herren Auge** (Snyder II/43)
STB, 2 vln, bc
Andere Kern-Sprüche, no. 9
Ed. Tunger, *Die Kantate* 162

R0182 **Siehe, eine Jungfrau ist schwanger** (Snyder IV/84)
SSATTB, 2 vln, 2 vla, 4 tbn, bc
Annunciation
D-Dlb Mus. ms. 1739-E-510 (Grimma U 251/U 51)
score and parts
DMA 3/1291

R0183 **So spricht der Herr: Beschicke dein Haus** (Snyder IV/85)
SATB, 2 vln, 2 vltta, bc
D-B Mus. ms. 18884, no. 9 (Bokemeyer)
score
DMA 44//144

R0184 **Te Deum laudamus** (Snyder IV/86)
SATB, 2 vln, 2 vla, clar, bsn, bc
D-B Mus. ms. 18882, no. 12 (Bokemeyer)
score
DMA 2/1817

R0185 **Tret her, die ihr voll Jammer seid** (Snyder III/5)
SSATB
Funeral of Regina Bose
Leipzig, 1654
Reich 244, 246
Ed. F. Hamel, *Acht Begräbnisgesänge zu fünf Stimmen* (Wolfenbüttel, 1930), no. 5

R0186 **Unser Trübsal, die zeitlich und leichte ist** (Snyder IV/87)
SATB, 2 vln, 2 vla, bsn, bc
D-B Mus. ms. 18884, no. 7 (Bokemeyer)
score
DMA 44//144

R0187 **Vater, ich habe gesündigt** (Snyder IV/88)
ATTB, 2 vln, vlne, bc
11th Sunday after Trinity
D-Dlb Mus. ms. 1739-E-503 (Grimma U 595/T 13) (1669)
parts
DMA 3/1292
D-Dlb Mus. Löb 53
score

R0188 **Wahrlich, wahrlich, ich sage euch** (Snyder IV/89)
SATB, 2 vln, bc
Andere Kern-Sprüche, no. 16
Ed. Tunger, *Die Kantate* 74

R0189 **Was hat der Mensch auf dieser Erden** (Snyder III/6)
SSATB
Funeral of Bartholomäus Hahn
Leipzig, 1650
Reich 237 (score)
DMA 34//33
Ed. F. Hamel, *Acht Begräbnisgesänge zu fünf Stimmen* (Wolfenbüttel, 1930), no. 2

R0190 **Was ist es doch** (Snyder III/7)
SSATB
Funeral of Polycarp Wirth
Leipzig, 1654
Reich 248 (score)
DMA 70//136
Ed. F. Hamel, *Acht Begräbnisgesänge zu fünf Stimmen* (Wolfenbüttel, 1930), no. 6

R0191 **Was stehet ihr hier müssig** (Snyder IV/90)
SATB, 2 vln, 2 vla, vlne, bc
Septuagesima
D-B Mus. ms. 18904 (Erfurt) (1679)
parts
DMA 37//147

R0192 **Weil wir wissen, daß der Mensch** (Snyder II/45)
ATB, 2 vln, bc
Andere Kern-Sprüche, no. 11
Ed. Tunger, *Die Kantate* 161

ROSENMÜLLER, Johann (*continued*)

R0193   **Welt ade, ich bin dein müde** (Snyder III/8)
SSATB
Funerals of Abraham Teller and of Johanna
   Elisabeth Teller
Leipzig, 1652 (composed 1649)
   Reich 243
   DMA 34//33
Ed. F. Hamel, *Acht Begräbnisgesänge zu fünf
   Stimmen* (Wolfenbüttel, 1930), no. 1
Ed. Straube, *Ausgewählte Gesänge des
   Thomanerchores zu Leipzig* II/19
   (Breitkopf & Härtel, 1924)
Ed. Doblinger
Vopelius Gesangbuch (1682)
Ed. A. Becker, *Musica sacra* (Bote & Bock),
   vol. 15, pp. 94-95
Das Chorblatt 143

R0194   **Wenn ich zu dir rufe** (Snyder IV/91)
SATB, 2 vln, 2 vla, bc
D-B Mus. ms. 18896 (Erfurt) (1677)
   parts
   DMA 42//31

R0195   **Wie lieblich sind deine Wohnungen** (Snyder II/46)
SSTTB, 2 vln, 2 vla, 2 cornettino, 3 tbn, bc
D-Dlb Mus. ms. 1739-E-502 (Grimma U
   519/T 33)
   parts
   DMA 3/1293

R0196   **Wo wollen wir einkehren**
See under Weckmann

ROSIER, Carl (1640-1725)

COLLECTIONS

In fletu solatium, cantiones sacrae (1667)
   RISM R2651 (parts)

Motetta, cantiones sacrae, op. 2 (1668)
   RISM R2652 (parts)
   manuscript score, with contents slightly
      rearranged: F-Pn Vm¹ 1002

WORKS

R0197   **Eamus properemus**
SATB, 2 vln, bsn, bc
In fletu solatium, no. 7

R0198   **Florete flores**
SAB, bc
Motetta, no. 4

F-Pn Vm¹ 1002, no. 4
   score

R0199   **Heu quare suspiras**
SAB, 2 vln, bsn, bc
In fletu solatium, no. 2

R0200   **In valle lacrymarum**
ATB, vln, 2 vla, bsn, bc
D-B Mus. ms. 30260, no. 19 (Bokemeyer)
   score
   DMA 2/904
F-Pn Vm¹ 1217
   score

R0201   **Io triumphe**
STB, 2 vln, bsn, bc
In fletu solatium, no. 3
Ed. Niemöller, pp. 218-29

R0202   **Missa à capella**
SATB, 2 vln, vla, bsn, bc
D-KNmi
   parts

R0203   **Missa (A)**
SSATB, 2 vln, vla, bsn, bc
D-KNmi
   parts

R0204   **Missa à 5 (c)**
SSATB, 2 vln, vla, bsn, bc
D-Bds Mus. ms. autogr. Ch. Rosier 7
   (1715)
   parts
D-KNmi
   parts

R0205   **Missa à 9 (G)**
SSATB, 2 vln, vla, bsn, bc
D-Bds Mus. ms. autogr. Ch. Rosier 3
   parts
D-KNmi
   parts

R0206   **Missa à 9 (b)**
SSATB, 2 vln, vla, bsn, bc
D-Bds Mus. ms. autogr. Ch. Rosier 5
   (1706)
   parts
D-KNmi
   parts

R0207   **Missa (a)**
SSATB, 2 vln, vla, bsn, bc
D-KNmi (1721)
   parts

R0208   **Missa (B-flat)**
SSATB, 2 vln, 2 vla, bc

D-KNmi
parts

R0209 **Missa (B-flat)**
SSATB, 2 vln, vla, bsn, bc
D-Bds Mus. ms. autogr. Ch. Rosier 6
parts
D-KNmi
parts

R0210 **Missa (F)**
SATB, 2 vln, 2 vla, bsn, bc
D-KNmi
parts

R0211 **Missa brevis**
SATB, 2 vln, vla, bsn, bc
D-Bds Mus. ms. autogr. Ch. Rosier 4
(1715)
parts
D-KNmi
parts
Ed. Niemöller (1957), pp. 230-36 (Kyrie only)

R0212 **Missa nativitatis**
SATB, 2 vln, vla, bsn, bc
D-KNmi (1711)
parts

R0213 **O dulcissime Jesu**
SSB, bc
Motetta, no. 2
F-Pn Vm^1 1002, no. 2
score

R0214 **O Maria spes**
STB, bc
Motetta, no. 5
F-Pn Vm^1 1002, no. 5
score

R0215 **O panis mellifluus**
SSB, vc, bc
D-Bds Mus. ms. autogr. Ch. Rosier 2
(1712)
parts

R0216 **Pater superni luminis**
STB, 2 vln, bsn, bc
In fletu solatium, no. 6

R0217 **Regina caeli**
S/TAB, bc
Motetta, no. 10
F-Pn Vm^1 1002, no. 9
score

R0218 **Salve regina**
SAT, bc
Motetta, no. 8

F-Pn Vm^1 1002, no. 12
score

R0219 **Salve regina**
SAT, bc
Motetta, no. 9
F-Pn Vm^1 1002, no. 11
score

R0220 **Sancta et immaculata**
SST, 2 vln, bsn, bc
In fletu solatium, no. 5

R0221 **Transfige dulcissime Domine**
SSB, bc
Motetta, no. 1
F-Pn Vm^1 1002, no. 1
score

R0222 **Veni Jesu et mirare**
SATB, 2 vln, vla, bc
Feast of Saint Theresa
D-KNmi

R0223 **Venite ad me, omnes**
STB, bc
Motetta, no. 3
F-Pn Vm^1 1002, no. 3
score

R0224 **Victimae paschali**
SAT, 2 vln, bsn, bc
In fletu solatium, no. 4

ROTH, Johann

R0225 **Unglück und lauter Schmerzen**
SATB
Funeral of Christian von Bülow
Leipzig, 1661
Reich 259

ROTHE, Wolf Ernst

R0226 **Der Kampf ist tot und ausgelitten**
SSATB
Funeral of Maria Krause
Weimar, 1682
RISM R2794, Reich 422 (score)
DMA 70//140
DdT 46/47, p. xii

R0227 **Nun wir gerecht sind worden**
SATB
Funeral of Regina Sophia Stieler
Jena, 1677
RISM R2793, Reich 166

RUBERT, Johann Martin (1614-1680)

COLLECTION

> *Musicalische Seelen-Erquickung* (1664)
> RISM R3031 (parts)

WORKS

R0228 **Gott der Herr**
SATB, 2 vln, 2 vla, vlne, bc
Musicalische Seelen-Erquickung, no. 4

R0229 **Herr, stärke mich**
SSB, 2 vln, bc
Musicalische Seelen-Erquickung, no. 10

R0230 **Ich weiß, mein Gott**
SSB, 2 vln, 2 vla, bc
Musicalische Seelen-Erquickung, no. 7

R0231 **Laudate Dominum**
SST, 2 vln, 2 vla, vlne, bc
Musicalische Seelen-Erquickung, no. 1

R0232 **Merk auf, mein Herz**
SSS, 2 vln, corn, bsn, bc
Musicalische Seelen-Erquickung, no. 5

R0233 **Wie Jonas der Prophet sich ließ ins Meer**
SSB, 2 vln, 2 vla, corn, bsn, bc
Musicalische Seelen-Erquickung, no. 9

S

SAILER, Fr.

S0001   **Litania**
     4 vv, 2 vln, 2 ob, 2 clar, timp, vlne, bc
     A-KR Ms. Kasten E, Fasc. 47, no. 119
     parts
     D-Mf 1211

SAILER (Seyler), Leonhard (1656-1696)

COLLECTION

     Cantiones sacrae (1696)
     RISM S316 (parts)

WORKS

S0002   **Ad mensam supernum**
     ATB, 2 vln, bc
     Maundy Thursday
     Cantiones sacrae, no. 8

S0003   **Ad sonos, ad cantus**
     SAB, 2 vln, bc
     Cantiones sacrae, no. 4

S0004   **Ave Jesu Christe**
     SSB, 2 vln, bc
     Cantiones sacrae, no. 2

S0005   **Das neugeborne Kindelein**
     ATB, 2 vln, bc
     New Year's Day
     Cantiones sacrae, no. 13

S0006   **Die Not mich zwingt**
     SATB, 2 vln, 2 vla, vlne, bc
     2nd Sunday of Lent

     D-F Ms. Ff. Mus. 456
     parts

S0007   **Durum cor**
     ATB, 2 vln, bc
     Cantiones sacrae, no. 10

S0008   **Eamus properemus**
     SATB, 2 vln, 2 vla, bc
     Epiphany
     Cantiones sacrae, no. 5

S0009   **Jesu, liebster Schatz der Frommen**
     SATB, 2 vln, 2 vla, bc
     D-Bds Mus. ms. 30268, no. 1 (Bokemeyer)
     score

S0010   **Nolite timere**
     ATB, 2 vln, bc
     Cantiones sacrae, no. 12

S0011   **O anima mea**
     ATB, 2 vln, vla, bc
     Cantiones sacrae, no. 7

S0012   **O caeli beati**
     ATB, 2 vln, bc
     Easter Sunday
     Cantiones sacrae, no. 9

S0013   **Siehe, meine Freundin, du bist schön**
     SATB, 2 vln, 3 vla, bsn, bc
     D-F Ms. Ff. Mus. 457
     parts

S0014   **Valete**
     ATB, 2 vln, bc
     Cantiones sacrae, no. 11

SANCES, Giovanni Felice (ca. 1600-1679)

Note: The following list comprises Sances's extant works in manuscript dating from after 1649, when he began working for the Viennese court. Works published in Venice are omitted.

S0015   **Audite sodales**
         SATB, 2 vln, 3 vla, vlne, bc
         Feast of a Confessor
         CS-KRa II, 26 (1676)
            parts
            microfilm: US-SY

S0016   **Beati pacifici**
         SATB, vla, vltta, vc, corn, 2 tbn, vlne,
            bsn, bc
         A-Wn Ms. 18999, no. 4
            parts

S0017   **Beatus vir**
         SATB, SATB, vlne, bc
         CS-KRa III, 37, no. 3
            parts
            microfilm: US-SY

S0018   **Beatus vir**
         SATB, 2 vln, 3 vla, vlne, bc
         CS-KRa III, 93, no. 3 (1674)
            parts
            microfilm: US-SY

S0019   **Cantate Domino**
         SATB, 2 vla, vltta, vc, vlne, bc
         4th Sunday after Easter
         A-Wn Ms. H.K. 649
            parts

S0020   **Clamaverunt ad te Domine**
         SATB, vln, 2 vla, vltta, vc, vlne, bc
         Feast of Saints Philip and Jacob
         A-Wn Ms. H.K. 694
            parts

S0021   **Conceptio est hodie Sanctae Mariae**
         See Nativitas est hodie Sanctae Mariae

S0022   **Confitebor pleno coro**
         SSAATTBB, 2 vla, bass vla, 4 vltta, vlne, bc
         CS-KRa III, 32
            parts
            microfilm: US-SY

S0023   **Confitebor tibi Domine**
         SATB, SATB, vlne, bc
         CS-KRa III, 37, no. 2
            parts
            microfilm: US-SY

S0024   **Confitebor tibi Domine**
         SATB, 2 vln, 3 vla, vlne, bc

CS-KRa III, 93, no. 2 (1674)
            parts
            microfilm: US-SY

S0025   **Confitebor tibi Domine**
         SATB, SATB
         5th Sunday of Lent
         A-Wn Ms. 19002
            parts

S0026   **Corde et animo Christo canamus**
         SATB, 2 vla, corn, 2 tbn, bsn, vc, vlne, bc
         Feast of the Conception or Christmas
         A-Wn Ms. 18997, no. 4
            parts

S0027   **Credidi**
         SATB, SATB, vlne, bc
         CS-KRa III, 37, no. 11
            parts
            microfilm: US-SY

S0028   **Cum complerentur dies pentecostes**
         SSATTB, 2 vln, 3 vla, 2 corn, 4 tbn, vlne, bc
         Pentecost
         CS-KRa II, 32
            parts (4 tbn missing)
            microfilm: US-SY

S0029   **Cum jucunditate conceptionem/Nativitatem**
         SATB, 2 vla, corn, 2 tbn, bsn, vc, vlne, bc
         Feast of the Conception or Christmas
         A-Wn Ms. 18997, no. 5
            parts

S0030   **Custodi me Domine**
         SATB, SATB
         Tuesday of Holy Week or Holy Saturday
         A-Wn Ms. 15732
            score
         A-Wn Ms. 19000
            parts

S0031   **De ore prudentis**
         SSATB, 2 vln, 2 vla, 2 clar, 3 tbn, vlne,
            bsn, bc
         Feast of a Confessor
         CS-KRa II, 58 (1676)
            parts
            microfilm: US-SY

S0032   **De profundis**
         SATB, SATB, vlne, bc
         CS-KRa III, 37, no. 15
            parts
            microfilm: US-SY

S0033 **Deus in adjutorium**
SATB, vltta/vln, vln, vla, vc, vlne, bc
11th Sunday after Trinity
A-Wn Ms. H.K. 670
parts

S0034 **Deus in loco sancto**
SATB, 2 vla, vltta, vc, vlne, bc
10th Sunday after Trinity
A-Wn Ms. H.K. 669
parts

S0035 **Dextera Domini**
SATB, SATB
Good Friday
A-Wn Ms. 15777; Ms. 17029; Ms. SA.67.G.74
score
A-Wn Ms. 19001; Ms. 19004
parts

S0036 **Dies irae**
SSATTB, 5 vla, 2 vltta, 4 tbn, vlne, bc
Funeral of Ferdinand III
A-KR Ser. E, Fasc. 2, no. 67(2) (1654)
parts (vltta I missing)

S0037 **Dixit Dominus**
SATB, SATB, vlne, bc
CS-KRa III, 37, no. 1
parts
microfilm: US-SY

S0038 **Dixit Dominus**
SATB, 2 vln, 3 vla, vlne, bc
CS-KRa III, 93, no. 1 (1674)
parts
microfilm: US-SY

S0039 **Domine Jesu Christe rex gloriae**
SSATTB, 4 vla, 4 tbn, vlne, bc
Requiem
A-KR Ser. E, Fasc. 2, no. 67(3)
parts

S0040 **Domine ne longe facias**
SATB, 2 vla, vltta, vc, vlne, bc
Palm Sunday
A-Wn Ms. H.K. 641
parts

S0041 **Domine probasti**
SATB, SATB, vlne, bc
CS-KRa III, 37, no. 13
parts
microfilm: US-SY

S0042 **Dominus dixit**
SATB, 3 vla, vc, vlne, bc

Christmas Day
A-Wn Ms. H.K. 623
parts

S0043 **Dominus fortitudo**
SATB, 2 vla, vltta, vc, vlne, bc
5th Sunday after Trinity
A-Wn Ms. H.K. 663
parts

S0044 **Dum clamarem**
SATB, 2 vla, vltta, vc, vlne, bc
9th Sunday after Trinity
A-Wn Ms. H.K. 668
parts

S0045 **Ecce Deus**
SATB, 2 vla, vltta, vc, vlne, bc
8th Sunday after Trinity
A-Wn Ms. H.K. 667
parts

S0046 **Ecce Maria genuit**
SATB, 3 vla, vc, corn, 2 tbn, vlne, bsn, bc
A-Wn Ms. 18998, no. 5
parts

S0047 **Eripe me**
SSAATTBB
Wednesday of Holy Week
A-Wn Ms. 19003
parts

S0048 **Exita furorem**
SATB
US-Wc M1490.M88, pp. 135-40
score

S0049 **Gentes plaudentes ite prodite**
SATB, 2 vln, 2 vla, bc
Feast of a Confessor
CS-KRa II, 1 (1670)
parts
microfilm: US-SY

S0050 **Germinavit radix Jesse**
SATB, 3 vla, vc, corn, 2 tbn, vlne, bsn, bc
A-Wn Ms. 18998, no. 4
parts

S0051 **Gloriosae Virginis Mariae ortum**
SATB, 2 vla, corn, 2 tbn, bsn, vc, vlne, bc
Feast of the Conception or Christmas
A-Wn Ms. 18997, no. 6
parts

S0052 **Hoc est praeceptum meum**
SATB, vla, vltta, vc, corn, 2 tbn, vlne, bsn, bc
A-Wn Ms. 18999, no. 1
parts

SANCES, Giovanni Felice (*continued*)

S0053 Improperium expectavit cor meum
SATB, bc
Palm Sunday
A-Wn Ms. 19005
parts

S0054 In convertendo
SATB, SATB, vlne, bc
CS-KRa III, 37, no. 12
parts
microfilm: US-SY

S0055 In exitu
SATB, SATB, vlne, bc
CS-KRa III, 37, no. 6
parts
microfilm: US-SY

S0056 In patientia vestra
SATB, vla, vltta, vc, corn, 2 tbn, vlne,
bsn, bc
A-Wn Ms. 18999, no. 5
parts

S0057 Inclina Domine
SATB, vla, vltta, vc, corn/vltta, 2 tbn/vla,
vlne, bc
14th Sunday after Trinity
A-Wn Ms. H.K. 673
parts

S0058 Jubilate
SATB, 2 vla, vltta, vc, corn/vltta, tbn/vla,
vlne, bc
3rd Sunday after Easter
A-Wn Ms. H.K. 648
parts

S0059 Justus es Domine
SATB, vla, vltta, vc, vlne, bc
16th Sunday after Trinity
A-Wn Ms. H.K. 675
parts

S0060 Laetatus sum
SSATTB, 5 vla, bass vla, bc
CS-KRa III, 34 (1674)
parts
microfilm: US-SY

S0061 Laetatus sum
SATB, SATB, vlne, bc
CS-KRa III, 37, no. 8
parts
microfilm: US-SY

S0062 Lauda Jerusalem
SATB, SATB, vlne, bc

CS-KRa III, 37, no. 10
parts
microfilm: US-SY

S0063 Laudate Dominum
SATB, SATB, vlne, bc
CS-KRa III, 37, no. 5
parts
microfilm: US-SY

S0064 Laudate, pueri
SATB, SATB, vlne, bc
CS-KRa III, 37, no. 4
parts
microfilm: US-SY

S0065 Litaniae Beatae Mariae Virginis
SSAATTBB, 4 vla, vlne, bc
CS-KRa V, 23 (1676)
parts
microfilm: US-SY

S0066 Litaniae Beatae Mariae Virginis
SATB, bc
CS-KRa V, 42
parts
microfilm: US-SY

S0067 Magnificat
SATB, SATB, vlne, bc
CS-KRa III, 37, no. 7
parts
microfilm: US-SY

S0068 Magnificat
SATB, SATB, vlne, bc
CS-KRa III, 37, no. 14
parts
microfilm: US-SY

S0069 Majorem caritatem nemo habet
SATB, vla, vltta, vc, corn, 2 tbn, vlne,
bsn, bc
A-Wn Ms. 18999, no. 2
parts

S0070 Memento Domine, David
SATB, SATB, vlne, bc
CS-KRa III, 37, no. 16
parts
microfilm: US-SY

S0071 Miserere mei, Domine
SATB, vln/vla, vla, vltta, vc, corn/vltta,
tbn/vla, tbn, vlne, bc
15th Sunday after Trinity
A-Wn H.K. 674
parts

S0072   **Miserere servorum morum**
    ATB
    US-Wc M1490.M88, pp. 38-41
    score

S0073   **Missa Benedictionis**
    SSATB, vln, 4 vla, vlne, bc
    CS-KRa I, 179
    parts
    microfilm: US-SY

S0074   **Missa Brevis et felix**
    SSATTB, 2 vln, 4 vla, vlne, bc
    CS-KRa I, 175
    parts
    microfilm: US-SY

S0075   **Missa defunctorum**
    SSATTB, bass vla, 4 vltta, 3 tbn, vlne, bc
    A-KR Ser. E, Fasc. 2, no. 67(1) (1654)
    parts

S0076   **Missa Gratiosa**
    SATB, vln, 2 vla, 3 tbn, bc
    CS-KRa I, 84
    parts
    microfilm: US-SY

S0077   **Missa In te confido (Requiem)**
    SATB, 3 vla, bc
    CS-KRa XIII, 2a
    score

S0078   **Missa Kyrie eleison**
    SATB, 3 vla, bc
    Palm Sunday
    H-PH
    parts
    Citation from Webhofer

S0079   **Missa Kyrie eleison**
    SSATTB, 5 vla, 4 tbn, bc
    CS-KRa I, 8
    parts
    microfilm: US-SY

S0080   **Missa Mater gratiae**
    SSATTB, 2 vln, tbn, vlne, bc
    CS-KRa I, 181
    parts
    microfilm: US-SY

S0081   **Missa Necessitatis**
    SATB, 2 vln, 2 vla, vlne, bc
    CS-KRa I, 245
    parts
    microfilm: US-SY

S0082   **Missa Pia**
    SSATB, 2 vln, bc
    CS-KRa I, 51
    parts
    microfilm: US-SY

S0083   **Missa Porta coeli**
    SSATB, 5 vla, vlne, bc
    CS-KRa I, 176
    parts
    microfilm: US-SY

S0084   **Missa Praesentationis**
    8 vv, 5 strings, 2 corn, 5 tbn, colascione, bc
    A-KR Ser. C, Fasc. 7, no. 652
    parts

S0085   **Missa Rosarum**
    SSATTB, 2 vln, 4 vla, 4 tbn, vlne, bc
    CS-KRa I, 180
    parts
    microfilm: US-SY

S0086   **Missa Sagittae**
    SSATB, 2 vln, 3 vla, vlne, bc
    CS-KRa I, 177
    parts
    microfilm: US-SY

S0087   **Missa Sances**
    SSATTB, 2 vln, 3 vla, 4 tbn, bc
    CS-KRa I, 127
    parts
    microfilm: US-SY

S0088   **Missa Sanctae Mariae Magdalenae**
    SSATTB, 2 vln, 4 vltta, 2 clar, 4 tbn, bc
    CS-KRa I, 25 (1665)
    parts
    microfilm: US-SY

S0089   **Missa Solicita**
    SATB, 2 vln, 2 tbn, vlne, bc
    CS-KRa I, 101
    parts
    microfilm: US-SY

S0090   **Missa Spedita**
    SSATTB, 2 vln, 4 vla, 4 tbn, bc
    CS-KRa I, 219
    parts
    microfilm: US-SY

S0091   **Missa Velocissima**
    SATB, 2 vln, 3 tbn, vlne, bc
    CS-KRa I, 195 (1666)
    parts
    microfilm: US-SY

SANCES, Giovanni Felice (*continued*)

S0092 **Nativitas/Conceptio est hodie Sanctae Mariae**
SATB, 2 vla, corn, 2 tbn, bsn, vc, vlne, bc
Feast of the Conception or Christmas
A-Wn Ms. 18997, no. 2
parts

S0093 **Nativitas gloriosae Virginis Mariae**
SATB, 2 vla, corn, 2 tbn, bsn, vlne, bc
Feast of the Conception or Christmas
A-Wn Ms. 18997, no. 1
parts

S0094 **Nisi Dominus**
SSATTB, 4 vla, bass vla, bc
CS-KRa III, 34 (1674)
parts
microfilm: US-SY

S0095 **Nisi Dominus**
SATB, SATB, vlne, bc
CS-KRa III, 37, no. 9
parts
microfilm: US-SY

S0096 **Nos autem gloriari**
SATB, vlne, bc
Good Friday
A-Wn Ms. H.K. 643
parts

S0097 **O admirabile commercium**
SATB, 3 vla, vc, corn, 2 tbn, vlne, bsn, bc
A-Wn Ms. 18998, no. 1
parts

S0098 **Omnes gentes**
SATB, 2 vla, vltta, vc, vlne, bc
6th Sunday after Trinity
A-Wn Ms. H.K. 665
parts

S0099 **Omnia quae fecisti**
SATB, 2 vla, vltta, vc, vlne, bc
19th Sunday after Trinity
A-Wn Ms. H.K. 678
parts

S0100 **Propter nimiam caritatem**
SATB, 3 vla, vc, corn, 2 tbn, vlne, bsn, bc
A-Wn Ms. 18998, no. 6
parts

S0101 **Protexisti me**
SATB, vln/vltta, 2 vla, vc, vlne, bc
Feast of St. George, martyr, St. Hermegild,
   martyr, or any martyr in Eastertide
A-Wn Ms. H.K. 720
parts

S0102 **Quam dilecta tabernacula**
SATB, 2 vla, vltta, vc, vlne, bc
13th Sunday after Trinity
A-Wn Ms. H.K. 672
parts

S0103 **Quando natus es**
SATB, 3 vla, vc, corn, 2 tbn, vlne, bsn, bc
A-Wn Ms. 18998, no. 2
parts

S0104 **Quasi modo geniti**
SATB, 2 vla, vltta/vln, vc, vlne, bc
1st Sunday after Easter
A-Wn Ms. H.K. 646
parts

S0105 **Regali ex progenie**
SATB, 2 vla, corn, 2 tbn, bsn, vc, vlne, bc
Feast of the Conception or Christmas
A-Wn Ms. 18997, no. 3
parts

S0106 **Requiem Ferdinandi III**
8 vv, 5 vla, 2 corn, 4 tbn, vlne, bc
A-KR Ser. E, Fasc. 2, no. 66
parts

S0107 **Respice, Domine**
SATB, 2 vla, vltta, vc, vlne, bc
12th Sunday after Trinity
A-Wn Ms. H.K. 671
parts

S0108 **Rubum, quem viderat**
SATB, 3 vla, vc, corn, 2 tbn, vlne, bsn, bc
A-Wn Ms. 18998, no. 3
parts

S0109 **Salus populi**
SATB, 2 vln, vc, tbn/vla, vlne, bc
18th Sunday after Trinity
A-Wn Ms. H.K. 677
parts

S0110 **Senex puerum portabat**
SATB, 3 vla, vc, corn, 2 tbn, vlne, bsn, bc
Purification of the Virgin Mary
A-Wn Ms. 18998, no. 7
parts

S0111 **Sette consolationi a Maria Virgine**
A-KR Ms. 153

S0112 **Sub tuum praesidium**
SATB, bc
CS-KRa V, 42
parts
microfilm: US-SY

S0113 **Suscepimus Deus**
SATB, 2 vla, vltta, vc, vlne, bc
7th Sunday after Trinity
A-Wn Ms. H.K. 666
parts

S0114 **Tradent enim vos**
SATB, vla, vltta, vc, corn, 2 tbn, vlne, bsn
A-Wn Ms. 18999, no. 6
parts

S0115 **Vesperae de confessore**
SATB, 3 vla, 3 tbn, vlne, bc
CS-KRa III, 15
parts (bc missing)
microfilm: US-SY

S0116 **Victimae paschali laudes**
SSAATTBB, 5 vla, 5 tbn, vlne, bc
Easter Sunday
CS-KRa II, 156 (1672)
parts
microfilm: US-SY

S0117 **Vos amici mei estis**
SATB, vla, vltta, vc, corn, 2 tbn, vlne,
bsn, bc
A-Wn Ms. 18999, no. 3
parts

SAYLER (Sauler), Johann Kaspar

S0118 **Ach, wie elend ist unser Zeit**
SATB, 2 vln, 3 vla, vlne, bc
F-Ssp
parts
DMA 3/372

SCHARMANN, Andreas

S0119 **Gedenke, Herr, wie es uns gehet**
SATTB, 4 vla, bc
Funeral of Wilhelm Ludwell
Altdorf, 1663
RISM S1310, Reich 6 (parts)
DMA 70//161
EdM 79, pp. 79-87

SCHEDLICH, David (1607-1687)

S0120 **Ach wie weh und überweh**
SATB
Funeral of Christoph Führer

Nürnberg, 1653
RISM S1318 (score)

S0121 **Alles macht der Tod zu schanden**
SATB, bc
Funeral of Matthaeus Keller
Nürnberg, 1662
RISM S1326 (score)

S0122 **Amen**
SSATB
D-Nla Spit. NR. 119
choirbook

S0123 **Benedicamus Domino (I)**
SSATB
D-Nla Fen. IV. 230. 2°
choirbook

S0124 **Benedicamus Domino (II)**
SATB
D-Nla Fen. IV. 230. 2°
choirbook
Ed. F. Hofmann, *Bayerisches Chorheft
1975* (Hänssler no. 2.054, 1974, p. 17)

S0125 **Benedicamus Domino (III)**
SATB
D-Nla Spit. NR. 119
choirbook

S0126 **Benedicamus Domino (IV)**
SATB
D-Nla Spit. NR. 119
choirbook

S0127 **Benedicamus Domino (V)**
SSATB
D-Nla Spit. NR. 119
choirbook

S0128 **Benedicamus Domino (VI)**
SSATB
D-Nla Spit. NR. 119
choirbook

S0129 **Benedicamus Domino (VII)**
SSATB
D-Nla Spit. NR. 119
choirbook

S0130 **Benedicamus Domino (VIII)**
SSATB
D-Nla Spit. NR. 119
choirbook

S0131 **Benedicamus Domino (IX)**
SSATB
D-Nla Spit. NR. 119
choirbook

SCHEDLICH, David (*continued*)

S0132 **Benedicamus Domino (X)**
SSATB
D-Nla Spit. NR. 119
choirbook

S0133 **Benedicamus Domino (XI)**
SSATB
D-Nla Spit. NR. 119
choirbook

S0134 **Deo gratias**
SATB
D-Nla Spit. NR. 119
choirbook

S0135 **Deutsche Magnificat (I)**
SSATB, 2 vln, 2 vla, bsn, bc
D-Nst E IIIa, no. 1a (1681)
parts and tablature

S0136 **Deutsche Magnificat (II)**
SSATB, 2 vln, 2 vla, bsn, bc
D-Nst E IIIa, no. 1a (1681)
parts and tablature

S0137 **Deutsche Magnificat (III)**
SSATB, 2 vln, 2 vla, bsn, bc
D-Nst E IIIa, no. 1a (1681)
parts and tablature

S0138 **Deutsche Magnificat (IV)**
SSATB, 2 vln, 2 vla, bsn, bc
D-Nst E IIIa, no. 1a (1681)
parts and tablature

S0139 **Deutsche Magnificat (V)**
SSATB, 2 vln, 2 vla, bsn, bc
D-Nst E IIIa, no. 1a (1681)
parts and tablature

S0140 **Deutsche Magnificat (VI)**
SSATB, 2 vln, 2 vla, bsn, bc
D-Nst E IIIa, no. 1a (1681)
parts and tablature

S0141 **Deutsche Magnificat (VII)**
SSATB, 2 vln, 2 vla, bsn, bc
D-Nst E IIIa, no. 1a (1681)
parts and tablature

S0142 **Deutsche Magnificat (VIII)**
SSATB, 2 vln, 2 vla, bsn, bc
D-Nst E IIIa, no. 1a (1681)
parts and tablature

S0143 **Deutsche Magnificat (IX)**
SSATB, 2 vln, 2 vla, bsn, bc
D-Nst E IIIa, no. 1a (1681)
parts and tablature

S0144 **Deutsche Magnificat (X)**
SSATB, 2 vln, 2 vla, bsn, bc
D-Nst E IIIa, no. 1a (1681)
parts and tablature

S0145 **Die mit Tränen säen**
SSB, 2 vln, bc
Funeral of Christoff Schnabel
Nürnberg, 1656
RISM S1321 (score)

S0146 **Domine ad adjuvandum (I)**
SSATB, 2 vln, 2 vla, bsn, bc
D-Nst E IIIa, no. 1a (1681)
parts and tablature

S0147 **Domine ad adjuvandum (II)**
SSATB, 2 vln, 2 vla, bsn, bc
D-Nst E IIIa, no. 1a (1681)
parts and tablature

S0148 **Domine ad adjuvandum (III)**
SSATB, 2 vln, 2 vla, bsn, bc
D-Nst E IIIa, no. 1a (1681)
parts and tablature

S0149 **Domine ad adjuvandum (IV)**
SSATB, 2 vln, 2 vla, bsn, bc
D-Nst E IIIa, no. 1a (1681)
parts and tablature

S0150 **Domine ad adjuvandum (V)**
SSATB, 2 vln, 2 vla, bsn, bc
D-Nst E IIIa, no. 1a (1681)
parts and tablature

S0151 **Domine ad adjuvandum (VI)**
SSATB, 2 vln, 2 vla, bsn, bc
D-Nst E IIIa, no. 1a (1681)
parts and tablature

S0152 **Domine ad adjuvandum (VII)**
SSATB, 2 vln, 2 vla, bsn, bc
D-Nst E IIIa, no. 1a (1681)
parts and tablature

S0153 **Domine ad adjuvandum (VIII)**
SSATB, 2 vln, 2 vla, bsn, bc
D-Nst E IIIa, no. 1a (1681)
parts and tablature

S0154 **Domine ad adjuvandum (IX)**
SSATB, 2 vln, 2 vla, bsn, bc
D-Nst E IIIa, no. 1a (1681)
parts and tablature

S0155 **Domine ad adjuvandum (X)**
SSATB, 2 vln, 2 vla, bsn, bc
D-Nst E IIIa, no. 1a (1681)
parts and tablature

S0156 **Hört, stellet euer Trauren ein**
SATB
Funeral of Tobias Peller
Nürnberg, 1651
RISM S1316, Reich 306 (score)

S0157 **In dem sich eben jetzt der rauhe Herbst einstellet**
SATB
Funeral of Wolff Jacob Walther
Nürnberg, 1640
RISM S1315 (score)

S0158 **Lauter Schmerzen, Angst, und Pein heget Kinder-Scheiden**
SATB, bc
Funeral of Leonhard Golling
Nürnberg, 1658
D-Nst
score

S0159 **Muß denn Nürnberg immer klagen?**
SATB
Funeral of Georg Abraham Pömer
Nürnberg, 1655
RISM S1319 (score)
DMA 70//159

S0160 **Nun lob, mein Seel, den Herren**
SAB, 2 vln, vla, vc, bc
Funeral of Gall, Freiherr von Räcknitz
Nürnberg, 1658
RISM S1322, S1323, Reich 316 (score)
Ed. H. Federhofer, *Musik alter Meister* 3,
pp. 4-13

S0161 **Nunmehr hat sich geendet**
SATB
Funeral of Maximilianae von Praunfalck
Nürnberg, 1653
RISM S1317 (score)
Ed. H. Federhofer, *Musik alter Meister* 3,
pp. 13-15

S0162 **O du schnöde, blöde Welt**
SAB, bc
Funeral of Gall, Freiherr von Räcknitz
Nürnberg, 1658
RISM S1322, S1323, Reich 316 (score)
Ed. H. Federhofer, *Musik alter Meister* 3,
p. 3

S0163 **Stehet still und schauet an**
SATB
Funeral of Hanns Adam Praunfalck
Nürnberg, 1655
RISM S1320 (score)
DMA 70//176

SCHEIFFELHUT, Jacob (1647-1709)

S0164 **Ach! allzustarker Donnerschlag**
SATB, bc
Funeral of Regina Barbara Ammann
Augsburg, 1686
Reich 28 (score)
DMA 70//111

S0165 **Du trübe Luft**
SSATB, bc
Funeral of Regina Welser
Augsburg, 1679
Reich 25 (choirbook)
DMA 70//176

S0166 **Fließ ab, du herber Tränen-Bach**
SSATB, bc
Funeral of Adolph Zobel von und zu Pfersen
Augsburg, 1678
RISM S1366, Reich 24

S0167 **O selig über selig sind, die in dem Herren sterben**
SATB
Funeral of Adolph Zobel von Pfersen
Augsburg, 1689
RISM S1371, Reich 30

S0168 **O süße Himmels-Herrlichkeit**
SSATB, bc
Funeral of Jakobina Hentschel
Augsburg, 1680
Reich 26

SCHELLE, Johann (1648-1701)

S0169 **Ach Gott und Herr, wie groß und schwer**
SSATB, vln, 4 vla, 3 tbn, bsn, bc
D-Dlb Mus. 1857-E-517 (Grimma U 356/N 89)
parts
Composer: J. S.
D-B Mus. ms. 30242, no. 9 (Bokemeyer)
score
Anonymous
Cf. Krummacher, *Mf* 16 (1963): 343

SCHELLE, Johann (*continued*)

S0170 **Ach, was erhebet sich die arme Erde**
SSATB, 4 vla, 3 tbn, bsn, bc
D-Dlb Mus. 1857-E-511, no. 1 (Grimma U
386/N 73)
score
Attributed in D-Dlb catalog

S0171 **Actus musicus auf Weihnachten**
See Vom Himmel hoch

S0172 **Alleluja, man singet mit Freuden**
SSATB, 2 vln, 2 vla, 2 corn, bsn, bc
lost; formerly Grimma U 184/V 42
Ed. Krüger, *Die Kantate* 39 (1966)

S0173 **Also hat Gott die Welt geliebet**
SSATB, 2 vln, 2 vla, 2 clar, timp, bsn, bc
Pentecost
D-B Mus. ms. 19780, no. 1 (Bokemeyer)
score
DMA 1/1627

S0174 **Aus der Tiefen rufe ich Herr zu dir**
SATB, 2 vln, 2 vla, bsn, bc
D-B Mus. ms. 19780, no. 2 (Bokemeyer)
score
DMA 1/1628

S0175 **Barmherzig und gnädig ist der Herr**
SSATB, 2 vln, 2 vla, bsn, bc
D-Dlb Mus. 1857-E-510 (Grimma U 270/U 70)
parts
DdT 58/59, pp. 207-18
Ed. Krüger, *Die Kantate* 166 (1966)

S0176 **Beatus vir qui timet**
SSATB, 3 vln, vc, bc
D-Dlb Mus. 1857-E-518 (Grimma U 260/U 61)
parts
D-Dlb Mus. 1739-E-516, no. 1
score

S0177 **Christus der ist mein Leben**
SSATB, 4 vln, 4 vla, bsn, bc
D-B Mus. ms. 19780, no. 3 (Bokemeyer)
(1693)
score
DMA 1/1629
D-Dlb Mus. 1857-E-514 (Grimma U 252/U 53)
(1716)
parts (title page attribution: Rosenmüller)
DMA 3/1280
Ed. Morris, M.A. thesis, 1971

S0178 **Christus ist des Gesetzes Ende**
SSAB, ATTB, bc

Funeral of Gottfried Eggers
Leipzig, 1684
RISM S1440, Reich 272 (parts)
DMA 70//170
Ed. Straube, *Ausgewählte Gesänge des
Thomaschors* II, no. 23 (Breitkopf &
Härtel no. 2686, 1929)
Ed. Buszin (Concordia no. 97-6297, 1958)

S0179 **Da die Zeit erfüllet war**
SSATB, 2 vln, 2 vla, bsn, bc
D-Dlb Mus. 1857-E-519 (Grimma U 423/P 23)
parts
Attributed in D-Dlb catalog

S0180 **Das ist meine Freude**
SSAB, ATTB, bc
D-Dlb Mus. 1857-E-513 (Grimma U 533/T 8)
score and parts
Composer: J. S.
Attributed in D-Dlb catalog

S0181 **Das ist mir lieb**
SSATB, 2 vln, 2 vla, bc
D-B Mus. ms. 19780, no. 7 (Bokemeyer)
score
DMA 1/1630

S0182 **Der Abgrund tut sich auf**
TB soli, SSATB, 2 vln, 2 vla, bsn, bc
D-B Mus. ms. 19780, no. 6 (Bokemeyer)
score
DMA 1/1631

S0183 **Der Gerechte, ob er gleich zu zeitlich stirbt**
SATB, SATB
D-B Mus. ms. 19788 (Erfurt)
parts
DMA 1/1632

S0184 **Der Segen des Herrn macht reich**
SSATB, 2 vln, 2 vla, bsn, bc
D-B Mus. ms. 19780, no. 5 (Bokemeyer)
score
DMA 1/1633

S0185 **Die auf den Herrn hoffen**
SSATB, 2 vln, 2 vla, bsn, bc
D-B Mus. ms. 19780, no. 8 (Bokemeyer)
score
DMA 1/1634

S0186 **Die Güte des Herrn ists, daß wir nicht gar aus
sind**
SSATB, 2 vln, 2 vla, bc
D-B Mus. ms. 19780, no. 9 (Bokemeyer)
score
DMA 1/1635

S0187 **Die Liebe Gottes ist ausgegossen**
SATTB, 2 vln, 3 vla, bsn, bc
D-B Mus. ms. 19780, no. 4 (Bokemeyer)
score
DMA 1/1636

S0188 **Durch Adams Fall**
SSATB, 2 vln, 2 vla, 2 corn, 3 tbn, bc
14th Sunday after Trinity
GB-Ob MS. Mus. Sch. C.31, fols. 69-84
parts

S0189 **Ehre sei Gott in der Höhe**
SSATB, 2 vln, 2 clar, timp, 3 tbn, bc
D-Dlb Mus. 1857-E-504 (Grimma U 263/U 63)
score and parts
Ed. Krüger, *Die Kantate* 90 (1960)

S0190 **Erkenne deine Missetat**
SSSSSS, 5 vla, vlne, bc
D-Dlb Mus. 1857-E-509 (Grimma U 269/U 69)
score and parts

S0191 **Eructavit cor meum**
SSSSAATTBB, 2 vln, 2 vla, 2 corn, 3 tbn, bsn, bc
D-Dlb Mus. 1857-E-505 (Grimma U 264/U 64)
parts

S0192 **Gesegnet ist der Mann**
SSS, 2 vln, 3 gamba, bsn, bc
D-B Mus. ms. 19780, no. 11 (Bokemeyer)
score
DMA 1/1638

S0193 **Gott segne dies vertraute Paar**
SSATB, 2 vln, 2 vla/tbn, 3 clar, timp, vlne/bsn, bc
D-B Mus. ms. 19780, no. 14 (Bokemeyer)
score
DMA 1/1639

S0194 **Gott sende dein Licht und deine Wahrheit** (A minor)
SATB, 2 vln, 2 vla, bsn, bc
D-B Mus. ms. 19780, no. 13 (Bokemeyer)
score
DMA 1/1640

S0195 **Gott sende dein Licht und deine Wahrheit** (A major)
SATB, 2 vln, 2 vla, bsn, bc
D-Dlb Mus. 1857-E-508 (Grimma U 267/U 67)
parts

S0196 **Habe deine Lust an dem Herrn**
SATB, SATB
D-Dlb Mus. 1857-E-515 (Grimma U 532/T 9)
parts

Composer: J. S.
Attributed in D-Dlb catalog

S0197 **Hemmt eure Tränenflut**
ATB soli, SSATB, 2 vln, 2 vla, 4 clar, timp, bc
D-B Mus. ms. 19781, no. 2 (Bokemeyer)
score
DMA 1/1642

S0198 **Herr, deine Augen sehen nach dem Glauben**
SSATB, 2 vln, 2 corn, 3 tbn, bc
D-B Mus. ms. 19781, no. 1 (Bokemeyer)
score
DMA 1/1643

S0199 **Herr lehre uns bedenken**
SSB, vln, gamba, vltta, bc
16th Sunday after Trinity
D-Dlb Mus. 1857-E-507 (Grimma U 266/U 66) (1683)
score and parts (2 sets)
DMA 34//32

S0200 **Heut triumphieret Gottes Sohn**
SSATB, 2 vln, 2 vla, vlne, bc
D-B Mus. ms. 19782 (Erfurt)
score (incomplete) and parts
DMA 2/1821
Ed. Morris, M.A. thesis, 1971

S0201 **Ich hielte mich nicht dafür**
SSATB, 2 vln, 2 vla, bc
D-B Mus. ms. 19781, no. 4 (Bokemeyer)
score
DMA 1/1644

S0202 **Ich weiß, daß mein Erlöser lebt**
SATB, SATB, bc
Funeral of Elisabeth Kaess
Leipzig, 1684
RISM S1441, Reich 273 (parts)
EdM 79, pp. 55-68

S0203 **In dich hab ich gehoffet, Herr**
SSATB, 2 vln, 2 vla, 2 clar, bc
D-B Mus. ms. 19781, no. 3 (Bokemeyer) (1694)
score
DMA 1/1645
Ed. Morris, M.A. thesis, 1971

S0204 **Komm, Jesu, komm**
SSATB
Funeral of Jakob Thomasius
Leipzig, 1684
Reich 274 (score)
DMA 70//140

SCHELLE, Johann (*continued*)

S0205 Lobe den Herrn, meine Seele
SSATB, SSATB, 2 vln, 2 vla, 2 corn, 4
clar, timp, 3 tbn, bsn, bc
D-B Mus. ms. 19781, no. 5 (Bokemeyer)
score
DMA 1/1646
DdT 58/59, pp. 122-66

S0206 Machet die Tore weit
SATB, 2 vln, 2 vla, 2 clar, timp, bsn, bc
D-Dlb Mus. 1857-E-501 (Grimma U 268/U 68)
parts

S0207 Magnificat
SSATB, 2 vln, 2 vla, 2 corn, 3 tbn, bc
GB-Ob MS. Mus. Sch. C. 31, fols. 1-26
parts

S0208 Meine Seele ist betrübt bis in den Tod
See under Anonymous

S0209 Nun danket alle Gott
SSATB, 2 vln, 2 clar, bc
D-B Mus. ms. 19781, no. 7 (Bokemeyer)
(1697)
score
DMA 1/1647
Ed. Morris, M.A. thesis, 1971

S0210 Nun gibst du, Gott, einen gnädigen Regen
SSATB, 2 vln, 2 vla, bc
D-B Mus. ms. 19781, no. 6 (Bokemeyer)
score
DMA 1/1648
D-Dlb Mus. 1857-E-512 (Grimma U 336/N 35)
parts

S0211 Salve
SSATB, 2 vln, 2 vla, 2 corn, clar, 3 tbn, bc
Feast of John the Baptist
GB-Ob MS. Mus. Sch. C. 31, fols. 49-67
parts

S0212 Schaffe in mir, Gott, ein reines Herz
SATB, 2 vln, 2 vln piccolo, 2 vltta, 2
cornettino, clar, vlne/bsn, bc
D-B Mus. ms. 19781, no. 8 (Bokemeyer)
score
DMA 1/1649

S0213 Siehe, es hat überwunden der Löwe
SATB, 2 vln, 2 vla, 4 tpt, timp, bsn, bc
D-Dlb Mus. 1857-E-500 (Grimma U 259/U 60)
parts

S0214 Und da die Tage ihrer Reinigung
SSATB, 2 vln, 2 vla, 4 gamba, 2 clar,
vlne, bsn, bc

D-B Mus. ms. 19784 (Erfurt) (1692)
parts
DMA 1/1650

S0215 Uns ist ein Kind geboren (I)
SSATB, 2 vln, 2 clar, 2 tbn, bc
D-B Mus. ms. 19781, no. 9 (Bokemeyer)
score
DMA 1/1651

S0216 Uns ist ein Kind geboren (II)
TTB, 2 ob/vln, bsn, bc
D-MÜG (1716)

S0217 Vom Himmel hoch (Actus musicus auf Weihnachten)
T solo, SSATTB, 4 vla, winds ad lib, bsn, bc
D-LUC 296A (1715)
score
DMA 3/373
Ed. Baselt (Bärenreiter no. 4444, 1965)
Ed. Wanek (Schott no. 5744, 1969)

S0218 Vom Himmel kam der Engel Schar
SSATB, 2 vln, 2 vltta, 2 corn, 2 clar,
timp, 3 tbn, bsn, bc
D-B Mus. ms. 19781, no. 10 (Bokemeyer)
score
DMA 1/1652
DdT 58/59, pp. 167-206

S0219 Was du tust, so bedenke das Ende
SSSB, vln, 2 gamba, bsn, bc
1st Sunday after Trinity
D-B Mus. ms. 19783 (Erfurt) (1692)
parts
DMA 3/375

S0220 Wie der Hirsch schreiet nach frischem Wasser
SAB, SATTB, bc
D-Dlb Mus. 1857-E-516 (Grimma U 534/T 7)
parts
Anonymous
Attributed in D-Dlb catalog

S0221 Wohl dem, der den Herrn fürchtet
SSATB, SSATB, 2 vln, 2 clar, 3 tbn, bc
D-B Mus. ms. 19781, no. 11 (Bokemeyer)
score
DMA 1/1654

SCHERER, Sebastian Anton (1631-1712)

COLLECTION

Musica sacra (1657)
RISM S1473 (parts)

WORKS

S0222 **Benedicam Domino**
SSATB, bc
Musica sacra, no. 4

S0223 **Confitebor tibi Domine**
SSAB, 2 vln, vla, gamba/bsn, bc
Musica sacra, no. 5

S0224 **Ich weiß, daß mein Erlöser lebt**
5 vv, bc
Funeral of Johann Ludwig Pöckh
Ulm, 1664
Taken from *New Grove* and MGG; not in
RISM or Reich

S0225 **In te Domine speravi**
SSATB, bc
Musica sacra, no. 3

S0226 **Jubilate Deo, gentes**
STB, 2 vln, vla, gamba/bsn, bc
Musica sacra, no. 9
S-Uu 86:39, fol. 1r-4r (Düben)
tablature
S-Uu 34:8 (Düben)
parts

S0227 **Missa à 5 (A minor)**
SSATB, bc
Musica sacra, no. 1

S0228 **Missa à 5 (G minor)**
SSATB, 2 vln, vlne, bc
Musica sacra, no. 2

S0229 **O Deus meus**
STB, 2 vln, vla, gamba/bsn, bc
Musica sacra, no. 7

S0230 **O quam mirabilia sunt**
STB, 2 vln, vla, gamba/bsn, bc
Musica sacra, no. 6
S-Uu 86:39a, fol. 3v-7r (Düben)
tablature
S-Uu 34:9 (Düben)
parts

S0231 **Omnes gentes plaudite**
SAB, 2 vln, vla, gamba/bsn, bc
Musica sacra, no. 8

SCHERZER

S0232 **Quidquid vivitur sub sole**
SATB, 2 vln, bc
D-Bds Mus. ms. 30268, no. 4 (Bokemeyer)
score

SCHIMMER, Johann

S0233 **Unser Wandel ist im Himmel**
SATB, 2 vln, 2 vla, bc
D-Bds Mus. ms. 30268, no. 5 (Bokemeyer)
score

SCHLACKE, Kaspar

S0234 **Tribularer si nescirem misericordias tuas**
SSATB, 3 vln, bc
S-Uu 66:3 (Düben)
parts

SCHMEERBACH

S0235 **Der Gerechte, ob er gleich zu zeitlich stirbt**
SATB
Funeral
D-Gs Cod. Ms. philos. 84e Schmeerbach 1
score and parts

S0236 **Der Mensch vom Weibe geboren**
SATB
Funeral
D-Gs Cod. Ms. philos. 84e Schmeerbach 2
score (incomplete) and parts

S0237 **Du hast nicht Lust an unserm Verderben**
SATB
D-Gs Cod. Ms. philos. 84e Schmeerbach 3
(1716)
score and parts

S0238 **Ich hab einen guten Kampf gekämpft**
SATB
Funeral
D-Gs Cod. Ms. philos. 84e Schmeerbach 4
score and parts

SCHMELZER, Johann Heinrich (ca. 1623-1680)

S0239 **Ad concentus o mortales ad triumphos**
SSATTB, 2 vln, 3 vla, 2 corn, 2 clar, 4
tbn, vlne, bc
CS-KRa II, 62
parts
microfilm: US-SY

S0240 **Compieta**
SATB, 2 vln, vc, corn, 2 tbn, vlne, bsn, bc
A-Wn 17328
parts
Includes: Cum invocarem, In te Domine, Qui
habitat in adjutorio, Ecce nunc benedicite,
Te lucis ante terminum, and Nunc dimittis

SCHMELZER, Johann Heinrich (*continued*)

S0241 Credidi
See Vesperae brevissimae de beatissimae virgine

S0242 Cum invocarem
See Compieta

S0243 Currite, accurrite, caeli et terrae
SATB, 2 vln, 3 vla, vlne, bc
Christmas Day
CS-KRa II, 124
parts
microfilm: US-SY

S0244 Die Stärke der Liebe
SSATT, 2 vln, bc
A-Wn 16883 (1677)
score
A-Wn 18572, no. 2
score (1 chorus only)

S0245 Dixit Dominus
See Vesperae brevissimae de beatissimae virgine

S0246 Domine probasti me
See Vesperae brevissimae de beatissimae virgine

S0247 Ecce nunc benedicite
See Compieta

S0248 Hodie lux tua, sancte fulgebit
SATB, 2 vln, 3 vla, bc
CS-KRa II, 169
parts
microfilm: US-SY

S0249 In convertendo
See Vesperae brevissimae de beatissimae virgine

S0250 In te Domine
See Compieta

S0251 Inquietum est cor meum
SATB, 2 vln, 2 vla, vlne, bc
CS-KRa II, 56 (1676)
parts
microfilm: US-SY

S0252 Laetatus sum
See Vesperae brevissimae de beatissimae virgine

S0253 Lauda Jerusalem
See Vesperae brevissimae de beatissimae virgine

S0254 Laudate, pueri
See Vesperae brevissimae de beatissimae virgine

S0255 Le memorie dolorose
SSATTTBB, 2 vln, 4 vla, 2 gamba, bc
A-Wn 16915
score

S0256 Magnificat
See Vesperae brevissimae de beatissimae virgine

S0257 Missa Dei patris benedicte
SSAATTBB, 5 vla, 2 clar, 3 tbn, vlne, bc
CS-KRa I, 27
parts
microfilm: US-SY

S0258 Missa Jesu crucifixi
SSAATTBB, 2 vln, 4 vla, 2 clar, vlne, bc
A-KR Ser. C, Fasc. 11, no. 684
CS-KRa I, 26
parts (incomplete)
microfilm: US-SY

S0259 Missa Mater purissima
SATB, 3 vla, corn, 3 tbn, vlne, bc
CS-KRa I, 29 (1677)
score and parts
microfilm: US-SY

S0260 Missa Natalis (Kyrie & Gloria only)
SSATTB, 2 vln, 2 vla, 2 clar, 4 tbn, vlne, bc
CS-KRa I, 129
parts
microfilm: US-SY

S0261 Missa Nuptialis
SSATTB, 2 vln, 4 tbn, vlne, bc
A-KR Ser. C, Fasc. 11, no. 683
DTÖ 49 (Jg. 28/2), pp. 48-73

S0262 Missa peregrina in honorem Sancti Rochi
SATB, 2 vln, 3 vla, 2 corn, 3 tbn, vlne, bc
CS-KRa I, 141
parts
microfilm: US-SY
CS-KRa I, 242 (1679)
score
microfilm: US-SY

S0263 Missa pro defunctis (Kyrie, Sanctus, Agnus)
SATB, 3 vla, bc
CS-KRa I, 242a (1679)
score
microfilm: US-SY

S0264 **Missa Sancti Joannis**
SATB, 2 vln, 2 vla, 3 tbn, vlne, bc
CS-KRa I, 31
parts
microfilm: US-SY

S0265 **Missa Sancti Spiritus**
SSATTB, 2 vln, 2 vla, 2 corn, 2 clar, 4 tbn, bc
CS-KRa I, 23
parts
microfilm: US-SY

S0266 **Missa Sancti Stanislai**
SATB, 2 vln, 3 vla, bc
CS-KRa I, 222
parts
microfilm: US-SY

S0267 **Missa Tarde venientium in honorem Sancti Wenceslai**
SATB, 2 vln, corn/tbn, 2 tbn, vlne, bc
CS-KRa I, 30 (1671)
parts
microfilm: US-SY

S0268 **Nisi Dominus**
See Vesperae brevissimae de beatissimae virgine

S0269 **Nos autem gloriari**
SATB, 3 vla, vc, vlne, bc
A-Wn H.K. 718

S0270 **Nunc dimittis**
See Compieta

S0271 **O Jesu, summa caritas**
SATB, 2 vln, 2 vla, theorbo, bc
S-Uu 34:11 (Düben)
parts
DMA 2/2284

S0272 **Qui habitat in adjutorio**
See Compieta

S0273 **Sileat misericordiam tuam, o bone Jesu**
SATB, vln, 3 vla, vlne, bc
CS-KRa II, 64
parts
microfilm: US-SY
D-Dlb Mus. ms. 1817-E-500 (Grimma U 288/U 89)
parts

S0274 **Te lucis ante terminum**
See Compieta

S0275 **Terra triumphans jubila**
SATB, 2 vln, gamba, vlne, bc

S-Uu 78:40 (Düben)
tablature
DMA 2/2285
S-Uu 46:8 (Düben)
parts (abridged version)
DMA 2/2285

S0276 **Vesperae brevissimae de beatissimae virgine et de apostolis**
SATB, 2 vln, vc, corn, 2 tbn, vlne, bsn, bc
A-Wn 17329
parts
Includes: Dixit Dominus, Laudate pueri, Laetatus sum, Nisi Dominus, Lauda Jerusalem, Credidi, In convertendo, Domine probasti me, and Magnificat

S0277 **Vesperae solemnis pleno coro**
SSAATTBB, 2 vln, 5 vla, 2 corn, 2 clar, 3 tbn, vlne, bc
CS-KRa III, 92
parts
microfilm: US-SY

SCHMEZER, Georg (1642-1697)

COLLECTIONS

Motettae sive cantiones sacrae (1671)
RISM S1662 (parts, incomplete)
DMA 51//37
Copy of most pieces in F-Pn Vm1 1309 (score)

Sacri concentus latini (1689)
RISM S1663 (parts)
DMA 2/1158

WORKS

S0278 **Ad te querelas/Ich ruf, Herr**
SATB, 2 vln, 2 vla, bc
Sacri concentus latini, no. 5

S0279 **Ah Domine Jesu Christi tibi vivo morior**
SSB, bc
Motettae sive cantiones sacrae, no. 5
S-Uu 34:12 (Düben)
parts
DMA 3/379

S0280 **Audite sancti, audite**
SSB, 2 vln, bc
Motettae sive cantiones sacrae, no. 13
F-Pn Vm1 1309, fol. 44r
score

SCHMEZER, Georg (*continued*)

S0281   **Betrübet euch nicht gar zu sehr**
        SSATTB, bc
        Funeral of Adolph Zobel von und zu Pfersen
        Augsburg, 1678
            RISM S1664, Reich 24

S0282   **Descende dilecte mi**
        SSATTB, SSATTB, 4 vln, 4 tbn, vlne, bc
        Wedding
        Sacri concentus latini, no. 13

S0283   **Domine salvum fac regem**
        SATB, 2 vln, 2 vla, bsn, bc
        Motettae sive cantiones sacrae, no. 20
        F-Pn Vm1 1309, fol. 90r
            score

S0284   **Du werte Musen Schar**
        SATB, bc
        Funeral of Regina Barbara Ammann
        Augsburg, 1686
            Reich 28 (score)
            DMA 70//111

S0285   **En! mutua concordia/Sieh, lieber Christ**
        SATB, 3 vln, 2 vla, bsn, bc
        Wedding
        Sacri concentus latini, no. 7

S0286   **Fahr hin, du Schatten dieser Zeit**
        SATB
        Funeral of Jakobina Hentschel
        Augsburg, 1680
            Reich 26

S0287   **Heu! quos dabimus miseranda**
        ATB, 2 vln, bc
        Motettae sive cantiones sacrae, no. 12
        F-Pn Vm1 1309, fol. 36r
            score

S0288   **Hinc evolandum**
        SATB, vln, 2 vla, bc
        Sacri concentus latini, no. 6

S0289   **Ich leb, aber nicht ich**
        ATB, 2 vln, bc
        S-Uu 34:13 (Düben)
            parts
            DMA 3/380

S0290   **Ich ruf, Herr**
        See Ad te querelas

S0291   **Jauchzet dem Herrn**
        See Jubila Jesu

S0292   **Jesu, pastor animarum/Jesu, treuer Seelen Hüter**
        SAT, 2 vln, bc
        Sacri concentus latini, no. 3

S0293   **Jesu, treuer Seelen Hüter**
        See Jesu pastor animarum

S0294   **Jubila Jesu/Jauchzet dem Herrn**
        SATB, 2 vln, vla, vla/tbn, 2 clar, tbn,
            bsn, bc
        Sacri concentus latini, no. 9

S0295   **Lasset ab, ihr meine Lieben**
        SSATTB
        Funeral of Regina Welser
        Augsburg, 1679
            Reich 25 (choirbook)
            DMA 70//176

S0296   **Magnus es Domine**
        SATB, 2 vln, 3 vla, bc
        PL-Kj 40129, no. 5
            tablature

S0297   **Miserere mei, o Jesu, secundum misericordiam**
        SSATB, 3 vla, vlne, bc
        S-Uu 83:33, fol. 22v-25r (Düben)
            tablature
            DMA 1/1657
        S-Uu 34:16 (Düben)
            parts
            DMA 1/1657

S0298   **Missa à 6**
        SSB, 2 vln, gamba, bc
        S-Uu 34:14 (Düben)
            parts
            DMA 3/381

S0299   **O adoranda Trinitas**
        SSATB, 2 vln, 2 vla/tbn, tpt, 2 clar, tbtta,
            bsn, bc
        Trinity Sunday
        Sacri concentus latini, no. 10

S0300   **O anima mea**
        ATB, bc
        Motettae sive cantiones sacrae, no. 7
        F-Pn Vm1 1309, fol. 24r
            score

S0301   **O felix felicitas**
        SAT/B, bc
        Motettae sive cantiones sacrae, no. 4
        F-Pn Vm1 1309, fol. 12r
            score

S0302   **O felix felicitas, jucunda jucunditas**
         SSB, 2 vln, 2 vla, bc
         S-Uu 34:18 (Düben)
         parts
         DMA 1/1659

S0303   **O quam pulchra es, amica mea**
         SSATB, 2 vln, bc
         Motettae sive cantiones sacrae, no. 17
         F-Pn Vm1 1309, fol. 68r
         score

S0304   **O vanitatis affecta**
         SATB, 2 vln, 2 vla, bsn, bc
         Sacri concentus latini, no. 8

S0305   **Qui sitit veniat**
         SAT, bc
         Motettae sive cantiones sacrae, no. 6
         F-Pn Vm1 1309, fol. 18r
         score

S0306   **Quicquid vivitur sub sole vanitatum vanitas**
         SATB, 2 vln, bc
         Motettae sive cantiones sacrae, no. 14
         F-Pn Vm1 1309, fol. 52r
         score
         S-Uu 70:3 (Düben)
         parts

S0307   **Sieh, lieber Christ**
         See En! mutua concordia

S0308   **Surgite cum gaudio**
         SSATTB, 2 vln, 2 clar, 4 tbtta, timp, 2
         tbn, bc
         Easter or Ascension
         Sacri concentus latini, no. 11

S0309   **Surgite cum gaudio**
         SSB, vln, vla, gamba, vlne, bc
         S-Uu 86:70, fol. 1v-5r (Düben)
         tablature
         DMA 3/382
         S-Uu 46:6 (Düben)
         parts (vln 2 missing)
         DMA 3/382

S0310   **Te Deum laudamus**
         SSATTB, 2 vln, 2 clar, 2 tbtta, timp, 4
         tbn, bc
         Sacri concentus latini, no. 12

S0311   **Tribularer si nescirem**
         SSATB, 2 vln, vla, bsn, bc
         Motettae sive cantiones sacrae, no. 19
         F-Pn Vm1 1309, fol. 84r
         score

S0312   **Wie war mir um Trost so bange**
         SATTB, bc
         Funeral of Reymund Egger von und auf
         Hamel
         Augsburg, 1696
         RISM S1668, Reich 31 (score)
         DMA 70//177
         EdM 79, pp. 10-12

SCHMID. *See also* **SCHMIDT, SCHMIEDT**

SCHMID

S0313   **Der Herr ist mein Hirte**
         SATB, 2 vln/ob, 2 vltta, 2 clar, bc
         D-Bds Mus. ms. 30268, no. 6 (Bokemeyer)
         score

SCHMID, David

S0314   **So wünsch ich nun ein gute Nacht**
         SATB5, bc
         Funeral of Dorothea Schmid
         Königsberg, 1683
         RISM J1695, Reich 205
         EdM 79, p. 8

SCHMIDT. *See also* **SCHMIDT, SCHMIEDT**

SCHMIDT, Johann Andreas

S0315   **Höret, die ihr annoch lebet**
         SSATB, bc
         Funeral of Petrus Herda
         Jena, 1675
         RISM S1747, IN197, Reich 165 (score)
         Composer given as "I.A.S.C.I." Reich
         attributes to Johann Andreas Schmidt,
         Cantor Isnanceni

SCHMIDT, Johann Christoph (1664-1728)

S0316   **Auf Gott hoffe ich**
         SATB, 2 vln, 2 vla, 2 fl, 2 clar, 2 tpt, bsn,
         theorbo, bc
         D-Bds Mus. ms. 30187, no. 10
         score

S0317   **Christe eleison, Kyrie eleison**
         SSATB, bc

SCHMIDT, Johann Christoph (*continued*)

    D-B Mus. ms. 30308, no. 6
    score

S0318 **Gott, du bleibest doch mein Gott**
    4 vv, 2 vln, 2 vla, bc
    F-Ssp

S0319 **Kyrie eleison**
    See Christe eleison

S0320 **Lobe den Herrn, meine Seele**
    5 vv, 2 vln, 2 vla, vlne, bc
    F-Ssp

S0321 **Missa (brevis)**
    SSATB, 2 vln, 2 vla, 2 ob, bc
    D-Bds Mus. ms. 30172, no. 2
    score

S0322 **Missa à 6 voci**
    SSATTB
    D-B Mus. ms. 1620, no. 3
    score

S0323 **Missa (brevis) à 12**
    SSATB, 2 vln, 2 vla, 2 ob, bc
    D-B Mus. ms. 19919
    parts (ob parts lacking)

S0324 **Schwing dich auf zu deinem Gott**
    SATB, 2 vln, 2 vla, vlne, bc
    F-Ssp
    parts
    DMA 2/912

S0325 **Sie ist fest gegründet auf den heiligen Bergen**
    SATB, SATB, 2 vln, 2 vla, 2 corn, 2 tpt, 2 tbn, bc
    D-Bds Mus. ms. 30268, no. 9 (Bokemeyer)
    score

S0326 **Wo ist solch ein Gott wie du**
    SSATB, SSATB, 2 vln, 2 vla, bc
    D-Bds Mus. ms. 30268, no. 8 (Bokemeyer)
    (1701)
    score

SCHMIEDEKNECHT, Johann Matthäus (1660-1715)

S0327 **Ein Diener soll in Freud und Leid**
    SSAATTBB
    Funeral of Georg Hesse
    Gotha, 1694
    RISM S1751, Reich 116

S0328 **Ihr meine Liebsten, gute Nacht**
    SATB

    Funeral of Susanne Sibylle Reichardt
    Gotha, 1697
    RISM S1752, Reich 117 (choirbook)
    DMA 74//117

S0329 **Wie manches Ungemach**
    SSATB
    Funeral of Magnus Saul
    Gotha, 1699
    RISM S1753, Reich 118 (score)
    DMA 70//3

S0330 **Wo Jesus lebt, da wird mein Geist**
    SATB
    Funeral of Anna Elisabeth Hesse
    Gotha, 1688
    RISM S1750, Reich 114 (score)
    DMA 70//204

SCHMIEDT. *See also* **SCHMID, SCHMIDT**

SCHMIEDT

S0331 **Die mit Tränen säen**
    SATB, 2 vln, 2 vla, bc
    16th Sunday after Trinity
    D-Gs Cod. Ms. philos. 84e Schmiedt 1
    score and parts

S0332 **Jauchzet dem Herrn, alle Welt**
    SATB, 2 vln, 2 ob, bc
    D-Gs Cod. Ms. philos. 84e Schmiedt 3
    (1722)
    score and parts

S0333 **Lobe den Herrn, meine Seele**
    SATB, 2 vln, vla, ob, 2 corn, bc
    D-Gs Cod. Ms. philos. 84e Schmiedt 4
    (1723)
    score and parts (bc)

S0334 **Wenn du es wüßtest, so würdest du auch bedenken**
    SATB, 2 vln, 2 vla, ob, bc
    10th Sunday after Trinity
    D-Gs Cod. Ms. philos. 84e Schmiedt 5
    (1718)
    score and parts (vla 2 & bc lacking)

SCHNELL, Johann Michael

S0335 **Schau! O Stadt, und faß zu Herzen**
    SSATB, bc
    Funeral of Friderich Ludwig von Janowitz
    n.p., 1673
    RISM S1898

SCHOBER, Johann (d. 1697)

S0336   **Denn die ihm vertrauen**
SATB, 2 vln, 2 vla, vlne, bc
5th Sunday after Trinity
D-F Ms. Ff. Mus. 460
score and parts

SCHOLTZ, Johann

S0337   **Muß es denn nun sein geschieden?**
SSB, 4 vla, bc
Funeral of Anna Sabine Stryke
Guben, 1677
RISM S2065, Reich 122 (parts)

SCHÖPPERLIN, Georg Wilhelm

S0338   **Meiner Seelen Schatz und Leben**
SSATB, bc
Funeral of Maria Frickinger
Ansbach, 1674
RISM S2057

SCHREINER, Conrad

S0339   **Zier der Rechten, Landes-Vater**
SATB
Funeral of Martin Wieland
Ulm, 1686
RISM S2121, Reich 418 (score)
DMA 70//170

SCHRÖTER, Johann Christoph

S0340   **Alleluja, denn der allmächtige Gott hat das Reich eingenommen**
B solo, SATB, 2 vln/ob, 2 vla, vlne, bc
Feast of Saint Michael
D-Gs Cod. Ms. philos. 84e, Schröter 1
score and parts

S0341   **Bleib bei uns, Herr, denn es will Abend werden**
SATB, 2 vln, 2 vla, vlne, bc
Easter Monday
D-Gs Cod. Ms. philos. 84e Schröter 2
score and parts

S0342   **Der Tod ist verschlungen in den Sieg**
SATB, 2 vln, 2 vla, bc
Easter Sunday
D-Gs Cod. Ms. philos. 84e Schröter 3
score and parts

S0343   **Gelobet sei der Herr**
SATB, 2 vln, 2 vla, vlne, bc
Feast of Saint John the Baptist
D-Gs Cod. Ms. philos. 84e Schröter 4
score and parts (vla 1 & bc lacking)

S0344   **Jerusalem, wie oft hab ich deine Kinder versammeln wollen**
SATB, 2 vln, 2 vla, bsn, bc
2nd Day of Christmas
D-Gs Cod. Ms. philos. 84e Schröter 5
(1715)
score and parts (bsn & bc lacking)

S0345   **Nun gibst du, Gott, einen gnädigen Regen**
SATB, 2 vln, 2 vla, bc
D-Gs Cod. Ms. philos. 84e Schröter 6
score and parts

S0346   **Uns ist ein Kind geboren**
SATB, 2 vln, 2 vla, vlne, bc
Christmas Day
D-Gs Cod. Ms. philos. 84e Schröter 7
score and parts (vla 1 & 2 lacking)

S0347   **Wo ist ein solcher Gott wie du bist**
SATB, 2 vln, 2 vla, bc
19th Sunday after Trinity
D-Gs Cod. Ms. philos. 84e Schröter 8
score and parts (vla 1 & 2 lacking)

SCHULTZE. *See also* **SCHULZE**

SCHULTZE, Christoph (1606-1683)

S0348   **Das bittere Leiden und Sterben Jesu Christi nach Lukas**
Leipzig, 1653
RISM S2336 (score)
Ed. J. Wolf in Hirsch *Veröffentlichungen* 10

S0349   **Furcht des Herrn**
8 vv
D-DL (1682)

S0350   **Geduldig und gar kurze Zeit**
Funeral of Gottfried Schultze
Listed in MGG and *New Grove*; unable to verify

S0351   **Ich harre des Herren**
SSATB, bc
Funeral of Christina Mayer
Leipzig, 1650
RISM S2335, Reich 238 (score)

SCHULTZE, Christoph (*continued*)

S0352   **Klingender neues Jahres Wunsch**
10 vv
D-DL (1662)
parts

S0353   **Lukaspassion**
See Das bittere Leiden und Sterben

SCHULTZE, David

S0354   **Heran, herauf, du ganze Schar**
SSB
Funeral of Dorothea Katarina zu Puttlitz
Lüneburg, 1670
RISM S2323, Reich 282

SCHULZE. *See also* **SCHULTZE**

SCHULZE, Christian Andreas (ca. 1660-1699)

S0355   **Ach Gott und Herr, wie groß und schwer**
SSATTB, 2 vln, 2 vla, 4 tbn, bsn, bc
F-Ssp
parts
DMA 2/1864

S0356   **Als der Tag der Pfingsten erfüllet war**
SAB, vln, corn, tbn, bsn, bc
D-Dlb 1696-E-512 (Grimma U 369/N 57)
parts

S0357   **Als der Tag der Pfingsten erfüllet war**
BBBB, 4 vln, bc
D-Dlb 1696-E-513 (Grimma U 283/N 76)
parts

S0358   **Also heilig ist der Tag**
SSATB, SSATB, 2 vln, 2 vla, 2 corn, 2
tbn, bsn, bc
D-Dlb 1696-E-510 (Grimma U 282/U 75)
parts

S0359   **Animae justorum in manu Dei sunt**
SSB, 2 vln, bsn, bc
D-Dlb 1696-E-505 (Grimma U 277/U 84)
parts

S0360   **Bessre dich, Jerusalem**
SSATB, 2 vln, 2 vla, bc
D-Bds Mus. ms. 30268, no. 14 (Bokemeyer)
score

S0361   **Das ist meine Freude**
ATB, 2 vln, 3 vla, bsn, bc

D-Bds Mus. ms. 30268, no. 12 (Bokemeyer)
score

S0362   **Das Wort ward Fleisch**
SSATTB, 2 vln, 3 vla, 2 ob, bsn, bc
Christmas Day
D-LUC (1740)
parts
F-Ssp

S0363   **Der Gott Abraham**
SSATB, 2 vln, 2 vla, 2 corn, 3 tbn, bsn, bc
Wedding
F-Ssp Ms. 102
parts
DMA 2/1845

S0364   **Der Tod ist verschlungen in den Sieg**
SSATB, 2 ob, 2 taille, bsn, bc
Easter
D-MÜG 66 (1715)
parts

S0365   **Duo seraphim stabant et clamabant**
SSATB, SSATB, 2 vln, 2 vla, 2 corn, 3
tbn, bsn, bc
D-Dlb 1696-E-501 (Grimma U 272/U 79)
parts

S0366   **Es sei denn, daß jemand geboren werde aus
Wasser und dem Geist**
SSATB, 2 vln, 2 vla, bsn, bc
D-F Ms. Ff. Mus. 462
parts
DMA 2/913

S0367   **Habt nicht lieb die Welt, noch was in der Welt ist**
SSATTB, 2 vln, 2 vla, bsn, bc
2nd Sunday after Trinity
D-F Ms. Ff. Mus. 463
score and parts
DMA 2/914

S0368   **Herr Jesu Christ, du höchstes Gut**
SSATB, SSATB, 2 vln, 2 vla, bsn, bc
F-Ssp
parts
DMA 2/1847

S0369   **Historia resurrectionis Domini nostri Jesu Christi**
SSATB, 2 vln, 2 vla/tbn, bsn/vlne/tbn, bc
Easter Sunday
D-Dlb 1696-E-511 (Grimma U 293/U 101)
(1686)
parts

S0370   **Ich schreie mit meiner Stimme zu Gott**
SSATB, 2 vln, 2 vla, bsn, bc
F-Ssp Ms. 126

parts
DMA 2/1848

S0371   **Laetatus sum**
SSATB, 2 vln, 3 vla, 2 shawm, 3 tbn, bc
D-Dlb 1696-E-507 (Grimma U 279/U 72)
parts

S0372   **Meine Lieben und Freunde stehen gegen mir**
SSATB, 2 vln, 2 vla, bsn/vlne, bc
D-Dlb 1696-E-516 (Grimma U 292/U 94)
parts

S0373   **Missa Alla breve**
SSATB, 2 vln, 2 vla, 2 corn, bsn, bc
F-Ssp

S0374   **Quum me pulsat aliqua turpis cogitatio**
ATB, 2 vln, bsn, bc
D-Dlb 1696-E-506 (Grimma U 278/U 85)
parts

S0375   **Seid böse, ihr Völker**
SSATB, SSATB, 2 vln, 2 vla, 2 shawm,
timp, 3 tbn, bsn, bc
D-Dlb 1696-E-502 (Grimma U 273/U 80)
parts

S0376   **Singet umeinander**
SSATB, SSATB, 2 vln, 2 vla, bsn, bc
D-B Mus. ms. 20377 (Erfurt)
score and parts (B1 lacking)
DMA 2/1849

S0377   **So wahr ich lebe, spricht der Herr**
SSATB, 2 vln, 2 vla, bsn, bc
3rd Sunday after Trinity
D-F Ms. Ff. Mus. 27
parts
DMA 2/915
D-F Ms. Ff. Mus. 464
score (incomplete)

S0378   **Te Deum laudamus**
SSATB, 2 vln, 2 clar, timp, 3 tbn, bsn, bc
F-Ssp Ms. 104
parts
DMA 2/1850

S0379   **Veni sancte spiritus**
SSATTB, 2 vln, 2 vla, 2 shawm, timp,
bsn, bc
F-Ssp Ms. 92
parts
DMA 2/1852

S0380   **Warum sollt ich mich denn grämen**
SSATB, 2 vln, 2 vla, bsn, bc
F-Ssp

parts
DMA 2/1853

S0381   **Was du tust, so bedenke das Ende**
SSATB, 2 vln, 2 vla, bsn, bc
D-Dlb 1696-E-515 (Grimma U 291/U 92)
score and parts (vln & vla lacking)

S0382   **Wer mich liebet, der wird mein Wort halten**
SSATB, 2 vln, 2 vla, vlne, bsn, bc
Pentecost
D-F Ms. Ff. Mus. 465 (1678)
parts
DMA 2/916

SCHULZE, J. A.

S0383   **Gott, du bist von Ewigkeit/Herr, vor deinen Angesicht/Jesus meine Zuversicht**
SATB, 2 vln, vla, vc, 2 ob, timp, 2 tbn, bc
D-Gs Cod. Ms. philos. 84e Schulze 1
score and parts (timp, bc lacking)

S0384   **Herr, vor deinen Angesicht**
See Gott du bist

S0385   **Ich aber will schauen dein Antlitz**
SATB
Funeral
D-Gs Cod. Ms. philos. 84e Schulz [*sic*] 2
(1719)
score

S0386   **Jesus, meine Zuversicht**
See Gott du bist

SCHWAB (Suevius), Felicien (1611-1661)

Note: Only three of his many published collections survive complete.
Since nearly all of his extant works pre-date 1650, he has been omitted.

SCHWEMMER, Heinrich (1621-1696)

S0387   **Ach! Ach! wie ist doch verdunkelt worden unser Angesicht**
SATB, 2 vln, 2 vla, bc
Funeral of Amalia von Stubenberg
Nürnberg, 1665
RISM S2508, Reich 333 (parts)
DMA 70//183

S0388   **Ach! was presset bittre Tränen?**
SATTB
Funeral of Johann Gottfried Winckler
Leipzig, 1661
RISM S2497, Reich 263 (score)

SCHWEMMER, Heinrich (1621-1696)

S0389 **Benedicamus Domino** (2 settings)
SSATB
D-Nla Fen. IV. 230
choirbook

S0390 **Der Gerechten Seelen sind in Gottes Hand**
SSATB, 2 vln, 2 vla, bc
Funeral of Johann Michael Dilherr
Nürnberg, 1669
RISM S2513, 1669⁴, Reich 337 (parts)
DMA 1/1475

S0391 **Deus, in nomine tuo salvum me fac**
SSATB, 2 vln, 2 corn, 3 tbn, bc
S-Uu 83:24, fol. 6v-10r (Düben)
tablature
DMA 2/1397
S-Uu 35:2 (Düben)
parts
DMA 2/1397

S0392 **Die hohe Zeder ist gefällt**
SATB
Funeral of Johann Wilhelm Kress von
Kressenstein
Nürnberg, 1658
RISM S2492, Reich 315 (score)

S0393 **Die Sonne ist der Finsternis gewichen**
SATB
Funeral of Anna Potentianna Jörcher
Nürnberg, 1656
Reich 309 (score)

S0394 **Halleluja. Hodie Christus natus est**
See Laetare Christe ecclesia

S0395 **Ihr Stirnen-Wächter, ihr**
SATB
Funeral of Maria Magdalena Winckler
Leipzig, 1661
Reich 325 (score)

S0396 **In meiner Jugend Jahren**
SATTB
Funeral of Esther Besserer
Nürnberg, 1661
RISM S2498, Reich 320 & 321 (score)
DMA 70//161

S0397 **Jauchzet Gott, alle Land**
SSATB, 2 vln, 2 vla, vlne, bsn, bc
D-B Mus. ms. 20555 (Erfurt) (1682)
parts

S0398 **Jedes Ding sucht seine Quelle**
SATB

Funeral of Caspar de Neufville
Nürnberg, 1673
Reich 352

S0399 **Komm, du Rat des Vaterlandes**
SSATB, 3 vla, bc
Funeral of Tobias Ölhafen
Nürnberg, 1666
Reich 334 (parts)
DMA 70//176

S0400 **Laetare Christe ecclesia devota pange cantica**
SSATB, 2 vln, 2 corn, 3 tbn, bc
S-Uu 66:7 (Düben)
parts
DMA 2/1398
Sometimes listed by title "Halleluja. Hodie
Christus natus est"

S0401 **Magnus es Domine**
SSATB, 2 vln, 3 vla, bc
D-B Mus. ms. 20556/6
parts

S0402 **Nun es kann nicht anders sein**
SATB
Funeral of Johann Andreas Endter
Sulzbach, 1670
RISM S2519, Reich 413 (score)
DMA 70//111

S0403 **Nun ich scheide aus dem Leide dieses Erd-
Getrümmels**
SATB
Funeral of Susanna Endter
Sulzbach, 1669
RISM S2514, Reich 412 (score)

S0404 **Nunmehr ist mir gar wohl geschehen**
SATB
Funeral of Susanna Endter
Sulzbach, 1669
RISM S2514, Reich 412 (score)

S0405 **O wie manchen Berg bin ich**
SSATB, 2 vln, 2 vla, bc
Funeral of Amalia von Studenberg
Nürnberg, 1665
RISM S2508, Reich 333 (parts)
DMA 70//183

S0406 **Schon lange plötzlich hat gesauft**
SATB
Funeral of Esther Besserer
Nürnberg, 1661
RISM S2498, Reich 320 & 321 (score)
DMA 70//161

S0407 **Scintilla vel pusilla**
SSATB, 2 vln, 2 vla, vc, bc
S-Uu 81:112, fol. 112v-114r (Düben)
tablature
DMA 2/1399

S0408 **Siehe! der Gerechte kommet um**
SSB, 2 vln, vla, bc
Funeral of Georg Imhoff
Nürnberg, 1659
RISM S2493, Reich 318 (parts)
DMA 45//234 & 42//117

S0409 **So geh zur Ruh**
SATB
Funeral of Burckhard Löffelholtz von
Colberg
Nürnberg, 1675
RISM S2523

S0410 **So hast auch du vollendet den Lauf der Sterblichkeit**
SATB
Funeral of Margarethe Agathae Arnschwanger
n.p., 1656
RISM S2488 (score)

S0411 **Surgite, populi, clangite, buccina**
SSATTB, 2 corn, 3 tbn, bc
D-B Mus. ms. 20556/4
parts
PL-Kj Mus. ms. 40129
tablature

S0412 **Victoria, plaudite coelites**
SSATB, 2 corn, 2 clar, timp, 2 tbn, bsn, bc
D-B Mus. ms. 20556/2 (1689)
parts and tablature
DTB 6, pp. 28-45

S0413 **Was ist das Leben doch**
SATB
Funeral of Johann Christoph Schmid
Nürnberg, 1667
RISM S2511, Reich 336 (score)

S0414 **Was mühet ihr die Ärtzte viel?**
SATB
Funeral of Susanna Endter
Sulzbach, 1669
RISM S2514, Reich 412 (score)

S0415 **Was war meine Freude, meine Lebens-Zeite?**
SATB
Funeral of Pancratz Pilgram
Nürnberg, 1659
RISM S2495, Reich 319 (score)
DMA 70//159

Parody of Johann Crüger's "Jesu meine Freude"

S0416 **Weil ich die mich geboren, so zeitlich hab verloren**
SATTB
Funeral of Thomas Antonio Besserer
Nürnberg, 1661
RISM S2498, Reich 320 & 321 (score)
DMA 70//161

S0417 **Wem kann doch auf dieser Erde**
SATB
Funeral of Pancratz Pilgram
Nürnberg, 1659
RISM S2495, Reich 319 (score)
DMA 70//159

SCHWENCKENBECKER, Günther (1651-1714)

S0418 **Magnificat**
SSATB, 2 vln, 2 vla, 2 ob, bsn, bc
D-Bds Mus. ms. 30268, no. 16 (Bokemeyer)
score

SEBASTIANI, Johann (1622-1683)

S0419 **Ad sacram mensam properate fideles**
SSATB, 2 vln, 2 vla, 3 tbn, vlne, bc
2nd Sunday after Trinity
S-Uu 84:11, fol. 3v-6r (Düben)
tablature
DMA 27//136
S-Uu 35:3 (Düben)
parts
DMA 27//136

S0420 **Das Leiden und Sterben unsers Herrn Jesu Christi nach Matthäus**
SATTB, 2 vln, 4 vla, bc
Königsberg, 1672
RISM S2642 (parts)
DMA 2/191
DdT 17, pp. 7-103

S0421 **Dennoch bleibe ich stets an dir**
B solo, SSAT, SATB, 2 vln, 4 gamba, bc
Funeral of Anna Catharina von Königseck
Königsberg, 1673
RISM S2643 (parts)
DMA 2/718

S0422 **Gott tu mit mir, was ihm gefällt**
SATTB, 4 vla, bc
Funeral of M. Christophori Schulz

SEBASTIANI, Johann (*continued*)

Königsberg, 1679
RISM S2650 (score)
DMA 2/721

S0423   **Herr, du nimmst dich unser an**
SATTB, 4 vla, bc
Funeral of Pierre de la Cave
Königsberg, 1679
RISM S2649 (score)
DMA 2/722

S0424   **Herr, es gehen deine Plagen**
SATTB
Funeral of Gottfried Augustin
Königsberg, 1667
RISM S2638 (score)
DMA 2/714

S0425   **Herr, vergnüge mit der Welt**
SATTB, 4 vla, bc
Funeral of Regina Scharffin
Königsberg, 1670
RISM S2640 (score)
DMA 2/715

S0426   **Herr, wie ist dein Gnad so gross**
SATTB, 4 vla, bc
Funeral of Friedrich Schröder
Königsberg, 1680
RISM S2653 (score)
DMA 2/726

S0427   **Ich bin ein armer Wanders-Mann**
SATTB, 4 vla, bc
Funeral of Gerhard Schröder
Königsberg, 1678
RISM S2646 (score)
DMA 2/720

S0428   **Ich habe einen guten Kampf gekämpfet**
SSATB, 2 vln, 2 gamba, bc
Funeral of Anna Catharina von Kreytzen
Königsberg, 1657
parts
DMA 72//143

S0429   **Ich komm, o Gott der Gnaden**
SATTB, 3 vla, vlne, bc
Funeral of Valentin Leitzmann
Königsberg, 1664
RISM S2636 (score)
DMA 2/712

S0430   **Mein Freund ist mein**
SATTB, 4 vla, bc
Funeral of Barbara Maria von Götzen

Königsberg, 1676
RISM S2645 (score)
DMA 2/719

S0431   **Mein Gott, ich sehe wie die Welt**
SATTB, 4 vla, bc
Funeral of Rosina von Dobenecks
Königsberg, 1663
RISM S2633 (parts)
DMA 2/190
S-Uu 35:4 (Düben)
tablature and parts
S-Uu version with text "Min Gudh Jagh
seer att denna wärd"

S0432   **Meine Seele, gib dich nun wiederum zufrieden**
SATTB, 4 vla, bc
Funeral of Johann Röling
Königsberg, 1679
RISM S2648 (score)
DMA 2/723

S0433   **Min Gudh Jagh seer att denna wärd**
See Mein Gott, ich sehe wie die Welt

S0434   **Mir fället, Jesu, immer ein**
SATTB, 2 vln, 2 vla, vlne, bc
Funeral of Hinrich von Oppen
Königsberg, 1663
RISM S2634 (score)
DMA 2/1161
Ed. Zahn

S0435   **Nun danket alle Gott**
SATB, SATB, SATB, 2 vln/clar/corn/tpt,
vla/tbn, timp, bsn/vlne, bc
D-Bds Mus. ms. 30272, no. 2 (Bokemeyer)
score

S0436   **Omnes sumus debitores et iniquitates**
SSATB, 2 vln, tbn/bsn, 2 bsn, bc
22nd Sunday after Trinity
S-Uu 84:28, fol. 25v-29r (Düben)
tablature
DMA 1/1666
S-Uu 35:5 (Düben)
parts
DMA 1/1666

S0437   **Promite laetifico**
SATB, SATB, 2 vln, 2 cornettino, 2 tbn, 2
bsn, bc
D-Bds Mus. ms. 30272, no. 1 (Bokemeyer)
score

S0438   **Sei gnädig mir, o Herr mein Gott**
SATTB, 4 vla, bc
Funeral of Anna Franckin

Königsberg, 1663
RISM S2635 (score)
DMA 2/1160

S0439 Soll ich, Jesu, diesem Leben
SATTB, 4 vla, bc
Funeral of Johann Georg Döpner
Königsberg, 1680
RISM S2652 (score)
DMA 2/725

S0440 Wer, o Jesu, deine Wunden
SATTB, 3 vla, vlne, bc
Funeral
Königsberg, 1666
RISM S2637 (score)
DMA 2/713
EdM, 2nd ser. (Ostpreussen & Danzig),
vol. 1

S0441 Wie selig ist doch, der allhier
SATTB, 2 vln/chitarrini, 3 vla, bc
Funeral of Boguslav Radziwill
Königsberg, 1670
RISM S2639, Reich 204 (score)

S0442 Wo soll mein Zuflucht hin gerichtet sein und bleiben
SATTB, 4 vla, bc
Funeral of Elisabeth Sophia Korffin
Königsberg, 1679
RISM S2651 (score)
DMA 2/724

SEDELMAIER

S0443 Magnificat
SATB, 2 vln, bc
D-Bds Mus. ms. 30088, no. 18
score

SEIDEL, (Johann) Georg

S0444 Viel tausend gute Nacht
SATB, bc
Funeral of Barbara Elisabeth Findekeller
Dresden, 1688
RISM S2712, Reich 61

SEIDEL, Martin

S0445 Ach Traurigkeit! Ach Leid und Schmerzen
SATB
Funeral

n.p., 1680
RISM S2713 (score)
DMA 66//50

SEIDEL, Samuel (ca. 1610-1665)

COLLECTIONS

Corona gloriae (1657)
RISM S2716 (parts)

Geistliches Seelen-, Paradies-, und Lust-Gärtlein
(1658)
RISM S2717 (parts)

WORKS

S0446 Alleluia, Lob und Ehre
SSAATB, bc
Geistliches . . . Lust-Gärtlein, no. 15

S0447 Barmherzig und gnädig ist der Herr
SSATTB, bc
Geistliches . . . Lust-Gärtlein, no. 13

S0448 Das ist je gewißlich wahr
SSATB, bc
Geistliches . . . Lust-Gärtlein, no. 5

S0449 Der Tod ist verschlungen in den Sieg
SSATB, bc
Geistliches . . . Lust-Gärtlein, no. 6

S0450 Der Wagen Gottes ist vieltausendmal tausend
SSATB, bc
Geistliches . . . Lust-Gärtlein, no. 7

S0451 Ei, du frommer und getreuer Knecht
SSAATB, bc
Corona gloriae, no. 13

S0452 Eins bitte ich vom Herren
SSATB, bc
Corona gloriae, no. 1

S0453 Fürwahr, er trug unsere Krankheit
SSATB, bc
Geistliches . . . Lust-Gärtlein, no. 4

S0454 Gott ist unser Zuversicht und Stärke
SSATTB, bc
Geistliches . . . Lust-Gärtlein, no. 9

S0455 Herr, wenn ich nur dich habe
SSATB, bc
Corona gloriae, no. 8

S0456 Ich habe einen guten Kampf gekämpfet
SSATB, bc
Corona gloriae, no. 9

SEIDEL, Samuel (*continued*)

S0457 **Ich harre des Herren**
SSATB, bc
Corona gloriae, no. 5

S0458 **Ich liege und schlafe ganz mit Frieden**
SSATB, bc
Corona gloriae, no. 11

S0459 **Ich weiß, daß mein Erlöser lebt**
SSATB, bc
Corona gloriae, no. 10

S0460 **Ich will dem Herren singen mein Leben lang**
SSATB, bc
Corona gloriae, no. 4

S0461 **Ich will meinen Geist ausgießen**
SSATB, bc
Geistliches . . . Lust-Gärtlein, no. 8

S0462 **Ich will mich mit dir verloben in Ewigkeit**
SSAATB, bc
Geistliches . . . Lust-Gärtlein, no. 12

S0463 **Jawohl, du lieber Freund**
SATB, bc
Funeral of Anne Margarete Brehme
Dresden, 1652
RISM S2715, Reich 51

S0464 **Kommet her und schauet die Werke des Herren**
SSATTB, bc
Geistliches . . . Lust-Gärtlein, no. 10

S0465 **Lobe den Herren, meine Seele**
SSATB, bc
Corona gloriae, no. 6

S0466 **Nun ist das Heil**
SSAATB, bc
Geistliches . . . Lust-Gärtlein, no. 14

S0467 **Schaffe in mir, Gott, ein reines Herz**
SSATB, bc
Corona gloriae, no. 3

S0468 **Sei nun wieder zufrieden, meine Seele**
SSATB, bc
Corona gloriae, no. 12

S0469 **Siehe, es kommt die Zeit**
SSATB, bc
Geistliches . . . Lust-Gärtlein, no. 2

S0470 **So spricht der Herr, der König Israel**
SSATB, bc
Geistliches . . . Lust-Gärtlein, no. 1

S0471 **Uns ist ein Kind geboren**
SSATB, bc
Geistliches . . . Lust-Gärtlein, no. 3

S0472 **Verlaß mich nicht, Gott, im Alter**
SSATB, bc
Corona gloriae, no. 7

S0473 **Wie lieblich sind auf den Bergen**
SSAATB, bc
Geistliches . . . Lust-Gärtlein, no. 11

S0474 **Zweierlei bitt ich von dir**
SSATB, bc
Corona gloriae, no. 2

SEPP, R. P.

S0475 **Missa**
SATB, 2 vln, vla, bc
D-Bds Mus. ms. 30272, no. 3 (Bokemeyer)
score

SLÖPKE, Mauritz

S0476 **Ich preise dich, Herr**
SAB, 2 vln, vla, bc
S-Uu 66:8 (Düben) (1685)
parts (autograph)

S0477 **Nun komm, der Heiden Heiland**
SSATB, bc
S-Uu 35:6 (Düben) (1681)
parts (autograph)

SPAHN, Johann Ernst

S0478 **Gott, du bist meine Zuversicht**
SATB, bc
Funeral of Johann Georg Butschky
Dresden, 1686
RISM S4035, Reich 59 (parts)
DMA 70//172

S0479 **Ich achte es alle für Schaden**
SATB, bc
D-Dlb Mus. 1911-E-500 (Grimma U 522/T 17)
parts

S0480 **Missa (brevis)**
SSAATTBB, bc
PL-Kj Mus. ms. 40040, no. 110 (1683)
parts

S0481 **Wir sind getrost und haben vielmehr Lust**
SSAATTB, bc
Funeral of Agnetissa von Schönberg
Dresden, 1693
RISM S4036, Reich 63 (parts)
DMA 69//152

SPAHN, D. F.

S0482 **Missa paschalis**
SATB, bc
D-Bds Mus. ms. 30272, no. 4 (Bokemeyer)
score

SPEER, Daniel (1636-1707)

COLLECTIONS

Evangelische Seelen-Gedanken I (1681)
RISM S4068 (parts)

Evangelische Seelen-Gedanken II (1682)
RISM S4069 (parts)

Philomela angelica (1688)
RISM S4073 (parts)

WORKS

S0483 **Ach Herz! ich steck im Elend voll**
SSATB, 2 vln, 3 vla, bc
3rd Sunday after Epiphany
Evangelische Seelen-Gedanken I, no. 15

S0484 **Ach liebe Seele, sieh**
SSATB, 2 vln, 3 vla, bc
Quinquagesima
Evangelische Seelen-Gedanken I, no. 23

S0485 **Ach sehet euch wohl von**
SSATB, 2 vln, 3 vla, bc
8th Sunday after Trinity
Evangelische Seelen-Gedanken II, no. 12

S0486 **Also hat Gott geliebet**
SSATB, 2 vln, 3 vla, bc
Time of Pentecost
Evangelische Seelen-Gedanken I, no. 41

S0487 **Andreas läßt sich nicht**
SSATB, 2 vln, 3 vla, bc
Feast of Saint Andrew
Evangelische Seelen-Gedanken I, no. 2

S0488 **Bist du der da kommen soll**
SSATB, 2 vln, 3 vla, bc
3rd Sunday of Advent
Evangelische Seelen-Gedanken I, no. 4

S0489 **Christi Glieder sagen frei**
SSATB, 2 vln, 3 vla, bc
4th Sunday of Advent
Evangelische Seelen-Gedanken I, no. 5

S0490 **Christi Werke, Macht, und Stärke**
SSATB, 2 vln, 3 vla, bc
19th Sunday after Trinity
Evangelische Seelen-Gedanken II, no. 27

S0491 **Christus der vor dreien Tagen**
SSATB, 2 vln, 3 vla, bc
Easter Sunday
Evangelische Seelen-Gedanken I, no. 30

S0492 **Christus Jesus, Gottes Sohn**
SSATB, 2 vln, 3 vla, bc
5th Sunday after Easter
Evangelische Seelen-Gedanken I, no. 37

S0493 **Christus muß um der Wahrheit**
SSATB, 2 vln, 3 vla, bc
5th Sunday of Lent
Evangelische Seelen-Gedanken I, no. 29

S0494 **Christus spricht, ich bin der Weg**
SSATB, 2 vln, 3 vla, bc
Feast of Saints Philip and James
Evangelische Seelen-Gedanken I, no. 33

S0495 **Das allerhöchste Gebot**
SSATB, 2 vln, 3 vla, bc
Evangelische Seelen-Gedanken II, no. 25

S0496 **Daß Gott allmächtig sei**
SSATB, 2 vln, 3 vla, bc
7th Sunday after Trinity
Evangelische Seelen-Gedanken II, no. 11

S0497 **Den Frommen geht zu Hand**
SSATB, 2 vln, 3 vla, bc
3rd Sunday after Easter
Evangelische Seelen-Gedanken I, no. 35

S0498 **Der Eltern Christi Gottes Furcht**
SSATB, 2 vln, 3 vla, bc
1st Sunday after Epiphany
Evangelische Seelen-Gedanken I, no. 13

S0499 **Der Geist der Wahrheit kommt**
SSATB, 2 vln, 3 vla, bc
Sunday after Ascension
Evangelische Seelen-Gedanken I, no. 39

S0500 **Der Herr, der Gott Israel hat erlöset**
SSATB, 2 vln, 3 vla, bc
Feast of John the Baptist
Evangelische Seelen-Gedanken II, no. 2

S0501 **Der Juden Knäbelein im alten Testament**
SSATB, 2 vln, 3 vla, bc
Circumcision
Evangelische Seelen-Gedanken I, no. 10

S0502 **Der liebe Jüngste Tag**
SSATB, 2 vln, 3 vla, bc
2nd Sunday of Advent
Evangelische Seelen-Gedanken I, no. 3

S0503 **Des Hauses Vater kommt**
SSATB, 2 vln, 3 vla, bc

SPEER, Daniel (*continued*)

Septuagesima
Evangelische Seelen-Gedanken I, no. 20

S0504 **Die Eltern Christi nimmt es Wunder**
SSATB, 2 vln, 3 vla, bc
Sunday after Christmas
Evangelische Seelen-Gedanken I, no. 9

S0505 **Die so etwas bitten wollen**
SSATB, 2 vln, 3 vla, bc
6th Sunday after Trinity
Evangelische Seelen-Gedanken II, no. 9

S0506 **Die so ihr im Schulden Spittel zur Bezahlung**
SSATB, 2 vln, 3 vla, bc
22nd Sunday after Trinity
Evangelische Seelen-Gedanken II, no. 30

S0507 **Die weisen Heiden reisen fern**
SSATB, 2 vln, 3 vla, bc
Epiphany
Evangelische Seelen-Gedanken I, no. 12

S0508 **Ecce annuncio vobis gaudium**
ATB, 2 vln, bc
Philomela angelica, no. 14

S0509 **Ecce concipies in utero**
ATB, 2 vln, bc
Philomela angelica, no. 13

S0510 **Ecce non dormitabit qui custodit Israel**
ATB, 2 vln, bc
Philomela angelica, no. 18

S0511 **Ecce nos relinquimus omnia**
ATB, 2 vln, bc
Philomela angelica, no. 19

S0512 **Ecce nunc benedicite Domino**
ATB, 2 vln, bc
Philomela angelica, no. 17

S0513 **Ecce oculi Domini**
ATB, 2 vln, bc
Philomela angelica, no. 21

S0514 **Ecce quam bonum et quam jucundum**
ATB, 2 vln, bc
Philomela angelica, no. 23

S0515 **Ecce quomodo moritur justus**
ATB, 2 vln, bc
Philomela angelica, no. 15

S0516 **Ecce sic benedicetur homo qui timet Dominum**
ATB, 2 vln, bc
Philomela angelica, no. 20

S0517 **Ecce sto ad ostium et pulso**
ATB, 2 vln, bc
Philomela angelica, no. 22

S0518 **Ecce venit Dominus in sanctis millibus**
ATB, 2 vln, bc
Philomela angelica, no. 24

S0519 **Ecce vicit Leo de tribu Juda radix David**
ATB, 2 vln, bc
Philomela angelica, no. 16

S0520 **Ein großes Abendmahl wird uns heut**
SSATB, 2 vln, 3 vla, bc
2nd Sunday after Trinity
Evangelische Seelen-Gedanken II, no. 5

S0521 **Ein jeder sei von Herzen**
SSATB, 2 vln, 3 vla, bc
4th Sunday after Trinity
Evangelische Seelen-Gedanken II, no. 7

S0522 **Es ist ja der Mensch im Leben**
SSATB, 2 vln, 3 vla, bc
16th Sunday after Trinity
Evangelische Seelen-Gedanken II, no. 22

S0523 **Es soll in dieser Welt**
SSATB, 2 vln, 3 vla, bc
17th Sunday after Trinity
Evangelische Seelen-Gedanken II, no. 24

S0524 **Es springen und singen mit süßem Geschöne**
SSATB, 2 vln, 3 vla, bc
Christmas Day
Evangelische Seelen-Gedanken I, no. 7

S0525 **Es wartet auf der Wach**
SSATB, 2 vln, 3 vla, bc
27th Sunday after Trinity
Evangelische Seelen-Gedanken II, no. 35

S0526 **Es will der Priester und Levit**
SSATB, 2 vln, 3 vla, bc
13th Sunday after Trinity
Evangelische Seelen-Gedanken II, no. 18

S0527 **Freu dich sehr, o meine Seele**
SSATB, bc
Funeral
Evangelische Seelen-Gedanken II, no. 54

S0528 **Freuet euch alle**
SSATB, bc
Christmas Day
Evangelische Seelen-Gedanken II, no. 43

S0529 **Frohlocket, ihr Völker, von Freuden**
SSATB, 2 vln, 3 vla, bc
Ascension
Evangelische Seelen-Gedanken I, no. 38

S0530 **Frommen Seelen Ehren-Preis**
SSATB, 2 vln, 3 vla, bc
Annunciation of the Virgin Mary
Evangelische Seelen-Gedanken I, no. 26

S0531 **Gehe in dein Kämmerlein**
SSATB, 2 vln, 3 vla, bc
11th Sunday after Trinity
Evangelische Seelen-Gedanken II, no. 16

S0532 **Gib uns, Herr, ein gesegnetes**
SSATB, bc
Christmas Day
Evangelische Seelen-Gedanken II, no. 45

S0533 **Gott einer Obrigkeit**
SSATB, 2 vln, 3 vla, bc
23rd Sunday after Trinity
Evangelische Seelen-Gedanken II, no. 31

S0534 **Gott, wie lang muß ich noch warten**
SSATB, bc
Funeral
Evangelische Seelen-Gedanken II, no. 47

S0535 **Gottlob die hochgewünschte Zeit**
SSATB, bc
Christmas Day
Evangelische Seelen-Gedanken II, no. 40

S0536 **Gottlob, die Stund ist kommen**
SSATB, bc
Funeral
Evangelische Seelen-Gedanken II, no. 49

S0537 **Gute Nacht, ihr Eitelkeiten**
SSATB, bc
Funeral of David Buttersack
Evangelische Seelen-Gedanken II, no. 46

S0538 **Herr, nun laß in Friede fahren Deinen aus der Welt**
SSATB, 2 vln, 3 vla, bc
Purification of the Virgin Mary
Evangelische Seelen-Gedanken I, no. 17

S0539 **Hier, hier ist gut zu sein**
SSATB, 2 vln, 3 vla, bc
6th Sunday after Epiphany
Evangelische Seelen-Gedanken I, no. 19

S0540 **Ich komm, o Jesu, jetzt**
SSATB, 2 vln, 3 vla, bc
3rd Sunday after Trinity
Evangelische Seelen-Gedanken II, no. 6

S0541 **Ihr, ihr seids, die ihr verblieben**
SSATB, 2 vln, 3 vla, bc
Feast of Saint Bartholomew
Evangelische Seelen-Gedanken II, no. 14

S0542 **Jerusalem, du Mörderin der heiligen Propheten**
SSATB, 2 vln, 3 vla, bc
2nd Day of Christmas (Feast of Saint Stephen)
Evangelische Seelen-Gedanken I, no. 8

S0543 **Jesulein, ich komm zu grüßen**
SSATB, bc
Christmas Day
Evangelische Seelen-Gedanken II, no. 41

S0544 **Jetzt ist die rechte Freuden Zeit**
SSATB, bc
Christmas Day
Evangelische Seelen-Gedanken II, no. 36

S0545 **Joseph liebster, Joseph mein**
SSATB, bc
Christmas Day
Evangelische Seelen-Gedanken II, no. 44

S0546 **Kein Stündlein geht dahin**
SSATB, bc
Funeral
Evangelische Seelen-Gedanken II, no. 53

S0547 **Komm, komm, du guter Geist**
SSATB, 2 vln, 3 vla, bc
Pentecost
Evangelische Seelen-Gedanken I, no. 40

S0548 **Komm, liebe Seele, komm**
SSATB, 2 vln, 3 vla, bc
Feast of Saint Matthew
Evangelische Seelen-Gedanken I, no. 21

S0549 **Komm, meine Seele, komm**
SSATB, 2 vln, 3 vla, bc
2nd Sunday of Lent
Evangelische Seelen-Gedanken I, no. 25

S0550 **Kommet her zur Krippen**
SSATB, bc
Christmas Day
Evangelische Seelen-Gedanken II, no. 37

S0551 **Laß ab von Sünden**
SSATB, 2 vln, 3 vla, bc
10th Sunday after Trinity
Evangelische Seelen-Gedanken II, no. 15

S0552 **Laßt das Trauren, liebe Brüder**
SSATB, 2 vln, 3 vla, bc
1st Sunday after Easter
Evangelische Seelen-Gedanken I, no. 32

S0553 **Leben voll Beschwerlichkeit**
SSATB, bc
Funeral
Evangelische Seelen-Gedanken II, no. 51

S0554 **Liebe Seele, es ist Zeit**
SSATB, 2 vln, 3 vla, bc
1st Sunday of Lent
Evangelische Seelen-Gedanken I, no. 24

SPEER, Daniel (*continued*)

S0555 **Liebster Jesu, komm doch bald**
SSATB, 2 vln, 3 vla, bc
21st Sunday after Trinity
Evangelische Seelen-Gedanken II, no. 29

S0556 **Man sieht den Verwüstungs Greul**
SSATB, 2 vln, 3 vla, bc
25th Sunday after Trinity
Evangelische Seelen-Gedanken II, no. 33

S0557 **Mein junges Leben hat ein End**
SSATB, bc
Funeral
Evangelische Seelen-Gedanken II, no. 50

S0558 **Merkt doch wie Christus klagt**
SSATB, 2 vln, 3 vla, bc
14th Sunday after Trinity
Evangelische Seelen-Gedanken II, no. 20

S0559 **O Christe, Schutz-Herz deinen Glieder**
SSATB, 2 vln, 3 vla, bc
Eastertide
Evangelische Seelen-Gedanken I, no. 31

S0560 **O du schnödes Weltgebäude**
SSATB, bc
Funeral
Evangelische Seelen-Gedanken II, no. 55

S0561 **O Jesu Christ, dein Kripplein ist**
SSATB, bc
Christmas Day
Evangelische Seelen-Gedanken II, no. 42

S0562 **O laßt euch zu Jesu führen**
SSATB, 2 vln, 3 vla, bc
12th Sunday after Trinity
Evangelische Seelen-Gedanken II, no. 17

S0563 **O meine Seele, sieh dich für**
SSATB, 2 vln, 3 vla, bc
5th Sunday after Epiphany
Evangelische Seelen-Gedanken I, no. 18

S0564 **O selig, selig sind**
SSATB, 2 vln, 3 vla, bc
3rd Sunday of Lent
Evangelische Seelen-Gedanken I, no. 27

S0565 **Schaut, wie der Himmels König**
SSATB, 2 vln, 3 vla, bc
20th Sunday after Trinity
Evangelische Seelen-Gedanken II, no. 28

S0566 **Schaut, wie der Satan hier**
SSATB, 2 vln, 3 vla, bc
Sunday after Circumcision
Evangelische Seelen-Gedanken I, no. 11

S0567 **Sehet Matthäum den Zollner und Sünder**
SSATB, 2 vln, 3 vla, bc
Feast of Saint Matthew
Evangelische Seelen-Gedanken II, no. 19

S0568 **Sei gegrüßt, mein Gnadenthron**
SSATB, bc
Christmas Day
Evangelische Seelen-Gedanken II, no. 38

S0569 **Simon Petro dem Bekennen**
SSATB, 2 vln, 3 vla, bc
Feast of Saints Peter and Paul
Evangelische Seelen-Gedanken II, no. 4

S0570 **So ihr wollt in Himmel kommen**
SSATB, 2 vln, 3 vla, bc
6th Sunday after Trinity
Evangelische Seelen-Gedanken II, no. 10

S0571 **Stimmet Hosianna in christlichen Chören**
SSATB, 2 vln, 3 vla, bc
1st Sunday of Advent
Evangelische Seelen-Gedanken I, no. 1

S0572 **Strahlet, ihr Lichter, Mond, Sternen, und Sonne**
SSATB, bc
Christmas Day
Evangelische Seelen-Gedanken II, no. 39

S0573 **Thomas, der ungläubig war**
SSATB, 2 vln, 3 vla, bc
Feast of Saint Thomas
Evangelische Seelen-Gedanken I, no. 6

S0574 **Wann des Menschen Sohn wird kommen**
SSATB, 2 vln, 3 vla, bc
26th Sunday after Trinity
Evangelische Seelen-Gedanken II, no. 34

S0575 **Wann diese arge Welt samt allen ihren Türken**
SSATB, 2 vln, 3 vla, bc
4th Sunday after Epiphany
Evangelische Seelen-Gedanken I, no. 16

S0576 **Was Christus hier zu seinen Jüngern**
SSATB, 2 vln, 3 vla, bc
Feast of Saints Simon and Jude
Evangelische Seelen-Gedanken II, no. 26

S0577 **Was dem Menschen auch tut fehlen**
SSATB, 2 vln, 3 vla, bc
24th Sunday after Trinity
Evangelische Seelen-Gedanken II, no. 32

S0578 **Was mein Gott will, das gescheh allzeit**
SSATB, bc
Funeral
Evangelische Seelen-Gedanken II, no. 48

S0579 **Was sorget ihr um Speise**
SSATB, 2 vln, 3 vla, bc
15th Sunday after Trinity
Evangelische Seelen-Gedanken II, no. 21

S0580 **Weil nun Christus Sünd und Tod**
SSATB, 2 vln, 3 vla, bc
4th Sunday after Easter
Evangelische Seelen-Gedanken I, no. 36

S0581 **Welcher Same fällt in Hecken**
SSATB, 2 vln, 3 vla, bc
Sexagesima
Evangelische Seelen-Gedanken I, no. 22

S0582 **Wenn Gott der Engel Schütz nicht hätte**
SSATB, 2 vln, 3 vla, bc
Feast of the Holy Angels
Evangelische Seelen-Gedanken II, no. 23

S0583 **Wer da saget, daß er liebet Gott**
SSATB, 2 vln, 3 vla, bc
1st Sunday after Trinity
Evangelische Seelen-Gedanken II, no. 3

S0584 **Wer im Namen Jesu Christ**
SSATB, 2 vln, 3 vla, bc
5th Sunday after Trinity
Evangelische Seelen-Gedanken II, no. 8

S0585 **Wer Jesum ladet ein auf sein hochzeitlich Fest**
SSATB, 2 vln, 3 vla, bc
2nd Sunday after Epiphany
Evangelische Seelen-Gedanken I, no. 14

S0586 **Wer sich so viel bemühet**
SSATB, 2 vln, 3 vla, bc
4th Sunday of Lent
Evangelische Seelen-Gedanken I, no. 28

S0587 **Wie gar gewiß ist doch der Tod**
SSATB, bc
Funeral
Evangelische Seelen-Gedanken II, no. 52

S0588 **Wir müssen all von nun geboren werden**
SSATB, 2 vln, 3 vla, bc
Trinity
Evangelische Seelen-Gedanken II, no. 1

S0589 **Wo find't sich solcher Hirt**
SSATB, 2 vln, 3 vla, bc
2nd Sunday after Easter
Evangelische Seelen-Gedanken I, no. 34

S0590 **Wohl dem, wohl dem der vorsichtig wandelt**
SSATB, 2 vln, 3 vla, bc
9th Sunday after Trinity
Evangelische Seelen-Gedanken II, no. 13

SPIRIDION, Pater (Johann Nenning) (1615-1685)

COLLECTIONS

Musica romana (1665)
RISM S1665[3] (parts)

Musica theo-liturgica (1668)
RISM S4118 (parts)

WORKS

S0591 **Missa (Kyrie, Gloria, Credo)**
SSB, 2 vln, bc
S-Uu 83:36, fol. 29v-38r (Düben)
tablature
DMA 2/2293

S0592 **Missa Sancti Alberti Carmelitae Confessoris**
SSATB, 2 vln, bc
Musica theo-liturgica, no. 4

S0593 **Missa Sancti Angeli Martyris Carmelitae**
SSATB, 2 vln, bc
Musica theo-liturgica, no. 2

S0594 **Missa Sancti Cyrilli Carmelitae**
SSATB, 2 vln, bc
Musica theo-liturgica, no. 3

S0595 **Missa Sancti Simonis Stock, Carmelitae Confessoris**
SSATB, 2 vln, bc
Musica theo-liturgica, no. 1

S0596 **Salve regina**
ATB, bc
Musica romana, no. 13

STEFFANI, Agostino (1654-1728)

COLLECTIONS

Psalmodia vespertina (1674)
RISM S4733 (parts)
DMA 84//5
Ms. score ed. by A. Einstein, "Madrigals of
the Sixteenth and Seventeenth Century,"
vol. 58A (Smith College)

Sacer janus quadrifons (1685)
RISM S4739 (parts)
Ms. score ed. by A. Einstein, "Madrigals of
the Sixteenth and Seventeenth Century,"
vol. 58A (Smith College)

WORKS

S0597 **Beatus vir**
SATB, SATB, bc
Psalmodia vespertina, no. 3

STEFFANI, Agostino (*continued*)

S0598 **Beatus vir**
SSB, 2 vln, bc
GB-Cfm Ms. 30.F2, no. 3, p. 51
score
GB-Lbl Add. Ms. 31481, no. 4, fol. 20r-31v
score

S0599 **Beatus vir**
8 vv, bc
I-Af MSS 322/4 (1676)
score (autograph)

S0600 **Cingite floribus**
STB, bc
Feast of a Virgin Martyr
Sacer janus quadrifons, no. 9
GB-Lbl Add. Ms. 31477, no. 12, fol. 46b-52v;
Add. Ms. 31481, no. 7, fol. 62r-81v
score (SSB, 2 vln, bc)

S0601 **Confitebor**
SATB, SATB, bc
Psalmodia vespertina, no. 2

S0602 **Confitebor tibi**
SSB, bc
GB-Lbl Add. Ms. 14398, no. 39, fol.
134b-143v (1709)
score
New Grove: doubtful

S0603 **Credidi**
SATB, SATB, bc
Psalmodia vespertina, no. 6

S0604 **Dixit Dominus**
SATB, SATB, bc
Psalmodia vespertina, no. 1

S0605 **Dixit Dominus**
SSATB, 2 vln, 2 vla, bc
D-Bds Mus. ms. 2755, no. 3
score
Ms. score by A. Einstein, "Madrigals of
the Sixteenth and Seventeenth Century,"
vol. 58A (Smith College)

S0606 **Domine probasti me**
SATB, SATB, bc
Psalmodia vespertina, no. 8

S0607 **Elevamini in voce tubae**
ATB, bc
Sacer janus quadrifons, no. 11

S0608 **Felices adae filii**
SAT, bc
Sacer janus quadrifons, no. 3

GB-Lbl Add. Ms. 31499, no. 4, fol. 23b-29v
score

S0609 **Flores agri**
SAB, bc
Feast of a Saint
Sacer janus quadrifons, no. 5
GB-Lbl Add. Ms. 31499, no. 6, fol. 36b-41v
score (SAT, bc)

S0610 **Fuge cara anima**
ATB, bc
Sacer janus quadrifons, no. 12

S0611 **In convertendo**
SATB, SATB, bc
Psalmodia vespertina, no. 7

S0612 **In exitu**
SATB, SATB, bc
Psalmodia vespertina, no. 5

S0613 **Laetatus sum**
SATB, SATB, bc
Psalmodia vespertina, no. 11

S0614 **Lauda Jerusalem**
SATB, SATB, bc
Psalmodia vespertina, no. 13

S0615 **Laudate Dominum**
SSSS, SSSS, bc
GB-Cfm Ms. 30.F2, no. 4, p. 91 (1673)
score

S0616 **Laudate Dominum, omnes gentes**
SATB, SATB, bc
Psalmodia vespertina, no. 9

S0617 **Laudate, pueri**
SATB, SATB, bc
Psalmodia vespertina, no. 4

S0618 **Laudate, pueri**
SSAT, SSAT
GB-Cfm Ms. 30.F2, no. 5, p. 115 (1673)
score

S0619 **Magnificat**
SATB, SATB, bc
Psalmodia vespertina, no. 14

S0620 **Memento Domine, David**
SATB, SATB, bc
Psalmodia vespertina, no. 10

S0621 **Motetto per ogni tempo**
4 vv, instr
I-Fc
Listed only in *New Grove*

S0622 **Nisi Dominus**
SATB, SATB, bc
Psalmodia vespertina, no. 12

S0623 **Pro Christo affligimur**
SSB, bc
GB-Lbl Add. Ms. 31477, no. 12, fol. 53r-54r;
Ms. 31818, no. 6, fol. 38b
score

S0624 **Qui diligit Mariam/filium/Dominum/Christum**
SSATB, bc
GB-Cfm Ms. 23.F2 (cat. no. 31), p. 136;
Ms. 24.F3 (cat. no. 43), section 2, p. 1
score
GB-Cfm Ms. 32.G 17 (cat. no. 160)
parts
GB-Lbl Add. Ms. 31499, no. 1, fol. 1v-11r;
Ms. 5054, no. 1, fol. 8b; Ms. 31409, no.
2, fol. 12; Ms. 31477, no. 1, fol. 3;
Add. Ms. 31481, no. 5, fol. 32r-40v
score
additional copies in GB-Lcm, GB-Ob,
B-Bc

S0625 **Qui pacem amatis**
SSB, bc
Sacer janus quadrifons, no. 2
GB-Lbl Add. Ms. 31477, no. 10, fol. 37r-41r;
Ms. 31476, no. 3, fol. 9; Ms. 31499, no.
3, fol. 17v-23v
score
B-Bc Wotquenne 211
score

S0626 **Reginam nostram**
SSB, bc
Any feast of the Virgin Mary
Sacer janus quadrifons, no. 1
GB-Lbl Add. Ms. 31477, no. 9, fol. 33r-36v;
Ms. 31818, no. 5, fol. 31b; Ms. 31499,
no. 2, fol. 11v-17v
score
DTB 11 (Jg. 6/2), pp. 150-61

S0627 **Sonitus armorum**
SAT, bc
Any feast of the Virgin Mary
Sacer janus quadrifons, no. 4
GB-Lbl Add. Ms. 31499, no. 5, fol. 30r-36r
score

S0628 **Sperate in Deo**
SSATB, bc
GB-Cfm Ms. 30.F2, no. 1, p. 1
score

GB-Lbl Add. Ms. 31481, no. 3, fol. 8r-19r
score

S0629 **Stabat Mater**
SSATTB, 2 vln, 3 vla, vc, bc
GB-Lbl Add. Ms. 31498; Ms. 5049, no. 2,
fol. 34
score
D-Hs M B/2510
parts
D-Hs M B/1761
score
Ed. C. K. Scott (Oxford Univ. Press, 1938)
Ed. H. Sievers (Moseler, 1956)

S0630 **Surge, propera, veni**
ATB, bc
Feast of a Virgin not a Martyr
Sacer janus quadrifons, no. 10

S0631 **Tandem adest**
SAB, bc
Feast of a Confessor Saint
Sacer janus quadrifons, no. 6
GB-Lbl Add. Ms. 31499, no. 7, fol. 42r-47r
score
DTB 11 (Jg. 6/2), pp. 162-73

S0632 **Triduanas a Domino**
SSAT, SSAT
GB-Cfm Ms. 30.F2, no. 2, p. 39 (1673)
score

S0633 **Venite, exultemus**
SAB, bc
Feast of Saint Vidius
Sacer janus quadrifons, no. 7
GB-Lbl Add. Ms. 31477, no. 11, fol. 41b-46v
score (SSB, bc)

S0634 **Videte gentes**
STB, bc
Feast of a Martyr Saint
Sacer janus quadrifons, no. 8
GB-Lbl Add. Ms. 31481, no. 6, fol. 41r-61v
score (SSB, 2 vln, bc)

STEINGADEN, Constantin (ca. 1618-1675)

COLLECTIONS

Flores hyemnales (1666)
RISM S5726 (parts)

Messe concertante (1666)
RISM S5727 (parts)

STEINGADEN, Constantin (*continued*)

WORKS

S0635 **Beatus vir**
SATB, 2 vln, bc
Flores hyemnales, no. 18
S-Uu 85:72, fol. 7v-9r (Düben)
tablature
DMA 2/2296

S0636 **Confitebor**
SATB, 2 vln, bc
Flores hyemnales, no. 17

S0637 **Dixit Dominus**
SATB, 2 vln, bc
Flores hyemnales, no. 16
S-Uu 85:70, vol. 1v-2r (Düben)
tablature
DMA 2/2297

S0638 **Domine salvum fac regem**
See under anonymous

S0639 **Estote fortes in bello**
SSB, bc
Flores hyemnales, no. 4

S0640 **Exaltabo te, Domine**
SSB, bc
Flores hyemnales, no. 6

S0641 **Hoc est praeceptum meum**
SSB, bc
Flores hyemnales, no. 5

S0642 **In exitu Israel**
SATB, 2 vln, bc
Flores hyemnales, no. 21

S0643 **Laudate Dominum, omnes gentes**
SATB, 2 vln, bc
Flores hyemnales, no. 20

S0644 **Laudate, pueri**
SATB, 2 vln, bc
Flores hyemnales, no. 19

S0645 **Magnificat**
SATB, 2 vln, bc
Flores hyemnales, no. 22

S0646 **Missa I Leopoldo**
SATB, 2 vln, bc
Flores hyemnales, no. 15
S-Uu 85:71, fol. 2v-8r (Düben)
tablature
DMA 2/2300

S0647 **Missa II**
SATB, 2 vln, bc
Flores hyemnales, no. 23

S0648 **Missa III**
SATB, 2 vln, bc
Flores hyemnales, no. 24

S0649 **Missa O per amor, o per forza**
SSATB, 2 vln, 2 vla, vc, bc
Messe concertante, no. 4

S0650 **Missa Pacta clara amicitia firma**
SSATB, 2 vln, 2 vla, vc, bc
Messe concertante, no. 3

S0651 **Missa per Angusta ad Augusta**
SATB, 2 vln, 2 vla, bc
Messe concertante, no. 1
S-Uu 85:75 (Düben)
tablature
DMA 2/2301

S0652 **Missa Sancti Pelagius**
SATB, 2 vln, 2 vla, bc
Messe concertante, no. 2
S-Uu 86:12, fol. 16v-22r (Düben)
tablature
DMA 2/2299

S0653 **Missa Viva Mörspurg**
SSATB, 2 vln, 2 vla, vc, bc
Messe concertante, no. 5

STOSS

S0654 **Bestelle dein Haus**
AAB, 3 vla, vlne, bc
D-Dlb 1907-E-500 (Grimma U 296/U 100)
parts

STRATTNER, Georg Christoph (ca. 1664-1704)

S0655 **Ach mein Vater, ich habe gesündiget**
SATB, 2 vln, 3 vla, vlne, bc
19th Sunday after Trinity
D-F Ff. mus. 516 (1689)
parts (B lacking) and score (incomplete)

S0656 **Aus der Tiefe**
SSATB, 2 vln, 3 vla, vlne, bsn, bc
D-F Ff. mus. 517 (1685)
parts (C1 lacking)

S0657 **Barmherzig treuer Gott**
SATB, 2 vln, 3 vla, vlne, bc
D-F Ff. mus. 518
parts

S0658 **Beatus vir qui timet**
See under Anonymous

S0659 **Die Welt, das ungestüme Meer mich trägt**
SATB, 2 vln, 2 vla, bsn, bc
D-F Ff. mus. 519
parts (B lacking)

S0660 **Drei sind, die da zeugen im Himmel**
ATB, 2 vln, vlne, bc
D-F Ff. mus. 520
parts

S0661 **Du Hirt Israel höre**
SATB, 2 vln, 3 vla, bass viol/bsn, bc
D-F Ff. mus. 521
parts

S0662 **Erstanden ist des Todes Tod**
SATB, 2 vln, 2 vla/tbn, 2 fl/corn, bass viol/bsn, bc
D-F Ff. mus. 522
parts

S0663 **Getreue Schöpfer, der du mich**
SATB, 2 vln, 4 vla, bc
D-F Ff. mus. 523
parts

S0664 **Gott, sei mir gnädig**
See under Anonymous

S0665 **Herr, auf dich traue ich**
SATB, 4 vla, bc
US-Wc M2020.S8807 case
score

S0666 **Herr, der du uns hast anvertraut**
SATB, 2 vln, 3 vla, bc
9th Sunday after Trinity
D-F Ff. mus. 524
score (voices, bc only) and parts

S0667 **Himmel und Erde werden vergehen**
SATB, 2 vln, 2 vla, bc
2nd Sunday of Advent
D-B Mus. ms. 21478/4 (1687)
parts

S0668 **Ich komm, o höchster Gott**
See under Anonymous

S0669 **Ich stelle mich bei meinem Leben**
SSATB, 2 vln, 4 vla, bc
D-F Ff. mus. 525 (1676)
parts

S0670 **Ich will den Herrn loben allezeit**
SSATB, 2 vln, 2 vla, vlne, bsn, bc
D-F Ff. mus. 526 (1690)
parts

S0671 **Ihr Himmelsfeste, höret doch**
SSATTBB, 2 vln, 3 vla, bc
16th Sunday after Trinity
D-F Ff. mus. 527 (1693)
parts

S0672 **In corde dixit fatuus**
ATB, 2 vln, vlne, bc
D-F Ff. mus. 528 (1675)
parts

S0673 **O Gott, du Ursprung aller Liebe**
SATB, 2 vla, 2 ob, vlne, bsn, bc
Wedding
D-F Ff. mus. 529
parts

S0674 **Sehet doch, ihr Menschenkinder**
SSATTB, 2 vln, 4 vla, bc
Passion
D-F Ff. mus. 530 (1692)
parts

STRUNGK, Delphin (1600/01-1694)

S0675 **Kommet und sehet die Werke des Herrn**
SSATB, 2 vln/corn, 2 vla/tbn, 4 tpt, tbn, bc
D-W Musica Hdschr. 252 (1671)
parts
DMA 1/395

STRUNGK, Nicolaus Adam (1640-1700)

S0676 **Christus resurgens ex mortius**
STB, 2 vln, bsn, bc
D-Bds Mus. ms. 30272, no. 14 (Bokemeyer)
score
DMA 15//82
D-Dlb Mus. ms. 1845-E-1, no. 2, pp. 27-36
score

S0677 **Cum invocarem exaudiet me Deo**
SATB, 2 vln, 2 vla, bc
GB-Lbl Mus. R.M.24.a.3 (7)
score (includes 2 vla parts)
DMA 54//72

S0678 **Es woll uns Gott genädig sein**
STB, 2 vln, 2 vla, vlne/vc, bsn, bc
D-LUC 302A (1714)
parts
DMA 2/2303
D-B Mus. ms. 30099, no. 9 (Bokemeyer)
score
Attributed to Bronner in D-B

STRUNGK, Nicolaus Adam (*continued*)

    S0679   **Höre, mein Volk**
        AAB, 2 vln, 2 vla, bsn, bc
        D-Bds Mus. ms. 30272, no. 16 (Bokemeyer)
           score
           DMA 15//82
        D-Dlb Mus. ms. 1845-E-1, no. 4, pp. 55-77
           score

    S0680   **Nun treten wir ins neue Jahr**
        SATB, 2 vln, bc
        D-Bds Mus. ms. 30272, no. 15 (Bokemeyer)
           score
           DMA 15//82
        D-Dlb Mus. ms. 1845-E-1, no. 3, pp. 37-54
           score

    S0681   **Siehe, meine Freundin, du bist schön**
        SSATB, 2 vln, 2 vltta, bsn, bc
        D-Bds Mus. ms. 30272, no. 17 (Bokemeyer)
           score
           DMA 15//82
        D-Dlb Mus. ms. 1845-E-1, no. 5, pp. 78-107
           score

STRUTIUS (Strutz), Thomas (ca. 1621-1678)

    COLLECTION

        Lobsingenden Hertzens-Andacht (1656)
           RISM S7006 (choirbook)

    WORKS

    S0682   **Ach Christen für den Anti-Christ**
        SATB, bc
        8th Sunday after Trinity
        Lobsingenden Hertzens-Andacht, no. 55

    S0683   **Ach danket Gott zu dieser Zeit**
        SATB, bc
        Trinity
        Lobsingenden Hertzens-Andacht, no. 47

    S0684   **Ach Herr! wes soll ich trösten mich**
        SATB, bc
        1st Sunday after Trinity
        Lobsingenden Hertzens-Andacht, no. 48

    S0685   **Ach Herr, wie lang**
        SATB, bc
        21st Sunday after Trinity
        Lobsingenden Hertzens-Andacht, no. 69[a]

    S0686   **Ach hilf, mein Gott, die Schmerzen sein**
        SATB, bc
        3rd Sunday after Epiphany
        Lobsingenden Hertzens-Andacht, no. 15

    S0687   **Ach hilf mir, lieber Davids Sohn**
        SATB, bc
        2nd Sunday of Lent
        Lobsingenden Hertzens-Andacht, no. 23

    S0688   **Ach höret Christen Herzen**
        See Laßt Freuden Lieder klingen

    S0689   **Ach Jesu, laß anblicken**
        SATB, bc
        25th Sunday after Trinity
        Lobsingenden Hertzens-Andacht, no. 71

    S0690   **Ach Kirch, ach armes Häufelein**
        SATB, bc
        4th Sunday after Epiphany
        Lobsingenden Hertzens-Andacht, no. 16

    S0691   **Ach lasse das Trauren aus dem Sinn**
        SATB, bc
        4th Sunday after Easter
        Lobsingenden Hertzens-Andacht, no. 40

    S0692   **Ach schauet wie des Höchsten Hand**
        SATB, bc
        10th Sunday after Trinity
        Lobsingenden Hertzens-Andacht, no. 57

    S0693   **Ach schöne Herr! nach scharfem Recht**
        SATB, bc
        11th Sunday after Trinity
        Lobsingenden Hertzens-Andacht, no. 58

    S0694   **Ach was für Pein, mein Jesulein**
        SATB, bc
        Good Friday
        Lobsingenden Hertzens-Andacht, no. 32
        Winterfeld II, pp. 55-56 (Suppl.)

    S0695   **Ach, was hat doch des Menschen Sohn**
        SATB, bc
        5th Sunday after Epiphany
        Lobsingenden Hertzens-Andacht, no. 18

    S0696   **Ach, was soll ich machen**
        SATB, bc
        2nd Day of Christmas
        Lobsingenden Hertzens-Andacht, no. 6

    S0697   **Ach welche schöne Stimme klingt**
        SATB, bc
        Whit Tuesday
        Lobsingenden Hertzens-Andacht, no. 46

    S0698   **Ach welche Zeit, wir armen Leut**
        SATB, bc
        Sunday after Ascension
        Lobsingenden Hertzens-Andacht, no. 43

S0699 **Ach wie ist der Mensch geplaget**
SATB, bc
2nd Sunday of Advent
Lobsingenden Hertzens-Andacht, no. 2

S0700 **Ach wo nehm ich hin meinen Lauf**
SATB, bc
3rd Sunday after Trinity
Lobsingenden Hertzens-Andacht, no. 50

S0701 **Als Christus wahrer Mensch und Gott**
SATB, bc
1st Sunday of Lent
Lobsingenden Hertzens-Andacht, no. 22

S0702 **Auf! auf! mein Geist danksage**
SATB, bc
Easter Sunday
Lobsingenden Hertzens-Andacht, no. 34

S0703 **Aus meines Jesu Munde**
SATB, bc
5th Sunday after Easter
Lobsingenden Hertzens-Andacht, no. 41

S0704 **Christ unser Herr und Gott**
SATB, bc
Quinquagesima
Lobsingenden Hertzens-Andacht, no. 21

S0705 **Da Jesus nun mehr wohl bedacht**
SATB, bc
Palm Sunday
Lobsingenden Hertzens-Andacht, no. 28

S0706 **Das ist die Stund**
SATB, bc
Annunciation to the Virgin Mary
Lobsingenden Hertzens-Andacht, no. 25

S0707 **Das ist ein teures wertes Wort**
SATB, bc
19th Sunday after Trinity
Lobsingenden Hertzens-Andacht, no. 67

S0708 **Den Völkern alles Licht gebricht**
SATB, bc
Christmas Day
Lobsingenden Hertzens-Andacht, no. 5

S0709 **Der eingeborne Gottes Sohn**
SATB, bc
Sexagesima
Lobsingenden Hertzens-Andacht, no. 20

S0710 **Der große Drach, die alte Schlang**
SATB, bc
Christmas Day
Lobsingenden Hertzens-Andacht, no. 13[a]
Winterfeld II, pp. 54-55 (suppl.)

S0711 **Der Herr, der Herr erschienen ist**
SATB, bc
1st Sunday after Easter
Lobsingenden Hertzens-Andacht, no. 38[a]

S0712 **Der wunderschöne Jacobs-Stern**
SATB, bc
Epiphany
Lobsingenden Hertzens-Andacht, no. 12

S0713 **Des grossen Richters Stimme**
SATB, bc
24th Sunday after Trinity
Lobsingenden Hertzens-Andacht, no. 70

S0714 **Durch Teufels Neid ist Sünd und Tod**
SATB, bc
3rd Sunday of Lent
Lobsingenden Hertzens-Andacht, no. 24

S0715 **Es ist doch nur ein Grund**
SATB, bc
5th Sunday of Lent
Lobsingenden Hertzens-Andacht, no. 27

S0716 **Gaudeamus omnes fideles**
STB, 2 vln, bc
Christmas Day
S-Uu 35:8 (Düben)
parts
DMA 1/1667

S0717 **Gib unserm Landesherrn**
See Verleih uns Frieden gnädiglich

S0718 **Gleich wie bei heißer Sommerzeit**
SATB, bc
Epiphany
Lobsingenden Hertzens-Andacht, no. 17

S0719 **Gott ist dein Behüter**
SATB, bc
Sunday after New Year
Lobsingenden Hertzens-Andacht, no. 10

S0720 **Gott sei Dank für das Lösegeld**
SATB, bc
Easter Tuesday
Lobsingenden Hertzens-Andacht, no. 37

S0721 **Gottlob! wir sind gesprungen gesund**
SATB, bc
New Year
Lobsingenden Hertzens-Andacht, no. 11

S0722 **Herr Jesu, Trost der Armen**
SATB, bc
Maundy Thursday
Lobsingenden Hertzens-Andacht, no. 29

STRUTIUS (Strutz), Thomas (*continued*)

S0723 **Hilf, Jesu, mir anheben**
SATB, bc
Septuagesima
Lobsingenden Hertzens-Andacht, no. 19

S0724 **Hilf, Vater, tragen diese Last**
SATB, bc
3rd Sunday after Easter
Lobsingenden Hertzens-Andacht, no. 39

S0725 **Ich girre, winsel', Herr hilf mir**
SATB, bc
14th Sunday after Trinity
Lobsingenden Hertzens-Andacht, no. 61

S0726 **Ich heb auf meine Hände**
SATB, bc
5th Sunday after Trinity
Lobsingenden Hertzens-Andacht, no. 52

S0727 **Ich preise deine Gütigkeit**
SATB, bc
2nd Sunday after Trinity
Lobsingenden Hertzens-Andacht, no. 49

S0728 **Ihr Häupter unter Gottes Volk**
SATB, bc
23rd Sunday after Trinity
Lobsingenden Hertzens-Andacht, no. 69[c]

S0729 **Jesu, meine Freuden Sonne**
SATB, bc
New Year
Lobsingenden Hertzens-Andacht, no. 9

S0730 **Komm, du werter Geist**
SATB, bc
Pentecost
Lobsingenden Hertzens-Andacht, no. 44

S0731 **Kommt her zu mir, ihr Kinderlein**
SATB, bc
1st Sunday after Epiphany
Lobsingenden Hertzens-Andacht, no. 13[b]

S0732 **Kommt, kommt, ihr zarten Kinder**
SATB, bc
Feast of Saint Michael
Lobsingenden Hertzens-Andacht, no. 63

S0733 **Laßt Freuden Lieder klingen**
SATB, bc
1st Sunday of Advent
Lobsingenden Hertzens-Andacht, no. 1
Same music serves the text "Ach höret
Christen Herzen," Advent III

S0734 **Meine Jesu, für dein Angesicht**
SATB, bc
Maundy Thursday
Lobsingenden Hertzens-Andacht, no. 30

S0735 **Mein liebster Vater, wie soll ich**
SATB, bc
17th Sunday after Trinity
Lobsingenden Hertzens-Andacht, no. 65

S0736 **Meine Seele sich erfreuet**
SATB, bc
15th Sunday after Trinity
Lobsingenden Hertzens-Andacht, no. 62

S0737 **Meine Seele, stehet sich nach Jesu**
SATB, bc
27th Sunday after Trinity
Lobsingenden Hertzens-Andacht, no. 75

S0738 **Merkt auf! es wird die Stunde kommen**
SATB, bc
26th Sunday after Trinity
Lobsingenden Hertzens-Andacht, no. 74

S0739 **Nisi Dominus aedificaverit domum**
STB, 2 vln, bc
S-Uu 35:9a (Düben)
parts
DMA 2/2305

S0740 **Nun ist vollbracht der Lebenslauf**
SATB, bc
Ascension
Lobsingenden Hertzens-Andacht, no. 42

S0741 **Nun lasset uns erheben**
SATB, bc
7th Sunday after Trinity
Lobsingenden Hertzens-Andacht, no. 54
Misnumbered 56 in collection

S0742 **Nun soll mein Herz, Sinn, und Mund**
SATB, bc
18th Sunday after Trinity
Lobsingenden Hertzens-Andacht, no. 66

S0743 **O himmelssüße Liebes Brunst**
SATB, bc
Whit Monday
Lobsingenden Hertzens-Andacht, no. 45

S0744 **O ihr lieben Kinder**
SATB, bc
20th Sunday after Trinity
Lobsingenden Hertzens-Andacht, no. 68

S0745 **O Mensch, Gott hat gesesset**
SATB, bc
9th Sunday after Trinity
Lobsingenden Hertzens-Andacht, no. 56

S0746 **O Menschen Kind, dir ist bewußt**
SATB, bc
22nd Sunday after Trinity
Lobsingenden Hertzens-Andacht, no. 69[b]

S0747 **O reicher Gott von Gütigkeit**
SATB, bc
4th Sunday after Trinity
Lobsingenden Hertzens-Andacht, no. 51

S0748 **O Traurigkeit, jetzt ist es Zeit**
SATB, bc
Good Friday
Lobsingenden Hertzens-Andacht, no. 33

S0749 **Resonet in laudibus**
SSB, 2 vln, bc
S-Uu 35:10 (Düben)
parts
DMA 1/770
Ed. B. Grusnick (Bärenreiter 3519, 1968)

S0750 **Schau an, o schnödes Menschen Kind**
SATB, bc
16th Sunday after Trinity
Lobsingenden Hertzens-Andacht, no. 64

S0751 **So kommt von Gott der Menschen Heil**
SATB, bc
13th Sunday after Trinity
Lobsingenden Hertzens-Andacht, no. 60

S0752 **Verleih uns Frieden gnädiglich/Gib unserm Landesherrn**
STB, 2 vln, bc
D-Dlb Mus. ms. 1914-E-500 (Grimma U 491/P 64 IV)
parts
DMA 2/2306

S0753 **Von meines Jesu Treue und Herzens**
SATB, bc
2nd Sunday after Easter
Lobsingenden Hertzens-Andacht, no. 38[b]

S0754 **Wach auf! vom Sünde schlaf**
SATB, bc
Easter Monday
Lobsingenden Hertzens-Andacht, no. 36

S0755 **Was bist du, armes Menschen Kind**
SATB, bc
4th Sunday of Advent
Lobsingenden Hertzens-Andacht, no. 4

S0756 **Was dem Gesetz unmöglich war**
SATB, bc
6th Sunday after Trinity
Lobsingenden Hertzens-Andacht, no. 53

S0757 **Was mein Gott macht**
SATB, bc
12th Sunday after Trinity
Lobsingenden Hertzens-Andacht, no. 59

S0758 **Wie freundlich muß der Herr doch sein**
SATB, bc
Maundy Thursday
Lobsingenden Hertzens-Andacht, no. 31

S0759 **Wie weißlich hat des Höchsten Hand**
SATB, bc
2nd Sunday after Epiphany
Lobsingenden Hertzens-Andacht, no. 14

S0760 **Wohl dem, dem seine Zuversicht**
SATB, bc
4th Sunday of Lent
Lobsingenden Hertzens-Andacht, no. 26

S0761 **Wohlauf, mein Geist**
SATB, bc
3rd Day of Christmas
Lobsingenden Hertzens-Andacht, no. 7

S0762 **Wunder von dem Wunderkinde**
SATB, bc
Sunday after Christmas
Lobsingenden Hertzens-Andacht, no. 8

STURM, Leonhard

S0763 **Ach grosses Herzenleid so leider wir erfahren**
SATB
Funeral of Heinrich Gottfried Gundelfinger
Ansbach, 1672
RISM S7097

S0764 **Ach laß von Trauren ab**
SSATB, bc
Funeral of Adam Frickinger
n.p., 1657
RISM S7090 (parts)

S0765 **Ach mein Gott**
SATB, bc
Funeral of Margarita Christiana Hauffen
Nördlingen, 1649
RISM S7085 (score)

S0766 **An den Blumen kannst du sehen**
SSATB
Funeral of Anna Maria Deitrich Onolzbach
Ansbach, 1663
RISM S7094 (parts)

STURM, Leonhard (*continued*)

S0767   **An mich macht sich schon zu würgen**
SSATB, bc
Funeral of Anna Barbara Wengen
n.p., 1660
RISM S7092 (parts)

S0768   **Du, du Menschenkind**
SATB, SATB
Funeral of Jacob Meyer
Ulm, 1647
RISM S7084 (parts)

S0769   **Es ist der Mensch der alte Bund**
SSATB, bc
Funeral of Elisabeth Steinlin
Ulm, 1659
RISM S7091 (score)

S0770   **Herr Gott muß dich dann verlassen**
SSATB, bc
Funeral of Franz von Weltz
Nürnberg, 1661
RISM S7093, Reich 324 (score)

S0771   **Ist dann kein Kräutlein nicht in aller Welt zu finden?**
SATB, bc
Funeral of Johann Klotzeisen
n.p., 1649
RISM S7086 (score)

S0772   **Job, ein Mann von vielen Plagen**
SSATB, bc
Funeral of Johann Konrad Gundelfinger

Ansbach, 1670
RISM S7095, Reich 17 (parts)
RISM S7096 (score)

S0773   **Leb ich, so leb ich meinem Gott**
SATB, SATB
Funeral of Caspar Adam
Ulm, 1655
RISM S7087 (parts)

S0774   **Machs mit mir, Gott**
SSATB
Funeral of Maria Susanna Westerfeld
Ulm, 1656
RISM S7089 (parts)

S0775   **Mein Heil und Gnaden**
SATB, bc
Funeral of Margarita Christiana Hauffen
Nördlingen, 1649
RISM S7085 (score)

S0776   **Mein Herr Jesu**
SATB, bc
Funeral of Margarita Christiana Hauffen
Nördlingen, 1649
RISM S7085 (score)

S0777   **Soll dieser werte Herr**
SATB
Funeral of Johann Marcelli Westerfeld
Nördlingen, 1678
RISM S7098 (parts)

SUEVIUS. *See* **Schwab**

T

TACK, Johann

T0001 **Rahel klagt in großem Schmerzen**
SSATB, bc
Funeral of Maria Elisabeth, Landgräfin zu
Hesse
Darmstadt, 1665
RISM T11, Reich 46 (choirbook)
DMA 70//178

T0002 **Wer ist doch die so kläglich rufe**
SATB
Funeral of Catharine Eleanora von Sellen
Darmstadt, 1675 (choirbook)
DMA 70//169

T0003 **Wer ist doch diese**
SATB
Funeral of Anna Margarethe Tack
Darmstadt, 1674
RISM T12, Reich 47

THEILE, Johann (1646-1724)

COLLECTION

Pars prima missarum (1673)
RISM T646 (parts)
DMA 2/1173

WORKS

T0004 **Beatus vir, qui timet**
SATB, 2 vln, 2 vltta, bsn, bc
D-B Mus. ms. 21822, no. 3 (Bokemeyer)
score
DMA 3/409

T0005 **Benedicam Domino in omni tempore**
SATB, 3 vln, 2 vltta, bsn, bc
D-B Mus. ms. 21822, no. 5 (Bokemeyer)
score
DMA 3/410
Mackey 1968, vol. 2, pp. 1-49

T0006 **Cum invocarem**
SATB, 2 vln, 2 vla, bsn, bc
D-B Mus. ms. 21822, no. 4 (Bokemeyer)
score
DMA 3/411

T0007 **Daran ist erschienen die Liebe Gottes**
SATB, 2 vln, 3 vla, bsn, bc
Christmas Day
S-Uu 35:16 (Düben)
parts
DMA 1/776

T0008 **Das Blut Jesu Christi**
STB, 2 vln, vla, vc, bc
D-B Mus. ms. 21825/1
parts
DMA 2/2309

T0009 **Denen die Gott lieben**
SATB, 2 vln, 2 vla, 3 ob, bsn, bc
D-B Mus. ms. 21825/3
parts
DMA 2/2310

T0010 **Dixit Dominus**
SATB, 3 vln, 2 vltta, bsn, bc
D-B Mus. ms. 21822, no. 1 (Bokemeyer)
score
DMA 3/412

THEILE, Johann (*continued*)

T0011   **Domine ne in furore tuo**
      SATB, 5 vla, bc
      D-B Mus. ms. 21822, no. 2 (Bokemeyer)
        score
      DMA 3/413

T0012   **Es ist in keinem andern Heil**
      SATB, 2 vln, 2 vla, vc, 2 ob, bsn, bc
      D-B Mus. ms. 21825/9
        parts
      DMA 2/2312
      Mackey 1968, vol. 2, pp. 50-83

T0013   **Es ist nichts Verdammliches**
      SATB, 2 vln, vla, vc, bc
      D-B Mus. ms. 21825/5
        parts
      DMA 2/2313

T0014   **Gott hilf mir**
      SSATB, 4 vla, vlne, bc
      S-Uu 66:11 (Düben)
        parts
      DMA 1/774

T0015   **Gott, sei mir gnädig**
      SATB, 2 vln, 2 vla, bc
      D-B Mus. ms. 21823, no. 2 (Bokemeyer)
        score

T0016   **Herr unser Herrscher**
      SSATB, 2 vln, 2 vla, 2 corn, 2 clar, timp,
        3 tbn, bsn, bc
      D-B Mus. ms. 21823, no. 4 (Bokemeyer)
        score

T0017   **Ich habe den Herrn alle Zeit**
      SATB, 2 vln, 2 vla, bc
      D-B Mus. ms. 21823, no. 9 (Bokemeyer)
        score

T0018   **Ich preise dich, Herr**
      SSATB, 2 vln, 2 vla, bc
      D-B Mus. ms. 21823, no. 6 (Bokemeyer)
        score

T0019   **Ich will den Herrn loben alle Zeit**
      SSATB, 2 vln, 2 vla, bsn, bc
      D-B Mus. ms. 21823, no. 8 (Bokemeyer)
        score

T0020   **Jauchzet Gott, alle Lande**
      SSATB, 2 vln, 2 vla, 2 clar, bsn, bc
      D-B Mus. ms. 21823, no. 5 (Bokemeyer)
        score

T0021   **Jubilate Deo**
      SATB, 2 vln, bc

      D-Bds Mus. ms. 30243, no. 9
        score
      Anonymous; attributed by Mackey

T0022   **Kyrie eleison (Litany)**
      SSATB, 2 vln, 2 vltta, bsn, bc
      D-B Mus. ms. 21823, no. 14 (Bokemeyer)
        score

T0023   **Laudate Dominum, omnes gentes**
      SATB, 2 vln, 3 vla, bc
      D-B Mus. ms. 21822, no. 7 (Bokemeyer)
        score
      DMA 3/414

T0024   **Missa**
      SATB, bc
      Pars prima missarum, no. 5

T0025   **Missa (Kyrie, Sanctus, Agnus Dei)**
      SATB
      D-Bds Mus. ms. theor. 913 (Musicalisches
        Kunstbuch)
        score
      DnM 1, pp. 65-74

T0026   **Missa**
      SSATB, 2 vln, 2 vla, 2 ob, 2 corn, bc
      D-Bds Mus. ms. 30172, no. 9
        score
      DMA 2/2316

T0027   **Missa brevis**
      SATB, bc
      Pars prima missarum, no. 1

T0028   **Missa (Kyrie only)**
      SATB, bc
      D-Bds Mus. ms. theor. 913 (Musicalisches
        Kunstbuch)
        parts
      DnM 1, pp. 88-96

T0029   **Missa brevis**
      SATB, bc
      Pars prima missarum, no. 2

T0030   **Missa brevis**
      SATB, bc
      Pars prima missarum, no. 3

T0031   **Missa (brevis)**
      SSATB, bc
      Pars prima missarum, no. 6

T0032   **Missa (brevis)**
      SSATB, bc
      D-B Mus. ms. 21822, no. 6 (Bokemeyer)
        score
      DMA 3/415

D-B Mus. ms. 21820, no. 1 (1680)
score
Das Chorwerk 16

T0033 Missa super Nun komm, der Heiden Heiland
SATB, bc
Pars prima missarum, no. 4

T0034 Passion nach dem Heiligen Evangelisten Matthaeo
TB soli, SSATB, 2 vla, 2 gamba, bc
Lübeck, 1673
RISM T647 (parts)
DMA 1/1484
DdT 17, pp. 105-99

T0035 Schaffe in mir, Gott, ein reines Herz
SATB, 2 vln, 2 vla, bsn, bc
D-B Mus. ms. 21823, no. 10 (Bokemeyer)
score

T0036 Triumph, alleluia
SSB, 2 vln, bc
D-B Mus. ms. 21823, no. 11 (Bokemeyer)
score

T0037 Tröstet mein Volk
SSATB, 2 vln, 2 clar, 3 tbn, bc
D-B Mus. ms. 21823, no. 12 (Bokemeyer)
(1679)
score

T0038 Warum toben die Heiden
SSATB, 2 vln, 2 vla, 2 clar, timp, bsn, bc
D-B Mus. ms. 21823, no. 13 (Bokemeyer)
score
Mackey 1968, vol. 2, pp. 84-122

T0039 Wirf dein Anliegen
SATB, 3 vla, bsn, bc
D-B Mus. ms. 21825/32 (1680), 21825/33
(Erfurt)
parts
DMA 2/2318-2319
D-Bds Mus. ms. 30177, no. 8
score

T0040 Wohl denen, die ohne Wandel leben
SATB, 2 vln, 2 vla, 2 ob, bsn, bc
D-B Mus. ms. 21825/30
parts
DMA 2/2320

THIEME, Clemens (1631-1668)

T0041 Beatus vir
SSATB, 2 vln, 2 vla, bsn, theorbo, bc
S-Uu 35:20 (Düben)
parts
DMA 1/1671

T0042 Befiehl dem Herren deine Wege
ATB, 2 vln, vla, bc
D-B Mus. ms. 30286, no. 11 (Bokemeyer)
(1695)
score

T0043 Danksaget dem Vater
ATB, 2 vln, bsn, bc
D-B Mus. ms. 30286, no. 12 (Bokemeyer)
score

T0044 Laetatus sum
SATTB, 2 vln, 2 vla, bsn, bc
D-B Mus. ms. 30286, no. 14 (Bokemeyer)
(1695)
score

T0045 Laudate, pueri, Dominum
SSATTB, 2 vln, 3 vla, bsn, bc
S-Uu 69:11 (Düben)
parts
S-Uu 82:34, fol. 7v-12r (Düben)
tablature (incomplete)
DMA 3/1792

T0046 Lobe den Herren, meine Seele
ATB, 2 vln, bc
D-B Mus. ms. 30286, no. 13
score
D-LUC ms. 1659, no. 124

T0047 Lobe den Herren, meine Seele
SSATTB, 2 vln, 4 vla, bc
D-B Mus. ms. 21831 (old no. 2239)
parts

T0048 Meine Seele erhebet den Herren
SSAATB, 2 vln, 5 vla, 2 clar, timp, 3 tbn, bc
D-B Mus. ms. 30286, no. 15 (Bokemeyer)
score

T0049 Missa (brevis) à 10
SSATB, 4 vla, bsn, bc
S-Uu 66:13 (Düben); 35:22 (Düben)
parts
DMA 1/2126

T0050 Missa (brevis) ex A
SSATB, 4 vla, bc
D-B Mus. ms. 21830 (Erfurt) (1674)
score and parts
S-Uu 85:74, fol. 10v-12r (Düben)
tablature (incomplete)
DMA 1/2127
S-Uu 35:21 (Düben)
parts (SATB, 3 vln, vlne, bc)

T0051 Nunc dimittis
SSTB, 4 vla, bsn, bc

THIEME, Clemens (*continued*)

S-Uu 66:12 (Düben)
parts
DMA 3/1793
S-Uu 85:61, fol. 3v-6r (Düben)
tablature
DMA 3/1793

T0052 **Schaffe in mir, Gott, ein reines Herz**
ATB, 3 vln, theorbo, bc
S-Uu 35:23 (Düben)
parts and tablature
DMA 1/1672
Tablature with Swedish text: Schapa i
migh, gudh

T0053 **Schapa i migh, Gudh**
See Schaffe in mir, Gott

THILL, Johann Gottlieb

T0054 **Ergießet euch, gerechte Tränen**
SSB
Funeral of Isabella Veronica Donauer
Regensburg, 1685
RISM T670, Reich 371

TITIUS, Erhard

T0055 **Ach du hochbetrübtes Sachsen**
SATTB, bc
Funeral of Johann Georg II, Kurfürst von
Sachsen
Dresden and Zittau, 1681
RISM T846, Reich 58 (score)
DMA 70//113

T0056 **Gottlob, es geht nun mehr zum Ende**
See under Anonymous

TOPF, Johann

T0057 **Alleluia. Fürchtet euch nicht**
SSATBB
USSR-KA Ms. 13661 (lost)
DdT 49/50, pp. 23-29

T0058 **Da die Zeit erfüllet war**
SSATB
USSR-KA Ms. 13661 (lost)
DdT 49/50, pp. 8-13

T0059 **Danket dem Herrn**
SSATTB

USSR-KA Ms. 13661 (lost)
DdT 49/50, pp. 72-80

T0060 **Das Wort ward Fleisch (I)**
SSATB
USSR-KA Ms. 13661 (lost)
DdT 49/50, pp. 30-35

T0061 **Das Wort ward Fleisch (II)**
SSATTB
USSR-KA Ms. 13661 (lost)
DdT 49/50, pp. 58-61

T0062 **Fürchtet euch nicht**
SSATB
USSR-KA Ms. 13661 (lost)
DdT 49/50, pp. 1-4

T0063 **Gott, du krönest das Jahr mit deinem Gut**
SSATB, 2 vln, 2 vla, 3 ob, vlne, bsn, bc
D-Gs Cod. Ms. philos. 84e Topff 1 (1720)
score and parts (incomplete)

T0064 **Jauchzet dem Herrn**
SSATTB
USSR-KA Ms. 13661 (lost)
DdT 49/50, pp. 144-52

T0065 **Lobet den Herrn auf Erden**
SSATB
USSR-KA Ms. 13661 (lost)
DdT 49/50, pp. 17-23

T0066 **Mit Fried und Freud ich fahr dahin**
SATB, vln, 2 vltta, ob, bc
D-B Mus. ms. 30286, no. 16 (Bokemeyer)
score

T0067 **Muß nicht der Mensch immer im Streit sein**
SATB
Funeral
D-Gs Cod. Ms. philos. 84e Topff 2
score and parts

T0068 **Nun danket alle Gott**
SSATBB
USSR-KA Ms. 13661 (lost)
DdT 49/50, pp. 138-43

T0069 **Preise, Jerusalem, den Herren**
SATB, 2 vln, 2 vla, 2 tpt, vlne, bc
D-Gs Cod. Ms. philos. 84e Topff 3
score and parts

TRÜMPER, Michael

COLLECTION

Geistlicher Kirchen-Weirauch (1656)
RISM T1298 (score)

WORKS

T0070 **Ach du mein frommer Herr und Gott**
SATB
2nd Sunday of Lent
Geistlicher Kirchen-Weirauch, no. 25

T0071 **Ach Herr, dein irrigs Schäfelein**
SATB
3rd Sunday after Trinity
Geistlicher Kirchen-Weirauch, no. 46

T0072 **Ach Herr, mein Hertz jetzt oft beklagt**
SATB
3rd Sunday after Easter
Geistlicher Kirchen-Weirauch, no. 35

T0073 **Ach Herr sehr hart leigt mir im Sinn**
SATB
3rd Sunday after Epiphany
Geistlicher Kirchen-Weirauch, no. 18

T0074 **Ach Herr, wie klein dein Häuslein ist**
SATB
Whit Tuesday
Geistlicher Kirchen-Weirauch, no. 42

T0075 **Ach Herr, wie seh ich in der Welt**
SATB
16th Sunday after Trinity
Geistlicher Kirchen-Weirauch, no. 59

T0076 **Allein du O Herr Jesu Christ**
SATB
2nd Sunday after Easter
Geistlicher Kirchen-Weirauch, no. 34

T0077 **Allhie lieg ich Herr Jesu Christ**
SATB
13th Sunday after Trinity
Geistlicher Kirchen-Weirauch, no. 56

T0078 **Behüt mich, Herr, vor stolzen Mut**
SATB
Feast of Saint Bartholomew
Geistlicher Kirchen-Weirauch, no. 85

T0079 **Bei deinem Volk, Herr Jesu Christ**
SATB
10th Sunday after Trinity
Geistlicher Kirchen-Weirauch, no. 53

T0080 **Billig dank ich, Herr Jesu**
SATB
Trinity
Geistlicher Kirchen-Weirauch, no. 43

T0081 **Billig soll ich dir Dankbar sein**
SATB
Feast of Andrew the Apostle
Geistlicher Kirchen-Weirauch, no. 71

T0082 **Das ist Herr Christ, mein größte Freud**
SATB
6th Sunday after Trinity
Geistlicher Kirchen-Weirauch, no. 49

T0083 **Das soll mein Herz viel quälen sich**
SATB
7th Sunday after Trinity
Geistlicher Kirchen-Weirauch, no. 50

T0084 **Dein Geist bezeugt in mir, Herr Christ**
SATB
Sunday after Ascension
Geistlicher Kirchen-Weirauch, no. 39

T0085 **Dein Jüngern, Herr, gibst zu verstehen**
SATB
4th Sunday after Easter
Geistlicher Kirchen-Weirauch, no. 36

T0086 **Dein Mutter, liebstes Jesulein**
SATB
Feast of the Purification
Geistlicher Kirchen-Weirauch, no. 77

T0087 **Der böse Geist, Herr, schleiche umher**
SATB
3rd Sunday of Lent
Geistlicher Kirchen-Weirauch, no. 26

T0088 **Der du, O liebstes Jesu**
SATB
Sunday after Christmas
Geistlicher Kirchen-Weirauch, no. 11

T0089 **Der Gerechten Seelen sind in Gottes Hand**
SATB, bc
Funeral of Magdalene Ludovici
Gotha, 1656
RISM T1299, Reich 95

T0090 **Der ist ein sehr unglücklich Mann**
SATB
Feast of Saint Matthew
Geistlicher Kirchen-Weirauch, no. 86

T0091 **Der Satan ist wie du, Herr, weist**
SATB
1st Sunday of Lent
Geistlicher Kirchen-Weirauch, no. 24

T0092 **Die klugen Welt-Kinder**
SATB
Feast of Matthew the Apostle
Geistlicher Kirchen-Weirauch, no. 78

T0093 **Die Zeit geht hin**
SATB
9th Sunday after Trinity
Geistlicher Kirchen-Weirauch, no. 52

TRÜMPER, Michael (*continued*)

T0094 **Du bist Herr Christ, wahr Mensch und Gott**
SATB
1st Sunday after Easter
Geistlicher Kirchen-Weirauch, no. 33

T0095 **Du edler König, Herr Jesu Christ**
SATB
1st Sunday of Advent
Geistlicher Kirchen-Weirauch, no. 2

T0096 **Du reicher Nährer allen Welt**
SATB
4th Sunday of Lent
Geistlicher Kirchen-Weirauch, no. 27

T0097 **Du siehst, Herr Christ, die Feinde mein**
SATB
4th Sunday of Advent
Geistlicher Kirchen-Weirauch, no. 5

T0098 **Du siehst wie ich heilig, O Herr**
SATB
19th Sunday after Trinity
Geistlicher Kirchen-Weirauch, no. 62

T0099 **Du weist, Herr Christ, wie viel der Feind**
SATB
Feast of Saint Paul's Conversion
Geistlicher Kirchen-Weirauch, no. 76

T0100 **Du zeigst mir wohl, Herr Christ**
SATB
18th Sunday after Trinity
Geistlicher Kirchen-Weirauch, no. 61

T0101 **Freilich weist du mein Gott vorhin**
SATB
22nd Sunday after Trinity
Geistlicher Kirchen-Weirauch, no. 65

T0102 **Freu dich, O werte Christenheit**
SATB
Ascension
Geistlicher Kirchen-Weirauch, no. 38

T0103 **Freuet euch, ihr Christen fromme**
SATB
Christmas Day
Geistlicher Kirchen-Weirauch, no. 7

T0104 **Freulich bistu Herr Christ gerecht**
SATB
5th Sunday of Lent
Geistlicher Kirchen-Weirauch, no. 28

T0105 **Gib mir, Herr Jesu, dein Genad**
SATB
15th Sunday after Trinity
Geistlicher Kirchen-Weirauch, no. 58

T0106 **Gott, der du schaffst, daß Sanct Johann**
SATB
Feast of John the Baptist
Geistlicher Kirchen-Weirauch, no. 81

T0107 **Gott, unsre Bitt für deinen Thron**
SATB
5th Sunday after Easter
Geistlicher Kirchen-Weirauch, no. 37

T0108 **Gottes und Marien Kind**
SATB
Epiphany
Geistlicher Kirchen-Weirauch, no. 15

T0109 **Groß Freud hab ich in meinem Gemüt**
SATB
Geistlicher Kirchen-Weirauch, no. 80

T0110 **Heil du allein, Herr Jesu Christ**
SATB
8th Sunday after Trinity
Geistlicher Kirchen-Weirauch, no. 51

T0111 **Herr, alle die dich und dein Wort lehren**
SATB
Feast of Saint John the Evangelist
Geistlicher Kirchen-Weirauch, no. 74

T0112 **Herr Christ, dein Jünger zeigen an**
SATB
Feast of Saints Peter and Paul
Geistlicher Kirchen-Weirauch, no. 82

T0113 **Herr Christ, der du zu jeder**
SATB
Feast of Saint Stephen
Geistlicher Kirchen-Weirauch, no. 73

T0114 **Herr Christ, der Kön'gisch bitten tut**
SATB
21st Sunday after Trinity
Geistlicher Kirchen-Weirauch, no. 64

T0115 **Herr Christ, mein Herz im Leib sich freut**
SATB
27th Sunday after Trinity
Geistlicher Kirchen-Weirauch, no. 70

T0116 **Herr Christe, dein Hilfreiche Hand**
SATB
12th Sunday after Trinity
Geistlicher Kirchen-Weirauch, no. 55

T0117 **Herr Christe, deiner Jünger zween**
SATB
Easter Monday
Geistlicher Kirchen-Weirauch, no. 31

T0118 **Herr Christe, du selbst zeigest an**
SATB
Quinquagesima
Geistlicher Kirchen-Weirauch, no. 23

T0119 **Herr, du bist mein Emanuel**
SATB
3rd Sunday of Advent
Geistlicher Kirchen-Weirauch, no. 4

T0120 **Herr Gott, die ganze Christenheit**
SATB
Septuagesima
Geistlicher Kirchen-Weirauch, no. 21

T0121 **Herr Gott, weil ohn dein heilsam Lehr**
SATB
1st Sunday after Epiphany
Geistlicher Kirchen-Weirauch, no. 16

T0122 **Heut bist du, zartes Jesulein**
SATB
New Year
Geistlicher Kirchen-Weirauch, no. 13

T0123 **Heut ist des Herren Sabbat-Tag**
SATB
17th Sunday after Trinity
Geistlicher Kirchen-Weirauch, no. 60

T0124 **Hilf, edler Heiland Jesu Christ**
SATB
Geistlicher Kirchen-Weirauch, no. 89

T0125 **Hilf, Herr, daß ich göttfürchtig sei**
SATB
Visitation of Mary
Geistlicher Kirchen-Weirauch, no. 83

T0126 **Hilf Herr, daß wir barmherzig sein**
SATB
4th Sunday after Trinity
Geistlicher Kirchen-Weirauch, no. 47

T0127 **Hilf mir, du frommer Gottes Sohn**
SATB
23rd Sunday after Trinity
Geistlicher Kirchen-Weirauch, no. 66

T0128 **Ich armer Sünder mit Begier**
SATB
11th Sunday after Trinity
Geistlicher Kirchen-Weirauch, no. 54

T0129 **Ich bin ein sündlich Evae Kind**
SATB
14th Sunday after Trinity
Geistlicher Kirchen-Weirauch, no. 57

T0130 **Ich bitt dich, allmächtiger Gott**
SATB
Feast of Saint Michael
Geistlicher Kirchen-Weirauch, no. 87

T0131 **Ich merk gar wohl, Herr Jesu Christ**
SATB
Feast of Saint Jacob
Geistlicher Kirchen-Weirauch, no. 84

T0132 **Ich plfege gern Herr Jesu Christ**
SATB
5th Sunday after Trinity
Geistlicher Kirchen-Weirauch, no. 48

T0133 **Ich steh', Herr Christ, in grosser Gfahr**
SATB
Feast of the Holy Innocents
Geistlicher Kirchen-Weirauch, no. 75

T0134 **Ich weiß es wohl, daß du Herr Christ**
SATB
Feast of Saint Thomas the Apostle
Geistlicher Kirchen-Weirauch, no. 72

T0135 **Ich weiß gar wohl, Herr Jesu Christ**
SATB
24th Sunday after Trinity
Geistlicher Kirchen-Weirauch, no. 67

T0136 **Jesu, du heilges Kindlein**
SATB
Christmas Day
Geistlicher Kirchen-Weirauch, no. 8

T0137 **Jetzt ist schon da die letzte Zeit**
SATB
25th Sunday after Trinity
Geistlicher Kirchen-Weirauch, no. 68

T0138 **Laß lieben mich allzeit, Herr Christ**
SATB
Feast of Simon Juda
Geistlicher Kirchen-Weirauch, no. 88

T0139 **Laßt uns ansingen**
SATB
Christmas Day
Geistlicher Kirchen-Weirauch, no. 6

T0140 **Man ruft Herr täglich in deinem Saal**
SATB
2nd Sunday after Trinity
Geistlicher Kirchen-Weirauch, no. 45

T0141 **Maria hört ihr Söhnelein**
SATB
Annunciation
Geistlicher Kirchen-Weirauch, no. 79

TRÜMPER, Michael (*continued*)

T0142   **O Gott, dein ist die ganze Welt**
SATB
5th Sunday after Epiphany
Geistlicher Kirchen-Weirauch, no. 20

T0143   **O Gott Vater im höchsten Thron**
SATB
2nd Sunday of Advent
Geistlicher Kirchen-Weirauch, no. 3

T0144   **O großer König, Herr Jesu Christ**
SATB
Palm Sunday
Geistlicher Kirchen-Weirauch, no. 29

T0145   **O Herr, du edler Schöpfer gut**
SATB
1st Sunday after Trinity
Geistlicher Kirchen-Weirauch, no. 44

T0146   **O Herr, du starker Helden-Mann**
SATB
Easter Tuesday
Geistlicher Kirchen-Weirauch, no. 32

T0147   **O Jesu Christ, du König aller Ehren**
SATB
1st Sunday of Advent
Geistlicher Kirchen-Weirauch, no. 1

T0148   **O Jesu, der du uns zu gut**
SATB
New Year
Geistlicher Kirchen-Weirauch, no. 12

T0149   **O Traurigkeit, O Herzeleid**
SATB
Funeral
Geistlicher Kirchen-Weirauch, no. 90

T0150   **Pflanz in mir, Herr, dein Göttlich Leib**
SATB
Pentecost
Geistlicher Kirchen-Weirauch, no. 40

T0151   **Schön singen uns die Engelein**
SATB
Christmas Day
Geistlicher Kirchen-Weirauch, no. 9

T0152   **Sehr freu ich mich**
SATB
26th Sunday after Trinity
Geistlicher Kirchen-Weirauch, no. 69

T0153   **Sollt mirs O Gott nicht tröstlich sein**
SATB
20th Sunday after Trinity
Geistlicher Kirchen-Weirauch, no. 63

T0154   **Uns ist bewust, Herr Jesu Christ**
SATB
1st [*sic*, i.e., 2nd] Sunday after Epiphany
Geistlicher Kirchen-Weirauch, no. 17

T0155   **Uns ist ein Kindlein heut geboren**
SATTB
Christmas Day
Geistlicher Kirchen-Weirauch, no. 10

T0156   **Unschuld muß immer leiden**
SATB
Sunday after New Year
Geistlicher Kirchen-Weirauch, no. 14

T0157   **Viel Unfalls, Herr, begegnet mir**
SATB
4th Sunday after Epiphany
Geistlicher Kirchen-Weirauch, no. 19

T0158   **Wenn ich komm an den Ort**
SATB
Sexagesima
Geistlicher Kirchen-Weirauch, no. 22

T0159   **Wir danken dir, du frommer Gott**
SATB
Whit Monday
Geistlicher Kirchen-Weirauch, no. 41

T0160   **Wir danken dir, Herr Jesu Christ**
SATB
Easter Sunday
Geistlicher Kirchen-Weirauch, no. 30

TUNDER, Franz (1614-1667)

T0161   **Dominus illuminatio mea et salus mea**
SSATB, 2 vln, bc
S-Uu 86:17, fol. 1r-7r (Düben)
   tablature
S-Uu 36:1 (Düben)
   parts
DdT 3, pp. 42-56

T0162   **Ein feste Burg**
SSTB, 2 vln, 3 vla, vlne, bc
S-Uu 78:75, fol. 75v-80r (Düben) (1665)
   tablature
S-Uu 36:2 (Düben)
   parts
DdT 3, pp. 142-57
Ed. M. Seiffert, *Organum* I, 15

T0163   **Helft mir Gotts Güte preisen**
SSATTB, 4 vla, vlne, bc

S-Uu 36:5 (Düben)
    parts and tablature
DdT 3, pp. 118-23

T0164 **Hosianna dem Sohne David. Jubilate et exultate**
    SSATB, 2 vln, 2 vla, vla/bsn, bc
    Advent
    S-Uu 36:6 (Düben)
        parts
    DdT 3, pp. 79-97
    Ed. Krüger, *Die Kantate* 47

T0165 **Nisi Dominus aedificaverit**
    SSB, 2 vln, bc
    S-Uu 81:80, fol. 70r-74r (Düben)
        tablature
    S-Uu 36:7 (Düben)
        parts
    DdT 3, pp. 33-41

T0166 **Nisi Dominus aedificaverit**
    SSATB, 2 vln, 2 vla, vlne, bc

S-Uu 81:69, fol. 70r-74r (Düben) (1665)
    tablature
S-Uu 36:8 (Düben)
    parts
S-Uu 86:56
    tablature (instr. parts only, without
        sinfonia)
DdT 3, pp. 57-78

T0167 **Streuet mit Palmen, ihr Schäfer und Hirten**
    SSATB, 2 vln, 2 vla, vlne, bc
    Palm Sunday
    S-Uu 36:12 (Düben)
        parts and tablature
    DdT 3, pp. 113-17
    Ed. Lillehaug (Concordia 97-6406, 1963)

T0168 **Wend ab dein Zorn**
    SSATTB, 4 vla, vlne, bc
    S-Uu 36:15 (Düben)
        parts
    DdT 3, pp. 124-41

U

ULICH, Johann (b. 1634)

    U0001   **Missa**
                SATB, 2 clar, timp, 3 tbn, bc
                D-Bds Mus. ms. 30307, no. 2 (Bokemeyer)
                    score
                    DMA 21//61

V

VETTER, Daniel (1657/58-1721)

V0001 **Alleluia, Christus von den Toden auferwecket**
SSATB, 2 vln, 2 corn, 4 clar, 3 tbn, bc
D-Dlb 1918-E-500 (Grimma U 300/N 8)
score and parts

V0002 **Heut freue dich, Christenheit**
SATB, 2 vln, 2 vla, bc
D-Bds Mus. ms. 30293, no. 5 (Bokemeyer)
score
DMA 3/1316

V0003 **Ich will dem Herren singen**
SATB, SATB
D-Dlb 1918-E-502 (Grimma U 302/N 10)
parts

V0004 **Veni Sancte Spiritus**
SSATB, 2 vln/corn, 3 vla/tbn, 4 clar,
timp, bc
D-Dlb 1918-E-501 (Grimma U 301/N 9)
parts (clar 1 lacking)

VISMARI, Filippo (before 1635-1706?)

V0005 **Dixit Dominus**
SSATB, 2 vln, 3 vla, 2 vltta, 2 corn, 3
tbn, vlne, theorbo, bc
CS-KRa III, 49
parts
microfilm: US-SY

V0006 **Missa Novella**
SSATB, 2 vln, 4 vla, 4 tbn, bc
CS-KRa I, 136
parts
microfilm: US-SY

V0007 **Salmo à capella**
SATB, bc
CS-KRa III, 39
parts
microfilm: US-SY

VOGEL, G.

V0008 **Alleluia! Freuet euch, ihr Christen alle**
SSATB, 2 vln, 2 vla/tbn, 2 clar, timp,
bsn/tbn, bc
Christmas Day
D-Dlb 1919-E-501 (Grimma U 529/L 17)
(1701)
score and parts

V0009 **Nun aber gibst du, Gott, einen gnädigen
Regen**
SSATB, 2 vln, 2 vla, 2 horns, bsn, bc
Pentecost
D-Dlb 1919-E-500 (Grimma U 299/U 93)
(1714)
parts (S1 missing)

W

WAGNER, Bernhard Christoph

W0001   **Nun gute Nacht, mein Jesus ruft**
SSATB, 2 vln, 2 vla, bc
Funeral of Benedict Christoph Wagner
Ansbach, 1695
   RISM W56, Reich 20 (score)

WAGNER, Michael

W0002   **Ach! ach! wie wird mein Herz**
SATTB, bc
Funeral of Hedwig Hahn
Leipzig, 1672
   RISM W61, Reich 267

W0003   **Hilf, treuer Gott! wie ist**
SSATB, bc
Funeral of Hedwig Hahn
Leipzig, 1672
   RISM W61, Reich 267

WALTER, Johann Chr.

W0004   **Ach, ich armer Sünden Knecht**
SATB, bc
D-Gs Cod. Ms. philos. 84e Walter 1 (1695)

WECKER, Georg Caspar (1632-1695)

COLLECTION

XVIII Geistliche Concerten (1695)
PL-Kj
(not in RISM) (parts)

WORKS

W0005   **Allein Gott in der Höh sei Ehr**
SSATTB, 2 vln, 2 vla, 2 corn, 2 tbn, bsn, bc
D-B Mus. ms. 22830
   parts
D-Bds Mus. ms. anon. 1037 (Erfurt)
   parts
PL-Kj Mus. ms. 40129, no. 6 (1656)
   tablature
DTB 10 (Jg. 6/1), pp. 46-68

W0006   **Der Gott unsers Herrn**
SS(or T)AB, 2 vln, 2 vla, vlne, bc
Pentecost
XVIII Geistliche Concerten, no. 10

W0007   **Dies ist der Tag**
SS(or T)AB, 2 vln, 2 vla, vlne, bc
Dedication of a church
XVIII Geistliche Concerten, no. 15

W0008   **Es segne uns Gott**
SS(or T)AB, 2 vln, 2 vla, vlne, bc
Trinity
XVIII Geistliche Concerten, no. 12

W0009   **Gnade sei mit uns**
SS(or T)AB, 2 vln, 2 vla, vlne, bc
Good Friday
XVIII Geistliche Concerten, no. 6

W0010   **Gute Nacht, es ist vollendt**
SATB
Funeral of Johann Andreas Endter
Sulzbach, 1670
   RISM W473a, IN48, Reich 413 (choirbook)
   DMA 70//111
   Attributed to C. G. W. in source

W0011 **Halleluia! Lobe den Herrn meine Seele**
SS(or T)AB, 2 vln, 2 vla, vlne, bc
Feast of Saint John the Baptist
XVIII Geistliche Concerten, no. 13

W0012 **Herr, du machest mich mit deinem Gebot**
SS(or T)AB, 2 vln, 2 vla, vlne, bc
Epiphany
XVIII Geistliche Concerten, no. 5

W0013 **Herr, enthalte uns dein Wort**
SS(or T)AB, 2 vln, 2 vla, vlne, bc
2nd Day of Christmas
XVIII Geistliche Concerten, no. 3

W0014 **Herr, ich warte auf dein Heil**
SS(or T)AB, 2 vln, 2 vla, vlne, bc
Christmas Day
XVIII Geistliche Concerten, no. 2

W0015 **Herr Jesu, zeuch mich dir nach**
SS(or T)AB, 2 vln, 2 vla, vlne, bc
Ascension
XVIII Geistliche Concerten, no. 9
DTB 6, pp. 69-79

W0016 **Herr! laß dein Antlitz leuchten**
SS(or T)AB, 2 vln, 2 vla, vlne, bc
Whit Monday
XVIII Geistliche Concerten, no. 11

W0017 **Herr mein Gott! sei mir freundlich**
SS(or T)AB, 2 vln, 2 vla, vlne, bc
Easter Monday
XVIII Geistliche Concerten, no. 8

W0018 **Herr! wende dich zu mir**
SS(or T)AB, 2 vln, 2 vla, vlne, bc
Feast of Saint Michael the Archangel
XVIII Geistliche Concerten, no. 14

W0019 **Ich weiß, daß mein Erlöser lebt**
SS(or T)AB, 2 vln, 2 vla, vlne, bc
Funeral
XVIII Geistliche Concerten, no. 18
DTB 6, pp. 80-92

W0020 **Ich werde nicht sterben**
SS(or T)AB, 2 vln, 2 vla, vlne, bc
Easter Sunday
XVIII Geistliche Concerten, no. 7

W0021 **Kommt her zu mir, alle**
SS(or T)AB, 2 vln, 2 vla, vlne, bc
XVIII Geistliche Concerten, no. 16

W0022 **Laetatus sum**
SATTB, 2 vln, 2 vla, bc
D-B Mus. ms. 22831
parts

W0023 **O Herr, hilfe**
SS(or T)AB, 2 vln, 2 vla, vlne, bc
1st Sunday of Advent
XVIII Geistliche Concerten, no. 1
D-Bds Mus. ms. 30282, no. 12 (1702)
score

W0024 **Schaffe in mir, Gott**
SS(or T)AB, 2 vln, 2 vla, vlne, bc
New Year's Day
XVIII Geistliche Concerten, no. 4

W0025 **Wohl dem, der den Herrn fürchtet**
SS(or T)AB, 2 vln, 2 vla, vlne, bc
Wedding
XVIII Geistliche Concerten, no. 17

WECHMAN, Jacob (1643-1680)

W0026 **Ein Tag in deinen Vorhöfen**
SAB, 2 vln, bsn, bc
D-Bds Mus. ms. 30293, no. 9 (Bokemeyer)
score
DMA 3/1320
S-Uu 85:53 (Düben)
tablature
DMA 2/1877

W0027 **Herr, warum trittest du so ferne**
STB, 2 vln, vltta, bc
D-Bds Mus. ms. 30293, no. 10 (Bokemeyer)
score
DMA 3/1321

WECKMANN, Matthias (1619-1674)

W0028 **Der Tod ist verschlungen in den Sieg**
STB, 2 vln, gamba, bc
Easter Sunday
D-Bds Mus. ms. 30293, no. 11 (Bokemeyer)
score
DMA 3/1322
DdT 6, pp. 101-07

W0029 **Dialogo von Tobias und Racel**
See Wo wollen wir einkehren

W0030 **Es erhub sich ein Streit**
SSATB, 2 vln, 2 tbn, bc
Feast of Saint Michael
D-Bds Mus. ms. 30293, no. 12 (Bokemeyer)
score
DMA 3/1323
DdT 6, pp. 29-57

WECKMANN, Matthias (*continued*)

W0031   **Herr wenn ich nur dich habe**
ATB, 2 vln, 3 gamba, bc
D-Lr Mus. ant. pract. KN 207/6, no. 3 (1663)
score
DMA 1/1192
Ed. Wetherwax (1978), pp. 31-66
Ed. Silbiger, RRMBE 46, pp. 70-87

W0032   **Weine nicht, es hat überwunden der Löwe**
ATB, 3 vln, 3 gamba, bc
Easter Sunday
D-Lr KN 207/6, no. 1 (1664)
score
DMA 1/1192
S-Uu 79:109, fol. 109v-115r (Düben)
tablature
DMA 3/1112
DdT 6, pp. 58-78
Organum I, no. 18
Ed. Silbiger, RRMBE 46, pp. 1-52

W0033   **Wenn der Herr die Gefangenen zu Zion**
SATB, 2 vln, 2 gamba, bc
D-Bds Mus. ms. 30293, no. 13 (Bokemeyer)
score
DMA 3/1324
Organum I, no. 2 (incorrectly attributed to
Jacob Weckmann)
DdT 6, pp. 79-100
Ed. D. Krüger, *Die Kantate* 170

W0034   **Wo wollen wir einkehren. Dialogo von Tobias
und Rachel**
ATB, 2 vln, bc
S-Uu 81:13, fol. 13v-18r (Düben) (1665)
tablature
DMA 2/526
Organum I, no. 21
Attributed to "J. R." in source, but generally
assigned to Weckmann, based on Seiffert

W0035   **Zion spricht: Der Herr hat mich verlassen**
ATB, 2 vln, 3 gamba, bc
D-Lr Mus. ant. pract. KN 207/6, no. 2 (1663)
score
DMA 1/1192
Organum I, no. 17
Ed. Silbiger, RRMBE 46, pp. 53-69

WEICHLEIN, Romanus (1652-1706)

COLLECTION

Parnassus ecclesiastico-musicus (1702)
RISM W500 (parts)

WORKS

W0036   **Missa Afflicti cordis**
SATB, 2 vln, 2 vla, vlne, bc
Parnassus ecclesiastico-musicus, no. 6

W0037   **Missa Bonae conscientiae**
SSATB, 2 vln, 2 vla, vlne, bc
Parnassus ecclesiastico-musicus, no. 7

W0038   **Missa Gloriosae Virginis in coelo**
SATB, 2 vln, 2 vla, vlne, bc
Parnassus ecclesiastico-musicus, no. 2

W0039   **Missa Joannis sub cruce**
SATB, 2 vln, 2 vla, vlne, bc
Parnassus ecclesiastico-musicus, no. 4

W0040   **Missa Praecursoris Domini**
SATB, 2 vln, 2 vla, vlne, bc
Parnassus ecclesiastico-musicus, no. 3

W0041   **Missa Rectorum cordium**
SSATTB, 2 vln, 2 vla, 3 clar, timp, 2 tbn,
vlne, bc
A-KR Kasten C, Fasc. 8, no. 668 (1687)
parts

W0042   **Missa Sanctissimae Trinitatis**
SATB, 2 vln, 2 vla, vlne, bc
Parnassus ecclesiastico-musicus, no. 1

W0043   **Missa Sanctorum auxiliatorum**
SSATB, 2 vln, 2 vla, vlne, bc
Parnassus ecclesiastico-musicus, no. 5

W0044   **Requiem**
See Responsoria brevia

W0045   **Responsoria brevia pro officia defunctorum**
SATB, 3 vla, vlne, bc
A-Sn XVIII, 4 and II, 8
parts
A-Sn II, 8 entitled "Responsoria I Noct.
Off. Mart."

W0046   **Responsoria I Noct. Off. Mart.**
See Responsoria brevia pro officia
defunctorum

W0047   **Tenebrae factae sunt**
SATB, vlne, bc
A-Sn III, 6
parts

WEILAND, Julius Johann (d. 1663)

COLLECTIONS

Deuterotokos: Sacratissimarum odarum (1656)
RISM W545 (parts)
DMA 1/279

Erstlinge Musicalischer Andachten (1654)
RISM W544 (parts)
DMA 1/278

WORKS

W0048 **Die starken bebürsen des Arztes nicht**
ATB, 2 vln, bc
Erstlinge Musicalischer Andachten, no. 21

W0049 **Factum est praelium magnum**
ATTB, 2 vln, bc
Deuterotokos: Sacratissimarum odarum,
no. 15
S-Uu 81:99, fol. 100r-103r (Düben) (1665)
tablature (SATTB)

W0050 **Habe deine Lust an dem Herrn**
ATB, bc
Erstlinge Musicalischer Andachten, no. 14

W0051 **Herr, lehre doch mich**
ATB, bc
Erstlinge Musicalischer Andachten, no. 17

W0052 **Herr wenn ich nur dich habe**
ATB, bc
Erstlinge Musicalischer Andachten, no. 13

W0053 **Ich rufte zu dem Herrn**
3 vv, 2 vln, bc
D-W
Library unable to locate or verify in 1983

W0054 **In te Domine speravi**
ATB, bc
Erstlinge Musicalischer Andachten, no. 15

W0055 **Jesu dulcis memoria**
STB, 2 vln, bc
Deuterotokos: Sacratissimarum odarum,
no. 12

W0056 **Laß dichs nicht irren**
ATB, bc
Erstlinge Musicalischer Andachten, no. 16

W0057 **Lasset die Kindelein zu mir kommen**
SSAB, bc
Erstlinge Musicalischer Andachten, no. 18

W0058 **Laudate Dominum, omnes gentes**
SSATTB, 2 vln, bc
New Year, Court of August, Herzog von
Braunschweig
Wolfenbüttel, 1662
RISM W548 (parts)
DMA 1/281

W0059 **Nun danket alle Gott**
SSAT, 4 vln, bsn, bc

New Year, Court of August, Herzog von
Braunschweig
Wolfenbüttel, 1661
RISM W547 (parts)
DMA 1/280

W0060 **Salve, o Jesu, mi dulcissime**
ATB, 2 vln, bc
Circumcision
Deuterotokos: Sacratissimarum odarum,
no. 13
S-Uu 77:59 (Düben) (1663)
tablature (no text)
DMA 47//9
S-Uu 45:13 (Düben) (1663)
parts
DMA 47//2

W0061 **Uns ist ein Kind geboren**
SSSSSATB, 2 vln, 2 vla, bc
New Year, Court of August, Herzog von
Braunschweig
Wolfenbüttel, 1663
RISM W549 (parts)
DMA 1/282

W0062 **Veni Sancte Spiritus**
ATB, bc
Erstlinge Musicalischer Andachten, no. 12

W0063 **Veni Sancte Spiritus**
ATB, 2 vln, bc
Pentecost
Deuterotokos: Sacratissimarum odarum,
no. 14
S-Uu 77:129 (Düben) (1664)
tablature (no text)
S-Uu 46:17 (Düben) (1664)
parts

W0064 **Wer wälzet uns den Stein**
SSATB, 2 vln, 2 vla, vlne, bc
D-Bds Mus. ms. 30293, no. 14 (Bokemeyer)
score
New Grove: authenticity doubtful

W0065 **Wohl dem, der ein tugendsam Weib hat**
SSTB, 2 vln, bc
Erstlinge Musicalischer Andachten, no. 22

WELTER, Johann Samuel (1650-1720)

W0066 **Ach, was ist doch unser Zeit**
SATB, 4 vla, vlne, bc
F-Ssp
parts
DMA 2/2327

WELTER, Johann Samuel (*continued*)

W0067 **Ach! will des Todes grimme Hand**
SATB
Funeral of Johann Friedrich Wibel
Schwäbisch Hall, 1703
RISM W727, Reich 394

W0068 **Aller Dinge Vater, Helfer und Berater**
SATB, vln, 3 vla, bsn/vlne, bc
F-Ssp
parts
DMA 2/2328

W0069 **Auf, auf ihr Gottes Hausgenossen**
ATB, 2 vln, 2 vla, bsn, bc
D-F Ff. Mus. 596 (1687)
parts

W0070 **Der Sünden Aussatz plaget mich**
SSATB, 4 vla, vlne, bc
F-Ssp
parts

W0071 **Gott sei uns gnädig**
SSATB, 2 vln, 2 corn, 3 tbn, bc
D-F Ff. Mus. 597
parts (2 sets)

W0072 **Herr, höre mein Gebet**
SSATB, 4 vla, vlne, bc
F-Ssp

W0073 **Herr Jesu Christ, du höchstes Gut**
SATB, 2 vln, 2 gamba, vlne, bc
F-Ssp
parts
DMA 2/2329

W0074 **Herr, wie du willst, so schicks mit mir**
SSATB, 2 vln, 3 vla, vlne, bc
F-Ssp
parts
DMA 2/920

W0075 **Jesu, meine Freude**
SATB, 2 vln, 2 vla, bsn/vlne, bc
F-Ssp
parts
DMA 2/2330

W0076 **Was betrübst du dich, meine Seele**
SATB, 2 vln, 2 vla, vlne, bc
D-F Ff. Mus. 598
score and parts

W0077 **Wer nur den lieben Gott läßt walten**
SATB, 2 vln, 2 gamba, vlne, bc
F-Ssp
parts
DMA 2/2331

WENZEL, Jakob

W0078 **In te spem figunt**
SSB, 2 vln, 2 vla, bc
D-Bds Mus. ms. 30293, no. 16 (Bokemeyer)
score
DMA 3/1329

WERCKMEISTER, Andreas (1645-1706)

W0079 **Wo ist der neugeborne König der Jüden?**
SATB, 2 vln, vla, bc
Epiphany
D-Gs Cod. Ms. philos. 84e Werckmeister 1
(1717)
score and parts

WESTPHAL, Philipp

W0080 **Ihr meine Lieben, hemmet euer Klagen**
SATB
Funeral of Martin Donike
Berlin, 1669
RISM W964, Reich 35

W0081 **Nun bin ich endlich kommen**
SATB
Funeral of Ursula Maria Gericke
Berlin, 1672
RISM W963, Reich 38

W0082 **Nun geh ich hin zu meiner Ruh**
SATB
Funeral of Elisabeth Hoppe
Berlin, 1669
RISM W962, Reich 36 (score)

WIEDEMANN, Michael (1659-1719)

W0083 **Durch einen Menschen ist die Sünde**
SSATB, 2 vln, 2 vla, 2 fl, vlne, bc
Funeral of Sigismund Heinrich von Biberau
und Modlau
Lauban, 1693
RISM W1053, Reich 211 (score)

W0084 **Es ist vollbracht, was mir mein Gott**
SATB, SATB, lute, bc
Funeral of Sigismund Heinrich von Biberau
und Modlau
Lauban, 1693
RISM W1055, Reich 211 (score)
Parts listed as in RISM; Reich gives SB
soli, SSATB, bc

W0085 **Siehe, der Gerechte kommt**
SSSATB, 3 vla, 2 fl, bc
Funeral of Sigismund Heinrich von Biberau
und Modlau
Lauban, 1693
RISM W1054, Reich 211 (parts)

WIERING

W0086 **Angeli plaudite**
SATB, 2 vln/ob, vla, bc
D-B Mus. ms. 30295, no. 3 (Bokemeyer)
score

W0087 **Dixit Dominus**
SATB, 2 vln, bc
D-B Mus. ms. 30295, no. 4 (Bokemeyer)
score

WIGLEB, Stephan Heinrich

W0088 **Die Worte gehen mir zu Herzen**
ATTB
Funeral of Agnesa Tilemann
Gotha, 1682
RISM W1060

W0089 **Es will die Zeit hierbei nun rücken**
SSAT
Funeral of Agnesa Tilemann
Gotha, 1682
RISM W1060

W0090 **So lebet und schwebet in ewigen Freuden**
SATB
Funeral of Agnesa Tilemann
Gotha, 1682
RISM W1060

WILHELMI, Johann Heinrich

W0091 **Miserere mei, Deus**
SSATTB, 2 vln, 2 vla, 2 corn, bsn, bc
D-Dlb Mus. 1799-E-500 (Grimma U 307/N 15)
(1682)
score and parts

WINTZER, Jacob

W0092 **Unser Wandel ist im Himmel**
SSATB, bc
Funeral of Maria Elisabeth Jahn
Coburg, 1650
RISM W1681, Reich 187

WITT, Christian Friedrich (1660-1716)

W0093 **Also hat Gott die Welt geliebet**
SATB, 2 vln, 2 vla, bc
Whit Monday
D-Nla Pfarrämter III (Rep 55) VII
Rentweinsdorf Nr. 4-40
parts

W0094 **Am Abend aber desselbigen Sabbats**
SATB, 2 vln, 2 vla, bc
1st Sunday after Easter
D-Nla Pfarrämter III (Rep 55) VII
Rentweinsdorf Nr. 4-32
parts

W0095 **Da aber Johannes im Gefängnis**
SATB, 2 vln, 2 vla, bc
3rd Sunday of Advent
D-Nla Pfarrämter III (Rep 55) VII
Rentweinsdorf Nr. 4-3
parts

W0096 **Da gingen die Pharisäer hin**
SATB, 2 vln, 2 vla, bc
23rd Sunday after Trinity
D-Nla Pfarrämter III (Rep 55) VII
Rentweinsdorf Nr. 4-68
parts

W0097 **Da Jesus vom Berg**
SATB, 2 vln, 2 vla, bc
3rd Sunday after Epiphany
D-Nla Pfarrämter III (Rep 55) VII
Rentweinsdorf Nr. 4-14
parts

W0098 **Da sie aber davon redeten**
SATB, 2 vln, 2 vla, bc
Easter Tuesday
D-Nla Pfarrämter III (Rep 55) VII
Rentweinsdorf Nr. 4-31
parts

W0099 **Da sie nun nahe bei Jerusalem waren**
SATB, 2 vln, 2 vla, bc
Palm Sunday
D-Nla Pfarrämter III (Rep 55) VII
Rentweinsdorf Nr. 4-25
parts

W0100 **Da war Jesus vom Geist in die Wüste geführt**
SATB, 2 vln, 2 vla, bc
1st Sunday of Lent
D-Nla Pfarrämter III (Rep 55) VII
Rentweinsdorf Nr. 4-20
parts

WITT, Christian Friedrich (*continued*)

W0101   **Danach fuhr Jesus über**
SATB, 2 vln, 2 vla, bc
4th Sunday of Lent
D-Nla Pfarrämter III (Rep 55) VII
Rentweinsdorf Nr. 4-23
parts

W0102   **Daran ist erschienen die Liebe Gottes**
SATB, 2 vln, 2 vla, vlne, bc
Christmas Day
F-Ssp
parts

W0103   **Das Himmelreich ist gleich einem Könige**
SATB, 2 vln, 2 vla, bc
22nd Sunday after Trinity
D-Nla Pfarrämter III (Rep 55) VII
Rentweinsdorf Nr. 4-67
parts

W0104   **Du kannst mich rüsten mit Stärke**
SATB, 2 vln, 2 vla, vlne, bc
F-Ssp
parts

W0105   **Er nahm aber zu sich die Zwölfe**
SATB, 2 vln, 2 vla, bc
Quinquagesima
D-Nla Pfarrämter III (Rep 55) VII
Rentweinsdorf Nr. 4-19
parts (1720)

W0106   **Es ging ein Sämann aus zu säen**
SATB, 2 vln, 2 vla, bsn, bc
Sexagesima
D-Nla Pfarrämter III (Rep 55) VII
Rentweinsdorf Nr. 4-18
parts

W0107   **Es kommt aber die Zeit**
SATB, 2 vln, 2 vla, bc
Sunday after Ascension
D-Nla Pfarrämter III (Rep 55) VII
Rentweinsdorf Nr. 4-38
parts

W0108   **Es naheten aber zu ihm allerlei Zöllner**
SATB, 2 vln, 2 vla, bc
3rd Sunday after Trinity
D-Nla Pfarrämter III (Rep 55) VII
Rentweinsdorf Nr. 4-46
parts

W0109   **Es sei denn, daß ihr euch umkehret**
SATB, 2 vln, 2 vla, vlne, bc

Feast of Saint Michael the Archangel
D-Nla Pfarrämter III (Rep 55) VII
Rentweinsdorf Nr. 4-61
parts

W0110   **Es sei denn eure Gerechtigkeit**
SATB, 2 vln, 2 vla, bc
6th Sunday after Trinity
D-Nla Pfarrämter III (Rep 55) VII
Rentweinsdorf Nr. 4-50
parts

W0111   **Es war ein Mensch, der machte ein groß Abendmahl**
SATB, 2 vln, 2 vla, bc
2nd Sunday after Trinity
D-Nla Pfarrämter III (Rep 55) VII
Rentweinsdorf Nr. 4-44
parts

W0112   **Es werden Zeichen und Wunder**
SATB, 2 vln, 2 vla, bc
2nd Sunday of Advent
D-Nla Pfarrämter III (Rep 55) VII
Rentweinsdorf Nr. 4-2
parts

W0113   **Fahret auf die Höhe und werfet eure Netze aus**
SATB, 2 vln, 2 vla, bc
5th Sunday after Trinity
D-Nla Pfarrämter III (Rep 55) VII
Rentweinsdorf Nr. 4-49
parts

W0114   **Fürchte dich nicht Maria**
SATB, 2 vln, 2 vla, bc
Annunciation to the Virgin Mary
D-Nla Pfarrämter III (Rep 55) VII
Rentweinsdorf Nr. 4-26
parts

W0115   **Fürchtet euch nicht**
SATB, 2 vln, 2 vla, 2 clar, timp, vlne, bsn, bc
Christmas Day
D-F Ff. Mus. 667
score (voices, clar, & bc only) and parts

W0116   **Gelobet sei der Herr, der Gott Israel**
SATB, 2 vln, 2 vla, 2 clar, bc
Feast of Saint John the Baptist
D-Nla Pfarrämter III (Rep 55) VII
Rentweinsdorf Nr. 4-45
parts

W0117   **Gleich wie der Blitz ausgehet**
SATB, 2 vln, 2 vla, bc
25th Sunday after Trinity

D-Nla Pfarrämter III (Rep 55) VII
Rentweinsdorf Nr. 4-70
parts

W0118 Gott ist getreu
SATB, 2 vln, 2 vla, vlne, bc
F-Ssp
parts

W0119 Gott ist offenbaret im Fleisch
SATB, 2 vln, 2 vla, 3 fl, 2 tbn, bc
D-B Mus. ms. 30295, no. 9 (Bokemeyer)
score

W0120 Herr, meine Tochter ist jetzt gestorben
SATB, 2 vln, 2 vla, bc
24th Sunday after Trinity
D-Nla Pfarrämter III (Rep 55) VII
Rentweinsdorf Nr. 4-69
parts

W0121 Herr wenn Trübsal da ist
SATB, 2 vln, 2 vla, vlne, bc
4th Sunday after Epiphany
D-F Ff. Mus. 668
score (voices & bc only) and parts

W0122 Ich bin die Tür, so jemand durch mich eingehet
SATB, 2 vln, 2 vla, bc
Whit Tuesday
D-Nla Pfarrämter III (Rep 55) VII
Rentweinsdorf Nr. 4-41
parts

W0123 Ich bin ein guter Hirt
SATB, 2 vln, 2 vla, bc
2nd Sunday after Easter
D-Nla Pfarrämter III (Rep 55) VII
Rentweinsdorf Nr. 4-33
parts (vocal parts lacking)

W0124 Ich danke dir, Gott, daß ich nicht bin
SATB, 2 vln, 2 vla, bc
11th Sunday after Trinity
D-Nla Pfarrämter III (Rep 55) VII
Rentweinsdorf Nr. 4-55
parts

W0125 Ihr werdet weinen und heulen
SATB, 2 vln, 2 vla, bsn, bc
3rd Sunday after Easter
D-Nla Pfarrämter III (Rep 55) VII
Rentweinsdorf Nr. 4-34
parts

W0126 Jesus sprach zu seinen Jüngern
SATB, 2 vln, 2 vla, bc
3rd Day of Christmas

D-Nla Pfarrämter III (Rep 55) VII
Rentweinsdorf Nr. 4-7
parts

W0127 Joseph lebet noch und ist ein Herr im ganzen Ägypten Lande
ATB, 2 vln, bc
Easter Monday
D-Gs Cod. Ms. philos. 84e Witte 1 (1715)
score and parts

W0128 Mich jammert des Volks
4 vv, 5 instr, bc
7th Sunday after Trinity
D-LUC (1715)
parts

W0129 O selig bist du, die du geglaubt hast
SATB, 2 vln, 2 vla, bc
Visitation of the Virgin Mary
D-Nla Pfarrämter III (Rep 55) VII
Rentweinsdorf Nr. 4-47
parts

W0130 Sagen wir nicht recht, daß du ein Samariter bist
SATB, 2 vln, 2 vla, bsn, bc
5th Sunday of Lent
D-Nla Pfarrämter III (Rep 55) VII
Rentweinsdorf Nr. 4-24
parts

W0131 Saget den Gästen: Siehe, meine Mahlzeit
SATB, 2 vln, 2 vla, bc
20th Sunday after Trinity
D-Nla Pfarrämter III (Rep 55) VII
Rentweinsdorf Nr. 4-65
parts

W0132 Saget der Tochter Zion
SATB, 2 vln, 2 vla, bc
1st Sunday of Advent
D-Nla Pfarrämter III (Rep 55) VII
Rentweinsdorf Nr. 4-1
parts

W0133 Sehet euch vor vor den falschen Propheten
SATB, 2 vln, 2 vla, bc
8th Sunday after Trinity
D-Nla Pfarrämter III (Rep 55) VII
Rentweinsdorf Nr. 4-52
parts

W0134 Seid untertan aller Menschen
SATB, 2 vln, 2 vla, bc
D-B Mus. ms. 30295, no. 8 (Bokemeyer)
score

W0135 Selig sind die Augen
SATB, 2 vln, 2 vla, bc

WITT, Christian Friedrich (*continued*)

13th Sunday after Trinity
D-Nla Pfarrämter III (Rep 55) VII
Rentweinsdorf Nr. 4-57
parts

W0136   **Setze mich wie einen Siegel**
SATB, 2 vln, 2 vla, bc
D-B Mus. ms. 30295, no. 10 (Bokemeyer)
score

W0137   **Siehe, dieser wird gesetzt zu seinem Fall**
SATB, 2 vln, 2 vla, bc
Sunday after Christmas
D-Nla Pfarrämter III (Rep 55) VII
Rentweinsdorf Nr. 4-8
parts

W0138   **Siehe, ein Mensch war zu Jerusalem**
SATB, 2 vln, 2 vla, bc
Purification of the Virgin Mary
D-Nla Pfarrämter III (Rep 55) VII
Rentweinsdorf Nr. 4-16
parts

W0139   **Siehe, es erhub sich ein groß Ungestüm**
SATB, 2 vln, 2 vla, bsn, bc
4th Sunday after Epiphany
D-Nla Pfarrämter III (Rep 55) VII
Rentweinsdorf Nr. 4-15
parts

W0140   **Siehe, ich sende zu euch Propheten**
SATB, 2 vln, 2 vla, bc
2nd Day of Christmas
D-Nla Pfarrämter III (Rep 55) VII
Rentweinsdorf Nr. 4-6
parts
F-Ssp 109
parts
DMA 2/922

W0141   **Sorget nicht für euer Leben**
SATB, 2 vln, 2 vla, bc
15th Sunday after Trinity
D-Nla Pfarrämter III (Rep 55) VII
Rentweinsdorf Nr. 4-59
parts

W0142   **Stehe auf und nimm das Kindlein**
SATB, 2 vln, 2 vla, bc
Sunday after Circumcision
D-Nla Pfarrämter III (Rep 55) VII
Rentweinsdorf Nr. 4-10
parts (1713)

W0143   **Und als er in einen Markt kam**
SATB, 2 vln, 2 vla, bc
14th Sunday after Trinity
D-Nla Pfarrämter III (Rep 55) VII
Rentweinsdorf Nr. 4-58
parts

W0144   **Und als der nahe an das Stadttor kam**
SATB, 2 vln, 2 vla, bc
16th Sunday after Trinity
D-Nla Pfarrämter III (Rep 55) VII
Rentweinsdorf Nr. 4-60
parts

W0145   **Und als sie daselbst waren**
SATB, 2 vln, 2 vla, bc
Christmas Day
D-Nla Pfarrämter III (Rep 55) VII
Rentweinsdorf Nr. 4-5
parts

W0146   **Und am dritten Tage war eine Hochzeit zu Cana**
SATB, 2 vln, 2 vla, bc
2nd Sunday of Epiphany
D-Nla Pfarrämter III (Rep 55) VII
Rentweinsdorf Nr. 4-13
parts

W0147   **Und da acht Tage um waren**
SATB, 2 vln, 2 vla, vlne/bsn, bc
Circumcision
D-Nla Pfarrämter III (Rep 55) VII
Rentweinsdorf Nr. 4-9
parts (vlne/bsn lacking)
F-Ssp 106
parts
DMA 2/921

W0148   **Und da acht Tage vollendet waren**
SATB, 2 vln, 2 vla, bc
1st Sunday after Epiphany
D-Nla Pfarrämter III (Rep 55) VII
Rentweinsdorf Nr. 4-12
parts

W0149   **Und da der Sabbat vergangen war**
SATB, 2 vln, 2 vla, vlne/bsn, bc
Easter Sunday
D-Nla Pfarrämter III (Rep 55) VII
Rentweinsdorf Nr. 4-29
parts (vlne/bsn lacking)

W0150   **Und da er wieder ausging**
SATB, 2 vln, 2 vla, bc
12th Sunday after Trinity

D-Nla Pfarrämter III (Rep 55) VII
Rentweinsdorf Nr. 4-56
parts

**W0151   Und da es nun Abend war, sprach der Herr des
          Weinbergs**
          SATB, 2 vln, 2 vla, bc
          Septuagesima
          D-Nla Pfarrämter III (Rep 55) VII
          Rentweinsdorf Nr. 4-17
          parts

**W0152   Und der Herr, nachdem er mit ihnen geredet
          hatte**
          SATB, 2 vln, 2 vla, bc
          Ascension
          D-Nla Pfarrämter III (Rep 55) VII
          Rentweinsdorf Nr. 4-37
          parts

W0153   Und es begab sich, daß er kam in ein Haus
          SATB, 2 vln, 2 vla, bsn, bc
          17th Sunday after Trinity
          D-Nla Pfarrämter III (Rep 55) VII
          Rentweinsdorf Nr. 4-62
          parts

W0154   Und Jesus ging aus von dannen
          SATB, 2 vln, 2 vla, bc
          2nd Sunday of Lent
          D-Nla Pfarrämter III (Rep 55) VII
          Rentweinsdorf Nr. 4-21
          parts

W0155   Und sie brachten zu ihm einen Gichtbrüchigen
          SATB, 2 vln, 2 vla, bc
          19th Sunday after Trinity
          D-Nla Pfarrämter III (Rep 55) VII
          Rentweinsdorf Nr. 4-64
          parts

W0156   Wahrlich, ich sage dir es sei denn
          SATB, 2 vln, 2 vla, bc
          Trinity
          D-Nla Pfarrämter III (Rep 55) VII
          Rentweinsdorf Nr. 4-42
          parts

W0157   Wahrlich, ich sage euch
          SATB, 2 vln, 2 vla, bc
          5th Sunday after Easter
          D-Nla Pfarrämter III (Rep 55) VII
          Rentweinsdorf Nr. 4-36
          parts

W0158   Warum taufest du denn
          SATB, 2 vln, 2 vla, bc
          4th Sunday of Advent

D-Nla Pfarrämter III (Rep 55) VII
Rentweinsdorf Nr. 4-4
parts

W0159   Was sind das für Reden
          SATB, 2 vln, 2 vla, bc
          Easter Monday
          D-Nla Pfarrämter III (Rep 55) VII
          Rentweinsdorf Nr. 4-30
          parts (B lacking)

W0160   Wenn aber jener der Geist der Wahrheit
          SATB, 2 vln, 2 vla, bc
          4th Sunday after Easter
          D-Nla Pfarrämter III (Rep 55) VII
          Rentweinsdorf Nr. 4-35
          parts

W0161   Wenn du es wüßtest
          SATB, 2 vln, 2 vla, bc
          10th Sunday after Trinity
          D-Nla Pfarrämter III (Rep 55) VII
          Rentweinsdorf Nr. 4-54
          parts

**W0162   Wenn ein starker Gewappneter seinen Palast
          bewahret**
          SATB, 2 vln, 2 vla, bc
          3rd Sunday of Lent
          D-Nla Pfarrämter III (Rep 55) VII
          Rentweinsdorf Nr. 4-22
          parts

W0163   Wenn ihr nicht Zeichen und Wunder seht
          SATB, 2 vln, 2 vla, bc
          21st Sunday after Trinity
          D-Nla Pfarrämter III (Rep 55) VII
          Rentweinsdorf Nr. 4-66
          parts

W0164   Wer kann des Höchsten Rat
          SSATB
          Funeral of Susanne Sibylle Reichardt
          Gotha, 1697
          RISM 1697[1], Reich 117 (choirbook)
          DMA 74//117

W0165   Wer mich liebet, der wird mein Wort halten
          SATB, 2 vln, 2 vla, bc
          Pentecost
          D-Nla Pfarrämter III (Rep 55) VII
          Rentweinsdorf Nr. 4-39
          parts

W0166   Wie denket euch um Christo
          SATB, 2 vln, 2 vla, bc
          18th Sunday after Trinity

WITT, Christian Friedrich (*continued*)

    D-Nla Pfarrämter III (Rep 55) VII
    Rentweinsdorf Nr. 4-63
    parts

W0167   **Wie hör ich das von dir**
    SATB, 2 vln, 2 vla, vlne, bc
    9th Sunday after Trinity
    D-Nla Pfarrämter III (Rep 55) VII
    Rentweinsdorf Nr. 4-53
    parts

W0168   **Wir müssen durch viel Trübsal**
    SATB, 2 vln, 2 vla, vlne, bc
    F-Ssp
    parts

W0169   **Wirf dein Anliegen auf den Herrn**
    SATB, 2 vln, 2 vla, vlne, bc
    F-Ssp (1703)
    parts

W0170   **Wo ist der neugeborne König der Juden**
    SATB, 2 vln, 2 vla, bc
    Epiphany
    D-Nla Pfarrämter III (Rep 55) VII
    Rentweinsdorf Nr. 4-11
    parts

W0171   **Zeuch mich nicht hin unter die Gottlosen**
    SATB, 2 vln, 2 vla, vlne, bc
    F-Ssp
    parts

WOLTZ, Georg Sebastian

W0172   **Da mein herzbetrübter Sinn**
    SST, bc
    Funeral Schwäbisch Hall, 1658
    RISM W1847, Reich 391

WRATZKE, Jacob

W0173   **Weil du, Herr Christ, erstanden bist**
    SSA, bc
    Funeral of Martin von Necker
    Stettin, 1658
    RISM W2161, Reich 400 (score)

W0174   **Zwar daß die Welt uns manche Plagen**
    5 vv, instr
    Funeral of Anna Maria von Tettawen
    Königsberg, 1661
    RISM W2162 (score)

Z

ZACHER (Zächer), Johann Michael (1651-1712)

Note: All works said by MGG to be in A-Wsp are no longer extant, according to Carl Rouland, *Katalog des Musik-Archives der St. Peterskirche in Wien* (1908). The following titles said by MGG to be in A-KR could not be located in that archive: "Missa," "Requiem," and "Vesperae à 5."

Z0001 **Beatus vir**
    See Vesperae de confessore

Z0002 **Confitebor tibi Domine**
    See Vesperae de confessore

Z0003 **Dico ego opera mea**
    See Gaudeamus omnes

Z0004 **Dixit Dominus**
    See Vesperae de confessore

Z0005 **Gaudeamus omnes**
    SATB, 4 vla, vltta, vc, corn, 2 tbn, vlne, bsn, bc
    Assumption or Annunciation of the Virgin Mary
    A-Ws (without shelf number) (1712)
    parts
    Text begins: "Dico ego opera mea"

Z0006 **Laudate Dominum**
    See Vesperae de confessore

Z0007 **Laudate pueri, Dominum**
    See Vesperae de confessore

Z0008 **Missa Sancti Stephani**
    SATB, 2 vln, 2 vla, 2 clar, 3 tbn, vlne, bc
    A-Kr Kasten C, Fasc. 8, no. 662 (1693)
    parts

Z0009 **Spiritus Domini replevit**
    SATB, 2 vla, vltta, corn, 2 tbn, vlne, bsn, bc

    Pentecost
    A-Ws (without shelf number)
    parts

Z0010 **Vesperae de confessore**
    SATB, 2 vln, 2 vla, 3 tbn, bc
    CS-KRa III, 114
    parts
    microfilm: US-SY
    Includes: Dixit Dominus, Confitebor tibi Domine, Beatus vir, Laudate pueri Dominum, Laudate Dominum

ZACHOW, Friedrich Wilhelm (1663-1712)

Note: "Chorus ille coelitum/Ich hab dich erhöret," "Danksaget dem Vater," "Herzlich tut mich verlangen," "Stehe auf meine Freundin," "Triumph," "victoria," and "Venite ad me omnes" are attributed to the composer ♃ in the Grimma collection sources. Although long assumed to indicate Zachow, the symbol probably represents not the letter Z but the astrological sign for the god Jupiter (Zeus) and the fifth day of the week (Thursday). In the same way that Jacobi designated Christian Liebe and Johann Krieger with the signs for Venus (i.e., Liebe) and Mars (i.e., Krieg), ♃ most likely stands for a composer whose identity has not yet been determined (ref. discussion with Ortrun Landmann, D-Dlb).

Z0011 **Ach Herr, mich armen Sünder straf nicht in deinem Zorn**
    SATB, 2 vln/ob & fl, 2 vla, bc
    D-Dlb Mus. ms. 2-E-545 (Grimma U 352/N 93)
    parts
    Organum I/12
    Anonymous; formerly attributed to Handel; *see* Krummacher (1963)

ZACHOW, Friedrich Wilhelm (*continued*)

Z0012 **Chorus ille caelitum/Ich hab dich erhöret**
See introductory note

Z0013 **Danksaget dem Vater**
See introductory note

Z0014 **Das ist das ewige Leben**
SATB, 2 vln, vla, 2 ob, bsn, bc
Trinity Sunday
D-B Mus. ms. 23445, no. 1 (Bokemeyer)
score
DMA 3/1333
D-Dlb Mus. ms. 2150-E-507 (Grimma a/w
38/T 99)
parts (vla & bc missing)
DdT 21/22, pp. 3-24

Z0015 **Die Apostel wurden alle voll des Heiligen Geistes**
SATB, 2 vln, vla, 2 clar, prin, timp, bc
Pentecost
D-Dlb Mus. ms. 2150-E-505 (Grimma U
314/N 21)
parts

Z0016 **Dies ist der Tag den der Herr gemacht hat**
STB soli, SATB, 2 vln, 2 bassonetti, 2
horn, bsn, bc
Easter
B-Bc 1008
score
DdT 21/22, pp. 236-59

Z0017 **Es wird eine Rute aufgehen**
SATB, 2 vln, 2 vla, 2 ob, 2 horn, bc
Christmas Day
B-Bc 1007
parts
DdT 21/22, pp. 204-35

Z0018 **Herr lehre mich tun nach deinem Wohlgefallen**
SATB, 2 vln, vla, 3 tbtta, timp, bc
D-Dlb Mus. ms. 2150-E-508 (Grimma U
319/N 25)
parts

Z0019 **Herr wenn ich nur dich habe**
SATB, 2 vln, 2 vla, harp, bc
D-Bds Mus. ms. 23445/10 (Bokemeyer)
score (Handel autograph)
DdT 21/22, pp. 25-40
Ed. Seiffert, *Organum* I/5 (1924)
Facs. of p. 1 in Müller-Blattau, *Händel*
(1933), p. 9
Facs. of pp. 1-2 in Rackwitz & Steffens,
Händel (1962), pl. 16

Z0020 **Herzlich tut mich verlangen**
See introductory note

Z0021 **Heut feiern wir das hohe Fest**
SATB, 2 vln, 2 vla, 2 ob, bsn, bc
D-Dlb Mus. ms. 2150-E-510 (Grimma U
305/N 13) (1714)
parts
Anonymous; attributed by Krummacher
(1963)

Z0022 **Ich bin die Auferstehung und das Leben**
SATB, 2 vln, vla, ob, bsn, bc
Easter
D-Dlb Mus. ms. 2150-E-502 (Grimma U
310/N 18)
parts

Z0023 **Ich hab dich erhöret**
See introductory note

Z0024 **Ich will mich mit dir verloben**
SATB, 2 vln, 2 vla, 2 clar, bc
Annunciation
D-B Mus. ms. 23445, no. 2 (Bokemeyer)
score
DMA 3/1334
DdT 21/22, pp. 41-53

Z0025 **Lehre mich tun nach deinem Wohlgefallen**
SATB, 2 vln, vla, 2 clar, prin, timp, vlne, bc
Pentecost
D-Dlb Mus. ms. 2150-E-503 (Grimma U
312/N 19)
parts (timp lacking)

Z0026 **Lobe den Herrn, meine Seele**
SSATB, 2 vln, vla, 2 ob, 2 horns, bsn, bc
B-Bc 1006
score
DdT 21/22, pp. 145-203

Z0027 **Missa (brevis) super Christ lag in Todesbanden**
SATB, bc
D-B Mus. ms. 30315 (formerly 23440)
score
DdT 21/22, pp. 304-10
Ed. Beckmann, *Monatsschrift für
Gottesdienst u. kirchliche Kunst* 19
(1914), pp. 136ff (Kyrie only, German
text)
(Hänssler no. 27.009)

Z0028 **Meine Seel erhebt den Herrn**
SATB, 2 vln, vla, 2 gamba, 2 corn, 2 fl, 2
ob, bc

Annunciation
D-Bds Mus. ms. 30199, no. 7 (formerly
ms. 199)
score (considered autograph by Thomas)
DdT 21/22, pp. 104-28

Z0029 Nun aber gibst du, Gott, einen gnädigen Regen
SATB, 2 vln, vla, 2 corni grossi, ob, bsn, bc
Pentecost
D-Dlb Mus. ms. 2150-E-504 (Grimma U
313/N 20)
parts

Z0030 Nun aber gibst du, Gott, einen gnädigen Regen
SATB, 2 vln, vla, 2 ob, 2 horn, bsn, bc
Pentecost
lost (formerly Berlin, Bibliothek der
Kaiserin Augusta, Charlottenburg)
DdT 21/22, pp. 269-303

Z0031 Preiset mit mir den Herren
SATB, 3 vln, vc, 3 ob, bsn, bc
New Year's Day
D-Dlb Mus. ms. 2150-E-506 (Grimma
Q/W 10/T 79)
parts

Z0032 Redet untereinander mit Psalmen
SATB, 2 vln, 2 vla, 2 clar, bc
Visitation of the Virgin Mary
D-LUC 365A
parts

Z0033 Ruhe, Friede, Freud, und Wonne
SAATTBB, 2 vln, 2 vla, 2 ob, taille, bsn, bc
Pentecost
D-B Mus. ms. 23445, no. 3 (Bokemeyer)
score
DMA 3/1335
DdT 21/22, pp. 54-89

Z0034 Siehe, das ist Gottes Lamm
SATB, 2 vln, 3 vla, 2 corn, bsn, bc
Feast of Saint John the Baptist
D-LUC 366A
parts

Z0035 Siehe, ich bin bei euch alle Tage
ATB soli, SATB, 2 vln, vla, 2 clar, bc
Ascension
D-Bds Mus. ms. 30199, no. 8 (formerly
199)
score (considered autograph by Thomas)
DdT 21/22, pp. 129-44

Z0036 Stehe auf, meine Freundin
See introductory note

Z0037 Triumph, victoria
See introductory note

Z0038 Uns ist ein Kind geboren
SATB, 2 vln, 2 vla, ob, bsn/vlne, bc
Christmas Day
D-Dlb Mus. ms. 2150-E-500 (Grimma U
308/N 16)
parts
Ed. Krüger, *Die Kantate* 247

Z0039 Venite ad me, omnes
See introductory note

Z0040 Vom Himmel kam der Engel Schar
SATB, 2 vln, 3 vltta, 4 clar, timp, bsn, bc
Christmas Day
D-B Mus. ms. 23445, no. 5 (Bokemeyer)
(1697)
score
DMA 3/1336
DdT 21/22, pp. 90-103

Z0041 Weg, nichtige Freuden
SATB, 2 vln, 2 vla, 2 ob, bsn, bc
D-Dlb Mus. ms. 2150-E-509 (Grimma U
536/T 4)
parts

ZEUTSCHNER, Tobias (1621-1675)

COLLECTIONS

Musicalische Kirchen- und Haus-Freude (1661)
RISM Z171 (parts)

Musicalischen Fleisses erster Theil (1652)
RISM Z169 (parts)

WORKS

Z0042 Ach Herr! Ach Herr meiner schöne
SAT, 2 vln, bc
Musicalischen Fleisses erster Theil, no. 6

Z0043 Benedicta sit Sancta Trinitas
ATB, 2 vln, bc
Musicalische Kirchen- und Haus-Freude,
no. 1
S-Uu 77:42 (Düben)
tablature
S-Uu 38:21 (Düben)
parts

Z0044 Beweise, Herr, deine wunderliche Güte
SSATB, 2 vln, bc
Musicalischen Fleisses erster Theil, no. 8

ZEUTSCHNER, Tobias (*continued*)

Z0045 **Confitemini Domino**
ATB, bc
Musicalischen Fleisses erster Theil, no. 4

Z0046 **Du großer Schmerzen-Mann**
SATB
D-Dlb Mus. Löb 53, no. 151
score
DMA 2/538

Z0047 **Es erhub sich ein Streit**
SSATB, 2 vln, 3 tbn, bc
Musicalische Kirchen- und Haus-Freude,
no. 6
S-Uu 77:84 (Düben)
tablature
S-Uu 41:4 (Düben)
parts

Z0048 **Es ist kein ander Heil**
SATB, 2 vln, 3 tbn, bc
Musicalische Kirchen- und Haus-Freude,
no. 2
S-Uu 77:44 (Düben)
tablature
S-Uu 45:8 (Düben)
parts
S-Uu copies have text "Quis est quem
metius"

Z0049 **Exaudi Domine justitium meam**
SSATB, 2 vln, bc
Musicalischen Fleisses erster Theil, no. 10

Z0050 **Gott, du Gott Israel**
SSATB, 2 vln, 3 tbn, bc
Musicalische Kirchen- und Haus-Freude,
no. 5
S-Uu 77:53 (Düben); 3:23 (Düben)
tablature
S-Uu 37:14 (Düben)
parts

Z0051 **Gott, sei mir gnädig**
SATB, 2 vln, bc
Musicalische Kirchen- und Haus-Freude,
no. 3
S-Uu 37:15 (Düben)
parts
S-Uu copy has text "Gudh war migh nadilig"
Ed. Herrmann, *Die Kantate* 260

Z0052 **Gott und Vater, reich von Güte**
SATB
Breslau, 1660
RISM Z170 (score)

Z0053 **Gudh war migh nadeligh**
See Gott sei mir gnädig

Z0054 **Herr, hebe an zu segnen das Haus**
SATB, 2 vln, 3 tbn, bc
Musicalische Kirchen- und Haus-Freude,
no. 4
S-Uu 77:49, fol. 49v-54r (Düben)
tablature
S-Uu 43:3 (Düben)
parts
S-Uu copies have text "Laetare nunc in
Domino"

Z0055 **Ich bin der Herr, der erste**
4 vv, 2 vln, bc
D-LUC

Z0056 **Jesu dulcis memoria**
STB, 2 vln, 5 vla, bc
S-Uu 77:57 (Düben) (1663)
tablature (no text)
S-Uu 42:4 (Düben)
parts

Z0057 **Laetare nunc in Domino**
See Herr hebe an zu segnen

Z0058 **Lauda Jerusalem**
SSATTB, 2 vln, 3 tbn, bc
Musicalische Kirchen- und Haus-Freude,
no. 8
S-Uu 69:10 (Düben)
parts

Z0059 **Laudate Dominum, omnes gentes**
SSATB, 2 vln, 3 tbn, bc
Musicalische Kirchen- und Haus-Freude,
no. 7
S-Uu 77:37 (Düben)
tablature
S-Uu 43:10 (Düben)
parts

Z0060 **Lobet den Namen des Herren**
ATB, bc
Musicalischen Fleisses erster Theil, no. 3

Z0061 **O Domine Jesu Christe**
SSATB, 2 vln, bc
Musicalischen Fleisses erster Theil, no. 9

Z0062 **Quis est quem metius**
See Es ist kein ander Heil

Z0063 **Resonent organa**
SSATB, 2 vln, 2 clar, 3 tbn, bc
Musicalische Kirchen- und Haus-Freude,
no. 9

D-B Mus. ms. 23585
 score (SSATB, 2 vln, 2 vla, vlne, bc)

Z0064 **Te Deum laudamus**
 SSATB, 2 vln, 2 clar, 3 tbn, bc
 Musicalische Kirchen- und Haus-Freude,
  no. 10
 S-Uu 85:92 (Düben)
  tablature (incomplete)

Z0065 **Unde animae meae salus?**
 SSATB, 2 vln, bc
 Musicalischen Fleisses erster Theil, no. 7

ZIEGLER, Johann Christoph

Z0066 **Laudate pueri, Dominum**
 SATB, 2 vln, 3 vla, 2 corn, bsn, bc
 D-Dlb Mus. 1916-E-500 (Grimma U 322/N 27)
  parts

Z0067 **O weh! ach Schmerz!**
 SATB, bc
 Funeral of Sophia Augusta, Fürstin zu Anhalt
 Wittenberg, 1681
  RISM Z185, Reich 429 (choirbook)
  DMA 70//3

*T*itle Index

Gleich wie der Adler **A0239**
Gleich wie der Blitz ausgehet **B0798, F0116, W0117**
Gloria et divitiae **M0272**
Gloria et honore **C0033, H0529, M0273-74**
Gloria in excelsis Deo **A0240, F0025, K0316, L0081, R0117-19**
Gloriabuntur in te **M0275**
Gloriosae Virginis Mariae **S0051**
Gloriosum diem **E0042**
Gloriosus Deus in sanctis suis **M0358**
Gnade, Gnade, Jesu, Gnade **L0082**
Gnade sei mit uns **W0009**
Gott alleine kann uns schützen **B0799**
Gott bauet selbst sein Himmelreich **P0139**
Gott, dein Weg ist heilig **H0089**
Gott, der da reich ist von Barmherzigkeit **A0432**
Gott, der du bist ein reines Wesen **B0800**
Gott, der du dein Kreuz getragen hast **A0039**
Gott, der du schaffst, daß Sanct Johann **T0106**
Gott der Götter, Herr der Herren **B0801**
Gott der Herr **R0228**
Gott der Herr, der Mächtige redet **B0504, B0802**
Gott des Segens, deinen Segen **B0803**
Gott, du bist derselbst mein König **M0224**
Gott, du bist meine Zuversicht **S0478**
Gott, du bist von Ewigkeit **S0383**
Gott, du bleibest doch mein Gott **S0318**
Gott, du Brunnquell aller Güte **K0317**
Gott, du Gott Israel **H0090, P0019, Z0050**
Gott, du Herrscher aller Dinge **K0018**
Gott, du krönest das Jahr mit deinem Gut **T0063**
Gott, du wahrer Amens **K0019**
Gott einer Obrigkeit **S0533**
Gott einen Tag gesetzet **N0076**
Gott, es ist mein rechter Ernst **H0571**
Gott fähret auf mit Jauchzen **B0804, B1370**
Gott, gib dein Gericht dem Könige **B0805**
Gott hat den, der von keiner Sünde **N0077**
Gott hat den Menschen geschaffen **M0025**
Gott hat Jesum erwecket **R0032**
Gott hat uns **C0133**
Gott hat uns nicht gesetzt zum Zorn **B0806, H0091**
Gott hilf mir **B1371, T0014**
Gott hilf mir, denn das Wasser gehet **B0807**
Gott im Himmel sei es geklaget **A0040**
Gott in der Höhe **A0041**
Gott ist dein Behüter **S0719**
Gott ist die Liebe **H0092, H0362, M0026**
Gott ist einem König gleich **P0140**
Gott ist getreu **W0118**
Gott ist offenbaret im Fleisch **W0119**
Gott ist unser Zuversicht **A0433, B1325, K0276, M0027, N0078, P0020-21, S0454**

Gott lieben ist die allerschönste Weisheit **M0028**
Gott liebet dieses Kind **K0277**
Gott, man lobet dich in der Stille **A0005, B0153, E0136**
Gott, mein Herz ist bereit **H0093, M0225**
Gott, mein Ruhm schweige nicht **B0808**
Gott segne dies vertraute Paar **S0193**
Gott sei Dank für das Lösegeld **S0720**
Gott, sei mir gnädig **A0241, A0435-36, B0389, B0809, K0155, N0079, S0664, T0015, Z0051**
Gott sei uns gnädig **H0289, P0022, W0071**
Gott sende dein Licht und deine Wahrheit **S0194-95**
Gott tu mit mir, was ihm gefällt **S0422**
Gott und Vater, reich von Güte **Z0052**
Gott unser Heiland **H0363**
Gott, unsre Bitt für deinen Thron **T0107**
Gott Vater, dessen Sohn **B0810**
Gott, warum verstößest du uns so gar **B0811**
Gott, wende dich von deinem Grimme **K0278**
Gott, wie dein Name, so ist auch dein Ruhm **L0113**
Gott, wie lang muß ich noch warten **S0534**
Gott will für alle seine Gaben **E0137**
Gott wird abwischen alle Tränen **F0117**
Gott Zebaoth, dich wende doch **B0812**
Gottes Geist bemüht sich sehr **P0141**
Gottes Name wird ewiglich bleiben **M0029**
Gottes und Marien Kind **T0108**
Gottlob die hochgewünschte Zeit **S0535**
Gottlob, die Stund ist kommen **S0536**
Gottlob, es geht nun mehr zum Ende **A0434, A0437, T0056**
Gottlob, es läuft uns schier zu Ende **N0015**
Gottlob! wir sind gesprungen gesund **S0721**
Gratias agimus **E0138**
Groß Freud hab ich in meinem Gemüt **T0109**
Groß und wundersam sind deine Werke **C0134**
Großer Gott du wohnst dort oben **B0813**
Grundgütigster Vater **B0814**
Gudh war migh nadeligh **Z0053**
Gustate **L0008**
Gustate et videte **L0111**
Gute Nacht, du eitles Leben **B0815-16**
Gute Nacht, es ist vollendt **W0010**
Gute Nacht, ihr Eitelkeiten **S0537**
Guter Hirt, der du dein Leben **B0817**
Gutes Kindlein Jesu, mußt du fliehen **B0818**

Habe deine Lust an dem Herrn **B0390, E0098, G0105, H0094, M0312, S0196, W0050**
Haben wir das Gute empfangen **J0022**
Habt nicht lieb die Welt, noch was in der Welt ist **S0367**
Haec dies **B0244, B0391, C0034**
Haec est dies quam fecit Dominus **G0069**

Nicht nur eines Todes Schrecken **K0036**
Nicht uns, Herr, sondern deinem Namen gibt Ehre **B1022**
Nichts soll uns scheiden **B1399**
Niemand fähret gen Himmel **B1023**
Niemand kann Jesum einen Herrn **N0096**
Niemand sage, wenn er versucht wird **M0046**
Niemand will dich leiden **A0305**
Nihil est quod timeam **E0054**
Nihil novum sub sole **R0162**
Nimm hin deine Thron, o Mutter mein **A0076**
Nimm von uns, Herr, du treuer Gott **B1400**
Nimm wohl in acht mein Herz **B1024**
Nisi Dominus **A0611-13, B0127, B0547-48, B0556, B1328,**
    C0070-71, F0036, F0200, G0193-95, H0460, M0102, M0388,
    P0185, R0163-65, S0094-95, S0268, S0622, S0739, T0165-66
Nolite timere **S0010**
Non est inventus **M0298**
Non omnis **B1299**
Non sunt condig **L0019**
Non timebus **B1300**
Nos autem gloriari **B0479, S0096, S0269**
Nos misereros peccatores **M0176**
Nu låt oß Gudh wår Herra **B1401, B1403**
Nulla scientia melior est illa **A0614**
Nun aber gehe ich hin **F0135, H0203**
Nun aber gibst du, Gott **N0097**
Nun aber gibst du, Gott, einen gnädigen Regen **V0009, Z0029-30**
Nun ade, du Jammer-Welt **A0488, B1025**
Nun bich ich endlich kommen **W0081**
Nun danket alle Gott **A0306, A0489-90, B0564, B1329, B1402,**
    F0136, H0303, K0182, K0290, N0098, P0047, S0209, S0435,
    T0068, W0059
Nun danket alle Gott, dem sich der Himmel **B1026**
Nun danket alle Gott, der große Dinge tut **B1027, H0542,**
    K0335
Nun empfind ich, daß es will **G0207**
Nun erfahre ich mit der Wahrheit **N0099**
Nun es kann nicht anders sein **S0402**
Nun freu sich, alle Christenheit **B1028**
Nun freuet euch **H0381**
Nun freut euch, lieben Christen gmein **K0183, R0037**
Nun geh ich aus der Jammer-Welt **D0022**
Nun geh ich hin zu meiner Ruh **W0082**
Nun gehe ich hin zu dem, der mich gesandt hat **P0186**
Nun gibst du, Gott, einen gnädigen Regen **R0166, S0210,**
    S0345
Nun gibet der Höchste den gnädigen Regen **A0307**
Nun Gottlob, es ist vollbracht **A0491, R0167**
Nun gute Nacht **A0492**
Nun gute Nacht, du Jammerwelt **A0493**
Nun gute Nacht, mein Jesus ruft **W0001**
Nun gute Nacht, o weltlich Wesen **K0202**

Nun gute Nacht! Ihr Allerliebsten mein **H0539**
Nun hab ich ausgehaucht **A0308**
Nun hab ich überwunden **B0032**
Nun hat das heilig Gottes Lamm **K0354**
Nun hat sich über uns **H0294**
Nun, Herr, wes soll ich mich trösten **A0494, N0100**
Nun ich scheide aus dem Leide dieses Erd-Getümmels **S0403**
Nun ist das Heil **S0466**
Nun ist des Satans Macht gefället **F0137**
Nun ist es billig, Jesu Christ **A0309**
Nun ist vollbracht der Lebenslauf **S0740**
Nun komm, der Heiden Heiland **B0565, H0204, S0477**
Nun lab und erquicke mein durstiges Herz **A0495**
Nun lasset uns erheben **S0741**
Nun laßt uns den Leib begraben **A0496**
Nun laßt uns Gott dem Herren **B1403**
Nun lob, mein Seel, den Herren **B1239, S0160**
Nun lob, mein Seele **B1029**
Nun mehr ist die Zeit vorhanden **A0077**
Nun muß ich nicht mehr sehn **D0023**
Nun, nun hab ich meinen Lauf erfüllt **B1030**
Nun ruhe, meine Seele, laß alle Arbeit liegen **B1031**
Nun so kehr doch ein zu mir **A0168**
Nun soll mein Herz, Sinn, und Mund **S0742**
Nun treten wir ins neue Jahr **S0680**
Nun weichet der Sonnen Zier **A0169**
Nun wir denn sind gerecht worden durch den Glauben **A0497**
Nun wir gerecht sind worden **R0227**
Nun wir sind gerecht worden durch den Glauben **B1032**
Nun wohlauf ihr Christen-Sinnen **B1033**
Nunc dimittis **B1028, B0298-305, H0628, R0168, S0270, T0051**
Nunc sciovere **B0480**
Nunmehr hat sich geendet **S0161**
Nunmehr ist mir gar wohl geschehen **S0404**
Nur immer selig so geendet **H0015**
Nur in meines Jesu Wunden **P0290**
Nur Kreuz und Not **R0169**

O admirabile commercium **S0097**
O adoranda Trinitas **S0299**
O aeternitas **A0078, G0196**
O altitudo **H0016, P0187**
O amantissime **L0020**
O amor, o timor **M0365**
O amor qui semper **C0202**
O Angst! O schwerer Fall! **A0079**
O anima mea **B0404, P0188, S0011, S0300**
O Anna, liebste Gemahlin mein **A0080**
O aurora **E0055**
O barmherziger Vater **H0205**
O beata benedicti **A0081, A0137**

O beata Trinitas **E0056**
O Beate Pater Francisce **H0415**
O beatum incendium **C0203**
O beatum virum **M0299, P0248**
O benignissime Jesu **K0184**
O blind-verstocktes Menschen Kind **G0222**
O bone Jesu **C0204, M0344**
O bone Jesu, o dulcedo cordis mei **F0680**
O caeli beati **R0008, S0012**
O caeli sapientia, Jesu, spes mentis unica **G0077**
O caelis cives **E0057**
O Christ, dir dank ich sehr **A0170**
O Christe, Schutz-Herz deinen Glieder **S0559**
O Christe, trautster Seelen Hort **K0037**
O cor meum **K0244**
O Corinth, du Zier der Welt **H0382**
O daß ich könnt ein Schloß an meinem Mund legen **B0057**
O des Schmerzen, O der Plagen **B1034**
O Deus meus **S0229**
O dilecte Jesu Christe **A0082**
O Domine Dominator **G0197**
O Domine Jesu Christe **A0310, E0103, H0206, Z0061**
O Domine Jesu Christe, adoro te **R0170**
O du allersüßester, allerfreundlichster **B1035**
O du hochdurchleuchtges Paar **O0017**
O du honigsüsser Mund **A0083**
O du König aller Erden **K0038**
O du kostbarliches Blute **A0084**
O du liebste Mutter mein **A0085**
O du liebstes Jesu Kindelein **A0086**
O du mein allerliebster Herr **A0087**
O du mein ganz betrübtes Herz **A0498**
O du mein lebendiges Brot **A0088**
O du mein liebstes Jesulein **A0089**
O du schnöde, blöde Welt **S0162**
O du schnödes Weltgebäude **S0560**
O du Stifter aller Zeit **K0039**
O du Sünder insgemeine . . . Hier bin ich verborgen **A0090**
O du Sünder insgemeine . . . Hier hang ich unschuldig **A0091**
O du Sünder insgemeine . . . Hier lieg ich im Stalle **A0092**
O du unschuldigen Jesu **A0093**
O dulcissima Virgo **A0094, P0249**
O dulcissime Domine **G0198**
O dulcissime Jesu **H0207, R0213**
O Erden, tu dich auf **A0095**
O Ewigkeit, grausame Zeit **A0499**
O felicissima dies **H0416**
O felix felicitas **E0058, S0301**
O felix felicitas, jucunda jucunditas **S0302**
O felix jucunditas **C0205**
O felix martyris triumphus **P0250**
O felix, o fausta dies **P0251**

O fideles, modicum sustinete tempus **P0085**
O Francisce, Vater mein **A0096**
O Freude und dennoch Leid **P0189**
O freundlicher **H0208**
O fröhliche Stunden, o herrliche Zeit **B1404**
O Gabriel, du getreuer Knecht **A0097**
O gaudium super gaudium **C0206**
O gloriosissima Virgo **B0481**
O Gott, dein ist die ganze Welt **T0142**
O Gott, der du im Paradies **A0098**
O Gott, der du uns hast gesandt **A0099**
O Gott, du Ursprung aller Liebe **S0673**
O Gott im Himmel, mein höchster Trost **A0100**
O Gott mein Heiland **A0101**
O Gott, nun lässest du mich hin **A0500**
O Gott! O Mensch! O Blut! **A0102**
O Gott Vater im höchsten Thron **T0143**
O Gott von sehr grosser Majestät **A0103**
O Gott, wir danken deiner Güt **B1405**
O grande mysterium **B1246**
O gravem dexteram **L0021**
O großer Gott, der du die Welt **B1036**
O großer König, Herr Jesu Christ **T0144**
O harter Schlag **M0321**
O harter Spalt! wenn Leib und Seel sich scheiden **H0017**
O Heiland aller Welt **L0095**
O Heiliger Geist **A0311**
O Heiliger Geist, du werter Hart **A0171**
O heiligster Vater **A0312**
O Herr, du edler Schöpfer gut **T0145**
O Herr, du starker Helden-Mann **T0146**
O Herr, gerechter Gott **B1037**
O Herr, hilf, wir verderben **H0209**
O Herr, hilfe **W0023**
O Herr Jesu Christ **H0210**
O Herr Jesu, mein Heiland **A0313**
O Himmels-Prinz **A0314**
O himmelssüße Liebes Brunst **S0743**
O honigsüsses Engel-Brot **A0104**
O ich elende Kreature **A0105**
O ich elende verdammte Seel **A0106**
O ich elender Sünder **H0211**
O ihr lieben Hirten, fürchtet euch nicht **H0212**
O ihr lieben Kinder **S0744**
O ihr schnöden Eitelkeiten **K0263**
O immensa bonitas entangit **A0501, G0078**
O Jammer, Elend, Angst, und Not **K0203**
O Jesu **L0022**
O Jesu, allmächtiger Held **G0223**
O Jesu amantissime, quem animam desiderat **G0079**
O Jesu Christ, dein Kripplein ist **S0561**
O Jesu Christ, du König aller Ehren **T0147**

O Jesu Christ, du machst es lang mit deinem Jüngsten Tage **B1038**

O Jesu Christe, Gottes Sohn **M0377**

O Jesu, cor meum **K0097**

O Jesu, der du uns zu gut **T0148**

O Jesu, du allersüßester Heiland **H0213**

O Jesu, dulcis dilectio **G0080**

O Jesu, fons purissime **A0108**

O Jesu, großer Friedens Held **A0172**

O Jesu, heilger Same **A0173**

O Jesu, Herzenkündiger **A0315**

O Jesu, höchste Gütigkeit **K0245**

O Jesu, Hoffnung wahrer Reu **K0246**

O Jesu, liebster Heiland wert **A0107**

O Jesu, mein Bräutigam **B1039**

O Jesu, mein Erlöser **H0214**

O Jesu, mein Heiland **H0215**

O Jesu, mein Jesu **H0216**

O Jesu mi dulcissime **A0615, B0176, B1406, C0207**

O Jesu mi dulcissime, spes suspiratis animae **P0086**

O Jesu, o König **N0028**

O Jesu, summa caritas **C0208, S0271**

O Jesu süß **C0209**

O Jesu süß, wer dein gedenkt **A0631**

O Jesu, wir wissen, daß du **H0217**

O Jesu, Wunder-König du **K0247**

O Jesulein **N0029**

O Joseph liebster, Joseph mein **A0109**

O jucunda dies, o fortunata dies **G0081**

O Juda, du Verräter verflucht **A0110**

O Judex inscrutabilis **A0111**

O komm, lieber Herr Jesu **H0218**

O König grosser Kraft und Ehr **K0248**

O laßt euch zu Jesu führen **S0562**

O Leicht geboren aus dem Leichte **A0316**

O lieber Vater im höchsten Thron **A0112**

O liebes Kind **F0011**

O liebste Jungfrau mein **A0113**

O liebste Schar, denkt nach **H0383**

O liebster Jesu mein **A0114**

O liebster Jesu, wie so heiß **A0115**

O liebstes Jesulein **A0116**

O lux beata Trinitas **A0317, C0072, R0171**

O Maria caeli decus **A0117, A0137**

O Maria, mater Dei **M0177**

O Maria, Morgenstern **A0118**

O Maria spes **R0214**

O mein Heiland, wie süß **K0249**

O mein Seel, fang gar schnell an zu loben **A0119**

O meine Seele, sieh dich für **S0563**

O Mensch, Gott hat gesesset **S0745**

O Mensch, in ganzen Leben **A0318**

O Mensch! O Kreuz! O lieber Gott! **A0120**

O Menschen Kind, dir ist bewußt **S0746**

O mich betrübtes Weibe **A0121**

O mich elenden Sündern **A0122**

O Michael, du berühmter Held **A0123**

O mortales **K0098**

O Mutter der Barmherzigkeit **A0124**

O Mutter Gottes Gebärerin **A0125**

O Mutter Maria, mein Herz ist zittern **A0126**

O nomen Jesu, nomen dulce **R0172**

O nova, o rara **B1301**

O panis mellifluus **K0099, R0215**

O Pater Augustine **A0127**

O patroni singulares **P0252**

O perfecta caritas **E0059**

O piissime Jesu, ad te o solus mea **G0082**

O plausus orantes jungemus **F0081**

O pulcherrima mulier **P0190**

O quales flores **B1302**

O quam dulcis, quam suavis **F0082**

O quam gloriosum **C0210**

O quam metuendus **E0060**

O quam metuendus est **H0502-03, P0253**

O quam mirabilia sunt **S0230**

O quam pulchra **L0023, S0303**

O quam suavis **A0128**

O quam suavis est Domine **B0306, R0052**

O quam vana est **F0037**

O quanta in coelis **B1303**

O quanta in coelis laetitia **B1330**

O reicher Gott von Gütigkeit **S0747**

O sacrum convivium **B0307, B1304, E0061**

O salutaris hostia **M0178**

O salvator Jesu dulcissime **M0345**

O sancta Trinitas **G0224**

O schöne Morgenröt **A0129**

O schweres Kreuz **A0130**

O selig bist du, die du geglaubt hast **W0129**

O selig ist ein solcher Mann **H0384**

O selig, selig sind **S0564**

O selig über selig sind, die in dem Herren sterben **S0167**

O sichre Welt **N0101**

O sichre Welt, wie lange willst du träumen **A0319**

O starker Löw von Juda **A0131**

O suavis aura **H0504**

O süße Himmels-Herrlichkeit **S0168**

O süßer Tag, nun wir der Geist **A0502**

O süßer, o freundlicher, o gütiger Herr Jesu Christe **H0219**

O tempus amatum **H0333**

O teuerer Fürsten-Geist **M0322**

O tiefster Grund! O Allmachts höchste **B1040**

O Tod, O Traurigkeit **A0320**

Wohl dem, der in Gottes Furcht steht **G0123**
Wohl dem, der nicht wandelt **B1218, F0162**
Wohl dem, der sich des Durstigen annimmt **B1219-21**
Wohl dem, der sich des Herrn erfreut **D0030**
Wohl dem, des Hilfe der Gott Jacobs ist **B1222**
Wohl dem hier die Übertretung ist vergeben **B1223**
Wohl dem Volk, deß der Herr ein Gott ist **B1224**
Wohl dem, wohl dem der vorsichtig wandelt **S0590**
Wohl denen, die ohne Wandel leben **D0031, T0040**
Wohl euch, o ihr zarten Seelen **B1225**
Wohl sind des rauen Herbstes Zeiten **A0549, L0030**
Wohlan alle, die ihr durstig seid **B1226-27, E0173**
Wohlan, mein liebster Mann **A0149**
Wohlauf, mein Geist **S0760**
Wohlher und lasset uns wohl leben **B1228**
Wollt ihr die gute Straße reisen **H0404**
Womit erfreuet Gott die Menschen am allermeisten? **G0043**
Womit kann ein Mensch im Himmel Freude anrichten? **G0044**
Womit kann man sich in Not und Tod recht kräftig trösten? **G0045**
Wunder von dem Wunderkinde **S0762**
Wunderkindlein groß und klein **B1229**
Wünschet Jerusalem Gluck **A0550**

Zeige mir, Herr, den Weg **D0032**
Zerreißet eure Herzen **A0375**
Zeuch mich nicht hin unter die Gottlosen **W0171**
Ziehet hin, ihr Liebsten beide **A0551**
Zier der Rechten, Landes-Vater **S0339**
Zion klaget aus der Maßen **B1230**
Zion spricht: Der Herr hat mich verlassen **B1231-32, H0286, W0035**
Zions Fürst aus Davids **A0376**
Zu deinem grossen Abendmahl **B1233**
Zu der Zeit da wieder viel Volks da war **H0619**
Zu derselbigen Stunde **H0620**
Zu Gott wir setzen ein Vertrauen **H0405**
Zu guter Nacht, du unbeständiges Leben **E0174**
Zuletzt da die Elfe **H0621**
Zum Frieden und zur Ruh **M0319**
Zum Haus der Herren wallen **B1234**
Zur selbigen Zeit wird dien Volk erlöset werden **B0415**
Zwar daß die Welt uns manche Plagen **W0174**
Zwar ich bin des Herren Statt **P0216**
Zweierlei bitte ich, Herr, von dir **B1235-36**
Zweierlei bitte ich von dir **B0066, B1237, G0124, H0287, M0064, O0046, S0474**
Zwingt die Saiten in Cithara **A0377-78**

Performing Forces Index

The first level of arrangement is by number of voices; the arrangement follows the normal distribution of voice parts on the modern staff; i.e., soprano(s), alto(s), tenor(s), bass(es). The second level of arrangement groups together all pieces with the same distribution of voices, with pieces that call for solo voices coming in each case at the end of the group. Each vocal subgroup then is ordered based on its use of instruments, as follows: 1) no instruments, 2) basso continuo instruments only, 3) one or more non-continuo instruments. Entries in the latter category fall according to the way in which they use the principal instruments, given here in the following order of priority: vln, vla, vltta, gamba (2 or more), other non-continuo strings, corn, tpt, clar, fl, ob, tbn (2 or more), other non-continuo winds. Thus, all pieces that include 1 or more violins precede those that do not, followed by those that include 1 or more violas but no violins, etc. Furthermore, entries with 1 violin precede those with 2, etc. For the purposes of this index, continuo instruments are considered to be the following: vlne, 1 gamba, vc, bass viola, org, lute, theorbo, bsn, 1 tbn, bombard.

3 vv H0482, M0238
3 vv, 2 vln, bc W0053
3 vv, 2 vln, vla, vlne, bc N0032

SSS H0489
SSS, bc C0129, E0016-17, E0022, E0066, E0072, G0198, G0203, M0281, M0285, P0054, P0185, P0194, R0129
SSS, 2 vln, bc B0159, E0044, E0078, E0080, E0098, L0001, L0003-15, L0017-18, L0021-22, L0025-27
SSS, 2 vln, 3 gamba, bsn, bc S0192
SSS, 2 vln, corn, bsn, bc R0232
SSS, 3 vln, bc P0098

SSA H0457, K0010-11, K0017, K0020, K0029, K0033, K0037, K0049
SSA, bc B0175, E0034, H0446, K0228, M0005, M0178, M0206, W0173
SSA, 2 vln, bc E0032, E0085, P0093
SSA, 2 vln, va, bc A0631
SSA, 2 vln, 2 gamba, vlne, theorbo, bc P0086
SSA, 2 vltta, 2 gamba, vlne, theorbo, bc P0086

SATTBB soli, SSA, bc L0043

SST A0482, H0478, K0001, K0003-05, K0007, K0012, K0014-16, K0018-19, K0024, K0026, K0028, K0030, K0035-36, K0039-41, K0044-47, K0050, K0052-53
SST, bc C0053, C0133, C0224, E0067, H0022, H0086, H0184, K0068, K0227, K0229, K0242, K0304, M0153, M0180, M0248, W0172
SST, tbn, bc H0213
SST, vln, bc P0271
SST, 2 vln, bc A0553, C0075, C0094, C0177, E0028, E0050, P0218, P0221, P0227, P0233
SST, 2 vln, vlne, vc, tbn, bc L0057
SST, 2 vln, gamba, bc G0080, P0064
SST, 2 vln, bsn, bc G0093, R0220
SST, 2 vln, tbn, bc C0147
SST, 2 vln, bombard, bc P0064
SST, 2 vln, vla, bc A0582
SST, 2 vln, 2 vla, vlne, bc R0231
SST, 2 vln, 2 vla, vltta, bc A0563
SST, 3 vln, bc K0302, M0235, P0096
SST, 3 vln, bsn, bc P0053
SST, 3 vla, vlne, bc P0135
SST, 4 vla, vlne, bc N0003
SST, 3 gamba, vlne, bc P0173
SST, 3 tbn, bc H0234, H0268
SST, 3 tbn, vlne, bc H0050

SSB   A0517, H0142, H0459, H0466, H0517, K0008, K0021, K0023, K0027, K0051, L0002, L0024, R0041, S0354, T0054

SSB, bc   A0293, A0573, A0575, B0162, B0170, B0172, B0391, B0557, B1298, B1311, B1345, B1354, C0020, C0043, C0074, C0085, C0092-93, C0130, C0158, C0162, C0213, E0018, E0073, E0082, F0059, F0077, F0092, G0077, G0196, H0060, H0123, H0131, H0274, H0300, H0422, H0448, H0490, H0630-33, H0635, H0637, K0103, K0243, K0246, L0117, M0116-18, M0147, M0270, P0091, P0188, R0008, R0035, R0078, R0111, R0124, R0213, R0221, S0279, S0602, S0623, S0625-26, S0639-41

SSB, vc, bc   R0215

SSB, tbn, bc   H0033, H0107, H0113, H0202

SSB, vln, bc   P0272

SSB, vln, vla, gamba, vlne, bc   S0309

SSB, vln, 3 vla, bc   E0070

SSB, vln, vltta, gamba, bc   S0199

SSB, 2 vln, bc   A0430, A0558, A0578, A0622, A0624, B0042-43, B0045, B0047-48, B0050, B0052-53, B0057, B0061, B0063-66, B0165, B0384, B0397, B1184, B1379, B1392, C0018, C0054, C0056, C0089, C0118, C0153-56, C0186-87, C0209, C0226, E0021, E0025, E0038, E0045, E0063, E0086, F0086, F0102, G0057, G0079, H0100, H0102, H0260, H0298, H0308, H0421, K0013, K0072, K0303, K0331, L0111, M0289, M0350, M0376, P0066, P0094, P0103, P0139, P0217, P0223, P0229-30, P0234, P0249, P0255-56, P0295, R0229, S0004, S0145, S0280, S0591, S0598, S0749, T0036, T0165

SSB, 2 vln, vlne, bc   A0463, B0038-41, B0044, B0046, B0049, B0051, B0054-56, B0058, B0060, B0062, B1353, B1375, B1376, B1382, B1396, B1406, B1409, B1421, G0054, G0086, G0089, P0061, P0181

SSB, 2 vln, gamba, bc   B0656, G0056, G0068, G0070, G0075, G0078, R0028, S0298

SSB, 2 vln, theorbo, bc   G0069, G0081

SSB, 2 vln, bsn, bc   B1329, B1375, B1385, B1409, B1423, C0131, C0146, C0220, G0099, H0288, K0207, K0213, M0314, M0318, P0059-60, P0099, P0101, P0282, S0359

SSB, 2 vln, tbn, bc   C0219

SSB, 2 vln, vla, bc   A0552, A0559, A0566, A0574, A0580, A0584, A0594, A0619, A0625-26, G0087, P0057, S0408

SSB, 2 vln, vla, vlne, bc   B1337, D0090

SSB, 2 vln, vla, theorbo, bc   G0092

SSB, 2 vln, vla, vltta, bc   A0572

SSB, 2 vln, vla, vltta, vlne, bc   A0621

SSB, 2 vln, vla, bass vla, 2 ob ad lib, bsn ad lib, bc   M0225

SSB, 2 vln, 2 vla, bc   A0617, C0008, F0100, F0119, F0132, F0147, K0073, O0046, R0230, S0302, W0078

SSB, 2 vln, 2 vla, vlne, bc   A0469, B1391, K0327

SSB, 2 vln, 2 vla, bsn, bc   B1274, B1361, K0214

SSB, 2 vln, 2 vla, corn, bsn, bc   R0233

SSB, 2 vln, 2 vla, 2 corn, 2 tpt, bsn, bc   B1370

SSB, 2 vln, 3 vla, bc   B1361

SSB, 2 vln, 3 vla, bsn, bc   C0105

SSB, 2 vln, 2 vltta, corn, tbtta, bc   R0140

SSB, 2 vln, 2 vltta, 2 corn, bc   R0140

SSB, 2 vln, 2 gamba, bc   K0211

SSB, 2 vln, 2 corn, 2 tpt, 2 tbn, bsn, bc   B1370

SSB, 2 vln, 2 corn, 3 tpt, bc   H0542

SSB, 2 vln, 2 tpt, bc   B1390

SSB, 2 vln, 3 tpt, 2 fl, bc   H0542

SSB, 2 vln, 2 tbn, vlne, bc   H0140

SSB, 3 vln, vlne, bc   B0037, B1350

SSB, 3 vln, vlne, org   G0074

SSB, 3 vln, bsn, bc   B1413

SSB, 3 vln, vla, bsn, bc   B1415

SSB, 3 vln, 2 vla, bsn, bc   A0401

SSB, 4 vln, bsn, bc   B1415

SSB, vla, bc   M0242

SSB, 2 vla, vlne, bc   P0210

SSB, 2 vla, bsn, bc   C0123

SSB, 2 vla, 2 clar, bc   M0260, M0262

SSB, 2 vla, 2 tromba marina, bc   M0260, M0262

SSB, 2 vla, 3 tbn, bc   H0460

SSB, 3 vla, bc   F0141, M0267

SSB, 3 vla, vlne, bc   P0176

SSB, 4 vla, bc   S0337

SSB, 4 vla, vlne, bc   G0076, P0143

SSB, 5 gamba, bc   B1414

SSB, 2 fl, 2 tbn, bc   H0073

SSB, 2 tbn, bc   H0124, H0220, H0270

SSB, 2 instr, bc   B0873

SSB, 3 instr, bc   B0994

SAT   H0456, K0006, K0022, K0025, K0034, K0038, K0048

SAT, bc   A0396, B0166, B1307, C0013, C0132, C0139, C0144, D0046, H0415, H0429, H0438, H0447, K0239-40, R0096, R0217-19, S0301, S0305, S0608, S0627

SAT, vln, bc   B0494

SAT, 2 vln, bc   A0627, C0119, C0225, E0047, E0087, G0103, P0219, S0292, Z0042

SAT, 2 vln, vlne, bc   F0082

SAT, 2 vln, gamba, bc   C0143

SAT, 2 vln, bsn, bc   K0178, P0284, R0224

SAT, 2 vln, tbn, bc   C0143

SAT, 2 vln, vla, bc   E0084

SAT, 2 vln, 2 vla, bc   H0176

SAT, 2 vln, 2 vltte, trbtta, bsn, bc   F0027

SAT, 2 vla, bsn, bc   P0070, P0073

SAT, 3 fl, tbn, bc   A0326

SAB   B0433, K0042

SAB, bc **B1281, B1300, B1380, C0142, H0418, K0064, K0245, K0247, K0312, M0166, R0198, R0217, S0162, S0301, S0609, S0631, S0633**
SAB, vlne, bc **F0076**
SAB, vc, vlne, bc **D0081**
SAB, vln, corn, tbn, bsn, bc **S0356**
SAB, 2 vln, bc **A0564, B0895, B1328, C0126-27, E0106, F0026, F0061, G0120, K0307, K0309, P0005, P0087, P0097, P0226, P0276, P0291, S0003**
SAB, 2 vln, vlne, bc **B0630, B1399, B1420, B1422, F0063, G0059, K0313, K0336**
SAB, 2 vln, vlne, gamba, bc **P0104**
SAB, 2 vln, vlne, theorbo, bc **D0082**
SAB, 2 vln, 3 vlne, bc **D0082**
SAB, 2 vln, gamba, bc **B0607, G0059, M0231**
SAB, 2 vln, gamba, theorbo, bc **F0083**
SAB, 2 vln, vc, bc **K0323**
SAB, 2 vln, vc, bsn, bc **K0338**
SAB, 2 vln, bsn, bc **G0096, K0344, P0283, R0199, W0026**
SAB, 2 vln, tbn, bc **B0766, B0962**
SAB, 2 vln, vla, bc **C0240, S0476**
SAB, 2 vln, vla, vlne, bc **F0080**
SAB, 2 vln, vla, gamba, bc **S0231**
SAB, 2 vln, vla, vc, bc **S0160**
SAB, 2 vln, vla, bsn, bc **S0231**
SAB, 2 vln, 3 vla, bc **C0095, F0090**
SAB, 2 vln, 3 vla, 2 corn, bsn, bc **R0139**
SAB, 2 vln, 2 vltta, bc **R0177**
SAB, 4 vln, 4 corn, 2 tpt, 2 fl, 3 tbn, 3 bsn, bc **B1395**
SAB, 2 vln, 2 clar, timp, bsn, bc **A0383**
SAB, 2 vla, bc **P0184**
SAB, 3 vla, 2 corn, bc **K0163**
SAB, 2 vla, 2 clar, timp, bsn, bc **G0094**
SAB, 4 vla, bc **K0197**
SAB, 4 vla, fl, theorbo, bc **R0038**
SAB, 2 clar, bass viol, bc **M0287**
SAB, 2 tbn, bc **H0216**

STB, bc **B0387, B0398, B0570, C0138, M0112, M0179, M0189, M0244, R0214, R0223, S0600, S0634**
STB, vln, bc **M0120**
STB, vln, vla, bc **H0017, H0021**
STB, vln, 2 vla, bc **F0154, H0010**
STB, 2 vln, bc **B0580, B0589, B0611, B0628, B0954, B1066, B1133, C0099, C0176, F0028, F0178-79, H0299, H0301, H0304, K0258, K0325, K0335, M0135, R0112, R0181, S0716, S0739, S0752, W0055**
STB, 2 vln, gamba, bc **W0028**
STB, 2 vln, vc, bc **O0005**
STB, 2 vln, bass vla, bc **M0255**
STB, 2 vln, bsn, bc **B0388, R0201, R0216, S0676**

STB, 2 vln, vla, bc **R0132**
STB, 2 vln, vla, vlne, bc **H0345**
STB, 2 vln, vla, gamba, bc **S0226, S0229-30**
STB, 2 vln, vla, vc, bc **T0008**
STB, 2 vln, vla, bsn, bc **S0226, S0229-30**
STB, 2 vln, vla, vc, 2 clar, timp, bc **M0224**
STB, 2 vln, 2 vla, vlne, bc **B1238, H0079, P0152**
STB, 2 vln, 2 vla, vlne, bsn, bc **S0678**
STB, 2 vln, 2 vla, vc, bsn, bc **S0678**
STB, 2 vln, 2 vla, bsn, bc **B1238**
STB, 2 vln, 5 vla, bc **Z0056**
STB, 2 vln, vltta, bc **W0027**
STB, 3 vln, bc **B0599**
STB, 2 vla, bass vla, bc **M0255**
STB, 2 clar, timp, bc **G0107**
STB, 2 instr, bc **B0600**

AAT, bc **C0015**

AAB, 2 vln, bc **E0083, K0099**
AAB, 2 vln, 2 vla, bsn, bc **S0679**
AAB, 3 vla, vlne, bc **S0654**

ATT, bc **M0246**

ATB **A0379, G0133-34, H0458, H0484, K0200, L0019-20, L0023, L0028, S0072**
ATB, bc **A0245, A0392, A0477, A0509, A0616, B0406, B1278-79, B1286, B1290-92, B1295-96, B1301-02, B1314, B1317, C0037, C0071, C0081, C0096, C0136, C0145, C0148, C0218, E0023, E0035, E0058-59, E0064, F0071, G0158, G0198-200, G0202, G0204-06, H0414, H0634, K0063, K0070, K0097-98, K0225, K0238, K0248, K0255, M0127, M0280, P0088, P0134, P0205, P0277, R0033, R0061, R0071, R0090, R0131, R0153, R0170, R0217, S0300, S0596, S0607, S0610, S0630, W0050-52, W0054, W0056, W0062, Z0045, Z0060**
ATB, vln, 2 vla, bsn, bc **R0200**
ATB, vln, 2 gamba, vlne, bc **O0039**
ATB, vln, corn, tbn, bc **C0214**
ATB, 2 vln, bc **A0189, A0201, A0233, A0282, A0332, A0375, A0412, A0441, A0460, A0467, A0474, A0534, A0620, B0174, B0394, B0411, B0698, B0825, B1046, B1085, B1093, B1349, B1383, B1416, C0079, C0106, C0114, C0122, C0134, C0141, C0181, C0227, E0020, E0054, E0069, E0076, E0092, F0081, F0087-88, F0126, F0151, H0242, H0267, H0269, H0337, J0034, K0233, M0313, N0007, N0009, N0012-14, N0016-17, N0021, N0024-25, N0027,**

ATB, 2 vln, bc—*continued*
  N0033, P0090, P0236, P0238-39, P0250, P0254, P0264,
  R0080, R0122, R0136, R0155, R0158, R0164, R0192,
  S0002, S0005, S0007, S0010, S0012, S0014, S0287, S0289,
  S0508-19, T0046, W0034, W0048, W0060, W0063, W0127,
  Z0043
ATB, 2 vln, vlne, bc B0578, B0979, B0982, B0986, B0988,
  B1043, B1070, B1087, B1096, B1389, B1411, F0079, K0352,
  P0286, S0660, S0672
ATB, 2 vln, gamba, bc A0385, B1052, B1348, F0074, K0184
ATB, 2 vln, bass vla, bc M0291
ATB, 2 vln, bsn, bc A0004, A0518, B1389, F0161, G0149,
  K0210, K0218, P0067, S0374, T0043
ATB, 2 vln, tbn, bc K0139, K0158
ATB, 2 vln, bomb, bc K0184
ATB, 2 vln, vla, bc A0555, A0590, A0612, A0623, B1167,
  B1227, E0033, G0149, K0158, S0011, T0042
ATB, 2 vln, vla, vlne, bc B1384, H0116
ATB, 2 vln, vla, 2 vltta, bc R0100
ATB, 2 vln, 2 vla, bc A0618, B0867, F0146, G0101, K0284
ATB, 2 vln, 2 vla, vlne, bc K0285
ATB, 2 vln, 2 vla, vlne, bsn, bc N0011
ATB, 2 vln, 2 vla, bsn, bc O0015, P0069, W0069
ATB, 2 vln, 2 vla, 2 corn, 2 clar, vlne, bsn, bc A0548
ATB, 2 vln, 3 vla, bc K0310
ATB, 2 vln, 3 vla, bsn, bc S0361
ATB, 2 vln, vltta, bsn, bc O0035, O0038
ATB, 2 vln, 2 vltta, bsn, bc R0100
ATB, 2 vln, 3 gamba, bc W0031, W0035
ATB, 2 vln, 2 corn, bc P0092
ATB, 2 vln, 2 clar, bc E0077
ATB, 2 vln, 4 tbn, bc A0366, A0378
ATB, 3 vln, bc C0238, F0148, K0355, L0113
ATB, 3 vln, theorbo, bc T0052
ATB, 3 vln, 3 gamba, bc W0032
ATB, vla, 2 corn, bc K0158, M0303
ATB, 2 vla, vla d'amore, bass vla, vlne, bc P0112
ATB, 2 vla, 2 clar, bc M0288
ATB, 2 vla, 2 tromba marina, bc M0288
ATB, 3 vla, tbn majore, bc A0295
ATB, 4 vla, bc A0419, C0100, C0110, C0117, C0124-25,
  C0202, C0205-06, C0210-11, C0215-16
ATB, 4 vla, vlne, bc H0265
ATB, 4 viol, bc C0179
ATB, 3 gamba, bc F0094
ATB, 2 corn, bc H0129, H0267
ATB, 2 corn, bsn, bc P0052
ATB, 2 corn, tbn, bc K0158
ATB, 2 cornettini, gamba, bc K0184
ATB, 2 cornettini, bomb, bc K0184
ATB, 3 tbn, tbn majore, bc A0295
ATB, 3 bomb K0192

TTT, bc E0017, E0022, E0066, E0072, G0198, G0203, M0201,
  M0241, M0285
TTT, 2 vln, bc L0001, L0003-15, L0017-18, L0021-22, L0025-27

TTB F0171, H0459, H0461, K0032
TTB, bc A0137, A0257, B0278, B1305, C0112, C0178, H0060,
  H0135, H0274, H0628, M0157, M0196, M0247, M0257,
  R0078
TTB, vln, bc M0107
TTB, vln, 2 gamba, bc B1267
TTB, vln, 3 gamba, vlne, bc B0001
TTB, 2 vln, bc A0191, B1021, C0104, C0118, C0140, F0108,
  H0002, R0081, R0120
TTB, 2 vln, gamba, bc M0312
TTB, 2 vln, gamba, bsn, bc O0044
TTB, 2 vln, bsn, bc S0216
TTB, 2 vln, 2 vla, vlne, bc A0205
TTB, 3 vla, bc M0267
TTB, 2 ob, bsn, bc S0216

TBB, bc H0048
TBB, 2 vln, vlne, bc B0059

BBB G0135
BBB, bc E0009, K0250
BBB, 2 vln, bc K0066

4 vv A0536, B0185, B0225, B0287-88, B0316, B0338, B0377,
  F0032, F0050, M0236, P0273
4 vv, bc B0196, B0201, B0204, B0226, M0251
4 vv, 2 vln, bc Z0055
4 vv, 2 vln, vlne, bc B0496
4 vv, 2 vln, vla, bc F0041
4 vv, 2 vln, 2 vla, bc S0318
4 vv, 2 vln, 2 vla, 2 clar, vlne, bc B1244
4 vv, 2 vln, 2 vla, 2 clar, 2 ob, timp, vlne, bc B0340
4 vv, 2 vln, vltta, bc R0016
4 vv, 2 vln, 2 clar, 2 ob, timp, vlne, bc S0001
4 vv, 3 vln, 2 vla, bsn, bc F0033
4 vv, 5 vln, bc H0541
4 vv, 3 vla, vlne, bc B1247
4 vv, 3 vla, 3 vltta, bc B0499
4 vv, 5 gamba, 2 ob, bsn, bc M0229
4 vv, 5 instr, bc W0128
4 vv, instr. B0286, H0483, S0621

SSSS, bc M0114, M0159

SSSA, bc **C0175**

SSSB, bc **P0075, P0172**
SSSB, vln, 2 gamba, bsn, bc **S0219**
SSSB, 2 vln, vlne, bc **G0053**

SSAA, 2 vln, vc, vlne, bc **L0036**

SSAT **B0177, G0136, H0488, W0089**
SSAT, 2 vln, 2 vla, bsn, bc **O0045**
SSAT, 4 vln, bsn, bc **W0059**
SSAT, 4 vln, bc **R0018**
SSAT, 3 tbn, vlne, bc **H0257**
SSAT, 3 instr, bc **R0021**

SSSAT soli, SSAT, 2 vln, vla, vlne, bc **L0055**

SSAB, bc **A0571, A0577, A0615, H0047, W0057**
SSAB, 2 vln, bc **H0203, P0263**
SSAB, 2 vln, tbn, bc **B0629, B1011, B1051**
SSAB, 2 vln, vla, bc **B1072**
SSAB, 2 vln, vla, vlne, theorbo, bc **A0511**
SSAB, 2 vln, vla, gamba, bc **S0223**
SSAB, 2 vln, vla, bsn, bc **S0223**
SSAB, 2 vln, 2 vla, bc **D0049, H0321**
SSAB, 2 vln, 2 vla, vlne, bc **B1404, W0006-09, W0011-21, W0023-25**
SSAB, 2 vln, 2 vla, 2 tpt, tbn, vlne, bc **B1366**
SSAB, 2 vln, 2 vltta, vlne, bc **B1407**
SSAB, 2 vln, 2 gamba, vlne, bc **A0465**
SSAB, 3 vla, vlne, bc **B1045**
SSAB, 3 tbn, bc **H0157**

SSTT, vln, 4 vla, 2 corn, tbn, bc **B0446**
SSTT, 2 vln, bc **A0244, R0125**
SSTT, 2 vln, vlne, bc **P0167**
SSTT, 3 vla, bc **P0160**
SSTT, 3 vla, vlne, bc **P0165**

SSTB **L0016**
SSTB, bc **H0538, P0107**
SSTB, tbn, bc **H0023, H0044**
SSTB, vln, 2 vla, bc **B0847**
SSTB, vln, 2 gamba, vlne, bc **P0136**

SSTB, 2 vln, bc **B0642, B0654, B0734, B0840, B0892, B01033, B1055, B1149, B1162, B1171, B1230, B1237, C0174, G0062, H0076, H0081, H0108, H0112, H0297, H0302, H0305, K0342, W0065**
SSTB, 2 vln, vlne, bc **B0725, B0920, G0066, P0138, P0153, P0158, P0175, P0196**
SSTB, 2 vln, gamba, bc **G0090**
SSTB, 2 vln, bsn, bc **G0117, H0303**
SSTB, 2 vln, vla, bc **B1210**
SSTB, 2 vln, 2 vla, bc **F0099, F0124, F0138, F0142, F0158**
SSTB, 2 vln, 2 vla, vlne, bc **A0007, B0775, B0845, M0223, P0127, P0141, P0146, P0149, P0156-57, P0170, P0195, P0208**
SSTB, 2 vln, 2 vla, vlne, theorbo, bc **G0072**
SSTB, 2 vln, 2 vla, 2 clar, bc **F0157**
SSTB, 2 vln, 3 vla, bc **D0083**
SSTB, 2 vln, 3 vla, vlne, bc **T0162**
SSTB, 2 vln, 2 ob, bc **B1239**
SSTB, 2 vla, bc **H0275**
SSTB, 2 vla, vlne, bc **P0191, P0199**
SSTB, 3 vla, vlne, bc **P0125, P0131, P0144, P0147, P0150, P0159, P0174, P0198, P0209, P0212, P0214, P0216**
SSTB, 4 vla, theorbo, bc **P0161**
SSTB, 4 vla, vlne, bc **P0213**
SSTB, 4 vla, bsn, bc **T0051**
SSTB, 3 gamba, vlne, bc **P0136**
SSTB, 2 corn, bc **H0076**
SSTB, 2 corn, 3 tbn, bc **B1029**
SSTB, 2 tbn, bc **H0104**

SSBB, bc **K0060, M0175, P0058**

SAAB **K0124**

SATB **A0010, A0012-17, A0021-24, A0028-34, A0036-46, A0048-60, A0062-64, A0075-80, A0082-93, A0095-116, A0118-27, A0129-36, A0139-40, A0142-43, A0147-49, A0153-70, A0173-74, A0176-77, A0179-80, A0183-86, A0195-96, A0198-99, A0203, A0210, A0213, A0216-17, A0225, A0227, A0234, A0237-39, A0242, A0248, A0251, A0253-54, A0266, A0268, A0270-72, A0276-77, A0280-81, A0304-05, A0314-15, A0319-21, A0325, A0328, A0334-35, A0337, A0340, A0351, A0358-59, A0367, A0372, A0380-81, A0386-87, A0389, A0391, A0408, A0410, A0423, A0427-28, A0449, A0452, A0457, A0459, A0471, A0497-98, A0505, A0508, A0512, A0538, A0541, A0549, A0628, B0005, B0148, B0151, B0160-61, B0163, B0173, B0180, B0182, B0184, B0186, B0190, B0194, B0235-36, B0262, B0267-74, B0279-81, B0290, B0295-96, B0298-305, B0331, B0334,**

SATB—*continued*

B0378-79, B0396, B0572, B0590, B0593, B0619, B0728,
B0752, B0837, B0854, B0856, B0887, B0899, B0922, B1030,
B1088, B1107, B1152-53, B1169, B1218, B1277, D0035,
D0037, D0041-42, D0080, D0086, E0090, E0126, E0131,
E0174, F0009, F0020, F0167-68, F0170, F0172-75, F0177,
G0207-11, H0003-05, H0008, H0011-12, H0014-15,
H0018-20, H0638, J0012, K0126, K0128, K0148, K0204,
K0215, K0257, K0260-64, K0267, K0271, K0277-78,
K0280-81, K0287-89, K0296, K0298-301, L0030-31,
L0104-06, M0301, M0320, N0042-43, R0010-11, R0013,
R0026, R0159, R0225, R0227, S0048, S0120, S0124-26,
S0134, S0156-57, S0159, S0161, S0163, S0167, S0235-38,
S0286, S0328, S0330, S0339, S0385, S0392-93, S0395,
S0398, S0402-04, S0406, S0409-10, S0413-15, S0417, S0445,
S0763, S0777, T0002-03, T0025, T0067, T0070-88,
T0090-154, T0156-60, W0010, W0067, W0080-82, W0090,
Z0046, Z0052

SATB, bc A0018, A0026, A0151, A0171-72, A0296, A0313,
A0354, A0402, A0415, A0461, A0500, A0532, A0546,
A0551, B0010, B0017, B0158, B0164, B0168-69, B0181,
B0183, B0191, B0195, B0202-03, B0205-07, B0210-12,
B0219-20, B0224, B0228-30, B0232-33, B0239-44, B0246,
B0248, B0250-54, B0256-57, B0264-65, B0306-12, B0314-15,
B0325, B0327, B0329, B0333, B0335, B0339, B0342-44,
B0346, B0349-52, B0354-55, B0358, B0361-63, B0365-76,
B0380-82, B0390, B0399, B0414, B0416-17, B0419-20,
B0422-23, B0426-27, B0430, B0434, B0436-38, B0443,
B0447-48, B0479-80, B0484-87, B0489-93, B0495, B0497,
B0502-03, B0542-43, B0553, B0585, B0595, B0602, B0606,
B0608, B0616, B0620, B0633, B0650, B0652, B0658, B0666,
B0676-77, B0679, B0681-82, B0687, B0692, B0694, B0699,
B0706, B0723, B0727, B0735, B0740, B0761-62, B0786-87,
B0789, B0792, B0798, B0851, B0871, B0880, B0883, B0888,
B0896, B0903, B0905, B0923, B0929, B0937, B0939,
B0943-47, B0949-50, B0951-53, B1007, B1012, B1028,
B1038, B1048, B1060, B1064, B1067, B1077-78, B1103,
B1121, B1123, B1125-26, B1129, B1132, B1136, B1180,
B1186, B1192, B1201, B1205, B1280, B1284-85, B1294,
B1299, B1306, B1309, B1310, B1313, B1316, C0031,
D0029-30, D0044-45, E0019, E0024, E0027, E0068, E0074,
E0103, F0017, F0022, F0075, F0096, F0200, G0051, G0137,
G0201, G0212-23, G0225, G0227-31, H0024-25, H0030,
H0046, H0109, H0166, H0171, H0182, H0205, H0210-11,
H0219, H0285, H0336, H0407, H0409-13, H0417, H0419,
J0018, J0020, J0024, J0026, J0030, K0057, K0100-01,
K0106, K0109, K0170, K0221, K0287, M0088, M0100,
M0103, M0105, M0109, M0111, M0113, M0121, M0123,
M0125, M0130, M0134, M0142-44, M0149, M0162, M0167,
M0169, M0176, M0183, M0190, M0197, M0202, M0214,
M0221, M0237, M0250, M0268, M0283, M0298, M0307,
M0332, M0389, P0042, P0046, P0192, P0200, R0027,
R0037, R0095, R0103, R0123, R0160, R0172, S0053,
S0066, S0112, S0121, S0158, S0164, S0284, S0444, S0463,
S0478-79, S0482, S0682-87, S0689-715, S0718-38, S0740-48,
S0750-51, S0753-62, S0765, S0771, S0775-76, T0024,
T0027-30, T0033, T0088, V0007, W0004, Z0027, Z0067

SATB, vlne, bc B0348, B0456, B0475, S0096, W0047

SATB, vc, bc B0341

SATB, vc, vlne, bc B0192-93, B0197-200, B0209, B0218,
B0221-23, B0231, B0234, B0247, B0258, B0261, B0275,
B0323-24, B0332, B0347, B0353, B0364

SATB, vln R0020

SATB, vln, tbn, bc B0713

SATB, vln, vla, bc B1202

SATB, vln, vla, vltta, vc, vlne, bc S0033

SATB, vln, vla, vltta, vc, corn, 2 tbn, vlne, bc S0071

SATB, vln, vla, 2 vltta, vc, 2 tbn, vlne, bc S0071

SATB, vln, 2 vla, bc S0288

SATB, vln, 2 vla, vlne, bc A0294, B1327, D0043, M0222

SATB, vln, 2 vla, vc, vlne, bc S0101, S0104

SATB, vln, 2 vla, bsn, bc L0099, M0319

SATB, vln, 2 vla, tbn, bc A0294, B1327

SATB, vln, 2 vla, vltta, vc, vlne, bc S0020

SATB, vln, 2 vla, vltta, vc, corn, tbn, vlne, bc S0071

SATB, vln, 2 vla, 2 vltta, vc, tbn, vlne, bc S0071

SATB, vln, 2 vla, 2 fl, 2 ob, vlne, bsn, bc M0226

SATB, vln, 2 vla, 4 ob, 4 harps, vlne, bc L0087

SATB, vln, 2 vla, 3 tbn, bc F0007, F0011, S0076

SATB, vln, 3 vla, bc H0428, H0431-32, H0435, H0440-41,
H0443, H0454, L0084, R0019

SATB, vln, 3 vla, vlne, bc B0016, S0273, W0068

SATB, vln, 3 vla, bsn, bc A0436, B0152, W0068

SATB, vln, 4 vla, bc B0488

SATB, vln, 2 vltta, ob, bc T0066

SATB, vln, 3 gamba, bc A0422, O0008

SATB, vln, corn, bc B1146

SATB, vln, corn, tbn, bsn, bc P0278

SATB, vln, ob, vlne, bc A0473

SATB, vln, 2 tbn, vlne, bc A0294, B1327

SATB, vln, 3 tbn, bc A0294, B1327

SATB, vln, 3 tbn, vlne, bc F0008

SATB, 2 vln M0310

SATB, 2 vln, bc A0204, A0256, A0265, A0278, A0298-300,
A0306, A0338-39, A0453, A0629, B0072-73, B0075-79,
B0081, B0084-85, B0087-89, B0098, B0100-01, B0106-07,
B0109-11, B0113, B0117-18, B0122, B0128, B0131, B0137,
B0145, B0171, B0179, B0575, B0596, B0610, B0615, B0618,
B0625, B0627, B0648-49, B0662-64, B0669, B0671-73,
B0683, B0685-86, B0689-91, B0697, B0702, B0704, B0707,
B0717-18, B0724, B0726, B0729, B0739, B0741, B0748,
B0751, B0770-71, B0776-77, B0797, B0799-800, B0811-15,
B0819, B0823, B0827, B0829, B0832, B0841, B0848-49,
B0858, B0860-61, B0869-70, B0875, B0877-78, B0884,

SATB, 2 vln, 2 vla, bc—*continued*

> G0043-45, G0132, H0289, H0310-13, H0316-20, H0322-26, H0329-30, H0420, H0427, H0430, H0433-34, H0436-37, H0439, H0442, H0449-53, H0543-44, H0545-60, H0562-70, H0572-621, K0317, N0004-06, N0008, N0010, N0015, N0018-20, N0022-23, N0026, N0028-31, N0034-41, O0003, O0020, O0027, P0083, P0258, R0085-86, R0194, S0008-09, S0049, S0233, S0278, S0331, S0342, S0345, S0347, S0387, S0651-52, S0677, T0015, T0017, V0002, W0093-101, W0103, W0105, W0107-08, W0110-14, W0117, W0120, W0122-24, W0126, W0129, W0131-38, W0140-46, W0148, W0150-52, W0154-63, W0165-66, W0170, Z0011

SATB, 2 vln, 2 vla, vlne, bc **A0178, A0435, A0439, A0443, A0496, A0521, B0013, B0282, B0284-85, B0291-94, B0393, B0452, B1347, B1356, B1387-88, B1425, C0237, E0121, E0148, F0093, G0004, G0128, G0130, K0055-56, K0119, K0196, L0071, L0074, M0216, M0333-49, P0051, P0169, P0171, P0244, P0245, P0257, R0053, R0191, R0228, S0006, S0081, S0251, S0324, S0336, S0341, S0343, S0346, W0006-09, W0011-21, W0023-25, W0036, W0038-40, W0042, W0075, W0076, W0102, W0104, W0109, W0118, W0121, W0147, W0149, W0167-69, W0171**

SATB, 2 vln, 2 vla, vlne, theorbo, bc **A0502, A0540**

SATB, 2 vln, 2 vla, vlne, bsn, bc **A0432, G0187, K0349, M0069-70, M0078-80, M0084-86, M0089-90, M0093, M0095, M0097-99, M0101-02, P0110, P0297**

SATB, 2 vln, 2 vla, vlne, tbn, bc **G0187**

SATB, 2 vln, 2 vla, vlne, bsn, calizon, vc, bc **G0129**

SATB, 2 vln, 2 vla, vc, bc **K0268, K0291, K0340, M0067, M0087, M0092, O0006, O0016, O0030**

SATB, 2 vln, 2 vla, theorbo, bc **C0113, S0271**

SATB, 2 vln, 2 vla, harp, bc **Z0019**

SATB, 2 vln, 2 vla, bsn, bc **A0514, A0519, B0013, B0282-85, B0291-94, B0563, B1268-69, B1271, C0006-07, C0009-10, C0014, C0016, C0022, C0024, C0026, C0036, C0038, C0049-52, C0057-59, C0062, C0063-70, C0149, D0084, E0109-10, E0112-13, E0118, E0120, E0121, E0123, E0125, E0128, E0135, E0140, E0142-44, E0146, E0149, E0151, E0159, E0162-63, E0166-67, E0169, E0173, F0055, F0121, F0160, G0004, G0105, K0157, K0186, K0259, K0345, L0073, L0080, L0083, L0098, L0103, L0114, O0032, O0036-37, O0040-41, P0111, R0001, R0007, R0063, R0065, R0070, R0073, R0087, R0106, R0168, R0186, R0210, S0174, S0194-95, S0283, S0304, S0344, S0659, T0006, T0035, W0075, W0106, W0125, W0130, W0139, W0147, W0149, W0153**

SATB, 2 vln, 2 vla, tbn, bsn, bc **K0306**

SATB, 2 vln, 2 vla, vltta, bc **A0599, A0608-10**

SATB, 2 vln, 2 vla, vla d'amore, 2 recorder, bc **R0030**

SATB, 2 vln, 2 vla, corn, bsn, bc **K0305**

SATB, 2 vln, 2 vla, corn, clar, bc **R0174**

SATB, 2 vln, 2 vla, 2 corn, bass viol, bc **S0662**

SATB, 2 vln, 2 vla, 2 corn, bsn, bc **S0662**

SATB, 2 vln, 2 vla, 2 corn, 2 tpt, timp, 3 tbn, bsn, bc **K0337**

SATB, 2 vln, 2 vla, 2 corn, 3 tbn, bsn, bc **P0102**

SATB, 2 vln, 2 vla, tpt, bc **E0157, G0038, G0042**

SATB, 2 vln, 2 vla, tpt, vlne, bc **E0147**

SATB, 2 vln, 2 vla, tpt, bsn, bc **E0147, K0305**

SATB, 2 vln, 2 vla, 2 tpt, bc **P0032**

SATB, 2 vln, 2 vla, 2 tpt, vlne, bc **T0069**

SATB, 2 vln, 2 vla, 2 tpt, bsn, bc **B0357, B0569, E0164**

SATB, 2 vln, 2 vla, 2 tpt, bsn, timp, bc **E0158**

SATB, 2 vln, 2 vla, 4 tpt, timp, bsn, bc **S0213**

SATB, 2 vln, 2 vla, clar, bc **B1339**

SATB, 2 vln, 2 vla, clar, vlne, bc **E0141**

SATB, 2 vln, 2 vla, clar, bsn, bc **R0184**

SATB, 2 vln, 2 vla, 2 clar, bc **W0116, Z0024, Z0032**

SATB, 2 vln, 2 vla, 2 clar, timp, vlne, bsn, bc **W0115**

SATB, 2 vln, 2 vla, 2 clar, vlne, bc **A0504, K0112, K0117, L0077**

SATB, 2 vln, 2 vla, 2 clar, bsn, bc **B1273, E0116, E0132, G0005, L0077**

SATB, 2 vln, 2 vla, 2 clar, bsn, timp, bc **E0134, S0206**

SATB, 2 vln, 2 vla, 2 clar, tbn, bsn, bc **S0294**

SATB, 2 vln, 2 vla, 2 clar, 2 tpt, 2 fl, bsn, theorbo, bc **S0316**

SATB, 2 vln, 2 vla, 2 clar, 2 ob, bc **B0336**

SATB, 2 vln, 2 vla, 2 clar, 3 tbn, vlne, bc **Z0008**

SATB, 2 vln, 2 vla, 3 fl, 2 tbn, bc **W0119**

SATB, 2 vln, 2 vla, ob, bc **S0334**

SATB, 2 vln, 2 vla, ob, vlne, bc **Z0038**

SATB, 2 vln, 2 vla, ob, bsn, bc **Z0038**

SATB, 2 vln, 2 vla, ob, bsn, vc, bc **K0319**

SATB, 2 vln, 2 vla, 2 ob, bc **B0337, B0345, G0014**

SATB, 2 vln, 2 vla, 2 ob, bsn, bc **B0567, K0083, T0040, Z0021, Z0041**

SATB, 2 vln, 2 vla, 2 ob, bsn, vc, bc **T0012**

SATB, 2 vln, 2 vla, 2 ob, 2 horn, bc **Z0017**

SATB, 2 vln, 2 vla, 2 ob, 3 tbn, bc **B0259**

SATB, 2 vln, 2 vla, 2 ob, 3 tbn, vc, bc **B0330**

SATB, 2 vln, 2 vla, 2 ob, taille, bsn, bassone, bc **A0406**

SATB, 2 vln, 2 vla, 3 ob, bsn, bc **T0009**

SATB, 2 vln, 2 vla, 3 ob, bsn, bassone, harp, bc **E0139**

SATB, 2 vln, 2 vla, 3 ob, bsn, db, harp, bc **E0137**

SATB, 2 vln, 2 vla, 4 ob, vlne, bc **K0054**

SATB, 2 vln, 2 vla, 2 fl, bass viol, bc **S0662**

SATB, 2 vln, 2 vla, 2 fl, bsn, bc **S0662**

SATB, 2 vln, 2 vla, 2 tbn, vlne, bsn, bc **B0357**

SATB, 2 vln, 2 vla, 3 tbn, bc **B0505-11, B0513-16, B0518-29, B0531, B0534-37, B0547-48, Z0010**

SATB, 2 vln, 2 vla, 3 tbn, vlne, bc **S0264**

SATB, 2 vln, 2 vla, 4 tbn, bc **F0193**

SATB, 2 vln, 2 vla, 2 tbtta, vlne, bc **B0926**

SATB, 2 vln, 3 vla, bc **B0389, B0459, B0473, B0556, C0157, E0006, F0051, G0008, K0222-24, K0226, K0230-31,**

K0234-36, K0241, K0244, K0249, K0251-53, K0256, K0269, K0275, K0329, K0343, M0065-66, M0071-73, M0075, M0081-83, M0091, M0094, M0104, M0168, P0168, R0099, R0134, R0142, R0165, S0248, S0266, S0296, S0666-67, T0023

SATB, 2 vln, 3 vla, vlne, bc **A0152, K0113, K0116, K0314, M0069-70, M0078-80, M0084-86, M0089-90, M0093, M0095, M0097-99, M0101-02, R0171, S0015, S0018, S0024, S0038, S0118, S0243, S0655, S0657**

SATB, 2 vln, 3 vla, vc, bc **K0285, K0294, K0334**

SATB, 2 vln, 3 vla, bass viol, bc **K0089, S0661**

SATB, 2 vln, 3 vla, bsn, bc **B0020, C0002, C0004-05, C0011-12, C0019, C0021, C0025, C0027, C0029-30, C0033, C0039-41, C0046-48, C0060-61, C0077, C0088, C0168, C0229, E0115, E0145, E0152, K0089, K0096, K0150-51, K0166, K0266, K0270, K0295, K0315, K0341, M0316, P0001, P0009, P0013, P0017, P0020, P0038, R0076, R0104, S0013, S0661, T0007**

SATB, 2 vln, 3 vla, tbn, bc **A0442**

SATB, 2 vln, 3 vla, 2 corn, vlne, bc **M0048**

SATB, 2 vln, 3 vla, 2 corn, bsn, bc **Z0034, Z0066**

SATB, 2 vln, 3 vla, 2 corn, 3 tbn, vlne, bc **S0262**

SATB, 2 vln, 3 vla, 2 corn, 4 tbn, bc **B0463**

SATB, 2 vln, 3 vla, 2 cornettini, 3 tbn, bsn, bc **K0188**

SATB, 2 vln, 3 vla, 3 tpt, bc **A0001**

SATB, 2 vln, 3 vla, 4 tpt, timp, bsn, bc **B0555**

SATB, 2 vln, 3 vla, 2 clar, bc **M0076, M0106**

SATB, 2 vln, 3 vla, 2 clar, timp, bc **E0119**

SATB, 2 vln, 3 vla, 2 clar, vlne, bc **B1242**

SATB, 2 vln, 3 vla, 2 clar, timp, bsn, bc **K0330**

SATB, 2 vln, 3 vla, 2 fl, vlne, theorbo, bc **B1321**

SATB, 2 vln, 3 vla, 2 ob, bc **A0397**

SATB, 2 vln, 3 vla, 2 ob, 3 tbn, vlne, bc **B0328**

SATB, 2 vln, 3 vla, 3 tbn, bc **K0059**

SATB, 2 vln, 3 vla, 3 tbn, vlne, bc **H0636**

SATB, 2 vln, 3 vla, 5 tbn, 5 bsn, bc **M0299**

SATB, 2 vln, 3 vla, 10 tbn, bc **M0299**

SATB, 2 vln, 8 vla, 5 tbn, bc **M0299**

SATB, 2 vln, 8 vla, 5 bsn, bc **M0299**

SATB, 2 vln, 4 vla, bc **R0088, S0663**

SATB, 2 vln, 4 vla, 3 tbn, vlne, bc **K0091**

SATB, 2 vln, 2 vltta, bc **E0124, E0156, O0014, R0183**

SATB, 2 vln, 2 vltta, vc, bc **O0029**

SATB, 2 vln, 2 vltta, bsn, bc **B1400, O0009, O0011, R0098, R0141, T0004**

SATB, 2 vln, 2 vltta, 2 clar, bc **S0313**

SATB, 2 vln, 2 vltta, tromba, bassono, bc **R0075**

SATB, 2 vln, 2 vltta, 2 vln piccolo, 2 cornettino, clar, vlne, bc **S0212**

SATB, 2 vln, 2 vltta, 2 vln piccolo, 2 cornettino, clar, bsn, bc **S0212**

SATB, 2 vln, vltta, bc **A0470**

SATB, 2 vln, vltta, vla bassa, bsn, bc **F0067**

SATB, 2 vln, vltta, bsn, bc **G0108**

SATB, 2 vln, vltta, 2 fl, gamba, vlne, theorbo, bc **C0150**

SATB, 2 vln, 2 vltta, bc **R0072**

SATB, 2 vln, 2 vltta, vlne, bc **B1362**

SATB, 2 vln, 2 vltta, 2 clar, timp, bsn, bc **C0239**

SATB, 2 vln, 2 vltta, ob, bsn, bc **R0024**

SATB, 2 vln, 2 vltta, tromba, bsn, bc **K0316, R0117**

SATB, 2 vln, 3 vltta, 4 clar, timp, bsn, bc **Z0040**

SATB, 2 vln, 4 vltta, 3 tbn, vlne, bc **B0458**

SATB, 2 vln, gamba, bc **C0111, F0085, H0307, K0339, K0347**

SATB, 2 vln, gamba, vlne, bc **A0501, S0275**

SATB, 2 vln, gamba, 2 fl, 2 ob, bsn, bc **R0029**

SATB, 2 vln, 2 gamba, bc **W0033**

SATB, 2 vln, 2 gamba, vlne, bc **W0073, W0077**

SATB, 2 vln, 4 gamba, bc **E0007**

SATB, 2 vln, corn, bc **G0001**

SATB, 2 vln, corn, tbn, bc **B0684**

SATB, 2 vln, corn, 2 clar, 3 tbn, bc **A0005**

SATB, 2 vln, corn, 2 tbn, vlne, bc **S0267**

SATB, 2 vln, corn, 2 tbn, vlne, bsn, vc, bc **S0240, S0276**

SATB, 2 vln, 2 corn, bc **F0044, P0028**

SATB, 2 vln, 2 corn, 2 clar, 2 horns, bc **A0458**

SATB, 2 vln, 2 corn, 2 tbn, bass viol, bc **S0662**

SATB, 2 vln, 2 corn, 2 tbn, bsn, bc **S0662**

SATB, 2 vln, 2 corn, 2 tbn, bsn, vlne, bc **M0039**

SATB, 2 vln, 2 corn, 3 tbn, bc **C0194**

SATB, 2 vln, 2 corn, 3 tbn, vlne, bc **M0027, M0039, M0048**

SATB, 2 vln, 2 cornettino, bc **A0513**

SATB, 2 vln, clar, bc **P0045**

SATB, 2 vln, clar, tbn, bc **L0089**

SATB, 2 vln, 2 clar, bc **B1003, G0131, K0274**

SATB, 2 vln, 2 clar, timp, bc **A0550**

SATB, 2 vln, 2 clar, bsn, bc **B1272, L0078, L0090**

SATB, 2 vln, 2 clar, 2 tbn, bc **R0150**

SATB, 2 vln, 2 clar, 3 tbn, bc **M0035, M0076, M0106**

SATB, 2 vln, 2 fl, vc, bc **L0100**

SATB, 2 vln, 2 fl, 2 tbn, bass viol, bc **S0662**

SATB, 2 vln, 2 fl, 2 tbn, bsn, bc **S0662**

SATB, 2 vln, 2 fl, 2 tbn, bsn, vlne, bc **M0039**

SATB, 2 vln, 2 fl, 3 tbn, vlne, bc **M0039**

SATB, 2 vln, 2 ob, bc **S0332**

SATB, 2 vln, 2 ob, taille, bsn, bc **L0072, L0096, L0102**

SATB, 2 vln, 2 tbn, bc **R0072**

SATB, 2 vln, 2 tbn, vlne, bc **S0089**

SATB, 2 vln, 2 tbn, vlne, bsn, bc **G0187, M0044, M0046, M0051, M0069-70, M0078-80, M0084-86, M0089-90, M0093, M0095, M0097-99, M0101-02**

SATB, 2 vln, 2 tbn, 2 vlne, bc **M0059**

SATB, 2 vln, 2 tbn, tromba, bsn, bc **R0117**

SATB, 2 vln, 3 tbn, bc **A0228, H0624, M0014, M0016, M0032, M0065-66, M0071-73, M0075, M0081-83, M0091, M0094, M0104, M0264, Z0048, Z0054**

SATB, 2 vln, 3 tbn, vlne, bc **G0187, K0114-15, M0008, M0021, M0025-26, M0031, M0044, M0046, M0051, M0054, M0059, M0061, M0063, R0058, S0091, S0267**

SATB, 2 vln, 3 tbn, vlne, bass viol, bc **K0085**

SATB, 2 vln, 3 tbn, vlne, bsn, bc **K0085**

SATB, 2 vln, 2 tbtta, bc **A0489**

SATB, 2 vln, 4 ob, bc **L0079, L0091**

SATB, 2 vln, 4 tbn, bc **A0301**

SATB, 3 vln, bc **C0150, F0109**

SATB, 3 vln, vlne, bc **B1355**

SATB, 3 vln, bsn, bc **B1355**

SATB, 3 vln, vla, 2 vltta, tbtta, bc **R0107**

SATB, 3 vln, 2 vla, bc **E0172**

SATB, 3 vln, 2 vla, vlne, bc **F0031**

SATB, 3 vln, 2 vla, vc, bc **K0272**

SATB, 3 vln, 2 vla, bsn, bc **S0285**

SATB, 3 vln, 2 vla, 2 clar, bsn, bc **E0136**

SATB, 3 vln, 3 vla, 3 tbtta, 4 tbn, bc **F0199**

SATB, 3 vln, 2 vltta, bc **F0030**

SATB, 3 vln, 2 vltta, bsn, bc **T0005, T0010**

SATB, 3 vln, 3 gambas, bc **B0504**

SATB, 3 vln, corn, vlne, bc **B1275**

SATB, 3 vln, 2 trba, timp, bc **E0005**

SATB, 3 vln, 3 ob, bsn, vc, bc **Z0031**

SATB, 3 vln, waldhorn, vlne, bc **B1275**

SATB, 4 vln, vla, bc **A0464**

SATB, vla, vltta, vc, vlne, bc **S0059**

SATB, vla, vltta, corn, 2 tbn, vlne, vc, bc **S0057**

SATB, vla, vltta, corn, 2 tbn, vlne, vc, bsn **S0114**

SATB, vla, vltta, corn, 2 tbn, vlne, vc, bsn, bc **L0061, S0016, S0052, S0056, S0069, S0117**

SATV, vla, 2 vltta, 2 tbn, vlne, vc, bc **S0057**

SATB, vla, 2 ob, bc **W0086**

SATB, 2 vla, bc **H0315**

SATB, 2 vla, vlne, bc **A0539**

SATB, 2 vla, vltta, vc, vlne, bc **S0019, S0034, S0040, S0043-45, S0098-99, S0101, S0102, S0104, S0107, S0113**

SATB, 2 vla, vltta, corn, tbn, vlne, vc, bc **S0058**

SATB, 2 vla, vltta, corn, 2 tbn, vlne, vc, bc **S0071**

SATB, 2 vla, vltta, corn, 2 tbn, vlne, bsn, bc **Z0009**

SATB, 2 vla, 2 vltta, vc, tbn, vlne, bc **S0058**

SATB, 2 vla, 2 vltta, vc, 2 tbn, vlne, bc **S0071**

SATB, 2 vla, corn, vlne, bc **A0294, B1327**

SATB, 2 vla, corn, tbn, bc **A0294, B1327**

SATB, 2 vla, corn, 2 tbn, bsn, vlne, bc **S0093**

SATB, 2 vla, corn, 2 tbn, bsn, vc, vlne, bc **S0026, S0029, S0051, S0092, S0105**

SATB, 2 vla, 2 corn, bsn, vlne, bc **G0187**

SATB, 2 vla, 2 corn, tbn, vlne, bc **G0187**

SATB, 2 vla, 2 tpt, bc **G0039**

SATB, 2 vla, 2 tpt, 2 ob, bc **G0014**

SATB, 2 vla, fl, ob, bc **Z0011**

SATB, 2 vla, 2 fl, vlne, theorbo, bc **P0207**

SATB, 2 vla, 2 ob, vlne, bsn, bc **S0673**

SATB, 2 vla, 2 tbn, bsn, vc, vlne, theorbo, bc **F0046**

SATB, 2 vla, 3 tbn, bc **B0249**

SATB, 3 vla, bc **A0493, E0011, G0082, H0294, H0509, H0511, H0516, P0043, P0285, S0077-78, S0263**

SATB, 3 vla, vlne, bc **A0630, B1386, D0093, F0187, K0162, W0045**

SATB, 3 vla, vc, vlne, bc **B0214, B0227, B0237-38, B0245, B0263, B0266, B0276, B0297, B0313, B0322, B0326, S0042, S0269**

SATB, 3 vla, vlne, bsn, bc **K0350**

SATB, 3 vla, bsn, bc **A0545, K0162, O0026, T0039**

SATB, 3 vla, tbn, bc **B0208**

SATB, 3 vla, vltta, corn, vlne, vc, bc **S0057-58**

SATB, 3 vla, vltta, corn, tbn, vlne, vc, bc **S0071**

SATB, 3 vla, 2 vltta, vc, vlne, bc **S0057-58**

SATB, 3 vla, 2 vltta, vc, tbn, vlne, bc **S0071**

SATB, 3 vla, corn, 3 tbn, vlne, bc **S0259**

SATB, 3 vla, corn, 2 tbn, vlne, vc, bsn, bc **S0046, S0050, S0097, S0100, S0103, S0108, S0110**

SATB, 3 vla, 2 corn, 5 tbn, 5 bsn, bc **M0299**

SATB, 3 vla, 2 corn, 10 tbn, bc **M0299**

SATB, 3 vla, 3 tbn, bc **B0451**

SATB, 3 vla, 3 tbn, vlne, bc **K0172, S0115**

SATB, 4 vla, bc **C0189, D0094, H0444-45, H0455, K0194, M0068, P0035, R0036, S0665**

SATB, 4 vla, vlne, bc **W0066**

SATB, 4 vla, vc, vlne, bc **B0277**

SATB, 4 vla, bsn, bc **E0171**

SATB, 4 vla, 4 org **B0550**

SATB, 4 vla, vltta, vc, corn, 2 tbn, vlne, bsn, bc **Z0005**

SATB, 5 vla, bc **A0542, D0092, F0042, R0173, T0011**

SATB, 5 vla, vlne, bc **F0056**

SATB, 8 vla, 2 corn, 5 bsn, bc **M0299**

SATB, 8 vla, 2 corn, 5 tbn, bc **M0299**

SATB, 2 vla d'amore, 2 gamba, bc **B1340**

SATB, vltta, 2 gamba, bc **A0525**

SATB, vltta, 2 gamba, bsn, bc **K0311**

SATB, 2 vltta, 2 corn, bc **R0072**

SATB, 2 vltta, 2 clar, bsn, bc **G0112**

SATB, 2 vltta, 2 clar, 2 ob, bc **S0313**

SATB, 2 vltta, 2 ob, vc, bc **O0029**

SATB, 2 vltta, 2 ob, bsn, bc **G0112**

SATB, 3 vltta, bc **K0069**

SATB, 2 gamba, bc **F0048**

SATB, 3 gamba, bc **A0400, A0447, O0021**

SATB, 4 gamba, bc **A0006**

SATB, 4 gamba, bsn, bc **P0044**

SATB, corn, 2 tbn, vlne, bc **A0294, B1327**

SATB, corn, 3 tbn, bc **A0294, B1327**

SATB, corn, 3 tbn, vlne, bc **E0012, F0008**

SATB, 2 corn, bc **H0212**
SATB, 2 corn, 2 clar, bc **H0251**
SATB, 2 corn, 2 clar, bsn, bc **F0189**
SATB, 2 corn, 2 tbn, bc **R0072**
SATB, 2 corn, 2 tbn, bsn, vlne, bc **G0187**
SATB, 2 corn, 2 tbn, tbn, vlne, bc **G0187**
SATB, 2 corn (schryari), 2 tbn, bc **F0012**
SATB, 2 corn, 3 tbn, bc **M0264**
SATB, 2 tpt, 2 ob, timp, bc **A0472**
SATB, 2 clar, timp, harp, bc **K0192**
SATB, 2 clar, 2 ob, bsn, bc **G0112**
SATB, 2 clar, timp, 3 tbn, bc **U0001**
SATB, 2 fl, vlne, bc **E0008**
SATB, 3 fl, 3 tpt, bc **F0045**
SATB, 2 ob, bc **K0216**
SATB, 2 ob, taille, bsn, bc **L0092, L0101**
SATB, 4 ob, bsn, bc **G0112**
SATB, 1 treble instr, bc **F0029**
SATB, 3 instr, bc **R0017**
SATB, 4 instr, bc **G0071**
SATB, 4 treble instr, bc **H0423**
SATB, 5 instruments (unspecified), bc **P0280**

S solo, SATB, bc **P0115**
S solo, SATB, vln, 2 gamba, vc, bc **M0234**
S solo, SATB, 2 vln, 2 vla, vlne, bc **A0003**
S solo, SATB, 2 vln, 2 vla, 4 clar, vlne, bc **B0383**
S solo, SATB, 2 vln, 2 vla, 2 harps, 2 fl, 2 clar, timp, bsn, bc
  A0533
S solo, SATB, 2 vln, vltta, vc, corn, clar, 2 tbn, vlne, bsn, bc
  L0045
S solo, SATB, vla, vltta, vc, corn, 2 tbn, vlne, bsn, bc **L0063**
S solo, SATB, 2 vla, vltta, vc, corn, clar, 2 tbn, vlne, bsn, bc
  L0039
S solo, SATB, 2 vla, vltta, vc, corn, 2 tbn, vlne, bsn, bc
  L0059
SA solo, SATB, 2 vln, 2 vla, vlne, bc **M0390**
SA solo, SATB, 2 vln, 2 vla, bsn, bc **M0390**
SATB soli, SATB **P0076**
SATB soli, SATB, bc **L0054**
SATB soli, SATB, 2 vln, vla, 2 clar, 2 tbn, bass viol, vlne, bc
  L0038
SATB soli, SATB, 2 vln, vla, 2 clar, 2 tbn, bsn, vlne, bc
  L0038
SATB soli, SATB, 2 vln, vla, 2 ob, bsn, vc, bc **M0232**
SATB soli, SATB, 2 vln, 2 vla, corn, 2 clar, bass viol, vlne,
  bc **L0038**
SATB soli, SATB, 2 vln, 2 vla, corn, 2 clar, bsn, vlne, bc
  L0038
SATB soli, SATB, 2 vln, 3 vla, 2 clar, bass viol, vlne, bc
  L0038
SATB soli, SATB, 2 vln, 3 vla, 2 clar, bsn, vlne, bc **L0038**

SATB soli, SATB, 2 vln, 3 vltta, 3 tbn, vlne, theorbo, bc
  L0052
SATB soli, SATB, 2 vln, corn, 2 clar, 2 tbn, bass viol, vlne,
  bc **L0038**
SATB soli, SATB, 2 vln, corn, 2 clar, 2 tbn, bsn, vlne, bc
  L0038
SATB soli, SATB, 2 vln, corn, 2 tbn, vlne, theorbo, bc
  L0041
SATB soli, SATB, 2 vln, corn, 2 tbn, vlne, vc, bsn, bc
  L0037, L0048, L0058, L0065-67
SATB soli, SATB, 2 vla, vltta, corn, 2 tbn, vlne, vc, bsn, bc
  L0062
SATB soli, SATB, 3 vla, 3 gamba, corn, 3 tbn, bass viol,
  vlne, theorbo, bc **L0042**
SATB soli, SATB, 4 vla, 2 vltta, 3 tbn, bsn, bc **L0050**
SATB soli, SATB, 4 vla, corn, 3 tbn, vlne, bass viol, theorbo,
  bc **L0032**
SATB soli, SATB, 5 vltta, 2 gamba, vlne, lyra, 2 baritoni,
  bass viol, bc **L0051**
STTB soli, SATB, bc **K0348**
STB soli, SATB, 2 vln, 4 vla, vlne, theorbo, bc **B0409**
STB soli, SATB, 2 vln, 2 bassonetti, 2 horn, bsn, bc **Z0016**
STB soli, SATB, 5 instr, bc **A0283**
SB soli, SATB, 4 instr, bc **F0058**
A solo, SATB, 2 vla, vltta, vc, corn, clar, 2 tbn, vlne, bsn, bc
  L0033
ATB soli, SATB, 2 vln, vla, 2 clar, bc **Z0035**
AB soli, SATB, 2 vln, vlne, bc **B0760**
T solo, SATB, 2 vln, 2 vla, 4 clar, vlne, bc **B0383**
T solo, SATB, 2 vln, vc, corn, clar, 3 tbn, vlne, bc **L0035**
B solo, SATB, 2 vln, 2 vla, vlne, bc **S0340**
B solo, SATB, 2 vln, 2 vla, bsn, bc **B0412**
B solo, SATB, 4 vln, bc **M0317**
B solo, SATB, 2 vla, 2 ob, vlne, bc **S0340**

STTB, bc **F0053, H0243, M0139, M0164**
STTB, 2 vln, bc **F0114, G0083**
STTB, 2 vln, vla, bc **B0767**
STTB, 2 vln, 2 vla, bc **F0128**
STTB, 2 vln, 2 vla, vlne, bc **P0177, P0189**
STTB, 2 vln, 2 vla, gamba, bc **F0192**
STTB, 2 vln, 2 vla, corn, bc **B0783**
STTB, 2 vla, vlne, bc **P0120, P0140**
STTB, 3 vla, vlne, bc **P0142, P0182**
STTB, 4 vla, vlne, bc **P0162**

AATB, bc **B1304, H0539**

ATTB **D0038, W0088**
ATTB, bc **H0408, M0243, M0304**

ATTB, 2 vln, bc **B1248, B1363, H0309, W0049**
ATTB, 2 vln, vlne, bc **R0187**
ATTB, 2 vln, vla, bc **B1266**
ATTB, 5 vla, bc **D0091**
ATTB, clar, bass viola, bc **M0290**
ATTB, tromba marina, bass viola, bc **M0290**

BBBB, bc **E0075, K0065**
BBBB, 4 vln, bc **S0357**

à 5 **F0014, F0021**
5 vv **A0390, B1176, E0014, F0169, F0180, K0009**
5 vv, bc **S0224**
5 vv, 2 vln, 2 vla, vlne, bc **S0320**
5 vv, 2 vln, 2 vla, bsn, bc **M0324**
5 vv, 2 vln, 3 vla, bc **H0508, H0518**
5 vv, 2 vln, corn, bc **B1320**
5 vv, 2 vln, 2 corn, 2 shawms, bsn, bc **L0097**
5 vv, 4 vla, 4 tbn, vlne, bc **R0057**
5 vv, instr. **W0174**
5 vv, 5 instr. **K0168**
5 vv, instr, bc **B0428**

SSSSS, bc **M0188**

SSSSA, 2 vln, bsn, bc **K0094**
SSSSA, 2 vln, tbn, bc **K0094**

SSSAT, bc **D0073**
SSSAT, 2 vln, 3 vla, bc **H0523**

B solo, SSSAB, 2 vln, vc, 2 corn, clar, vlne, bsn, bc **L0046**

SSSTB, 2 vln, bc **H0261**
SSSTB, 3 vla, vlne, bc **P0202**

SSATT, 2 vln, bc **S0244**

SSATB **A0150, A0388, A0399, A0420, A0446, A0488,**
A0491-92, B0155, B0401, B0560, B0564, B0722, B0859,
B1190, D0033, D0036, D0040, D0087, D0089, E0001-02,
E0114, F0001-03, F0176, G0007, H0290, H0331, H0534,
K0002, K0134, K0201-03, L0060, L0107, N0001, N0048,
O0007, P0004, P0106-08, R0012, R0067, R0157, R0167,
R0169, R0185, R0189, R0190, R0193, R0226, S0122-23,
S0127-33, S0204, S0329, S0389, S0766, S0773, T0058-60,
T0062, T0065, W0164
SSATB, bc **A0192, A0206, A0255, A0263, A0308, A0374,**
A0434, A0437, A0481, A0524, A0543, B0007, B0018,
B0149, B0176, B0178, B0187, B0189, B0598, B0631, B0638,
B0645, B0660, B0674, B0716, B0744, B0753, B0756, B0773,
B0778, B0793, B0816, B0850, B0898, B0904, B0909, B0931,
B0942, B0959, B0964, B1023, B1049, B1071, B1073-75,
B1090, B1134, B1182, B1188, B1193, B1235, B1283, B1287,
B1293, B1297, B1303, B1308, B1312, B1398, D0013,
D0022-23, D0026, D0034, E0057, E0094, F0188, G0048-50,
G0192, H0031, H0039, H0042, H0052, H0058, H0058,
H0063-65, H0069, H0087, H0089-91, H0094, H0105,
H0110, H0114, H0118, H0121, H0126-27, H0130, H0134,
H0137, H0139, H0141, H0144, H0163, H0165, H0173,
H0183, H0185, H0206-08, H0214-15, H0218, H0221,
H0226-27, H0230-31, H0235, H0237-38, H0240, H0247,
H0262, H0276-77, H0284, H0286-87, H0291-93, H0406,
H0495, J0004, J0008, J0021, J0027, J0032, K0058, K0062,
K0129, K0283, L0047, L0076, L0108-10, M0108, M0124,
M0131, M0138, M0146, M0152, M0154, M0161, M0171,
M0182, M0185-86, M0191, M0193, M0195, M0199,
M0207-10, M0215, M0245, M0321-22, N0002, P0190,
P0267, R0023, S0165, S0166, S0168, S0222, S0225, S0227,
S0315, S0317, S0335, S0338, S0351, S0448-50, S0452-53,
S0455-61, S0465, S0467-72, S0474, S0477, S0527-28, S0532,
S0534-37, S0543-46, S0550, S0553, S0557, S0560-61, S0568,
S0572, S0578, S0587, S0624, S0628, S0764, S0767, S0769,
S0770, S0772, T0001, T0031-32, W0003, W0092
SSATB, bc **L0064**
SSATB, vlne, bc **G0182**
SSATB, vln, vlne, tbn, theorbo, bc **A0417**
SSATB, vln, tbn, bc **B0703**
SSATB, vln, 2 vla, bc **M0263, M0295**
SSATB, vln, 3 vla, vln piccolo, cornettino, 3 bombarde, bc
K0135
SSATB, vln, 4 vla, bc **B1246**
SSATB, vln, 4 vla, vlne, bc **S0073**
SSATB, vln, 4 vla, 3 tbn, bsn, bc **S0169**
SSATB, 2 vln, bc **A0330, A0418, A0485, A0614, B0068,**
B0096, B0099, B0103, B0121, B0123, B0125-26, B0132,
B0135-36, B0141, B0147, B0624, B0646, B0661, B0678,
B0693, B0700, B0708-10, B0714, B0719, B0746, B0754-55,
B0784, B0795, B0801, B0803, B0810, B0817-18, B0821,
B0839, B0842-43, B0853, B0866, B0872, B0876, B0901,
B0915, B0935, B0938, B0955, B0957, B0996-97, B1037,
B1042, B1047, B1057-59, B1076, B1106, B1110, B1112,
B1116, B1137, B1139, B1145, B1151, B1163, B1185, B1199,
B1226, B1229, B1233, B1343, C0108, C0182-83, C0192,
F0054, F0101, F0104, F0118, F0122, F0129, F0133, F0143,

F0159, G0088, H0054, H0101, H0119, H0152, H0159,
H0181, H0190-91, H0193, H0217, H0229, H0249-50,
H0258, H0272, H0280-81, J0005, K0081, K0130, M0110,
M0122, M0194, M0217-18, M0306, P0040, P0242, P0246,
R0093-94, R0101, S0082, S0303, S0592-95, T0161, Z0044,
Z0049, Z0061, Z0065
SSATB, 2 vln, vlne, bc   B1344, B1360, B1364, B1378, B1405,
B1408, B1412, G0181, H0028, H0032, H0035-36, H0045,
H0051, H0071, H0082, H0088, H0106, H0120, H0128,
H0147-51, H0154-56, H0174-75, H0179-80, H0225, H0228,
H0232, H0248, H0259, L0069, M0351-52, M0354,
M0362-63, M0367, M0369-74, S0228
SSATB, 2 vln, vc, bc   F0025
SSATB, 2 vln, gamba, bc   A0554
SSATB, 2 vln, bsn, bc   F0127, G0116
SSATB, 2 vln, 2 bsn, tbn, bc   S0436
SSATB, 2 vln, 3 bsn, bc   S0436
SSATB, 2 vln, tbn, bc   B0609, B0626, B0647, B0804, B0911,
B1143
SSATB, 2 vln, bomb, 3 tbn, bc   H0334
SSATB, 2 vln, vla, bc   B0742, B0747, B0774, B0831, B1015,
B1083, B1100, B1117, B1131, B1200, B1220, B1232, K0173
SSATB, 2 vln, vla, vlne, bc   A0438
SSATB, 2 vln, vla, gamba, vlne, org   G0063
SSATB, 2 vln, vla, bsn, bc   R0203-07, R0209, S0311
SSATB, 2 vln, vla, tbn, bsn, bc   K0297
SSATB, 2 vln, vla, vltta, bc   A0604, A0607
SSATB, 2 vln, vla, vltta, gamba, bc   A0557, A0560, A0567-68,
A0581, A0583, A0585, A0587, A0589, A0591-92, A0595-96,
A0613
SSATB, 2 vln, vla, 2 vltta, bc   R0144
SSATB, 2 vln, vla, 2 gamba, bsn, bc   P0016
SSATB, 2 vln, vla, 2 gamba, 4 tpt, timp, bc   P0031
SSATB, 2 vln, vla, 2 gamba, 4 tpt, timp, bsn, bc   P0033
SSATB, 2 vln, vla, 2 tpt, 2 fl, bc   A0429
SSATB, 2 vln, vla, 2 ob, 2 horns, bsn, bc   Z0026
SSATB, 2 vln, vla, 2 tbn, bsn, vlne, bc   G0184
SSATB, 2 vln, 2 vla, bc   A0529, B0002, B0636, B0644, B0653,
B0785, B0826, B0862-63, B0868, B0970, B0981, B1032,
B1068, B1098, B1104, B1196-97, B1212, C0243, F0018,
F0103, F0107, F0110-11, F0116, F0123, F0125, F0130,
F0135, F0145, F0152-53, G0110, G0113, G0118, H0007,
H0009, H0495, K0067, K0082, K0326, L0085, O0004,
O0017, O0022, O0031, O0033, P0259-60, R0052, R0115,
R0128, R0208, S0181, S0186, S0201, S0210, S0360, S0390,
S0405, S0605, T0018, W0001
SSATB, 2 vln, 2 vla, vlne, bc   A0218, A0267, A0291, A0475,
B0154, B1089, B1346, B1359, B1381, D0074, H0160,
H0333, J0001, J0007, M0020, N0044-47, N0049-70, N0072,
N0074-100, N0103-21, P0203, P0220, R0044-46, R0055,
R0082, R0116, S0200, S0369, S0372, T0166-67, W0037,
W0043, W0064

SSATB, 2 vln, 2 vla, vlne, bsn, bc   G0173, G0175-76,
G0177-80, G0183-84, K0318, K0351, M0023, M0029,
P0279, S0382, S0397, S0670
SSATB, 2 vln, 2 vla, vlne, tbn, bc   G0173, G0175-76,
G0177-80, G0183, M0012
SSATB, 2 vln, 2 vla, bass viol, bc   K0084
SSATB, 2 vln, 2 vla, bass vla, bc   K0110
SSATB, 2 vln, 2 vla, bass vla, gamba, vlne, bc   P0274
SSATB, 2 vln, 2 vla, vc, bc   B0395, E0003, K0321, S0407,
S0649-50, S0653
SSATB, 2 vln, 2 vla, vc, bsn, bc   K0328
SSATB, 2 vln, 2 vla, bsn, bc   A0404, A0424, A0462, A0484,
B0008, B0154, B0157, B0554, B0559, B0561, B1365, C0231,
F0134, F0162, G0095, G0097, G0102, G0106, G0109,
G0115, G0121-24, H0333, H0462, H0464-65, H0470,
H0479, H0520, J0007, K0084, K0110, L0070, L0082,
M0377, O0025, P0089, P0114, R0004-05, R0176, S0135-44,
S0146-55, S0175, S0179, S0184-85, S0366, S0369-70, S0372,
S0377, S0380-81, T0019, T0164
SSATB, 2 vln, 2 vla, bsn, theorbo, bc   T0041
SSATB, 2 vln, 2 vla, tbn, bc   S0369, M0045
SSATB, 2 vln, 2 vla, vltta, vlne, bc   A0531
SSATB, 2 vln, 2 vla, vltta, 2 corn, 3 tbn, vlne, bc   K0137
SSATB, 2 vln, 2 vla, 4 gamba, 2 clar, vlne, bsn, bc   S0214
SSATB, 2 vln, 2 vla, 2 corn, bc   K0071
SSATB, 2 vln, 2 vla, 2 corn, vlne, bc   M0233
SSATB, 2 vln, 2 vla, 2 corn, bsn, bc   S0172, S0373
SSATB, 2 vln, 2 vla, 2 corn, clar, 3 tbn, bc   S0211
SSATB, 2 vln, 2 vla, 2 corn, 2 clar, bc   F0165
SSATB, 2 vln, 2 vla, 2 corn, 2 clar, 3 tbn, vlne, bc   P0078
SSATB, 2 vln, 2 vla, 2 corn, 2 clar, timp, 3 tbn, bsn, bc
T0016
SSATB, 2 vln, 2 vla, 2 corn, 2 ob, 2 taille, 3 tbn, vlne, bsn,
bc   K0132
SSATB, 2 vln, 2 vla, 2 corn, 3 tbn, bc   K0205, S0188, S0207
SSATB, 2 vln, 2 vla, 2 corn, 3 tbn, vlne, bc   R0178
SSATB, 2 vln, 2 vla, 2 corn, 3 tbn, bsn, bc   B0562, S0363
SSATB, 2 vln, 2 vla, cornettino, clar, vlne, bc   G0186
SSATB, 2 vln, 2 vla, 2 cornettini, bsn, vlne, bc   G0185
SSATB, 2 vln, 2 vla, 2 cornettini, tbn, vlne, bc   G0185
SSATB, 2 vln, 2 vla, 2 cornettini, 4 clar, timp, 3 tbn, bsn, bc
K0190
SSATB, 2 vln, 2 vla, 2 cornettini, 3 tbn, bsn, bc   P0063
SSATB, 2 vln, 2 vla, tpt, 2 clar, tbtta, bsn, bc   S0299
SSATB, 2 vln, 2 vla, 2 tpt, vlne, bc   B1368, B1373-74, R0040
SSATB, 2 vln, 2 vla, 2 tpt, bsn, bc   A0478, B1373
SSATB, 2 vln, 2 vla, 4 tpt, tbn, bc   S0675
SSATB, 2 vln, 2 vla, 2 clar, bc   A0526, F0137, F0149, R0025,
S0203
SSATB, 2 vln, 2 vla, 2 clar, vlne, bc   G0085-86, P0071
SSATB, 2 vln, 2 vla, 2 clar, vlne, bsn, bc   G0185
SSATB, 2 vln, 2 vla, 2 clar, vlne, tbn, bc   G0185

SSATB, 2 vln, 2 vla, 2 clar, gamba, bc **P0292**
SSATB, 2 vln, 2 vla, 2 clar, gamba, vlne, bc **G0061**
SSATB, 2 vln, 2 vla, 2 clar, bsn, bc **P0109, P0292, O0042, O0043, T0020, V0008**
SSATB, 2 vln, 2 vla, 2 clar, timp, bsn, bc **L0075, S0173, R0015, T0038, V0008**
SSATB, 2 vln, 2 vla, 2 clar, tbn, timp, bc **V0008**
SSATB, 2 vln, 2 vla, 2 clar, 2 tbn, bsn, bc **K0144**
SSATB, 2 vln, 2 vla, 2 clar, 3 tbn, vlne, bsn, bc **S0031**
SSATB, 2 vln, 2 vla, 2 clar, 3 tbn, timp, bsn, bc **K0145**
SSATB, 2 vln, 2 vla, 3 clar, timp, vlne, bc **S0193**
SSATB, 2 vln, 2 vla, 3 clar, timp, bsn, bc **S0193**
SSATB, 2 vln, 2 vla, 3 clar, 3 tbn, bc **K0121**
SSATB, 2 vln, 2 vla, 4 clar, timp, bc **R0009**
SSATB, 2 vln, 2 vla, 4 clar, timp, bsn, bc **K0142**
SSATB, 2 vln, 2 vla, 2 fl, vlne, bc **A0382, A0495, W0083**
SSATB, 2 vln, 2 vla, 2 fl, 3 tbn, vlne, bc **K0164**
SSATB, 2 vln, 2 vla, ob, 2 tailles, bsn, bc **A0445**
SSATB, 2 vln, 2 vla, 2 ob, bc **S0321, S0323**
SSATB, 2 vln, 2 vla, 2 ob, bsn, bc **S0418**
SSATB, 2 vln, 2 vla, 3 ob, vlne, bsn, bc **T0063**
SSATB, 2 vln, 2 vla, 4 ob, bsn, bc **A0466**
SSATB, 2 vln, 2 vla, 2 piff, timp, bsn, bc **B0156**
SSATB, 2 vln, 2 vla, 2 horns, bsn, bc **V0009**
SSATB, 2 vln, 2 vla, 2 tbn, bc **A0455**
SSATB, 2 vln, 2 vla, 3 tbn, vlne, bc **S0419**
SSATB, 2 vln, 2 vla, 3 tbn, vlne, bsn, 3 org **B0517**
SSATB, 2 vln, 2 vla, 3 tbn, bsn, bc **K0191**
SSATB, 2 vln, 2 vla, 3 tbn, theorbo, 2 org **B0546**
SSATB, 2 vln, 2 vla, 3 tbn, 3 org **B0546**
SSATB, 2 vln, 2 vla, 2 tbtta, vlne, bc **G0052**
SSATB, 2 vln, 2 vla, 4 tbtta, timp, bsn, bc **K0198**
SSATB, 2 vln, 3 vla, bc **A0499, E0015, E0026, E0029, E0031, E0036-37, E0039-43, E0046, E0048-49, E0053, E0055, E0060-62, E0065, E0071, E0079, E0088-89, H0469, H0471, H0475, H0491-92, H0498, H0505, H0521, K0324, M0096, M0325-31, M0353, M0356-57, M0359-61, M0365-66, M0368, P0268, R0151, R0162, S0401, S0483-507, S0520-26, S0529-31, S0533, S0538-42, S0547-49, S0551-52, S0554-56, S0558-59, S0562-67, S0569-71, S0573-77, S0579-86, S0588-90, T0164**
SSATB, 2 vln, 3 vla, vlne, bc **G0139-48, G0150-57, G0159-72, G0184, G0188-91, G0193-95, K0273, M0133, S0086, W0074**
SSATB, 2 vln, 3 vla, vlne, bsn, bc **S0656**
SSATB, 2 vln, 3 vla, vc, bc **E0138**
SSATB, 2 vln, 3 vla, bsn, bc **B0407, E0127, K0169, P0006-07, P0011, R0077**
SSATB, 2 vln, 3 vla, bassone, bsn, bc **R0084**
SSATB, 2 vln, 3 vla, 2 vltta, 2 corn, 3 tbn, vlne, theorbo, bc **V0005**
SSATB, 2 vln, 3 vla, 2 corn, bsn, bc **P0037**
SSATB, 2 vln, 3 vla, 2 corn, 3 clar, vlne, bc **H0334-35**

SSATB, 2 vln, 3 vla, 2 corn, 3 tbn, bsn, bc **K0156**
SSATB, 2 vln, 3 vla, 2 corn, 3 tbn, bombard, bsn, bc **K0199**
SSATB, 2 vln, 3 vla, 3 tpt, 2 clar, timp, 3 tbn, vlne, bc **B0544**
SSATB, 2 vln, 3 vla, 4 tpt, timp, bsn, bc **P0010, P0025**
SSATB, 2 vln, 3 vla, 4 tpt, 2 clar, timp, 3 tbn, vlne, bc **R0054**
SSATB, 2 vln, 3 vla, 5 tpt, 2 fl, harp, timp, tbn, bc **P0029**
SSATB, 2 vln, 3 vla, 2 clar, vlne, bc **G0067**
SSATB, 2 vln, 3 vla, 2 clar, bsn, bc **E0165**
SSATB, 2 vln, 3 vla, 2 clar, 3 tbn, bc **E0081**
SSATB, 2 vln, 3 vla, 2 clar, 3 tbn, bc **E0081**
SSATB, 2 vln, 3 vla, 2 clar, 3 tbn, vlne, bc **R0048**
SSATB, 2 vln, 3 vla, 4 clar, timp, bc **K0232, V0004**
SSATB, 2 vln, 3 vla, 2 ob, bsn, bc **P0026, P0030, P0034, P0037**
SSATB, 2 vln, 3 vla, 2 shawm, 3 tbn, bc **S0371**
SSATB, 2 vln, 3 vla, 3 tbn, bc **B0552, H0500**
SSATB, 2 vln, 3 vla, 3 tbn, tiorbo, org **B0546**
SSATB, 2 vln, 3 vla, 3 tbn, 2 org **B0546**
SSATB, 2 vln, 4 vla, bc **B0386, E0160, S0669**
SSATB, 2 vln, 4 vla, bsn, bc **M0323, P0014**
SSATB, 2 vln, 4 vla, timp, bsn, bc **P0022**
SSATB, 2 vln, 4 vla, 2 corn, 3 tbn, bc **K0176**
SSATB, 2 vln, 4 vla, 2 corn, 4 tbn, vlne, bc **D0075**
SSATB, 2 vln, 4 vla, 2 tpt, 2 clar, bomb, timp, bsn, bc **K0149**
SSATB, 2 vln, 4 vla, 2 bomb, 3 tbn, bc **K0176**
SSATB, 2 vln, 4 vla, 4 tbn, bc **V0006**
SSATB, 2 vln, vltta, tbn, vlne, bc **K0118**
SSATB, 2 vln, 2 vltta, vlne, bc **F0078**
SSATB, 2 vln, 2 vltta, vla basso, bc **O0023**
SSATB, 2 vln, 2 vltta, bsn, bc **O0024, S0681, T0022**
SSATB, 2 vln, 2 vltta, 2 corn, 2 clar, timp, 3 tbn, bsn, bc **S0218**
SSATB, 2 vln, 2 vltta, 2 clar, 2 fl, timp, bsn, bc **K0131**
SSATB, 2 vln, 3 vltta, 2 clar, timp, 3 tbn, bsn, bc **K0171**
SSATB, 2 vln, 4 vltta, 2 clar, timp, 3 tbn, bc **K0171**
SSATB, 2 vln, 2 gamba, bc **E0105, S0428**
SSATB, 2 vln, 2 gamba, vlne, bc **B1369**
SSATB, 2 vln, 2 gamba, bsn, bc **B1369**
SSATB, 2 vln, corn, clar, vlne, bc **A0601**
SSATB, 2 vln, corn, 2 tpt, 2 fl, vlne, bc **A0414, A0468**
SSATB, 2 vln, 2 corn, bc **F0006**
SSATB, 2 vln, 2 corn, vlne, bc **A0556, A0561-62, A0565, A0569-70, A0576, A0579, A0586, A0588, A0593, A0597-98, A0600, A0603, A0611**
SSATB, 2 vln, 2 corn, 2 tpt, vlne, bsn, bc **B1402**
SSATB, 2 vln, 2 corn, 2 clar, 2 prin, timp, 2 tbn, bsn, vlne, bc **M0015**
SSATB, 2 vln, 2 corn, 2 clar, 2 prin, 3 tbn, vlne, bc **M0047**

SSATB, 2 corn, 2 clar, bc **A0454**
SSATB, 2 corn, 2 clar, 2 tbn, timp, bsn, bc **S0412**
SSATB, 2 corn, 2 clar, 3 tbn, bc **A0403, M0296**
SSATB, 2 corn, 2 clar, 3 tbn, 4 tbtta, bc **M0265**
SSATB, 2 corn, 4 clar, 3 tbn, timp, bc **V0004**
SSATB, 2 corn, 2 tbn, bsn, vlne, bc **G0176, G0183**
SSATB, 2 corn, 3 tbn, bc **A0440, M0292, P0113, R0162**
SSATB, 2 corn, 3 tbn, vlne, bc **G0176, G0183**
SSATB, 2 cornettino, 2 tbn, bsn, vlne, bc **G0173**
SSATB, 2 cornettino, 3 tbn, vlne, bc **G0139-48, G0150-57,**
 G0159-73, G0188-91, G0193-95
SSATB, 2 fl, bc **H0245**
SSATB, 2 ob, 2 taille, bsn, bc **S0364**
SSATB, 2 tbn, vlne, bc **K0127**
SSATB, 3 tbn, bc **K0127, M0261**
SSATB, 7 tbn, bc **A0252**
SSATB, 5 str, bc **R0069**
SSATB, 5 instr, bc **M0305**
SSATB, instr, bc **K0153**

SSATB soli, SSATB, 2 vln, 2 vla, vc, 2 corn, 2 clar, 2 tbn,
 vlne, bsn, bc **L0049**
SSATB soli, SSATB, 4 vla, corn, 3 tbn, vlne, theorbo, vc, bc
 L0068
SSATB soli, SSATB, 4 vla, 2 corn, 2 tbn, vlne, bsn, bc
 L0056
SSATB soli, SSATB, 4 vla, 2 corn, 3 tbn, vlne, bc **L0053**
SSB soli, SSATB, 3 gamba, 2 vltta, bc **P0084**
ST soli, SSATB, 2 vln, 2 vla, vlne, bc **H0049**
ST soli, SSATB, 2 vln, 2 tbn, vlne, bc **H0283**
ATB soli, SSATB, 2 vln, 2 vla, 4 clar, timp, bc **S0197**
ATB soli, SSATB, 2 vln, bombard, vlne, bc **R0127**
ATB soli, SSATB, 2 vln, bombard, bsn, bc **R0127**
T solo, SSATB, bc **H0136**
T solo, SSATB, 2 vln, bc **B0894**
T solo, SSATB, 2 vln, 2 clar, bc **R0062**
TT soli, SSATB, bc **H0075, H0161**
TT soli, SSATB, 2 vln, vlne, bc **R0154**
TTB soli, SSATB, 2 vln, 2 vla, bc **R0114**
TB soli, SSATB, 2 vln, 2 vla, bsn, bc **S0182**
TB soli, SSATB, 2 vla, 2 gamba, bc **T0034**
B solo, SSATB, 2 vln, 2 vla, vlne, bc **A0476**
B solo, SSATB, 2 vln, 2 vla, bsn, bc **A0476**

SSTBB, 2 vln, vlne, bc **P0122**

SSTTB, bc **P0129**
SSTTB, 2 vln, bc **B0574, B0833, B0925, B1206, G0055**
SSTTB, 2 vln, vlne, bc **K0157, P0126, P0183, P0186**

SSTTB, 2 vln, gamba, vlne, bc **P0128**
SSTTB, 2 vln, 2 vla, bc **F0095, F0097, F0120, P0133**
SSTTB, 2 vln, 2 vla, vlne, bc **B0670, B0749, P0132, P0137,**
 P0148, P0155, P0193, P0211
SSTTB, 2 vln, 2 vla, bsn, bc **K0183, K0209**
SSTTB, 2 vln, 2 vla, 2 cornettino, 3 tbn, bc **R0195**
SSTTB, 2 vln, 2 vla, 2 clar, vlne, bsn, bc **G0064**
SSTTB, 2 vln, 2 gamba, bc **P0124**
SSTTB, 2 vla, vlne, bc **P0118, P0145, P0163-64, P0166**
SSTTB, 3 vla, vlne, bc **P0119, P0121, P0151, P0179-80, P0215**
SSTTB, 4 vla, bc **M0311, P0187**
SSTTB, 4 vla, vlne, bc **P0154, P0178**

SST soli, SSTTB, 2 vln, vla, gamba, vlne, bc **P0130**

SAATB, bc **K0061, M0148, M0158, M0174, M0192**
SAATB, 2 vln, bc **B1016**
SAATB, 2 vln, 3 vla, bc **K0140**
SAATB, 2 vln, 3 vla, vltta, bsn, bc **E0097**
SAATB, 3 vla, bc **M0150**

SATTB **A0393, B0021, B0255, B0402, B1034, D0088, H0536,**
 K0031, K0043, M0002, S0388, S0396, S0416, S0424, T0155
SATTB, bc **A0297, A0310, B0006, B0011, B0029, B0036,**
 B0705, B1054, B1203, B1261, B1265, B1282, B1288-89,
 C0234-35, H0526-28, H0530-31, H0535, H0623, J0029,
 K0104, L0086, M0004, M0077, M0128, M0165, M0181,
 M0187, S0312, T0055, W0002
SATTB, vlne, bc **B0030**
SATTB, vln, 4 vla, bsn, bc **L0088**
SATTB, 2 vln, bc **B0688, F0106, F0113, F0131, M0140,**
 M0155, M0219, M0254
SATTB, 2 vln, bsn, bc **F0105, K0094**
SATTB, 2 vln, tbn, bc **K0094**
SATTB, 2 vln, 2 vla, bc **A0507, F9156, R0059, W0022**
SATTB, 2 vln, 2 vla, vlne, bc **B0031, K0208, S0434**
SATTB, 2 vln, 2 vla, bsn, bc **H0506, K0160, K0217, T0044**
SATTB, 2 vln, 2 vla, 2 clar, bc **F0136**
SATTB, 2 vln, 2 vla, 2 ob, bc **B0400**
SATTB, 2 vln, 2 vla, 2 tbtta, bsn, bc **P0293**
SATTB, 2 vln, 3 vla, bc **F0197, K0333, M0074, S0441**
SATTB, 2 vln, 3 vla, vlne, bc **K0086**
SATTB, 2 vln, 3 vla, bsn, bc **K0086, K0146, S0187**
SATTB, 2 vln, 3 vla, 2 cornettini, 3 tbn, bsn, bc **K0165**
SATTB, 2 vln, 4 vla, bc **B0467, B0474, S0420**
SATTB, 2 vln, 4 vla, 4 tpt, timp, bsn, bc **B0009**
SATTB, 2 vln, 4 vla, 4 tbn, vlne, bc **B0469**
SATTB, 2 vln, 4 vltta, 4 tbn, vlne, bc **B0457**
SATTB, 2 vln, 2 corn, bsn, bc **B1325**

SATTB, 2 vln, 2 clar, 3 tbn, vlne, bc **C0199**
SATTB, 2 vln, 2 tbn, bc **A0507**
SATTB, 2 vln, 2 tbn, bomb, bc **G0226**
SATTB, 2 vln, 3 tbn, bc **H0468, H0504, M0074**
SATTB, 2 vln, 4 tbn, bc **B0467, B0474**
SATTB, 3 vln, 5 vla, bc **M0276**
SATTB, 2 vla, 2 corn, bc **A0507**
SATTB, 3 vla, bc **A0544**
SATTB, 3 vla, vlne, bc **K0090, S0429, S0440**
SATTB, 3 vla, bsn, bc **K0090**
SATTB, 3 vla, 2 chitarrini, bc **S0441**
SATTB, 4 vla, bc **E0095-96, L0029, S0119, S0422-23,**
    S0425-27, S0430-32, S0438-39, S0442
SATTB, 4 vla, vlne, bsn, bc **G0224**
SATTB, 5 vla, bc **K0105**
SATTB, 5 vla, 4 tbn, vlne, bc **E0013**
SATTB, 3 gamba, bc **H0013**
SATTB, corn, 2 tbn, bc **B0022**
SATTB, 2 corn, bc **M0254**
SATTB, 2 corn, 2 tbn, bc **A0507**
SATTB, 2 tbtta, 3 tbn, bc **A0200**
SATTB, 5 instr, bc **A0421**

SA soli, SATTB, 2 vln, 2 vla, vlne, bc **A0220**
SATTB soli, SATTB, 6 vla, 2 corn, 4 tbn, bc **M0277**

SATBB, bc **B0415, J0017, K0107, R0056, S0314**
SATBB, 2 vln, 2 vla, vlne, bc **B0435**
SATBB, 3 vln, 2 vla, bsn, bc **F0036**
SATBB, 2 vln, 2 vla, 2 ob, bc **F0023**
SATBB, 2 vln, 2 vltta, bsn, bc **O0010**
SATBB, 2 vla, 2 vltta, 3 ob, 2 bsn, bc **O0002**

S solo, SSATB, 2 vln, 2 vla, bsn, bc **G0119**
S solo, SATTB, 4 vla, bsn, bc **B0408**
S solo, SATTB, 5 vla, bc **B0408, C0241**

SATB5, 2 vln, bc **B0067, B0069-71, B0074, B0080, B0091,**
    B0094-95, B0102, B0104, B0112, B0114-16, B0119, B0127,
    B0130, B0133, B0134, B0138-40, B0146, B0830, M0200

ATTTB, bc **A0286**

TTTTB, 2 vln, 2 tbn, bc **M0253**

à 6 & 12 **F0004**

6 vv **H0295**
6 vv, 2 vln, 3 vla, gamba, vlne, bc **B1241**

SSS, SSS, 3 vln, 3 vln rip **K0191**
SSSSSS, 5 vla, vlne, bc **S0190**

SSSSSA, bc **D0067**

SAB, SSS, bc **E0010**

SSSATB, 2 vln, 2 vla, bsn, bc **P0074**
SSSATB, 2 vln, 3 vla, 2 clar, timp, 3 tbn, bsn, bc **P0077**
SSSATB, 3 vla, 2 fl, bc **W0085**
SS, SATB, 4 gambas, bc **C0180**

SSSTTB, 2 vln, 2 vla, vlne, bc **P0201**

SSAATT, bc **A0011**
SAT, SAT, 2 vln, 2 vla, bc **R0145**

SSAATB, bc **A0019, B0738, S0446, S0451, S0462, S0466, S0473**
SSAATB, 2 vln, 2 vla, bc **D0070**
SSAATB, 2 vln, 2 vla, bsn, bc **G0114**
SSAATB, 2 vln, 2 vla, 2 piffari, bsn, bc **A0516**
SSAATB, 2 vln, 5 vla, 2 clar, timp, 3 tbn, bc **T0048**

SSATTB **B0341, B0603, B1168, D0066, D0072, E0170, F0185,**
    G0046-47, H0539, N0071, N0073, N0101-02, S0295, S0322,
    T0059, T0061, T0064
SSATTB, bc **A0182, A0188, A0207, A0230, A0236, A0246-47,**
    A0260, A0302, A0317, A0331, A0377, B0033, B0584,
    B0597, B0604, B0667, B0897, B1150, B1173, B1204, B1256,
    B1258, B1260, D0005, D0085, E0004, F0043, F0057,
    F0181-82, H0026-27, H0029, H0034, H0037, H0041,
    H0043, H0053, H0056-57, H0059, H0066, H0068, H0070,
    H0072, H0074, H0077, H0080, H0085, H0092-93, H0095,
    H0097-99, H0111, H0117, H0122, H0125, H0132, H0138,
    H0145, H0153, H0158, H0162, H0167-70, H0178, H0186,
    H0187-89, H0204, H0222, H0224, H0233, H0236, H0239,
    H0253, H0263, H0266, H0279, J0028, K0125, K0177,
    K0195, M0278, M0297, S0281, S0447, S0454, S0464
SSATTB, 2 vln, bc **B0612-13, B0928, C0151, H0194-95, K0077,**
    K0093, M0220, W0058
SSATTB, 2 vln, tbn, vlne, bc **B0460, S0080**

SSATTB, 2 vln, vla, 4 instr, bc **F0065**
SSATTB, 2 vln, 2 vla, bc **K0087**
SSATTB, 2 vln, 2 vla, vlne, bc **H0571**
SSATTB, 2 vln, 2 vla, vlne, gamba, bc **F0060**
SSATTB, 2 vln, 2 vla, vlne, spinetto, bc **F0060**
SSATTB, 2 vln, 2 vla, bsn, bc **K0206, S0367**
SSATTB, 2 vln, 2 vla, vltta, vlne, bc **B0478**
SSATTB, 2 vln, 2 vla, 2 vltta, clar, 2 corn, 4 tbn, bc **B0453**
SSATTB, 2 vln, 2 vla, 2 gamba, bc **C0222**
SSATTB, 2 vln, 2 vla, 2 corn, bc **H0485**
SSATTB, 2 vln, 2 vla, 2 corn, bsn, bc **W0091**
SSATTB, 2 vln, 2 vla, 2 corn, 2 clar, 4 tbn, bc **S0265**
SSATTB, 2 vln, 2 vla, 2 corn, 2 tbn, bsn, bc **W0005**
SSATTB, 2 vln, 2 vla, 2 corn, 3 tbn, vlne, bc **P0083**
SSATTB, 2 vln, 2 vla, 2 cornettini, 2 tbn, bc **P0062**
SSATTB, 2 vln, 2 vla, 2 corn, 2 fl, tbn, bc **C0236**
SSATTB, 2 vln, 2 vla, 2 clar, 4 tbn, vlne, bc **S0260**
SSATTB, 2 vln, 2 vla, 3 clar, timp, 2 tbn, vlne, bc **W0041**
SSATTB, 2 vln, 2 vla, 2 shawm, timp, bsn, bc **S0379**
SSATTB, 2 vln, 2 vla, 3 tbn, vlne, bsn, bc **E0175**
SSATTB, 2 vln, 2 vla, 4 tbn, bc **R0182**
SSATTB, 2 vln, 2 vla, 4 tbn, bsn, bc **S0355**
SSATTB, 2 vln, 3 vla, bc **K0182, P0079**
SSATTB, 2 vln, 3 vla, vlne, bc **E0101**
SSATTB, 2 vln, 3 vla, vc, bc **S0629**
SSATTB, 2 vln, 3 vla, bsn, bc **G0100, K0161, P0082, P0294, T0045**
SSATTB, 2 vln, 3 vla, 2 gamba, bc **C0101**
SSATTB, 2 vln, 3 vla, 2 corn, bsn, bc **C0115**
SSATTB, 2 vln, 3 vla, 2 corn, tbn, bc **C0115**
SSATTB, 2 vln, 3 vla, 2 corn, 2 clar, 4 tbn, vlne, bc **S0239**
SSATTB, 2 vln, 3 vla, 2 corn, 2 fl, bsn, bc **A0486**
SSATTB, 2 vln, 3 vla, 2 corn, 2 fl, tbn, bc **A0486**
SSATTB, 2 vln, 3 vla, 2 corn, 3 tbn, bsn, bc **K0193**
SSATTB, 2 vln, 3 vla, 2 corn, 4 tbn, vlne, bc **S0028**
SSATTB, 2 vln, 3 vla, 2 corn, 4 tbn, vlne, bass vla, bc **K0111**
SSATTB, 2 vln, 3 vla, 2 corn, 4 tbn, vlne, bsn, bc **K0111**
SSATTB, 2 vln, 3 vla, 2 cornettini, 4 tbn, bsn, bc **K0185**
SSATTB, 2 vln, 3 vla, 3 tpt, 2 clar, 4 bomb (3 piff, bsn), timp, bc **K0143**
SSATTB, 2 vln, 3 vla, 2 clar, vlne, bc **R0060**
SSATTB, 2 vln, 3 vla, 2 clar, timp, vlne, bc **L0081**
SSATTB, 2 vln, 3 vla, 2 clar, 3 tbn, vlne, bc **R0047, R0050**
SSATTB, 2 vln, 3 vla, tromba, bc **R0138**
SSATTB, 2 vln, 3 vla, 2 ob, bsn, bc **S0362**
SSATTB, 2 vln, 3 vla, 4 tbn, bc **R0043, S0087**
SSATTB, 2 vln, 4 vla, bc **S0674, T0047**
SSATTB, 2 vln, 4 vla, vlne, bc **S0074**
SSATTB, 2 vln, 4 vla, 2 cornettini, bc **P0062**
SSATTB, 2 vln, 4 vla, 2 clar, 4 tbn, vlne, bc **B0471**
SSATTB, 2 vln, 4 vla, 4 tbn, bc **F0190, S0090**

SSATTB, 2 vln, 4 vla, 4 tbn, vlne, bc **S0085**
SSATTB, 2 vln, 5 vla, bc **K0180**
SSATTB, 2 vln, 5 vla, 2 clar, 4 tbn, vlne, bc **R0049**
SSATTB, 2 vln, vltta, vlne, bc **B0460**
SSATTB, 2 vln, vltta, 3 tbn, bc **B0425**
SSATTB, 2 vln, 2 vltta, vlne, bc **E0107**
SSATTB, 2 vln, 2 vltta, 2 gamba, bc **H0016**
SSATTB, 2 vln, 3 vltta, gamba, bc **E0093**
SSATTB, 2 vln, 4 vltta, 2 clar, 4 tbn, bc **S0088**
SSATTB, 2 vln, 2 gamba, bc **E0100**
SSATTB, 2 vln, 2 corn, 3 tbn, bc **R0113**
SSATTB, 2 vln, 2 corn, 3 tbn, bsn, bc **C0115**
SSATTB, 2 vln, 2 corn, 4 tbn, bc **C0115, R0119**
SSATTB, 2 vln, 3 tpt, bsn, bc **B0558**
SSATTB, 2 vln, 2 clar, 2 tbn, timp, bsn, bc **K0154**
SSATTB, 2 vln, 2 clar, 3 tbn, bc **H0339**
SSATTB, 2 vln, 2 clar, 2 tbtta, timp, 4 tbn, bc **S0310**
SSATTB, 2 vln, 2 clar, 4 tbtta, timp, 2 tbn, bc **S0308**
SSATTB, 2 vln, 3 tbn, bc **A0490, B1108, H0198, Z0058**
SSATTB, 2 vln, 3 tbn, vlne, bc **B0482**
SSATTB, 2 vln, 4 tbn, bc **H0199, H0502, K0212, M0252**
SSATTB, 2 vln, 4 tbn, vlne, bc **S0261**
SSATTB, 2 vln, 4 tbn, bsn, bc **J0002**
SSATTB, 2 vln, tbtta, timp, bc **A0431**
SSATTB, 2 vln, 3 tbtta, bc **B1108**
SSATTB, 2 vln, 4 instr, bsn, bc **F0065**
SSATTB, 3 vln, bc **A0456**
SSATTB, 3 vln, 2 vla, vlne, bc **R0156**
SSATTB, 3 vln, 3 tpt, 3 tbn, cym, vlne, bc **B1424**
SSATTB, vla, 2 vltta, bc **F0049**
SSATTB, 3 vla, bc **D0058**
SSATTB, 3 vla, vlne, bc **E0104**
SSATTB, 3 vla, 2 vltta, bsn, bc **P0296**
SSATTB, 3 vla, 2 corn, vlne, bc **B1332**
SSATTB, 3 vla, 3 fl, vlne, bc **B0432**
SSATTB, 3 vla, 3 tbn, bc **H0510, H0513**
SSATTB, 3 vla, 3 tbn, vlne, bc **H0519**
SSATTB, 4 vla, bc **D0055, D0068, E0102, E0108**
SSATTB, 4 vla, vlne, bc **B0481, T0163, T0168**
SSATTB, 4 vla, bass vla, bc **S0094**
SSATTB, 4 vla, 2 tbn, bc **F0013**
SSATTB, 4 vla, 4 tbn, vlne, bc **S0039**
SSATTB, 5 vla, bc **C0137**
SSATTB, 5 vla, bass vla, bc **S0060**
SSATTB, 5 vla, 2 vltta, 4 tbn, vlne, bc **S0036**
SSATTB, 5 vla, 3 tbn, vlne, bc **B0404**
SSATTB, 5 vla, 4 tbn, bc **S0079**
SSATTB, 6 vla, bc **P0290**
SSATTB, 6 vla, vlne, bc **B0439**
SSATTB, 4 vltta, 3 tbn, bass vla, vlne, bc **S0075**
SSATTB, 2 corn, 3 tbn, bc **S0411**
SSATTB, 2 corn, 4 tbn, bc **M0252**

SSATTB, 2 clar, 3 tbn, bc **B1108, H0271**
SSATTB, 2 clar, 3 tbtta, bc **B1108**
SSATTB, 5 instr, bc **C0116**
SSATTB, 6 instr, bc **H0503**

SSATTB soli, SSATTB, 2 vln, vla, vltta, vc, corn, 2 clar, 2
 tbn, vlne, bsn, bc **L0034**
SSATTB soli, SSATTB, 2 vln, 2 vltta, vc, 2 corn, 2 clar, 2
 tbn, vlne, bsn, bc **L0044**
SSATTB soli, SSATTB, 3 vltta, gamba, 2 corn, 2 tbn, vlne,
 bsn, bc **L0040**
T solo, SSATTB, 4 vla, winds ad lib., bsn, bc **S0217**

SSATBB **T0057, T0068**
SSATBB, bc **B0541, H0209**
SSATBB, 2 vln, bc **G0197**
SSATBB, 2 vln, 2 vla, vlne, bc **B1371, F0191, P0204**
SSATBB, 2 vln, 2 vla, 2 corn, 2 clar, tbn, vlne, bc **M0030**
SSATBB, 2 vln, 2 vla, 2 corn, 4 clar, timp, bc **F0163**
SSATBB, 2 vln, 2 vla, 2 tpt, 3 tbn, bc **B1243**
SSATBB, 2 vln, 2 vltta, ob, vlne, bc **O0018**
SSATBB, 2 vln, corn, 3 tbn, bc **F0052**
SSATBB, 2 vln, 2 corn, 2 clar, 3 tbn, vlne, bc **M0030**
SSATBB, 4 vla, bc **C0190**
SSATBB, 4 vltta, 2 trombe basse, 2 ob, 3 tbn, vlne, bsn, bc
 B0551

SSTTBB, 2 vln, 2 vla, bc **A0425**

SAATTB, 2 vln, 3 vltta, bc **E0091**

SATTBB, 2 vln, bc **M0010**

SATBBB, 2 vln, 2 clar, 2 tbn, timp, bsn, bc **A0520**

AATTBB, 3 vla, 2 bsn, bc **C0107**

à 7 **F0019**

SSB, SSSB **A0537**

SSSAATT, bc **M0249**

SSSAATB, 2 vln, 2 vla, bc **D0048**
SSSAATB, 2 vla, bc **D0047**

SSSATTB, bc **H0192**
STB, SSATB, vln, vla, 3 tbn, bc **H0164**
SSSATTB, vln, 2 vla, bc **D0071**
SSSATTB, 2 vln, 3 vla, bc **D0056**
SSSATTB, 2 vln, 3 vla, 2 clar, 2 tpt, timp, bsn, bc **C0135**
SSSATTB, 3 vla, bc **D0061**

SSB, SATB, 2 vln, vlne, bc **D0001-04, D0006-12, D0014-21,
 D0024-25, D0027-28, D0031-32**
SSB, SATB, 2 vln, bsn, bc **D0001-04, D0006-12, D0014-21,
 D0024-25, D0027-28, D0031-32**
SB, SSATB, 2 vln, 2 vla, bc **A0384**
SSB, SATB, 2 vla, 2 clar, bc **M0294**
SSB, SATB, 2 vla, 2 tromba marina, bc **M0294**

SSST, TTB, bc **B1250**

SSAATTB, bc **A0258, A0344, S0481**
SAT, SATB, bc **A0342**
SSAATTB, 2 vln, 4 vla, bc **D0053**
SSAATTB, 2 vln, 5 vla, bc **K0179, K0181**
SAT, SATB, 2 vln, 2 tbtta, bc **A0264**

SSATTTB, bc **J0023, M0184**
TT, SSATB, 2 vln, 3 tbn, bc **H0040**
TT, SSATB, 2 corn, 3 tbn, bc **H0040**

SATB, SAB, bc **B0213**
SSATTBB, 2 vln, bc **C0120, C0121, C0184**
SATB, STB, 2 vln, vla, vlne, bc **A0444**
STB, SATB, 2 vln, 2 vla, bsn, bc **P0056**
SSATTBB, 2 vln, 2 vla, 5 tbn, vlne, bc **R0068**
SSATTBB, 2 vln, 3 vla, bc **S0671**
SSATTBB, 2 vln, 3 vla, 2 clar, 4 tbn, vlne, bc **R0051**
SSATTBB, 2 vln, vltta, bsn, bc **F0037**
SSATTBB, 2 vln, 2 vltta, tbn, bc **B0498**
SSATTBB, 2 vln, 2 vltta, 2 fl, bsn, bc **O0012**
SSATTBB, 2 vln, 2 vltta, 2 ob, bsn, bc **O0012**
SSATTBB, 3 vln, 3 vltta, bsn, bc **O0034**
SSATTBB, 4 vln, 2 vla, 4 gamba, bsn, bc **F0150**
TB, SSATB, 3 gamba, bc **R0179**
SSATTBB, 2 vla, 2 corn, 5 tbn, vlne, bc **R0068**

SSTTTBB, 2 vln, 2 vla, 2 corn, 5 tbn, theorbo, vlne, bc **R0166**

SSTTTBB, 2 vln, 2 vla, 2 corn, 5 tbn, spinett, vlne, bc **R0166**

ATB, SATB, 2 vln, 2 vla, vlne, bc **H0561**

SAATTBB, 2 vln, 2 vla, 2 ob, taille, bsn, bc **Z0033**

ATB, SATB, 2 vln, 2 gamba, 2 ob, bsn, bc **L0112**

SAATTBB, 3 vla, 3 tbn, bsn, bc **D0052**

TB, SATTB, 3 vla, vlne, bc **C0242**

à 8 **F0016**

8 vv **S0349**

8 vv, bc **H0507, S0599**

8 vv, 5 vla, 2 corn, 4 tbn, vlne, bc **S0106**

8 vv, 5 instr. **B1330**

8 vv, 5 strings, 2 corn, 5 tbn, colascione, bc **S0084**

SSSS, SSSS, bc **S0615**

SSSSSATB, 2 vln, 2 vla, bc **W0061**

SSAT, SSAT **S0618, S0632**

SSSAATTB, bc **M0160, M0213**

SSAT, SATB, bc **M0279**

B solo, SSAT, SATB, 2 vln, 4 gamba, bc **S0421**

SAB, SSATB, 2 vln, vla, vlne, bc **A0311**

SSST, ATBB, bc **H0146, H0201**

SSAT, STBB, 2 tbtta, 2 tbn, bc **H0244**

S solo, SSST, ATTB, 4 bsn, bc **A0235**

SSTB, STTB, bc **B1254**

ATT, SSATB, 2 vln, 2 vla, 2 gamb, timp, bsn, bc **B0153**

SATB, SATB **A0066-73, A0547, B0012, B0014, B0024-25, B0317-21, H0525, S0025, S0030, S0035, S0183, S0196, S0768, S0773, V0003**

SATB, SATB, bc **A0020, A0025, A0027, A0035, A0047, A0061, A0065, A0074, A0094, A0128, A0138, A0141, A0144-46, A0241, A0322, A0336, A0343, A0369, B0015, B0019, B0028, B0032, B0167, B0188, B1249, C0232, F0184, H0115, H0133, H0143, H0223, H0246, H0264, H0282, H0494, H0524, H0529, H0533, H0537, H0626, J0010-11, J0014, J0016-17, J0022, J0025, J0031, K0147, M0119, M0141, M0156, M0203-05, M0258, M0272-73, M0302, M0308, P0002-03, P0018, P0021, P0024, P0027, P0047-50, S0202, S0597, S0601, S0603-04, S0606, S0611-14, S0616-17, S0619-20, S0622**

SATB, SATB, vlne, bc **H0625, S0017, S0023, S0027, S0032, S0037, S0041, S0054-55, S0061-64, S0067-68, S0070, S0095**

SATB, SATB, lute, bc **W0084**

SATB, SATB, vlne, bc **M0145**

SATB, SATB, vln, corn, bc **R0110**

SATB, SATB, 2 vln, bc **A0480, B0082-83, B0086, B0090, B0092-93, B0097, B0105, B0108, B0120, B0124, B0129, B0143-44, H0062, M0137, M0151, M0170, M0173, R0092, R0130**

SATB, SATB, 2 vln, tbn, bc **H0463**

SATB, SATB, 2 vln, vla, bc **M0129**

SATB, SATB, 2 vln, vla, vlne, bc **A0261**

SATB, SATB, 2 vln, vla, vltta, 2 corn, 3 tbn, bc **R0126**

SATB, SATB, 2 vln, vla, 2 vltta, bc **R0175**

SATB, SATB, 2 vln, vla, 2 vltta, 2 corn, 3 tbn, bc **R0105, R0137, R0149, R0152**

SATB, SATB, 2 vln, vla, timp, 3 tbn, bc **K0290**

SATB, SATB, 2 vln, vla, 2 clar, bc **M0355, M0358, M0364, M0375**

SATB, SATB, 2 vln, 2 vla, bc **R0163**

SATB, SATB, 2 vln, 2 vla, vlne, bc **B1336, K0122**

SATB, SATB, 2 vln, 2 vla, vc, bc **K0265**

SATB, SATB, 2 vln, 2 vla, bsn, bc **C0195, F0183, P0080, R0006**

SATB, SATB, 2 vln, 2 vla, 2 corn, 2 tpt, 2 tbn, bc **S0325**

SATB, SATB, 2 vln, 2 vla, 2 corn, 2 tpt, 2 fl, timp, 3 tbn, harp, cymbals, bsn, vc, bc **K0279**

SATB, SATB, 2 vln, 2 vla, 2 corn, 4 tpt, 3 tbn, timp, bc **H0514**

SATB, SATB, 2 vln, 2 vla, 2 corn, 4 tpt, timp, 3 tbn, vlne, bc **B0512, B0533**

SATB, SATB, 2 vln, 2 vla, 2 corn, 4 tpt, timp, 3 tbn, bsn, bc **R0031**

SATB, SATB, 2 vln, 2 vla, 2 corn, clar, 3 tbn, bsn, bc **R0135**

SATB, SATB, 2 vln, 2 vla, 2 corn, 2 clar, 3 tbn, bc **H0499**
SATB, SATB, 2 vln, 2 vla, 2 corn, 2 clar, 3 tbn, vlne, bc
 B0540
SATB, SATB, 2 vln, 2 vla, 2 corn, 3 tbn, bsn, bc **R0109,
 R0133**
SATB, SATB, 2 vln, 2 vla, 2 corn, 3 tbn, tbtta, bsn, bc
 R0161
SATB, SATB, 2 vln, 2 vla, 2 tpt, bsn, timp, bc **E0133**
SATB, SATB, 2 vln, 2 vla, clar, 3 tromba, bc **B0359**
SATB, SATB, 2 vln, 2 vla, 2 clar, 3 tbn, bc **B0360**
SATB, SATB, 2 vln, 2 vla, 3 tbn, vlne, bc **B0532**
SATB, SATB, 2 vln, 3 vla, bc **H0467, H0474**
SATB, SATB, 2 vln, 3 vla, vltta, vlne, bc **B1326**
SATB, SATB, 2 vln, 3 vla, tbn, vlne, bc **B1326**
SATB, SATB, 2 vln, 3 vla, corn, 2 cornettini, 5 tpt, timp, 3
 tbn, bc **K0189**
SATB, SATB, 2 vln, 3 vla, 2 corn, 4 tpt, 3 tbn, timp, bc
 B0539
SATB, SATB, 2 vln, 3 vla, 2 corn, 6 tpt, timp, 3 tbn,
 theorbo **B0538**
SATB, SATB, 2 vln, 3 vla, 2 corn, 2 clar, 4 tbn, vlne, bc
 B0476
SATB, SATB, 2 vln, 3 vla, 2 corn, 2 tbn, vlne, bsn, bc
 P0206
SATB, SATB, 2 vln, 3 vla, 2 cornettini, tpt, 2 clar, 2 tbn,
 bsn **K0167**
SATB, SATB, 2 vln, 3 vla, 2 ob, 4 tbn, bc **K0108**
SATB, SATB, 2 vln, 5 vla, 2 tpt, 3 tbn, bc **B0530**
SATB, SATB, 2 vln, vltta, 2 corn, bc **R0118**
SATB, SATB, 2 vln, vltta, 3 tbn, vlne, bc **B1326**
SATB, SATB, 2 vln, 2 vltta, tbtta, violoncino, bc **R0147**
SATB, SATB, 2 vln, 6 vltta, bsn, bc **K0332**
SATB, SATB, 2 vln, 2 corn, 2 clar, 3 tbn, vlne, bc **H0627**
SATB, SATB, 2 vln, 2 corn, 3 tbn, bc **H0481, H0486**
SATB, SATB, 2 vln, 2 cornettino, 2 tbn, 2 bsn, bc **S0437**
SATB, SATB, 2 vln, 2 clar, bsn, bc **M0355, M0358, M0364,
 M0375**
SATB, SATB, 2 vln, 2 tbn, bsn, bc **F0183**
SATB, SATB, 2 vln, 3 tbn, bc **H0474**
SATB, SATB, 2 vln, 4 tbn, vlne, bc **B1326**
SATB, SATB, 3 vln, 2 tbn, vlne, bc **B1335**
SATB, SATB, 3 vln, 3 tbn, bc **B1323**
SATB, SATB, 4 vln, vla, 4 vltta, bc **R0074**
SATB, SATB, 4 vln, vltta, bsn, bc **F0040**
SATB, SATB, 2 vla, 2 corn, bsn, bc **F0183**
SATB, SATB, 2 vla, 4 tbn, bc **H0522**
SATB, SATB, 3 vla, bc **B0216**
SATB, SATB, 3 vla, vc, vlne, bc **B0217**
SATB, SATB, 3 vla, 2 corn, bc **H0474**
SATB, SATB, 3 vla, 2 clar, 3 tbtta, 4 tbn, vlne, bc **H0515**
SATB, SATB, 4 vla, 2 corn, 3 tbn, bc **H0497**

SATB, SATB, 4 vla, 2 corn, 3 tbn, org **H0473**
SATB, SATB, 4 vla, 3 tbn, vlne, bc **H0629**
SATB, SATB, 3 vltta, bc **B0215**
SATB, SATB, 4 vltta, 4 tbn, bc **B0477**
SATB, SATB, 2 corn, bc **R0089**
SATB, SATB, 2 corn, 2 tbn, bsn, bc **F0183**
SATB, SATB, 2 corn, 3 tbn, bc **H0474**
SATB, SATB, 2 tbtta, bc **A0290**
SATB, SATB, instr, bc **K0079**

SS soli, SATB, SATB, 2 vln, vla, 6 vltta, bsn, bc **R0083**

SSAATTBB **S0047, S0327**
SSAATTBB, bc **A0494, F0005, G0127, S0480**
SSAATTBB, vlne, bc **B0500**
SSAATTBB, 2 vln, bc **C0196, C0201, K0075**
SSAATTBB, 2 vln, vlne, bc **B0442**
SSAATTBB, 2 vln, 2 vla, vlne, bc **P0247**
SSAATTBB, 2 vln, 2 vla, bsn, bc **R0146**
SSAATTBB, 2 vln, 2 vla, 2 corn, 3 tbn, vlne, bsn, bc **B0466**
SSAATTBB, 2 vln, 3 vla, 2 corn, 3 tbn, bsn, bc **K0152**
SSAATTBB, 2 vln, 2 vla, 2 corn, 4 tbn, vlne, bc **B0466**
SSAATTBB, 2 vln, 2 vla, clar, 3 tbn, bc **H0425**
SSAATTBB, 2 vln, 2 vla, 4 tbn, vlne, bc **K0095**
SSAATTBB, 2 vln, 3 vla, bc **B1322**
SSAATTBB, 2 vln, 3 vla, vlne, bc **B0450**
SSAATTBB, 2 vln, 3 vla, 2 clar, timp, bsn, bc **A0411**
SSAATTBB, 2 vln, 3 vla, 2 clar, 3 tbn, bc **B1240**
SSAATTBB, 2 vln, 4 vla, gamba, 2 corn, 2 clar, 4 tbn, vlne,
 bc **F0198**
SSAATTBB, 2 vln, 4 vla, 2 corn, 3 tbn, vlne, bc **B0454**
SSAATTBB, 2 vln, 4 vla, 2 corn, 5 tbn, vlne, bc **B0470**
SSAATTBB, 2 vln, 4 vla, 2 clar, vlne, bc **S0258**
SSAATTBB, 2 vln, 4 vla, 4 tbn, bc **B0464**
SSAATTBB, 2 vln, 4 vla, 4 tbn, vlne, bc **B0461**
SSAATTBB, 2 vln, 5 vla, 2 corn, bsn, vlne, bc **B0466**
SSAATTBB, 2 vln, 5 vla, 2 corn, tbn, vlne, bc **B0466**
SSAATTBB, 2 vln, 5 vla, 2 corn, 2 clar, 3 tbn, vlne,
 bc **S0277**
SSAATTBB, 2 vln, 5 vla, 7 tbn, bc **K0138**
SSAATTBB, 2 vln, 2 vltta, 3 tbn, bc **B0431**
SSAATTBB, 2 vln, 2 vltta, 4 tbn, theorbo, bc **B0465**
SSAATTBB, 2 vln, 4 vltta, 2 corn, 2 clar, 5 tbn, bc **B0472**
SSAATTBB, 2 vln, 2 gamba, 2 corn, 3 tbn, vlne, bc **B0501**
SSAATTBB, 2 vln, 2 corn, bc **C0198**
SSAATTBB, 2 vln, 2 tbn, vlne, bc **B0421**
SSAATTBB, 2 vln, 3 tbn, bc **B0468, B1322**
SSAATTBB, 4 vln, 2 clar, bc **C0221**
SSAATTBB, 2 vla, bc **D0062**
SSAATTBB, 2 vla, 4 vltta, vlne, bass vla, bc **S0022**

SSAATTBB, 3 vla, 4 tbn, bc **B0444**
SSAATTBB, 4 vla, bc **C0191**
SSAATTBB, 4 vla, vlne, bc **S0065**
SSAATTBB, 5 vla, 2 clar, 3 tbn, vlne, bc **S0257**
SSAATTBB, 5 vla, 5 tbn, vlne, bc **S0116**

SSATB, ATB, 2 vln, vla, vlne, bsn, bc **E0168**
SSATB, ATB, 2 vln, vltta, 3 tbn, bc **K0123**
SSATB, ATB, 2 corn, bc **H0255**
SSATB, ATB, 2 tbtta, bc **H0255**

SAB, SATTB, bc **S0220**

SSAB, ATTB, bc **A0187, A0287, A0329, A0357, A0363,**
A0368, A0373, B1262, B1263, P0105, S0178, S0180
SSAB, ATTB, 2 vln, 2 tpt, 3 tbn, trombone grosso, bc
B1324
SSAB, ATTB, 2 tbtta, bc **A0333**

SSAT, ATTB **H0532**
SSAT, ATTB, bc **B0003, B1251, B1252, B1255, B1257, B1259,**
B1264, C0230, H0061, H0103, M0001
SSAT, ATTB, 2 clar, 2 gamba, bc **A0394**
SSAT, ATTB, 2 tbtta, 2 gamba, bc **A0394**

SSATTTTB, 2 vln, 2 vla, 2 tbtta, 2 corn, 2 tbn, bc **F0015**

SSATB, TTB, bc **B1253, H0067, H0078**
SATB, STTB, 2 vln, bc **M0126**
SSATTTBB, 2 vln, 4 vla, 2 gamba, bc **S0254**

SSTB, ATBB, bc **H0273**

SATB, ATTB **B0027**
SATB, ATTB, bc **B0023, B0026, B0034**
SATB, ATTB, 4 instr, bc **H0622**

à 9 **F0010**
9 vv, 9 inst in 3 groups **B0403**

SSSAB, SATB, bc **D0077**

SSSAAATTB, 4 vla, gamba, bc **D0054**

SATB, SSATB, bc **B0571, H0278**
SSATB, SATB, 2 vln, bc **K0074**
SSATB, SATB, 2 vln, 2 vla, 2 corn, 4 tbn, bsn, bc **B0385**
SSATB, SATB, 2 vln, 2 vla, 3 tbn, bsn, bc **A0487**
SSATB, SATB, 2 vln, 2 corn, 4 tbtta, 3 tbn, vlne, bsn, bomb,
bc **B1352**

SSSATTTBB, vln, 4 vla, bc **D0057**
STB, SSATTB, 2 corn, 2 tbn, bc **H0256**

SSSATTBBB, 3 vla, bc **D0063**

SSATB, ATTB, bc **H0254**
SSATTB, ATB, bc **B0004, B0035**
SATB, SATTB, bc **J0033**
SSATB, ATTB, bc **H0254**
SATB, SATTB, 2 vln, vla, bc **M0136**
SSAATTTBB, 2 vln, 3 vla, bc **D0051**

SSABB, ATBB, bc **H0083**

10 vv **S0352**
10 vv, TB soli, 3 vln, 3 tbn, bc **M0259**
10 vv, TB soli, 3 corn, 3 tbn, bc **M0259**

SSB, SSB, SATB, 2 vln, bc **A0506**

SSATB, SSATB **A0510**
SSATB, SSATB, 2 vln, 2 vla, bc **S0324**
SSATB, SSATB, 2 vln, 2 vla, bsn, bc **S0368, S0376**
SSATB, SSATB, 2 vln, 2 vla, 2 corn, 4 clar, timp, 3 tbn, bsn,
bc **S0205**
SSATB, SSATB, 2 vln, 2 vla, 2 corn, 2 tbn, bsn, bc **S0358**
SSATB, SSATB, 2 vln, 2 vla, 2 corn, 3 tbn, vlne, bc **B0392**
SSSSAATTBB, 2 vln, 2 vla, 2 corn, 3 tbn, bsn, bc **S0191**
SSATB, SSATB, 2 vln, 2 vla, 2 corn, 3 tbn, bsn, bc **S0365,**
S0392

SSATB, SSATB, 2 vln, 2 vla, ob, 2 taille, bc **A0395**
SSATB, SSATB, 2 vln, 2 vla, 2 shawm, timp, 3 tbn, bsn, bc
     S0375
SSATB, SSATB, 2 vln, 3 vla, bsn, bc **P0036**
SSATB, SSATB, 2 vln, 2 vltta, 2 corn, 3 tbn, bsn, bc **B0410**
SSSSAATTBB, 2 vln, 2 vltta bassono, 2 corn, 3 tbn, tromba,
     bc **R0148**
SSATB, SSATB, 2 vln, 2 clar, 3 tbn, bc **S0221**
SSATB, SSATB, 3 gamba, bc **A0503**
SSATB, SSATB, 3 gamba, bc **A0503**
SSATB, SAATB, bc **J0015**
SSSAAATTBB, vln, 2 vla, 3 gamba, 2 baryton, bc **D0065**

SSSAATTTBB, bc **D0079**
SSATB, SATTB, bc **J0019**
SSSAATTTBB, 2 vln, 2 vla, 2 corn, 4 tbn, 5 tbtta, vlne, bc
     B0455

SSSAB, ATTBB, bc **A0289**

STBBB, SSATB, 2 vln, 2 vla, bsn, bc **A0448**

SSAATTTTBB, 2 vln, 2 vla, 4 clar, 3 tbn, vlne, bc **B1245**

SSATB, ATTBB, bc **A0345**

11
SSAATTB, SSSA, vln, 4 vla, 6 lute, bc **D0064**

SATB, SATB, SSA, 4 tbn, bc **A0240**

SSATTBB, SATB, 2 vln, vlne, bc **H0006**

12 vv **B1332**

SSATTB, SSATTB, bc **M0269, M0275**
SSATTB, SSATTB, 2 vln, 2 vla, bc **M0378**
SSATTB, SSATTB, 2 vln, 4 tbn, bc **M0266, M0271**
SSATTB, SSATTB, 4 vln, 4 tbn, vlne, bc **S0282**

SSATTB, SSATTB, vla, bc **M0239**
SSATTB, SSATTB, 2 corn, 4 tbn, bc **M0266, M0271**
SSATTB, SSATTB, 2 corn, 4 tbn, 6 bsn, bc **M0309**
SSATTB, SSATTB, 6 instr, 4 tbtta, bc **M0256**

SSSAAAATTTBB, vln, 4 vla, bc **D0069**
SSSAAATTTBBB, bc **F0047**
SATB, SATB, SATB, bc **H0241, M0274**
SATB, SATB, SATB, 2 vln, vla, timp, vlne, bc **S0435**
SATB, SATB, SATB, 2 vln, vla, timp, bsn, bc **S0435**
SSAB, SATB, ATTB, 2 vln, vla, 2 corn, 2 tbtta, timp, 4 tbn,
     vlne, bc **B1334**
SATB, SATB, SATB, 2 vln, 3 vla, 2 corn, 3 clar, 3 tbn, vlne,
     bc **K0080**
SATB, SATB, SATB, 2 vln, tbn, timp, vlne, bc **S0435**
SATB, SATB, SATB, 2 vln, tbn, timp, bsn, bc **S0435**
SATB, SATB, SATB, vla, 2 corn, timp, vlne, bc **S0435**
SATB, SATB, SATB, vla, 2 corn, timp, bsn, bc **S0435**
SATB, SATB, SATB, vla, 2 tpt, timp, vlne, bc **S0435**
SATB, SATB, SATB, vla, 2 tpt, timp, bsn, bc **S0435**
SATB, SATB, SATB, vla, 2 clar, timp, vlne, bc **S0435**
SATB, SATB, SATB, vla, 2 clar, timp, bsn, bc **S0435**
SATB, SATB, SATB, 2 corn, tbn, timp, vlne, bc **S0435**
SATB, SATB, SATB, 2 corn, tbn, timp, bsn, bc **S0435**
SATB, SATB, SATB, 2 tpt, tbn, timp, vlne, bc **S0435**
SATB, SATB, SATB, 2 tpt, tbn, timp, bsn, bc **S0435**
SATB, SATB, SATB, 2 clar, tbn, timp, vlne, bc **S0435**
SATB, SATB, SATB, 2 clar, tbn, timp, bsn, bc **S0435**

13
SATB, SATB, SATB, B, 2 vln, vla, vlne, bc **A0522**

14
SSATTB, SSAATTBB, bc **C0233**
SATB, SATB, SSATTB, 2 corn, 3 clar, 5 tbtta, 4 tbn,
     bc **M0240**
SATB, SATB, SSATTB, 2 corn, 4 tbn, bc **M0282**

SSAATTB, T, SATBBB, 2 vln, 3 vla, 2 gamba, 2 fl, 2 corn, 2
     clar, bsn, bc **C0090**

15
SSATB, SSATB, SSATB (echo choirs) **P0116**

16
SSSAATTTBB, SAB, SSA, 2 vln, vltta, bc **D0050**

SSTTBB, SSATB, SSATB, bc **D0059**

SSATTB, SSATTB, SATB, corn, clar, 4 tbtta, 8 tbn, bc
  M0284

SSAATTBB, SSAATTBB, 4 vln, 8 vla, 4 rec, 2 ob, 2 corn,
  2 tpt **B0545, B0549**

18
SSATTB, SSATTB, SSATTB, 2 vln, 4 tbn, bc **M0300**
SSATTB, SSATTB, SSATTB, 2 corn, 4 tbn, bc **M0300**

20
SATB, SATB, SATB, SATB, SATB, bc **M0286**

Liturgical Occasions Index

SUNDAYS AND RELATED LITURGICAL OCCASIONS ARRANGED BY
LITURGICAL CALENDAR, OTHER OCCASIONS ALPHABETICALLY

*M*anuscript Sources Index

A-GÖ (Benediktinerstift, Furth bei Göttweig, Austria **B0550,**
K0109, R0016, R0019-20, R0023, R0025

A-H (Chorherrenstift, Herzogenburg, Austria) **B0552**

A-KR (Benediktinerstift, Kremsmünster, Austria) **B0316,**
B0416-17, B0419-20, B0422-23, B0426-27, B0430, B0434,
B0436-38, B0443, B0447-48, B0461, B0470, B0477,
B0479-80, B0484-87, B0489-93, B0495, B0497, B0502-03,
B0538, B0544, D0074-75, F0193, H0499, H0501, K0080,
K0085, K0087, K0095, S0001, S0036, S0039, S0075, S0084,
S0106, S0111, S0258, S0261, W0041, Z0008

A-Sca (Museum Carolino Augusteum, Salzburg, Austria)
B0545, B0549

A-Sd (Dom-Musikarchiv, Salzburg, Austria) **B0421, B0435,**
B0482, B0517, B0530, B0546, B0550-53, H0503, H0508,
H0518, K0067, K0071, K0110-11, M0236

A-Sn (Benediktiner-Frauenstift Nonnberg, Salzburg, Austria)
H0516, W0045, W0047

A-Ssp (St. Peter Benediktiner-Erzabtei, Salzburg, Austria)
B0553

A-SEI (Benediktinerstift, Seitenstetten, Austria) **B0541-42**

A-Wgm (Gesellschaft der Musikfreunde, Vienna, Austria)
B0021, B0030, B0032, B0185, B0196, B0279, B0307, B1377,
L0041, L0050-51, L0062

A-Wm (Minoritenkonvent, Vienna, Austria) **K0106**

A-Wn (Musiksammlung, Österreichische Nationalbibliothek,
Vienna, Austria) **B0191, B0206-07, B0210, B0213, B0216,**
B0221, B0224, B0229, B0232-33, B0242-44, B0246,
B0249-50, B0252-54, B0259-60, B0265, B0277, B0279-81,
B0290, B0295-96, B0306-07, B0309, B0311-12, B0314,
B0321, B0328-30, B0335-37, B0342-46, B0350-52, B0356-57,
B0359, B0361-62, B0371, B0375-76, B0379-80, B0446,
D0046-59, D0061-73, D0077, D0079-82, F0046-47,
L0032-68, R0017-18, R0021, S0016, S0019-20, S0025-26,
S0029-30, S0033-35, S0040, S0042-47, S0050-53, S0056-59,

S0069, S0071, S0092-93, S0096-105, S0107-10, S0113-14,
S0117, S0240, S0244, S0255, S0269, S0276

A-Ws (Schottenstift, Vienna, Austria) **Z0005, Z0009**

A-Wsp (Musikarchiv, St. Peter, Vienna, Austria) **Z0001**

B-Bc (Conservatoire Royal de Musique, Brussels, Belgium)
S0624, S0625, Z0016, Z0017, Z0026

B-Br (Bibliothèque Royale Albert ler, Brussels, Belgium)
B0539, B0545

Bokemeyer Collection **A0008, A0383, A0412, A0631, B0392-93,**
B0395, B0412, B0504, B0555-56, B0559, B0561-63,
B0565-68, B1238-39, B1246, B1267-69, B1271-76, B1347,
B1374, B1379, B1415-16, C0095, C0105, C0114-15,
C0124-25, C0134-35, C0137, C0151, C0157, C0177, C0183,
C0193, C0195, C0220, C0225-26, C0229-31, D0084, E0003,
E0006, E0095, E0098-99, E0104, E0106, E0119, E0124,
E0136, E0141, E0146-47, E0150-52, E0154, E0156, E0159,
E0165, E0172, F0023-28, F0036-37, F0040, F0055, F0059,
F0067, F0084, F0093-139, F0141-65, F0189, F0200, G0091,
G0093-124, H0013, H0288, H0543, J0034, K0069,
K0076-77, K0081, K0096, K0130-31, K0138, K0144,
K0149-52, K0156, K0158-59, K0161, K0163-64, K0170,
K0178, K0182-83, K0193, K0197-99, K0205-06, K0208-10,
K0212-14, K0218-19, K0222-24, K0226, K0230-37, K0241,
K0244, K0249, K0251-53, K0258-59, K0265-66, K0268-69,
K0272, K0275, K0291, K0305, K0308, K0309, K0311-12,
K0315-16, K0320, K0323-25, K0329, K0332, K0337-38,
K0340-46, L0081, L0085, L0100, L0113, M0311-19, M0323,
M0376-77, O0002-46, P0053-54, P0057, P0059, P0062,
P0067, P0071, P0077, P0080, P0090, P0092, P0095, P0097,
P0099, P0101, P0103, P0114, P0127, P0132, P0153, P0281,
P0283, P0285, P0292, P0296, R0024, R0029, R0031,
R0065-66, R0070-79, R0082-83, R0085-91, R0098, R0100,

A0442, A0445-46, A0448, A0462, A0464, A0466, A0470-71, A0473, A0479, A0494, A0514, A0516, A0519-20, A0523, A0527, A0533, A0546, A0550, B0037, B0156-57, B0498, C0111, C0244, D0044, E0109-10, E0112, E0116, E0118, E0121, E0123, E0127-28, E0130, E0134-135, E0139-40, E0142-45, E0147, E0149, E0162-63, E0166-67, E0169, E0171, E0173, E0175, F0008, F0017, F0080, G0050, G0204, G0226, H0306-07, H0333-34, H0337, H0561, J0010-12, K0054, K0131-33, K0135, K0142-43, K0145-46, K0149, K0153-55, K0160, K0162, K0165-67, K0169, K0171, K0176, K0184-86, K0188-90, K0192, K0196, K0198, K0284, K0303, K0306-07, K0309, K0314, K0322, K0355, L0070, L0072-73, L0075-76, L0078, L0086-88, L0090, L0095, M0390, P0046, P0052-56, P0058, P0060, P0063-64, P0066, P0069-70, P0072-73, P0077, P0084-85, P0087, P0089, P0091, P0095-96, P0098-100, P0102, P0109-11, P0276, P0289, R0015, R0063, R0071, R0077, R0084, R0121, R0135, R0158, R0162, R0164-65, R0174, R0178, R0182, R0187, R0195, S0169-70, S0172, S0175-77, S0179-80, S0189-91, S0195-96, S0199, S0206, S0210, S0213, S0220, S0273, S0356-59, S0365, S0369, S0371-72, S0374-75, S0381, S0479, S0654, S0752, V0001, V0003-04, V0008-09, W0091, Z0011, Z0014-15, Z0018, Z0021-22, Z0025, Z0029, Z0031, Z0038, Z0041, Z0066

H-PH (Szent Benedekrend Központi Fokönyvtára, Pannonhalma, Hungary **S0078**

I-Af (S. Francesco, Assisi, Italy) **B0225, B0338, S0599**
I-Bc (Civico Museo Bibliografico Musicale, Bologna, Italy) **B0208, B0213, B0226, B0286-88, B0295, B0377**
I-Fc (Conservatorio di Musica Luigi Cherubini, Florence, Italy) **S0621**
I-Rsm (Archivio Capitolare di S. Maria Maggiore, Rome, Italy) **B0167**

PL-GD (Biblioteka Polskiej Akademii Nauk, Gdańsk, Poland) **B1320, B1332, M0222, M0226, M0229, M0232**
PL-Kj (Biblioteka Jagiellońska, Kraków, Poland) **C0122, C0126, C0191, C0204, F0051, H0006, H0016, H0090, K0075, S0296, S0411, S0480, W0005**
Pölchau Collection **C0149, C0228**

S-L (Universitetsbiblioteket, Lund, Sweden) **G0001**
S-Uu (Universitetsbiblioteket, Uppsala, Sweden) **A0006, A0382, A0385, A0398, A0400, A0416-17, A0421, A0424, A0430, A0447, A0460, A0463, A0475, A0483-84,**

A0487, A0493, A0495, A0499, A0501-02, A0511, A0513, A0529, A0535, A0540, A0553, A0557, A0559, A0563, A0572, A0574, A0587, A0614, A0618, A0620-22, A0629-30, B0384-87, B0391, B0393, B0397-98, B0403-04, B0406-09, B0411-12, B0415, B0431, B0478, B0570, B1321-26, B1328, B1335-36, B1338, B1343-56, B1358-72, B1375, B1378-92, B1395-96, B1398, B1400, B1402-14, B1418-19, B1421-23, C0095, C0097, C0099-103, C0108-10, C0113, C0116, C0123, C0125, C0127-28, C0150-51, C0159-60, C0163-64, C0166, C0169, C0171-73, C0175, C0181, C0185, C0187, C0189-90, C0192, C0197, C0200, C0207, C0210-11, C0213, C0215-17, C0222-23, C0225, D0083, D0090-94, E0007-08, E0091-94, E0096-97, E0099-100, E0102-05, E0107-08, F0012, F0018, F0053, F0056, F0059-61, F0063-67, F0070-71, F0074-88, F0090-92, F0178-79, F0194, G0053-90, G0092-93, G0224, H0001-02, H0010, H0321, H0337, H0406, H0622, J0001, K0073, K0157, K0174, K0191, K0207, K0217, K0220, K0230, K0273, K0284, K0304-05, K0313, K0318, K0327, K0335-36, K0338, L0045, L0111, M0223-25, M0231, M0234-35, M0325-26, M0329, M0350, N0011, P0052, P0058, P0061-62, P0074, P0077, P0086, P0088, P0094-95, P0099, P0104, P0118-33, P0135-71, P0173-84, P0186-87, P0189, P0191, P0193, P0195-99, P0201-04, P0206-16, P0223, P0251, P0276-80, P0282, P0284, P0286, P0290-91, P0293-95, P0297, R0027-28, R0030, R0033-38, R0040, R0061, R0080, R0115, R0134, S0226, S0230, S0234, S0271, S0275, S0279, S0289, S0297-98, S0302, S0306, S0309, S0391, S0400, S0407, S0419, S0431, S0436, S0476-77, S0591, S0635, S0637, S0646, S0651-52, S0716, S0739, S0749, T0007, T0014, T0041, T0045, T0049-52, T0161-68, W0026, W0032, W0034, W0049, W0060, W0063, Z0043, Z0047-48, Z0050-51, Z0054, Z0056, Z0058-59, Z0064

Tenbury Collection **P0006-07, P0009-11, P0013-17, P0020, P0022, P0025, P0028-34, P0036-41, P0045**

US-Bp (Boston Public Library, Boston, Massachusetts, USA) **R0130**
US-Cn (Newberry Library, Chicago, Illinois, USA) **A0508, A0512**
US-CHH (University of North Carolina, Music Library, Chapel Hill, North Carolina, USA) **F0059-92**
US-SY (George Arents Research Library, Syracuse University, Syracuse, New York, USA) **A0001-02, B0426, B0432, B0439, B0442, B0444, B0449-76, B0478, B0481, B0488, B0500-01, B0512, B0532-33, B0542, B1240-45, B1247, C0120, C0184, C0199, E0009-13, F0052, F0190-92, F0195-99, H0467, H0469, H0471, H0473-75, H0481, H0485-86, H0490-98, H0500, H0502, H0509-11, H0513-15,**

H0519, H0521-22, H0623-27, H0629, H0636, K0091, K0095, K0112-23, L0029, M0168, M0216, P0078, P0083, P0093, P0267-68, P0270-72, P0274, R0009, R0041-60, S0015, S0017-18, S0022-24, S0027-28, S0031-32, S0037-38, S0041, S0049, S0054-55, S0060-68, S0070, S0073-74, S0076, S0079-83, S0085-91, S0094-95, S0112, S0115-16, S0239, S0243, S0248, S0251, S0257-60, S0262-67, S0273, S0277, V0005-07, Z0010

US-Wc (Music Division, Library of Congress, Washington, D.C., USA)   **B0433, F0140, S0048, S0072, S0665**
USSR-KA (Oblastnaya Biblioteka, Kaliningrad)   **B0024, B0033, E0131, E0170, N0042-43, N0048, N0071, N0073, N0101, T0057-62, T0064-65, T0068**

Wenster Collection   **G0001**

About the Author

DIANE PARR WALKER *is Music Librarian at the University of Virginia. She has directed the U.S. RISM Libretto Project, centered at the University of Virginia, and serves on the RISM Subcommission on librettos. She is a member of the Board of Directors of the Music Library Association and has previously held positions in the music libraries of the State University of New York at Buffalo and the University of Illinois.*

PAUL WALKER *is a musicologist specializing in German and Italian music of the 16th and 17th centuries, and he is currently completing a book on the history of the theory of fugue. He is director of the University of Virginia Collegium Musicum and of the Charlottesville-based early music ensemble Zephyrus. His articles have appeared in the* Schütz Jahrbuch *and the* Bach Jahrbuch, *and he is editor of* Church, Stage, and Studio *(UMI Research Press), a collection of articles on 17th century German music. In addition to the present appointment at the University of Virginia, he has held faculty positions at Yale University and the University of Chicago.*